The Crown Jewels Conspiracy

John Paul Davis

The Crown Jewels Conspiracy
First Edition

© John Paul Davis 2017
ISBN: 978-1979955621

The right of John Paul Davis to be identified as the author of this work has been asserted in accordance with sections 77 and 78 of the Copyright Designs and Patents Act 1988.

The following tale is a work of fiction. All names, people, locations and events are either the product of the author's imagination or else used fictitiously. Any similarity to people, living or deceased, events, organisations or locales not otherwise acknowledged is coincidence.

This book or eBook is sold subject to the condition that it shall not, by way of trade or otherwise, be resold, lent, hired out or otherwise circulated without the author's prior consent in any form of binding or cover other than that in which it is published and without a similar condition, including this condition, being imposed on the subsequent purchaser.

For my father, Mike . . .

Praise for The Templar Agenda

Can't wait for the new one...
Richard Doetsch, international bestselling author of *The Thieves of Heaven*

John Paul Davis clearly owns the genre of historical thrillers.
Steven Sora, author of The Lost Colony of the Templars

A well-researched, original and fascinating work – a real page-turner
Graham Phillips, international bestselling non-fiction author

If John Paul Davis wrote the phonebook, we'd all be reading it!
Keith Houghton, #1 bestselling thriller author

Books by John Paul Davis

Fiction

The Templar Agenda
The Larmenius Inheritance
The Plantagenet Vendetta
The Cromwell Deception (a prequel to this novel)
The Bordeaux Connection (a White Hart prequel)
The Cortés Trilogy: Enigma, Revenge, Revelation
The Crown Jewels Conspiracy

Non-Fiction

Robin Hood: The Unknown Templar (Peter Owen Publishers)
Pity For The Guy – a Biography of Guy Fawkes (Peter Owen Publishers)
The Gothic King – a Biography of Henry III (Peter Owen Publishers)

For more information please visit

www.johnpauldavisauthor.com

And

www.theunknowntemplar.com

In Medieval England the defence of the realm in times of need rested on the shoulders of twelve men – a secret brotherhood of knights, who answered only to the ruler of England . . .

They were called the White Hart . . .

As they are now . . .

The Crown Jewels Conspiracy

John Paul Davis

*Here, by ye Permission of Heaven,
Hell broke loose upon this...city*

Inscription once located at the site of Thomas Farriner's bakery, Pudding Lane

Prologue

The Tower of London, London, England, 1 September, 21:53, Present Day

The ceremony took place at the same time every night. It had been that way for at least six centuries.

According to those in charge, it was the oldest ongoing event of its kind anywhere.

The time at which the proceedings would commence could be affected by a number of factors. One of the most important was the weather – like all outdoor ceremonial events, it was easier to conduct in the dry.

Another was the fitness of those taking part, especially the person in charge. An experienced man marching the same route three nights a week for over fifteen years could train himself to ensure everything ran like clockwork, but even the smallest unplanned incident or injury could result in delay.

Of most importance was the identity of the participants themselves. The walking time of two men over the well-trodden and long-established route, even if they started out together and were of near-identical size and fitness, could still differ by up to forty-five seconds. The start time had never been important.

All that mattered was when they finished.

The decision about who would lead the proceedings on any particular evening was made from a roster of six that included the Chief Yeoman Warder and his deputy, the Yeoman Gaoler. Four Queen's Guards would be selected to provide an escort.

No more than fifteen would be involved in the ceremony at the same time.

The three factors that came into play on this occasion differed little from the usual. The evening air was warm but slightly moist, a light drizzle showing up most clearly under the nearby wall lights. The man in charge was neither injured nor young; in his earlier years, he would have set off slightly later. Tonight, responsibility had been placed on the shoulders of the Chief Yeoman Warder, the man of the greatest experience. In nine years, he had conducted the ceremony over a thousand times and never been late.

Only once in its entire history had the ceremony not finished on time.

At precisely 21:53 and 35 seconds, the Chief Yeoman Warder appeared through the main door of his lodgings in the Byward Tower, just as he had done on each previous occasion. Picking up his four-man escort from below the archway of the Bloody Tower, he took the familiar route along Water Lane and over the coming minutes proceeded to lock each of the Tower's outer gates.

* * *

The sentry had been posted at the usual place, close to the point where the ceremony would end. The man on duty, although taking part for the first time, had already gone through two rehearsals earlier that day.

Like every member of the Queen's Guard presently stationed at the Tower, he was also a regular spectator.

Standing to attention in the shadows of the Bloody Tower, he heard the collective noise of heavy marching along Water Lane, exactly as he had expected. He waited until the ghostly shadows of soldiers in the uniforms of old danced across the illuminated stonework below a small wall light on the steps close to St Thomas's Tower before stepping forward, his rifle raised.

"Halt!"

The leader of the escort ordered his men to comply; their feet fell silent.

"Who comes there?" the sentry resumed.

"The keys," the Chief Yeoman Warder replied.

"Whose keys?"

"Queen Elizabeth's keys."

The sentry backed down. "Pass, Queen Elizabeth's keys. All is well."

The party moved on beneath the archway of the Bloody Tower. On reaching the other side, they marched swiftly along the walkway between the White Tower and Tower Green, where the main guard was already assembled at the top of the Broadwalk Steps.

On the orders of their leader, the escort and the Chief Yeoman Warder again came to a halt.

The leader of the main guard marched forward, the noise of his footfalls echoing across the castle's Inner Ward. In a harsh, booming voice, he commanded the gathering to present arms, and each man snapped to it.

The Chief Yeoman Warder took two paces forward and raised his Tudor bonnet from above his head.

"God preserve Queen Elizabeth."

The guard answered as one, "Amen!"

The clock chimed ten.

With the hour past and the chimes fading, a deathly silence ensued as the duty drummer raised his bugle to his lips to sound the "Last Post". Over the next few minutes, the chief returned the keys to the Queen's House, at which point the guard was dismissed. At precisely 22:05, the final visitors were escorted to the main exit overlooking the remains of the old menagerie.

The Tower of London was secure for another night.

Among the small gathering of onlookers, the man with the darkest hair complied with the instructions of the watchman as he departed from the Tower, heading towards the Welcome Centre. He kept moving till he was in sight of Tower Hill, the noises of the Underground and the nearby road now overwhelming that of traffic on the river.

The visit had been enlightening for many reasons. Seeing the ceremony with his own eyes had been an experience unlike any other, an insight into the actions of others. It was like looking into the past, only different.

He knew that the true significance of what he had just seen transcended time.

Two men were waiting for him by the old city wall, both dressed in leather jackets, the red glow of their cigarettes lighting up faces of similar features and hair colour.

The older of the two spoke first. "My uncle rang only moments ago. The helicopter will be waiting for us in ten minutes."

The newcomer nodded, neither surprised nor concerned. He lit a cigarette of his own and exhaled. "Then let us not waste any more time."

Edinburgh Castle, Edinburgh, Scotland, 22:00

Over three hundred miles north of London, a similar ceremony was taking place away from the gaze of public onlookers.

Standing on parade in the Upper Ward close to the Royal Palace, where the Crown Jewels of Scotland had been on display for the last two hundred years, four armed guards stood to attention as two of their colleagues marched at quick time away from the entrance of the palace, coming to a halt before the man standing at the centre of the escort.

Unlike the four who surrounded him, the man's ceremonial attire was notably illustrious.

The guard with the keys saluted him. "I return these keys, being perfectly convinced that they cannot be placed in better hands than those of the Lord Provost and Councillors of my good City of Edinburgh."

The Lord Provost nodded as he accepted the keys before being escorted safely to the castle's main exit.

The Louvre, Paris, France, 23:00

Close to the north bank of the River Seine, there had been no such ceremony. The museum had been closed for several hours, the last visitors, staff and employees long since departed. At this hour, the majority of the illumination was external to the grand hallways, lighting up the famous façade like the rising of a great moon. Even from a distance the lights were clearly visible, reflecting off the calm waters and the iconic glass pyramid that was now arguably as famous as the building to which it was adjoined.

Like its cousins north of the channel, all the usual precautions had already taken place, the key areas secured.

The next people to see the Crown Jewels of France would do so at dawn.

Bordeaux, France,
02:00

The limousines had been arriving at regular intervals throughout the last hour. Though none of the models were exactly the same, each was of identical colour, handpicked by the building's owners to ensure the guests arrived in a manner befitting the property.

Ever since their invention, such grandiose limos had been used to transport the participants to these meetings. While in recent years it had become generally accepted, despite the lavish trappings of wealth and grandeur that pervaded the area, that being chauffeured was no longer an essential requirement, any need for more fundamental change was still to be considered worthy of more extensive discussion by the owners. In common with the other vehicles that had recently made their way up the impressive driveway, there was more to them than matters of transport.

Like the men who drove them, the limos had been handpicked to meet every requirement.

Should an outsider watching on have presumed that the use of such vehicles was a luxury that went with the social standing of the occupants, they were unlikely to need correcting, yet on this occasion comfort was only one consideration. As always, the passengers were banned from arriving in their own vehicles as well as from carrying anything that could offer any clue to their true identities. Under no circumstances could the limos be traced to their passengers. Even if the models were registered to the property, each new addition would meet that same requirement.

The dark glass and paintwork were the perfect way to ensure anonymity.

As the final limousine made its way through the large metallic gateway, its classical design an ostentatious prelude to what lay beyond, the distinguished passenger gazed quietly through the tinted glass as over three acres of unlit greenery gave way to something altogether more imposing. Beyond the trees that peppered the immense gardens like a dehesa in the plains of Spain, a gravelled forecourt surrounded a house that an outsider might describe as palatial. The 19th-century chateau, although not old compared to many in France, instead had other claims to fame, perhaps older still. In the absence of any opportunity to conduct thorough research, even the most eminent historians or archaeologists would struggle to find evidence in the floodlit stonework of anything of genuine ancient pedigree. In truth, the meaningful clues were to be found not in the material fabric but in the people. Despite being rebuilt many times throughout its history, the same family had always overseen it.

An unbroken chain that, legend had it, dated back to before any great fortress.

Leaving the limousine as it stopped at the foot of a four-step entrance that preceded a neo-gothic façade, the well-dressed occupant took one final opportunity to smarten his appearance in the vehicle's spotless glass exterior before proceeding through the open door. Unlike the attendees who had already arrived, his stylish suit-shirt combination had a youthful feel that suited his handsome face and designer hairstyle. As the limo disappeared, the sound of tyres on gravel fading, he entered the main hallway, coming face to face with the ageing butler, whose appearance was equally impeccable.

"Is everything all right, sir?" The old man addressed the visitor warmly. "I was rather under the impression your uncle was expected."

The young man smiled as he shook his head. "Even the hounds of Hell would struggle to rouse my uncle before dawn. Rest assured, though, the duke will make his presence known in his own good time."

The butler nodded and stepped aside to allow the final visitor access. From here, the young man needed no further instruction. Though several years had passed since his previous visit, he remembered the layout as if the property were his own, the experience of taking that first step on the immaculate marble floor causing an unexpected release of forgotten feelings that threatened to take his breath away.

Ignoring the sound of soft chatter and the movement of plates and cutlery coming from the servants' areas, he crossed the hallway quickly, continuing up the grand stairway. Like the opulent furnishings and artwork that decorated his own ancestral home, the pieces he saw were notable for their rarity; some were almost exact replicas. Through a career in the art world, he had acquired an enviable knowledge on the history and value of such pieces, but he knew the reason for the similarities went deeper than the owners' personal tastes.

But for the differences in clothing, looking into the oval frames, he could have almost convinced himself that he was looking into a series of mirrors.

As the stairway ended and the luxurious carpet gave way once more to marble flooring, a narrow corridor of identical wall colouring contained less in the way of artwork and ended with double doors, whose appearance heralded an entrance to a room of great importance. Two suited men stood rigidly to attention at either side of the doors; they closed behind him as he entered. On another occasion, knowing he was the last to arrive might have indicated that he was guilty of being late.

Today he knew his arrival had been achieved with exemplary punctuality.

As the sound of the closing doors faded, he moved slowly towards the centre of the room, observing its features for the first time. Although other parts of the chateau were familiar to him, he had now entered the one room that throughout his youth had been perpetually off-limits, an area not meant for children. In his mind, he sensed himself becoming reacquainted with memories of the past – booming voices engaged in heated discussion, a great mystery taking place behind the doors. His father had once referred to it as the room where kingdoms would rise and fall.

Only in recent years had he learned the truth behind those words.

Similar to the parts of the chateau with which he was already familiar, the ceiling was high, gilded in a rare stuccoed style that any well-informed visitor would instantly associate with past nobility. Light cyan walls surrounded them on every side, their continuity broken by ornate neo-gothic windows that at the late hour were all draped, absorbing the low candlelight glow of two large crystal chandeliers. As in the previous rooms, the acoustics were strangely amplified, causing the volume of his footsteps to sound unnaturally loud on the oak floor. The artwork again consisted primarily of portraits, the faces of illustrious warlords watching on from all sides, their features also noticeably similar to those of the latest visitor, whose attention now focused on the room's final feature. Located in the centre, surrounded by chairs arranged in equal spacing, a grand table was occupied by twenty-three men.

Only one seat remained vacant.

Without further delay, the final attendee took his place and turned his attention to the far end of the room. While those at the table, all men of varying ages and appearances, sat in a manner that implied equilibrium, at the head of the room parity gave way to status. Seated on a raised platform in a manner of an overlord, a final man was greater not only in age but all other things. Unlike the chairs of the twenty-four, the design of those on the raised platform were unique to the room, but not so the world beyond the walls. The man he was looking at was a king. A ruler. The latest of a long line.

The newcomer bowed before him as he took his seat.

The man on the throne smiled cautiously as he watched the final attendee take his seat. Though many years had passed since their last encounter, the facial resemblance was clear – something shared with every other person present. Under no circumstances would an alternative be accepted. It was a tradition that predated the castle and the portraits, one whose origins were lost in the mists of time. It had survived many wars, not only in France. While tradition had it that one of the kings whose portrait adorned the wall had once claimed that in war one couldn't be too choosy of one's bedfellows, in the eight centuries since, the lessons of such mistakes had been learnt. Never would they need to be relearned. Instead, it told an undeniable truth.

In times of war, the only people worthy of trust are family.

The man on the throne rose slowly to his feet; within seconds, all present followed.

"Gabriel." The old man faced the nearest of the twenty-four, of all present the man whose facial similarities suggested the closest family link. "The pledge."

All present bowed their heads as the younger man recited a predetermined speech from memory. None of the words that were spoken would mean anything to anyone outside this select circle.

Nor since the organisation's creation had any unfortunate enough to hear them lived long enough to attempt to learn of their dreadful truth.

Once the speaker had finished, the twenty-four returned to their seats. With one notable exception, every seat in the room was now taken. Located to the left of the throne, the vacant chair equalled it both in importance and appearance.

As the silence returned, the man on the throne cast his eye over the gathering, spending sufficient time only to take in the faces of those present, which was a struggle to his ageing eyes, even with the aid of heavy varifocal lenses. In keeping with the remainder of his features, his eyes were deep set, his bony sockets of a sunken, gaunt appearance that, although offering little indication of his true age, were enough to confirm he had experienced a long life.

"Bizu!" He addressed a dark-haired man among the twenty-four. "Let us begin."

The dark-haired man nodded, needing no further direction beyond the soft uttering of his name. "Everard Payet was buried yesterday in a private ceremony in the hometown of his grandparents. For the purpose of avoiding undue attention, the ceremony was a small affair; the only visitors were close friends and family. Due to the sensitive circumstances surrounding his death and his previous confinement overseas, it has been necessary that details up until now have remained undisclosed. Now that he has been put to rest, it is only right that I offer you all the opportunity to share in our grief."

The remaining twenty-three looked quickly from side to side, the expressions of most clearly revealing shock and surprise. For a time nobody spoke.

"Has his wife and brother-in-law been informed?" asked a white-haired man seated about midway along the table. In common with the others, a smart suit complemented a face of aristocratic features.

"Every member of his immediate family was there, including myself," the same man replied. Unlike the majority of the group, whose faces and hair colour largely resembled those of the white-haired man, the speaker's features were aquiline, yet mysterious, his hair darker, though not necessarily younger. His face bore the marks of character and experience but was not devoid of charisma, comparable perhaps to a well-known celebrity seeking to conceal the ever-increasing ravages of advancing years from an adoring public. Whereas most present came from the same part of France, his ancestry was from further north.

In certain circles he was known as the Anjouvin.

"I apologise, of course, if any here wished to attend," he continued.

"Such is the way of the world," said another white-haired man in his late sixties seated at the opposite end from the thrones. "Everard was a good man and a good soldier. Dare I say, he was a friend of everyone here. Ever since I was a young boy, I have often felt it to be the saddest aspect of our business that again we must carry our grief in silence." Several heads nodded in agreement. "How long has he been dead?"

"Three weeks," the Anjouvin replied.

"What happened?" the first white-haired man asked.

"What His Lordship said moments ago is quite correct. Everard was an honourable man and an able soldier. He understood, as we do, that our cause will always be bigger than one's own life."

All in the group paused for thought. None of them needed official confirmation that the signs pointed to suicide.

"The chapel at Angers is big enough for many." A man of balding grey hair and bearded features in his late fifties spoke for the first time. "Why not bring his body there? Perhaps then we can all mourn together."

In the seat closest to the throne, the man who had led them in taking the pledge was less impressed. "The chapel at Angers is for royalty and nobility only, Philippe; you know this as well as any. Never has a yeoman been buried in a house of kings."

Silence fell, this time clearly judgemental. Philippe cleared his throat, a dense, awkward cough that suggested neither good health nor comfort. "Forgive me, sir, I do not wish to be insubordinate. It just pains me to think that my loyal kinsmen could give so much only to pass without honour."

"Ah, but what is honour?" the man on the throne asked, the sagging skin around his mouth relaxed as though he were lost in deep contemplation. "Surely, it is only by learning to serve in a way where your first thoughts are to your cause that one can really possess full integrity. Remember, it was said in the gospels: blessed are those who are persecuted because of righteousness. For theirs is the Kingdom of Heaven."

The twenty-four watched and listened attentively as the man on the throne joined the conversation for the first time since the pledge, the atmosphere in the room changing notably with his involvement.

"Under the circumstances, it was decided the only sensible course of action would be for Everard to be laid to rest under the loving eyes of his family." The Anjouvin nodded sombrely. "In an ideal world, perhaps together we may all have participated in adding soil to the ground. Only in a loving world would it be safe for us to all stand together as one."

Heads nodded in agreement.

"How is Randek?" the first white-haired man asked.

"Why don't you ask him yourself?" The Anjouvin gestured to the man alongside him. In contrast to the majority, Randek's hair was short and blond, his age less than half that of most of them.

"Fabien?" The final attendee spoke for the first time, completely shocked by Randek's appearance. "I'm so sorry, cousin, I never would have recognised you as a blond."

"Nor I you, dressed with a tie." Randek smiled at his distant cousin, bringing soft laughter. "We really must try to catch up more, François."

François smiled slyly; though several minutes had passed since his arrival, his heart was still pounding beneath the luxurious fabric of his suit. "How is your sister?"

"Coping. The circumstances are, of course, unwelcome to her."

"I should imagine losing the father of her young child would break the heart of even the strongest." François nodded. "And her current location?"

"With her husband dead, the world is no longer a safe place for her and her son." The Anjouvin's words were unequivocal. "Especially with another soon to join them."

It was clear from the facial reactions that this was news to the majority.

"So she's in hiding?" François pressed.

"She is currently under the protection of those who love her most deeply." The Anjouvin nodded. "There she must stay. At least until her safety can be assured."

François's gaze alternated between the Anjouvin and Randek, his eyes a fixed stare from across the table. "You are aware, I assume?"

"My sister is a daughter of France and the mother of my nephew," Randek replied. "She may not be a soldier, but she is no less a patriot than any at this table. She did not request to be a burden. For that, I take the responsibility, including the guarding of her few secrets."

"Even from dear old cousins?"

A wry smile. "A bond between a brother and sister is most sacred, *mon ami*. My loyalty to her can never be questioned. Even if it means laying down my own life."

The man on the throne smiled as he adjusted his glasses, quietly remembering why for almost seven centuries such meetings had never included those from outside the family circle.

"What of the others?" His attention returned to the Anjouvin. "The men captured from the gallery in Paris?"

"Also dead," the Anjouvin replied.

"Circumstances?" The first white-haired man spoke again.

"In truth, something of a mixture. Thuram and Petit took the honourable route together on the eve of their torture. The rest had already succumbed to their wounds outside the Musée d'Orsay."

"Torture?" The man shook his head, venom oozing. "I thought the British denied use of such things."

"Just because one denies use of it doesn't make the punishment any less painful," Gabriel said.

The man on the throne nodded, remembering the details of the events six months earlier. "Then that leaves only you, Fabien."

Randek nodded. "Everybody dies eventually. Everard and the others accepted what I accept. As do their replacements."

"With this in mind, let us move on to the here and now. Let us not forget the true reason we are here this evening." Gabriel looked around the table before turning his attention to the Anjouvin. "Bizu?"

The Anjouvin took a contemplative breath and nodded. "Gentlemen, as everybody here is well aware, on this night over three hundred years ago, our predecessors sat in the same room of the castle that once stood where we are now, preparing for what history would later view as the greatest accident of all time. What thoughts would be going through their minds right now, we can only imagine. Only I'm sure that they would be those of pride!"

"Perhaps it is the thoughts of those that are living that should be of greater concern," the second white-haired man said, his eyes fixed in firm concentration. "What news from London?"

"The plans we have discussed for so long have now all been put in place," the

Anjouvin replied, his aquiline features cold and poised. "All that now remains is for a light to be put to the fuse. Tomorrow I plan to be there myself. In a supervisory capacity, of course."

François laughed quietly. "Where is the location?"

"That is not of concern."

The young art director's gaze remained unflinching. "But you have seen it yourself?"

"I have seen much, young one."

"That doesn't really answer my question."

"I seem to recall your uncle once said the same thing."

Soft laughter echoed around the table.

"Well, soon you will have the opportunity to tell my uncle yourself. In the meantime, perhaps you'll ease my curiosity?" François pressed.

"It is the same plan we have been through many times." Randek took over.

"Plans are subject to change, cousin. Until tonight, I was unaware your brother-in-law was even dead."

Randek met François's gaze, delaying his response in order to dispel any passing bitterness. "The plans are sound, their secrecy secure; they have been for some time. Ever since the politician's wife acquired the manuscript from the house in the English countryside, the way in has never been in question. The only surprise was what additional bonuses it provided."

Quiet consternation engulfed the group. François was clearly not the only man in the dark.

"May we hear of these bonuses?" Gabriel asked. "Don't tell me they're also to be laid to rest with their grandparents."

On this occasion the laughter that met the man's words was louder.

"The actions of our predecessors were legendary," Randek relented, still unwilling to give too much away. "Only once in history has a whole city been obliterated in one strike of a match."

"A remark like that can demonstrate only alarming overconfidence or an appalling grasp of history," the first white-haired man said, humour now absent. "Our predecessors may have succeeded in putting light to a match, but they also failed in rebuilding what was there to be rebuilt. Because of this, for over three hundred years we, the Descendants of the Gemini, have been playing catch up." His gaze centred on the Anjouvin. "What of Edinburgh?"

"There is little new to report, at least little different from London. For over six months now, we have had eyes inside the castle and out. The loyalty of the Queen's Guard has never been in doubt; after tomorrow, perhaps this will change. The way in is known to all who are willing to use their eyes to see. The same is true of London."

The man on the throne adjusted his glasses. "So the rumours are true? All these years, beneath the ground."

"In Edinburgh, the existence of the streets beneath the city has long been known. In London, evidence of its dark past is perhaps less obvious. Nevertheless, both can be entered through the correct doors. Thanks to Monsieur Raleigh and the family from Scotland, neither is a secret to us."

The man on the throne nodded. "And what of closer to home?"

Randek smiled. "Thanks to the elegance of the artwork acquired from the Musée d'Orsay, the museum in Paris is no longer a problem. Nor will it be necessary to inflict damage on any of the city's beautiful buildings."

François smiled. "I never had you down as a romantic, cousin."

"I claim no genius. However, I spit on the Frenchman who denies his own patriotism."

The man on the throne smiled warmly. "My friends, I see in your eyes the love and loyalty that would warm each remaining drop of blood in my ever-failing heart. And for that, you humble me. Tonight we sit in old chairs around old tables. We walk in old footsteps, footsteps even our predecessors once believed were haunted by the spirits of the past. When a great disease afflicts a great city, an even greater remedy must be required. Just like that which came by permission of heaven on the godless city three hundred years ago, tomorrow heaven gives us permission again. To right the wrongs of the past and remedy them with the blessings of a brighter future."

The expressions of all present varied from sombre pride to those impatient for malice. As the room again fell silent, the Anjouvin took over.

"The failings of the past are famous, but the future begins tonight. By this same permission, a second wave will be unleashed on the godless city, and the mistakes of the past, including those of our own predecessors, will be swept away forever. All of which is to be put into operation precisely nineteen hours from now."

1

The Brecon Beacons, South Wales, Twenty-Four Months Earlier

Lieutenant Mike Hansen adjusted the straps on his SAS-style bergen rucksack and casually tossed it over both shoulders before checking his appearance in the tinted glass of his car window. The lower bodywork of his 57-reg Ford Fiesta had seen better days, but it was no longer his number one car. Behind the glass, the muddy interior matched much of the exterior.

It was always the car he took to the great outdoors.

His own appearance was consistent with that of the car. The fabric of his camouflage-patterned combat uniform had become slightly frayed with use and there were some marks that even the strongest detergent couldn't shift. Over the years, he'd tried a number, but these days there was something about the stains he liked. They were a sign of use and experience, reminding him of the words of his first staff sergeant.

"You don't join the forces to keep your trousers clean."

He gave himself the once-over, saving the vanity of his handsome face till last. Dirt aside, his appearance was similar to that of most soldiers out on manoeuvres, any lack of wrinkles and other outward signs of the hard wear and tear of operational experience largely explainable by his relatively young age. Though he'd never formally applied to join the Special Forces, he admired the stories he'd heard from his colleagues about days spent operating overseas in secret. His driving aim was to prove to himself that he was capable of making the grade.

Including passing the near-impossible tests.

The SAS selection process was legendary, though more so among civilians than the military. In certain circles, reports seemed to possess something of a mythical quality: god-like heroes traversing the ground almost undetectably before vanishing without a trace, destined only to return in their country's hour of greatest need. He'd heard more concrete reports from those who had been there and done it, usually before the ISIS days. He remembered the first time he'd tried it himself.

Even as a veteran of the 1st Battalion of the Parachute Regiment, never before had he experienced such anguish.

The most notorious part of the fitness challenge was a speed march up the highest mountain in South Wales. He remembered visiting the area as a kid, but it wasn't until he tried it himself, he realised what Mother Nature really had in store. Officially, Pen y Fan stood at 886m elevation, including over 660m of actual climbing, but that told only part of the story. There were four mountains in the vicinity; an active tourist out trekking for pleasure could walk eighteen kilometres full circle, and that was a stretch even at leisure. The SAS route centred on Pen y Fan, but in full combat gear.

And the participants had to do it twice.

The bergen was usually the deal breaker. The first time he walked it, succeeding without particular difficulty; even at a run, he was satisfied his fitness was up to the challenge. Doing it twice was a bigger strain, even without the extra weight. A fully packed bergen weighed approximately sixteen kilograms, maybe twenty depending on who set the challenge. Though running with it was never easy, in the last six months he'd come a long way towards achieving the required standard.

If the test ever came about in real life, he knew he was capable of handling it.

The early sun was a distant fireball, its rays casting off the nearby cloud that today was almost as pale as the sky. It was one of those days where the sun was more decorative than warm. A sharp frost had enveloped the greenery, enhancing the drama of the rugged landscape. It was a sight the locals had become accustomed to, cherished even.

It was a different story for those out on manoeuvres.

Even in the cold the National Park could be a popular tourist spot, but today the numbers were sparse. It was still early, and much could change, especially if the rain kept away. Too often September brought the grey as well as the warm; the forecast promised the same later.

If all went to plan, it wouldn't come until after they left.

Among the few who had ventured out, one man in particular was a reluctant observer. He remembered attempting to climb the mountain for his own reasons – succeeding, though with some difficulty. The same was true of the man of Asian features alongside him, who breathed impatiently into his camouflage snood, inwardly anticipating the moment the dreary early autumn scene would be swapped for a warming soup in the nearby half-timbered surroundings of the village pub.

He gazed at the first man. "Shouldn't he have started by now?"

The dark-haired man alongside him nodded. "He's late. If our paths do ever cross, I may have to hold it against him."

While both men continued their mild banter, a third man wore an altogether more serious expression. Though he suffered worst from the cold, of the three he also had the most to learn.

He lowered his field glasses and breathed visibly into the misty air. "I think our man has arrived."

Mike had parked in the usual car park and made his way along the nearest pathway that started in an area of woodland before meandering in a jagged course through the hillside. Although the faint remnants of frost still covered the greenery, reflecting a sparkling glow in the low sunlight, he knew it wouldn't take long for the temperature to rise.

He quickened his pace as the landscape became more open and started the timer on his wristwatch at the first checkpoint. It was lonely out, isolated; a thick mist enveloped the nearby peaks, which were still devoid of people, a blessing under the circumstances. Although the SAS march involved a double sprint up Pen y Fan, today he'd decided to experiment. Neglecting the usual left turn up the mountain at the bottom of the valley, he started with a right and continued to the top of the bizarrely named Fan y Big. He'd promised his former sergeant he'd take a selfie if he ever did it. Apparently that was another military tradition.

Every soldier in the Regiment must take at least one selfie atop the Big Fanny.

He descended Fan y Big at near sprint speed and used the extra momentum to start a charge up Pen y Fan, taking extra care to avoid losing his footing on the muddy pathway. He took another selfie where the National Trust had erected a sign marking the pinnacle, doing his best to avoid complacency at the satisfaction he'd felt at the previous summit. Allowing himself a two-minute break, he followed the path down and up Corn Du and finally Cribyn, the last of the four. He checked his watch. Three hours, twenty-one minutes. Excellent!

If all went to plan, he'd be back at the car park within five hours of starting out.

The most senior of the three onlookers lowered his field glasses as his target re-emerged through a thick area of woodland close to the reservoir. Though the lad was still to finish, he'd seen everything he needed to.

Everything matched what he'd read in the reports and so far they had all been exemplary. The man was twenty-seven years old, a five-year veteran of the 1st Battalion of the Parachute Regiment on the back of a degree at Loughborough. Like most of his type, his military motivations were largely unspecified, only that he had designs on a captain's position as soon as possible and that his original desire to sign up had been deeply instilled by family. That much he didn't doubt. He'd met the man's uncle, served with him, attended his wedding. He had seen the lad before, long ago.

Much had changed in seventeen years.

The man turned to his two companions, his nose now raw from so long out in the cold.

"What say we discuss this somewhere warmer?"

2

London, England,
2 September, 20:23, Present Day

The Anjouvin walked slowly to the foot of the Monument and breathed in as he took in the sights. The usual hubbub of people gathering primarily to the west was far less tonight than he'd witnessed in previous days. The evening air was still, the light fading. The two bars located on the corners of Monument Street and Fish Street Hill were busy but far from buzzing. Several couples sat inside, mainly at two-seater tables, enjoying a quiet drink, maybe bar food, while small groups of men propped up the counters, some gathering by the doors to enjoy a quick cigarette. A premier league game was being shown live on the multitude of big screens, but it wasn't clear from the lack of sound who was playing unless one was paying close attention. The majority were happy to keep themselves to themselves; few seemed on a mission to get drunk.

It was Wednesday night in the city and that was sufficient explanation.

Outside the bars and east along Monument Street, the atmosphere was typical of a weekday evening, quiet yet strangely surreal. The 311-step monument, which had towered above the crossroads since 1677, cast its usual pointed shadow over the grey concrete, imposing but still a long way from achieving peak effect. The night-time floodlights were now on, but the final rays of the evening sun were still setting behind the city skyline to the west; he knew from previous visits that within twenty minutes its effect would be far greater. It was still early.

Too early.

East of the Monument, the evening air seemed calmer still, the silence broken only by the nearby traffic that moved steadily along Lower Thames Street. The public toilets at the bottom of Monument Street were closed for the night; he had been the last to use them before they were locked. The nearby buildings were apparently deserted, the isolated glow of an interior light a rare addition to the street lighting.

He focused on the largest of the nearby buildings, a typical glass-fronted shell with a large corporate sign confirming the name *Faryners House* accompanied by the title Lloyds Banking Group above the main doors. Even without the sign, he would have known the building now belonged to a bank. In the past, many other businesses had occupied the site.

Most famously a bakery.

At 20:25, the Anjouvin looked across the concrete paving with renewed interest as the main door to the Monument opened, a staff member offering him access. Despite being officially closed for the day, his arrival was expected – a special privilege from the correct people.

He smiled at the man and shook hands as he entered, making his way up the first of the 311 steps.

The Welcome Centre, The Tower of London, 20:27

The distinguished academic shuffled the thick sheaf of papers in his hands and cast an enquiring gaze over the crowd. The sight of a busy lecture theatre, strangers of various ages, creeds and character sprawled out across the red padded seats, was a far cry from the dozy expressions he was used to from the majority of his undergrads, clearly nursing light heads and hangovers. There was a buzz of anticipation in the air, different from the classes he usually taught. While the University of Nottingham was regarded as one of the best in the country, a place where the most talented of the generation would study in preparation for distinguished careers, he knew the modern mindset was often one of debauchery over dedication, especially among the first-years. The crowd he saw now was older, more mature. Unlike the students who attended his university lectures, he knew entry tonight was an all-ticket affair and the audience was delighted to be there.

He shuffled again through his notes, forming a picture in his mind of the proceedings that would soon follow. The occasion was billed as once in a lifetime, a fact more due to the date than the subject matter. It was the anniversary of a famous event in England's history. It was an honour to be asked.

Especially at such a special location.

Placing his papers down on the lectern, he moved towards his laptop and examined the presentation, checking how it appeared on the big screen.

Satisfied, he returned to the lectern.

Assistant curator of the Tower of London was just the latest of many official job titles Emily Fletcher had held in less than six years working at the Tower. Though her list of duties rarely involved anything to do with the education department, tonight's event was so unmissable, she'd have happily attended for free.

She remembered from her time at Nottingham that Professor David Champion had a rare capability of capturing an audience's attention, even if the subject matter was less appealing. There was something about his enthusiasm and knowledge that was simply infectious.

Tonight she already sensed she was in for a treat.

The lecture had been her idea, which was also rare. The education officer had posed the idea through a group email months earlier about how to honour the anniversary of the Great Fire; at the time replies had been slow. It wasn't till weeks later that she remembered her favourite lecturer at university had written a book on the subject.

The opportunity had been too good to miss.

Sitting one row from the back, her hazel eyes panned quickly over the big screen as the experienced academic skimmed through his PowerPoint presentation in preparation for the event. She smiled as she caught his attention before finishing up her own arrangements. As the most senior employee present, she had agreed to the education officer's request to write a blog for the website, including taking photographs.

She heard a voice in her ear, courtesy of a small communications device she regularly used for lectures, asking how it was looking.

"Perfect," she replied via a similar device, her smile radiating almost as wide as the stage. "Just one piece of advice. I didn't realise this was on Waterloo!"

Realising the PowerPoint presentation was the wrong one, Champion smiled. "My dear, what would I do without you?"

Putting on her dark-framed, geek-chic-style glasses, she closed the A4-sized ring binder on the stand in front of her and laughed quietly as she adjusted herself in her seat.

As she glanced to her right, she noticed a late arrival settle into the far seat of the final row.

Captain Michael Hansen wasn't used to being late. In his profession, it simply didn't happen. As a soldier with more than seven years' experience, he had learned the hard way that timing was often everything. It was a career where punctuality was a prerequisite of the job, quite often the difference between life and death.

As a member of arguably the world's most secretive, elite Special Forces group, it was an honour of a select few.

The last few hours had been hectic. Working for an organisation tasked with the safety of the realm, security threats were far from rare, but recent intel was disturbing. A surge of reports had come to light regarding a possible threat, this time north of the border. He remembered something similar had taken place six months earlier. The attacks on Edinburgh had occurred suddenly, completely from left field. The rebuild had been ongoing ever since; in some locations it was still to properly begin. The culprits were dead save one.

Still, he longed for the day when Fabien Randek would return to his life.

Settling into his seat on the back row and placing his black rucksack down by his feet, he glanced around the lecture theatre, more out of curiosity than concern. The twenty-plus rows of red padded seats, he guessed adding up to a total of perhaps 120, were presently occupied to at least two-thirds capacity and looking fairly busy the way people were spread out. He remembered from his own time at university that attendances at these lectures could vary between almost empty and full to overflowing, usually depending on the subject matter and the lecturer. Of tonight's subject matter, he had neglected to enquire.

All he knew was that it was being delivered by the best.

Turning his attention to the front, he saw the imposing frame of David Champion making his way along the walkway like a senior politician waiting to approach the podium. Though several months had passed since their last meeting, it was impossible not to recognise him. His familiar healthy head of greying, silver hair was combed to the usual smart side parting, the colour complemented by a stunning silver suit that hung tightly to his slightly plump physique and caught the overhead lights, bringing out the best of his sharp eyes that always appeared keen and focused. The man was famed both home and abroad for his kindly nature and charismatic enthusiasm that Mike's parents had always claimed ran in the family. A brightly coloured wristwatch also caught the light as Champion checked the time before looking up in the direction of the final row, clearly registering Mike's presence. For now, a smile and subtle nod was enough to offer mutual recognition. Later the embrace would be more befitting, more familial. Now was not the time for sentiment.

It was 20:30.

Time for the lecture to begin.

The Anjouvin took a deep breath as he reached the final step, finally allowing his tired body a moment to relax. The narrow stairway had wound in a clockwise direction; had he not seen the pinnacle from the outside, he could have conned himself into believing it could go on forever.

While the climb to the summit of the Monument was certainly steep, it did little to compare to its designer's more famous accomplishment.

He walked through the open doorway that separated the stairwell from the observation level and began to take in the sights. Once upon a time, the platform had provided some of the best views in London, but these days it was greatly restricted by the surrounding buildings and mesh caging. It was ironic, he mused as he looked out. A great irony.

According to hearsay, the site had been responsible for more suicides than the deaths caused by the disaster that it commemorated.

He began by looking to the south before moving swiftly on to the east. The Lloyds bank in Faryners House seemed far less imposing viewed from above, its glassy façade and thick walls dominated by its neighbours. Further afield, Tower Bridge glowed a radiant purple and green like a rainbow from a fantasy novel, its exotic hues mixing with the quiet flow of the Thames. Left of the bridge, the Tower possessed a similar, dominating aura, its impenetrable walls basking in the glow of nearby floodlights.

Just as in the tales of old, it still stood guard over the kingdom.

The Anjouvin removed his iPhone from his pocket and started to photograph the view. Satisfied, he did the same for the west side, his attention on one building in particular. Like the structure he had just climbed, it encapsulated the legacy of a great man.

And an even greater event.

Professor Champion approached the lectern as the house lights dimmed and a round of applause went up from the crowd. He sipped from his glass of water before adjusting the microphone, looking at his audience as he began.

"Here by ye permission of heaven, hell broke loose upon this protestant city from the malicious hearts of barbarous papists, by ye hand of their agent Hubert, who confessed, and on ye ruines of this place declared the fact, for which he was hanged, that here began that dreadful fire, which is described and perpetuated on and by the neighbouring pillar."

Champion clicked his mouse a couple of times and the pictures on the big screen changed. Replacing the title screen, the instantly recognisable image of the famous painting of the Great Fire of London as seen on the third day from St Katharine Docks, a new slide displayed a photograph of what appeared to be a stone tablet broken in two.

"While the Great Fire of London may not have been actually delivered by permission of heaven, in the days following the fire it was the view of most in positions of authority that the fire was at the very least by permission of someone. Everyone from the Dutch to the Lutherans to the papacy themselves were included in the dark utterings. However, in the eyes of many of its citizens, no finger of *j'accuse* was pointed more strongly than at the French. As most historians will agree, the man responsible for this powerful statement, Sir Patience Ward, then mayor of the city, was not only a man of his time but, just like his predecessors, a man with an agenda. A man with a very real question that needed a clear answer.

"What had caused the destruction of his city, and why?"

Emily watched with rapt attention as the sixty-two-year-old professor settled quickly into his stride. She smiled to herself as he made a joke about cakes, and took a few photos with her DSLR camera, recalling the request from the education officer to provide some for the website.

The professor's tone was smooth, familiar, the experience far more relaxing since she knew she didn't have to memorise what she was hearing for an exam that could potentially shape her future. She recalled nearly crying after taking the one for his module, fearing the worst.

Either by permission of the teacher or heaven, she'd come out with a 2:1.

As the professor's attention turned to the next part of the presentation that was illustrated by famous paintings of the Great Fire in its early hours, her own was drawn briefly to the back row and the newcomer in the final seat on the opposite side. Like the man taking the lecture, his features were pleasant but strong, reminding her of an RAF bomber pilot from the Second World War who only called upon his strengths in times of crisis. She sensed from his appearance there was something of a military background – knew it even. Though years had passed, the dark hair was still close-cropped, and the well-defined blue eyes still displayed a teasing, mysterious quality, visible even in the half-light of the lecture theatre. She smiled to herself.

She recalled his name was Mike Hansen.

Mike laughed for a second time in as many minutes as Champion recited an anecdote by the then mayor that the original bakery fire could have been "pissed out by a woman". He had heard the same joke before, only from a different person and in very different circumstances.

He wondered where Kit Masterson really got his material.

What had started as a strident diatribe against conspirators of ill intent, be they Englishmen or foreigner, had moved on to an in-depth discussion of the practical problems of tackling the blaze itself. The images in the slideshow presented a clear picture of mass panic, widespread destruction. At school he had learned the same story. Even the smallest mistake could lead to a catastrophe. A negligent business owner. A badly planned city layout.

Looking at the scale of the blaze now, it seemed hard to believe that it hadn't been a terrorist attack.

Champion took a further sip of water and waited for the next image to come up.

"While many of London's terrified citizens could be excused for concentrating their efforts on self-interest and preservation, we are most fortunate to the endeavours of many for their own hurried correspondence, which today offers us a deeply insightful window into this drastic series of events, thus helping us to truly understand what was going through the minds of the people whose lives were being brought to ashes along with their property. To none are we more indebted than to this man." He pointed at the famous wigged, dandy-esque face of Samuel Pepys, whose portrait now appeared on the screen.

"Along, perhaps, with that of Anne Frank, Pepys's diary is without question one of the most famous first-hand documentary accounts of a major historical event, providing a contemporary, rich and often brutally frank insight into the trials and tribulations that beset the people living in London at that time. For Pepys and his contemporaries, the fire posed a very real terror.

"One that threatened to destroy the city they knew and loved, and possibly even the nation as they knew it."

The Anjouvin left the stairway at a far easier pace than he'd climbed it and re-emerged on to Monument Street at ground level. The night air was cooler than it had been. The two bars to the west had quietened considerably; had it not been for the internal lights, it would no longer have been clear whether they were still open.

He moved slowly past the public toilets and loitered outside the building on the corner of Monument Street and Pudding Lane, his attention firmly on the walls. A plaque had been erected on the side of Faryners House, dated 1986.

He knew that at one time something far older had existed there.

Returning to the Monument, he circled it slowly, checking his watch for the first time since leaving the stairwell. Like the plaque he had just read on the nearby building, two inscriptions had been engraved into the north and south sides, cataloguing the tale of how the catastrophe began and was dealt with, while a third above the entrance on the east side described the intricate process of the Monument's own creation. Looking up from the base, the epic column reminiscent of a pillar from a Greek temple, he recalled that at an earlier time a church had stood on the site.

The first notable victim of a great tragedy.

Allowing himself a moment to admire the architecture, his focus turned to the top of the column. It had been built to a height of precisely 202 feet, the exact distance of the Monument from where the tragedy struck. At the very summit, visible only from further away, was a gilded metal urn.

Representing fire.

"Declarations of faith," Champion explained, "may have been wide reaching and long lasting at the time of the fire, but within eleven years of the destruction of the city, the Lord Mayor and his cronies were at last able to claim responsibility for something far brighter. The Monument located at the site of old St Margaret's Church at Fish Street Hill is famous for many reasons." He clicked the mouse and the picture of Pepys was replaced by one of the Monument as it had appeared in the early 1700s. "This famous singular Doric column with its representation of destruction may have been erected as an acknowledgement of loss, but, just like others by the same designer, it also represented something far greater – rebirth. The inscriptions confirm that there were actually two sides to the fire. It is interesting to know that in Wren's initial design, at the top would have been a phoenix – depicting rebirth from ashes. While the statue itself never saw the light of day, in truth, Wren's phoenix would soon become visible all around him. It survives to this day." The image on the screen changed again, now showing photographs of the present city, notably St Paul's Cathedral. "If the great tragedy that befell the city really was meant by permission of heaven, by the turn of the next decade, so it would appear, hell had at last been quietened. And the light of heaven was ready to shine once more over the city."

The lecture theatre broke into applause and the houselights came on. Mike grinned with quiet satisfaction as Champion drained his water glass and spoke once more into the microphone.

"Ladies and gentlemen, it is my pleasure to welcome you all this evening to Her Majesty's Tower of London to launch the Tower's autumn lecture program. Over the course of the next hour you will all be welcome to join me on a guided tour of the building next door, which will include the Jewel House and an opportunity to observe the famous Ceremony of the Keys – an English institution that, so we believe, remains unbroken right back to the days of the building's founders." His words brought about further applause. "If you could all make your way to the aisles, we shall start the tour and continue the lecture afterwards."

***

The Anjouvin raised an eyebrow, suddenly distracted. He knew that the emergence of people from the bar to the north-west was always likely, but under the circumstances he still found it unsettling. Three men had emerged, possibly drunk.

He knew if they stayed where they were, they would soon receive the shock of their lives.

He checked his watch for the umpteenth time, his mind counting down the seconds. As they reached single digits, he headed for the north side, his focus once more on the Latin inscription. While he knew the words would mean little to the typical passer-by, the engraving told a familiar story. Horror raining down on an old city, the like of which would never be repeated.

Could never.

He checked his watch again. Five seconds. Four.

Taking a deep breath, he walked round to the west side, pulling his sleeve back down as his watch confirmed the hour.

Exactly 202 feet away from the Monument, a fire was seen coming from the site where there had once been a bakery in Pudding Lane.

3

Somewhere in Suffolk

The call went out at 21:03. Precisely ten people heard it. Throughout history it had meant only one thing.

And it was rarely good!

To the residents of the private, circular-shaped estate in the village of Charlestown, its purpose was self-explanatory. Like a ringing bell at a fire station, its significance was relevant only to those who were on duty.

In the case of the residents of the twelve Tudor-style houses, there was never a time to be off duty.

As those currently inside the houses received the message, outside, the leafy courtyard retained its usual façade of calm and tranquillity. Even in the busy periods, it was never the liveliest of areas. Most of the comings and goings were coordinated as single events, often involving a people-carrying transit vehicle. On occasions when the driveways were occupied, motors ranging from modest hatchbacks to luxury sports cars and 4x4s, it was never obvious whether the homeowners were in. Should an inquisitive onlooker have witnessed one of the handsome, well-built occupants carrying out routine tasks around their properties, it was unlikely they would learn anything of significance. For those familiar with the area, a little knowledge went a long way.

Behind the calm exterior, a different story was already well under way.

One by one, with military efficiency, male residents from ten of the twelve houses made their way across the picturesque manicured lawns and through the heavy stretch of ancient woodland that adjoined them at the rear. As always they made their way in single file, the pace set by the first out, the rest following at intervals of around ten metres. Just like when out on manoeuvres, the reason was more of precaution than fitness. Should one man go to ground, a victim of a surprise attack, at least the effects of the attack would be limited.

Never in their history had an entire unit been taken out in one movement.

Once the first of the ten had made his way across the acre-wide area of woodland, following a muddy footpath that required stepping over a wooden stile, he then moved through a second area of open field in the direction of an isolated building that from the path appeared non-accessible to motor vehicles. Despite the clear presence of lights shining through the windows on the ground floor, he knew that nothing about their arrival would attract attention. Even if they were witnessed by those already frequenting the building, it mattered not; those already present had run the same paths many times and in similar numbers. If one were to make eye contact, there was unlikely to be any significant acknowledgement; a half-hearted salute at best, maybe just a thumbs-up.

The only thing guaranteed was the raising of pint glasses when the job was done.

As the leader of the ten approached the ancient building, its purpose clearly identified by its external signs and gable as a 17th-century coaching inn, he took a detour towards a quiet area at the rear, finding a remote, original doorway that opened without the need of a key. Taking the doorway into what, at first sight, appeared to be a lightless enclosure, the new arrivals descended the dusty stone steps into a typical storage area cluttered with beer kegs and other sundry items one would immediately associate with a pub. Should an outsider have stumbled upon the room by chance, there was no reason for them to view the tired, run-down draughty cellar as anything other than it outwardly appeared.

Yet within this otherwise typical cellar was something that defied explanation – something those familiar with the building knew only too well offered the greatest clue to their true identity. While three surrounding walls were heavy in soot and cobwebs and clearly provided an essential part of the building's foundations, the fourth inexplicably opened, offering access into something that would seem impossible to exist in such a location. In stark contrast to the dark pub-like clutter, this previously hidden room was brightly illuminated by a highly sophisticated lighting system. Several splashes of colour, images – some moving, some not – seemingly floated against a clear white backdrop like a semi-translucent projector screen. Flanking the centre of the room, where the lighting was at its brightest, an array of telephones and computers occupied a series of desks along with other high-tech equipment of less easily identifiable purpose. Even to an outsider, the focus was clearly military.

But in what capacity only one clue existed.

Located at the centre of the room, a circular table was currently not in use. In contrast to the whiteness of the walls, the tabletop was decorated with the same forestry animal portrayed in the image that was hanging from the freestanding pole outside the inn, inlaid in an almost three-dimensional design against an archery board-style backdrop of twelve equal green and white colourings. There was no name. Just a solitary symbol.

A white deer.

More specifically a hart.

Surrounding the symbol, within the equally spaced set of green and white colourings, could be found words handwritten in the style of a bygone time. The wooden chairs contained the same words, all of which were names. Though many had sat there, the names had never changed. They were the names of twelve knights. The original knights:

Thomas, Earl of Warwick
Ralph, Earl of Stafford
William, Earl of Salisbury
Roger, Earl of March
John, Baron Beauchamp
Sir Hugh de Courtenay

Sir Miles Stapleton
Jean de Grailly, Captal de Buch
Sir Richard Fitz-Simon
Sir Henry Eam
Henry of Grosmont, Earl of Lancaster

Of the twelve, one seat was distinctly more grandiose, more revered than the others. Like the eleven, it belonged only to one man: historically the king's commander in the field. At this table he was known as Edward.

In history and legend, the Black Prince.

In the case of the men who sat there today, these were not their names of birth but the names of an older group. A group in whose footsteps they followed.

An ancient order whose origins were shrouded in secrecy.

Entering the room, the ten made their way directly to their seats. According to their birth certificates and military records, their names were as follows:

Captain Robert 'Sandy' Sanders
Captain Marcus 'Trev' Wilcox
Captain Anthony 'The Chief' Pentland
Captain Jack 'Jackie' Dawson
Captain Tommy 'The Caramel Barrel' Ward
Captain Danny 'Fever' Pugh
Captain Andrew 'AC' Chambers
Captain Jamal 'Jay' Iqbal
Captain Kristoffa 'KKR' Rawlins
Captain Sean 'Spiky' Cummins

Two members of the full group of twelve were missing:
Captain Michael 'The Honey Badger' Hansen.
And the man who now sat in the seat once occupied by the Black Prince.
Captain Christopher (Kit) 'TBP' Masterson.

While the king's leader in the field was unavoidably absent, the man whose status in the eyes of the assembled group equalled that of a king looked on with unwavering concentration as the ten took their seats. Unlike the kings of old attired in the trimmings of ancient regalia, his appearance was low key, his manner and suited appearance nevertheless confirming his position to be among the most important of the important. Instead of a crown or a beret of officer status, his head was bare, revealing the same impeccable crew cut of once-brown hair that had gone silver with time and experience. Yet while age had taken its toll on his hair and forehead, there were other things it had blessed him with – most notably experience. If there were anyone better placed to lead this strange group, he had probably already done so. Throughout history, this man had no name. If any dared utter it, they knew the consequences. In honour of the order, he could be addressed as Mr White.

The twelve called him sire.

"Reports during the last half hour indicate that the intelligence we recently received about the preparation of an undefined threat has unfortunately now proven to be accurate; after the events of earlier today, this should be nothing new to anybody," the Director of the White Hart began. "The only surprise, if there is one, is the location. Within the last few minutes, further reports have emerged on the grapevine of threats close to the river. The prime minister has been alerted. It is time for us to move out."

Seated in between the two empty seats, the brown-haired Captain Sanders was the first to speak. "What do we know?" he asked calmly, a hard expression crossing his bearded face. In the absence of Masterson, he was the most senior man on parade.

"Right now, not a lot. At precisely 21:00 hours, a fire broke out at a building close to the Great Fire Monument near Pudding Lane. In the interests of public safety, the top brass and the suits are already reporting it as a gas explosion – though I fear for their chances of maintaining that stance for much longer." The Director circled the table slowly.

"Unfortunately, the location and the date are particularly against them. The location, so the historians tell me, is on the site of the same bakery where over three hundred and fifty years ago the greatest tragedy in the city's history began. And tonight being the anniversary of the beginning of the Great Fire, it's unlikely to be long before links start to be drawn and questions asked."

Around the round table, questions were already being prepared.

"I'm guessing none of this has made the news channels?" the blond-haired Captain Wilcox asked, seated next up from Sanders. "Being honest, I haven't been watching."

"You have a phone, don't you?" Captain Jamal Iqbal said, a ghost of a grin crossing his handsome face that as usual was flanked by smart, designer facial hair. "Or maybe you only use it for Tinder."

As usual, Mr White let the humour slide. "Not yet, but inevitably it will only be a matter of time before the media does get on to it. The location and the event are famous the world over. Sky is already commentating on reports of an explosion; it's unlikely to be long before they get a visual. From that perspective, there's no reason to suggest it's anything more than a minor repeat of the 2011 riots."

"How about eyewitness reports?" Iqbal spoke up again, his tone more serious than before. "Presumably if it is a gas leak, the signs of the fire would be consistent with burning gas."

"Interesting point." Mr White brushed his index finger against his nine-inch tablet and the pictures on the semi-translucent screen to the east of the round table instantly changed. "Despite the strength of the blaze, no reports of an actual explosion have been reported, nor was anyone seen in the vicinity of the building at the time. There were some indications from the nearby establishments that the ground shook, but nothing that can presently be confirmed. The fire service, of course, has wasted little time in making their way to the scene."

"So it's out?" Sanders asked.

"No. Worse still it seems to be spreading. No victims – only empty buildings. The main concern of our friends in the local authorities at the present time is to ensure no harm comes to the Monument."

The ten watched as the pictures continued to change. What began as a series of still photographs was replaced by video footage, possibly a live streaming, of several buildings ablaze in the heart of the city. As the footage played out, none among them failed to recognise the 202-foot-high monument located close to Monument Tube station.

So far the fire was yet to touch it.

Sanders was first to break the silence. "Any leads?"

Mr White tapped quickly at his tablet and the pictures changed again. The location was clearly the same but before the fire – the calm before the storm. As the clock at the bottom of the screen reached 21:00, a raging inferno erupted from one of the buildings, spreading quickly along the north side of the street.

The images from the cameras indicated that the locality had been largely deserted.

"Here." Mr White paused the footage and began to zoom in. The area close to the bottom of Pudding Lane was uninhabited, the headlights of passing cars driving along Lower Thames Street offering a regular supplement to the illumination from the streetlights. Further north, the area around the public toilets was also deserted; the only obvious signs of life were further west. There were two bars on the corners of Monument Street and Fish Street Hill; the sudden blaze had already caught the attention of their patrons; interestingly the glass of their windows was still intact.

Even more of interest, so were those of the adjoining building.

The Director of the White Hart rolled the footage on slightly, stopping again and zooming in further. A solitary figure was walking across the west side of the Monument, his wiry frame deep in shadow. The man appeared to look briefly at the blaze before disappearing south along Fish Street Hill.

"Well, at least one person saw everything." Iqbal's eyes were on the mysterious tourist. As best he could tell, the man had played no part in starting the blaze.

Wilcox was also curious, a hostile scowl crossing his unshaven face. "I don't suppose we have footage to suggest why he was hiding behind the Monument?"

"Actually, it seems our man was paying particularly close attention to the inscription on the north side as the fire began, which is a little surprising, as it's written in Latin." Mr White brought up a second window of footage, split screen. "As Phil has already reminded me, there are English translations found there. Clearly our man didn't need them."

Jay bit his lip, his curiosity piqued. "I'm guessing we already have an ID."

The pictures changed again. A profile photo, accompanied by several others.

"Bizante Sergio Patrice Blanco." Mr White read the caption aloud as it appeared on the screen. "Known in certain circles as the Anjouvin. His biggest claim to fame was for playing a very minor role in the French Connection. However, of more recent intrigue, he's Fabien Randek's uncle."

The revelation left a sore spot, especially for Sanders and Iqbal. Both vividly recalled chasing Randek along the River Seine after his botched escape from the Musée d'Orsay six months earlier.

"I'm guessing this can't be a coincidence?" Sanders posed.

Mr White touched his tablet and the picture of Blanco disappeared. "Gentlemen, as we've discussed many times in the last six months, sightings of Randek have been rare to say the least. There's plenty of conjecture, but that's usually when the trail goes cold. He was apparently seen in Bordeaux within twenty-four hours of the business in Paris; the most recent sighting was Goa. I've heard a rumour that he recently attended the funeral of his sister's boyfriend."

"So Payet is dead?" Sanders asked.

"Official confirmation unfortunately has been almost impossible to come by – which is rare, even for us. Needless to say, the Foreign Secretary has enough on his plate without dealing with the cock-ups of his predecessor." The Director took a breath, recalling in his mind the challenges of six months earlier and the mental scars it had left on his men. A terror attack in Scotland, another at Covent Garden, the curtain coming down in Paris. Even now, a full explanation for what had secretly been dubbed the Bordeaux Connection was still to be found.

"But there was a funeral?" Jay pressed.

"Our sources tell me there was a service, although precise details are sketchy to say the least. Since being captured after that nasty business in Paris, Payet was never let out of solitary confinement. Off the record, it's doubtful he ever saw the sun again. If he did die, he took his own life and, if so, he did it recently. As I'm sure you'll appreciate, his family would have received no telegram in the post."

"So the funeral was purely symbolic?"

"I've heard rumours of a cremation and a parcel being sent to the residence of his late grandparents, who hail from near Crécy – ironic, all things considered. If there is any truth in the rumours, it certainly wasn't us who sent the package. Nor do we endorse such tomfoolery."

Sanders was almost lost for words. "You suggest a conspiracy?"

"I suggest nothing. Nor does it do any good to consider anything except the known facts. A fire is raging in London on the anniversary of the city's most famous disaster and the man's girlfriend's uncle was recently seen near the site."

"Reading inscriptions in Latin?" Jay posed.

"Who is this Anjouvin?" Pentland spoke for the first time, his soft features distorted by an expression of intense interest. "As far as I remember, his name wasn't mentioned six months ago."

"If he was there, he was probably watching from the sidelines," Sanders answered. "I certainly never shot at him."

"Nor did Mike or Kit," Jay added. "Remember, Kit never forgets a face."

"I assure you, none of you fired at him," Mr White confirmed. "Until recently, MI6 were beginning to think he'd met his maker. And not at their hands either. For the last five years he seems to have fallen off the face of the earth."

"Any history with us?" Wilcox asked.

"Nothing that would get the Black Prince excited. Or even Beauchamp for that matter," he said of the bearded Tommy Ward, who smiled on hearing his codename. "His claims to fame till now have predominantly been local to Marseille. And even then rarely so antagonistic."

"Why the Anjouvin?" Jay asked. "A long way from Marseille."

"In truth, we're back to dealing with hearsay. I've heard some rumours; again nothing that would stand up in court. Like most of his family there are cousins from the Angers region, but none of particular significance for us. Most of them are respected art dealers. As far as I'm aware, there's little relevance to the modern day."

"How about Randek?" Sanders pushed.

"Randek was the son of the man's late brother; incidentally he had no such nickname. Other than the attacks earlier this year, as far as I'm aware, Randek and Payet have no record of misdemeanours north of Aquitaine."

"You make it sound so medieval. Is that important?" Wilcox asked.

"Not necessarily, but the family lineage is far from modern. The Angers line goes back a long way; rumour has it there's even royal blood in there. Not that it does them much good now."

"Except in their own heads." Jay raised his eyebrows wryly.

"The business with Payet, if confirmed, could throw some light on things here. Assuming he's really dead, the appearance of Blanco is unlikely to be a coincidence. If Payet's ashes were sent back to France, the possibility can't be ruled out that the attacks tonight are in some way connected. Revenge would be a clear motive."

"Why Monument?" Pentland asked. "The bakery site is now just a bank. Or was, anyway."

"Nevertheless, it is the site and today is the anniversary," Mr White confirmed. "We don't exactly need to take Randek in for questioning to know he'd quite happily see the city burn to the ground a second time. Even if he has no involvement tonight, he clearly has no love for us."

Jay grimaced, his eyes returning to the semi-translucent screen. Throughout the briefing, footage of the blaze had continued, along with reruns of the start. Blanco's appearance confused him.

"Let's assume – as we suspect – that this isn't an accident. We've been briefed all day about a potential threat. Is this flesh to the bones, or are we talking something from left field?"

Mr White pressed his index finger against his tablet and the semi-translucent screen disappeared.

"Perhaps when the sparkies have managed to put out these fires, we'll be able to figure out what in God's name we're dealing with."

With trademark precision, the ten highly trained operatives boarded the camouflaged military-style helicopter that had been hovering over the open greenery for the last twenty seconds. As usual, its arrival had been achieved with impeccable timing. If one of the inn's regulars had seen or heard the double-bladed helicopter arrive suddenly and loiter briefly, its blades kicking up a minor dust storm that swept across the nearby car park, none among them would have posed further questions. Even if the inn's patrons were unfamiliar with the exact model, chances were they'd travelled aboard one of its predecessors.

Standing at the front of the cargo hold, the Director of the White Hart watched with a hard expression as the doors closed and the helicopter rose swiftly into the air. As soon as it had reached a safe height, the roofs of local buildings fading into the distance as the pilot followed a course over the surrounding woodland, he removed a second, smaller electronic tablet from his jacket pocket and a second semi-translucent screen emerged against the fuselage. Once again the images revealed scenes of utter chaos: a blazing inferno that was becoming ever more extensive.

In less than twelve minutes the entire street had become engulfed in flames.

The Director brought up a second screen carrying a video link; the recipient was an attractive, impeccably made up and suntanned woman with jet-black hair done up in a ponytail.

"Maria, what's the latest on Masterson?"

"GPS places him at Covent Garden. Apparently the theatre."

An ironic location, all things considered. "Get in contact as soon as you can. If we're lucky, he'll be there when we arrive."

"Understood. The PM's secretary has already been on the line. We've got a clear line guaranteed the moment you set down."

"By which time, we might actually have something to tell her. I want every CCTV camera in the city searched to get a trace on Blanco. And when you can, also get in touch with our newest member."

4

The Tower of London, 21:14

The noise of the fires hadn't been audible inside the auditorium. Even in the areas surrounding the Tower there was little indication anything was amiss. A small gathering of tourists loitered near the benches close to the information signs overlooking what was once the moat; most of the walkways on the riverside were now off-limits, the gates locked. Further afield, the piers were deserted; those still out ambling the walkways, most of them heading in the direction of one of the trendy evening spots at St Katharine Docks, were doing so in the usual manner, seemingly unaware of the breaking news. As always, illumination of the area came primarily from an array of ground-level floodlights, the majority of which were pointed directly at the famous structure in front of them.

Just as it had done a thousand years ago, the Tower dominated the site like a king holding court.

Mike Hansen moved swiftly through the excitable crowd as he departed the lecture theatre and accelerated into a relaxed jog once outside. The visitor centre had been empty except for some of the Tower staff and those attending the lecture; the nearby food vendors whose fare he'd personally sampled a year earlier were now closed for the day, the shutters down, the employees and queues departed.

Champion was leading the crowd towards the main entrance to the Tower, assuming the role of a jocular tour guide. He smiled at two on-duty staff members as the party approached the remains of the 13th-century Lion Tower, stopping briefly for a chat.

Mike slowed to a walk as one of the staff members asked to check his rucksack. Keeping the straps where they were, he removed his wallet from the left pocket of his jeans and flashed a security card. Unlike his driving licence, the name read Matthew Paris, the year of his birth ten months later than the true date. After checking the card, the guard allowed him access.

Mike caught up with Champion. "Uncle Dave."

Champion's face beamed on seeing him. "Mike Hansen, you old rascal. How lovely to see you."

"For a moment, I thought I'd have to miss you." The pair shook hands; under the circumstances Mike decided against a hug. "I forgot how amazing this place looks at night."

"Far more so to us than to any of its famous residents, I'm quite sure." Champion released his hand. "Though I have no doubt that prison life under the light of its fiery torches would have been an extremely intimidating experience.

In a way, I've always thought it's one of history's strangest paradoxes, how the mighty edifices somehow seem to take on a life of their own under modern illumination."

"Least we don't have to put up with the smells!" Mike smiled as they headed for the barbican-style Middle Tower, preparing to cross the bridge over the now-empty moat. "I'll never forget the last time I came here. One of the Beefeaters made a joke that when the tide came in, it took the sewage all the way to Normandy."

The professor laughed cheerfully. "Quite inaccurate, though most entertaining nonetheless. Quite a skill it is for any man to accurately follow the tides, but I've always thought it a much greater challenge to be a Yeoman Warder. It takes a certain kind of mettle to be charming to those who crave it, humorous to those who enjoy it, obedient to those who command it and dominant over those who require it." He looked around, remembering his words were capable of being overheard. "Then again, of course, you know more about that sort of thing than me."

Emily Fletcher had been among the last to leave the auditorium. She'd smiled her approval at Champion from a distance before having a chat with the man in charge of the projector.

The man at the back had already disappeared with the crowds.

She locked the Welcome Centre after switching off the lights in reception, knowing no one else would enter it before morning. The lecture party had moved on, the majority following the lecturer towards the bridge.

Lagging behind, she started to run.

Mike checked his iPhone as he walked, taking advantage of the conversation with his uncle being joined by an oriental couple, clearly excited by their visit. Also in his pocket, his specially designed White Hart satellite phone had emitted a short, sharp buzzing sound; a solitary LED flashed amber. There were five colours in total: green, yellow, amber, red and purple, all indicating various levels of terror alert. He was used to amber, but red and purple were the trouble colours. He hadn't seen either for over six months.

He prayed that situation wouldn't change in a hurry.

The amber light wasn't surprising. Since leaving Whitehall an hour earlier, rumours that had been spreading about a possible threat had seemingly quietened. Using his satellite phone to log in to the White Hart secure network, he saw there were no messages other than those he would normally expect. Pulling up the GPS navigation system, he saw a series of white dots somewhere in Suffolk, confirming most of the knights were together. Kit Masterson was in London, inside the Royal Opera House; he assumed Sharon was on his mind more than the opera. A circular amber dot was flashing less than a mile away – north of the river, close to the Monument.

Feeling a nudge in his back, he closed his phone.

"Of course, one of the most common inaccuracies about the Great Fire is that it eradicated the Great Plague," Champion said, taking the conversation off at a tangent. "The plague itself, records now clearly show, began to subside as early as February, almost seven months before the fire. Furthermore, most of the later cases involving the Great Plague occurred in the suburbs. The fire, as we all very well know, was only in the city itself."

"Now there's a fact I never did know," an English woman said in a humoured tone. "How come you never mentioned that in any of your lectures?"

Glancing to his left, Mike noticed that the woman he'd previously seen in the row in front of him had made it quickly to the front of the crowd, her mission clearly one of duty as much as being sociable. Her made-up cheeks were dimpled on both sides, complementing the warmth of her smile that was more than a little affected by recent shortness of breath. At around five feet six she compared to most women he knew, with a weight that was neither thin nor fat, and a face and complexion that could be considered naturally pretty without the need for heavy layers of make-up. Without her glasses, her hazel eyes appeared extra bright, intensified by her raven-coloured hair that seemed to possess an ironic connection with the building they were about to enter. He smiled at her as she looked him in the eye inquisitively, almost certainly asking the same question mentally as he did of her.

Where do I know you from?

"Just because one chooses not to retain knowledge does not mean it was never there." Champion beamed in his response. "Though fortunately for you, Miss Fletcher, I do not recall the question was ever on any exam in recent years."

The woman laughed. "It's a shame more of your exams weren't on tonight's topic. I think I'd have aced it."

"A shame indeed; though I do recall it has made an appearance in more recent years. Not that there is much room for improvement on a first class honours degree."

"Wish the same could be said of a 2:2." Mike smiled wryly, replacing his satphone in his pocket and using the opportunity to enter the conversation. "Weren't you in my class at Nottingham?"

"Actually I think it was Loughborough. I dropped out at the end of my fresher year." She looked at him, her stare questioning and possibly bordering on a point beyond friendliness. "I was never cut out to be a sports scientist."

"I guess that explains why you're currently out of breath." Mike gave her a cocky smile. "So presumably after leaving Lufs, you did history at Nottingham?"

"You're very perceptive. It was there that I met this amazing gentleman."

Champion dismissed her comment.

"So, judging by your arrogance, I'm guessing you think you're in better shape?"

Mike's smile widened. "Well, I kinda have no choice, it's in my job description. I guess there's less call for it as assistant curator of the Tower."

She stared at him, suddenly curious. "How do you know my job?"

"Even sports scientists know how to read an ID tag."

***

Champion brought proceedings to a halt as they crossed the moat, stopping near the Byward Tower. Close to the walls, the imposing stonework of the identical barbican-style secondary entrance seemed to take on new heights as the shadows of the surrounding crowd moved beneath the lights.

"Ladies and gentlemen, once again may I offer you a warm welcome to Her Majesty's Tower of London to mark the start of the autumn lecture programme," Champion began. "In a few moments, we will continue our tour along Water Lane, where we will be granted rare and privileged access to the famous Inner Ward. Now, if you would like to follow me."

The walk resumed, Champion leading. He spoke briefly to those close to him as they made their way along Water Lane, the eerie glow of the nearby wall lights providing a convincing illusion of lanterns from a bygone time. He led them past the entrance to St Thomas's Tower, stopping briefly for a talk close to Traitors' Gate before passing the thick round walls of the Wakefield Tower, heading for Henry III's Watergate.

It was 21:18 and Mike realised they were getting a tour first.

Emily walked alongside him, clearly captivated. "So what exactly happened to you? I'm guessing you weren't cut out for sports science either if you also ended up at Nottingham?"

"Actually, I did graduate. I did a history master's at Nottingham part time after I joined the forces."

"There much call for historians in the forces?"

A wry smile. "Actually, my motivation was kinda two-fold."

"Meaning?"

Champion smiled as he rejoined the conversation. "I think what the old boy is trying to say, Miss Fletcher, is that he probably wouldn't have done so had his boring old uncle not nagged him into doing it in the first place."

5

Covent Garden, London,
21:19

Kit Masterson hadn't expected to be called into action that evening. After the briefing he'd received from the Director earlier in the day, he knew that an imminent terrorist attack somewhere in the UK was a possibility, but he'd heard the same threats before, and they were usually false alarms. A casual discussion between minor terror suspects, often showing up in the form of vague, unconfirmed cryptic messages intercepted by an intelligence operative at GCHQ headquarters in Cheltenham, where the eyes and ears of the UK had existed since before he was born, were usually taken care of without the need for it to reach the top.

As the captain in the field of the White Hart, he was at the top of the top.

In practice there was no such thing as a day off. As one of twelve field operatives of the nation's most secretive elite military organisation – if not the entire world's – social time was virtually non-existent, particularly at a time when the terror threat was continuously high. He remembered the Director had warned him on his arrival that to join the White Hart demanded a responsibility to carry the burden of the nation on his shoulders. Even to this day he remembered his exact response.

It's a small price to pay for being the best.

The nearest thing he'd had to a day off in what seemed like months had begun at 14:00 at Trafalgar Square. It had started with a leisurely stroll around the National Gallery, admiring the masterpieces. By 17:00 he had moved on to Leicester Square and dinner in one of the finer pubs. He remembered spending much of his previous life in the same place, only now with a different person. As usual she looked beautiful, the striking elegance of her subtle turquoise dress and the bright sparkle of her lovely eyes every bit the perfect prelude for an evening of opera followed by a night at the Ritz, courtesy of the firm.

As on his last trip to Leicester Square, he never did get round to ordering dessert.

At 21:25 he was sitting in a padded seat, watching what appeared to be a large Russian singing about ecstasy. It wasn't his first trip to the Royal Opera House at Covent Garden. However, it was his first since the reopening.

The first since the bomb went off.

Seated in a private four-seater box on the first tier, his attention was drawn away from the stage to a similar box on the opposite side. Unlike his own, all of the seats were occupied; two banks of two, none of which were permanently attached to the floor. The door behind was closed, allowing no light to enter from the corridors. Removing his high-powered, high-spec opera glasses from his inside pocket, he adjusted the settings of the lenses to obtain an X-ray vision of everything around him, concentrating on the area behind the unlit box.

Unlike Mike Hansen's experience six months earlier, he saw no sign of liquid explosives.

A soft touch from his left returned him to the moment. While six months earlier his reward for a morning's sleuthing in the Cabinet Office on Whitehall had been floor seats near the back with Captain Hansen, tonight his reward was something far more appealing. A soothing fragrance of sweet perfume drifted softly from his fiancée's elegant neck, partially covered by long, silky and slightly curly chestnut hair that tonight complemented the natural radiance and softness of her delicate skin, which glowed softly in the diffused lighting. She smiled at Kit as she tenderly touched his hand, her eyes playfully spellbinding like a siren on a mission to entice a lost sailor into deep waters.

"We don't have to stay if you don't want to."

While Kit savoured the feeling of her calming touch on his hands, elsewhere he felt uneasy. Though his thick, dark brown hair, tonight styled to his usual flamboyant quiff, was as smart as ever, matching his tailor-made tuxedo that Jamal Iqbal once joked would make James Bond jealous, his eyes for once let him down. The usual look of self-assurance that had brought him time and again to the peak of performance was tonight plagued by doubt. He knew exactly what had caused it. Seventeen had died. All within sight of where he was currently sitting.

He was looking at the rebuilt shell of what six months earlier had been his first failure.

His only failure.

A sharp buzzing sensation vibrated through the right pocket of his smart trousers. Removing his unique White Hart standard operative satphone, he glanced at the screen, squinting slightly. A message showed up clearly.

He looked at his fiancée, allowing their hands to remain joined as long as possible.

She knew the change in his eyes was the only apology she would receive.

The Monument to the Great Fire was located in easy reach. According to the Maps app on his phone, the journey was typically eight minutes by car, eleven in current traffic. Despite being on the same side of the river, it was slower by Tube – seventeen minutes, not including getting to the station. Realistically that left only one option.

Sprint it.

The reports he'd read on logging in to the White Hart portable server via his satphone were as erratic as those he was hearing through the news apps. The first thing he'd noticed on the Sky News app was a report of a fire close to Monument. He remembered Mr White mentioning earlier that day that tonight was the anniversary of the Great Fire.

He had never believed in coincidences.

Taking the route south, he moved at speed along the Strand and east towards St Clement Danes. As he crossed the street, taking advantage of a fortunate break in the traffic, he felt a strange sense of déjà vu. It wasn't something he'd seen before but merely heard about – many times. The incident at the Royal Opera House six months ago had been chaotic; had it not been for Mike's intervention, Kit knew he might have been killed. While Everard Payet made his getaway, Kit had been forced to labour in the corridors, limping his way into the toilets to make contact with the Foreign Secretary. As Payet attempted to flee, it had been up to Mike to pursue.

He was following the exact same route Mike had done for Payet.

Safely across, he followed the Strand east, doing his best not to attract too much attention. The street was busy with traffic and pedestrians; it was London, and that was explanation enough. On passing Somerset House, he remembered Payet had caught a train from Temple; thanks to the timing of the arrival, he had boarded without Mike being able to follow.

Tonight Lady Luck was smiling. After taking the Underground at Temple, he alighted four stops later at Monument. In total, he'd been on the train six minutes.

Even before leaving the concourse, he was able to smell the smoke.

6

South of the River Thames,
21:22

The Anjouvin had been running since leaving the danger zone. Thirty-eight years in the business had been time enough to learn not to start running before the action started. Any idiot could look conspicuous if they allowed themselves to act in a guilty manner. In a city under constant surveillance, he knew it wouldn't take long before a connection was made.

The last thing he wanted to do was draw attention too soon.

The fire had begun exactly where he'd expected, the moment of ignition surprisingly quiet. The first sounds hadn't come until later, a secondary impact.

He surmised that the fire had probably caught a gas line.

The first people to appear had been the duty staff at Monument. Under orders from their superior, they had worked late that night.

It wasn't long till they had company.

The masses had congregated around the Monument; few dared get any closer to the building itself. Most had previously been in the bars on the west side; as the flames edged higher, more came from the north and east. Traffic had stopped intermittently on Lower Thames Street to the south; it was already crawling on Eastcheap. Most of the tailbacks were caused by astounded onlookers rather than any problems on the road.

He was pleased to see the curiosity of the sheep had already been piqued.

He disappeared south as the crowds began to swell, ignoring the temptation to take the Underground. The inevitable echo of sirens was already in full force by the time he reached King William Street; amidst the chaos he'd heard frantic voices claim an explosion had been detectable even on the Tube. On crossing London Bridge, what he saw was closer to normality; even in the course of a terror attack, Londoners still had homes to get to. South of the water, he stopped and stared northward.

Even from over a mile away, it was clear the fire was spreading.

By the time he reached City Hall, the cacophony of sirens had become almost deafening; there could have been hundreds on that side of the water alone. On entering Potters Fields Park, the number seemed to have doubled again; strangely, the roads were quiet.

A black cab was parked just off Potters Fields, its yellow sign unilluminated. He got into the back seat nevertheless.

Randek was seated behind the wheel alongside François.

"I must say this was hardly what I expected," Blanco began on entering the car. "Where on earth did you get it?"

"Vehicles such as this are easy enough to acquire if you know where to look.

Under the circumstances, I thought its use might avoid suspicion." Randek smiled, a light air of quiet humour pervading. "You might say I took your advice for once."

"The best way to get lost is in a crowd, you mean?" The Anjouvin considered his recent journey. Only by feigning dread and fear at the ensuing chaos did he know he was unlikely to arouse suspicion. "You're showing off new talents, Fabien. In truth, I'd expected something far more rudimentary."

"Let's not get carried away." François lit a cigarette. "The London taxis may be many in number and pleasing to the eye, but their supply is not easily exhaustible. Any idiot with a phone may obtain one from the correct vendor; however, few would be unusual enough to make the purchase in the first place. However, under the circumstances, I prefer them to the limousines." He observed Blanco via the rear-view mirror. "Were you seen?"

The Anjouvin stared back hard. "You expected me to cross a mile of London invisible?"

François blew smoke. "Let me rephrase the question."

"The fires, as we have already discussed, were started away from the enquiring gazes of passers-by. Had a curious policeman asked my name at the time, unless I'd been carrying the lighted matches in my hand, the only evidence he would have been able to find would have been circumstantial. However, I'm sure it won't take long before the powers that be ensure connections are made – even false ones."

"The plans, it would appear, you still understand better than I." The young art director's voice tinged with aggression. "Unless you would finally care to fill us in fully?"

"Answers to all your questions and more will be given in due course. For now, all you need to know is they are under control."

François remained unimpressed. "My uncle is a patient man, not to mention a careful one. Had this been planned a year earlier, perhaps he'd have been less concerned. There is too much at stake for fate to be left to its own devices. Tell me, where did you plant the bombs?"

"I myself planted nothing, nor did I ever mention anything about bombs. Accept the words I say. The plans are tight – the locations are secure."

"So there's more than one?" Randek pressed.

François's face remained stern. "The news channels are already reporting that the fire is spreading. It will not take long before a pattern emerges. Buildings will be searched; further mishaps avoided. Reassure my troubled mind. If you love my uncle, you will not wish him any further suffering."

"Your uncle's mind remains with his body. Whether it be troubled or not, it remains a long way from here. Hear me now and hear me well. The source of the fires will not be found. Even if there is a pattern."

François concentrated on his cigarette, troubled by Blanco's comment about never mentioning explosives or bombs. "The inferno that engulfed this city is legendary. Even a child can see the pattern. If we're not careful, the effects, though great, may be short lived."

"Who says we weren't careful?" The Anjouvin eyeballed François, his hard, yet noble features tinged with sweat. "By permission of heaven, a great catastrophe indeed washed over the old city. It is within the ruins of history itself, the truth remains hidden."

François glared back at him through the mirror in the sun visor, his handsome face growing ever more annoyed. "You reassure me with puzzles?"

"The sirens are becoming louder; it will not be long until they begin to close the roads." Randek breathed in the second-hand smoke, briefly regretting his promise to his sister he would kick the habit. "The surveillance footage may fail to catch a criminal in the act, but it will not take long for assumptions to be made. If the English can pass sentence without trial, they will do so willingly – especially if the only thing at stake is the life of a Frenchman. Let us move out. Whatever happens tonight in the old city will be something only its ghosts will see."

While the black cab with its unlit sign made its way on to Tooley Street, heading south-east away from the mayhem, over 300 miles away a man whose face was unknown in the City of Edinburgh cast a watchful eye over a far different outlook. As a child, he remembered becoming captivated with the incredible amalgamation of the manmade and the natural; tonight, his experienced mind was once again blown away by the sheer imposing magnificence of the legendary Arthur's Seat. According to tradition, it had once been the throne of a great king.

Today it offered a perfect view of the city.

Night was drawing in, the daylight fading into twilight. The last rays of sunlight would soon disappear into the western sky; darkness had already descended in the east. If there were stars above him, they were no longer visible; even outside the city, the cosmos offered little opposition to the glare of the electronic age.

Beyond the coastline, the sea was an oily pool, ironic considering the signs of great industry that existed there. Below it, the floodlights of the Hibernian football club's stadium stood out sharply against the surrounding darkness; he knew that there was a match against Hearts tonight – another irony, all things considered. To the west, the great castle cast a dramatic silhouette; like its famous neighbours below, its iconic shape was instantly identifiable, even without the aid of binoculars. There would be movement behind its walls, he mused. Subtle, but significant.

Like the repeating of history, an old rule was about to be replaced.

He looked out at the horizon, an icy chill now piercing his chest where before he'd sensed only heat. As the seconds passed, he felt sweat despite the cold, tightness where there was earlier calm. The quiet of the night was about to be disturbed for good.

Unlike the practice run six months earlier, tonight was the real thing.

* * *

Close to the famous museum north of the River Seine, two men whose faces were similarly unknown in the city alighted the Métro at Temple. While most of the passengers headed up to the concourse, some crossing to the next platform in preparation for boarding another train, the two tourists loitered briefly by a vending machine, acquiring extra sustenance. As the next train came and went, they disappeared through a door marked *Staff Only*.

The next time they would appear on surveillance, there would still be no evidence to connect them with the biggest robbery in the city's post-war history.

7

Inner Ward, The Tower of London, 21:29

Mike followed the crowd past the Lanthorn Tower, taking his time to explore the sights. Though he'd visited the Tower twice before, it felt different at night. The surrounding towers cast imposing shadows on the concrete, their eerie presence an ominous complement to the distant crowing of the ravens.

Emily was walking alongside him again; he'd noticed she'd come and gone several times in recent minutes.

"I can't believe he's your uncle!" she resumed as the tour took them between the south lawn and the New Armouries Restaurant, to the north of the White Tower. Champion was talking intermittently, mostly in private conversation. "You're actually being serious?"

Mike shrugged. "Either that or my parents have been lying to me all these years."

The assistant curator's face was a picture. Despite now accepting the family connection, she found it hard to believe both men had been cut from the same cloth. Throughout his career, Champion had lived up to his name: his clothes and posture were that of a dying breed, like a great poet or statesman who would eventually be glorified in prose and statue.

The man alongside her was different. Though he walked with a swagger of confidence and indifference, any hallmarks of distinction were far less developed.

Mike noticed she'd gone quiet. "I hope I haven't spoiled your perception of my uncle?"

Emily noticed he said that with a smile.

"It's okay, you don't have to explain. Everyone says it. Uncle Dave is this incredible uni professor, accolades galore, the walls of his study chock full of degrees and diplomas, invites to the palace. Then you dig a little deeper, and you see all these black sheep coming out of the closet."

"You have a farm in your bedroom?"

He smiled, quietly visualising the look on her face if she ever saw his unique bachelor pad in the quiet village of Charlestown. "Trust me, you wouldn't believe it if you saw my bedroom."

Emily's jaw dropped; Mike's smile widened.

"I'm sorry, do I keep offending you?"

"You can cut the sweet talk, mister. I've heard it all before. Even in the days I saw your uncle every day, I never really fell for any of that stuff."

"Wow, I almost don't know what to say; I never knew Uncle Dave had it in him." He paused until he was satisfied he was making a mark. "Nevertheless, I was right. You did expect something different."

"Take a look around you, Uncle Dave's nephew. We're currently walking around one of the most enigmatic buildings in England; the place where history was made and still is; where even to this day the secrets of the past continue to be revealed." She looked him in the eye. "You work in a place like here long enough, modern life runs out of things to surprise you with."

The cocky grin was now permanent. "In that case, you should definitely meet my brother."

Champion led them north and west, completing a full circuit of the White Tower. The brightness of the floodlights was especially brilliant on the north side, the iconic structure creating a familiar, yet imposing silhouette across the nearby greenery on which a monument had been erected in commemoration of ten executions, mainly of noble and royal status, that had occurred within the Tower's walls. Yeoman Warders and a detachment of the Queen's Guard marched efficiently from wall to wall, stopping intermittently as they went through their highly practised routine.

Mike watched on, both intrigued and respectful. Champion, meanwhile, resumed his lecture.

"Beyond the steps to your left, we come to this, the Bloody Tower, so renamed after the alleged deaths of the two princes here in 1483 – the name itself we believe to be a response to the building's immortalisation through the works of William Shakespeare." Champion led them past what remained of the Inmost Ward to where the Bloody Tower arched over the nearby walkway, the rounded stonework of the Wakefield Tower looming large alongside it. "Prior to that time, the tower had in fact been named the Garden Tower due to its close proximity to what was once the constable's garden. Much has changed since that time."

Mike waited till Champion stopped talking and spoke in Emily's ear. "You know, I read a book once that claimed the princes actually survived and their descendants still live somewhere up in Yorkshire. Was a pretty good read; I think the author's name was Davis."

"Interesting knowledge for a sports scientist." She turned to face him, her glasses once again shielding her eyes. "Wait, I'm sorry, you did say you did a history master's?"

"Among other things."

"You know, you never did answer my question about whether they have much call for historians in the forces." For once Champion's words passed her by. "So which of the services do you actually work for? I'm guessing from your brashness it might be the RAF."

"You got something against the RAF?"

"No, but I can tell I've hit a mark."

"Matter of fact, I'm officially Parachute Regiment. It's not technically the RAF, but usually involves a plane."

"So what do you do all day, jump out of planes?"

A wry smile. "Do you want the short answer or the long-winded one where I avoid the question?"

She rolled her eyes and walked away.

The scene Kit saw was one of utter chaos. Thick, billowing smoke obscured any view of the sky above the local buildings, causing traffic to stop and people to gather. Large groups packed the pavements on every side, where a sizeable police presence had been established close to the Monument.

Predictably it had done little to deter public interest.

A fire truck was blocking the way along Monument Street; five more were wedged in on the other side and a further six along Fish Street Hill. As best Kit could tell, at least five more had made their way along the west side of Monument Street; the front three of which were tackling the blaze at Faryners House.

Though all of the buildings on the north side were still burning, the tremendous heat causing his skin to perspire, he sensed it was starting to come under control.

Two duty police sergeants were trying to direct traffic away from the Monument. He thought about making contact with them and asking who was in charge, but immediately decided against it.

Tonight, he knew his task was to be neither seen nor heard.

Turning away from the fires, he continued back west along Monument Street. Once he was far enough away, he logged back in to the White Hart secure database with his specially assigned satphone and brought up the GPS tracking system.

A large red dot was flashing over Faryners House, identifying it as the core of the trouble zone. A series of white dots occupied different areas of the map. Several were moving quickly, approaching London from the north-east.

He knew that meant ten of the twelve were travelling at speed.

Only one was separate, also in London. Taking a moment to ensure he was alone, he closed the database and put through a call to Mike Hansen.

Champion completed a short talk on the Princes in the Tower and brought the tour back in the opposite direction, stopping outside the entrance to the Waterloo Block. Mike stood at the rear of the group, admiring the double-towered entrance.

Like most areas of the Tower, it was big enough to be a castle on its own.

"I am sure you all are already aware that the Tower's greatest claim to fame, in addition to being a noted place of incarceration, concerns the things that are kept here even now." Champion pointed to the Jewel House. "The building behind us, though redecorated in recent times, is the latest of a long line of homes for the Crown Jewels that have adorned the bodies of the monarchs since the seventeenth century. By special invitation of the governor, I'm delighted to welcome you all to view them. But, before we enter, I must remind you all that photography is strictly forbidden. So please also switch off your mobile phones."

8

Horse Guards Parade, 21:37

Putting out fires had never been an official part of the job description for members of the White Hart. In their earliest days, their role had been similar to that of a typical knight, especially on the battlefield.

Over the years, it had always adapted with the times. What began at Crécy, with the unleashing of the most advanced knightly unit of the age, had already achieved legendary status among the inner circles by the Tudor period. Like the Grail Knights, the Order of the Round Table had their own Arthurian connotations, even more so, depending on who was asked or told. When the Protectorate was over, the ashes of the once mighty order rose from the flames like a phoenix, the old aims and values re-established. Throughout history, the order had thrived in times of war. By the time Lawrence began his crusade over Arabia, only one significant difference was easily identifiable.

The machine gun really was mightier than both the pen and the sword.

Only with the outbreak of the Second World War did the role finally begin to come up to speed with that of the modern day. What had once taken place on the battlefield had given way to black ops; the tales of Percival to Higgins. Only once in their seven-hundred-year history had they been called upon to help put out a fire.

Coincidentally it had happened on that same night over 350 years earlier!

Less than two miles from where an inferno in Pudding Lane was once again wreaking havoc, the twin-engined military helicopter descended quickly over Horse Guards Parade. It was quiet out despite the warm weather, the surrounding floodlights causing heavy shadows as the chopper landed on the famous parade ground. Within seconds the doors opened, its occupants spreading out like wildfire in the direction of the palatial-style building to the north. On reaching the entrance, they disappeared inside.

By which time the helicopter was already heading west over St James's Park.

Inside the chateau-like building whose grand corridors and chambers had once been the setting of meetings of high importance between politicians and famed naval personnel, the image of the night differed significantly from that seen during the day. What in the day was commonly a hive of intense activity, employees of various ethnicities and pay grades carrying out duties ranging from admin to military, government relations to project management, their conversations littered with unique jargon that made sense only to those who worked inside the walls, at night was a picture of solitude. Along the corridors, every room was deserted, some locked, the dim glow of desk lamps or the patterns of screensavers the only lighting. Despite its historical significance as a site associated with national government, the Old Admiralty Building was no longer renowned for dealing with matters of imminent importance.

Tonight that was to the benefit of those charged with the task of catching those responsible for the fires.

Along one of the grand corridors, a number of aging but fully functional lifts from the building's heyday were maintained ready for use. Entering quickly, the ten military uniformed men and their suited leader waited with disciplined anticipation as the dated motors and cable mechanisms took them to the bottom level. As the doors opened to a pinging sound, the motors fell silent; even compared to the corridors above it was quiet. Gone was the noise of the local traffic: cars along Whitehall, the Mall or the roads around St James's Park; even the echoes of the Underground were few, so good was the insulation.

As the new arrivals left the lift, hurrying in formation along the passages of the subterranean complex, they came to a halt outside one of many doors that in appearance might have formed part of a cellar – an impression not entirely inaccurate.

Like the strange undercroft in Charlestown, no one seeing it could possibly have determined its true significance from the outside alone.

Behind the door, the interior of the room was unlike anything ever seen, or expected, in the building, be it night or day. As in the mysterious room below the Suffolk inn, the walls glowed from the reflected lights of futuristic technology and hummed with the collective sounds of the people they were spying on. A large round table, with historic features, was located precisely in the centre – differing only from the one in the room in Charlestown in the number of chairs. Instead of thirteen, designated solely for the field operatives and the king, as inspired by the knights of legend, today there were sixteen, three of which were already occupied.

One by a bearded individual in casual dress and another by a sharp-looking woman in her early thirties with jet-black hair done up in a ponytail; their names were Phil and Maria.

The third individual was far smarter, his crisply pressed suit matching that of the Director's. Once the Undersecretary of State at the Ministry of Defence, he was now Deputy Director of the White Hart.

His name was Ian Atkins.

Directly opposite the largest chair, its design resembling that of a throne from the medieval period, a large flat-screen television was set up for a videoconference. With everyone settled into their seats, the Director nodded at Phil to switch on the big screen. As the screen illuminated, a picture emerged of another table, this one plain and devoid of any heraldic markings, with a recently varnished, mirror-like surface at which was seated a middle-aged woman of firm, possibly aristocratic, features, looking back at him with a gaunt expression rather like a headmistress about to reprimand a pupil for poor punctuality. In truth, the Director knew the parallel, though not strictly accurate, was also not inaccurate. She was the only person to whom he was inferior. His only boss.

She was the Prime Minister of the United Kingdom.

"The fire at Faryners House is all but extinguished," the Director began, gripping the wooden armrests that had been touched by many before him, his gaze remaining focused on the screen despite the movements of his men. "One of our men is already at the scene; I expect to speak with him imminently. All of the fires have been in close proximity to the first building. With today being the anniversary of the Great Fire, the rationale for the choice of location seems obvious."

The prime minister's expression remained unchanged. "That may well be so, Director, but I fear that your confidence that the fire is under control may be misplaced. Downing Street received this message at 8:59 this evening. It ended at the exact moment the fire began."

The prime minister nodded at an unseen person off camera and an audio message played.

"My Dear Prime Minister,

"Here, by ye permission of heaven, hell will break loose on this godless city from the humble hearts of loyal redeemers, by ye hand of their agent Everard, who did willingly give his life and, on ye ruins of this place, declared the fact for which he was murdered, that he began this dreadful fire, the like of which is described and perpetuated on the neighbouring pillar."

The message ended abruptly. On screen, the prime minister sat quietly, her hands joined together in contemplation. Beneath the Old Admiralty Building, everyone sat in silence.

"That same message appeared on the original plaque at Faryners House," the bearded man of non-military appearance began, recognising the wording.

"It is. Only it's been contemporised," Deputy Director Ian Atkins added, from his seated position alongside Mr White. "Everard – that can only refer to one person."

"While I have always respected the fact in recent times there is much more to a prime minister's life than individual terror suspects, I fear, Prime Minister, you have not been entirely open with me. Nor for that matter have your colleagues." The Director spoke with clear purpose. "I know Payet is dead; what I don't know is how. Nor did I suspect it was already common knowledge."

"Everard Payet was found dead in his prison cell three weeks ago by one of his captors," the prime minister replied, her icy gaze becoming colder still, as though the temperature had been further lowered at the mention of that name. "His personal involvement in tonight's event clearly isn't possible."

"That may be so, but nor should one underestimate the importance of association. This man was caught on CCTV, loitering around the Monument at the exact moment the fire began." The Director pulled out his portable tablet and a semi-translucent screen appeared behind him, visible to the PM. The Director waited until he was certain the prime minister had obtained a clear picture of the man's face before continuing. "The man's name is Bizante Blanco – uncle of Fabien Randek. Whether Everard was alive tonight or not, the identity of the culprits confirms a clear familial link."

The Director rose to his feet, his fingers again moving quickly across his tablet, causing the pictures on the screen to change once more. Several faces appeared, ID shots; many had red Xs through their name.

"Six months ago, Fabien Randek and Everard Payet were two of only six survivors from an original group of eight who we believe to have been responsible for the attacks in Edinburgh, Covent Garden and subsequently a successful theft from the Musée d'Orsay," the Director resumed. "The other survivors also committed suicide in their cells; we know two of their names as Patrice Thuram and Jordan Petit. Prior to this, their only crimes seem to have been local to the city of their births. Only one evaded arrest." He looked seriously at the prime minister. "This really isn't the time to withhold secrets, Prime Minister. What happened to Payet?"

"The fate of Everard Payet is exactly as I have already told you. The man was found hanged – he'd been locked up alone. Since his extradition with the help of the French government, he never left prison in England."

Inwardly the Director sensed that wasn't the whole truth. "Be that the case or not, news of his death has clearly spread. My intelligence sources tell me that there was a funeral near his ancestral home in Crécy. If there was a leak, it certainly didn't come from us. Worse, and to the point, if there was a funeral, they had something to bury."

"If you're suggesting we deliberately set out to antagonise our enemies, then I assure you you're quite mistaken." Behind the unchanged façade, the PM was clearly livid. "I don't know what kind of people you're used to dealing with, Director. In my government we do things by the book."

"I assure you, Prime Minister, I was making no such claims directly. Nevertheless, be it by carelessness or intent, news of Payet's death has clearly spread. And the mention of his name and the presence of Blanco in close proximity to the danger zone itself tells a powerful story." He glanced at Phil before returning his gaze to the screen. "Ma'am, may I ask you to play the message again?"

Everyone listened quietly as the message was played again, during which time Phil made a second recording. The voice, though speaking clear English, had an obvious French twang.

"Any sign of voice recognition?" The Director turned to Phil.

"I can do some tests, see if we get a match," the IT specialist confirmed.

The Director nodded before returning his gaze to the prime minister. "The presence of Blanco should not be overlooked. If he was indeed responsible for sending the message, chances are it was pre-recorded." He brought up the video footage of Blanco at Monument on the floating screen behind him. "I suggest a lockdown on every road within a three-mile radius. Only by following the cameras will we be able to trace him."

"You are aware you're asking for the power to close every road in the busiest city in Europe?"

"The words of the recording fail to rule out the possibility more can come," the Director pressed, quietly praying he was wrong. "If that's the case, closing roads will be necessary anyway."

The PM watched the footage as she listened. "Do what you must, Director – you know what powers I give you. Even if he was in some way connected, from what I've just seen, he was unlikely to have been the guilty party. After all, I saw no detonator in his hand."

"Just because he doesn't light the fuse, Prime Minister, doesn't mean he is exonerated of guilt."

"You may dispense with the logistics lesson, Director." Her expression had become increasingly drawn. "As you've recently pointed out, the message clearly does not rule out the possibility of more of the same. Strangely nor did it contain any demands. Worse still, I'm also hearing of a second attack in Edinburgh."

That was news to the Director.

"How long until you can trace Blanco?"

"From the information we have at present, it's unlikely he's left the city. I'll set up communications with all the key players at the JIC; we already have access to the cameras. It might take some close attention. Right now I'd say the main problem is avoiding panic."

"My main problem, Director, is dealing with a national security breach – and I'm afraid your discussions with the JIC will have to wait until they're done with me. They're all on their way to COBRA now."

Mr White recognised the table from the famous briefing room at 70 Whitehall. "Very well. In the meantime, priority must go to finding Blanco and ensuring the safety of the surrounding area. As far as we're aware, the fire has not yet spread further afield. And even if that is their intention, things have changed since 1666. I have ten agents right here; another is already at the scene. If Blanco was indeed responsible, you can rest assured we will find him."

"Concern yourself first with your firefighting skills, Director. After that, spare anyone you can to help in Edinburgh!"

Within moments of the conference call ending, the double-bladed helicopter reappeared over Horse Guards and three of the ten made their way on board.

Captain Rawlins waited until Pentland and Pugh had boarded before removing his dark balaclava, his shaven head reflecting the glow of the overhead lights.

As before, a second semi-translucent screen appeared against the fuselage.

The Deputy Director's face appeared instantly. "The fire in Edinburgh appears to have begun in a small alleyway just off the High Street. From what Phil tells me, it was this same location where the original Great Fire of Edinburgh broke out in November 1824."

Rawlins raised an eyebrow. "Sounds like another copycat."

"Exactly. Incidentally, the opposite was true six months ago. It seems as though someone is trying to confuse us."

"Any leads?"

"CCTV footage is strange. At one point it shows a visitor in one of the shops earlier in the day; apparently the firm has been having problems with their electrics. Still to get positive ID."

To Rawlins that made perfect sense. "What are our orders?"

"We'll worry about that when you get there. Right now, let's just pray it's down to faulty wiring."

At the same time, the remaining seven departed the Old Admiralty Building through the front door leading on to Whitehall. A large 4x4 awaited their arrival, pulling away at high speed within seconds of them getting in.

Inside, Jamal Iqbal talked quietly with the Director via his Bluetooth headset before relaying the commands to the others. Their mission was to stop Blanco and the fires.

How they did so was entirely up to them.

9

Borough of Tower Hamlets, London, 21:38

The taxi pulled up just off Wapping Lane, close to the High Street. Taking Tower Bridge at rush hour would have been a significant risk; after the episode at Monument, Blanco refused to contemplate it.

The drive east had taken them into Rotherhithe and then north over the river through the tunnel along the A101. Randek had followed Blanco's orders to the letter; as usual, the Anjouvin had been vague when it came to details.

Soon he realised why.

Randek parked near one of the historic pubs located close to the riverside gardens. No sooner had they disembarked, two men emerged from there; on Blanco's orders one of them drove off in the taxi.

The second man led them through the gardens, the walk taking place in silence. A second car was waiting off one of the side streets; it took them to St Katharine Docks. The locality was lively; he remembered as much from his past visits to the city.

From here all appeared well in London.

The driver led them to the heart of the marina, where a fine white yacht was moored. On climbing aboard, the three visitors were led in silence below deck through a maze of elegant corridors that culminated in a fine stateroom with decorations of a style that resembled former French royalty. More than fifty men were seated around an impressive dining table; the feast, so it appeared, was already over.

The majority of those present, Randek recognised.

François, less so.

Most of the attendees sat in silence, their appearance and bearing indicating they were military men, each of similar rank. At the head of the table sat the one exception, whose position and appearance seemed somewhat regal. An expensive suit fitted tightly to a well-maintained body, while his clean-cut face, more linear than curved, and well-chiselled jawline created the impression of a sculpture by a Renaissance artist commissioned to portray perfect angularity. His flamboyant, once dark brown, typically Poitevin hair, which he seemed to share with the figures in the portraits of his ancestral home, had become a pristine silver in recent years, occurring, seemingly, at the same rate that his equally pristine forehead had become deepened with lines. Yet unlike the lightening of his hair, the lines had less to do with age. Behind his noble features was wisdom and experience. After his father, he had been the second most important resident at the chateau in Bordeaux; heir not only to the chateau, but also to what had once been a dukedom.

And if the manuscripts that lined the shelves of his family library were to be believed, the heir to something far more important still.

His name was Gabriel de Fieschi.

Fieschi wiped his mouth with a serviette before placing it down on the empty plate in front of him; immediately, a servant took it away. While every other person present had stood to acknowledge the visitors' arrival, this man had remained seated.

"My friends, you are most welcome." He gestured with his hands. Without further instruction, the servants came with flagons of wine.

"No alcohol!" Randek's response was stern. "The master craftsman never touches a drop till the job is done."

"Admirable sentiments." Fieschi nodded, reserving his eye contact solely for the Anjouvin. "So, gentlemen, noble cousins. Do I detect from your words, it is not done?"

"As you are no doubt already aware, the plan has been put into operation. Judging by the time, I'd guess the same is true of other places." Blanco checked both his wristwatch and the gilded antique clock that hung from the main wall. Though his eyes displayed anger, his response was calculated and calm. "Or perhaps hope would be the better phrase. I do not wish for my assumptions to be based on falsities."

"Why don't you see for yourself?" Fieschi picked up a television remote and pointed it at the only item in the room whose invention post-dated the gilded ceiling and 19th-century furnishings. The flat-screen television was showing live news footage from London; at a press of a button, the sound returned.

The Sky News presenters described a similar situation in Edinburgh.

"The first fire was witnessed in Edinburgh exactly thirty minutes after the first in London; you might say it all went off like clockwork." He smiled at his own joke and muted the sound. "As you can see, your guess wasn't far wrong after all."

"Nevertheless, there is still much work to be done!" Blanco bit his lip and nodded. "As my nephew says, setting fire to a couple of buildings in London can hardly be considered a job done."

Fieschi waited for the nearest servant to refill his wine goblet using the same flagon that had been offered to the other three. He swirled it for several seconds, his expression pensive.

"Then what's stopping you?"

"For a man who talks so much about clocks, you as well as any should be familiar with our schedule." Blanco folded his arms, his expression hardening. "Right now, we are not even in the correct place."

Fieschi looked at the men of dark military attire occupying the surrounding seats. "You are all aware of the task at hand?"

All of them nodded in confirmation.

"In that case, you may retire."

The Anjouvin watched as the soldiers departed, the closing of the double doors a prelude to an awkward silence. Fieschi broke it again by unmuting the sound on the television, on which the news footage continued to play out.

The fires in Pudding Lane were spreading and already threatening to engulf the Monument. As expected, the blaze at Faryners House was now under control but, in less than an hour, the surrounding street had become a raging inferno.

The main problem for the authorities would be preventing new outbreaks.

"In Edinburgh the fire of 1824 began in a small alleyway off the High Street, just as it did tonight. In Paris, of course, we have no such conflagrations; nor would we consider such action. Even if France has changed for the worst, we are still patriots, after all." Fieschi changed channel, Sky News giving way to Canal+. "A few hours from now, unconfirmed reports will begin to circulate of an attempted break-in at the Louvre. The reports will be denied; the story of the jewels will never be made known. Within thirty minutes from now, every item should have been replaced; as far as the people of Paris will know, their beloved jewels remain safe and untouched." Fieschi smiled at Blanco. "Let me show you something."

He led the three newcomers to the far side of the room, where an antique side table had been placed close to a redundant fireplace and covered by a white tablecloth. Removing it, he took a step back. Of the four, Fieschi was the only person whose face illustrated little surprise.

They were looking at what appeared to be the Crown Jewels of England.

Randek merely gasped. "How is this possible?"

The Anjouvin shook his head. "Such a feat deserves little in the way of appreciation." He looked at the jewels in disgust and then at the heir to the historical Dukedom of Aquitaine. "I must say I am disappointed. I thought we had agreed there would be no duplicates made, no slipping in quietly unseen. Yet now I see my faith was misplaced."

"What you see is no forgery." François's lips ghosted into a smile. "Really, Gabriel, however did you persuade my uncle to part with them?"

Fieschi also smiled. "Not part, cousin, merely borrow. He agreed, as do I, that the mere sight of their return could bring great motivation to our cause."

For Blanco, the penny dropped. "You mean?"

Fieschi grasped the Anjouvin's shoulders tightly. "Yes, Bizu. Yes."

Blanco studied the contents of the table, a cold shiver running down his spine. He counted over twenty items, some showing clear signs of age and decay. Of particular interest were four crowns.

One stood out above all others.

"The Diadem of St Edward." He looked at François. "How?"

"I could tell you the story and you might smile," François began, his mind wandering back to his own experiences learning of the deception of Oliver Cromwell two years earlier. "But even though you may smile, I'm quite sure you would not believe me."

"The story, so I've been told, is actually rather a thrilling one." Fieschi's demeanour had noticeably lightened. "The chest was found back in England, following clues left behind by the former Lord Protector. I also understand there were a few priceless works of art involved; needless to say they've since been returned to their rightful owners. I'll leave it to François to fill you in."

Blanco glared at François. "You never told me!"

"You know now; as far as I was aware, the contents of the hoard found in England were in no way related." He lit a cigarette and smoked quietly. "Perhaps I'm missing something."

"You are. Until recently, I'm sorry to say, so was I." Fieschi paced the room. "Gentlemen, as you now know, recent history has been kind to us, and the heirlooms that were once enjoyed by our ancestors have found their way home. This is good news. A sign, perhaps, that almighty God himself has once again bestowed his blessing on us, paving the way that his rightfully anointed may return for what is theirs. Destiny, it seems, is with us – just as it should have been on that September night in 1666 when heaven gave us permission. Tonight, it gives us permission again."

Randek watched Fieschi with suspicious eyes. Till now he'd been quiet. "Most of the jewels worn by our ancestors have been found. I agree, that is a blessing I'd never dreamed possible till now." He studied the jewels briefly, the recently cleaned crowns sparkling their reflection in his eyes. "The modern jewels, however, were never in any way connected to our kin. Their creation was much more modern."

"That is not entirely true. And even in the case of those that are modern, they are not entirely inconsequential."

The answer only infuriated Randek further. "Why risk life and limb? The City of London is burning, but the city of the past was smaller than the giant of today. Destroying everything is impossible."

"Who said anything about that?"

Fieschi returned to the table, kneeling down before it. Three large holdalls had been left beneath it.

He placed them alongside the jewels.

"Everything you require tonight is here." He unzipped the first holdall, taking a step back as the trio examined the contents in silence. As he'd expected, Blanco showed the greatest interest. "The people of Great Britain will never know what secrets its royal buildings truly hide beneath the ground. Instead, they will know only of the failings that surround them; for that they can blame their own protectors. Our ambition was never war with our own people."

"Then why the great charade?" François beat the others to a response. He placed the crown of Alfred the Great on his head. "Same size." He removed it and tried on the diadem of Edward the Confessor. "Wish I could say the same about this one."

"Many years ago, it was said to my ancestor the Tower holds the key," Fieschi resumed. "When the son of our great usurped ancestor returned home one rainy night from our homeland, on entering the Tower, he found his way unguarded. Tonight the same will be true for us. At 21:53 the ceremony will begin. Tonight, however, it will not end on time."

The Anjouvin zipped up the final holdall, satisfied by the contents. "The plan itself is ingenious. But plans count for nothing unless properly executed. As I said before, we are not yet done."

"Soon you will be. The tunnels are close. I have seen them with my own eyes;

they will lead you to the heart of where you need to go." Fieschi returned to the table and picked up the first of the holdalls. "Take what has been created only recently and take back what replaced those of long ago."

"And what if things don't go to plan?"

Fieschi held Randek's gaze, his pause only momentary. "As one plan is subject to change, so can the next be – this also has been discussed. The taking of the Tower will alone act as a sign: one that the past and the present are coming together. If history has told us one thing, it is this:

"Whoever holds the Tower of London, holds England!"

10

The Monument to the Great Fire, 21:40

Kit hurried from King William Street to Lower Thames Street, the nearest he could get to completing a full circuit of the Monument. The fire at Pudding Lane was under control now, but there was evidence to the north the flames had spread beyond Eastcheap.

From a distance the scene was strange; the fire was growing but not naturally. The buildings north of the Tube station were separated by open road.

What the hell is happening?

He'd made two attempts to contact Mike on his satphone without success. After seven years in the White Hart, he knew that the satellite communications equipment they used was the best available, but tonight he was concerned that the conditions would cause problems.

The city was practically in lockdown.

Failing to contact Mike through official channels, he tried his iPhone; no better. After another minute of failure, he finally got a response from HQ.

A woman's voice.

"Maria, it's Edward."

Alone in the heart of the large room, Maria listened through a sleek Bluetooth headset while simultaneously watching footage of the fire on the semi-translucent screen. On hearing the name Edward, Kit's codename, in addition to receiving visual confirmation of his position from the GPS tracking system, she was in no doubt who it was. "Was hoping you'd show up at some point. What can you see?"

Tonight Kit let the insult slide. "Traffic. Lots of it. Warm out this evening; you'd like it. Where are you? What the hell's been happening?"

Inside the subterranean complex beneath the Old Admiralty Building, Maria now sat alone at an iMac computer, one of many positioned on a series of desks close to the Round Table. "Court has been assembled at the Rook. PM's just got off the big screen. The Director's ordered a complete lockdown. Suspect was last seen heading south."

Stopping at the bottom of Monument Street, Kit now had an unrestricted view back up towards the Monument. While the pencil-like pillar was clearly still intact, the inferno threatened to close in; most recently it had engulfed the bars on Fish Street Hill. Beyond the sounds of buildings burning, the roar of spraying water and sirens filled the air.

"What do we know?"

"Only his name. Bizante Blanco. Uncle of Fabien Randek."

Kit felt the wind leave his sails. "You're joking."

"If I am, that's two of us who don't think it's funny." Maria sent him a profile picture direct to his satphone. "He was seen near the Monument at the time of the blaze; right now, the visuals confirm nothing more than association."

Kit saw the picture. "Meaning what exactly?"

"Meaning probably what you've just heard. This isn't like the incident at the opera – Blanco carried no detonator in his hand." She tapped quickly at her keyboard, bringing up a selection of CCTV images. She saw Kit close to the road, successfully evading the panicked crowds. "That reminds me, how was the opera?"

"Captivating. Not to mention great seats. Where is the bastard now?"

"Somewhere south of the water. We saw him board a taxi. Still tracking it."

"How hard can it be?"

"You really want to know? Last I saw, it was entering the Rotherhithe Tunnel. We should get something on the way out. Unfortunately, we're getting an information overload at this point."

"Explains why the phone's barely working." Kit started moving again, east then north. Even close to St Mary-at-Hill the heat was almost unbearable. Traffic was stopping sporadically there too, while north on Eastcheap flames were encroaching on to the road, both from the fires to the south and seemingly from beneath the tarmac itself.

"What are my orders?"

"Everything we know so far, I'm sending through – you should have it imminently. I suggest you head for where the newest flames are burning."

"Understood. Where is everyone? My circuit's temperamental."

"They all are. Everyone bar you and Grosmont are currently heading out now. The Director is briefing them."

"I tried Grosmont but didn't get a reply."

"That's no surprise. He's currently at the Tower of London – according to the GPS, he's just entered the Jewel House."

"Why's that important?"

"Because it's one of the only places in the country our signal can't penetrate."

While Kit made his way back to Monument, beneath the Old Admiralty Building in the strange room visually reminiscent of the underground cellar in Charlestown, Lieutenant Maria Lyons moved to the workstation next to her own, from where she was able to view a series of computer screens.

Everything she saw was security related; the present pictures were from the immediate vicinity of the Monument.

The time was 20:59. And fifty-five seconds.

"Play that out," she requested, taking a seat alongside Phil, her eyes reserved solely for Blanco. The Frenchman had been standing west of the Monument, shielding himself from the blaze. As the inferno erupted, he paused for a moment, taking what appeared to be an exaggerated interest in what he saw before slipping away.

She followed his progress on the screens.

In a large office directly above the main hub, the former undersecretary of the MoD looked thoughtfully at the artwork on the wall from his leather chair at his oak desk. The office was one of only two in that part of the building, designated solely for the Director and Deputy Director of the White Hart.

Atkins answered, "Come in," to a knock on the door and saw Phil standing in the doorway.

"Sir, our cameras have tracked Blanco to the south side of the water. He took an unlit cab before heading east."

The Deputy Director nodded. "Keep track of him and see if you can find the registration of the taxi."

"Already ahead of you. The taxi was sold privately less than three weeks ago. Unfortunately it was bought cash in hand."

"Surely it's registered to someone?"

"Enquiries to the DVLA are still to come up with anything."

"Keep trying. These things often take time."

Phil departed, leaving the Deputy Director deep in thought. In an industry that thrived on action, the room was a rare oasis of calm in a desert of chaos.

Visually, Atkins' office was similar to the Director's. A smaller version of the flat videoconferencing screen had been positioned above a state-of-the-art, twenty-seven-inch iMac computer that was currently logged in to the White Hart's secure server. The GPS confirmed the helicopter had already reached the outskirts of London. The seven in the transit were way behind, battling the traffic, heading east towards Monument. Kit Masterson was already there; he could picture his animated frame moving from side to side. Only one was absent.

Curiously the white dot placed him inside the Tower of London.

Directly in front of him, his attention again became drawn to the wall art, the only things that covered the otherwise white walls. One was a copy of a famous piece, a 17th-century painting by an unknown artist in honour of the greatest tragedy in the city's history. The second was a reproduction of a famous photograph, another night when the city was on fire.

One building appeared in both.

Gazing at the scenes before him, the Deputy Director felt a twinge of anticipation. At one time, the city had fallen; the second it had survived.

He feared again London's resolve was about to be tested.

11

The Brecon Beacons, Twenty-One Months Earlier

The pattern continued: three months, nine visits; one route then the other. Conquering all four mountains in one stint was tougher than Pen y Fan twice, Mike decided, especially with the bergen. The march up the Big Fanny, down then up Pen y Fan, down and up Corn Du was as big a mental challenge as physical; even on a full stomach, it was an easy place to become light-headed.

The route down was complicated, especially when ending with Cribyn. He remembered the first time he'd tried it with his former staff sergeant. Instead of finding the correct path, they'd shimmied down through woodland. The area was suffering the effects of deforestation; today he decided to accept the challenge. The latest route added an extra hour to the march.

Five hours, forty-five minutes.

He'd experienced the toughest yet.

As the veteran of the parachute regiment returned to his car, the permanent mud patches on his combats joined by several new additions, his muscles aching from cold and stress, he sensed something; the experience was new, though not altogether unique. He had felt it before, recently. It had started exactly three months ago.

Someone, somewhere, was watching him.

No.1 Parachute Training School, RAF Brize Norton

The Lockheed C-130K Hercules was flying at the correct altitude and had been for some time. The plane, a four-engined turboprop transport craft favoured by both the US Air Force and the RAF since its creation in the mid-1950s, bounced gently as it caught minor turbulence. Lieutenant Mike Hansen had experienced the same thing many times; after five years in the job, it was a comforting feeling.

Enthralling even.

He remembered the day he'd arrived for his training. P Company had been the most gruelling experience of his life: five days of constant challenges ranging from stretcher carrying to route marches with a sixteen-kilogram bergen. The training that followed had been a doddle by comparison. His grandfather had told him many times that even in his day a willing participant had to successfully undertake at least eight jumps, the first of which was from a barrage balloon. The balloon had now been replaced with a

Skyvan, but it was the final two that remained the most demanding.

Only by completing two jumps fully equipped at the lowest heights yet out of the plane in which he currently rode would a red beret earn his 'wings'.

He gazed across the cargo hold, studying the faces of the eight young men alongside him. Satisfied, he smiled wryly.

Now he was the teacher, not the student.

Convinced none of them were in danger of vomiting or asking to stand down, he turned his attention to the nine unopened parachute sacks lying against the fuselage doors. He'd spent most of the morning overseeing their being packed in the main hangar, ensuring everything was ready. As he'd done so, he'd remembered other words his grandfather had told him.

'Once I put all of my faith in God. Now, I put just as much in the man who packs the chute.'

He waited for the pilot's instruction to come through his headphones before ordering the trainees into position. He smiled at the man alongside him.

"Scared, Parker?"

The fresh-faced recruit from somewhere on the south coast shook his head and yelled against the sounds of the motors. "No, sir."

A pause preceded Mike's reply. His eyes said he was, but the hell with it anyway.

"Just remember the words my grandfather once told me. First you crap yourself; then it's all rather enjoyable."

Satisfied the joke had raised spirits, Mike made the final preparations; all that remained was to open the doors.

"Just remember. I'll be right here behind you all!"

Mike moved swiftly across a combination of short mown grass and tarmac before coming to a halt outside the nearest hangar. He recognised his commanding officer, the stern-faced Air Commodore Markins, with more than a look of quiet indignation in his eyes as he gazed at Hansen from beneath the peak of his officer's cap.

"Sir, I'm happy to announce all present completed their jumps successfully. Every beret has earned his wings." Mike stopped within speaking distance and saluted his commanding officer. Replacing the combat headwear and windproof overalls that had recently accompanied his parachute, the single layer of camouflaged military dress with the airborne forces' patch of Bellerophon riding Pegasus on the right shoulder, complementing the famous cap badge pinned elegantly to his maroon beret, formed an imposing shadow against the sun-drenched pavement.

The CO saluted and nodded. "Excellent, Hansen. Fall the men in and I'll address them in person." He lowered his hand. "Once you're done, you have my permission to stand down. I've just been informed you have a visitor from London."

That surprised him. "For me, sir?"

"I assure you, I know less about it than you do. Report to the mess as soon as the men are fallen in. I'll take over from here."

"Yes, sir."

***

The mess was deserted, which was usual for 11:00. Most of the permanent staff who worked there during the week stayed overnight, especially the unmarried ones who otherwise faced a long commute.

Mike usually did the same unless he had a specific reason not to.

The dining area also contained two bars, which was one of the reasons he liked it. All of the tables were currently deserted; a dark jacket had been left on the back of one of the chairs. There was no sign of anyone in the kitchen either, which was strange, as the kettle was boiling. He considered helping himself to a brew, but decided against it.

The signs suggested company was imminent.

"I'll never forget the first time I entered this room," a voice said from behind him. "Of course, it all looked a lot different back then. A colonel from the US came over back in the late seventies. Real heartthrob; looked a bit like James Dean. I think his name was Jennings."

"Jenners," Mike corrected, his focus turning to the man standing opposite. The man was jacketless, his appearance otherwise suited with a black tie and spotless white shirt, crisply ironed, as though tailor-made to emphasise his already perfect posture. Though his hair was thinning on top, his expression was full, no nonsense. He stared at Mike through rimless spectacles.

"I'm pleased to see you know your history. After Jenners returned home, his, shall we say, colourful banter about his stay made a mark on the folks back at Fort Bragg. Not the most likeable of people by all accounts. Nevertheless, the CO at the time decided to seize the opportunity to spruce things up a bit." He looked around. "Can't say I disapprove. The old place was really rather ghastly."

The visitor walked a few paces forward, eyeing Mike like a distant uncle recently returned after several years away from home. "It's not impossible, of course, your own grandfather knew Jenners personally. I met him myself, you know – before the nonsense with Argentina. Even back then, he was proud to say he came from a long line of military men." He paused to adjust his spectacles. "I understand you've been here since P Company?"

"That's right," Mike answered. Though he had never spoken to the man before, he knew who he was. "I actually recall meeting you myself, sir, though back when I was much younger."

"Your memory serves you well. A wedding, I seem to recall, possibly your uncle's. Things were much different then."

"I'm sorry to say the marriage barely lasted longer than the wedding." Mike nodded, his expression offering little hint of emotion. "Forgive me, sir. While I feel I know who you are, I make it a habit never to talk too much to strangers while on duty. My grandfather always warned me about careless talk."

"I should think so, too." The civilian smiled and delved into his pocket, then showed Mike an identity card. "My name, as I'm sure you know, is Atkins. Former Undersecretary of State for the Ministry of Defence. Recently retired.

As you can see, I still have the clearance to be here."

Mike examined the man's security tag in his right hand. Though the photograph depicted a younger man, it was clearly the same person.

"Just as I remembered, Mr Atkins. I'm assuming your being here has something to do with the latest recruits?"

"Not exactly."

Mike was surprised. "Well, in that case, would you mind if I asked you why you are here?"

Atkins disappeared into the bar area and returned with an empty cocktail glass and what appeared to be the essence of a cocktail. He shook the canister and poured a drink over broken ice. Mike raised an eyebrow, stunned.

He was looking at a pink gin.

"Perhaps we should discuss this somewhere more private."

Atkins led Mike into the kitchen located just off the bar. He boiled the kettle a second time and offered Mike a tea. "One sugar. No milk. I understand that's how you take it?" He showed only indifference to Hansen's surprise. "Alternatively you're most welcome to consume the gin."

A wry smile. "You know, back in 1942, at least so my grandfather tells me, he was actually tempted into one of the newly formed regiments with a vodka martini. I always thought the whole recruitment over a pink gin was just a myth."

"Matter of fact, the drink is interchangeable; if the stories I hear are correct, your grandfather might just so have happened to have been in the company of one of the lads responsible for the growth of MI6. I know another young chap in their midst who loved a vodka martini. Probably not the chap you're thinking of."

Mike laughed. "Whether it was MI6 or not, I couldn't tell you. Other than it was definitely one of the evolving agencies. Not that they had much luck – even without the gin."

"A tough man to please, I think it was fair to say. Then again, the boys who attempted to conscript him were never renowned for their charm and wit. Even if they were useful under fire."

"Why did they use pink gin? I'd have thought back then the officers would have been against anything bad for discipline."

"It depended really on the circles. Like many a commando officer, it's possible your grandfather was also approached for recruitment over such a drink at White's Club by Lieutenant Colonel Laycock, not that it would have done him much good. In the early days, most of the North Africa raids were complete washouts."

"So the purpose of this is recruitment?" Mike finally accepted the tea. All the while his eyes never left the former undersecretary.

"You often find in vocations such as ours, the paths we take are those carved out for us as opposed to the ones we make ourselves, especially in situations such as yours. Your family has a long history in the military.

Grandfather at Dunkirk. D-Day. Operation Market Garden. The Bulge. Your great-grandfather also served, did he not?"

"General Edmund, sir. Killed just before the Armistice."

Atkins adjusted his glasses. "And on the other side also?"

"Sergeant T.K. Booth, my mother's grandfather. Died at the Somme." Mike was confused by the clearly emerging pattern. "Forgive me, sir, I'm due to give a lecture on capture behind enemy lines at 14:00 hours and I'm still to prepare. Would you mind if we cut to the chase and tell me which government agency I'm being touted for so I can tell you, in the kindest possible words, why I'm not interested."

Atkins placed his tea down on the nearest coaster. "You seem particularly certain, which I suppose is important for someone dropped by parachute as often as you are. It was similar men who established the new forces to begin with. When the SAS was founded, it was the view of the originators that the old ways needed to be replaced by something that relied more on guile. Less on tradition and formality. Even these days, the Regiment isn't exactly renowned for its ability to salute."

Mike's eyes narrowed, the penny beginning to drop. "So it was you who was watching me in the Brecon Beacons?"

"Me? No. At least not personally. But that's not to say you haven't been watched. I checked your records. You're still to apply to the Regiment."

"No, sir. And being honest, I'm still to find a reason to."

"You feel unready for selection?"

"Not at all; based on my recent visits, I'd have said if anything, I've found the process even more enjoyable than I did P Company. To tell you the God's honest truth, I'm just not sure the SAS, the SRR or even the SBS would make best use of my combined strengths. Not that a desk job would either."

A soft smile formed on the civilian's lips, which Mike found slightly unsettling. "As I've mentioned before, you often find in our business, it isn't the man that finds the role, but the role that finds the man. You're familiar with your grandfather's days after the war?"

"I know he served briefly in the commandos before watching the close of play back in London. Quite possibly with one of these in his hand." He spoke of the feminine cocktail.

"He told you about his stint in Suffolk?"

"Suffolk?"

The civilian's smile widened. "I thought not. Even in the tightest circles, there are some places from which even the nearest and dearest are excluded." He finished his tea and put on his jacket.

"Come, I think it's time you reacquainted me with the rest of the old place. As we walk, let me tell you a few stories that your own grandfather was unable to tell you himself."

12

Inner Ward, The Tower of London, 21:45

Mike checked his phone for a second time as the gathering moved into the Jewel House. He waited till last to ensure what he was doing didn't attract attention, temporarily pleased that Emily had again wandered off towards his uncle.

The server had updated since he'd last looked, yet there was clear evidence of a time lag. The ten Harts back in Charlestown had all moved out; judging by the GPS, they had already reached London. Kit had also left the opera; the white dot that tracked his movements was close to the amber one – he recognised the area as Monument. *Monument*, he mused.

A strange coincidence.

He followed the tour through the grand entrance and into the first room on the left, where emerald green walls were interrupted by illustrations of past kings from the Middle Ages to those of the Tudor era. Continuing into the next room, the decorations changed to an epic video display with running commentary on the history of the jewels against the stirring sounds of classical music.

He walked on quietly, doing his best to keep up. The light was dimmer than before, the glow of two artificial lanterns doing little more than create silhouettes of those around him. Despite the relative privacy, he realised making a phone call inside would be difficult.

He entered last into a third section, the way accessible via a similar archway and illuminated by identical lantern-style lighting. As the noise of the music and commentary from the previous room faded, he noticed a second video display on a screen at the end of the corridor, where some of the group were sitting down. As the video began, he checked his satphone.

Instantly he regretted it.

"'Ere, can't you read the signs? No mobiles in here. Same goes for photos."

A Yeoman Warder was waiting by the far doorway, his stocky build creating a round shadow against the royal blue walls.

Mike locked the display and smiled. "Sorry, I can't read. I have to look at the pictures."

The Beefeater laughed.

The tour resumed in the next room. The lighting improved on reaching a long corridor where a smart collection of maces, swords and trumpets from the 17th century were accompanied by informative displays. As he entered the main section, he saw the door was more imposing, the chamber clearly capable of being instantly sealed off.

Beyond it, a display case to his right housed a pre-reformation coronation spoon, alongside the ampulla and three ceremonial swords. A second display case was located adjacent the first, occupied by a further sword, titled the Sword of Offering and Scabbard. The imperial dress was in a third case, the layout causing hard shadows against the ground as it caught the overhead lights.

Mike realised from the descriptions that the items he was seeing were among the oldest in the collection.

Emily had made it to the main room, where the crowns were displayed in a long sequence of display cases, on either side of which people stood on moving travellators. Momentarily forgetting about contacting the White Hart, he caught her up, viewing the famous jewels as they moved from left to right.

"You know, I heard a rumour once that these are just props and the real jewels are located in a secure chamber somewhere beneath the city." He looked at her. "But you wouldn't know anything about that, would you, Miss Fletcher?"

Standing alongside him, Emily gave nothing away. "Even if I did, do you really think I'd tell you?" She hid a smile, her eyes focused on the crowns.

"I'll have you know I happen to be very trustworthy. Come to think of it, you think they'd even tell you?"

"Probably not." She left the moving walkway. "But if they are fake, you have to admit they're pretty amazing."

Champion had been talking from a small podium that overlooked the crowns, the sound of his voice drowning out the background chatter. As the tour moved on, he made his way down the steps, stopping briefly before the glass displays that housed the gilded altar plate and wedding banquet. He waited till last before following the crowds along the next section of the walkway, where the walls had taken on an increasingly purple hue.

The colour of royalty.

Mike took a passing interest in the exhibits, saving his greatest attention for the last. The display case Champion stood beside included only one crown.

He recognised it instantly.

"What we have here is the Imperial State Crown – one of the most important of the current collection and instantly recognisable worldwide as a symbol of the sovereignty of the monarchy," Champion began. "Standing at just over a foot tall at thirty-one point five centimetres and weighing just over a kilogram, note the four fleurs-de-lis and crosses pattée supporting two arches topped by the usual orb and a further cross pattée at the summit. Notice also the purple velvet cap trimmed with the famous items of heraldry. The frame consists of gold, silver and platinum and is decorated by over two thousand eight hundred diamonds, two hundred and sixty-nine pearls, seventeen sapphires, eleven emeralds and four rubies.

"Unlike the first crown that we saw among its smaller cousins" – Champion pointed back towards the main section – "the Imperial Crown has never been used for the crowning of the monarch. The crown of St Edward, used for that ceremony, was created in 1661, allegedly with gold from its predecessor that had been smelted down by Oliver Cromwell following the execution of Charles I. Prior to the Protectorate, St Edward's Crown was considered to be something of a holy relic, because of its connection with Edward the Confessor, and kept in the saint's shrine at Westminster Abbey, removed only to perform part of the anointing ceremony. Whereas the modern crown of St Edward was recreated for the coronation of Charles II after the Lord Protector's death, the Imperial State Crown here, though created as a replacement for its predecessor in 1937, has, unlike the others in this collection, existed in one form or another since the fifteenth century. In a sense, therefore, it predates the Protectorate."

Slowly Champion circled the display case. "At the top of the crown is embedded St Edward's Sapphire – allegedly once part of the coronation ring of Edward the Confessor, recovered following his reinterment at Westminster Abbey in 1163. Notice also the Black Prince's Ruby on the front cross – a quite alluring gift given to the eldest son of Edward III back in 1367 in Bordeaux."

Mike raised an eyebrow, suddenly intrigued. He remembered learning on his initiation in the White Hart how the famous jewel had once been in the possession of the order's founder.

"Other jewels of relevance include the Stuart Sapphire and the three-hundred-seventeen-carat Cullinan II, famously the second-largest clear-cut diamond in existence."

"Imagine having that on your finger."

Emily looked at Mike and walked away.

Champion brought his hands together and smiled. "Ladies and gentlemen, the time is now 9:49. With that in mind, may we now make our way to the Broadwalk Steps and the Ceremony of the Keys!"

Mike joined in the applause as the lecture came to an end, at which point people began to make their way into the next room. He waited till the majority had passed by before circling the Imperial State Crown, examining the ruby for the first time. He saw it at the front of the frame, its shape defying easy description.

He was still unsure of its exact history.

He rejoined the crowds as they headed outside. Champion was lingering by the ice cream kiosk, speaking quietly to a group of four. The external floodlights still shone down brightly, illuminating the nearby stairs to the Martin Tower, outside which were several statues of connection to the former menagerie.

He felt his satphone vibrate; checking it, he gazed in horror at the display.

The colour on the screen had changed from amber to purple.

13

The River Thames, 21:47

The skipper pulled back slowly on the yacht's throttle as they approached Tower Bridge. Widely famed as one of the world's most iconic water crossings, the Victorian-age combination of bascule and suspension engineering and architecture again stood out in an array of colours, the reflections of which danced brightly on the waters. It was calm on the river, less so on the bridge.

It was evening in London and traffic, as always, was heavy.

The skipper waited till the yacht began to drift before speaking into the intercom.

"Tower Bridge, this is the *Kestrel*. Request permission to raise the bridge. Over."

On hearing the request, the bridge operator gazed through his window at the impressive-looking yacht. Though it wasn't the largest he'd seen, it was still tall enough to pose a possible clearance problem. On a typical summer's day, he could be called into action no less than twenty times, letting things through as large as freighters.

Today, so far, had been far quieter.

Checking the facts at his disposal, he realised the correct request had been made over twenty-four hours earlier. "*Kestrel* from Tower Bridge, we've received your request. The bridge will be raised in moments. Please remain where you are and await further instruction."

The skipper waited patiently as the Victorian mechanisms were slowly put into action, preparing to allow him passage. He saw road traffic come to a halt on both sides, reassuring him it was only a matter of time.

A voice spoke a second time. "*Kestrel* from Tower Bridge, I will raise the bridge to forty-five degrees. Prepare to pass."

The yacht drifted to a standstill at Old Billingsgate, close to the headquarters of the *Daily Express*. It was low tide on the Thames; at this late hour, the banks were largely deserted.

From a position so close to the large buildings on the north bank, the fire was no longer visible.

In the stateroom below deck, Randek, François and Blanco leaned over a peculiar piece of paper that appeared to be a modern photocopy of something far older. The heir to the Dukedom of Aquitaine was still alongside them, now seated.

All of the jewels had disappeared.

"Once upon a time, a clear marker would have existed where the passage starts." Randek turned to his uncle as he spoke while simultaneously scanning the Maps app on his mobile phone. "Whatever existed, exists no longer."

The Anjouvin studied the photocopy; though he had seen it many times, he felt a familiar tingling sensation as he reminded himself he was looking at something known only to very few.

"The passage exists. We have seen it with our own eyes. Still you have no faith."

"The author was a genius – even as an English pirate, credit must be given where it is due," Randek replied, still trying to read his uncle's thoughts. "No man, however, has the gift of seeing the future. For all we know, the passage has now been blocked."

The Anjouvin stared back hard, pointing at the photocopy. "The map is clear. Its knowledge was intended only for those who know how to use it. Only through bravery will it lead us to the end."

He checked his watch and glanced at Fieschi. "It's time."

Within moments, the three men departed the yacht, along with the large body of soldiers who had earlier vacated the stateroom. As they disembarked close to the banks, the attention of the customers and staff of the local bars and eateries fixed on evening meals and refreshments, their movements went unseen as they headed north past St Magnus House and across Lower Thames Street.

14

The Byward Tower,
21:53 and 35 Seconds

The Ceremony of the Keys began at the usual time. Once again, responsibility fell on the shoulders of the Chief Yeoman Warder. Even if he was aware of news of a fire spreading beyond the building, nothing would get in the way of the completion of the ceremony.

Even during the Blitz, it had taken place every night without fail.

Within the walls itself, there was little reason to see the evening as different from any other. It was cloudy, but not raining – drier than the night before. There were no changes in personnel from the night before either, nor had any of the participants been afflicted by recent injury. Just as they'd rehearsed earlier that day, all was scheduled to end on time.

Exactly twenty-four hours after he had done the night before, the Chief Yeoman Warder emerged through the door of the Warders' Hall and picked up his four-man escort from below the Bloody Tower opposite Traitors' Gate.

There, they began the familiar march along Water Lane.

Mike jogged towards the statues of the animals, pleased to find Champion now alone. "Listen, Uncle Dave, I'm really sorry, but I'm afraid duty calls. I have to head off."

"Not for the next twelve minutes, I'm afraid you're not." Champion pulled back his sleeve to check his watch. "The time of reckoning is nearly upon us."

Mike realised he was talking about the Ceremony of the Keys. "Be that as it may, unfortunately I was just summoned. How can I get out?"

"At 22:05 all of us will be asked to make our way towards the exit. In the meantime, I'm afraid there's nothing you can do other than enjoy the ceremony. In just over ten minutes, we shall all leave together."

Mike bit his lip, knowing he probably had no choice. Emergency or not, he was unlikely to dissuade the Yeoman Warders and the Queen's Guard from delaying the Ceremony of the Keys.

"All right. You go on without me. I need to make a phone call."

Maria scanned the screens in front of her, confused. The footage on the CCTV, though clearly visible, simply didn't make sense.

The taxi had headed east from Tooley Street, continuing along the same route till it reached the Rotherhithe Tunnel. Traffic was bad inside the tunnel; it was unclear for now whether it was a direct consequence of the fires.

A second taxi had appeared in the outside lane, travelling at a similar speed until the traffic stopped. Once it did, the occupants of both swapped over.

On leaving the tunnel, each went their separate ways.

After crossing Lower Thames Street, the party headed east, within sight of the flames. Blanco was the first to cross, giving orders in a low voice. François and Randek both followed, as did the others.

Of all present, only Blanco knew where he was going.

They headed north up the narrow St Dunstan's Hill. There was greenery ahead of them, several buildings shrouded in darkness. Close by, a gateway was locked; they broke the lock and entered, spreading out among ruined walls.

Within seconds, all of them had disappeared from sight.

Champion led the large group of tourists to a quiet area west of the White Tower. The main guard had already assembled on the Broadwalk Steps, the leader strutting the stonework like a drill sergeant. Despite his regular visits to the Tower, this was the first time Champion had witnessed the ceremony first-hand.

He checked his watch as the leader stopped marching. 21:56.

Meaning in three minutes the remainder of the party would enter from below the Bloody Tower.

Mike headed straight for the toilets close to the Brick Tower, stopping on reaching the sink. He double-checked he was still alone before logging in to the White Hart server using his satphone.

His heart palpitated wildly as the connection took forever to load.

The GPS had updated since his last log in. Three of the white dots were now travelling at speed – Rawlins, Pentland and Pugh were heading north, apparently to Edinburgh. Iqbal had taken Ward and Chambers to Monument; Kit was already there, south of the flashing purple dot. The other four were moving at speed close to the river.

Clearly they were using some form of transport.

The purple dot at Monument had increased dramatically in size, indicating the problem area was expanding. On close inspection, something similar was true of Edinburgh.

Bringing up the satellite visuals, he saw there were buildings on fire.

He put a call through to the main switchboard, his phone now pressed firmly to his ear. Seconds later he hung up.

No contact.

Emily waited until the tour group had left before heading back into the heart of the Jewel House. Being alone in the midst of such incredible riches always caused her heart to skip, a reminder that she was paid less than £40,000 a year to be partly responsible for arguably the most priceless treasure in the world.

The Crown Jewels were always cleaned at night; it was the only opportunity to do so without incurring the wrath of disappointed visitors. The Crown Jeweller had waited until the group had left before making his way along the now switched off travellator, his eyes momentarily on the Crown of St Edward.

As usual, he was accompanied by a quartet of armed security.

Emily smiled at them, her eyes on the Jeweller. "You might want to start at the other end. I think I saw a few mucky fingerprints on the glass."

The way in had been located in the north section of the gardens, somewhere below the paving stones and block tiles. It wasn't obvious from the layout whether anyone in the modern day would even be aware of it.

Randek guessed the answer would be no.

It was cold underground, dark, desolate. The walls were old and constructed of stone, like a corridor chiselled out of the earth. He knew from the secret instructions in the sailor's manuscript, they had been created in the 1200s, when Henry III had designs on creating the greatest castle known to man.

Rumour had it they had once served his queen as escape tunnels.

He waited till his squad had completed their descent before planning his own. François and Blanco were alongside him, their slick combats and automatic weapons creating imposing shadows as their bodies moved across the path of their torches.

"Where does it lead?" Randek asked, shining his own light in his uncle's face.

Blanco placed his hand on the torch, lowering it. "Patience. I have told you before. Just because you haven't seen it does not mean it no longer exists."

Randek broke free of his uncle's grip, his eyes like those of a hawk in the torchlight. "Then after you."

Mike tried the same number twice more, failing both times. The main switchboard of the White Hart was never fixed to any one location.

In fast-developing situations like tonight, it was able to move at a moment's notice.

Mike placed his phone against the nearest sink and splashed water on to his dry face. Exhaling hard, he glanced up at the mirror, his reflection looking back almost mockingly in the dim light. Somehow even in his casual jeans and jacket, he still looked like a soldier. Whether it was the way he carried himself, the short back and sides or something more subconscious, it seemed there was no mistaking it. He smiled to himself as he thought of Emily. The enemy had chosen the worst possible time to show up, not that he expected otherwise. The cake had been warming nicely, he mused.

He'd regret not having the chance to sample it.

Picking up his satphone, he tried the same number again. After getting no response at Charlestown, he tried the Rook; same result. Next he tried Kit Masterson.

All he heard was interference.

The sentry was standing in the correct place, deep within the shadows of the Wakefield Tower. After making his debut the night before, the veteran of the Queen's Guard was far more relaxed than he'd been on the previous occasion.

He heard the collective noise of heavy footsteps along Water Lane, following which the ghostly shadows again manifested into something more physical.

"Halt!"

The leader of the escort ordered his men to comply.

"Who comes there?"

The Chief Yeoman Warder replied, "The keys."

"Whose keys?"

"Queen Elizabeth's keys."

The sentry backed down. "Pass Queen Elizabeth's keys. All is well."

Emily was leaving the Jewel House at exactly the same moment Mike passed in front of her. She stared at him from across the walkway, her expression indicating she was annoyed.

He put it down to his effect on her.

"What on earth are you still doing here?"

"Inspecting the royal privies." He decided against being truthful. "I never knew they had urinals back in King Henry's day."

"The ceremony will be over soon." She led him south-west past the Martin Tower, heading towards the front of the Jewel House. The strong walls of the White Tower again loomed above them, its white stonework glowing mysteriously pale under the floodlights.

"So why exactly do they call it the White Tower?"

Seeing him grin, she decided not to answer.

Blanco came to a halt without warning, infuriating Randek.

"What is it now?"

The rays of Blanco's flashlight had gone from being directed at the ground and surrounding walls to a point overhead.

Above them, wood could be seen embedded within the stonework.

Blanco looked earnestly at Randek. "Come. Let us hope it has not been covered over."

Back on the yacht, the lower deck was practically deserted. While earlier that evening it had been the scene of a sumptuous dinner attended by a number of guests, followed by a short, though highly important meeting, now only a solitary figure remained, seated with studied concentration in front of a laptop.

The security system at the Tower of London was among the most sophisticated he'd ever come across. It had taken over two years to become fully acquainted with all of its capabilities.

Nothing was controlled by one sole area or console; the area was far too diverse for that. Some of the surveillance equipment was non-operational, installed to create a misleading impression of the true extent of observation; to monitor every screen would have required a workforce of thousands. It was always possible mistakes could be made, but he had taken every possible precaution. Everyone agreed that obstacles would inevitably be encountered at some stage.

The best he could hope for was to delay them as long as possible.

Hunched over the laptop, footage via the infrared cameras that each of the intruders had placed close to their head torches confirmed entry would be imminent. Typing quickly on the keyboard, he finished off by pressing the return key.

All he could do now was wait.

15

The White Tower,
21:59

Randek came up in an area of paved flooring; penetrating it had been extremely tough. Whatever the exact materials that surrounded him, the slabs had been solidly sealed.

He sensed something else had been weighing them down.

Above the secret tunnel, there was darkness on all sides; in the absence of light, nearby sounds seemed particularly sharp. Switching on his torch, the first thing he saw left him speechless.

He was staring into the mouth of a cannon.

Hearing a voice from beneath him, he pointed the torch downwards and saw Blanco.

"Quickly! The ceremony will be over soon!"

Randek exited the void swiftly, reaching down to pull Blanco up. With the extra light, he realised they had entered near the foot of a wooden staircase in the heart of a military exhibition.

"What is this place?" Randek remained where he was to help François.

"The cellar of the White Tower. Once upon a time this would have been the storehouse." Blanco hurried on, passing the various displays and heading through the gift shop before taking a wooden stairway to the floor above. He proceeded towards the main door, hoping the technician back on the yacht had done his job properly.

Mike heard the sound of voices carried by the wind, reminiscent of soldiers practising drill. It wasn't clear to him exactly where it had come from; he sensed the acoustics were misleading, especially outside and at night.

Emily walked alongside him, the echo of her shoes interfering with his thought process. She looked cute.

Too cute.

She sensed he was glancing at her. "Do you really have nothing better to do?"

He smiled.

The door opened without triggering an alarm; the only sounds that followed were those of footsteps.

Blanco was first to pass beyond the door. He looked carefully in all directions before moving fully into the open, his eyes now fixed on the entrance to the Jewel House. An armed guard in his famous redcoat uniform was providing the usual solitary vigil, the features of his clean-shaven face lost in the darkness and beneath the coverage of his tall bearskin hat.

Raising his weapon, he fired quickly, causing the guard to slump instantly to the hard ground.

Randek was next to emerge from the gift shop.

"Come on."

Champion thought he heard a noise coming from behind him, strange under the circumstances. The escort was approaching from the other side of the Inner Ward; he saw them appear from beneath the archway of the Bloody Tower.

He glanced quickly over his shoulder, looking towards the Jewel House, which was partially obscured by the walls of the White Tower.

Seeing nothing obviously amiss, he turned his attention back to the Broadwalk Steps.

Mike's actions were instinctive. He grabbed Emily's hand and pulled her behind the east wall of the White Tower, stopping with their backs to the stonework.

Emily was appalled. "Just what the hell do you think you're doing?"

"Shhh!" Mike put his finger to his lips, his eyes on hers before edging towards the north-east corner. Cautiously, he peered along the north wall, his eyes on the area between the White Tower and the Jewel House.

At least forty armed men in dark combat uniforms had emerged from inside the White Tower.

Emily was standing within inches of him, stunned. Her lips quivered. "Oh my God."

He looked at her, noticing the heightened sound of her breathing; on this occasion, he ignored the temptation to make a joke about fitness. Rationally what he saw made no sense, but instinct and training immediately began to kick in.

He knew it was no coincidence that what he was witnessing was occurring within a mile of the Monument.

"Where exactly is the ceremony taking place?" He looked at her, gripping her shoulders tightly. "Emily?"

She shook her head, struggling to talk. "The Broadwalk Steps. It's the other side of the White Tower."

"Show me!"

The Chief Yeoman Warder and his military escort marched swiftly through the archway of the Bloody Tower, finding the main guard waiting on the Broadwalk Steps.

On the leader of the escort's orders, the party came to a halt.

The tour group watched with intense anticipation as the leader of the main guard walked forward, the echo of his heavy footfalls for now the only sound. He ordered the gathering to present arms.

As one, they snapped to it.

Mike wasted no time. Every person he'd seen emerging from the White Tower's north wall had headed west.

Judging from the direction of their movements, they were heading for either Tower Green or the Broadwalk Steps.

Staying close to the east wall, he grabbed Emily's hand and moved south. Reaching the remains of the great Wardrobe Tower, he looked west across the grassy area by the White Tower's south wall. There were shadows moving beyond the ruined wall of the Inmost Ward, close to the site where the great hall of the medieval palace had once been; the same area was now used to house the ravens. The figures seemed to be coming from the arch of the Bloody Tower, voices echoing in the wind.

Right on time, the Ceremony of the Keys was coming to an end.

He took cover behind the ruined wall; alongside him, Emily did the same, her pretty face frozen with fear.

"What was that door they came out of?" Mike asked.

"What door?"

"The one on the other side of the White Tower; where does it lead?"

Emily shook her head, her mind blank. Suddenly nothing made sense. "I don't know!"

"Think, dammit! You work here every day!"

She racked her brain, trying to remember. *The arsenal*, she thought to herself. They had come from the White Tower.

"It's a gift shop. The main entrance is up those steps." She pointed quickly along the south wall of the White Tower, where a wooden stairway rose above the south lawn. On the far side of the White Tower, she heard the leader of the military escort bark out the word *halt*.

Followed by silence.

Neither of them saw any sign of movement.

Mike's mind was now in overdrive. "What time does this place close?"

Again Emily had to consider her response. "Five thirty, unless you live here. Tickets for the ceremony are separate."

"How does someone get into the gift shop? This place must have been deserted for four hours."

"The gift shop is the main exit from the White Tower. The entrance is there." She pointed to the wooden stairway in front of them.

"There's CCTV everywhere here. Where's the main security room located?"

"The Waterloo Barracks. It's part of the same building where the jewels are. Also where the military are stationed."

"Who are they exactly?"

"British Army."

"Which regiment?"

"Varies. I think presently it's the Scots Guards."

Mike nodded. "What about the Beefeaters?"

She shook her head. "They're more ceremonial. Most of them live over there beside the Queen's House."

Mike stared hard beyond the Bloody Tower at the area where Emily was pointing, a block of predominantly country-style black and white houses with bright blue doors. He guessed they dated from the Tudor period.

Edging closer to the south-east corner, he considered his next move.

On the other side of the White Tower, voices could again be heard.

The Chief Yeoman Warder took two paces forward and raised his Tudor bonnet from above his head.

"God preserve Queen Elizabeth."

All of the guards answered, "Amen!"

Silence fell, broken when the clock struck ten. Mike listened intently as the dying chimes gave way to the melodious tones of a brass instrument; from what Champion had told him, the ending of the ceremony would be heralded by the sound of a bugle played by the duty drummer. Once that finished, the chief would return the keys to the Queen's House and the guard would be dismissed. As the pitch-perfect rendition of the "Last Post" ended, the final notes drifting out across the deserted Inner Ward, he heard the sound of marching.

Before the courtyard erupted with the sound of screaming.

Edinburgh Castle, Edinburgh, Scotland, 22:00

In the Scottish capital, a similar, though not identical ceremony was taking place, just as it had done the night before.

In the Upper Ward close to the Royal Palace, the four armed guards making up the escort for the Lord Provost waited patiently as their two colleagues, in similar attire, marched quickly across the stone concourse before coming to a halt.

The guard with the keys stood to attention and addressed the Lord Provost. "I return these keys, being perfectly convinced that they cannot be placed in better hands than those of the Lord Provost and Councillors of my good City of Edinburgh."

The Lord Provost nodded as he accepted the keys.

Within seconds, the four guards opened fire.

The Louvre, Paris, France, 23:00

North of the River Seine, the museum had been closed for over an hour. The only people still present were those employed to keep the nightly vigil over the national treasures.

In a quiet room, reputedly once the bedroom of the King of France, the two intruders moved slowly from their concealed positions within the fireplace. Quickly they made their way into an adjacent room where, earlier that day, a locked glass display case had been the centre of interest for most of the visitors.

The leader of the two spoke rapidly to the other before focusing his attention on the contents.

He knew he was looking at possibly the most valuable jewels in all of France.

16

The Inner Ward,
22:00

What happened next didn't register clearly with Mike. Grabbing Emily's hand, he headed rapidly across the line of the old Roman city wall and dived on reaching the Lanthorn Tower. Rolling, he checked on Emily and released her hand.

He could tell from her expression that she was in a state of stunned silence.

West of the White Tower, the sounds of panic were increasing in volume, each new scream causing his heart rate to quicken. Due to the position of the White Tower, it was unclear exactly what was happening on the other side, but from the appearance of the intruders in black, he feared the sudden commotion was a consequence of muffled gunfire.

Rising to his feet, he led the way west, heading down a set of stone steps. There was a gift shop on the right, opposite a takeaway food area close to Henry III's Watergate; Mike remembered enjoying a Cumberland sausage there a couple of years back. The walkway led to a dead end; on the lawn to his right, he saw cages where the ravens were housed beyond low metal railings, accompanied by several visual displays. To his left was a series of niches set into the castle's inner wall that connected the Lanthorn and Wakefield towers.

Under the circumstances it seemed as good a place to hide as any.

Close to the White Tower the distraught cries continued, louder than before. Within the general uproar he was able to make out specific voices.

"Get down!" Mike ushered Emily to the ground, clutching her body tightly to his. He looked her in the eye, observing the same intense fear that she had shown before; once again she had removed her glasses. "Keep still."

He kept low for what seemed an eternity before slowly rising to his feet. Beyond the raven cages, he saw movement close to the west wall of the White Tower, the same figures as before, clearly armed. There were bodies sprawled out across the Broadwalk Steps, close to which bright streaks of yellow broke the dark stillness. Apart from the screams, he heard no other sound, seemingly confirming his suspicion that the shooting involved the use of silencers.

None of the Queen's Guard appeared to still be alive.

He pulled himself over the railing and slowly skirted the ravens' cages, ensuring he remained hidden from sight. The intruders were moving beyond the Broadwalk Steps; some had gathered outside the Jewel House. He heard gunfire for the first time, a sudden flash of yellow emanating from the upper windows of the Waterloo Block. No less than twenty figures in black had assembled close to the entrance; Mike estimated half the total intruders.

The majority of the others were closing in on the Queen's House.

He took off his rucksack and removed his USP45 semi-automatic pistol from the main pocket. Under the circumstances, he was glad he'd brought it with him.

Emily had joined him by the ravens' cages.

"I told you to stay out of sight."

Distracted by the gun, Emily asked, "What's happening?"

"Keep down!" Mike lay down flat, doing his best to ignore the distraction of the assistant curator alongside him. Close to the White Tower, the tour group had been ordered into a tight circle; some had attempted to run off in fear. At least three lay lifeless on the floor.

Mike feared the worst.

He saw Champion among the crowd, his hands raised.

At least he was still alive.

Champion heard a second set of orders coming from the figure directly in front of him, prompting him to retreat closer to the nearest wall. Having already witnessed the strange group responsible for taking out every participant of the Ceremony of the Keys do the same to three members of his tour group, the last thing he needed was further persuasion. Although he was certain of what he'd just seen, his mind failed to accept it. Logically, it should never have happened. The Tower of London was impenetrable; he'd just witnessed the ceremony famous for ensuring its security. Only once in its illustrious history had it ever finished late.

For the first time in the Tower's history, he was looking at complete failure.

The sound of new voices carried again on the wind, some from further afield. Though the instructions he'd heard so far had been in English, he detected a second language reserved for private conversation, possibly French. Most of the gunfire had been inaudible except for the sounds of impact, physical evidence of which now peppered the surrounding stonework. A fine dust polluted the nearby air where the ground and walls had been disturbed.

He prayed that was the only thing that would be disturbed.

Another voice spoke from far nearer. Though his veiled appearance largely matched that of the others, Champion sensed that this man was the leader. Doing his best to hold his nerve, he complied with the latest orders and joined the others along the west wall of the White Tower.

Blanco fired without consideration, emptying his first magazine. Beside that aimed at one solitary window in the upper level of the Waterloo Barracks, the recent gunfire had been aimed at no particular person, its purpose solely to ensure the compliance of the hostages. The plan itself had gone off like clockwork.

Phase one was complete.

The short burst of audible gunfire from one of the upper windows of the Waterloo Block had ceased almost as soon as it had begun; a large stain discolouring the broken glass indicated his aim had been accurate. Blanco reasoned that further gunfire was unlikely as long as the hostages were held in close proximity.

Below the window, fifteen or more of his men had already entered the barracks.

He strutted up and down the Broadwalk Steps with an air of calmness, his eyes on the hostages. The seven who had earlier made up the ceremonial guard were lying lifeless, their blood pooling across the medieval stonework. The Chief Yeoman Warder also lay in a heap, his four-man escort close by. His uniform had been torn to pieces, his hat decimated.

Randek was barking orders at the tour group; another man did the same on Tower Green. The second detachment had already taken control of the area outside the Queen's House, their burly frames making their way quickly past the lifeless body of the silent guard. A series of bangs reverberated against the front door, following which it opened.

Blanco knew further conflict was unavoidable.

He moved towards the assembled tour group, ignoring the bodies of the three people who had been caught in the crossfire. In truth, he was unsure which bullets had killed them.

"All right, nothing will happen to you," he addressed the frightened crowd. "Now do exactly as I tell you. Very calmly, but very quickly, make your way towards the entrance of the Queen's House. It is very important you comply. Right? Move!"

Mike heard every word clearly. He sensed from the sound of the most dominant voice that the group were primarily Europeans; as the man was wearing a balaclava, it was impossible to see his facial features. The same was true of the man alongside him, the only other man he'd heard speak. This man, he didn't need to see first-hand.

"Randek!"

Emily was confused. "What?"

Mike ignored her, keeping his eyes on the hostages. Champion was okay, albeit startled; he'd clearly received no physical injuries. As best Mike could tell, none of the hostages had.

At least those who were still alive.

His satphone vibrated; fortunately the noise didn't carry. Quietly he blessed the Beefeater who'd insisted he put it on silent.

He made his way to the other side of the ravens' cages and answered quickly, his back to the ruined wall of the Inmost Ward. Ensuring Emily had followed, he placed the call on hands-free. A quick glance at the screen had been enough to see it was Kit.

"I can't really talk right now, Edward."

* * *

At the other end, the scene was one of chaos. Kit was still on the north side of the Monument, where King William Street met Cannon Street. The fires near Monument had spread, heading north along Gracechurch Street. Several tall buildings were now ablaze.

Once again traffic had ground to a halt.

Kit heard every word Mike said, despite the combination of static interference and background noise. "Well, in that case just listen. There's a situation brewing north of the Thames. The city's on fire."

Listening to every word, Mike glanced through a gap in the stonework and saw the hostages being marched up the steps towards the Queen's House. The man he believed to be Randek had hurried to the front.

Sure enough, the hostages were being ordered inside.

"Grosmont?"

"I hear you, Edward!" Mike lowered himself to a seated position, back to the stonework, his eyes on the Wakefield Tower to his right. Out of the corner of his eye he saw Emily move in alongside him, gazing beyond the wall towards Tower Green. He grabbed her arm.

"I said keep down!"

At the other end, Kit was confused. "What?"

Mike pulled Emily to the ground. "Never mind that. There's a situation brewing here."

"Well, there's an even bigger one brewing here. Half of London is on fire. The attacks started at Monument." Kit's face sweated from the intensity of the nearby heat that had already done noticeable damage to his previously smart tuxedo. "Have you spoken to the Rook?"

"Not recently."

"It's impossible to describe what I'm seeing here. It's as though the Great Fire of London has restarted."

Mike's heart skipped a beat. He recalled the subject matter of Champion's lecture, the date on the calendar; it already seemed like years had passed since he'd been seated in the auditorium.

"What?"

"Things are getting out of hand. The emergency services are fully stretched. The early fires are already out, but new ones are breaking out all over the place. We've ordered an evacuation of the surrounding area; everything that's been searched has come up with nothing. There's been no sound of explosions, no evidence of tampering. It's as if the fires are springing up by spontaneous combustion."

Mike couldn't believe what he was hearing. "Where are you?"

"Just north of Monument; it's the only place that doesn't feel like a sauna. Traffic is tailing back everywhere; pretty soon there's a real danger it'll extend beyond the bridge." He gazed across King William Street where the congestion was at its peak. The fires were encroaching steadily on the stationary cars, prompting some of the occupants to desert their vehicles and run off in various directions. The overcrowding on the Underground was close to the exhausting point. "Water alone isn't going to cure this one." He heard nothing beyond the nearby blaring of sirens. "Grosmont?"

Mike had returned to his feet, standing alongside Emily and looking once more beyond the ruined wall of the former great hall. Most of the hostages had already entered the Queen's House; Champion had disappeared.

So had Randek.

"Grosmont?" Kit repeated.

"Listen, I can't talk too loud right now. Something just as crazy is happening here."

"Where are you?"

"Tower of London."

"What on earth are you doing there?"

"It's a long story; just be glad I am."

"Grosmont?"

"Look, I don't have time to explain right now, but I just saw at least forty armed gunmen come out of the White Tower just as the Ceremony of the Keys was ending; my uncle was giving a lecture and tour, ironically on the Great Fire. All the guards are dead, as is the Chief Yeoman Warder."

"What?"

"It gets worse. They've also got hostages."

François looked on, clearly satisfied, as sounds of consternation gave way to quiet order. In single file a number of men, aged anything from early twenties to mid-forties, in full military attire but stripped of their weapons, were marched down the nearby stairs, their hands clutched tightly to the back of their heads. Their facial expressions clearly revealed their disdain for their captors.

The captain of the Queen's Guard came last.

François blocked his path. "A moment of your time, Captain." He walked him to a closed door in the heart of the Jewel House, its hard, vault-style solid steel casing alone confirmation it guarded something of significant value. "I will need you to open the door."

Standing with his hands clutched to his head, the blond-haired captain showed no emotion. "You think they would trust me with the keys? Only the Jeweller is allowed access to this room after dark. Our job is solely to guard the perimeter."

"I understand the jewels are cleaned at night." François's gaze was stern. "Where is the master craftsman?"

"Absent. The jewels are cleaned weekly, not daily."

The Frenchman removed a firearm from his jacket pocket, pressing it uncomfortably into the officer's midriff. "You're lying, Captain."

The captain bit his lip, remaining silent as the armed gunmen led him to the main door. Outside the Jewel House, Tower Green was deserted. The only signs of life were close to the doors of the Queen's House.

"Captain?"

Resistance was useless. "Take us captive if you want. Either way, you're wasting your time. The job of guarding the Jewel House is charged specifically to a private firm. Only they can open it."

François snatched the handheld transmitter from the captain's belt and held it up to him.

"Contact them."

The leader of the four-man escort heard the captain's request come through clearly. Though contact from the barracks was rare, it was not unheard of.

Answering immediately, the leader of the four led his men up the staircase that connected the jeweller's workshop to the jewel rooms and headed for the exit to the barracks.

17

The Inner Ward,
22:04

"How many hostages?" Kit pressed, detecting a further time lag in Mike's response. On this occasion, he sensed it had nothing to do with the static interference.

"Not sure exactly, possibly over sixty," Mike replied, suddenly distracted by the re-emergence of about twelve of the masked gunmen from the Jewel House, followed by what appeared to be further disquiet from several other houses scattered round Tower Green. A door had opened; shouts of panic and surprise sounded out from deep inside.

Mike struggled to see from his present location how many gunmen had entered.

The lodgings of the Yeoman Warders were located either east or west of Tower Green, in a series of character buildings distinguished by their elegant façades and light blue front doors, or in the outer ring along Mint Street. While most served as comfortable apartments, another building against the outer wall on the castle's riverside served a different purpose.

The Yeoman Warders' Club was the only remaining drinking establishment at the Tower. Separate from the various shops, eateries and food vendors, access was prohibited to the public.

Even the Queen herself could enter only by special invitation.

The situation in the club was typical of almost any evening. More than half of the Beefeaters were there, most relaxing over a drink at the bar or sitting in one of the comfortable red padded seats. A series of wooden plaques commemorating the various branches of the Yeomanry that had served the Tower during its long and distinguished history occupied pride of place on the predominantly white walls, alongside other ornaments, artwork and items of historical memorabilia. In a corner of the room was a locked glass cabinet containing thirty-seven iconic tankards, each designated for a particular person and used for the secret ceremonial dinners.

Tonight none were in use.

The main door opened with a thunderous crash, accompanied by loud shouting. Those already inside looked on in stunned silence as no less than twelve armed intruders stormed the pub.

* * *

THE CROWN JEWELS CONSPIRACY

Mike watched with rising concern as over twenty Beefeaters emerged from the north side of the White Tower, each man clearly flustered, their hands raised in surrender.

"Better make that over eighty," Mike added as he watched their every move, striving to obtain a good view while remaining concealed behind the ruined wall. "Three hostages are dead, along with everyone involved in the ceremony. We could be looking at a minimum of fifteen."

"Jeez!" Kit replied.

"My uncle's among the hostages. He's just been led into the Queen's House."

"What's there?"

"I'm not sure. Apparently the resident governor uses it. The silent guard is also dead."

"Who's in charge?"

"Not sure exactly. The constable doesn't live on site; as far as I'm aware he's not here."

"Any visuals on the intruders?"

"Uniforms are standard black ops; firearms sure look the part. Their faces are covered." He watched with rising hatred as the final intruder disappeared inside the Tudor mansion. "I'm pretty sure one of them is Randek!"

Almost a mile away, Kit came to an abrupt halt. He knew he didn't need Mike to clarify. "Have you spoken to Camelot?"

"Negative. I tried calling and got nothing but static."

"Camelot has been assembled at the Rook. The knights are already split up. Though we're still to get confirmation on who started the fires, CCTV cameras confirm Randek's uncle was in the vicinity."

Mike thought he was hearing things. "His what?"

"It's a long story, not particularly fascinating. His name's Bizante Blanco. Nicknamed the Anjouvin."

"Where's he now?"

"That's a good question. CCTV footage showed him crossing London Bridge on foot before making his way to a park south of the river. Reports indicate he was last in a taxi close to where you are now."

"Pound to a penny he's the guy calling the shots."

"What's Randek doing?"

"Best I can tell, he seems to be the number two." Mike lowered his voice as a second group of Beefeaters were escorted at gunpoint into the Queen's House. At the same time, three gunmen ran across the south lawn, their dark frames creating fast-moving shadows on the illuminated walls of the White Tower.

"Keep down!" he whispered to Emily, noticing her expression was now somewhere between an annoyed frown and a frightened glare. "Three more have just passed us," he said to Kit before addressing Emily a second time. "What's over there?"

Emily saw Mike was pointing beyond the Bloody Tower in the direction the gunmen were heading. "Most of the Yeoman Warders who don't live off Tower

Green live along Mint Street near the main entrance. The Chief and the Yeoman Gaoler live in the Byward Tower with their families." She looked sadly in the direction of the deceased escort. "Did."

"Something tells me that's exactly where they're heading." He returned his thoughts to Kit. "Where's everyone else?"

"Everyone who isn't tailing Blanco is here or heading to Edinburgh. Reports are coming through of trouble there as well!"

Mike swore beneath his breath. "I can't hold the baby on my own, Edward. Right now, I'd say at least forty fully armed and highly trained operatives stand in the way of me leaving here. The Yeomanry is all tied up, the Queen's sentries are either dead or been captured; I can't see beyond the barracks, but from what I can tell, chances are that's already compromised."

Back near Monument, Kit removed the handkerchief from the outer pocket of his tuxedo and wiped away patches of sweat from his brow. Gazing at his shirt, now covered with dirt and heavy patches of sweat from the intense heat, he wondered how 007 ever managed it. "Well, unfortunately I've got my hands tied right now. Where exactly are you?"

"By one of the south walls, close to the ravens. The hostages are all inside the Queen's House."

"Sit tight and stay where you are. If you can, try to rouse the guard – at least what's left of it. Better yet, get into the security area."

"Not gonna be easy. There's gunmen everywhere."

"I guess you'll have to take the long way, then. If you can't get there following the maps, you might have to learn that layout quickly."

He glanced at Emily. "I'm on it."

Mike replaced his phone in his pocket and grabbed Emily's hand, setting off across the grass and through the archway to Henry III's Watergate. Stopping briefly beneath the stone archway, he glanced quickly along Water Lane. Although he could hear voices in the distance, he saw no sign of life.

He backtracked slightly and moved north as far as the Lanthorn Tower. West of the White Tower, all had gone quiet.

"Get down!"

Four silhouettes moved suddenly beyond the north wall of the White Tower; it wasn't clear where they'd come from.

Emily hit the ground alongside him. "Oh my God, there's hundreds of them!"

Mike strained his vision as far as was humanly possible, watching the figures until they moved out of sight. "They seem to be heading for the rear of the Jewel House." A whole series of thoughts entered his mind. "Where's the main security area here?"

"The Waterloo Block. It's where most of the main offices are."

"What's the best way to get there?"

"We need to get out of here!"

Mike grabbed her shoulders. "There are over eighty hostages currently being held here; not to mention the fact the guys responsible for locking the gates are now dead. It's my duty to get them out."

He released her and took her hand, hurrying to the other side of the ruins of the Wardrobe Tower, heading back towards the White Tower.

He stopped on reaching the east wall.

The four intruders had made their way as far as the Martin Tower, close to the toilets Mike had used on leaving the Jewel House. At that same moment, five more appeared from the Queen's House, heading down the steps and across the south lawn. Mike watched them make their way up the wooden stairway into the White Tower.

He waited till both groups had disappeared before releasing Emily's hand. "All right. I need you to talk me through this. What's the best way into the barracks?"

Tears rolled down her cheeks; failing to respond, she wiped them away. Mike placed his hands against her face, holding her firmly.

"I know you're scared right now, but I promise we can do this. There's nothing here I haven't seen before, but I really need your help on this. You must trust me."

She looked at him, desperately trying to process what she'd seen and heard. Over fifteen had died. More could be about to follow. *There's nothing here I haven't seen before.* No one used phrases like that.

She shook her head. "Who are you?"

18

Berkshire, England, Twenty-One Months Earlier

The black hatchback moved steadily along the A404, making its way through the heart of the countryside. Though equipped with bulletproof glass and a heavily reinforced exterior over five times thicker than that of any ordinary hatchback, the vehicle was, to all outward appearances, unremarkable, blending in unnoticeably with most of the cars travelling that traditionally busy stretch of road.

Nothing suggested it had been specifically constructed for special military purposes.

As the driver concentrated on the road ahead, behind him the two smartly dressed passengers travelled in silence. While Ian Atkins had made the same journey many times before, often in the trusted and capable hands of the present driver, for Lieutenant Mike Hansen it was an entirely new experience. Since their initial meeting at RAF Brize Norton seven days ago, the questions posed then had remained unanswered.

Whatever the reason for the ceremony of the pink gin, Mike was sure that it related to nothing with which he was currently familiar.

As the hatchback exited the dual-carriage of the A404, heading on to the triple lanes of the M4 and from there on to the A332, several imposing buildings to the east caught Mike's attention.

"Windsor Castle," Mike said, quietly awed by the sight of the famous towers as they crept above the surrounding woodland. Though he had never actually visited the castle, the stone built regal towers were instantly recognisable. "I've always wanted to go there."

Seated alongside him, Atkins showed far less enthusiasm. "In that case, you might find your luck is about to change for the better."

The journey ended within the castle walls, in the shadow of the great Round Tower. Captivated by the surroundings, Mike quickly got out of the car and followed Atkins across the Middle Ward towards the Henry III Tower.

"The historical homes of the Royal Family haven't always been open to the public," the former undersecretary said, again showing no obvious interest in his surroundings. "I daresay there are many people inside government circles who would be only too satisfied if the same were true today."

Mike viewed the statement as odd. "What's to stop them?"

"You try telling that to the Great British public – not to mention her foreign cousins. Even in the days of Elizabeth I's father, it was enough of a challenge keeping the nosy parsons at bay. Since the invention of the Android, it's become almost impossible."

The walk continued in silence as Atkins led the way into the Lower Ward. Despite the developing brightness, the early rays of the rising sun creeping above the outer defences and casting long shadows across the medieval courtyards, Mike sensed a certain loneliness about the place, rare for a site open to the public.

"Where are the crowds?" he asked, noticing from his watch that it was 09:00.

"The semi-state rooms often close around the twelfth of December; though the main doors will open in about an hour. Despite what I just told you, even in this day and age, there are still certain areas that remain closed."

They came to a halt near the Horseshoe Cloisters, close to St George's Chapel. In the surrounding quiet, Mike could hear a melancholy echo of Gregorian-style chanting from within its walls; he guessed heralding the beginning of a service. Moments later, three burly men, each dressed in sharp suits, emerged quietly through the main doors, walking confidently in their direction. As a five-year veteran of the forces, Mike detected they were of a military background.

Atkins addressed them as they approached. "Gentlemen, I would like to introduce you to Lieutenant Hansen, 1st Battalion Parachute Regiment – Special Forces Support Group. As I'm sure you'll appreciate, this will be his first trip to the Tower."

Mike raised an eyebrow, unsure whether the comment was intended to be taken seriously. As a schoolboy educated in the stories of England's bloody past, he'd learned to associate the expression with the famous structure in London. While the appearance of the three newcomers was hardly that of gaolers or kidnappers, at close quarters Mike could see that they each carried a highly sophisticated semi-automatic pistol only partially hidden behind their slick jackets. Whereas two of the three were bearded, one worn thickly by a white man of a possible fatherly bearing, and the second more designer and covering a face of Asian features, the third displayed no facial hair, his jawline harbouring a hard and intense expression that suggested even the slightest pimple or hair out of place would be reason enough to put his firearm to good use. Though facially his handsomeness was arguably the most boyish of the three, even a few short seconds in the man's company was enough to detect he was the leader.

Mike studied the newcomers closely, listening carefully as Atkins continued to address them. Almost immediately one feature caught his attention: emblazoned on their jackets at breast height, a small emblem or symbol that reminded him of the Pegasus logo synonymous with the parachute regiment. Rather than a winged horse, however, this was clearly a forest animal.

A white hart.

Once Atkins finished talking, the leader of the three removed what appeared to be a black head sack from his inner pocket. "Shall we begin, sir?"

Atkins checked his watch and took a couple of measured footsteps towards

Mike. "Lieutenant, if you'd be so kind, I'm afraid this is one area of the tour where I must ask you to avert your gaze."

It took a few seconds for his sight to adjust to the new light; even after such a short period of time, his eyes struggled to take in the new surroundings. As the clarity of his vision returned, he realised he was standing in a historic chamber that he could now see was far larger than he had judged from the sounds alone.

The wood flooring, the source of the creaking sounds created by his footsteps, was laid out in a perfect circle, as if to replicate the sun or a clock face. The oak walls were richly decorated in a fine glossy overcoat covered at regular intervals by a series of artwork, the majority oil-based portraits. Although Mike was aware of the rich collection of paintings housed in the castle above, many of them famous portraits of former residents of the palace, whose lives and deeds had helped shape the course of history, none of the faces that he saw now were familiar.

The same was true of their dress, which appeared strangely consistent despite clear evolution over the centuries. Each man wore a unique set of robes, noble yet also unquestionably military, as though inspired by the religious orders of the Crusader period. Like the men who accompanied him, an identical deer-like symbol was emblazoned on to their white and green mantles, providing a possible clue to their identity, which he could now see was almost certainly linked to an impressive table at the very centre of the room.

What thoughts entered his mind at that moment were difficult, if not impossible, to put into words. While his expectation on receiving the pink gin had been of possible recruitment to an operational government unit, perhaps associated with the Special Forces, he now realised the truth was something far different. The footsteps that Atkins had spoken of had been walked not for decades, but for centuries. Any lingering element of ironic humour in his mind from the recent reference to the Tower had dissipated immediately on seeing what lay before him. It seemed to predate the days of the princes, perhaps even the walls themselves.

Those who had first walked these steps he was now sure had been the founders of a secret and famous order. One whose very existence had long been lost in the mists of time. History was laid bare before him, the answer to several questions – to every question. It was there in the form of the table that, like the room itself, was round.

And surrounded by twelve chairs.

19

The White Tower,
22:07

Blanco made sure the thick outer door was closed and those beyond it bolted before proceeding inside the White Tower. The plan was that the outer stairway would be used several times that night. Only in exceptional circumstances would anything be changed.

He made his way forward in near darkness, the dual light of his torch and the flashlight app on his phone revealing a wooden floor that he secretly believed didn't date back to when the tower was first constructed. He remembered learning once that the reason for the White Tower's height was largely psychological: the original ceiling was high, but almost a third lower than the surrounding walls, the purpose of its exterior to send out a clear message to the outside world.

Mess with us at your peril!

He navigated his way through a series of visual displays and came to an opening at which point electronic lighting illuminated a large impressive area surrounded by thick stone walls that matched those on the outside, and what could have been thousands of suits of military armour designed for both humans and animals. As he studied the information on the displays, he realised he was looking at things that had once been property of the kings of England.

Usurpers.

He removed his handheld transmitter from his belt and put a call through to Randek as he examined the heavy armoured suit once used by Henry VIII.

Alongside him, the four gunmen carried the same holdalls Fieschi had given him on board the yacht.

Randek had waited till the door to the White Tower was closed before making his own journey in the opposite direction. Entering the Queen's House, the intruders spread out quickly, guns at the ready. The wooden panelling he saw was different to that of the surrounding towers, the décor instead more akin to the luxury chateau he had visited in the early hours of the previous morning.

The governor had been in the dining room with his family, gathered round an illustrious dining table set with authentic tableware and surrounded by walls decorated with artwork of relevance to the Tower's past. Each resident's family had already been bound and gagged, their frightened faces revealing shock at their incarceration.

One by one, the Beefeaters joined them, each bearing angry and irritated expressions. Randek knew from his research that the Yeoman Warders, although all retired military and once of no less than warrant officer rank, rarely carried firearms, despite being capable of firing them. The only armed military were those that had been stationed in the Waterloo Barracks.

To hold all of the hostages would require a much larger room.

Randek heard his uncle's voice echo through the static.

"Queen's House is clear," he answered immediately. "Every man presently accounted for is currently in the dining room. The same is true of the governor's family."

Blanco heard Randek's response clearly. "What of the Yeoman Warders?"

"They are currently being brought in. Most were in the tavern."

"How many did you count?"

"Twenty-nine."

At the other end, Blanco was furious. "That leaves eight unaccounted for."

"Six. Two were involved in the Ceremony of the Keys, and are now dead. The lodgings in the Byward Tower and along Mint Street are being searched as we speak."

A relieved smile crossed the Anjouvin's lips. "How silly of me. For a moment, I'd forgotten. Where is François?"

"He is where he needs to be. The Waterloo Barracks have also now fallen."

Blanco's face was a picture of satisfaction. Both factions of the Tower's military had been stifled; he estimated the operation had taken less than three minutes. The only remaining obstacle was the Tower security, which was carried out by a private security firm.

He anticipated they would prove less of a problem.

He walked the corridors of the armoury, his footsteps causing a heavy echo as he trod the wooden boards. The lights against the nearby armoury caused imposing shadows in front of him, creating the illusion they had company.

Returning his attention to Henry VIII's body armour, he called to the nearest gunman. "Legend has it, after his death, the fat king's body exploded before it even made the crypt. Start with him. Let history repeat itself!"

20

The Inner Ward,
22:09

Mike grabbed hold of Emily's hand and ushered her along the White Tower's east wall. There were figures moving outside the Jewel House; he recognised the hardware they carried but was still unable to see their faces.

"AK-47s," Mike muttered under his breath, quietly wondering if there was a terrorist organisation in the world that didn't use such weapons. Failing again to connect to the central hub, he phoned Kit using his satphone.

"Getting to the barracks via the front might be a problem," he said on receiving an answer. "Practically all of these bastards are clocking Heckler & Kochs and AKs."

Kit had returned to the Monument, where Iqbal, Chambers and Ward were attempting to organise incoming fire trucks. All three had false IDs attached to their heavy, dark overalls that gave them some protection from the burning heat.

"Well, they were hardly likely to be carrying plastic cutlery, were they?" Kit came to a halt as he witnessed another fire come under control, the framework of the building sinking under the combination of heat and water. "What's happening in the Queen's House?"

"Seems quiet. I haven't seen anyone leave since Blanco. He's just entered the White Tower; he took four gunmen with him. Three more are on patrol outside the Jewel House. Whatever these guys are planning, they're clearly leaving nothing to chance."

"Can you see inside?"

"Hold on a sec." Mike led Emily south again, stopping close to the remains of the Wardrobe Tower. On his instructions they darted across the south lawn, his eyes briefly lingering on the wooden stairway where he'd last seen the man he believed to be Blanco.

The door to the White Tower was closed.

He stopped close to the ravens before instructing Emily to hide below the ruined wall. He paused briefly by the south wall of the White Tower before heading towards the Broadwalk Steps. The bodies of the main guard and the escort were still spread across the steps, blood pooling.

Keeping low, he gazed across Tower Green at the exterior of the Queen's House, where he'd recently seen a large crowd being escorted at gunpoint. The famous front door was closed.

Outwardly all seemed well.

"Can't see anything beyond the door," he said. Besides the forlorn crowing of the angry birds, he heard nothing. "Looks like everyone else has gone inside."

"How about Randek?"

"Haven't seen him since he entered the Queen's House." He looked around in every direction, focusing on the former scaffold site located outside the Beauchamp Tower and the royal chapel of St Peter ad Vincula. The site where the lives of seven of history's key figures had been ended with a swift blow of a sword or axe was shrouded in a strange ghostly mist; he put it down to water from the Thames.

He heard a different sound, voices, more rugged; it seemed to be coming from outside the Jewel House.

Shouting echoed through the darkness.

Looking over his shoulder, he saw Emily by the wall of the former great hall.

"Stay down!"

François waited until the main door opened, at which point the first of the four-man escort emerged. Evidently none were prepared for what awaited them.

Watching from a window on the ground floor of the Queen's House, Randek saw the security men emerge clearly, heading towards the Queen's House. Reaching for his binoculars, he gazed as best he could through the small square window frames.

He raised his HT to his lips and contacted Blanco. "The vault has been breached. They have made it into the jewel room!"

Mike didn't stop till he'd passed the ravens again, sprinting to the south wall of the former great hall. He came down alongside Emily, rolling over.

"What the hell's happening?"

"Shhh!" Ignoring her concern, Mike rose to his feet. There were figures moving north of the White Tower. While a further three uniformed guards were being escorted at gunpoint towards the Queen's House, the remaining gunmen disappeared inside the Jewel House.

He turned to Emily. "Where exactly does that lead?"

Emily also watched the figures head left on entering the Jewel House. "That door leads to the exhibition into the jewel room," she said, reality dawning on the possible reason for the intrusion. "You think they're here for the jewels?"

"I doubt they just came out to the gift shop for a souvenir." He eyed her, his own thoughts racing. "What's the security like here?"

"The room where the main jewels are kept is the most secure in the whole Tower. Any breach of security and it goes into automatic lockdown."

Mike nodded, remembering seeing the room himself not twenty minutes earlier. "Counts for little when there's no one around keeping guard."

Emily was stunned. "Do you have any idea what safeguards we have here, mister? The new security system is state of the art – it took over three years to install and all for good reason. The jewels themselves are protected by two-inch-thick, shatterproof glass, to say nothing of the fibre optics. The security room has cameras watching over everything."

Mike bit his lip and repeated his earlier thought, "Well, let's just hope it holds out when there's no one around to check up on them."

He skirted the ravens' cages along the right side, doing his best to remain low. As far as he could tell, movement close to the Jewel House entrance had ceased.

Emily moved alongside him once more.

"Whoever these guys are, they clearly aren't amateurs. They've already taken out the military; after that, security should be a doddle." He looked around, his face locked in a grim expression. A disturbing thought had occurred to him.

"You said the jewels are cleaned at night?"

"That's right."

"Who by?"

"The Crown Jeweller; he's the only person allowed to touch the real things."

"Where?"

"His workshop is below the Jewel House. He only comes once a week."

"Is he here tonight?"

Considering the question, Emily placed her hand to her mouth in horror.

Failing again to connect to the White Hart's server, Mike put through another call to Kit.

"Even if they are looking for the jewels, no one could possibly know that. Even I don't know his exact schedule," Emily said. "Getting them out is impossible."

"That's exactly what they said about sinking the *Titanic*." Mike held his satphone to his ear, waiting for an answer. The thought was astounding.

While London burned, no one would notice twenty billion pounds' worth of jewels slip away.

Kit was sprinting west, away from the fires, when he heard his phone ring again. Stopping close to the Underground, he answered.

"What's happening?"

Mike heard him clearly. "Hate to say it, but I have a nasty feeling we've just seen the end of the Tower Guard. Terrorists are closing in on the jewels."

Masterson slowed his pace, the thought lingering. "You're sure?"

"Sure as I can be." Mike edged his way across the south lawn, chancing exposure. On approaching the Broadwalk Steps, he saw sixteen bodies piled unceremoniously, the colours of thirteen confirming rank and regiment.

None had been spared.

Randek continued to look out the nearest window, keeping a vigilant eye across Tower Green. The number of prisoners had increased in recent minutes; as far as he could tell the only news was good.

He contacted François over the airwaves. "Where are you?"

"The armed guard has been disarmed. We have just entered the main exhibit," the art director replied, wandering the corridors where the jewels were kept. "These really will look most extraordinary back in our family home."

"What is it you see?"

"Swords." François looked up at the display case in front of him where the three ceremonial swords from the Plantagenet days reflected the overhead lights. "Not to mention artistry of the finest nature – it could only have originated from the motherland."

Randek rolled his eyes. "Are you alone?"

"For now." He continued quietly, the three gunmen following close behind. Treading softly, he made it to the beginning of the travellator, observing the illustrious crowns before looking beyond the far end.

There was sound coming from the next room.

"I think we've come just in time for a spring clean!"

Randek reattached his HT to his belt and returned his attention to the view beyond the window. The main door of the Jewel House had closed again; it was unclear whether François's armed guard had made it inside.

Turning to his right, he saw subtle movement close to the Broadwalk Steps. The figure was dressed casually, mostly in black; as far as he could tell, he carried no machine gun.

Nevertheless, he was clearly armed.

Moving away from the window, Randek hurried up the narrow stairway to the first floor, his heavy footsteps causing a pronounced echo as they pounded the wooden steps. He stopped at the first window he came to, staring out across the Inner Ward.

Someone other than one of his own men was walking the grounds.

21

The Broadwalk Steps,
22:11

Mike knelt down alongside the nearest body, taking a moment to inspect the features. The man was of oriental leanings, his face revealing shock rather than discomfort.

Mike sensed it was unlikely he'd known much about his death.

Further down the steps lay the bodies of the escort, their iconic greatcoats riddled with bullet holes. The blood on the steps was beginning to dry, staining the stonework like paint.

Like many of the victims of the Tower's bloody past, they had been executed in cold blood.

He knelt down for a third time where the bodies of two Beefeaters lay together, a sad, resigned look on his face.

"Edward, this is really bad. Turns out the deputy was also part of the ceremony."

Kit replied while simultaneously receiving an update from the server. According to the map, the fire in Edinburgh was also spreading. "Meaning what exactly?"

"Meaning both the Chief and the Yeoman Gaoler are now dead. Now I still don't know much about the security this place has, but one thing I do know is that at the start of the night they had thirty-seven Yeoman Warders and the top two have both been taken down. Even if the others are still alive, it leaves them without a leader."

"What about the barracks?"

"Still to get anywhere near it, but based on what I saw earlier, most of the Queen's Guards are now either dead or inside the Queen's House."

Randek watched from the upstairs window as the mysterious figure moved among the bodies of the dead. He saw him kneel down briefly close to one of the tourists, then again close to the Yeoman Warders.

The man seemed strangely inquisitive.

He removed his smart pair of field glasses from the inside pocket of his dark jacket, adjusting the setting to night vision. The man was around six feet, he mused; he carried himself well, almost certainly military or secret service. The gun he carried appeared semi-automatic; he guessed a USP, but he couldn't be sure.

Resetting his glasses to ordinary zoom and focusing on the man's face, he immediately felt more confident in his guess.

He'd seen this man before.

***

A series of sparks went up off the concrete, then more from the wall in front of him. Despite the silence, Mike instinctively knew what he was dealing with.

Gunfire.

Rolling to his left, he bolted down the Broadwalk Steps and beneath the archway of the Bloody Tower. Lunging into a summersault, he hit the ground with force.

He felt blood all the way up his back.

Holding his satphone to his ear, Kit heard what sounded like panicked movement. Though he'd heard no gunfire, he feared the worst.

"Grosmont?"

Mike came to a stop directly below the archway, his skin grazed from landing heavily against the brick paving. He found himself staring up at a combination of rounded and straight stone walls; it took him a moment to regain his bearings.

He recognised the imposing façade of the Wakefield Tower to his left; Champion had referred to the area to his right as Water Lane. It was the area where the tour had begun.

As he rolled to one side, he noticed the body of a uniformed soldier lying dead alongside him.

The sentry.

"Grosmont?" Kit's voice bellowed in his ears.

"I'm okay!"

Kit breathed a sigh of relief. "What the hell just happened?"

Mike gritted his teeth, doing his best to move. The skin on his back was warm, tingly; he felt blood trickling down his neck. The same was true of his arms, hands and face.

He sensed it wasn't all his.

"Grosmont?"

He heard Kit's voice speak clearly in his ear, and replied, "I think I just had a narrow escape."

"What happened?"

"I'm not sure. All I saw were sparks."

Kit raised an eyebrow on hearing the word *sparks*. "Well, I do hope you haven't been starting fires. We've got enough of them as it is."

"Well, when we're all through with this, we'll have to get together and compare notes. All the gunfire has been muffled. I think it came from the Queen's House."

"Randek?"

"Either that or whoever's babysitting him."

"Where are you now?"

"Just past the Bloody Tower." Mike raised himself cautiously to his haunches before finally ascending to his feet. He hurried back beneath the archway, hoping for a better view.

Due to the raised wall to his left, he could see no obvious signs of life.

"Listen to me. You need to find a way into the barracks. Find the security system and maybe you might finally see what's going on."

"It's gonna be a little tricky crossing Tower Green if someone's shooting at me."

"Look, there's a reason there's only twelve of us – if you can't find a way, you make one."

Skirting the round walls of the Wakefield Tower, Mike decided he was right.

"I'm on it!"

He ended the call and sprinted east along Water Lane, beneath the Salvin Bridge that connected the Wakefield Tower to St Thomas's Tower and then left, Henry III's Watergate. He prayed Emily hadn't moved.

He found her at the top of the steps, close to the Lanthorn Tower.

"Come on, stay low."

Emily covered her head, on this occasion showing no objection as Mike grabbed hold of her hand. On reaching Traitors' Gate, he released her.

As before, Water Lane was devoid of people.

She stared at him. "What the hell just happened?"

"I think I had a narrow escape."

They continued west along Water Lane, keeping watch for any sign of life. As they approached the gift shop close to the Byward Tower, Mike felt himself guided to the walls of the Bell Tower, suddenly wary that company could be imminent.

He remembered seeing three gunmen disappear past the water gate while Champion and the others were being escorted inside the Queen's House.

"We need a new plan if we're gonna get to the barracks undetected." The recent gunfire confirmed Randek had the Inner Ward covered. Mike assumed if he had his bearings correct, the only other way to the Jewel House was to head east then north, skirting the outer walls till they reached the Martin Tower. Getting there undetected would be a risk. "You know this place better than me. What are our options?"

"There's a second entrance from the rear. Getting there won't be easy."

"Is there any other way besides going round the outside?"

"Not unless you have your parachute tucked away in that rucksack."

He grimaced, concerned. "In that case, you best be showing me the way."

Kit heard a voice in his earpiece at the exact moment he ended his conversation with Mike. Unlike his recent use of the satellite communications technology, he knew any incomings through his earpiece were by way of encrypted radio waves.

"Talk to me."

"What else did you think I had in mind?"

He smiled wryly. *Maria.*

"The fires at Monument are under control, but they're starting to spread beyond Eastcheap," Kit replied, for once struggling to control the alarm in his voice. Further buildings had caught fire north of King William Street; more vehicles were being abandoned as the wind took the flames across the roads, making it almost impossible for the fire trucks to pass. "I've just spoken to the emergency services; they're trying to get help coming in from the air. The traffic's gridlocked. People are starting to panic."

"Is there any way you can get water there from the river?"

"What the hell are we supposed to do? Line up in rows and pass buckets?"

"I wish I could tell you I had a better idea." Maria shook her head, doing her level best to keep calm. "How are things looking to the south?"

Kit hurried south, returning to Monument. On both the north and south sides of Monument Street, the charred remains of destroyed buildings slowly began to cool off, a white steam rising as the white-hot metal made contact with the regular dowsing of nearby hoses. Even now the heat was tremendous.

In just over one hour, Pudding Lane had been obliterated.

"Fires around the Monument are practically out. Wish I could say the same about the smell."

"Any casualties?"

"A couple injured, but nothing worse that I know of." He coughed as he inadvertently breathed in the choking air. "Everyone else has moved north, but we're not helping anyone just standing here. Request permission to move to the Tower of London?"

Seated alone in the main office of the Rook, Maria stared at her iMac. Though she was aware from the GPS that Mike remained at the Tower, she was still to successfully make contact with him.

"Why?"

"I just spoke to Grosmont. The Tower's security has been compromised. Surely you've spoken to him?"

Maria raised an inquisitive eyebrow. "As a matter of fact, I've kinda got enough on my plate talking with everyone else without one guy out sightseeing! As I told you before, it's one of the few places our service is temperamental. What's happened?"

"The Ceremony of the Keys was compromised. The Chief Yeoman's dead, as are most of the Queen's Guards."

"What?"

"It gets better. He's certain he just saw Randek."

"He recognised him?"

"He also shot at him."

Maria was stunned. "This makes no sense. What possible business could Randek have with the Tower?"

"Can you really not think of anything?"

Maria moved her hand across her mouth. "Oh my God."

22

The Jewel House,
22:12

The position of Crown Jeweller was one of the most secretive in the Royal Household. Appointed directly by the British Monarch, it was a job defined by two key responsibilities: maintenance and, at times the jewels were absent from the Tower, ensuring their security. Since creation of the role by Queen Victoria in 1843, the Jeweller was officially on call day or night to fulfil their responsibilities, some of which could arise at very short notice. The present occupant had never forgotten the day the job description was explained to him by his predecessor.

Wherever the jewels go, you go!

The Jeweller waited until he was sure he was alone before getting to work on the article in front of him. Tonight, only one of the crowns would require maintenance; to work on everything in the collection would require more manpower and hours than he currently had at his disposal.

As the official Crown Jeweller, he was the only person alive trusted with the task of working on the jewels.

Though his workshop was technically part of the Jewel House, it was a room the public never got to see. Located below the main exhibition in a secluded space that could only be found with the appropriate direction and security clearance, it was visually unspectacular. Like the adapted garage at his own residence near Guildford, it lacked the trimmings of the room above, its many tables and shelves instead stocked with items that had been updated far less frequently than other parts of the building. The long, narrow work desk that had become almost a second home in recent years had been in place since the days of his predecessor, as had most of the tools.

Having once served as the man's understudy, he could now almost carry out the work blindfolded.

Tonight, his concern was solely with the crown generally viewed as the most important in the collection. With an upcoming ceremony imminent, the Imperial State Crown would soon leave its two-inch-thick shatterproof display case and make its way to Buckingham Palace, where it would adorn the head of the monarch.

Which left him only three days to complete the job.

The crown had been on the table for over ten minutes. It would stay there until the armed guard returned.

He wasn't expecting their return for at least an hour.

Concentrating on the area that required the most attention, he removed a fresh cotton bud from the previously unsealed pack and slowly doused it in liquid from the nearby container. The secret compound was a mystery to all except himself and his predecessor; only his replacement would learn the exact ingredients. Cleaning the Crown Jewels was more of an art than a science. The biggest threat to its appearance was for moisture to become trapped behind the precious stones, particularly significant in a crown that contained several thousand.

Finishing the first part of the job, he went over the same area with purified water before drying it carefully. Satisfied, he picked up his polishing cloth and set about rotating the crown.

François waited till he was sure they were alone before giving the command to move on. He recognised the Crown of St Edward the moment he laid eyes on it; after his experience in Cambridgeshire two years earlier, it felt like looking at a long-lost sibling.

He led the way along the now switched off travellator, doing his best to avoid the temptation to become distracted by the precious items in front of him. On passing the section that housed the gold altar plate, he found the final display case had recently been opened, its contents vanished.

Smiling, François turned to the leader of the armed police. "Take us to the workshop."

The Jeweller paused as he prepared to resume work on the opposite side of the crown. There were footsteps on the stairs outside his workshop, light, subtle, strangely startling. The armed guard was under strict orders not to disturb him.

He squinted in the direction of the door, removing his near-vision glasses for a better view. The leader of the four appeared in the doorway.

The Jeweller was unimpressed. "I told you before, I cannot work with interruptions."

A quick flash of yellow appeared from the other side of the doorway and the security man dropped lifelessly to the floor. Before the gunfire had a chance to register, four men entered the workspace, the leader a handsome, dark-haired man in his mid-to-late thirties.

"Mr Phillips! Please do not be alarmed. Nobody is here to harm you." François addressed the Jeweller, smiling warmly as he picked up the Imperial State Crown. "I do, however, have a matter with which I require your assistance."

Mike saw movement close to the outer doors of the Byward Tower, accompanied by the sound of terrified voices.

"Quickly!"

On this occasion it was Emily who grabbed his hand, guiding him towards the outer wall. He saw her take the first of the stone steps that led to the front door of St Thomas's Tower, stopping immediately.

Lying down flat, they held their breath.

Figures in black passed them quickly, their voices inaudible. In their present location, the walls reflected more light than they absorbed, a blessing under the circumstances. Among the figures, he also saw lighter colours, heard fewer foreign sounds. There were women present, children.

Mike realised they were the families of the Yeoman Warders.

Keeping low, he felt Emily move to his right, her frightened face now buried deep against his torso. Biting his lip, he held her tightly, doing his best to remain still.

The gathering passed without noticing them, disappearing through the archway beneath the Bloody Tower.

Mike breathed out a sigh of relief and released Emily.

"Come on." Emily began up the steps, climbing them quickly. Mike remembered from his previous visits that the way to St Thomas's Tower marked the beginning of the wall walks.

They came to a door: wooden, heavy. Pushing it, he discovered it was locked.

"Wait!" Emily removed a set of keys from her jacket pocket, trying to find the correct one. She inserted it into the keyhole and turned.

The door opened.

They entered quickly, Emily locking it again from the inside. Within moments of passing a second locked door, the room was filled with light, the surroundings becoming visible for the first time.

Mike looked around, speechless.

He was looking at the remains of the medieval palace.

23

Windsor Castle, Twenty-One Months Earlier

"They were called the White Hart," Atkins said with a clear air of triumph in his voice as he led Mike along another seemingly endless corridor that extended right through the heart of the incredible underground facility. "Formed as the Order of the Round Table in 1344 and allegedly inspired by the then King of England's devotion to the twelve apostles, the order played a key, albeit not always obvious, role in the Hundred Years' War before being formally patronised by his successor as a military order in their own right. In the early days, they served predominantly as the king's personal bodyguards. Aside from their valour on the battlefield, the original knights were also famed for their ability to hunt down enemy spies, weeding out critical information and contributing effectively to the planning of military campaigns – campaigns, I might add, that would see England become a dominant force in medieval Europe."

Walking alongside the former undersecretary of the MoD, his footsteps again echoing like a lonely drumbeat in the vast enclosure, Mike listened without offering any response. Since leaving the first chamber with its abundant artwork, the majority of which he now understood portrayed people who had played a significant part in the organisation's past, and a table that would have looked at home in the great hall of the mighty Camelot, what he had seen had been very different.

The sight of dusty walls – illuminated by dimly glowing candelabra-style wall lights whose designs had clearly changed little since the discovery of electricity, and decorated in chivalric emblems and tapestries that he guessed had some connection with the castle above – had since given way to something more modern.

Replacing the lowly lit, cellar-like rooms was an area that had more the appearance of a top-secret nuclear bunker, the walls no longer lined by oak but lead. At the far end, shielded by walls of coloured glass, which obscured the features of the people within, a vast workspace had been fitted with highly sophisticated modern, if not futuristic, lighting from which could be heard the light humming of a large bank of computers and the mixed sounds of numerous telephone conversations.

For Mike, the strange clash of architecture made it impossible to decide if he was dealing with something from the distant past or the not-too-distant future.

Directly in front of them, the three men in suits led the way. The leader of the three seemed to have acquired a habit of speaking whenever Atkins wasn't, but unlike the former undersecretary, his words were purposely vague. The only thing Mike had managed to pick up on was that his name was Masterson.

And his partners Iqbal and Sanders.

The walk ended with them leading Mike through the last of the subterranean chambers and into something far older. Entering through wide, stable-like oak doors, Mike gazed in awe at a hall-like assembly room that was rich in tapestries and clearly dated back to the Middle Ages. The tapestries and decorations all depicted knights jousting.

"At one time, this was used as the tournament room," Atkins said. "Every year, usually at Whitsun, the king and many of his relatives in the castle above would host a great weekend of feasting, during which members of the order would compete in a series of challenges. Only the most worthy were allowed the privilege of sitting at the Round Table."

Mike listened, fascinated. Seeing was believing, yet the more he heard, the less possible it seemed. Even though he had seen it himself.

Surrounded by twelve chairs.

"King Arthur?"

Atkins adjusted his glasses, a calculated pause. "Whether a king of that name ever really existed during the days of Roman England and sat at a table of the same shape, we can even now only speculate. The one thing that is known for sure is that when the very historical Edward III heard tales of the dalliances of his grandfather Edward I and of the jousts he'd held at Winchester, the young king became captivated. Inspired by the tales, in 1344 the young warlord endeavoured to create his own brotherhood, one that would exist to replicate the ways of the knights of legend. One that would strive to adhere to similar ideals."

Mike nodded, intrigued but no longer in disbelief. "But I thought Edward never actually formed the Order of the Round Table. The tower here was abandoned midway through; four years later, he formed the Order of the Garter instead."

"I told you he was an expert in history, sir," Masterson told Atkins.

Atkins smiled wryly. "Not abandoned exactly, merely relocated. The round tower Edward had begun above the ground was never intended as anything more than a cover. The tower itself was not only completed, but remains in use to this day. Matter of fact, you're currently standing in it."

Mike was speechless. The concept was simply incredible! Yet strangely, the explanation made sense of everything he'd seen.

"So why the deception? If Edward wanted the organisation to be a secret, then why announce it in the first place?"

"Answers to those questions and more can only be understood with a lengthy study of the circumstances of the time," the former undersecretary continued. "The best place to start is to go back to the earliest days, most notably the antics of his son. Within a year of the order's birth, Edward's army had already mounted its first attack on French soil. For the original knights, it's likely their first action was at Crécy; though back then they were still to be known as the White Hart. If anything, the change in warfare made the deception all the more vital. When Crécy was conquered, Edward's armies became feared; his generals targeted. After all, the greater the fame of the individual, the more susceptible he was to attack."

Mike nodded, quietly satisfied that what he was hearing contained at least a kernel of truth. "So who were these originals? I'm guessing it was their names I saw painted on the Round Table?"

"If you're hoping for a precise retelling, perhaps you're asking the wrong person. Like the men of Camelot, dare I say much of the early tales have been lost to legend. When Edward the Black Prince died a year before his father in 1376, it was feared among the newest of the knights that the order would fail to survive longer than the king. By that time, all of the original members had died and been replaced by younger men. England was in a precarious state, the new king far too young to govern in his own right. Ironically, this very uncertainty would ensure the order's future. When the young king came to the throne, it was the success of the second wave of knights in foiling the Peasants' Revolt and later staving off the Appellants that helped maintain Plantagenet rule. It is to Richard, not his father, to whom the order owes its name."

Mike nodded, again satisfied by the former undersecretary's answers. He was already aware Richard II's emblem was a white hart.

"Based on everything that followed, I'm surprised the order had any chance of surviving at all. I'd have thought what with all the turmoil, the Wars of the Roses would have put an end to it."

Atkins led them across the grand hall. "In some ways, it possibly did – but no man lives forever. When a king of England died or became dethroned, such was the complex, yet intricate nature of English politics, the order had a tendency to reinvent itself – after all, their oath was always to the Crown, never the individual. After the nonsense of the cousins' war was over and the rule of England was defined more by blood succession, the order that had been patronised by Richard II continued to evolve almost unaffected until the beheading of Charles I. Rather than disband the order, Cromwell merely rebranded them. The twelve in action at the time, some new, others who had once fought for Charles, were now enlisted as part of his New Model Army. When the Protectorate ended and the son of the executed king came to the throne, the White Hart was once again patronised with the seal of the monarch. With the exception of the inevitable evolution in personnel, you might say normal service resumed."

Mike was confused. "You suggest it was continuously reorganised? Sounds to me like it never had a solid core."

"Not exactly. Over the years, the order obtained much in the way of capital and properties, usually in the form of donations, not to mention inheriting the estates of deceased knights in their wills. As the order was originally patronised as a Christian order, our headquarters was also considered something of a pilgrimage site."

Atkins led the way across the medieval flooring and exited the hall into a short, dark corridor that led to a small chapel. Beyond a gathering of pews, Mike saw a ruined altarpiece surrounded by three walls of continuous fresco.

Behind the damaged stonework on the altar were painted wooden panels including a figure clearly representing Richard II seated as one of the Apostles.

Mike was in complete shock. "The Diptych?"

"Not the original, but a pretty shrewd observation, it must be said." Atkins smiled as he leaned against the rear pew, allowing Mike an unrestricted view of the ruined altarpiece. "The piece itself was lost many centuries ago – in the eyes of mainstream historians, it still is. It was actually retrieved from the English College in Rome. Not that it should ever have been taken away in the first place."

Mike moved in for a closer look, feeling the texture of the hinged panels and surrounding medieval masonry with his fingertips. He felt lost for words, realising that the more he learned, the more the truth about the existence of the White Hart became shrouded in fog.

"So who exactly are you? I didn't know the British government funded any religious orders. Nor advocated the use of royal bodyguards."

"Who says we do either?" Atkins removed his glasses and polished them with a handkerchief. "Once upon a time, of course, religion and the state were interchangeable; these days much has changed. These rooms are most imposing, but perhaps more so for their historical appeal than their present use. As I'm sure you'll agree, it's important never to forget one's past."

"So if you're not government owned, who is responsible?" Mike asked, still intrigued by the ruined altarpiece. "You saying you're privatised? What are we talking here? Self-serving vigilantes or the Local Defence Volunteers?"

"If anything, I'd say more like the Knights Templar; self-reliant might be the correct term, though certainly not self-serving. When Archduke Ferdinand was shot and war broke out in Central Europe, it was clear to the powers that be of the time that, unlike the previous wars, conquest of our enemies would depend on effective planning as much as sending men by the tens of thousand over the top. Victory in a conventional war may depend hugely on the effectiveness of the front line, but it is every bit as much the quiet unsung heroes we must thank for making the most decisive contributions." He replaced his glasses.

Mike nodded, slowly finding himself able to see through the fog. He remembered learning that organisations like the SAS and MI6 had evolved in similar ways to keep one step ahead of the enemy.

"So who do you report to? I'm guessing something of this magnitude can't be completely independent if it exists beneath the home of the royals. I assume we're talking black budget."

"There's a reason you haven't heard of us, if that's what you're getting at?" Atkins replied. "There's also a reason that none of your commanders in the 1st Battalion have either. If you look in the correct cabinet of the correct office, you'll find the paperwork, but dare I say such things are easily missed if you're unsure what you're looking for. Not that you'll get much help discovering where to look."

"Presumably those you recruit show up somewhere?" Mike cast his eye over the three men by the door. "I mean it's not like one day someone is recruited over a pink gin and he simply vanishes off the face of the earth."

"As far as you're concerned, that would be exactly the case. A pay cheque, of course, comes as usual; but when it does, you'll see no reference to us. If an auditor from the city or a civil servant at Whitehall does decide to look a little closer than normal into a file, all he'll learn is the man received his promotion, but stayed on at the same place. Again you might say business as usual. If you're looking for medals for gallantry, you'll be sure to receive them, not that those dishing them out will necessarily know what they're for. Yet you'll find nothing of the cause will be mentioned in despatches – not that we're looking for the type who require it. If one of our men dies overseas, you can be sure he'll get the recognition he deserves, only perhaps in a more personal way. You'll never appear on the Six O'clock News. On the plus side, any mistakes you make will be made in silence. They'll be no disciplinary tribunal or appearance in front of a beak."

"So basically you're just like MI6? Either that or I was right the first time. You're just the SAS under an old banner."

"In practice we're talking about neither one nor the other. Only when it comes to the crunch, we're all on the same side."

Mike brushed his fingers and thumb against his recently shaved face and pondered the scene in front of him. The chapel was old, steeped in ruin and history, its position, like the hidden tower, strangely allegorical.

Old. Existing in darkness. Without edges.

Strangely permanent.

"There's one thing I still don't understand. Twelve seats. No organisation in the world is so select."

"At least none you know of," Atkins responded. "Like most organisations of our type, the support we receive is outstanding, and when we do need to recruit, we look closely to ensure every box is ticked. In seven hundred years we have never expanded nor contracted."

"In that case, why am I needed?"

When the head sack was removed, Mike found himself again standing in broad daylight, his sensitive eyes staring out across the castle's Lower Ward, the early rays of daylight now hidden behind thick rain clouds.

The only thing that remained unchanged was the sound of singing from inside St George's Chapel.

Doing his best to ignore the seemingly endless laughing of Sanders and Iqbal, and the threatening gaze of Masterson, he walked alongside Atkins to the main entrance of the 14th-century, cathedral-like gothic building that was famous worldwide as the main point of worship for principal members of the royal family.

Atkins entered first, holding the door for Mike, who went second on Masterson's insistence. Once inside, the angelic singing of what he had originally assumed to be an all-boys choir gained extra volume and clarity as a large congregation boomed out the opening line of "I the Lord of Sea and Sky".

What he saw couldn't have been more different to what he'd expected. Rather than entering a near-deserted chapel, perhaps a family affair involving key members of the royal family, he found himself as one of several hundred attendees of a service of clear importance.

Beyond the medieval quire with its wooded seating occupied by males aged ten to eighty, dressed in the apparel of a local choir, was a large coffin draped in a Union Jack, watched over by a large number of clergymen and a congregation that was at least partly military. Though suits were in the majority, neither Mike nor those with whom he'd entered looked out of place. Dressed, as instructed, in casual battle dress, he knew his appearance was respectable.

They took up positions behind the final row, five of many who were deprived of a seat. As the four-hundred-strong congregation sang the famous hymn seemingly in direct competition with the organ, Mike focused on the medieval quire. Directly above where the forty-plus choir sat in their finely carved wooden seating, a series of heraldic-style banners all matched the pattern and logo he'd seen decorating the strange table below where he was standing.

The symbol of the White Hart.

Mike glanced to his left, suddenly uneasy. Atkins' head was buried in a hymnbook, words of song reverberating strongly from his larynx. To his right, the Asian man named Captain Iqbal was the only attendee not singing.

"Who was he?" Mike asked.

Iqbal replied with a soft smile, "His name was Captain James Fenway. He was your predecessor."

The service had a strange dreamlike quality, but unlike any dream Mike had experienced before. Among the large gathering of military men, suited VIPs and women of varying heights and hat styles, he saw faces he recognised, names he knew well. Among those he'd met in person, military commanders of the highest rank stood smartly alongside their partners or lifelong friends, many taking the opportunity to chat to present and past cabinet ministers, the majority of whom watched on with tactful expressions he had learned to associate with professional decorum.

He guessed from what he'd seen of the strange facility minutes earlier, the man's true military exploits would remain a mystery to the majority.

While Mike had come across some of those in attendance before, several of political fame stood out further still, one in particular. Dressed in an impeccable black dress, the like of which he had witnessed many times, the prime minister of the UK wore a solemn expression, the focus of her attention reserved for a small group of humble-looking people he immediately assumed to be the deceased soldier's family.

Among the crowd of friends and family, kind expressions masking the tears of the parents, a pretty woman with a veil to match her hair kept a low profile, her eyes reserved for her two young sons. Mike paid close attention to how the

PM spent extra time with her, cupping her hands kindly before allowing a small glimpse of warmth and joviality for the children, both of whom Mike guessed were too young to truly understand. While the PM had spoken both in private and from the lectern, others of more flamboyant dress had been far quieter. Despite the location, he felt an overriding surprise that the proceedings had been overseen by the Prince of Wales and the Duke of York.

As the mourners vacated the chapel, making their way out into the Lower Ward, the coffin of the soldier, agent, son, brother, husband, father-of-two was placed ceremoniously into an impressive-looking hearse, and Atkins led him back to the same military-style vehicle he had travelled in earlier that day. Without prior intention, Mike found himself in between Sanders and Masterson in the back, Iqbal at the wheel.

"You mind if I ask what that was all about?" Mike asked, growing ever more disturbed by his inclusion in the ceremony. As far as he was concerned, the pink gin was still to be consumed.

Atkins glanced into the mirror on the sun visor on the passenger side. "Answers to this and more will be revealed soon enough. But for now, Lieutenant, I'm afraid this part of the journey is another not for the eyes of outsiders."

He awoke suddenly in the back of the same car. It was bright without the head sack; he blinked instinctively.

He found himself alone, the strange armoured vehicle parked among many in what appeared to be a church car park. Among the plethora of modern hatchbacks that lined the gravel parking bays, he recognised the same hearse he had earlier seen outside the chapel at Windsor.

Atkins was leaning against a nearby wall close to the bonnet, his focus on the surrounding greenery. Mike got out of the car and moved alongside him.

There was no sign of the other three.

"The Church of Our Lady and St Benedict is located in Suffolk," Atkins said, not bothering to meet Mike's confused gaze. "More precisely, the quaint little village of Charlestown. You might say the place where it all began."

To Mike, the name meant nothing. "I've never heard of it."

"It appears on no map, you can rely on that," the civilian replied, his dynamic eyes looking Mike over for the first time. Despite his two-hour involuntary nap, Mike felt worse for it. "There's a tap over there. I suggest you make use of it."

Mike followed his directions and found a rusty nozzle attached to the north wall of the church, accessible through a small lychgate that pealed like an antique bell as it opened on its hinges. Mike allowed the cold water to flow over his skin, hoping at the very least it might dust away a few cobwebs.

"How can a place appear on no maps? You make it sound like Rendlesham Forest."

"In a way, yes. We're not alone, even in this green and pleasant land. Like the military camps in Virginia, it can be found by those who know where to look; dare I say, it can also be found by those who are completely lost. Most of the residents keep themselves to themselves; there are no secrets between us. Most are older than you and I. Nearly all served through either the dark days or the troubles."

Mike understood the reference to World War Two and Northern Ireland. "Sounds to me more like the Curse of the Black Pearl."

Atkins' face remained unflinching. "It's a beautiful place when one looks closely. The only thing that surrounds us is life itself. Just listen to the birds, the sea, the sounds of nature. We're quite alone here."

Mike sensed there was more to it than that. "You say where it all began? I thought the Round Table was founded by Edward at Windsor."

"I suppose if we're being grammatically precise, a better description might be the place where it all resumed. When the armies returned from war, it was never likely they were to stay inside Windsor itself – even the son of the king had his own residence. When the curtain came down, whether on a campaign or a fine career, it was only fitting the worthy knight had his own castle to call his own. The original location was in Clare, the lands forfeited by Lionel of Antwerp when he died at far too young an age. Charlestown was actually once named Antwerp. When the Restoration was complete and Charles II took the Protector's seat on the throne, the re-emerging order named this small village in honour of its new patron."

Mike raised an eyebrow, still intrigued by what he was learning. As his senses continued to adjust to the strange surroundings, he could hear voices breaking the silence.

People were emerging through the front doors of the nearby church.

He found himself walking through the churchyard, Atkins matching him stride for stride. The grass was muddy from recent rain, the nearby tombstones enveloped in a slippery coating. The dates on the stones varied from the height of the Middle Ages to within the last five years. Alongside the inscriptions, Mike noticed symbols engraved into the stonework, matching what he had seen earlier that day.

Even out in the open, he could have easily missed them had it not already been on his mind.

A burial was taking place somewhere close to the south transept, the group of mourners far smaller than the ceremony in Berkshire. He recognised some of those attending, most notably the soldier's widow and parents. The children, he noticed, weren't present.

As the seconds passed, he saw further movement. Masterson reappeared in the company of ten others, including Sanders and Iqbal. All eleven were attired in identical battle dress; the three men he had met earlier that day had all changed since leaving the car. Ten of the eleven moved to Masterson's commands, his words joined by another, clearly more senior.

The new man was dressed wholly in black, his silver, closely cropped hair unruffled by the strength of the wind. As proceedings continued, the civilian took centre stage. All eleven now stood to attention with automatic weapons in the present arms position; on the civilian's commands, they aimed them at the sky.

Mike watched in silence as they fired a five-round salute.

With the ceremony over, the congregation slowly began to disperse, the majority taking the time to convey their final condolences to the soldier's widow. Mike sensed she was struggling to keep her emotions in check.

"From the very beginning there have always been twelve seats at the round table. When one falls vacant, it is always filled quickly. For every master, there is always an apprentice. That is simply the way of things."

"Who was he?"

"Captain Fenway was a hero and a patriot." Atkins locked eyes with Mike, his expression altogether more reserved than before. "Like yourself, he once served as a red beret. He died for reasons that need not concern you."

Mike guessed that meant he'd died in the line of duty – duty for an order that officially didn't exist. "Presumably he has something written on his official record – if only for closure?"

"Even for the very best there are sometimes, unfortunately, challenges that can get the better of us. The service you have just seen is a reminder of this. Even the original twelve proved no less mortal than the rest of us. Had his life been different, you would not be here."

The civilian walked with light footsteps, stopping directly in Mike's line of view. "The path presented before you, if you choose to accept it, will mean there is no going back. I can't promise it will be easy; more truthfully it almost certainly will not be. To find the chambers you saw this morning and the village in which you stand now can't be done without knowing precisely where to look. It is both an honour and a privilege to be offered access; more still to be regarded as the best of the best. It is an altogether different affair, pitting your wits against the challenges that we consistently face."

Mike shook his head, his expression sombre. "I told you at Brize Norton, Undersecretary, I was never really interested in the SAS. All I ever wanted was to serve my country and maybe feel alive once in a while when I did it." He met the civilian's gaze. "I'm sure if you broaden your search beyond Wales and Oxfordshire, you'll find many better qualified than me."

"Oh, let's stop pretending, shall we? You decided you were in the moment you saw the cocktail." He moved slightly closer. "To be a member of the White Hart is not about climbing mountains with twenty-kilogram bergens or demonstrating outstanding technical skill in firing off bullets at a glorified dartboard. Nor is it just about being a good soldier. When the Round Table was founded, it was the intention of the king that all who sat there would possess the same qualities and embrace the same values as the men of legend; in a thousand years, the ideals of chivalry have changed very little, even if the uniforms have. To become one of the knights involves much more than simply kneeling before the monarch; it means being able to stand side by side with your brothers, knowing that you would die for them and they for you. Even in this day and age, such dedication is rarely found."

Mike saw the undersecretary move to one side, allowing him a clear view across the churchyard. While the majority of the mourners had departed, the eleven remained together, their arms interlocked in a group huddle.

Together they formed a perfect circle.

Atkins moved alongside Mike, his breath visible as he exhaled in the cold air. "It's a simple decision, Lieutenant. Agree to start the training now that could one day lead to you joining this circle, or I can ask Captain Masterson to replace that bag over your head."

24

St Thomas's Tower, 22:16

The door took them into St Thomas's Tower, the first part of the medieval palace. The second door was wooden framed with stained-glass panels, far less sturdy than the first.

"You have keys to everything in this place?" Mike asked, gazing at his surroundings. The atmosphere felt less oppressive with the lights on. The previously unlit and ill-defined void, which in the darkness might have been anything from a small hidey-hole to a great hall, could now be seen to be a large chamber housing various displays and educational presentations for visitors about Henry III and Edward I's medieval palace.

"Over two million people visit the Tower every year. As Tower officials, it's our job to make sure everything runs smoothly." She looked at him, replacing her glasses. "It's not just the Yeoman Warders who sometimes have to work late."

Mike smiled, continuing to take everything in. Beyond the entrance, the nearest parts of the wooden flooring were covered in rugs, the only evidence of warm texture, whereas the cold stone walls matched the tower's exterior and radiated the present temperature. As curiosity led him to the right side of the room, a series of narrow windows provided views across the Thames.

Strangely, the room immediately brought back memories of his first visit to Windsor.

Emily was standing near a large video presentation close to a series of text boards that in the day would educate its visitors on the state of the palace in the Middle Ages. Beyond it, he saw surrounding wooden frames that divided the room in two; behind her, a stairway led to an area off-limits to the general public.

"Are there cameras in this room?"

"Of course. There are cameras everywhere."

"In that case, turn off the lights."

"What?"

"Don't argue. Just do it."

Emily returned to the entrance, tentatively at first. Within moments, the overhead lights went out, leaving the great chamber illuminated solely by external sources filtering in through the surrounding panes of glass.

"If Randek has control of the Tower, they're probably watching us in the surveillance room. Even if they don't have keys, chances are they know where we are."

Emily was confused. "Who's Randek?"

"Just one of your typical visitors; you'd really love him." Mike hurried into the second half of the room, finding it fitted out similarly with numerous visual aids. To his right, two open doorways provided access to the opposite side of the chamber where the outer walls were lined with further windows. Peering through the glass, he saw the Thames flowing in its usual calm manner, the lights of several buildings reflecting off the surface.

From that view alone, all seemed well in London.

They continued into the next area of the palace, finding themselves in what appeared to be a grand bedroom. A large four-poster bed was surrounded by wooden furniture that matched the flooring. An equally imposing fireplace had been set into the far wall, the surrounding tiles decorated with the patterns of Plantagenet heraldry.

Mike was confused. "These areas aren't inhabited, are they?"

"You don't get out very often, do you, Captain?" Emily's expression suggested light humour beyond her more general demeanour of being unimpressed. "What you see was once the heart of the medieval palace; before the Queen's House was built, this would have been the bedroom of the king. The layout is designed to replicate the era of Edward I."

Mike nodded, realising that what he saw put the displays he'd seen in the previous room into a meaningful perspective. As the seconds passed, he recalled visiting the room as a tourist and witnessing actors dressed in costume.

"We need to get to the security room, ASAP."

"You've already made that quite clear. The security room is in the heart of the barracks. It's separate from the medieval palace."

"What's the nearest we can get to it?"

"I guess that depends."

"Depends on what?"

"Whether you want to risk returning outside."

Mike looked at her, noticing her skin was looking ghostly pale in the eerie light. As in the previous room, the only light came through the chapel-like windows that cut deep into the floral wall patterns.

"Listen, you know this place better than me. Even in the dark we're not entirely invisible. The City of London is under attack; as far as we know, we're the only people here unaccounted for. If the person responsible is who I think he is, he'll soon make his intentions far more widely known." He touched her shoulders, tightening his grip. "We have to keep moving."

She pointed to a doorway in the wall in front of them. "Through this is the Wakefield Tower. If we follow the wall walk, it'll take us to the other side of the Tower, but eventually we'll have no choice but to risk exposure outside."

Mike nodded, biting his lip; an ironic thought entered his mind as he realised that as long as he remained within any of the Tower's thick walls, he would be operating between the proverbial rock and a hard place. He tried contacting the White Hart on his satphone, again finding little in the way of clear reception.

"Come on. If we stay low and out of the light, that might at least buy us some time."

***

Randek headed out on to Tower Green, wary that the figure he had just shot at might still be alive on the other side of the Bloody Tower. Close by, the bodies of the slain lay where they had fallen. He gritted his teeth in concentration as he knelt down close to the Yeoman Gaoler, double-checking that every spare key had been removed before rising once more to his feet with a satisfied smile.

His uncle's reputation for efficiency was built on solid foundations.

He moved slowly past the bodies, keeping his eyes focused on the imposing towers and the walkway beyond. He saw another body in uniform on the opposite side of the archway; again he saw no sign of anything about his person.

Nor was there any sign of the elusive figure he'd just shot at.

He made his way onward beneath the archway of the Bloody Tower, the last area of shelter before reaching Water Lane. Keeping close to the walls, he inched his way left, seeking the shelter and seclusion of the deep shadows of the Wakefield Tower to minimise the possibility of being observed. Water Lane was clear; the warm glow of the wall lights confirmed it was devoid of human activity. In the distance he heard voices: female, clearly frightened.

As the seconds passed, he saw the terrified families of the Beefeaters being escorted from their homes on Mint Street.

Seeing no sign of the mysterious figure, he contacted Blanco.

Blanco had reached the top floor of the White Tower when he heard his nephew's voice. Witnessing the sight of the nation's once great arsenal assembled on the timber flooring in the manner of a museum display provided a unique sense of power as he considered what had come before and what would soon follow. The suits of armour, in particular, were unquestionably authentic; they had covered the bodies of powerful men, almost certainly in war against his countrymen and kin.

Overseeing their destruction would indeed be satisfying.

Blanco barely flinched as a sudden burst of static interrupted the calm air. He answered immediately. "What is it?"

Randek continued to advance west along Water Lane, staying close to the Bell Tower. "It seems British Intelligence moves faster than we expected. They are already here within the walls."

Walking the flooring with heavy boots, Blanco came to an abrupt halt. "What?"

"A figure was moving just now among the bodies; I shot at him, but making the kill from that distance was nearly impossible in the darkness."

Blanco relaxed slightly. "A missed resident perhaps. Or maybe an employee. Even at this late hour there may be some who walk these grounds, ignorant of the threats that await them." He laughed under his breath. "The tourists in particular have delicate stomachs for the English sausage."

At the other end, Randek wasn't laughing. "How many of them carry the weaponry of the Servants?"

Blanco's heart missed a beat. "Who?"

"Though it was dark, the weapon in his hand was clear."

The Anjouvin gazed coldly across the otherwise deserted museum as the three gunmen alongside him continued to remove the contents of the three holdalls, laying them out at strategic intervals. Finishing, he directed them to the stairs.

"The way inside is a secret few will ever know or understand. You know the details as well as any, the risks that we have had to take. Tell me, Fabien, what exactly did you see?"

"The figure was dressed in black; perhaps more like a soldier off duty rather than one assigned to combat dangerous terrorists. The weapon he carried was recognisable anywhere. You, Uncle, as well as I know who carries such firearms."

Standing in silence, Blanco leaned against the nearby stonework, allowing himself time to absorb the information he was being given. The plan had gone off like clockwork; nothing had been left to chance. The call would be put through on the hour, not before.

Any hint of alarm would have come recently.

Too recently.

"The security room in the barracks has monitors that observe everything within these walls. I suggest you use them. Use them and find him.

"And when you do, kill him!"

25

The Jewel House,
22:18

The jeweller's workshop was accessible from a small stairway that connected to the final room that made up part of the jewels display. Having already used it once, François was beginning to recognise its features.

After climbing the stairs and passing the now empty display case that usually housed the Imperial State Crown, the young art director progressed beyond the cases containing the wedding banquet and the altar plate, into the heart of the main jewel room, enjoying the sight of each crown as he walked along the travellator. The room was quiet with the motors off, quieter still without the crowds.

With the lights on, the reflection of his handsome face in the glass provided the only close company.

A sudden surge of static invaded the silence, accompanied by Blanco's voice. He answered immediately.

"*Allô?*"

"Where are you now?"

"If I told you what I was looking at, it would answer the question for you," François replied. "The Jeweller was most insistent he grant me a personal tour of his belongings."

Blanco smiled to himself. "Where is the master craftsman now?"

François looked to his left, where the Jeweller awkwardly watched on. Four gunmen surrounded him, their dark, black ops-style clothing intentionally chosen to ensure their features wouldn't stand out at night.

"He is cooperating, but not exactly fluent in French."

"You have seen the jewels?"

"I am carrying one of them right now." François gazed at the Imperial State Crown. "The rest can only be released from their cases by activation of a switch in the security room."

"Then do it!"

Two floors above, the larger of the two gunmen stared vigilantly at one of the banks of seemingly innumerable television monitors mounted on the far wall of the main security room. Entry to the room had been easier than anticipated. The Queen's Guards had been unarmed at the time, making capture easy. The door itself had required the entering of a code; convincing an unarmed guard to provide it had not been difficult.

The layout of the room was exactly as it had been described in reconnaissance reports. Over 10,000 security cameras had been installed at various points, overseeing everything from the public areas of the Tower to those where the wood was cracking.

All of which were relayed back to the wall of screens in front of them.

A large number were directed on the Jewel House, where no less than five of his accomplices had gathered. In one of the monochrome images, he saw François put his handheld transmitter to his lips for the second time in as many minutes.

Sure enough, the man's voice came through at his end.

"I am about to pass you on to the Jeweller. Forgive him, he speaks only English."

The Jeweller viewed the handsome Frenchman with renewed trepidation as François passed him the handheld transmitter.

"Monsieur Phillips, I understand there is only one way to access the displays before me. Please, monsieur – the code."

The abject look of defeat in the man's eyes showed no signs of abating.

"Monsieur, one of your cases has already been opened." François removed his firearm from his pocket. "Please do not make it necessary to sacrifice your own life in addition to such fine glasswork."

Randek had reached the bottom of Mint Street when Blanco contacted him again. All of the apartments had been checked; the street was deserted.

He answered, "*Oui?*"

"Where are you?"

"The apartments in the west wall have all been cleared. Their residents are being escorted to the governor's house as we speak."

"In that case, I suggest you join them. They will make far better company than the Tower's ghosts."

Randek lingered briefly outside the exhibition on Mint Street, his eyes on the off-limits passageway that circled the inner wall connecting the Bell and Beauchamp towers. "What about the Servant?"

"I've told you already, cameras cover every inch of this castle," Blanco responded, his deep voice revealing clear frustration. "The dining room in the Queen's House is getting crowded. I suggest it's time to relocate our guests."

26

The Wakefield Tower,
22:19

The open doorway revealed a small stairway that wound upwards from right to left. The stairway was blocked off directly below and then again further up. The only option was to take it up one storey and follow the narrow passageway of the Salvin Bridge in between two locked doors.

Mike waited as Emily unlocked the first, his attention immediately turning to one of two narrow windows on the left side. Immediately he ducked.

Directly below him, Fabien Randek was sprinting furiously along Water Lane.

"Keep still!" Mike lowered himself to his haunches, ensuring every inch of his body was out of Randek's possible sight line. He waited a few seconds, enough time he judged for the terrorist to have passed. Rising to his feet, he looked again through the window before doing the same through one on the other side.

Nothing.

He looked at Emily.

"What was that all about?"

"I'll have to tell you some time." Mike followed Emily through the now unlocked second door, exploring the surroundings as best he could in the poor light. A large, ornate fireplace, located to the left of another currently unused presentation screen, glowed with the flames of an artificial fire; directly above it, a large royal coat of arms, replicating the design used during the Plantagenet era, decorated the exterior. The light given off by the flames was enough to confirm only that they had entered a round chamber, its appearance not unlike those in the previous tower.

The circular shape brought back further memories.

To the left of the fireplace was what appeared to be a medieval throne. Mike approached it, his footsteps echoing off the wooden flooring. He stopped on reaching the roped partition, making a quick survey of the area behind it. Scanning a nearby information sign, he learned an answer to the next question.

They'd entered Henry III's throne room.

"This can't be real!" Mike said, concentrating on the throne before taking in more of the nearby surroundings. Though the stone walls and wooden boarding was consistent with what he imagined had existed in the distant past, its condition seemed clean, and possibly modern, by comparison.

"The room itself has been remodelled. Back then it was probably used as his council chamber," Emily replied. "Obviously, we've reconstructed the throne."

Mike looked around, suddenly sceptical. "Looks more like a chapel."

THE CROWN JEWELS CONSPIRACY

"Actually Henry III was very religious. There is a chapel right there."

Mike followed the direction of her hand, observing a small separate area beyond a painted timber screen, the door again adorned with the symbol of the Plantagenet rulers. He headed towards it and opened it.

"Are there cameras here?"

"I told you before, there are cameras everywhere."

"Get inside. Hopefully they might have missed us."

Emily entered first and Mike closed the wooden door behind them, immediately lowering himself to his haunches. The chapel was cramped. A small altar was located barely a metre inside the door, its surface lit up in an array of ghostly shapes as light shone in through a stained-glass window.

"Get down."

Emily moved in alongside him, confused. She noticed he was opening his rucksack while at the same time removing his jacket. "Just what the hell are you doing?"

"If they haven't seen us yet, at least this might buy us some time." He looked at her, noting her scepticism. "Unless you have a better plan?"

She crouched down, doing her best to keep her space. Her hair had become frizzy from running, her breath short, her skin perspiring.

Signing up for the lecture now seemed the worst idea she'd ever had.

"All right. Hiding is good. I mean, for all we know, they don't have anyone in the security room. By the time they find us, it's only a matter of time before the Queen's Guards regain control."

"I hate to break it to you, but the Queen's Guards aren't going anywhere for a while." Concentrating on changing his clothes, he remained silent till he had removed his jeans, noticing the appalled expression on Emily's face.

"What?"

"What the hell are you doing?"

"My jeans were starting to chafe me!" Replacing them, he pulled on his classic ops suit before doing the same for his boots. The last thing he'd expected at the start of the night was that they'd be necessary.

"What exactly is this thing?" he asked, struggling with the tight space.

"As I told you before, Henry III was very religious; he liked to pray in between council meetings!"

"I'm guessing it's famous."

"Matter of fact, Henry VI was allegedly murdered here."

He glanced at her, detecting from her expression it wasn't a joke. "Let's hope we're not!"

He pulled on the remainder of his black ops suit and tied up his boots, at the same time pushing his other clothes into his rucksack.

Looking the part – at least he felt better prepared.

He rose slowly, high enough to look beyond the timber screen, familiarising himself with the room. A second thick wooden door was presently closed; he guessed it led to another passageway or stairway. Another door was located inside the chapel, also locked. The wooden partition was large enough to hide behind, but hardly bulletproof.

What he needed was a plan.

He lowered himself and removed his satphone, logging in once again to the White Hart server and connecting the phone to a strap on his left arm. The service was slightly better here. While updating himself with the images as they appeared on the GPS, he attached a slick Bluetooth headset around his ear, adjusting the setting as he connected it with the inbuilt facility on his night-vision goggles.

Immediately he saw his position on the GPS facility.

"Where exactly are we?"

Emily glanced at his phone, amazed at what she was seeing. "Just who the hell are you?"

"We can get to that later." He knew the equipment she saw would seem like something from a video game. "Show me exactly. Where are we?"

"We're in the heart of the Wakefield Tower." She pointed to the screen.

"Where are the barracks from here?"

"Here."

Mike looked at the area beyond her finger. They still had half the Tower to cover.

"What are our options?"

"The door there leads out on to the south wall." She pointed beyond the timber screen. "Following it takes us here, the Lanthorn Tower."

"That's outside?"

"Unfortunately."

Mike bit his lip, considering their options. Apart from staying exactly where they were, he realised his only choices were going forward or back.

He tapped quickly on the keypad on his satphone, bringing up a host of commands. Within seconds, a new voice broke the silence, speaking directly in his ear. A glance at the display was enough to see it was HQ.

He answered, "Grosmont?"

At the other end, Maria exhaled in relief as Mike's voice came in over the radio waves. "Thank God, I thought I was going to have to get Edward as your go-between."

Mike felt similar relief on hearing her voice. "Listen, Maria. I don't have time to explain. Reception is limited, so I guess we're gonna have to make do with what we can."

Maria smiled as she listened, temporarily pleased that the White Hart personal role radio set up now far exceeded the standard British Army Bowman. "Fortunately you don't need to. Edward's already told us everything."

"I bet he didn't tell you the best bit. I just saw Randek sprinting along Water Lane. Looked pissed."

Back at the Rook, Maria was less surprised. "Where are you now?"

"The Wakefield Tower. Something called the Throne Room. Doesn't exactly look like a palace." Again he glanced behind him, his eyes focused between the throne and the two locked doors. "Tell me, Maria, you're a nice cultured girl. What do you know about the Tower of London?"

"I know it costs more to enter than Windsor."

"I'll be sure to pass that on to Edward. We need to make it to the security room."

"What's stopping you?"

"Try Fabien Randek and about forty armed terrorists. Not to mention about two hundred metres of wall that possesses almost zero shelter."

"How did you even get inside the Wakefield?"

Mike glanced to his right, aware Emily could hear everything. "I had some help."

"A warder?"

"Not exactly," Emily answered.

Maria heard a female voice, clearly within earshot. "Please identify yourself."

She looked at Mike; he nodded. "Her name's Emily Fletcher, she's assistant curator at the Tower."

"Acting head, actually. The curator's on paternity leave."

"He sure picked a great time," Mike added. "Listen to me, Maria, the Chief Yeoman and the Gaoler are both down; not to mention everyone else involved in the Ceremony of the Keys. From what I saw, no less than twenty Beefeaters and half as many Queen's Guards were escorted at gunpoint into the governor's house; I'm guessing they've got him too. Along with over sixty civilian hostages."

Maria delayed, an involuntary pause. "Your uncle?"

"Yeah, afraid so." He felt his heart skip as he answered. "One of the other guys entered the White Tower along with four others; seemed to be carrying some pretty heavy bags – could be explosives. From what Edward tells me, it could be Blanco."

"Highly unlikely. Last we saw, Blanco was making his getaway in the other direction. Not that he's without connection."

"What's the latest with the fires?"

"Still cold in the Rook. Not that I'd want to be much nearer. Reports indicate they've spread across Eastcheap. The others are keeping an eye on things."

"Let's hope they can spare the other eye as well. Not that I'd object to trading places."

"Well, right now, it doesn't look as if you have much choice. Whatever Randek's plans, it's unlikely to be long before reinforcements arrive."

"You think he gives a damn about that? He's got hostages, Maria, maybe a hundred."

Maria bit her lip. "Unfortunately for him, history tells us these situations never end well for the antagonist; unless he's on a suicide mission."

"Even if he isn't, it rarely ends well for the hostages either!" Again Mike tried to take his mind off Champion. "Maybe what happened to Payet sent him over the edge?"

"Right now, let's focus on what we do know, and more importantly what we can do. What can you see?"

"Stone. Windows. Our only way out is back the way we came or out on to the walls. Either way, we risk exposure."

Maria tapped quickly into her keyboard, bringing up a variety of new windows on the nearest screen. "I've got something here. According to this, when the old palace was built, Henry III and Edward I both put in escape tunnels in case the Tower was ever attacked from the river. According to the old architect's plans, the nearest is in the medieval palace."

"Where's that?"

"They're the rooms we just came from!" Emily joined the conversation. "Look, whoever you are, I assure you there are no tunnels. That rumour was merely a myth, probably from one of the Victorian romances."

"According to what I'm seeing here, there's dozens of them, hidden at various points throughout the Tower." Again Maria clicked rapidly at her mouse, her eyes focusing on the 3D plan of the castle as it came up on the nearby screen. "One runs directly from the king's bedroom down to the old water gate. Can't promise it'll be dry!"

Emily was confused. "Who told you this?"

"What you're hearing, Miss Fletcher, is of direct concern to the security of the realm. Just because you're employed to maintain the castle's treasures doesn't mean you're in a position to know all its secrets."

Emily was speechless; Mike beat her to a response.

"Where exactly do we need to look?"

"Try the fireplace. Either that or under the bed."

Mike wasted no time in getting to his feet. Leaving his rucksack by the altar, he opened the door to the chapel and hurried across the round chamber to the door that led to the passage back to St Thomas's.

"Come on! Leave everything you don't need."

Removing her designer handbag, Emily rushed behind him, key in hand. "Who was she?"

"She's an operations director in Whitehall." He looked at her as she delayed.

"What?"

Emily unlocked the door, opened it and closed it behind her. By the time she'd relocked it, Mike had already reached the other side of the footbridge.

This time there was no sign of Randek or anyone else on the walkways below.

Emily followed him, her hair askew, her cheeks puffed. Mike sensed anger in her.

"What is it?"

"Who exactly are you?"

"I've told you, I'm technically Parachute Regiment."

"Look, just stop a minute. Just stop. Less than an hour ago you were here on a tour with your uncle. You said you knew me from Loughborough. You were a captain in the Parachute Regiment. Since then, I've been shot at, seen at least forty people in black rush out of the White Tower, over ten people killed, and now someone is telling me there's a secret passage in a fireplace." She looked at him with a fierce glare. "You need to start answering some questions or else I will not take another step."

Mike looked at her: her face, her posture, her eyes, her hair. He could tell she meant what she said.

Only she was rattled.

"What parachutist turns up with a rucksack full of black ops gear?"

"All right, look. I promise if we make it out of here, we'll get to that. Right now, all you need to know is I'm your best bet to get out of here. And if there is a passageway, it's gonna be right where she said it is."

Taking a deep breath, Emily looked at him, her expression softening. She inserted the correct key into the door and headed back down the stairway and into St Thomas's Tower.

The fireplace was located on the far side of the bedroom, an area off-limits to tourists. Mike went first, wasting no time examining the layout. Several emblems and matching floral patterns marked the mantelpiece around another Plantagenet coat of arms. Like the one in the throne room, it was set up to replicate a medieval fireplace but, unlike the one in the throne room, it wasn't lit.

Mike got down on one knee, removing the wooden logs from the fireplace. Emily knelt down alongside him, her attention fixed on the tiles. Together they attempted to move them.

"Keep trying. I'll check the bed."

Emily watched on in disbelief as Mike hurried over to the bed, looking closely at the floor. The four legs were all raised up from floor level on a wooden platform that didn't appear designed to move.

"Come on, help me out."

Emily left the fireplace, taking up a position at the foot of the bed. She considered telling him the bed wasn't intended to be moved but decided better of it.

"What exactly are we looking for?"

"Not sure. Just help me move it."

Emily pulled hard while Mike pressed his shoulder against the nearest post, throwing away the cushions. Once the bed was a clear distance from the wall, he gazed down at the floor in disbelief.

"Wow!"

Emily hurried over and joined him. Wooden boarding continued beneath where the bed had been.

Set within it was a trapdoor.

27

Tower Green,
22:21

Randek re-entered the Queen's House through the front door, ignoring the sounds of consternation that appeared to be coming from the dining room. Blanco's orders had been specific.

He would carry them out to the letter.

The dining room was overcrowded with hostages, the majority of whom were seated uncomfortably on the floor. After failing to interrupt the general noise of desperate chatter, he got their attention with a gunshot.

The atmosphere changed to stunned silence as plaster fell down from the ceiling.

"General Yates." Randek stared at the governor. "Please. It is very crowded in here. It would be a good idea, yes, to allow more comfort."

Seated at the head of the table, the balding, bespectacled governor of the Tower looked back across the dining table with an expression of repressed fury. Unlike his appearance in full military dress in the many photographs that had been put up on the walls, he was dressed more casually in a white shirt and trousers.

"Tell me, Governor, of the room once used by St Thomas."

The governor was confused. "I'm sorry. The room of which you speak does not exist."

The Frenchman laughed. "Do not waste my time with pointless prevarication, General. As a man of great experience, you should be wise enough to understand the penalties of lying to your captor. Please, it is crowded in here. I do not wish to ease the overcrowding by other means." He reloaded his gun.

Realising he had no alternative, Yates led them to an area rarely seen by tourists. The governor stopped on reaching a heavy door, locked with an iron key, before opening it at Randek's command.

A small stairway led to a dank, star-shaped chamber in which the stone walls magnified both the cold and the noise. Randek was the first to enter.

"When the king who married six times built the house next door as a present for the queen he would one day behead, he also put in instructions to include a vast chamber that even his deadliest enemies would fear." Randek looked around, his attention falling on the vaulted ceiling, the design of which, coupled with the empty archway-style spaces, reminded him of a gothic church. "Legend has it that the martyr Sir Thomas More stayed here before he died. In honour of his bravery, I offer you all the same luxury."

Champion entered the chamber on the gunmen's orders, taking his time before lowering himself to the ground in between a Yeoman Warder and one of the women from his tour group. He remembered reading accounts of More's time in the chamber, but because of its remote location within the Queen's House in the 12th-century Bell Tower, he'd never seen it before.

He guessed its bare appearance had changed much since the former chancellor had occupied it.

He glanced briefly at his captors, careful not to make eye contact. No less than twelve gunmen had kept guard during the blond man's absence; like the others, he sensed this man was also French.

Again the blond-haired villain reserved the majority of his interest for the governor.

Champion thought back over what had happened in the last half hour: visiting the Crown Jewels, the Ceremony of the Keys – such little time had passed, reality was still to sink in. Exactly what the terrorists wanted remained a mystery.

Among the hostages, he'd heard rumours of fires in the city.

As he shuffled for comfort against the cold stone wall, his eyes remaining on the hard, dirty floor, his mind wandered back to what his nephew had told him – his apology that duty called. Though he'd never been exactly sure what that duty involved, being part of the same family often meant knowing when not to ask questions. His nephew had disappeared around 21:50, apparently to make a phone call in preparation for a speedy departure. Only two things he was now sure of. First, the warning was almost certainly of connection.

Second, Mike Hansen was definitely not currently in the same room.

Blanco left the White Tower via the same door he'd used less than fifteen minutes earlier. It was darker out than it had been. The area around Tower Green was now deserted, the atmosphere heavy with a quiet, melancholic air. He remembered on his previous visit learning how the site had become notorious as the location where several key executions had taken place.

Perhaps tonight it would do so again.

Heading south, he veered across the south lawn until he reached the ravens' cages. There were eight inside in total, the majority of which were still awake, some hopping from perch to perch. A biography of each had been attached to the outside of the cages, mentioning everything from their ages to their names.

There was a famous story that when the first astronomer to the king set up his observatory in the White Tower, he complained to the king that the birds had become a hindrance, regularly obstructing his views to the heavens. On receiving permission to dispense with the birds, the Chief Yeoman Warder reminded the king of an old legend that if the ravens were ever to leave the Tower, the Tower would fall. Blanco smiled as he recalled the second part of the legend, words he associated with the famous conqueror.

If the Tower should ever fall, so too should the kingdom.

* * *

In the main control room beneath the Old Admiralty Building, Maria watched with a confused expression as the first of the two taxis came to a stop in Wapping, north of the Thames. Over the coming seconds, she saw three men emerge; two others approached from nearby.

One headed off in the taxi.

For the next few minutes, she watched as the other man led the trio on a walk through the nearby gardens to a second vehicle parked on the other side. She traced it as the journey headed west.

Terminating after only three minutes.

Watching what followed, she put through a call to the Deputy Director.

28

St Thomas's Tower,
22:24

Emily was shell-shocked. The existence of the trapdoor, the wooden exterior matching that of the surrounding floor and cut into it as though part of the original design, simply didn't seem real despite what the woman from Whitehall had already told her. For more than five years, she'd been employed by the Tower to ensure rooms like the one she currently saw remained up to scratch, that every secret existing within its walls was accounted for and studied in detail.

She was looking at something she hadn't known was there.

Under the circumstances, she was glad she was wrong.

She moved quickly alongside Mike, kneeling down by his side. He had removed a torch from his belt and was shining it deep into the void.

He spoke into his headset. "You're more than just a pretty face, Maria."

Maria heard Mike's voice the moment she ended her conversation with Atkins and laughed. "Bet you wouldn't have said that if Edward were here."

Mike smiled. "Well, seeing what we're dealing with, I'm sure Sharon will excuse him for missing the opera." He gazed again beyond the hatch. "What I'm seeing here is actually quite something."

"What does it look like?"

"Kinda tough to describe from here."

"Give me that." Emily took possession of the torch and lowered her head into the dark space, managing to get slightly deeper than Mike. She estimated the gap to be less than a metre in width. Almost immediately, she raised her head. "Hope you don't mind getting wet!"

"Trust me, I'm used to it." Mike spoke again to Maria. "Where are we heading?"

"The original plans show you're heading into what was once a drainage area," Maria replied. "Fortunately for you it's no longer part of the royal privies. When you get below the Cradle Tower, you should be faced with a choice of right or straight on. Right will take you into the Thames."

"Which do we want?"

"I guess that depends on whether you want to leave the Tower or not?"

Mike bit his lip, knowing the decision was pivotal. Until now he was still to seriously consider personal escape. Rule number one of soldiering: never desert your post.

"Where does straight on take us?"

"Follow the drain, you should come up in the Well Tower. It was put in by the same king to protect the new river frontage."

Mike glanced down at Emily as he listened, seeing no obvious sign she was about to open up a scholarly debate. "Is the well still in use?"

"No!" Emily said. "But it still exists."

"All right. Let's try it."

Mike ended the conversation and edged towards the trapdoor, taking back the torch. The darkness below was so dense that the light did little other than confirm movement.

Flowing water.

Mike raised an eyebrow. "How far are we heading?"

"The Well Tower is part of the same walled complex as this one; it's the second most south-east of the towers, one on from the Cradle Tower. If your friend is right, we should know when we reach it."

I never said she was my friend. He looked again towards the bottom; with so little light, it was impossible to calculate the distance of the drop. On the other side of the room, he saw one of the wooden logs on the floor. He dropped it and after a few seconds heard a splash.

It sounded a long drop.

"Lower me in." Emily removed her glasses, placing them into her jacket pocket. Mike avoided the temptation to make a quip about taking a designer jacket into the drain. "Come on."

Mike grabbed her hands and slowly lowered her, waiting till the last possible moment before letting go. He heard a splash, far louder than before.

"You okay?"

A few seconds later he heard a stuttered response. "Really is awfully chilly down here!"

Maria watched the screen in front of her as the GPS dot denoting Mike's position moved several inches in a matter of seconds. She deduced from its sudden movement from the king's bedroom in the old palace to at least one level lower down, Mike had taken the plunge and was now battling his way through the previously hidden waters.

All that training with the Navy SEALs in Hell Week would come in handy, she mused.

Mike held his breath as he entered the water with a loud splash before becoming fully submerged. He felt his body go limp as the icy waters crept up around him, covering his head and getting into his ears and nostrils.

Breathing was suddenly impossible.

A series of sensations hit him all at once, memories coming flooding back. In the darkness, he felt completely trapped, as though he'd entered a pool from which there was no escape. As the seconds passed, the memories became stronger, surrounding him like the cold. He felt himself revisiting a past experience, one that continued to haunt him to this day. His first visit to hell.

Only once in his life had he experienced cold like it.

29

Charlestown, Suffolk, Twenty-One Months Earlier

The knock on the door came at precisely 19:30. Although Atkins had provided no definite indication of when training would begin, Mike had been expecting that it would not be long delayed. He remembered having a beer with a Navy SEAL before undergoing P Company, passing the time listening to the man from the Deep South describe the rigours of what the SEALs called Hell Week. It started with shocks to the system: false times, false promises . . . anything to break the usual routine and get the potential recruit out of their comfort zone. When P Company began, he'd experienced his own version.

If he ever ran into Sergeant Folkes again, he knew he owed the man a beer.

He'd spent the night in a quiet inn, apparently located in the same village as the church where Fenway had been buried. The building was reminiscent of some that he'd seen in Charlestown: half-timbered in a black and white Elizabethan style. The room was cosy, the bed a small double, the views from the window limited. As best he could tell, he was indeed looking at a part of Charlestown, but where and what exactly was a mystery. He'd spent the evening doing his best to find it on Google; intriguingly, he was still to lose access to his phone. Google had failed him; not that he expected anything different. Even if there were references, he guessed the White Hart – if that was their real name – was quietly keeping tabs on him.

The village appeared sleepy; it was as though he had landed either in the distant past or in a village created specifically to create that illusion. Most of what he saw belonged in the past: it reminded him of Shrewsbury, only smaller – perhaps part of Coventry before the Blitz. The people were distant, even in the inn; the only thing he'd learned was that it was called The White Hart.

Whatever its exact history, he knew there could be no coincidence.

It wasn't until he heard the knock at the door that he realised he'd been dozing. It was dark outside, the vague glimmer of Christmas lights in the distance heralding the approach of 25 December – that even in places off the map, Yuletide, the time of celebration, was upon them. The television was on in the corner of the room; the news had finished, The Hangover Part III *just* started. Alan was driving a convertible with a giraffe in tow to the sound of Hanson's "MMMBop".

He saw from the clock that he'd been asleep for almost an hour.

He rolled off the bed and opened the door; Captain Iqbal was waiting with a broad smile.

"Lieutenant Hansen, my man." The Asian captain shook his hand and offered him a man hug. "What's this? A family reunion?"

Hansen grinned, noticing the coincidence. "I thought it would help get me in the mood for what's to come."

"Just be happy Kit isn't here to see you." He spoke of Masterson. "He doesn't need a reason to get on a recruit's back."

"I hadn't noticed." Another grin. "So let me guess, one of you bastards has a nice cold bath in store for me?"

"All I know is I've been asked to collect you and to make sure this is placed tightly on your head." From his pocket he removed the same black head sack that Mike had already become acquainted with. "I can either do it now or Captain Masterson is waiting at the bottom of the stairs."

Mike found himself in what he guessed was a people carrier, the windows wound down despite the cold. Unlike at Windsor there had been no lifting or carrying; he sensed from the lack of noise that he had been escorted out the back way.

The sound of the engine ceased after less than three minutes; he heard Iqbal's voice as he was guided out. After thirty steps, the head sack was removed, his eyes once again struggling to adjust to new brightness. He found himself standing on a grassy parade ground flanked by a small military camp that was illuminated by bright floodlights. Fourteen people were standing looking at him, including Masterson and Sanders.

Iqbal soon made it fifteen.

Mike, meanwhile, was standing alone, the eyes of all present focused firmly on him. The sensation was strange; he'd never experienced a parade ground alone. Twelve of the fifteen he recognised, the eleven Harts the most obvious. Atkins was standing as the central figure, his serious face partially obscured by his rimless spectacles. A thirteenth was dressed in more casual attire, his bearded, potbellied appearance ruling him out as a field agent.

Mike placed him somewhere in IT.

The final two were also dressed in combat uniform, the colours clearly different. The sandy camouflage made them stand out; Mike was still unsure whether it was a good thing. The leader of the two was unshaken, a light stubble visible below his cap, his expression no nonsense. Alongside him, the next man was clearly older; a pair of dark sunglasses hid the colour of his eyes.

He didn't need a written itinerary to know the two men at the forefront were Navy SEALs.

The man with the stubble stepped forward, with calculated poise. Like the man Mike had met five years earlier, a star-spangled banner was stitched into his cap.

"How ya doing? You feeling okay?"

The question caught Mike off guard. "Good. Thank you, sir."

The Navy SEAL smiled. "Now, I'm already aware of the circumstances that have led to you being here with us tonight. We know that in the eyes of those who surround you, you are currently touted among the UK's best at what you do. But there's one thing that you need to understand. We don't give a shit about anyone else here or about what you've done in your life. We were asked to come over here for one reason and one reason only: to weed out the weak. We are here to see if, in our opinion, you're up for selection. I kid you not, I've heard a lot of things so far today, and already I'm not so sure."

A bluff. It had to be. Everything the man said contradicted the words Atkins had told him. He guessed, unlike himself, the SEAL had seen no Round Table.

"Now we may be retired, but unlike you, we've seen it all, done it, and even come back for dessert. For twelve years I served with the cream of the crop. Twelve years! There's a reason there's only about two thousand of us at any time. Soon you're gonna find out exactly why." The SEAL edged slightly closer. "Now, when I ask you a question, you are going to answer me with hoo-yah. It's a simple word; you might not have heard of it over here in England. But remember, Lieutenant. You're not in England now – you're in my battlefield. You understand me?"

"Hoo-yah!" Mike barked back.

"When you hear a command, we expect you to jump to it. Is that clear, Lieutenant Hansen?"

"Hoo-yah!"

"For purposes of this process, my name is Dennis Webbs; in case you're wondering, my primary function was kill house. The man on my right is Larry Mister, or as he'll be known to you – Mr Larry." The SEAL paused, his expression irritated. "You find something funny, Lieutenant Hansen?"

Though inwardly he did, Mike knew he'd kept a straight face. "Sir, no, sir."

"Larry doesn't say an awful lot, but believe me, he has a gift for knowing who has what it takes. Throughout this process, Larry and me are going to give you orders. Now I want you to watch what happens when you fail me."

The Navy SEAL blew sharply on his whistle and the eleven Harts joined the parade ground, lining up either side of Mike.

Larry barked at the Harts for the first time, "Drop down. Heads down. Backs straight. Come on, ladies, we're just getting started." He looked at Mike. "Come on, Hansen, what are you waiting for, you wanna be part of this bullshit?"

Mike jumped on to his front and joined in the press-ups, the commands echoing in his ears. "Down, up."

"One," the Harts' response boomed in unison.

"Down, up."

"Two."

As the press-ups continued, Webbs embarked on another of his monologues. "Back where we come from, for the guys lucky or unlucky enough to be selected for Hell Week, we stay awake for five days straight – five days. You're gonna get cold; you're gonna hurt; you're gonna get tired; you're gonna get thirsty; you're gonna wrestle both mentally and emotionally with every demon in your head, and if that's not enough, I am personally gonna beat the living snot out of you."

"Down, up."
"Twenty-five."
"On your feet."
"You've had a taste. A small taste of what's coming your way," Webbs resumed. "Now, when out on manoeuvres, the average Navy SEAL can burn up to fifteen thousand calories in a single day, so when you eat, it's important to eat good. It's now approaching 21:00 hours. We'll be heading off at 08:00 hours; for all you know this may be your last meal for some time. So eat while you can. Lights out at 22:00 hours."

Precisely four hours later, Mike awoke to the sound of shells going off; there were voices shouting, instructions aimed at him. He'd slept in full gear, minus only his jacket and boots. He unzipped his sleeping bag and pulled his boots on before heading out on to the parade ground.

The floodlights were on again; the camp had been pitch black when he'd retired. On leaving the tent, the gunfire faded; all he heard now was Larry's voice.

All of the Harts were back on parade, watching on intently. The SEALs, like before, were calling the shots.

The first thing Mike saw was a water pool; it was obvious from the lack of steam it was far from boiling. Before he'd even had the chance to enter, he felt cold water.

Masterson was spraying him with a pressure hose.

Webbs was shouting at him. "Get wet!"

He followed Larry's command and dived headfirst into the icy water, the cold bracing even by comparison to the hose. Leaving the water, he found himself negotiating a minor assault course that hadn't been there before he went to bed. He followed Larry's guidance: pole, pool, pole, pool, tarpaulin, rope ladder, pole, pool. He heard Webbs shout something about 'Do it for the Queen'.

He completed the course and made a beeline for the Harts, all of whom were watching on. Atkins had also appeared; his eyes appearing uncharacteristically tired.

"The first thing you gotta realise is, succeed or fail, you do it as a team. Mess up, it's them that suffer." Webbs pointed at the eleven men Mike had first seen huddled by the gravesite. "Come on now, let's see some push-ups – move!"

Mike followed the American's orders: up and down, hold, up. After fifteen minutes of press-ups, the same followed in sit-ups.

The cold was becoming unbearable.

"Cold enough for you?" Webbs bellowed.

Mike replied, "Hoo-yah!"

"Okay, Hansen, on your feet." This time the command came from Larry. "Okay, what say we wipe that grass off your face real quick?" He watched on while Mike complied. "Oh, looking good. Looking good. Yeah, looking real good. You mighty fine piece of ass. Hey, Masterson, you seen this?"

Kit emerged from the line, looking Mike over. Despite trying in vain not to shiver, his drenched clothes coupled with the near freezing temperature made it impossible.

Kit took his temperature with an ear gun. "Thirty-nine point three." *He looked at Mike.* "Would you care to visit the warming tent?"

Mike answered with chattering teeth, "No, sir. I'll go where I'm told."

Webbs was speaking again through a megaphone. "In the SEALs, we have a saying, die first, then quit. You see that bell, Hansen?" *He pointed to a gold-plated ornamental bell that looked from a distance like something from a 1940s fire truck.*

"Yes, sir."

"You want to quit, all you gotta do is ring that bell. You sure you don't want to quit?"

"Sir, no, sir!"

Larry walked towards Mike, now carrying the megaphone. "In times like this, we rely extra hard on teamwork. Camaraderie. It helps us through the day." *He offered it to Mike.* "What are you going to sing for us, Hansen?"

Mike was confused. "Excuse me?"

"Sing. What's it gonna be?"

For the first time since the exercise began, Mike was genuinely unprepared. "Do you have any requests?"

"Do I look like I have any requests? Come on." *The volume of his voice rose inexplicably.* "First thing that comes into your head."

Mike hesitated for several seconds and sang the first words that entered his head, the same song that had been playing when Jay entered his room. The words seemed to almost squeeze from his lips, the tone of his voice becoming less affected by the cold as he continued. While Larry held the megaphone, the Harts watched on, their expressions displaying nothing but mild hysteria.

Except for Masterson.

The expressions of the Harts lightened further, Iqbal's laugh audible from a distance. As Mike began the fifth line, Jay began to clap in time to the beat; by the sixth, all but Masterson had joined in.

"Enough!" *Webbs took the megaphone and handed it to Masterson, who barked press-up orders. Mike dropped to his chest.*

"Down, up."

"One."

Iqbal could barely contain himself. As the parade fell silent, he began singing the chorus.

The nine Harts alongside him erupted into laughter. Holding his position, arms at full length to Masterson's orders, Mike failed to hide a grin.

"Hold!" *Kit knelt down beside him, his lips so close Mike could feel the warmth of his breath. His expression again was like thunder.* "I assume you want to remain in the process?"

"Yes, sir."

"Then believe me, Hansen, you'd better start taking this seriously or in an Mmmbop you'll be gone!"

30

Beneath the Tower's Outer Wall, 22:28

Mike rose quickly to the surface, the bottom providing a good springboard as the soles of his feet made contact with it. He exhaled on resurfacing, fighting hard to adjust to the sudden cold. Unlike his experience with the Navy SEALs, the black ops suit was designed for such conditions.

Alongside him Emily was shivering.

He activated his night-vision goggles and quickly studied his surroundings, immediately satisfied the hazy green backdrop was having far greater effect than the circular rays of his torch. The tunnel was of heavy stone construction, the style and shade again matching the tower's exterior.

There was no doubting what he saw had existed for centuries.

He looked again at Emily. "Which way?"

"East," Emily replied through chattering teeth.

Mike led the way, doing his best to find east with the GPS on his phone, choosing to swim as an alternative to walking. Although the water level was becoming shallower as they continued, the force made walking difficult.

After a couple of minutes they found Maria's fork; Mike realised they had a decision to make. His illuminated goggles revealed passages that led straight on or to their right. Only there was a problem.

The one straight ahead was blocked off.

Emily appeared alongside him, looking with dismay at what lay in front of them. While the passage to the right appeared unrestricted, iron bars blocked the other one, its appearance rather like a primitive storm drain.

"What is this?" Mike was confused.

"The drain was probably put in to prevent capture during siege," Emily guessed. "My God, this could actually rewrite the Tower's history."

"I thought it was put in as an escape passage."

"It was. Only the king probably used it to actually escape."

Mike laughed, instantly realising that the route to the right appeared to be accessible. Doing his best to shut out the cold, he swam towards the grate. The bars were strong, but with signs of corrosion at the top.

Emily looked at him, confused. "What are you doing?"

Delving deep into his belt, Mike removed a small stick of plastic and attached it to the rusty bar. Almost instantly he retreated.

"Stand well back."

* * *

Maria saw the white dot come to an area below the Cradle Tower. For the first time since going into the drains, it had stopped moving.

"Grosmont, do you copy?" She failed to get a response. "Grosmont?"

All she heard was static.

Walking the grounds close to the Lanthorn Tower, two gunmen came to a sudden halt. The ground moved slightly around them, almost like a minor earthquake.

Confused, they looked at one another, deliberating for a few seconds before heading back to the Queen's House.

Emily felt herself become submerged the moment Mike dived on top of her. A sudden rise in the water level caused it to flood into her mouth, causing a choking sensation in her lungs.

Once again, his movements had caught her off guard.

As they returned to the surface, the cold water was expelled and her senses cleared. She picked up on a dense smell in the air, different to what had been present before. It was like fire, only less harsh.

As her vision cleared, she saw smoke.

Mike had already reached the storm drain. Catching him up, she saw that one of the bars had been completely removed.

Mike spoke into his headset, counting his blessings his equipment was waterproof. "Maria, didn't I tell you you're more than just a pretty face?"

Staring at the screen, Maria breathed a sigh of relief. "I was worried you'd got trapped."

"Better luck next time. You can say the same thing to Phil."

Terminating the transmission, Maria clicked rapidly on her mouse, watching the pictures change in front of her. While Mike's white dot moved quickly on the 3D map, among the city's security cameras, no less than a dozen had caught the second vehicle carrying Bizante Blanco and his two associates heading in the direction of St Katharine Docks.

Mike moved on ahead, with some difficulty, through the narrow space previously covered by the iron grate. The water was deeper on the other side; it seemed to be pooling from somewhere.

He guided Emily through the gap and began to explore the area directly above, noticing a clear change in the patterns of the architecture. The ceiling was ribbed, vaulted; it was like entering catacombs.

"Norman architecture. Just like the White Tower." Emily studied the patterns with her torch, stunned. "This could be one of the oldest constructions at the Tower."

Aided by his night visions, Mike focused dead ahead, detecting the tunnel was getting wider. "Well, let's just hope it leads where we want it to. Otherwise, this might be a real short trip!"

31

The Jewel House,
22:29

Blanco made his way directly to the main jewel room, ignoring the temptation to check up on Randek or address the governor first-hand. The hour had passed only twenty-nine minutes earlier; he wasn't due to make any dramatic announcement before Big Ben chimed again. If the rumours turned out to be false, one wouldn't be necessary at all.

Any deviations from the plan would be minor.

He entered the Jewel House and negotiated his way through the early rooms to the previously locked steel door, offering only the briefest acknowledgement to the gunmen, the black of their combat outfits distinguishing them clearly from the usual staff. He showed little interest as he passed the bodies of the recently deceased security personnel, reserving his greatest attention for the historic items, the earliest of which dated from before the Protectorate.

Like the antique furniture he'd seen on his cousin's yacht, he knew they were the few among the collection that dated back to the days of his forebears.

Over three hundred miles north in the Scottish capital, the leader of the four intruders inserted the correct key into the main door of the crown room and entered. The room was dark with the lights off, the famous display case only visible from the reflection of the torchlight on the glass.

Within seconds, the overhead lights came on.

The room was small compared to its equivalent in England, the walls enclosed, the ceiling far lower. A heavy smell of mahogany gave off a calm, studious atmosphere that suited the age of both the room and the jewels.

The Honours of Scotland were officially the oldest of their type in the United Kingdom. Used for the first time for the coronation of Mary Queen of Scots at Stirling Castle in 1543, they predated the English equivalents by over a century.

Coincidentally, their last official use was during the coronation of Charles II, the man for whom the present English jewels had been set.

The leader of the four circled the display case while his three accomplices took up positions by each possible entrance. Concentrating on the job in hand, he looked out the correct key and entered it into the smallest of the four glass panes, opening the case.

In Paris, the two thieves alighted the Métro at Quai de la Rapée, showing no obvious sign of nerves as they carried their recently filled dark holdalls through the sparse crowd to the station exit. On reaching the pavement, the warm, late summer air moistened by a calm wind blowing in off the Seine, they took the nearest stairway to the water's edge, taking great care not to catch the moving holdall against the wall.

A large yacht was floating close to the bank, its many lights creating reflections off the river. As it reached the walkway, the two thieves climbed aboard, heading straight to the main entrance.

And down the stairs into the galley below.

Blanco found François in the heart of the jewel room, leaning against the podium that overlooked the key display area. The Jeweller stood alongside him, fear etched across his ageing features.

Surrounding him on all sides, the four gunmen continued to monitor his every move.

The longest of the display cases was open; one crown had already been removed. A second lay on a white cloth on the floor, close to his feet.

Blanco realised he'd arrived just in time.

He took up a position alongside François, deciding against distracting him. The young expert, meanwhile, eyed the crown in his hands with unbreakable concentration, his left eye scrunched tightly shut as he examined the finer details through his special eyepiece.

After several seconds of silence, he lowered his hand and Blanco finally broke the silence.

"Well?"

In Edinburgh, the first thing to be removed was the Sword of State, whose handle was nearest the open glass. The intruder was aware from its history that it had been presented to James IV in 1507 by the same Pope responsible for forming the Swiss Guards. The famous break in the sword was clearly visible, causing a broken glint as he moved it.

Rumour had it, the break had occurred when the jewels were smuggled out of Dunnottar Castle in 1652.

Next came the sceptre, another item dating from the reign of James IV. According to its official history, it had also been presented to the Scottish King by the Vatican and later remodelled for the coronation of James V.

The third item was the crown itself, situated prominently atop a red cushion. Taking it out had been a delicate process, so great were the obstacles in front of it. Once safely removed, only three items remained: the Stone of Destiny in the same case and the Stewart and Lorne jewels lying against a backlit cyan fabric on the far side of the room.

The leader of the four took the crown to the far side of the room to a wooden table. Placing it down carefully, he closely inspected the exterior through a near-identical eyepiece to that of his accomplice in London, concentrating on the main jewels.

After seeing everything he needed to see, he prepared to put through a call to London.

In the main galley of the yacht, the two thieves handed over the three holdalls to the famed Parisian antiquarian. With shaking hands, he opened the first and placed the key pieces on the table in front of him before eyeing them with the correct equipment.

Within moments he'd made his conclusion.

Blanco stood with folded arms, his anticipation at fever pitch. A sudden onset of frustration overwhelmed him as he feared the silence had lasted too long. He saw no joy in his accomplice's eyes.

"François?"

François turned to face him, his face livid. "They're fake!"

32

Below the Well Tower,
22:31

The water level was rising and had been for some time. The increase had been gradual, like taking a bath with the taps dripping. Only recently had Mike started to become concerned.

For every second the water was rising, the low ceiling was getting nearer to the top of his head.

Maria had told him the Cradle Tower was roughly halfway between St Thomas's Tower and the Well Tower, indicating that the well should be close. Emily backed up the theory.

The only problem was she'd never seen it from the bottom.

Through his coloured lenses, Mike could see brightness somewhere up ahead. Focusing on the area above him, he noticed a clear change in the patterns, suggesting something of architectural importance. The walls were grander, the engravings better defined; to reach the source of the light, a swim underwater would be required.

He reasoned the end of the passage was in sight.

He waited till Emily was close at hand before risking the dive beneath the surface. Holding his breath, he struggled against the steady current, pushing himself through the cold towards the source of the light. The ceiling had become noticeably higher; a round void existed above and around them.

Light shone down in circular rays.

He emerged quickly above the water; fresh air had never felt so good. Emily surfaced alongside him, gasping for breath; her eyes appeared disoriented in the green light.

He pulled her towards him, supporting her. "You okay?"

She nodded, for now incapable of speaking. Mike waited till he was sure she was in control of her movements before relaxing his grip.

They'd come up in the centre of a well, its circular walls surrounding them evenly on all sides. Pulling up his goggles, he switched on his torch and saw the top was within touching distance. He reached out and pulled himself over.

Once out, he reached back to help Emily.

The cold was bracing, even out of the water; his black ops suit clung tightly to his body like an extra layer of skin. Doing his best to take his mind off the cold, he shone the light on the surroundings. Like those of the previous towers, the walls were medieval, constructed of stone; a clutter of barrels and wooden tables from a bygone era intensified the historical feel. Exploring the area above him, Mike realised the ceiling was ribbed in an ecclesiastical style.

His instinct told him he'd entered a crypt.

"What is this place?"

"When Edward I extended the medieval palace, he put in two shafts to draw up fresh water," Emily answered with chattering teeth. "The supporting walls were designed to protect it from the river."

Mike nodded. The description made sense of the water, less so the gothic, chapel-like design. Hearing a sharp noise in his ear, he answered, "Maria?"

"Glad to have you back. What can you see?"

"Pretty much what you predicted. Only it looks more like a crypt than a well."

"Unfortunately there are parts of the Tower than aren't open to the general public. Either that or I just missed it on the tour."

"You don't miss a thing." He walked around the room, shining his torch in every direction. For now he saw no obvious exit. "Where do we go from here?"

"The plans show a second water shaft; it should be in the next chamber to you."

Mike looked at Emily. "That make sense to you?"

She nodded, her face illustrating her unwillingness to go through further cold. "The second well is located in a different part of the tower. Unfortunately that one's covered up."

Maria heard every word. "Well, I'm afraid your only option might be to uncover it. Either that or come out the front door."

"I'll pass," Mike said. "How are the others?"

The fire had spread north along Gracechurch Street, devouring everything in its path. Kit had seen it all with his own eyes, breathed the smoke, felt the heat on his skin.

Recent blazes had escalated into an inferno.

He heard Mike's voice come through on the standard frequency; he'd heard every word since Mike had put on his black ops suit.

"Peachy!" he replied to Mike's question. "The fires at Monument are all out, but it's getting worse to the north. Fenchurch Street is also ablaze."

The name meant more to Maria than Mike; again she saw as much on the screens in front of her. "How are things looking to the west?"

"Nothing yet, but if this is anything to go by, it may only be a matter of time." Kit's eyes focused on the crossroads where Gracechurch Street met Fenchurch Street to the east and Lombard Street to the west. The traffic there had also ground to a halt, cars blocking the box junction, delaying the arrival of new fire engines.

Though some drivers had left their cars, most hadn't ventured far.

"I can't fight this on my own, Maria; I'm not a fireman."

"You don't have a truck either." Maria's response was ice cold. "How many street fires do you see?"

For Kit, the question was difficult to answer. "Everything is out south of Eastcheap and King William. From here, I'd say three streets are affected, but I might be wrong. With the traffic as it is, the sparkies can't break through."

"All the more reason to encourage panic." Mike was stunned by what he'd heard. Collectively, the symptoms of the problem indicated a clear disease. "They're launching a bosson attack."

"What?" Emily asked, eavesdropping.

"Like hitting us with a battering ram. Attacking on every front."

Kit frowned; at the Rook, Maria's expression was similarly morbid. "That's impossible. Even Randek doesn't have that kind of capability."

"You mean the kind to attack Edinburgh twice in six months, nearly blow up an opera theatre, rip off a Parisian gallery before infiltrating the Tower of London and setting fire to half the city?" Kit posed.

The last thing Mike wanted was to be right. "Think about it. The city's in flames; over forty men have stormed the Tower. It's the perfect three-pronged attack."

Maria was confused. "What are the three?"

"Information, transport, financial," Kit confirmed. "Like pounding every gate."

"That hasn't happened. All they've done so far is start the fires."

Looking across the roads at the scenes of panic, Kit checked his watch. "Maybe. But it's barely half-ten yet."

Away from the fires of London, in the 19th-century chateau near the River Garonne in the heart of Bordeaux, the man who two centuries earlier would have been addressed as the Duke of Aquitaine ended the phone conversation with his distant cousin and replaced the receiver. Within seconds, he pointed the remote control at the TV, reactivating the sound.

The news from London was dire. Fires had spread over two hundred metres since the initial blaze, taking out over thirty buildings. With the traffic at gridlock, fighting them was becoming a major concern.

The pictures reminded him of a scene from the Second World War.

Within a minute of ending the previous call, the phone went again.

"*Allô?*"

"The great home of the former lord has fallen," the voice said calmly. "I hadn't intended to witness the moment myself. However, under the circumstances, I thought it only fitting."

The duke recognised his son's voice. "There are many I know who would see what you did as difficult to understand. Others merely refuse to open their minds." The old man took in the scenes on the news. "You are safe?"

"Everyone departed the yacht at the agreed time; even the operator of the bridge saw no reason to delay us. Under the circumstances I almost felt the need to reward him, but I digress. The schedule is intact. Soon we shall receive confirmation from the Tower."

Seated at the head of the twenty-four-man table, the old man moved uneasily. "You anticipate problems?"

"I anticipate only what has already been discussed." At the other end Fieschi checked his watch. "I expect a call immediately. If the news is bad, they already know the correct course of action."

"The fires in the city have already caused much economic damage. I should fear for the city should another step be necessary."

"Soon we shall have our answer. In the meantime, you must rest. Perhaps in a few hours there will still be something of the old city to gaze over."

33

Whitehall,
22:33

The Director of the White Hart left his office, returning to the main hub. Maria was in the same place, Phil seated alongside her.

For the last half hour, they'd been the only people present.

"What's the latest?" he asked, descending a spiral stairway that connected the door of his office to the circular room.

"The fires have spread as far as Fenchurch Street; the early ones are all out." Maria blew up the images on her iMac, sharing them with the large semi-translucent pictures that seemingly floated over the heart of the room. A two-way conversation remained open over the airwaves with Mike and Kit, photos of them both appearing in profile.

Neither man showed up live.

"However, unfortunately we have a second situation brewing at the Tower."

Mr White stopped alongside Maria and placed a headset over his ears. "Grosmont, this is the King."

In the cellar of the Well Tower, Mike heard the Director's voice come through clearly. "Come in, sire."

"What's happening?"

"Security at the Tower's been compromised. At least forty men in black stormed out of the White Tower exactly as the Ceremony of the Keys ended. The Queen's Guard and the Beefeaters have been taken hostage. Along with several civilians."

The Director couldn't believe what he was hearing. "Any casualties?"

"At least fifteen dead, including the Chief Yeoman and his deputy; perhaps over eighty hostages." He avoided the temptation to mention his uncle. "The terrorists have taken control of the governor's residence; I'm guessing he was inside. Among them was Randek."

Though mention of the name evoked feelings of intense hostility, it was far from a surprise. "You're quite sure?"

"Quite sure," Mike replied. "There are others with him; all wore ski masks. Based on what I'm hearing, I wouldn't be surprised if the bastard you saw at Monument was one of them."

"Any news on Blanco?" The Director's question was for Maria.

"One of the taxis was last seen heading out of the city, possibly to Kingston. The other headed west. Searches remain ongoing."

The Director's attention returned to Hansen. "Where exactly are you?"

"In something called the Well Tower, off the radar. The security room is in the same building that houses the Crown Jewels. Getting there isn't exactly straightforward."

"There are passages beneath the surface." Maria showed the Director on the screen. "If they follow what we're seeing here, it should bring them out in the Constable Tower."

"Who's they?"

"He's with the assistant curator."

The Director took a moment to digest what he'd just heard. If one thing compromised a mission, it was outsiders. "You listen to me, Grosmont. Whatever happens tonight, under no circumstances can Randek be allowed to break free. He's already slipped the net once. We cannot allow that to happen again."

"Yes, sir."

"Keep in regular contact. I'll be in touch again when I can."

"Roger that." Mike ended the transmission.

The Director turned his attention to Maria. "Where is everyone else?"

"Most of the knights are currently at Monument; Grailly has been overseeing the damage. Unless you want them to continue posing as firefighters, there's nothing else for them to do. Unless, of course, the PM has other plans."

"The PM is in conference with the COBRA Committee – believe me, I'm expecting her back on the line the moment she's finished. In the meantime, make sure the area to the north is sealed off and the roads are cleared no matter how. And keep an eye on Blanco and Randek. The sooner those bastards are in custody, the better."

Mike followed Emily's directions into the adjacent chamber. In keeping with the last, it was church-like in design and had a forlorn atmosphere. The well had been covered over with an iron grate.

Mike guessed it would be accessible with tools.

He removed a small high-powered laser from his belt and in less than a minute had cut through the corroded metal grate. Not for the first time, Emily was speechless.

"You were right about the second shaft." Mike waited until the Director signed off before reopening the conversation with Maria. "Where exactly is this taking us?"

"The architectural drawings show that it starts out towards the Develin Tower directly east. After that it should take you left, north." Maria double-checked the route on the screen. "Look for something above you after about one hundred metres. According to this, there's something in the Constable Tower."

"Roger that." Mike examined the well as the conversation ended, the light of his torch dancing on the water below. "That mean anything to you?"

"The Constable Tower dates from about the same era. If the architecture is consistent, it's not impossible there's something below the ground."

Mike smiled at her, taking momentary pleasure in her appearance. Even freezing cold and soaked to the skin, her face somehow radiated warmth.

"I really hope there's air down there."

Emily perched herself on the side of the well, preparing to enter. "If there isn't, it's sure gonna be a short ride!"

Mike leaned over the side, lowering her in; the sound of a splash occurred far sooner than expected.

She confirmed immediately she was okay.

Mike spoke again into his earpiece transmitter. "Hey, Edward, you there?"

Making his way towards the nearest fires, Kit responded, "What is it?"

"You remember my initiation in Wales, I said that was the coldest thing I'd ever experienced."

"Yeah!"

"I take it back. This is definitely worse."

Amidst the panic around him, Kit felt the urge to smile. "Well, maybe you'll find some sand down there to do sugar cookies in."

Jay got the call within moments of Maria ending her conversation with Mike.

"The Director has instructed all the knights to join Edward north of Eastcheap," Maria began. "Fires are spreading."

Standing within the shadow of the Monument, what Jay saw was a sorry sight. With the exception of the famous column, everything had turned to rubble. "The emergency services said it might take thirty minutes before reinforcements can get through. Everywhere we go, the streets are gridlocked."

"Same in every direction. The RAF is preparing to bring six choppers in, but unfortunately it might take them a while. What about the trucks already there?"

Jay analytically observed the chaotic scene around him. Along Pudding Lane up to Monument Street, five of his accomplices were engaged in conversation with various branches of the emergency services. "Same problem."

"Make sure the area remains sealed; tell the bobbies they can start making arrests on the spot if necessary."

"I'm sure they'd love to. Question is, where do they take them?"

Maria realised he had a point. "Right now, I guess they're gonna just have to improvise. Fires are starting all over the place. If this is what we think it is, it's only a matter of time before they spread."

"What exactly do we think it is?"

Maria bit her lip. "If this is a repeat of what London saw in 1666, what we've seen so far could just be the very beginning."

34

Below the Tower's Outer Wall,
22:39

The water was freezing, just like before. In his mind, Mike had felt it engulfing him like an inescapable prison even prior to going into the well.

The passage was narrow, the walls barely distinguishable even with the aid of his night visions. With his hands numbed by the cold, the touch of the stone walls was almost unnoticeable.

Again, he remembered a time he'd encountered something far worse.

The leader of the SEALs took up a position at the front of his posse of eyewitnesses at the summit of the largest sandy knoll overlooking the shoreline. Mike stood alone.

"This is our playground – our home ballpark," Webbs began, barking his orders gruffly with a voice that was already showing the effects of shouting. "This is what we do. This is who we are."

Mike looked back with cold eyes, cold feet, cold hands . . . everything but a cold mind. He didn't need a history lesson to know the former SEAL commander was telling the truth. It was the look in his eyes, an aura of self-assurance that offered clear confirmation.

You're on my turf.

"There's an old saying, the ocean makes cowards of us all. The sea is unforgiving. The sea is ruthless. She is a bitch. My bitch. And I love her for it.

"Now this is the bit I love the most. We're gonna pay our respects to the ocean. And we're gonna keep doing it till the sun goes down tonight. You understand me, Hansen?"

"Hoo-yah, sir."

"Good. Now I'm gonna ask these gentlemen alongside me to join you in the water. Then I want all of you to link arms. We're gonna take you surfin' USA."

It sounded a lot better than it was, not that Mike expected better. The concept was simple, legendary. All eleven of the Harts entered together; Mike was in the middle, he sensed deliberately. They lowered themselves on Masterson's orders; he was floating on his wet behind to Mike's left. Their arms were now interlocked, his voice echoing in Mike's ears.

He closed his eyes, attempting to overcome the shock.

The water was freezing; he guessed less than ten degrees. It was Christmas Eve and the reasons were self-explanatory. The first half hour was the hardest; there was no work involved, only cold. His body floated as he caught the waves; the sound of the lapping tide drowned out the sound of the SEALs as they bellowed in the morning light.

"Does everybody hate me yet?" Webbs cried.

"Hoo-yah!"

Mike waited until the passage turned north before stopping to concentrate on the area ahead. The first turn had come almost exactly at the point Maria had indicated.

If his bearings were correct, they were now beneath the Develin Tower.

The channel was wider than it had been, the surrounding walls and cavernous ceiling curiously impressive. It was now possible to walk rather than swim.

Unlike before, there was evidence of silt banks.

Webbs smiled as they were led to the top of the largest sandy knoll in easy reach; Mike guessed it was over thirty feet in elevation. Standing alongside Masterson and Sanders, he looked down from above, his eyes on the angle of the slope.

He shivered. As did the others.

"Life in the SEALs is all about risk-reward," Webbs resumed. "We do what we do so that others don't have to. It's also about reward and punishment. Do you think you've been punished enough?"

The Harts remained silent.

"All right then." The leader of the SEALs grinned; Mike could tell the silence was the correct answer. "What we've got here is called Sugar Cookies. Our way of giving you a reward. Now, imagine you're a kid again. Rolling in the sand. Dawson, Chambers, you're up."

Mike watched as the two men rolled down the sandy slope, nearly colliding. Both men laughed, frolicked. Sand stuck to their training gear like sugar.

"Hansen, Masterson, get going."

Mike rolled down the slope, keeping his eyes on Kit to ensure they didn't collide. His body was still numb, his arms almost out of control.

Nevertheless, he felt warmer than before.

"Feel better, Hansen?"

"Hoo-yah, sir."

"Once you're finished, roll to your side. I want to see sand angels when you're done."

Removing his night visions, Mike saw Emily emerge from the water close behind.

In the torchlight, she looked alarmingly pale.

Mike grabbed her hand and guided her to his right, the area nearest the docks. Leaving the water, he lay down on the bank and began rolling around on the silt.

Emily was confused. "What are you doing?"

"It's called sugar cookies." Mike smiled at her. "Come on, it'll help you keep warm."

Still confused, but unwilling to argue, Emily lay down alongside him, following his lead. The texture was soft yet grainy. It reminded her of sand.

She spat it out as some got into her mouth. "Who taught you that?"

"Little trick I learned from a guy who used to be a Navy SEAL. Whenever they're cold out on manoeuvres, they do it to keep warm." He lay on his back, moving his arms and legs from side to side. "Try this too. It's called a sand angel."

Emily followed his advice, allowing the silt to find its way into her clothes and stick close to her body. Though she was still shivering, she noticed a slight improvement.

"Better?"

Her teeth chattering, she nodded. "Any other great advice?"

One of the Harts was injured; he'd cut his shin on a concealed rock. While Captain Rawlins was ordered to the medic, Mike and the other Harts sat in line, rowing-boat style. Each man rubbed the shoulders of the man in front; he'd learned the same in P Company – one of the core values of brotherhood often required shared bodily warmth. Iqbal was behind him, his soft hands shaking as they massaged Mike's arms. Mike did the same for the Hart in front of him; he placed him in his mid-thirties with a slowly receding hairline.

He'd learned his name was Captain Pentland.

Larry reappeared from inspecting Rawlins' injury. "Cold, Hansen?"

"Yes, sir." He somehow avoided answering with chattering teeth.

"Sometimes out on manoeuvres, we get so cold that we literally have to piss to keep each other warm. You know that? Literally, you hold out your hand, cup it and throw it over each other. Sometimes all you can do is improvise. The important thing is to hang in there."

Mike moved behind Emily and began rubbing her arms quickly with both hands. He remembered from his experience with the SEALs that in times of extreme cold, shared bodily warmth was sometimes the difference between life and death.

As the seconds passed, he sensed her becoming warmer, the hard pinpricks on her arms receding, replaced by her usual soft skin. With chattering teeth, he saw her looking at him, their eyes fleetingly locked.

Slowly, he rose to his feet.

"Come on. If Maria's correct, it's only another fifty metres."

Emily reached out and grabbed his hand, reluctantly re-entering the water. Following Mike's lead, they made their way onwards through the waist-deep stream. After approximately fifty metres, the light above changed again.

They came up in an area of heavy stonework and boarded in wood. Rather than a similar chamber to the previous one, what greeted them was a brightly illuminated castle wall.

Mike sensed he'd seen it before.

He scrambled out on to the nearby walkway and rolled across the wood underfoot, water dripping from his body and clothing. Once safely out, he offered his hand and pulled until Emily's whole body emerged above the strange timber platform.

The way up had been easy compared to leaving the well. On reaching the point that Maria had described, the passage upwards had proceeded at a forty-five-degree angle, making it climbable.

Albeit slippery.

"Where the hell are we?" Mike rose to a crouching position to look around at the new surroundings without giving away evidence of their position. Along the wall in both directions he saw imposing stone towers, yellow stonework mixed with white. As the seconds passed, he realised they had made it to the upper levels.

He was looking at the medieval walls.

"We're at the top of the inner east wall," Emily said, her designer suit now wet and ruined. Amidst the cold she managed a smile. "Whoever created this was a genius."

Mike was confused. "Care to elaborate?"

"The towers either side of us were built by Henry III as part of the inner curtain wall. From a defensive perspective, they're as strong as any here. It's possible the Constable Tower got its name because the Constable once had his lodgings there. Having an extra escape route alongside his lodgings was perfect planning."

Mike couldn't fault the logic. He placed his hand through his wet hair and followed her quickly north. The east side of the Tower was darker than most areas he'd seen, the nearby windows a black void; he learned most were now used as offices. Beneath his feet and lining the west side of the wall, the wooden boarding extended both alongside and above him, offering ample shelter. Through gaps in the wood, he saw the backs of two large buildings and beyond that the imposing outline of the White Tower casting its familiar outline over the Inner Ward. From there, it wasn't clear whether the bodies that had earlier soaked the Broadwalk Steps with innocent blood had since been removed. All that was clear was that the similarly well-trained men, presently circling the White Tower, were also carrying identical weapons to those who had been responsible for their killings.

Mike contacted Maria. "This is Grosmont, you copy?"

Maria heard his voice clearly. "How's the view from up there?"

"This time you were only nearly right. Came up on the east wall. Right between the Constable Tower and the Broad Arrow." Mike bit his lip, his attention on the gunmen patrolling the Inner Ward. "All in all, I guess it could've been worse."

"You're safe?"

"The walkway's covered in timber. It's really rather quaint, almost like a gazebo." He looked around, concerned there were cameras nearby. He doubted every area was manned, but he knew he couldn't be sure.

"Send me a picture. You never know, it might give me ideas."

"Doubt it'll do much good if the bullets start firing. Then again, I've never met a Frenchman yet who can see through wood. What are our options?"

Maria typed quickly on her keyboard, bringing up the same 3D map of the Tower she'd been studying for the past fifteen minutes. "Afraid the nearest underground passage is on the other side. You got keys to the towers?"

He looked at Emily, who was shivering head to toe; despite the cold, it was obvious to Mike she was still in control of her thoughts.

"Yes."

"Head inside the Constable Tower; after that, you come to the Martin Tower. It's the same one where the jewels used to be kept. As a matter of fact, they still have some."

"Anything of value?"

"Why are you asking me? You've got the curator alongside you."

"Acting curator." Emily stared at him.

Mike laughed.

"If you can get past the displays of the royal beasts, you should be able to find your way down from the Flint Tower. After that it will be an easy hop, step and a jump to the barracks."

"Roger that. How's Edward?"

A second voice joined the conversation. "Not deaf for a start."

A wry smile. "You been eavesdropping this whole time?"

"You do realise you have the facility to do the same to me?" Kit's eyes were now fixed on the area beyond Fenchurch Street where incoming fire trucks were at last beginning to tackle the flames. Within the constant onslaught of heavy smoke, a light spray took the edge off the close heat. "Then again, I shouldn't be too harsh on you. I know you struggle with the cold at the best of times."

"Well, fortunately we're out of that now. I guess a second with you we'd both be bone dry." Mike paused, suddenly concerned. "How is it over there?"

"Did Bennett ever tell you about the Blitz?"

"To be truthful, I never asked."

"Well, get down here, you might save yourself a question."

Mike nodded, contemplating the scene. He remembered watching a documentary on the Blitz once about a soldier returning home on leave, ignorant of the true horrors till his return. The soldier's parents had been killed by a bomb that had penetrated the Anderson shelter in which they had taken cover during an air raid. He later found his sister and little brother in the nearby wards.

In seventy years, the brother never spoke of the event.

"Maybe if I get out of here in time, I'll get to see it for myself," Mike said.

"Let's not get ahead of ourselves. You know the drill; always focus on the next step."

"Any ideas?"

"Just one. Remember what else you learned from the SEALs."

They reconvened on the parade ground, the Harts taking their usual place behind Webbs and Larry.

Again Mike stood alone.

"You've had a very interesting thirty-six hours. In that short time, Lieutenant, we've seen you grow and we've seen you progress. On the first

night, we showed you the true meaning of hell. We got you cold. We got you wet. We deprived you of sleep. We pushed you hard. You could have gone to the medics; you could have gone to the warming tent – you didn't. That's a hoo-yah from me to you."

Mike nodded, his eyes locked with Webbs. It was clear the compliment was genuine.

"Our time with you is coming to an end. You've still got a long road in front of you, brother. Now you know what it means to be a SEAL. From me to you, I believe you've got what it takes to live in our world."

Mike disconnected the call and moved quickly to where the boardwalk ended, stopping outside the door of the Constable Tower. He smiled at the sight of a metallic dummy in the shape of a Norman soldier, remembering a time when he had seen it before and laughed far harder. Emily was shivering again, the keys dangling in her hands. He held her gently.

"It's okay. We'll have you warm soon."

Quickly unlocking the door, Emily let them in, locking it behind her. In the available light, Mike saw a display case immediately to his right, the glass reflecting the white walls opposite; once again he refused to switch on the lights. He held her as he looked at the model building of the Tower on display behind the glass. Chancing the light of his phone, he asked, "What is that?"

"It's how the Tower looked at the time of the Peasants' Revolt. The layout's changed since then."

Mike realised she was right. The Jewel House and the Fusiliers' Museum on the north and east sides were missing; instead the area was occupied by smaller dwellings, far more primitive.

"Where are we now?"

"Here." She pointed to the Constable Tower, one of many among the inner wall. "We need to get to here." She referred to the area where the barracks now stood. "It's gonna be impossible without exposure."

"Looks as if we don't have much choice." Mike looked at her, again pitying the fact she was operating in such cold. As he did, he remembered another lesson from the Navy SEALs. "Put a song in your head. It'll help take your mind off it."

He led her to the far door, waiting for her to unlock it. No sooner had she done so, he closed it.

"What is it?" Emily's face was now cold with concern.

"I thought I just heard voices."

Seated alone in the heart of the security room, the gunman noticed something strange in St Thomas's Tower. The opulent bed, apparently put in to replicate that used by former kings, had been moved slightly, a clear gap noticeable between it and the wall.

Zooming in, he picked up his HT and put a call through to downstairs.

He was sure its position had changed since his arrival.

35

The Inner Ward,
22:42

Blanco left the Jewel House and stormed across the paved walkway, furious. The news he'd just heard, although long recognised as a possibility, still refused to sink in. It was as though a gun had gone off, aimed close to his heart, the shot intended to wound rather than kill. He'd experienced enough in life to know one needed to be prepared at all times, but there were some things even the most stringent training couldn't prepare for.

Especially involving a lifelong dream.

He passed the White Tower and headed across Tower Green, his eyes on the cottage-style building that ordinarily housed the governor and his family. If the news he'd received from his relative was correct, it still did.

Along with many others.

He put through a call to Randek via his HT; within seconds he saw his nephew's muscular frame emerge through the main door. He walked quickly, showing little concern for the possibility of his face being visible for the first time.

Nor damaging the fraudulent object he carried in his right hand.

Randek saw Blanco approach from the north. He'd used the delay to light up a cigarette, momentarily forgetting the promise he'd made to his sister that he would kick the habit. He eyeballed Blanco from across Tower Green, confused at what he saw.

Blanco carried the Imperial State Crown in his hand.

"Where is the governor?" Blanco shouted, the volume so loud Randek realised he was too angry to care about being overheard.

"The general is entertaining his guests in the accommodation of the martyr, as discussed." Randek took a drag of his cigarette and exhaled. "What's wrong?"

Blanco tossed him the crown, causing him to drop his cigarette as he caught it. "Bring the governor to me now. There are questions I wish to ask him."

Randek re-entered the Queen's House after treading out the stub of his first cigarette in weeks, and escorted Blanco through the original Tudor entrance hall. He changed direction as his uncle entered the dining room, making the short journey into St Thomas's room.

He found the governor seated among the hostages, his ageing frame partially shielded by the imposing shadows of the chapel-like room that the low lighting was far too weak to fully illuminate.

Randek stopped in front of him. "General Yates, I have urgent need of you."

The governor looked up, stern faced. "Whoever you are, you're never going to get away with this."

Randek removed his gun and fired at the ceiling, damaging some of its artistic fittings and causing new concern among the hostages.

"Do not test my patience, General. Next time, refusal to comply will carry a different type of penalty."

The governor marched to Randek's pace, well aware of the likely penalty for refusal to comply. As a retired officer, formerly of the Queen's Guard, his role as resident governor up till now had concerned the usual duties of office, a largely administrative and often ceremonial role that had little in common with that of his predecessors of long ago. Since leaving the Army, active combat had become a thing of the past, replaced largely by far less hazardous responsibilities. It seemed like years since he'd last engaged in battle.

Inwardly, he feared the present situation would prove beyond him.

He led the way through the dim Tudor corridors, taking a sudden turn into a well-lit room with wooden décor and grand tableware. A second stranger was seated in his usual seat at the head of the table, his elbows sprawled heavily across the wooden exterior, his fists supporting a face that bore the expression of someone carrying the weight of the world. Feelings of shock came over him as he saw the item before him.

The Imperial State Crown of George VI rested delicately on the varnished surface, its magnificent jewels reflecting the overhead lights.

"General Yates?"

The governor almost cringed on hearing his name. "What is the meaning of this?"

Blanco slammed his fist down hard on the table, the impact causing the crown to move. A fierce stare radiated from Blanco's brown eyes, a silent communication that uttered four simple words.

Don't mess with me!

"Governor, I am a patient man, yet tonight, every question I ask must be met with a simple and honest answer. Do you understand?"

"Who are you?"

Another thump on the table. "Do you understand?"

"Yes!" The general kept a stiff upper lip.

"Where are the Crown Jewels of England?"

The governor was confused. "Are you blind? The crown is there before you."

Blanco picked up the largest of the twelve knives set out as though in preparation for a grand banquet and slammed it deep into the purple lining. He eyed the governor with developing malice.

"Do not exhaust my patience, General. I asked you a question."

For what seemed like an eternity, Yates felt that air was no longer capable of entering or leaving his lungs. It was all a dream – it had to be. A nightmare. Even just a well thought out practice drill. He'd heard rumours of similar things having occurred in the distant past, tales from the Middle Ages. He recalled one particular account of how appalled Edward III had been on his return from France by the relaxed attitude shown by the Tower Guard after he'd entered his own castle without detection. As far as Yates knew, the same had never been repeated.

"Governor?" Blanco's penetrating stare continued to intensify. "I asked you a question."

Shaking his head, Yates felt his resolve strengthen. "Have you any idea what you've just done?"

A wry smile, softer now. Blanco knew he needed ask no further questions. He was looking at an honest man.

Honest and ignorant.

Blanco rose to his feet, turning his attention to Randek. "Count out six hostages, as well as the Ravenmaster. Tell him his expertise will come in handy."

Champion heard the creaking of the door for the third time in ten minutes. The blond-haired villain he had seen escort the governor back to the main house had returned, his trademark scowl seemingly intensified by a clear unwillingness to exercise patience. Keeping his gaze low, Champion decided to put his trust in his other senses, taking in the sound of the man's voice, the musk from his neck.

He associated both with the Gascony region of France.

Randek had stopped in the middle of the room, beginning a conversation in his native language with one of the gunmen; Champion knew enough French only to make out he was looking for one specific individual. The standout word was *corbeau*.

Raven.

The Ravenmaster was one of thirty-seven Yeoman Warders employed at the Tower. Dressed in the same attire as his comrades, protocol confirmed he was a military veteran with over twenty-two years' experience on active service.

Randek ended the conversation with the gunman and turned to the far wall, where most of the Beefeaters sat, their famous uniforms giving away their identities.

"Which of you is the Ravenmaster?" he asked to no response. "Speak."

"I am, sir." One of the prisoners raised his hand. Like most of them, the man was muscular but slightly portly, his cheeks framed by a masculine beard; Champion placed him in his early fifties.

Randek walked towards him, looking him over from head to toe. "How does one become Ravenmaster of the Tower?"

The Ravenmaster delayed offering a reply. "After eight years, the old Ravenmaster announced he was retiring. One day, he said to me, the birds might like me."

Randek's expression remained unchanged. "Do they?"

The Ravenmaster considered the question. "I suppose the important thing is I like them."

Randek folded his arms, his eyes examining him like a demon. "Come with me." He looked around, picking out six hostages at random.

Champion lowered his head as the door swung shut for the fourth time, the room now seven hostages lighter. A feeling of foreboding overcame him as he saw the absentees' families overwhelmed by tears, fearing their loved ones would not return.

Taking a deep breath, he tried to regain control of his thoughts and shut out the sounds around him. Only once in the history of the building above had it ever been successfully taken.

And that was over six hundred years ago.

The Director of the White Hart was in his office, finishing on the phone. He heard the sound of knocking at his door.

Maria entered.

"I've managed to trace Blanco. The taxi terminated at Wapping; three men got out. I've managed to get an ID on two of the three."

Mr White raised his eyebrows. "Go on."

Maria carried her own portable tablet. She brushed her fingers against the screen; three faces appeared as if floating in mid-air.

"Randek!" The Director leaned forward, short of breath but not in the least surprised. "So Hansen was right."

"Not impossible he was right about Blanco now being at the Tower."

"Who's the third man?"

"Unclear. So far there hasn't been a good enough view of his face."

The Director raised an eyebrow. "What became of the taxi?"

"Interesting. Two others met them; one drove off in it. Another walked them to the water gardens, where they were picked up by a second vehicle."

"Registration?"

"Searches remain ongoing."

"Where did it take them?"

"It stopped at the marina. All four then continued on foot to a luxury yacht moored in St Katharine Docks. It's registered to an Emmanuel Leboeuf. A retired antique dealer from Paris."

The Director rose to his feet. "Keep tabs on it. In the meantime, tell the knights it's time to split up!"

36

The Queen's House, 22:46

Randek left the Queen's House on Blanco's orders, heading in the direction of the White Tower. While Blanco prepared to take the six hostages and the Ravenmaster across the south lawn, he took another three gunmen and one of the most senior of the remaining Beefeaters up the stairs to the wall that connected the Constable and Martin towers.

He led the way to the Martin Tower at the north-east corner and waited patiently outside the door, using the delay as an opportunity to finish the cigarette he'd earlier been deprived of. The familiar sensation felt soothing on his throat and lungs, satisfying the three-week craving he'd had since his last. The news his uncle had broken moments earlier, though not a complete surprise, was still a major setback, the type that could easily compromise a mission. What at best case was a quick in-and-out job was now worst case a daylong siege.

He expected further bad news.

He watched the frustrated Yeoman Warder insert the correct key from a chain of many and push the door open. Extinguishing his dying cigarette, he followed him inside, ordering the Beefeater to put on the lights.

Illuminating a grand chamber filled with precious artefacts.

Mike waited until what seemed a significant amount of time had passed before opening the door for a second time, taking desperate care to ensure that the deep-pitched creaking sound would not be overheard.

The next section of the medieval wall could be seen immediately in front of him, the left side significantly higher than the right as the stonework matched the height of the tower for a further ten metres. A series of displays had been put up on the right side, each concerning wartime executions and espionage. The irony wasn't lost on him as he saw the door to the Martin Tower slightly ajar, the sounds of several voices talking in a foreign language carrying in the night air.

Within seconds the door closed again, bringing quiet.

Mike edged forward, gesturing Emily to follow him. He kept his eyes on the entrance to the Martin Tower, concerned the intruders might reappear; on this occasion, he instructed her not to lock the door behind them.

He stopped where the wall to his left ended, gun at the ready. Beyond the wall, metal fencing connected to a modern stairway.

He reasoned the villains had recently used it.

The Waterloo Block was visible now, immediately beyond the wall to his left. He considered the possibility of using the steps and making a run for the rear entrance. If he had his bearings correct, a door would be found on the north side; he estimated he could make it in twenty seconds. Still he had a problem.

Neither of them knew if they were being watched.

"Where does that lead?" Mike asked, gesturing in the direction of the entrance to the tower in front of him, still on his guard in case the door reopened. He'd counted five men; one of whom was dressed in the attire of a Yeoman Warder. One voice he recognised.

Randek.

"The Martin Tower," Emily replied, her body and hair still dripping wet. "It used to be the place where the jewels were kept."

Mike raised an eyebrow, recalling his recent conversation with Maria. "But not anymore?"

"It houses an exhibition on how the crowns were created," she said, her breath heavy, her body shivering. "It still contains five redundant crowns."

"What do you mean redundant?"

"The crowns are no longer used; they've all had their diamonds removed."

Mike nodded, realising all that mattered was getting to the barracks as soon as possible. He glanced again at the stairs, calculating his next move. Even though the barracks were in sight, he knew taking the stairs would be a risk.

"Come on!"

They moved on quickly, keeping to the right side of the wall, taking partial shelter close to the wartime displays. Mike felt a surge of adrenaline as he prepared for the door to open, calmed by a sense of relief when it didn't.

He moved to one side, allowing Emily access. With shaking fingers, she unlocked it, this time more slowly than before. Behind it, Mike saw a winding stairway, the way up barred.

The only option was to go down.

He descended slowly, ensuring each sound was kept to a minimum. After five steps he stopped on hearing voices speaking in the darkness.

Randek allowed himself a moment for his eyes to adjust to the new brightness before examining his surroundings more carefully. As a former tourist, he recalled the white décor and extensive array of glass display cases imbued the area with a museum-like quality, albeit far less intense than that of the large building adjacent. The red-carpeted flooring, subtly lit by the nearby wall lights, reminded him of a hotel atrium, somewhat similar to what he'd seen on Fieschi's yacht.

He wondered whether or not that was a coincidence.

He explored the room slowly, perusing the diamond and crowns' exhibition that began in the main room and continued into a second. He counted five crowns in total, the earliest from the reign of George I. There were also replicas of the stones cut from the Cullinan II diamond in the Imperial State Crown, over twelve thousand diamonds on loan from another museum and a sapphire from Victoria's crown.

His men followed him in turn.

"You have the keys?"

The Yeoman Warder shook his head. "The display cases are separate. Most likely the staff have them."

Randek nodded. "In that case, break the glass."

Back on the yacht, the dark-haired man viewed activity on his laptop. An alarm had gone off, apparently in the Martin Tower.

He moved the mouse quickly, clicking it a couple of times.

Then all was returned to normal.

Mike nearly lost his balance. His ears rang with the sounds of an alarm; it was as though a bank had been robbed, the metal bars about to come down, locking everyone inside. He feared for a moment that he'd been the cause; that their actions had just given the game away. Within seconds, the high-pitched noise ended. Randek was talking to someone, possibly over a radio link.

Again all was well.

Controlling his breathing, Mike inched his way further down the stairs, stopping at a point where the stairway levelled out before beginning to ascend. The end was in sight, the voices louder now.

Over the talking, he heard the sounds of glass breaking.

Randek waited until the final case had been emptied before putting through a call on his HT.

"François?"

Back in the workshop beneath the Jewel House, the young art director gazed at the now imprisoned Jeweller as he sat petrified in his chair. Even without the tightly tied cords that bound him to his work chair, the barrels of two AK-47s aimed directly at his torso ensured escape was impossible.

He heard his name being called across the airwaves. Removing his radio from his belt, he turned his attention away from the sight of the seven, apparently fake, crowns that had all been removed from their display cases and laid out evenly across the worktable.

"What is it, cousin?"

"The last crown has been collected as you requested – along with the remaining jewels. Where are you?"

François looked again at the Jeweller, remembering another occasion where he'd witnessed a man's spirit broken so quickly. The experience had also been in London, two years ago, involving one of its famous art galleries and the curator of 17th-century art. He had contacted the man on the pretence of seeking advice for an upcoming exhibition, a generous donation the potential reward.

Had the man known the full truth, he would not have even taken the first call.

"Bring everything to the Jewel House. Once there, I will send someone to meet you. It is best we carry out our inspection away from the sight of others."

Mike waited until Randek stopped talking before moving to obtain a view of what lay ahead. The stairway ended at an open doorway that led into a grand chamber, its white walls presenting an image of cleanliness, more like a stately home or fine hotel than a typical museum. Figures were moving quickly, some visible only as shadows. A further stairway led up to the second floor, clearly designated *Staff Only*. For the first time Mike was able to make out faces, no longer hidden by thick ski masks.

One of the intruders he recognised.

Retreating back up the stairs, he spoke quietly into his headset. "I just got confirmation. Randek."

The response came from Kit. "You see him?"

Mike peered out again, acutely aware that one ill-timed glance in his direction might result in all hell breaking loose. Perhaps it was better that way. Shoot the thug now and many debts would be settled. Rubbing the nozzle of his semi-automatic USP45, he exhaled slowly, remembering another lesson from his training.

Impatience never commanded success.

"Just about," Mike replied.

"What's he doing?"

Retreating further up the stairs, he watched out of the corner of his eye as Randek called his men together and headed for the exit. Once outside, he ordered the Yeoman Warder to lock the door, the sound of a key turning audible within seconds of their disappearance.

Then, as all fell silent, he heard a gunshot.

Mike felt soft hands grip tightly against his shoulders.

"He and three others have just left the Martin Tower, carrying five other crowns."

At the other end, Kit was confused. "What do you mean other crowns?"

"There were five other crowns on display; I understand from the assistant curator they're now redundant."

"Acting curator." He heard Emily's voice behind him.

"Apparently they're unlikely to offer much in the way of monetary value."

Kit listened carefully. "Keep tabs on him. As far as I'm aware, there's still to be any contact since the message to Downing Street."

"I'm on it."

Ending the conversation, Mike grabbed Emily's hand and rapidly left the stairs, heading for the door.

On reaching it, Emily veered off in the opposite direction.

"What are you waiting for?"

She headed for the display cases, searching each one in turn. After passing the first two, she entered the adjoining room, finding an almost identical situation. Every case had been broken and emptied, their glass showering the floor like an ice storm. Every item that had previously been kept there was described in printed lists attached to the cases.

To Mike, the names meant nothing.

"Ignorant fools!" Emily gasped, shaking her head and rubbing her arms both in exasperation and for warmth. "If they'd have checked the desk, they'd probably have found the keys they needed."

Mike guessed that wouldn't have featured in Randek's decision-making process. "You maybe want to get a move on. We're in a hurry."

Emily looked at him, alarmed. "You're going after him?"

"Not without you unlocking the door, I'm not."

"Are you mad? We're outnumbered. We'll both be killed."

He looked around, examining the second stairway connecting to the floor above. He took it, finding nothing except offices. Noticing a map on one of the walls, he compared it to the GPS on his satphone.

"Where are we now?"

"Back when the jewels were kept here, this was used as lodgings for the guards." Emily moved alongside him, pointing to the north-east tower. "The nearest entrance to the barracks is here." She moved her finger. "Getting there requires the same journey as before."

Mike nodded, rubbing his chin, the firm bristles of his light stubble scratching against his skin. "Is there any way to avoid the wall walk?"

"Not unless your friend knows something I don't."

He spoke into his headset. "Maria, you listening?"

"Every word. And sorry, not that I'm aware of. If there is anything, it's not on the original plans."

"Could really do with a satellite pickup down here."

Back at the Rook, Maria was looking at a bird's-eye view of the Tower. "Randek and his cronies have headed straight for the front of the Jewel House. Blanco has entered the White Tower."

Mike raised an eyebrow. "That's the second time he's done that."

"He made a stop off first near the raven cages. There were hostages with him."

Suddenly Mike felt panicked. "You recognise anyone?"

"It wasn't your uncle if that's what you mean?"

You know me too well. "Any word on reinforcements?"

"We've got a detachment of SAS coming in from Gloucestershire now along with several regulars, not to mention others arriving by river. Of course, the priority is still the fires."

"Any breaks in the traffic?"

"Negative. Even if there were, they'd just fill up again."

Mike nodded, gesturing to Emily he was ready to leave. "I really wanted to let rip just now, Edward."

"And deprive me of the chance?" Kit replied. "I hope you're not getting ahead of yourself, Grosmont."

"Just thinking about still being alive. I'm sure they've got cameras in this place somewhere."

"You learn anything new?"

"About Randek? Only that he came for the crowns and didn't care too much for the guy with the key."

"What would Randek want with the jewels? It's too obvious."

"Matter of fact, to me it makes perfect sense."

"How do you mean?"

"Remember earlier this year – the Raleigh manuscript and the Deputy PM's wife; that episode at the Musée d'Orsay. I'm beginning to think we've been giving this guy too much credit. He's just a French Thomas Crown with crap hair."

At the other end, Kit stopped at the corner of Gracechurch and Lombard streets, seemingly a million thoughts rushing through his mind. "Maybe, but something still doesn't sit right. Why would someone involved in all this simply look for a payday? It's not his style."

In the jeweller's workshop deep below the Jewel House, François awaited the arrival of Randek. As expected, between him and his men they carried five objects.

"Normally I'd say congratulations are in order. Not that I'm expecting miracles."

The young expert rose to his feet and took possession of the first crown, dated from the reign of George IV. "Well, the diamonds are already missing." He knew that was no surprise. The same was true of all the redundant crowns.

Retrieving his eyepiece from his pocket, he cleaned the glass and focused first on the replica diamonds from the Cullinan II.

Next he examined the sapphire.

"Just as I suspected."

Mike waited till Emily unlocked the door before inching it open just enough to obtain a view. Sure enough, the wall walk continued as before, the left side offering no shelter.

"Looks like the guys who built this didn't plan on helping us out," Mike said.

Standing behind him, Emily showed equally little enthusiasm. "I guess if you ever make it to purgatory, you could take it up with Henry III personally."

He smiled, recognising the reference from Dante. "Personally, I've never been one for limbo."

He inched the door open further, taking in what little the external lights allowed. On the right side of the walkway, the outer wall continued; to his left, metal railings offered little shelter. He saw a sign for the next tower, indicating a royal beasts exhibition. By the door, he noticed a ladder to the roof.

Under different circumstances, he'd happily have considered it.

"If there's watchers out, I estimate we've got less than four seconds to make it across. Get the key ready."

Searching her keyring, Emily jangled the heavy pieces of iron together, finding the correct one. She looked at him, brushing her still-soaked hair behind both ears. Finally, she offered a weak smile.

"Ready?"

She nodded.

Mike spoke into his headset. "Hey, Edward, you ever seen the beasts exhibition here?"

"Yes, but even if I hadn't, I'd still offer you the same advice."

"What's that?"

"Don't run into an ambush!"

37

The White Tower,
22:54

Blanco turned to his right on passing the White Tower, once again showing total indifference to the sight of the murdered soldiers piled up close to the Broadwalk Steps. He glanced at the Jewel House as it disappeared to his left, silently wondering how his nephew was faring in the Martin Tower.

After François's conclusions on examining the crowns, he no longer expected miracles.

He headed to the south side of the White Tower, leading the way on to the grass towards the only area within the grounds that still contained wildlife. Even from a distance, the sound of demonic crowing was audible; somehow it sounded far worse at night. Across the lawn, a strange mist was rising, reminiscent of vapour off the river. He was familiar with the rumours associated with the Tower: spectres of executed lords, headless queens roaming the grounds in the dead of night, their timeless entities frightening the living daylights out of anyone unfortunate enough to see them.

Like the legend of the ravens, he viewed the tales with total disdain.

He stopped on reaching the ravens' cages, examining them for the second time that evening. Traditionally no less than six would be kept at any one time.

As a precaution the number was currently eight.

On this occasion, one appeared to be missing.

He turned to his group of hostages, saving his attention for the man dressed in the attire of a Yeoman Warder. "Open it!"

The Ravenmaster was reluctant. "If the birds get out, it'll be almost impossible to get them all back in. These creatures are a menace at night."

"It wasn't a request." Blanco removed his firearm, pressing it deep into the Beefeater's torso, his eyes pulsating with venom. "However, as a small token of my respect, I will let you choose which one you remove."

The Ravenmaster remained unmoved, his best attempt at showing no fear. As a military veteran of almost forty years, he had been engaged in operations many times.

At the age of fifty-eight, he'd hoped those days were behind him.

Blanco watched as the expert opened one of the cages, successfully calling the nearest one to him. He loved the way the bird hopped readily onto his outstretched hand, as if expecting a treat.

Placing him inside a portable cage, the Ravenmaster closed the main door.

"Excellent. Let's continue," Blanco demanded.

Seated in the stateroom of his luxury yacht, Fieschi heard the telephone on the table in front of him begin to ring. In keeping with the practices of his forebears, there were always two lines in operation at any one time. Both for business; both encrypted.

He answered, knowing only three people were familiar with that number. "*Allô?*"

At the other end, Blanco had made it up the wooden stairway that led to the entrance of the White Tower. After one visit already, he was familiar with the layout.

"I'm afraid the news is as we feared."

Fieschi leaned back in his hardback chair, irritated by the uncomfortable upholstery. As he did so, he remembered his favourite saying.

Hard times create strong men. Strong men create good times.

"Where are you now?"

Blanco negotiated a path through the armour of old, the body shape of Henry VIII somehow instantly recognisable even without the accompanying description. "The Tower of the Conqueror. The Ravenmaster was most insistent on giving me the tour."

Fieschi smiled, equally familiar with the raven legend. It had been created long ago, almost certainly by one of his forebears. He, as well as any, knew of its significance.

"We always knew this would be possible. Under the circumstances, one could almost consider it a blessing. Let us continue with what we discussed. It is time to implement plan B."

Mike looked both ways before leaving the door of the latest tower, again relieved to find no gunmen awaited his arrival. He looked around carefully, his senses fully alert as Emily locked the door behind them.

Once again, he struggled to digest what he'd seen.

The Flint Tower was one of the oldest in the Tower of London. Originally built by Henry III between 1238 and 1272 as part of the outer defences, it was one of a number that had been adapted for modern warfare in the 20th century.

The last thing Mike had seen before leaving had been a display describing its role in World War One.

The wall walk continued outside the door, the area to his right offering far more protection than the left. Moving swiftly towards the Devereux Tower at the far end, he took Emily's advice and headed left on reaching a stairway. Adjoining the flat roof on which the first part of the stairway ended, the royal Chapel of St Peter ad Vincula cut a forlorn outline, its gothic walls creating sharp shadows under the light of nearby lampposts. Several puddles had formed on the flat area, close to the stairway, that was liberally populated with plant pots. The surrounding walls provided effective concealment from possible surveillance.

Again Mike assumed someone, somewhere, was watching surveillance footage.

He made it to the bottom of the steps and paused, looking out over the paved surface through a surrounding archway. The Waterloo Barracks were close now; the way apparently unguarded. There were two secure doors in the west wall and no obvious means of accessing them.

"How the hell do we get in?"

Emily was unsure. "The main door is code operated."

"Do you know it?"

She nodded. "It's also the headquarters of the education centre."

Taking his eyes off the nearest doors, further afield he saw a larger main door in the rear wall to the north. Seeing Emily was okay, he spoke into his headset.

"Maria, we're near the barracks. What can you tell me?"

"Blanco is still in the White Tower; Randek the Jewel House," Maria replied, pausing briefly. "Hang on a second."

"What is it?" Mike asked, suddenly unnerved.

"Someone seems to be moving on the roof."

Blanco ended the call and immediately contacted Randek. "Where are you?"

Standing hunched over the jeweller's worktable alongside François, Randek heard the question clearly.

"The workshop beneath the Jewel House," he replied, his eyes still taking in the fraudulent works before him. "I'm afraid it's as we expected."

Blanco was less surprised. "When you're finished, join me atop the White Tower. It's time for the illumination to commence."

The stairway ended at a locked door, accessible with the same keys that had once been the property of the Chief Yeoman Warder. Though Blanco was aware this area existed, he was still to see it with his own eyes. They'd been watching the building for months now, years including primary preparation; even in the modern day, it carried the same aura as it had throughout the centuries.

It almost saddened him to think soon it might no longer exist.

He stepped through the final door, bracing himself as he took the first step outside. The current roof had been added in the 15th century, the iron girders many centuries later. The centre was lead based, the outer rim the only area that was designed to be walked on. He recognised the four famous turrets shooting up above the battlements, reminiscent of something from the age of chivalry.

It felt strange touching them with his own hands.

The roof of the White Tower was the highest point in the castle, the tallest building for quarter of a mile. Walking the west side, he gazed out across the city. Beyond London Bridge, an array of flames danced brightly above the distant buildings, some reaching enormous heights. If history was repeating itself, he felt blessed to be part of it.

He knew within moments worse was to come.

"The roof of the White Tower is rarely open to the public." Blanco addressed the hostages as he walked. Under the circumstances, his unarmed followers showed little joy. "It is a rare privilege to be offered access."

Down below he saw movement across Tower Green; Randek and François were approaching the entrance. Next, he put through a second call to the yacht.

"Is everything set?"

Seated alone in front of his open laptop, the dark-haired figure clicked rapidly at his mouse before typing into his keyboard. The configuration was almost complete.

"*Oui!* Contact is imminent."

38

Cabinet Office Briefing Room A (COBRA), 70 Whitehall,
22:59

The Prime Minister of the UK sipped her coffee as she contemplated the words she had just heard. The meeting, as expected, had been heated but useful, the preliminary steps agreed and implemented. Every member of the Joint Intelligence Committee had spoken once, most only briefly. All roads heading into the city had been closed, the traffic lights set permanently to red; congestion was finally starting to clear on those close to the fires. Emergency services had been brought in from all of the Home Counties; more too would arrive soon from those further afield. All the key military branches had been placed on standby.

There were even promises of help from abroad if needed.

"What's the latest in Edinburgh?" the PM asked, finishing her coffee and brusquely instructing a nearby aide to provide a refill.

The Home Secretary spoke first. "The emergency services have clearly identified the source; we believe the fire may have been caused by an electrical fault. The owner of the shop, of course, was adamant the service was secure."

"So he's offered no apology or remorse?" the fifty-two-year-old Foreign Secretary, Martin Colson, said, his greying, once-dark hair slightly askew and plagued by sweat. "Not that anyone can necessarily blame him."

"On the contrary, the man is most distressed. The inspection by the energy company was one he believed to have been conducted entirely appropriately. It was not until the fire spread that he began to appreciate the probable link."

The PM nodded, the explanation making sense. As the granddaughter of an Edinburgh seamstress, she remembered hearing the tale many times as a girl of how the fire of 1824 had begun off a side alley.

"The fires clearly are developing in a similar pattern. They're spreading as if connected by wood." She looked along the table at the faces of her colleagues. "The question is how?"

The door to the room opened; a man in a suit entered without invitation. "Forgive the intrusion, Prime Minister. We have contact on the big screen."

The PM didn't bat an eyelid, gesturing for the chief of staff to continue. He activated the screen she had previously used to conduct a videoconference with the Director of the White Hart, and the pictures came to life.

They were looking at an outdoor scene, four men of varying dress and descriptions standing at the top of a tall building instantly recognisable as the White Tower. Three of the men were armed, their dark attire reminiscent of military personnel conducting a mission of connection to national security. The man at the front was older, his face more austere, with the bearing of a military commander of great experience and seniority. Though his clothing showed no obvious sign of office or status, the PM was aware that she was looking at a man of definite purpose.

The stranger walked towards the camera, his face displaying a confident smile, yet mixed with something far darker.

Frustration.

"Prime Minister, by now you're undoubtedly aware of the grave afflictions that have recently befallen your capital cities." He picked up the camera and turned it 180 degrees, the view now covering the city west of the Tower. From there, the impact of the fires appeared particularly great; it was near, yet of huge scale, seeming somehow all the more threatening viewed from somewhere so instantly recognisable.

"In August 1666, a week before hell broke loose, a famed fireworks maker had claimed to those who knew him that a great fireworks display would take place, and that it would culminate with a pure body of flame higher than St Paul's." The man returned the camera to its original position, his face again the central feature on the screen. "It is beautiful in its own way, no?"

Beneath her cool exterior, the PM felt her blood begin to boil. "Who are you?"

An ironic laugh. "Perhaps a better question might be to ask me who we were."

The PM's expression remained unmoved. "Perhaps a better one still might be to ask what you hope to achieve. You've clearly made no attempt to disguise your face."

Blanco's scowl developed into a wide smile. "Every year, tourists flock from all over the world to cast their eyes over what has long been kept in the building adjacent. The jewels are famous worldwide. Some say they possess the symbol of a great kingdom: that behind their beautiful exteriors lie the scars time will never forget." He looked deep into the camera, his eyes appearing almost demonic in the strange lighting. "How would these same people feel if they knew what they saw were worthless trinkets?"

He moved to one side and picked up the Imperial State Crown, displaying it clearly. "It is convincing, no? Who but the most qualified would know the difference?"

"Unless you desire an international incident, I suggest you return that to its rightful place immediately," the PM demanded. "The Crown Jewels are far from trinkets. I'll save you the indignity of informing you how much it's worth."

"This?" Blanco moved the crown clearly into view. "I know exactly of its value."

He removed his firearm from his pocket and shot the crown several times before tossing it over the battlements. Once finished, he picked up the camera and followed its path as it crashed to the ground, shattering on impact, to the horror of all at the meeting.

Blanco's face reappeared. "The trinkets on display in the Jewel House are imitations. What interests me are the originals."

The PM's expression hardened. The sight of the stranger in black throwing what appeared to be the Imperial State Crown over the edge of the White Tower was still to register, despite having seen it with her own eyes. "Are you quite out of your mind? The items on display are unique. Do you have any idea what you've just done?"

"You think I would be so foolish to throw away an original?"

"Whether you're foolish is not my concern. What does concern me is the well-being of my nation's citizens, not to mention its national treasures."

"Let me assure you, any items that you might consider to be national treasures are not to be found in the building nearby. The jewels on show exist for display only. Perhaps it was I who was naïve enough to imagine the Crown Jewels of England would be kept in such a position of prominence." He leaned in close to the lens. "So susceptible to outside hands."

In spite of the man's words, the PM knew few places in the capital were better equipped for the keeping of Her Majesty's jewels. "You honestly think we would be foolish enough to attempt such deception?"

"You may dispense with the pretence, Prime Minister. As I've told you once already, only a man ignorant of the art of jewellery would be taken in by such obvious duplicates. It is unfortunate for you it was necessary for me to access the location after hours to obtain a proper view. Now the matter is clear, we have a different problem. Where are the originals?"

"Are you quite out of your mind? I keep telling you, you were just looking at one of them."

"I heard once, a man of wisdom never throws out his only pair of socks." He moved towards the camera. "Unless you care to witness the continued destruction of your city, I suggest you take this matter seriously."

"The Crown Jewels are one of a kind; replicating something so famous worldwide would be almost impossible."

The Anjouvin raised his eyebrows. "Have it your way."

Blanco turned to the nearest gunman and issued orders sharply in French. As the man brandished his machine gun, six previously unseen hostages emerged behind him.

Each was stripped to the waist with rope hanging around their necks.

Around the table in Whitehall, all of the ministers and officials watched on with stunned expressions.

Blanco's face reappeared at the heart of the big screen, his eyes looking deep into the lens that from his view clearly displayed the long table at the COBRA.

"Are you hearing me now, Prime Minister?"

"Who are you?" The words left the mouth of the Foreign Secretary.

"Ask me who I was!"

"Enough of this madness!"

Again Blanco grinned. "On 4 August 1347, eleven months to the day after the beginning of the siege of Calais, the King of England made an offer to the town that he would spare the lives of its people in exchange for the voluntary deaths of six hostages. Little did the king know, among the six was one of the Cardinal's Boys." He glanced at the modern-day hostages. "These six have agreed to die so their fellow prisoners will not."

The PM held her breath; her colleagues responded with varying gestures. All watched on as the Frenchman eyed the six one at a time. "I wonder who here will be the first to volunteer."

"I've told you before," the PM pressed. "The jewels are real."

"In 1940, the Crown Jewels, along with many other important things, were removed from the Tower in anticipation of the Blitz. Perhaps when they were to be returned, something else was put forward in their place." Blanco returned his attention to the prisoners. "Who here will volunteer?"

"I will!" The offer came from the Ravenmaster, who had been standing out of camera shot. Blanco looked at him and smiled sombrely.

"Your offer is noted; perhaps later I will give it consideration." Again he addressed the six. "Who?"

A man stepped forward. "I will!"

"Dad, no!" The man's son was distraught.

Blanco nodded. "Very well."

The Frenchman guided the volunteer forward, ensuring his face was clearly visible to the COBRA Committee. The rough strands of the man's hair and beard looked dishevelled after an hour in captivity.

He waited until he was satisfied the image had its desired effect.

"It was written in the chronicle of the great Jean Froissart that Edward III received many requests to spare the men, all of which fell on deaf ears." He picked up the camera, pointing it as he attached the other end of the rope to the battlements. He ordered the man to take the first step, waving his gun in his back. With tears in his eyes, the man stepped forward.

"Only when his queen urged him to see reason did he finally stop."

Seated on the edge of her chair, the PM's eyes were open as wide as seemed humanly possible. The sight of the fires seemed almost inconsequential by comparison.

She was looking at murder in its committal.

"Will you show this man no pity?"

"You've heard it yourself!" the head of MI5 barked, his masculine face eyeing the screen through rimless glasses. "The jewels are original. What is it you want?"

Blanco looked at the hostage, preparing to push him over the edge.

"At the eleventh hour, at last the king showed mercy!" Blanco pulled the man back, throwing him to the ground. "I offer that same mercy."

He turned the camera back to his face. "Unless the genuine jewels are returned, the hell that broke loose in 1666 shall be repeated down to the last moment. The fireworks display witnessed then shall again be visible before us." He pointed the camera once more over the city, zooming in on the fires beyond the walls. "Captured forever on film."

The PM took a deep breath, trying to remove the recent pictures from her mind. The man had six hostages, possibly more from the way he was talking. The fires in the city were spreading; soon they would be brought under control.

The problem was preventing new ones.

"Surely you don't honestly believe you're capable of getting away with this?"

Even if the jewels are fake, and I have absolutely no reason to believe they are, getting out of the Tower alive will be almost impossible. The fires will be extinguished; within five minutes I can have that Tower surrounded. If necessary, I'll even starve you out."

"Perhaps you are forgetting, Prime Minister, I have already entered once without detection. Over one hundred hostages currently occupy the residence of the governor, in addition to the six who join me here. I have demonstrated I am a man capable of mercy."

"I assure you we're all very grateful for that."

"Do not test my patience." Blanco looked hard into the camera. "There is an old legend that when the Tower was established, it became a paradise among wildlife. Conspiracies of ravens would nestle here; in time, many became permanent residents."

He took the small cage from the Ravenmaster and opened it.

"Tradition has it that if the ravens should ever leave this place, the building on which we stand shall tumble to the ground. With that, so will the kingdom." He looked again deep into the camera, aimed his gun and fired.

The raven fell to the ground.

The screen went dead.

Seated among the hostages in the room once used by Sir Thomas More, David Champion detected a strange shift in the atmosphere. A light trembling feeling thudded beneath the floor, accompanied by a series of sounds external to what he heard in the room: sharp, heavy. It reminded him of a construction site – perhaps destruction. He closed his eyes in mild terror.

It was the sound of masonry falling.

39

North-West of the Inner Ward, 23:02

Mike saw the walls shake, at the same time experiencing a series of tremors moving swiftly through the ground. He felt his legs begin to wobble, the feeling penetrating deep into his spine. No sooner had it started, it stopped; he timed the weird sensation as lasting less than three seconds.

Then, inexplicably, he heard an almighty crash.

He hit the ground hard, his momentum taking him close to the nearby wall. Guided by instinct, he'd aimed left of the archway, protecting himself from avoidable injury. Behind him, Emily had moved in the opposite direction, heading for a second stairway that provided access to the inner west wall.

She stood with her hand to her mouth, gazing at a point somewhere beyond the walls. "Oh my God, the Middle Tower."

Staying low, Mike hurried up the steps behind her, struggling initially for balance. On reaching the battlements, he looked out in the same direction.

The bridge that connected the Middle Tower to the Byward Tower had crumbled into the moat.

"Get down."

A second noise followed, this time directly in his ear. As he caught his breath, he realised the latest noise was panicked speech.

Maria.

"Maria, there's been an attack."

Maria was watching the Tower via satellite footage coming through on the screen in front of her, struggling to believe what she'd just seen. "I just saw it. The approach bridge beyond the main entrance has been destroyed."

His eyes on the main entrance, Mike saw the previously immaculately presented moat was now packed with rubble, the structure of the Middle Tower beyond it also clearly damaged. Crowds of onlookers had appeared around it, figures barely visible beneath the distant streetlights.

As far as Mike could tell, no one had been hurt.

He grabbed Emily's hand and hurried back down the stairs before sprinting to the bottom of the main stone stairway. He took shelter behind the wall close to the archway, his focus again on the rear of the Waterloo Block. Over the coming moments, Mike heard what sounded like a second explosion, the impact far less heavy than before.

"What's happening?"

"The second entrance has also been destroyed." On this occasion Maria's voice was calmer.

Mike recalled the two bridges on the south side were far smaller, one for the use of the holders of designated group tickets. "Any sign of the culprit?"

"There are figures moving on the roof of the White Tower." Her eyes on the satellite footage, Maria attempted to zoom in, seeing nothing except clothing and outlines. "There are people up there, some are practically naked. I think I see Blanco."

Mike turned his attention to the roof of the White Tower, suddenly considering the possibility there might be surveillance from up high. Directly in front of him, the way to the barracks was unoccupied; a quick dash and they'd make it.

"What are my chances?"

Maria searched the Inner Ward rapidly. "The walkways are free. Your only threat is from the windows."

The only threat. Mike bit his lip; from his current hiding place, the surrounding buildings gave nothing away.

"It's a big chance to take, Maria."

At that moment the sound of a third explosion echoed beyond the walls. He turned and looked Emily in the eye.

"Come on!"

The screen went dead as soon as the raven hit the ground, the image of the PM's face replaced by blackness. Behind Blanco, the Ravenmaster was seething with anger, his eyes focused on the body of the bird.

His pet.

"You monster!"

Blanco's expression had hardened. "In war, many things are unavoidable. Perhaps next time you'd prefer the honour of doing it yourself."

"You bastard!"

Blanco fired into the air, the noise so near it had an almost deafening effect on those around him. "Your superior is dead; as is the gaoler. Do not forget to whom you speak!" The Anjouvin's stare was penetrating, a steely concentration evident in his demeanour. He held his gaze until the Ravenmaster looked away; to the former soldier's credit, he'd been reluctant to show submission. "Alternatively, perhaps you would prefer to honour your word and go first?"

The Ravenmaster frowned. Under the circumstances, the possibility seemed almost a blessing.

Blanco gestured to the surrounding gunmen. "Take this gentleman back to the Queen's House. And tell the governor I request his company."

As the gunmen disappeared, Blanco removed his HT from his belt and put through a message to a man in another part of the city. Getting a signal was difficult, a rare occurrence in his experience.

He put it down to the city's wider problems.

Nevertheless, a man answered. "*Allô?*"

"It is time."

A delay preceded the reply. "Everything is set."

Within seconds of ending the transmission, Blanco adjusted the frequency on the transmitter and spoke a second time, to a man in Edinburgh. Finally he used his satellite phone to make a call to the yacht.

"It is done."

Seated as before, Fieschi smiled thoughtfully, his reflection gleaming off the recently polished surface of the nearby table. "How was the prime minister?"

"Less happy than she'd be if we were dead."

The heir to the historical Duchy of Aquitaine's smile widened. "Did she agree to our terms?"

"The British always reject the first demand; it is as predictable as the sun going down. Even in their darkest hours, their pride can be their undoing."

"I hope for their sake, it doesn't take too long for their resolve to weaken."

"Our intentions are known. In an hour, we shall make things clearer still. I expect an answer in four."

"I hope for your sake you're right."

"When you've experienced as much in life as I have, you begin to see patterns. By three o'clock we shall have our answer; even the British aren't so stupid as to wait for their entire city to burn. With the walkways destroyed, entry to the Tower is now impossible by ordinary means. If anyone attempts to do so the long way round, he shall show up soon enough on camera."

"And if you're wrong?"

Blanco detected curiosity in his relative's voice. "Since the day we are born, each one of us is slowly dying. Some sooner than others. When the good lady realises her city is beyond salvation, it will leave her no choice." He smiled and checked the time. "Believe me. You experience these things as much as I, you can set your watch to it."

Less than a mile from the White Tower, the silhouetted figure made his way down a medieval stairway and into a crypt of similar age. He waited for less than thirty seconds before returning the same way.

Careful to avoid being seen, he looked both ways before emerging back out on to the main road.

He paid no attention to the sudden cloud of billowing smoke behind him.

In the City of Edinburgh, a man of almost identical build made a similar journey, but without the need to enter a crypt. Although most of the underground vaults in the Scottish capital were famous, he knew that the place he'd just visited had not been seen in recent years.

Less than a mile from the hidden vault, François's brother, Alain, watched from Arthur's Seat as new fires began to spread. Satisfied everything had gone to plan, he put through a call to Blanco.

"The fires are spreading to the east. Soon they will reach the Royal Mile." He looked down at the items by his feet, the false honours of Scotland discarded like spare parts. "Our escape from the castle went exactly to plan – just like in London, it seems the tunnels the manuscript told of haven't changed very much. What shall we do with the jewels?"

Blanco paused as he heard the sound of the door opening, heralding the arrival of his nephew and Alain's brother. He avoided the temptation of allowing them a familial greeting.

"For all I care, you may put them on the fire."

Through the window on the right side of the cargo hold in the fast-moving, double-bladed helicopter, Rawlins had the best view of the three. It was dark in every direction but one: in front of them, the Edinburgh skyline was bathed in the pale glow of artificial lighting supplemented on this occasion by a more intense red and yellow haze.

The fires in the distance were small in relation to the size of the city, and far less developed than those he had seen in the images streamed from London. The problems faced by Edinburgh were relatively minor.

Yet relativity meant different things to different people.

Amongst the unaffected areas close to the rocky outcrop where the famous castle overlooked the city, Rawlins noticed a second orange glow; it hadn't been there moments earlier.

Grabbing the attention of Pentland and Pugh, he pointed to the fires. "What do you make of that?"

Pentland left his seat for a better view, the lights of the city reflecting from his eyes as he studied the scene in front of him. After several seconds of concentrated thought, he replied, "I think someone's arse is in for a kicking."

40

The Waterloo Barracks, 23:04

Exactly how the decision was made didn't register clearly to Mike. It was as though the dual effect of Maria's voice coupled with the third explosion and the piercing sound of rubble falling from far nearer than either of the previous impacts had brought about a flight-or-fight reaction. Exactly what was going on behind the nearby windows was out of sight from his present position; he guessed that the offices were probably unmanned. Of the gunmen he had seen enter the Jewel House, all had made their way through the front door; their destination almost certainly the Crown Jewels.

Either way, it was too late to turn back.

He set off at a blistering pace, keeping as low as possible. In his mind, he imagined he was under fire; that even the slightest delay could be the difference between life and death. He felt Emily's hand slip free of his, the penetrating cold of their recent plunge into the watery depths still evident even several minutes later. He knew they'd need to change clothes soon.

At least she was still with him.

Access to the area at the rear of the barracks was restricted. Hurdling a chained fence, Mike headed directly for the main door, its location clearly designated by a sloped approach flanked by iron railings. He ducked as he squeezed between the railings, rolling hard into the doorway. The heavy stone archway provided a degree of shelter; there were two small doors either side of the main one, which was of strong wood construction, painted black like the entrance to a medieval prison. Frantically, Emily inserted the code.

And pushed the door open.

Kit was the first of the knights to hear the latest explosion. Though he was yet to pick up on any movement beneath his feet, he could tell the sound had reached him too slowly to have any connection with the developments that Maria and Mike had described at the Tower.

The fires beyond the road were still spreading north of King William Street. Sprinting west, crossing Gracechurch Street where it met Eastcheap, he saw further smoke coming from the buildings close to Clement's Lane.

There were flames inside St Clement's Church.

Champion glanced instinctively to his right as the door to the dank chamber reopened, heralding the return of one of the gunmen. He saw the Ravenmaster emerge behind him, his stocky figure immediately falling to the stone floor as he was pushed by the same pair of hands that had opened the door. There was sadness in the man's eyes, his energy drained.

He noticed none of the other hostages were with him.

The gunman walked quickly across the chamber, his heavy footsteps creating multiple echoes as he stepped on different areas of ground. He stopped alongside Champion, his eyes on the governor.

"General, the boss once more requests your assistance."

The Waterloo Barracks were among the more modern buildings at the Tower. Constructed 1845–52 on the orders of the then Constable, the Duke of Wellington, and named after his most famous of conquests, it had been built on the site of the original grand storehouse that had been gutted by fire four years earlier. Designed as a permanent barracks for a company of up to 1,000, it was now famed for its secondary purpose.

To provide a safe haven for the Crown Jewels of England.

Mike entered first, gun at the ready, and took a stairway to the floor above the Jewel House. It was quiet inside; under the circumstances he wasn't sure whether that was a good thing or bad.

It didn't look like a barracks. The neo-gothic façade and architecture had the appearance of a Victorian castle, more like the residence of the duke than a domicile for common soldiers. The carpeted, walled corridors were ornately decorated with paintings and memorabilia that combined business themes with military tradition.

He went into the first room on the left: a well-presented office.

He spoke to Maria. "We're in."

From her position in the Rook, Maria had watched them enter via the satellite transmission. "Great work. What do you see?"

"Offices." Mike raised an eyebrow, quietly thinking about the type of people who were recruited as guards. During his time in the Parachute Regiment, he'd met many of the Scots Guard. The regiment had a great reputation for bravery, yet the present silence was eerily out of character. "Where are we heading?"

Maria sensed the reception was in danger of failing. "The main security room is on the top floor – directly above the Crown Jewels. To get there you'll need to take the main stairway."

"No side doors?"

Maria checked the plans as they came up on the screens. "Matter of fact, you might just be in luck. There's an other ranks' stairway in the kitchen on the far side. Right now, only enemies seem to be in the security room or in the Jewel House. If reception goes, you'll have to face them yourself."

"Roger that!"

Mike wasted no time before heading along the corridor. He checked each open door as he passed, ensuring there were no signs of life, friend or enemy. It was quiet on the first floor, the atmosphere unreal, even with the lights on. Passing the priceless artwork, the faces of many of history's great and good looking on, he couldn't help feel a strange sense of anticipation. He'd entered a building that had been designed to keep out outsiders at all costs.

Tonight, he was witnessing its only failure.

He stopped on reaching the main stairway, taking shelter in the nearest doorway. There were voices on the stairs. Emily was sticking close to him; once again he sensed she was shivering.

Droplets of water stained the carpet.

"On any other day, I'd so be getting the sack for that."

A wry smile. "Somehow tomorrow, I'm guessing you might be getting something far better."

"If we're still here."

He looked at her, choosing silence as the best answer. "Maria, which way?"

The response was intermittent as Maria considered the best options. "Continue to the west end. The kitchen should be on the left."

He entered quickly, finding it in darkness. Avoiding the temptation to put on the lights, he followed Maria's instructions to the far side, finding an area less modern and un-renovated.

"You recognise any of this?" he asked Emily.

"The barracks are off-limits. Even if I dated a soldier, it'd be frowned upon."

Mike raised an eyebrow. "You say that like it's a bad thing."

They continued up the stairs, finding them exactly as Maria had described. Opening the first door at the top, Mike looked both ways and found himself in a long corridor, again devoid of human activity.

"Keep close!"

He headed left through the middle section, ignoring the temptation to look at what was behind the many doors. As he reached the area opposite the main stairs, he noticed a distinct change in the nearby exterior; the door was far sturdier and protected with a digital lock, accessible only by inserting the correct code on a keypad.

"Don't suppose you have anything for this on your keyring?"

Emily's face illustrated her despondency. "Not exactly."

"Well, I don't particularly care for knocking." He looked around, darting into the nearest doorway, finding a communal bedroom that was clearly being used by some of the Queen's Guards. He checked the drawers and bedside cabinets for ammo, finding only a towel. Rubbing it against his wet head, he tossed it to Emily.

"Who's in charge here ordinarily?"

"The main security is divided between the Queen's Guard and a private security firm." She dried her hair vigorously. "The Chief Yeoman's office is on this floor."

A series of thoughts entered Mike's mind. "Show me."

Maria entered the Director's office just as he ended another videoconference.

"I've managed to track the yacht to Old Billingsgate. No less than fifty men disembarked."

The Director looked back with a perplexed expression, assuming she was about to provide further information. "Where are they now?"

"Unclear at this point. The men were later seen heading north across Lower Thames Street. Last visual was in the gardens of St Dunstan-in-the-East."

"And the yacht?"

"Still there."

The Director nodded, placing his hand to his clean-shaven chin. A thought entered his mind.

Cut off the brain, the body will fall.

"Get Iqbal and Sanders on standby. It's time to move out."

Jay was north of King William Street at the time the message came through. On Kit's orders, they'd moved on from the Monument.

"The yacht the terrorists took to get to the Tower has just showed up north of the water," Jay said. "It's only a short run from here."

Kit was standing outside St Clement's, his face darkened from smoky dirt. "You're not still believing Mike was being serious, are you?"

A wry smile; Jay had served in the White Hart long enough to know humour was a tool the older generation had used to keep their chins up during the war. "Maria traced Blanco to a yacht at St Katharine Docks; it anchored close to Old Billingsgate. Apparently they even got the bridge to go up."

Kit raised an eyebrow. "I suppose one must admire their fortitude."

Wilcox and Sanders were hurrying across the street, a few metres separating each man. "We just heard the order from the Rook." Sanders joined the conversation. "The yellow helmets are damping down the fires in this area. We shouldn't have any problems south of the road."

Even from there, it was clear to Kit the original fires were done and dusted. "All right, you and Jay do what you have to do. Wilcox, come with me."

Jay and Sanders hurried south across the main road, timing their movements to find gaps in the traffic. Passing the Monument, they made their way beyond the imposing façade of St Magnus the Martyr, relieved that for the present it remained undamaged.

Heading east along Lower Thames Street, they stopped at an entrance to a car park, close to the headquarters of one of the tabloid newspapers. On reaching the water, they saw the yacht at anchor some distance from the riverbank.

It was unclear if anyone was aboard.

They headed to the far side of the car park and down on to the gravel bank that at this hour was partially submerged by the high tide. The yacht was within ten metres now, its pristine white stern undulating rhythmically on the water. Entry was possible.

Only not without getting wet.

***

Kit and Wilcox ran north of the church along Clement's Lane. The temperature immediately outside the main door of the church had been in excess of boiling point; Kit could sense the interior was already beginning to melt.

If the doors exploded, the impact could possibly take out everything in its path.

Finding a safer place to stand, he focused on his surroundings. The adjoining buildings remained safe for now, not that it would last long. A strange thought occurred to Kit as they passed.

The buildings were all so close together it was like being back in time.

Ward met them from the other direction. "North side of the street is now totally evacuated; problem is it's too goddamn narrow. Even if the fire engines get in, there's still little room to work."

Kit rubbed his face, staring at the nearby buildings in deep contemplation. So far, the only water had come from fire engines parked on King William Street. Because of the traffic, just two had made it close enough to begin tackling the blaze.

"How about further afield?"

"According to Maria, the streets are closed up to the Strand – the problem now is traffic heading the other way."

"How about further out?"

"Everyone who's headed into the city is trying to turn around to find an alternative route. All these three-point turns are only making things worse."

"I'm only surprised the traffic lights haven't screwed up," Wilcox said.

Kit bit his lip, hoping Mike's suggestion of a bosson attack was premature.

"If we have any chance of stopping this from spreading, the ground attack has to commence immediately – the firefighters can drive up the pavements for all I care."

"The RAF has six choppers coming in right now. Once they get in sight of the water, they'll have free rein. Even without the trucks, this could be out in twenty minutes."

"That may be so," Kit agreed. "But there's a bigger problem."

"What's that?"

"What happens when the next one begins?"

Seated at the control hub of the security room in the Waterloo Barracks, the French gunman froze. Two figures were moving along the corridor outside his door, heading for one of the offices.

He looked again, blinked, making sure he wasn't imagining things.

Someone, somehow, had infiltrated the barracks.

On the roof of the White Tower, Blanco made no acknowledgement as Randek and François made their way through the door of the nearby turret. Standing in silence, both men concentrated on the view overlooking the battlements.

Beyond the wall to the west, the fires burned steadily, engulfing no less than four separate streets. At 23:03, a second series of flames became visible, slightly north of the others. A church was on fire, as well as other buildings.

The sky was becoming more brightly lit by the minute.

At 23:06 they heard the door opening a second time; of the three, Blanco was the only man who didn't look. He watched the city until he'd fully assessed the scale of the developing inferno, picturing in his mind the looks of horror on the faces of nearby onlookers as the buildings tumbled.

For the first time that evening, he wished he were closer.

At 23:08, he turned away from the battlements and looked penetratingly at the governor.

"Now, General, I'm afraid I have a few more questions I need to ask you. Think carefully before you reply. The last thing you want is for me to question your integrity."

41

The Waterloo Barracks, 23:08

Mike opened the door of the Chief Yeoman Warder's office, pleased to find it wasn't locked. Entering quickly, he headed for the main desk, paying passing attention to the wider surroundings. Like most of the rooms he'd seen in the barracks so far, it was distinctly military in flavour, the historical decorations blending well with the neo-gothic stonework. Yeoman Warder memorabilia affixed to the walls ranged from framed photographs to items of clothing.

It suited the personality of a Beefeater.

"Maria?" He spoke into thin air, realising the connection had failed. He looked at Emily. "Why does that keep going?"

"Communications here are famously bad; I think it's to do with security for the jewels."

He found a landline phone on the desk, the display confirming it had both external and internal lines. After failing again with his satphone, he dialled the number for the Rook from memory, sensing he had a far better chance of getting a response using a landline.

Maria heard the phone ring, the first call she'd received apart from those from the knights. The caller ID was pulled from a vast database that had apparently been established during the 1970s.

The database equated it with the office of the Chief Yeoman Warder.

"We have contact from inside the Tower!" Maria said, getting the attention of Phil.

"Put it through."

She picked up. "Lieutenant Lyons."

"You know, for a minute I'd actually forgotten your second name."

Maria breathed out, smiling. "I take it from your present location, my directions came in handy."

"Better. Now my hair's no longer wet." Mike hunched over the desk, simultaneously checking it for anything that might come in useful. "Control room requires a code. Any ideas?"

"Have you asked your friend?"

A wry smile. Glancing to his left, he knew her words were unlikely to be overheard. "Trust me, I've exhausted every possibility at this point."

"Did you run into anyone?"

"Negative. There were voices on the ground floor; based on what I saw earlier, there's unlikely to be more than ten in the building at present and most of them could be in the Jewel House." He glanced at the door, praying it wouldn't open any time soon. "Nevertheless, I'd really appreciate a satellite link-up right about now."

Maria tapped rapidly at her keyboard, the pictures coming into focus. Seeing nothing on the satellite footage beyond the building's roof, she changed the specifications to infrared. "I see you. You're four doors down from the security room."

"I counted five, but under the circumstances I'm prepared to let you off."

"One of them is box sized. It could be a linen cupboard."

"I guess that would explain it." He looked at Emily as he continued to search the drawers. "Check the cabinets. See if there's anything we can make use of."

"Like what?"

"Like bullets, knives, a spare pair of clothes, a whiskey flask." He guessed the Yeoman Warders were unlikely to carry firearms. "Listen, Maria, I'm gonna need to come up with a plan and fast; I'm doing no good just skulking in here."

"Access code for the security room is out of our arena. How do you feel about causing a scene?"

"Pretty good. Only I'd hate to ruin the artwork."

"All right, you've got three in the security room and eight more on the floor below. Best I can see, the Jewel House is empty; however, it's possible there are rooms even we can't see."

"How figure?"

"Rumours have been flying around for centuries that the Crown Jewels on display aren't the real ones. Real ones are in a vault below."

"Your boyfriend tell you that?" He smiled, noticing the comment got a stare from Emily.

"Actually it was a Beefeater; though even if they weren't legit, it's unlikely the entire staff would know."

Secretly Mike recalled his own comment back in the Jewel House. "Any sign of Randek?"

"There are still figures moving on the roof of the White Tower; as far as we can tell, no one has left the Queen's House recently. Of course, we can't totally rule out people are moving between towers."

"Roger that. You honestly think there's any truth in those rumours?"

"What rumours?"

"About the jewels."

"Does it matter?"

"Well, someone came here for a reason, and I highly doubt destroying part of the masonry was part of it if all they intended was a quick robbery."

"You think they discovered the jewels were fake?"

"Well, if they did and they don't know where the originals are, the thought occurs that they might be here for quite some time."

Seated at the security console, the leader of the three gunmen kept his eyes fixed on the screens showing the corridor behind him as the two unidentified figures hurriedly made their way from room to room before ending their journey in the office of the Chief Yeoman Warder. The male, he deemed to be of military bearing.

The woman, though a mystery, seemed more at home in the present surroundings.

He spoke quickly with the men alongside him, ruing the fact the visuals weren't accompanied by something to pick up the phone conversation the man was now having via the chief's phone. Whatever the subject matter, potentially the ramifications were disastrous.

Taking his HT, he contacted the men two floors below.

Mike hung up the phone and finished searching the desk, finding nothing of value. In one of his more optimistic moments, he had almost wondered whether the chief had the code written down.

Then he dismissed the idea.

"If the door can only be opened from the outside, we're going to need help to get in," said Emily.

"You think I don't already know that?" Mike attempted to gather his thoughts. After fifteen minutes out of the water, he'd begun to adjust to the new temperature; his clothing was still wet but his body no longer shivered. Had they still been outside, he knew that there would have been an imminent risk of hypothermia.

At least for now they were back in the warm.

Mike hurried to the nearby door, edging it open and finding the corridor once again deserted. He counted the doors – five, all closed; working on Maria's suggestion that one of them might be a linen closet, he entered it, finding towels.

"Take this." He passed Emily a fresh one, the warm feeling comforting against her face. Approaching the security room, gun at the ready, he considered knocking, then decided against it. For a moment, he thought he heard sounds nearby, possibly from the floor below. He turned his gaze to the stairway, alarmed.

Gunfire!

Maria disconnected the call with Mike, her thoughts immediately turning to other matters. As she sought to contact Masterson, she heard Phil's voice from alongside her.

"We're getting an incoming from COBRA."

Maria looked up. "Call the Director."

Mr White entered just as the images on the screen changed. What had previously been a series of minimised pictures streamed live from everywhere from the Tower to the city centres of London and Edinburgh was replaced by the sight of the prime minister seated among many in the COBRA Committee.

"I'm sorry to report that further fires have appeared north of the original ones," the Director addressed her on returning to the hub. "With severe destruction to the roads and the traffic the way it is, our only choice is to tackle them from the air."

"I only wish it were that simple, Director." The PM's expression was cold. "I'm afraid we've just had a development."

The PM looked at an unseen face out of camera shot. "Play the footage."

The Director folded his arms as the pictures on the screen changed to outdoor footage. Over the coming sixty seconds, he watched it in its entirety, alarmed by what he heard and saw. The location was instantly recognisable.

Worse still, so was the man in view.

42

The Waterloo Barracks, 23:14

The first sign of life came from down the hallway on the far side. The stairs were grand, ornate, immaculately carpeted, the furnishings identical to those that lined both the corridor he now walked and the one on the floor below.

Again, it had more in keeping with the building's exterior than its original purpose.

Mike counted three men; he hadn't had time to take in their every feature. Each had been dressed in black, all definitely armed.

The gunfire had come from the stairs.

"Get down!"

Mike dived through the air to his right, coming down hard on the carpet. The luxurious texture was briefly soothing; his arms tingled as his wet skin made contact with the expensive fabric. Bullet marks appeared on the wall opposite, ruining a painting; Mike guessed the duke wouldn't have been impressed. The voices on the stairway had become louder.

Then the door to the security room opened.

"Get back inside!" Mike rushed to the nearest doorway, his eyes quickly on Emily. He saw her scramble in the opposite direction to the gunfire, heading back to the office. With no chance of getting there, she dived through the nearest open door, closing it behind her.

Now Mike was particularly glad that the corridor had come with a linen cupboard.

A fourth gunman appeared from the security room, firing immediately. Taking shelter in the doorway, Mike turned sharply and fired back, hitting him in the centre of the chest. Two more had appeared at the head of the stairway. He fired twice, narrowly missing.

With his back to the doorway, Mike ejected the empty magazine from his semi-automatic pistol and reloaded.

The gunfire resumed, recent impacts disturbingly close. Large chunks were being ripped from the nearby walls, ruining the paintwork. When the chaos died down, Mike turned again, keeping low. Two of the gunmen were fast approaching. He fired twice.

Both fell to the ground.

More gunfire followed immediately, this time from further afield. Looking over his shoulder, he saw two more gunmen appear at the top of the stairs followed by a rapid volley of gunfire in his direction. Rummaging through his pockets, he found a smoke bomb, activated it and threw it across the carpet. Within seconds the corridor was awash with smoke.

He waited till the gunfire stopped before chancing exposure, pleased to see movement accompanied by coughing. Aiming quickly, he fired.

Each of the remaining men hit the floor.

He looked to his left and saw the linen cupboard door reopen.

"Stay down!"

Immediately the door closed.

He moved quickly towards the first body, checking for any sign of life. As the smoke cleared, he did the same for the others, all the while inching ever closer to the security room. Maria had told him there had been three inside; he knew he'd shot one of them.

The door was once again closed.

The final gunman was still alive, albeit struggling. His firearm had become detached from his hand; Mike kicked it away and aimed his gun at him.

"You know the code for the door?" He knelt down, speaking clearly into the wounded man's ear. "You know the code?"

The gunman spat at him.

Mike pressed his hand deep into his wound, causing the gunman to writhe in agony. "Tell me the code!"

Inside the security room, the second gunman had risen to his feet, preparing to leave.

"No!" The first gunman shook his head. "Our orders are to remain here."

Ruefully, the second gunman prepared his weapon, aiming it at the door. If it opened, he would have a clean shot.

Emily waited until she heard her name being called before opening the linen cupboard door a second time. When she did, she found the once appealing corridor shrouded in smoke and littered with bullet holes. Seven men in dark combat gear lay flat out on the floor, their bloodstains mixed with watery footprints.

Mike stood hunched over one of them.

"Check the pockets. See if there's anything useful."

"Like what?"

"Bullets. Ammo. Communications devices."

"A flask of whiskey?" Emily raised her eyebrows.

Frisking the fifth man fiercely, Mike found the energy to smile. Satisfied the man was no longer armed, he pulled him to his feet. "Make yourself useful and pick up their guns. All that ammo could come in handy."

She stared at him, impressed by the idea, less so by his manner. "Yes, sir."

Mike carried the wounded gunman as far as the door. Reaching it, he told him to insert the code.

The man dithered.

Mike pressed his gun hard against his back. "What did I just tell you?"

Watching the screens, both gunmen saw the scene unfolding outside the door. Reloading their own weapons, they knew the second it opened, the mystery man would walk right into their trap.

"Stay here!" Mike gestured to the nearby wall, noticing Emily had been preparing to stand behind him. Gun at the ready, he watched the Frenchman insert the code.

The door opened.

Gunfire.

Mike pushed the injured man forward and spun away to his left. As the gunfire stopped, he returned the way he came, arms extended, and fired.

The injured man had caught a volley in the chest, killing him instantly. The second gunman fell to the floor slowly, a vacant gaze that had once possessed life. A third man was still seated at the screens.

Mike aimed at him. "Don't even think about it."

Emily entered behind him, closing the door. The security room was exactly as she remembered it, the surrounding décor bare aside from three walls covered in surveillance screens.

Mike lowered his gun and rotated the gunman's chair, pushing him out of the way.

"Help me tie him up."

Again Emily stared at him. "Yes, sir."

Mike hunched over the main console and began searching the screens for signs of activity. A small group of gunmen had been stationed near the main doors to the Queen's House; others were clearly inside, close to a small stairway that Mike guessed led down to a cellar. There was movement inside the White Tower, figures descending stairs.

Again he recognised Randek.

"Bastard!"

"What is it?" Emily asked; in the corner of the room, the gunman was now tied to a chair.

"Nothing." He looked at the gunman. "How'd you do that so quick?"

"I removed his shoelaces."

Mike smiled. "Gonna have to keep my eye on you."

Emily leaned in alongside him, placing her hand through her hair that had become tangled after being wet for so long. She clicked a few times on the mouse of the main computer console, bringing up the Jewel House.

"The Imperial State Crown is gone!" She removed her glasses from her jacket pocket, put them on and carefully observed the images of the other display cases. "They've taken everything."

Mike leaned in closer, his eyes on the display cases. "There's stuff still there." He noticed the altar plate, the swords and many of the minor pieces remained untouched. As far as he could tell, the things missing were the Imperial State Crown and most of the crowns from the main case.

He looked at Emily. "What happened to your handbag?"

"I left it the same place as your rucksack."

The chapel in the Wakefield Tower, he suddenly remembered. "Maybe if we get out of here, they'll compensate me."

He took a seat, now concentrating on the screens covering the White Tower. Six hostages were being held at gunpoint on the top floor; three others were standing on the roof, their gazes on the surrounding flames.

This was the first time Mike had seen the fires.

"Jeez Laweez."

Emily had noticed it too. From the current angle, the scene reminded her of the famous paintings of 1666.

"See if you can zoom in on their faces," Mike said, still confident that one of the men was Randek. Emily clicked the mouse rapidly, making the images move slightly.

For now, all they could see was the backs of their heads.

Mike returned his attention to the other screens, concentrating on the hostages. Indeed there were six.

Only six.

"I wonder where they're keeping the others." Mike saw no sign of Champion. "See if there's anything of the Yeoman Warder's lodgings."

"The lodgings themselves are strictly off-limits." She brought up the empty scene of the ravaged pub. "Wherever they are, they're not in there."

Mike leaned to his right, his hand gripping the nearby telephone. He called the same number as before.

Maria answered.

"Guess who."

"You know, I was actually starting to miss you!" She'd already noticed the call had come from a landline, the caller ID different than before. Same building. "I take it you had no trouble?"

"Nothing outside the line of duty. What's new?"

"A lot. PM's on the conference call. Blanco's made contact."

"What?"

"Just saw it with my own eyes. He made a video call direct to COBRA. He claimed the Crown Jewels were fake and demanded the originals."

Mike looked at Emily; clearly listening, the acting curator stared back blankly. "What happened?"

"Blanco's got six hostages on the roof of the White Tower. He threatened to kill one of them, but didn't."

"What else did he say?"

"Strange, actually. Made reference to London being illuminated before mentioning something about an event in Calais in 1347 when Edward III ordered the execution of six men. Apparently the king showed mercy."

"Sounds like Everard at St Mary le Strand." Mike thought back to his pursuit of Randek's brother-in-law six months earlier. "What's so significant about Calais and 1347?"

"I remember your uncle mentioned that once," Emily said. "The Burghers of

Calais. It was in the Hundred Years' War. Edward only gave mercy at the request of his queen."

Mike held his breath, distracted slightly at the mention of his uncle.

"Where did he make the call from?"

"From the footage it looked like the roof of the White Tower; not sure exactly what happened," Maria resumed. "The Director's on the line to the PM now. What are you seeing?"

"Surveillance screens." Mike looked around; counting them was impossible without more time. "We could be talking thousands."

"Anything specific?"

"Well, sure enough there's six hostages inside the White Tower; Blanco might have spared them for now, but I wouldn't rate their chances." Mike scanned the screens in front of him, returning his attention to those on the White Tower. The six hostages remained in the same place, securely bound and watched over by three gunmen.

"I've got something on the roof."

"Probably Blanco."

"If it is, he has company. How long ago did this happen?"

"On the hour. Try to zoom in on their faces."

"Right now they've got their backs to the camera." Mike found himself focusing on the flames beyond. "Tell you what, this whole thing sure seems real from up here."

"I hear you. Any sign of the others?"

"Negative. Not that there are cameras everywhere." He watched on as Emily continued to go through them. "Best I can see, the passages we've already seen aren't covered."

"They wouldn't be. Tower security is only concerned with high-value areas, especially those open to the public."

To Mike that made sense. "If the hostages are anywhere, they're probably still in the Queen's House. Anything that exists beneath the floor?"

Maria checked the 3D outline. "I've got something. Maybe basement level. It's tough to tell from here."

"More's room," Emily suggested. "It's the place Thomas More was held before his execution. It's directly behind the Queen's House."

"Any other way in?"

"Not that I know of."

"All right, right now let's focus on that. Maybe when the Director's off the phone, he'll be able to give us a better idea of what Blanco's demands are."

43

Edinburgh,
23:16

The helicopter came down in Princes Street Gardens, in the shadow of the castle rock. Over a hundred feet away, the famous stone edifice loomed above them like a lookout guard; though from a distance all seemed well, Rawlins knew it had been the scene of earlier discord.

To the east, the fires were spreading; watching them had been easy from the air. The map had pinpointed Old Assembly Close as being an alleyway just off the High Street, barely forty metres from St Giles' Cathedral.

Thankfully, the area around the cathedral had already been sectioned off.

They left via the hatch within seconds of touching down, heading east across the grass. Once Pentland and Pugh had joined him, they put through a call to the Rook.

"Fitz-Simon here," Rawlins began. "We're in position."

At the other end, Maria saw the call come through on the main circuit. Wasting no time, she got Atkins on the internal line.

"We've just received contact from Edinburgh. Pegasus II has landed."

"Put them through," the Deputy Director responded before taking the call on a personal headset. "How's it looking up there?"

"Worse from the air!" Rawlins replied while on the run; from the ground the fires were presently out of sight. "I've made contact with the chief of police. The key sites have been sealed off. Unfortunately fires are spreading up the High Street."

"In what direction?"

"East, I think. So far it's heading away from the cathedral."

"Interesting. Both fires seem to be following the historical routes. As there is no obvious physical conductor, it could be we're dealing with some form of remote detonation."

"The First Minister has already got SWAT teams combing the buildings. If it's above the surface, we'll find it."

"You think we're looking for something underground?"

"Well, I don't know about London, sir, but Edinburgh's famous for its subterranean passageways. Just the place to detonate something without drawing attention."

"You might have a point. When you make contact with the First Minister, tell her to extend the search."

"Will do. What are our orders?"

"Head to the cathedral. Make sure whatever is starting this doesn't escalate."

* * *

Within moments of disconnecting the call, the three Harts left the park, taking the pathway south-east, passing the National Gallery. Heading south along North Bank Street, the instantly recognisable features of St Giles came into view, the famous façade towering above the wet streets like the doors to the kingdom of heaven.

The roads were closed in both directions; unlike in London the traffic had largely cleared. There was a foul stench in the air, distant yet somehow near.

Along the High Street, Rawlins saw the flames.

Pentland and Pugh stood close behind him.

"According to this, Old Assembly Close is just beyond those buildings there." Pentland pointed east to a slightly cluttered area off the High Street, famously profuse in classical architecture. The early fires were fading, replaced by others further east. Though traffic was absent, the street was busy with fire engines. "Gonna hazard a guess, the yellow helmets won't appreciate our assistance."

Rawlins bit his lip, the nearby fires causing a hard shadow across his shaven head. As Kit had already said, the job of the White Hart wasn't to put out physical fires.

"Atkins said the fires are following their historical paths. Maybe if we can't put them out, we can at least stop what happens next."

In the capital of France, the luxury high-powered yacht made its way south-east along the Seine. Once away from the bright lights, the antiquarian put through the call he had never wanted to make.

"*Allô?*"

"Sir, it is Sébastien."

"Where are you?"

The man delayed, afraid of giving away anything incriminating.

"Are you safe?" the duke corrected.

"We are safe. The operation was a success."

At the other end, the old man rose to his feet; despite his ailments, he felt incapable of sitting. "And?" he asked, moving closer to the famous table. "Your conclusions?"

The antiquarian paused. "They are good."

On hearing those words, the duke felt a twinge of anticipation extend throughout his very soul. It was like being blessed by an angel, a feeling that could never be described in human words. "Bravo, Seb!"

"What are your instructions?"

The old man eased himself down into the nearest of the twenty-four seats, collecting his thoughts. Indeed, the job was only half done.

"Remain in the yacht. Continue out of the city. There you will await further instruction."

44

Whitehall,
23:19

Mr White left his office after the latest videoconference with the PM came to an end. He descended the banistered stairway back into the heart of the Rook, any tension from the recent call hidden behind his usual calm façade.

"What's the latest?" he asked, seeing Maria and Phil were the only people present.

"Fires have spread further north of King William Street; Kit says he first saw flames coming from inside St Clement's. He's currently tidying up the mess with Wilcox, Ward, Chambers, Cummins and Dawson. Rawlins and the others have landed in Edinburgh."

"How bad's the damage there?"

"Looks worse from the air, but not as bad as here." Maria brought the pictures up on the screen. "In both cases, they're following the historical patterns. Right now, St Giles is safe."

"The police have cordoned off every area within a quarter of a mile of Old Assembly Close." Atkins re-entered the room via the opposite, identical staircase. "Unlike here, the traffic has been well marshalled."

"At least that's something." The Director's eyes were fixed on the screens. "Where are the others?"

"Iqbal and Sanders have located the yacht; it hasn't moved since arriving at Old Billingsgate. They should be boarding anytime."

"What about Hansen?"

"He's made it to the security room."

"Do you have a secure line?"

"Hansen put through a call from a landline. Our satellites and radios can't breach it."

"Try to get him back."

Maria pressed recall on the terminal in front of her and heard the dialling tone in her ear.

Almost immediately it connected.

Mike and Emily heard the call come through from the phone they'd just used. Mike guessed it was either friend or foe.

He answered, "Grosmont!"

"Grosmont, this is the King."

Mike breathed a sigh of relief. "Come in, sire."

"What's happening there?"

"We've made it to the control room in the Waterloo Barracks, not that getting here was easy. At least seven gunmen had the place secure. One of them's still alive; right now, he's not going anywhere."

The Director listened carefully. "The PM received visual footage less than twenty minutes ago; I've just got off the line. Blanco's there. In exchange for calling off the fires, he's demanding the Crown Jewels of England."

"Maria just gave me the gist." Mike continued to watch the wall of screens, hoping the three figures currently on the roof of the White Tower would reveal a clear view of their faces. "I've got Blanco and two others on the security screens. As far as I can see, there's nothing here to do facial recognition."

"You got your decoder with you, Honey Badger?" Phil asked.

The decoder. A small device, the size of a flash drive, capable of infiltrating any technological system in the known world – at least according to Phil.

"You know I don't go anywhere without my belt, Phil."

"Insert it into the main terminal. Once you do, you should see a code."

Mike loosened his belt, finding three zip-up sections; he rummaged through the one on the left side. His actions confused Emily.

"Honey Badger?" She looked at him, receiving little in the way of a response. "You have hacking tools in your belt?"

Mike smiled, deciding against filling her in. He removed the device and began searching for a flash drive port.

He found one and inserted it. Immediately the device began to flash.

"I got a number: 54603812."

Phil inserted the number into his laptop and waited for a response. Within seconds, the images on the big screen changed.

"We're in."

The Director looked at the semi-translucent screen, recognising sights within the Tower's walls. The footage was wide ranging. It seemed live.

"Show me the White Tower."

Phil clicked rapidly at his mouse, finding several views of the famous Norman structure. Among the hundreds, he found live footage from the White Tower's roof.

Three figures were facing the battlements, their eyes on the burning city.

"That's him all right." The Director recognised the dark-haired man with angular features he'd seen on screen moments earlier. "And his nephew."

"Facial recognition will only work with a clear view," Maria said. "The third man is still a mystery."

Finally he moved.

"Freeze there!" Maria asked, immediately getting a response. Alongside her, the Director leaned forward for a closer view.

"Who is he?"

The results came up immediately. "François de Haulle. An art director and expert from the City of Angers," Maria confirmed, reading his bio. "Interestingly, he's of similar heritage. His father was the curator of art at the museum in Angers – a role now filled by the man's younger brother. Rumour has it, he's of royal lineage – in England too!"

Mr White's eyes narrowed, his intense focus now reserved for the handsome man in his mid to late thirties, his nicely styled jet-black hair further indication of his ancestry. "Why does that name ring a bell?"

"Remember a couple of years ago that business at the National Portrait Gallery with the van Dyck?"

"Of course. I remember the Director nearly had kittens when that went missing."

"Rumour has it Jérôme de Haulle was behind the theft. I'm not sure of any reason."

"I think you all know my opinion on coincidences." The Director examined the stranger's face with a pensive expression. "Grosmont, can you hear me?"

"Loud and clear, sir."

"The Thomas More room in the Bell Tower is located behind the Queen's House. The only entrance is in the house itself."

"Getting there won't be easy. At least forty gunmen emerged from beneath the White Tower; even taking away the ones I've killed, we could still be looking at over thirty. As best we can tell, the Beefeaters and the Queen's Guard are out of the equation. I can't do this alone."

"You have a better suggestion, Captain?" The Director's expression was hard; Mike could feel it despite not being in his presence. "The fires in London are spreading; they're also getting worse in Edinburgh. Blanco has warned of the penalties should military action be considered; worse still, I understand he's taken out every entrance."

"Presumably they got in from somewhere."

"I assure you as soon as his path becomes known to us, you'll have all the reinforcements you need. Right now, you're just going to have to make do."

Resigned, Mike nodded. "Yes, sir."

"Keep in regular contact. And whatever you do, make sure that bastard doesn't get away."

The Director walked away from the main desk, navigating his way through the futuristic-looking room. Though the hour was still relatively early, he felt his legs threaten to buckle with even the slightest contact with the furniture.

"Phil, get me some coffee. Half and half, you know how I like it." He prayed the long-awaited caffeine intake would solve at least one of his problems. "Maria, get me when possible the head of security at the Louvre and the French foreign secretary. The French president has already spoken to the prime minister. Rumours from north of the Seine say they might also have been the target of a heist."

Atkins was seated on the far side of the room, confused. "There are no reports of fires there, are there?"

"Not yet, but that doesn't mean they're not still to come." He accepted the coffee as soon as Phil brought it, prepared to endure the excessive heat on his tongue. "Also, get me our opposite number north of the border. And, if possible, contact with Rawlins, Pentland and Pugh."

"I just spoke with Rawlins," Atkins confirmed. "There's already been contact with the chief of police."

"Good." The Director took another sip, blowing on it first. "What do we know about the yacht?"

"Not much." Maria brought the vessel up twice on screen; the first a profile picture, the second live footage from security cameras overlooking the river at Old Billingsgate. "Further enquiries show Leboeuf died six months ago; he was also uncle to one of the victims of the Bordeaux Connection."

The Director raised an eyebrow. "Who owns it now?"

"Unclear. Only that it was moored in Bordeaux not six weeks ago. Was first seen in St Katharine Docks three weeks ago."

"Keep checking; see if we can't see who was responsible for bringing it here. How about Iqbal and Sanders?"

Maria expanded the pictures on screen, showing further live footage of the yacht. Two figures were making their way quietly through the water, preparing to board it.

"I think we're looking at them right now."

Jay was first to climb aboard. A metallic ladder overhung the port side; for some reason, the boat was facing the opposite way. Taking his time before putting his foot on the deck, he hurried towards the helm, seeking partial shelter behind the wheel.

Within seconds, Sanders joined him.

There were lights on down below, the only signs of life. Beyond the yacht, sounds drifted from across the water, light noise of numerous conversations from within the nearby restaurants the main disturbance to the silence. Further afield, the noise of sirens mixed with others yet more distant generated a pulsating echo, common in the city but discordant in the present opulent setting.

There was no sign of life on board.

Sanders picked up on the loneliness. "I don't like this, Jay. It's too quiet."

Iqbal smiled. "Geezer, you've been watching too many cowboy movies. Looks to me like the place is deserted."

"My thoughts exactly." Sanders focused on the door that led down to the galley, feelings of anxiety slowly building. His overwhelming feeling was one of guarded concern.

They were walking into a trap.

Jay spoke quietly into his headset. "Rook, this is Grailly."

The Director took the response. "Come in, Grailly."

"We're on the yacht." He looked around, wondering whether the reason for the lights below would soon become apparent. "Request permission to enter."

"Request granted, Grailly. Any sign of life, get the heck out of there."

"Roger that."

* * *

Less than a mile from the yacht, a helicopter of far different appearance to that which had recently touched down in a park in Edinburgh landed on a helipad above a block of luxury apartments south of the Thames. As the motors stuttered to a halt, the sole occupant alighted and made his way across an immaculate rooftop garden and through French doors into a luxuriously furnished living area.

Another person was already present, seated on a fine antique settee that matched what the newcomer had earlier witnessed on his yacht. Like the visitor, the man was French by birth and of ancestry that in a different time and place might have been considered either noble or royal. His age of 72, though difficult to determine from appearances, was young in comparison to his experience, of which he was well regarded. His neatly trimmed beard and well-chiselled jaw, complemented by dark eyes and a strong nose, were reflected in the glass table along with his well-groomed white, typically Anjouvin hair. Though many years had passed, the newcomer recognised the man instantly.

His name was Jérôme de Haulle, nominally Duke of Normandy and Count of Anjou.

"1869 – a marvellous year for the City of Bordeaux." The well-groomed man held up an unopened bottle of claret.

Gabriel de Fieschi, historically heir to the Dukedom of Aquitaine and County of Poitou, smiled at him. "One hundred and fifty years is a long time to wait."

Jérôme uncorked the wine and poured it into two crystal goblets. "I have been saving it for a special occasion. In one of my weaker moments, I decided to make do with one of its lesser cousins after my triumph with the Protector's jewels. Tonight, I will make no such mistake."

"Delicious!" Fieschi nodded, sampling it. Taking a seat, he removed his portable tablet from his inner pocket and tapped quickly at the display. "You won't object if I use your phone?"

Jérôme had no objection. "Be my guest."

About a mile downstream, a dark-haired figure sat quietly as he watched the north bank from close to Blackfriars. The view of the city was almost perfect, the immaculate façade of St Paul's brightly illuminated against the dark sky like a half moon, its epic dome basking in the glow of nearby floodlights. Further to his right, he noticed a different kind of glow.

Contemplating the view, he remembered the famous stories associated with the Great Fire.

He felt a vibration in his trouser pocket, followed by the sound of his ringtone. The caller ID suggested it was a local number.

"*Allô?*"

"Are you safe?"

He recognised Fieschi's voice. "I am downstream. The yacht is now deserted."

Inside the luxury apartment, Fieschi studied the pictures on the screen. The dark-haired man who had previously been in a reception room, close to the stateroom, was now absent.

But others were now present.

"Did you follow my instructions?"

"To the letter."

Fieschi smiled, his focus still on the screen. Two men in dark combat uniforms trod the luxury carpet of his late relative's yacht, clearly on guard for imminent contact.

"Good. You may detonate."

Jay ventured first through the doors of the stateroom, waiting until he was sure it was empty before taking a moment to inspect the quality. The walls and ceiling were gilded on every side, the long dining table reflecting the light of a crystal chandelier that illuminated the room.

"Imagine living in a place like this," Sanders said.

Jay raised an eyebrow, the thought occurring that the owner's permanent residence was probably smarter still.

He spoke through his headset. "Rook, this is Grailly."

Maria answered, "How's it looking in there?"

"We've searched this place top to bottom. There's no one here."

"Copy that, guys. Come ashore as soon as you're done."

Seated at the helm of his small cabin cruiser, the dark-haired man reopened his jacket pocket, removing the same device he had programmed not twenty minutes earlier. It seemed a shame, all that history and grandeur.

Nevertheless, the call was never his.

Gripping the small detonator in his right hand, he placed his thumb over the main button.

Slowly he pressed it.

Alongside Jérôme de Haulle, Fieschi felt the narrowest twinge of remorse. Some of the yacht's fittings had been in the family over two centuries.

Now, in one swift move, it had been obliterated.

"You know, I really should have saved the chandeliers."

Jérôme eyed him while preparing to sip the wine. "I recall the same was said of St Paul's three centuries ago. Remember, out of great destruction comes great opportunity."

Glancing at Jérôme, Fieschi nodded. "You know, you're quite right."

45

Whitehall,
23:23

A stunned silence descended on the Rook as the four present stared at the pictures in front of them. The luxury yacht, floating noiselessly on the calm waters of the Thames only seconds earlier, had been obliterated before their very eyes, vanished behind heavy smoke.

Maria placed her hand to her mouth. "Oh my God!"

Flaming wreckage was everywhere, the lighter objects floating on the surface whilst those of greater weight sank quickly to the bottom. The hull was damaged on both sides, the majority of the debris coming from the cabins. As the smoke began to clear, they saw it had capsized and was resting on its right side.

A second explosion followed.

The latest noise sparked new life into the Director. "Get Masterson and the others. I want a salvage op immediately. If they're still alive, every second could count." He looked at Phil. "Try to get a line direct to Grailly and Warwick."

Phil tried Jay while Maria contacted Kit. Phil shook his head. "No connection!"

Maria got through to Kit. "Edward, this is the Rook. We need a SWAT team to head south immediately. Orders of the King."

Standing in sight of the blaze at St Clement's, Kit was confused. "We're kind of tied up right now, Maria."

"Unfortunately there's been a change of plan. The yacht exploded. Grailly and Warwick were aboard."

Kit noticed deep concern in her voice. "What?"

"We saw it just now via CCTV. The yacht was planted. There's nothing left."

At the other end, Kit felt as though the air had left his lungs, his skin cold despite the nearby heat. "Maria?"

"If they're still alive, every second could count. Don't waste your talents. You said it yourself, you're not firefighters."

As the transmission ended, Kit sprinted south, finding Ward and Wilcox along the way.

"What is it?" Ward asked.

"There's no time to explain. I'll tell you when we're there!"

***

Blanco felt a quick vibration in his right pocket, preceding the sound of his ringtone. Removing his satphone from his pocket, he saw the caller was Fieschi.

He answered.

"I'm pleased to report that plan B has been implemented as planned. The prime minister was most displeased on hearing of our arrival."

"That will teach her to put her trust in medieval resources for modern-day warfare, won't it?" Fieschi sucked on the cigar Jérôme had recently lit for him. "On a related subject, phase two has also been necessary."

The Anjouvin considered what he'd just heard, recalling the plan from days earlier. His escape route had been compromised.

"I'm most sorry to hear that."

"Fortunately my uncle was insured. It will please you, I'm sure, to hear it took a couple of roaches with it."

Blanco smiled, aware that members of only one group would have been on board. "Pity. With my share of the jewels, I had been hoping to convince your uncle to part with it."

"A shrewd move perhaps, in another time. Then again, my uncle was never the keenest when it came to parting with his possessions."

"I was thinking more about the history. Speaking of which, that is where we must now concentrate. If the prime minister refuses to comply, we still have much work ahead of us. The original jewels are unlikely to reveal themselves."

"Your lack of patience is your undoing, Bizu; my father has told you this many times. Give the good lady time to consider the option. You said yourself, these things have a tendency to follow past courses."

"Be that as it may, tonight is not one in which we can put our trust in God alone." He gazed once again out across the burning city. "The building itself may be irreplaceable, but the possibility cannot be ruled out that its destruction will bring us new problems. You know my theory on what other secrets it contains."

Fieschi flicked ash into the nearby ashtray, recognising the family crest on the side. "Perhaps I should have guessed your appreciation for your ancestor's construction would render you impotent on such matters."

Blanco let the insult slide. "If the Tower falls, it falls. Masonry comes up and crumbles. That is the way of things. However, if the tunnel exists, it exists here. That is where our attention must lie."

"In that case, I suggest you be about it. After all, six hours is a lot to kill."

"My thoughts exactly."

Blanco picked up his HT within seconds of hanging up on Fieschi. "Christophe, do you copy?"

In the security room, a sudden burst of static caught Emily unaware. Mike noticed it had come from the device attached to the prisoner's belt.

Mike looked at him. "Don't even think about it."

At the other end, Blanco's frustrations were continuing to rise. "Christophe, do you copy?"

Mike grabbed the HT from the gunman's belt. "Christophe can't come to the phone right now. May I take a message?"

Blanco flinched at the sound of the unrecognisable voice. "Marcel?"

"Wrong again, jackass! For your next guess, you might want to consider someone outside your organisation."

Blanco's delay caught the attention of François and Randek; Randek was first to enquire. Blanco lowered his hand, ordering still. "Who is this?"

"Right now, how about you just call me sir. After that we can worry about whether or not I let you leave this place alive." Mike's gaze continued to focus on the screens. "I'm guessing it must be pretty cold up on that roof. It's a pity heat doesn't travel that far."

"The glow of the fires for now is all the comfort I need, though may I thank you for your concern. I really must congratulate you. The rest of your comrades were not so quick to evade the expertise of my men. However, I'm afraid I must warn you they are no longer in a position to help you. In less than two minutes, you will be joining them. If, indeed, you are still alive."

"From what I've seen so far, your own men seem to have a rather high mortality rate." Mike glanced to his left at the captured gunman and covered the mouthpiece to whisper to Emily, "You think you can shut him up?"

"You got any ideas?" Emily asked.

Mike returned to the HT. "Listen, jackass. You may not know who I am, but I know exactly who you are. I know Randek and de Haulle are with you. Now, you may have evaded capture so far; in truth, I tip my hat. It's a shame Payet wasn't so quick when escaping the Musée d'Orsay."

Listening at Blanco's left, Randek was furious. "So it was you my nephew saw on the Broadwalk Steps. A most fine feat of evade and escape. I'm almost sorry it was a complete waste of time."

"I remember a John Lennon quote. Time enjoyed spent wasted isn't time wasted at all."

"A most talented musician. You'll recall another of his. Give peace a chance."

A wry smile. "I guess that one must have been lost on you. What is it that you want?"

"The Crown Jewels of England are legally the property of the City of Angers. I'm quite sure for a soldier such as you the name will mean very little. Sadly, very few people take the time to learn where they truly came from. You might say it was the place where it all began."

"Sounds to me as if you have a different sort of anger issue."

Blanco laughed. "A most witty remark; I must try to replicate it sometime. However, unfortunately you are unlikely to be around to hear it."

"Captain!" Emily pointed at the screen, her voice heavy with apprehension. Sure enough, the footage confirmed there were gunmen leaving the Queen's House.

"My loss, I'm sure." Mike saw on the screen that Randek and François were listening in alongside Blanco, Randek speaking on his own HT. "If it's the jewels you want, why are you still here? I see you've already accessed the display cases."

"Opened them, examined them, dismissed them. As you are undoubtedly already aware, the jewels are fakes."

"You honestly think the British government would put duplicates in a place under the watchful eye of so many? Come on, Blanco, even they're not that stupid!"

"On the contrary. If I were wearing a hat, I might even make the effort to tip it myself. The honours of both England and Scotland are worth a pretty penny to the interested collector; I have heard figures ranging up to thirty billion dollars. Only a fool would put them in sight of the gathering masses."

"I guess the same must be true of the Magna Carta and the Bill of Rights." Mike grimaced on seeing eight gunmen descending on the entrance to the Jewel House. He knew in under sixty seconds they'd have company. "I must say I'm surprised at you. All this work just to commit petty theft."

"The rightful return of my family's lost heirlooms is only one consideration. As a soldier, I will spare giving you the lesson in something you could never possibly begin to understand."

"Your family's reputation precedes you in many ways. Last I checked, you weren't even top dogs in Marseille."

"You can dispense with the pleasantries. They are unnecessary. In just under six hours, our mission will be over. Either the Gemini will have what we seek or the city will turn to ash. One way or another the jewels will be found."

"Who are you?"

"Ask me who we were."

"You got selective memory now?"

"Perhaps I should ask the same question of you. I thought the Order of the Servants had died out long ago."

Mike raised an eyebrow, automatically equating the phrase with the White Hart's motto – 'I serve'. "What?"

Randek tried to take possession of the HT. "My nephew is most insistent on a word; however, under the circumstances, I think it would be unwise," Blanco resumed. "In my experience, many an old feud can become deadly in the wrong circumstances."

"I understand his brother-in-law is dead now. How was the funeral?"

Randek tore the HT from Blanco's hand. "You bastard."

"I was beginning to think you'd undertaken a vow of silence. I must admit you pulled a number on us back in Paris. Pity for Payet he couldn't do the same."

"So it was you I wrestled with on the boat?"

"No, but trust me, he's also got a good memory."

The Frenchman laughed wryly. "Of course, I hear it in the voice now. You are far less refined, yet similarly arrogant."

"A shame the same can't be said of your brother-in-law."

"What kind of man would take joy in such things? Particularly when it involves family?"

"Perhaps when the man who died was himself responsible for so many innocent deaths."

"It will grieve you, I'm sure, to know the same is true of your friends."

Mike raised an eyebrow, sensing a bluff. "What are you talking about?"

"The two men aboard the yacht near the Tower. A most foolish move. Sadly for them, there is no longer anything left."

Mike's concern was growing. "Nice try, jackass."

"You think I lie?"

"Pretty soon, you'll be able to tell me face to face. Personally, I've never cared much for conversation over the phone."

"Do not get too comfortable. Your time is running out."

Emily was tugging at Mike's arm. "We have to get out of here."

He glanced at the screens, seeing movement outside. Eight gunmen had entered the barracks, heading for the main stairs.

Contact was imminent.

"I heard a rumour once that the jewels had actually been shipped back to France. But I guess you wouldn't know anything about that, would you?"

"Do not test my patience, Servant. Over one hundred hostages are currently being kept at gunpoint below the governor's house. I would hate for you to have their deaths on your conscience."

Mike scowled, angry at the thought.

"Captain?"

Picking up on Emily's concern, he glanced again at the screens, seeing movement on the stairs. "Who exactly are you?"

Blanco retook the HT. "Ask me who I was."

"Who were you?"

Blanco's lips curled into a broad smile. "That is a question only Her Majesty can answer."

46

The Waterloo Barracks, 23:26

Mike stared hard at the screen, with a sense of increasing trepidation. The words he'd just heard, though vague, had a ring of truth about them.

If an explosion had taken place, it wouldn't be difficult to confirm.

He hurried over to the left side of the room, where the captured gunman was seated on the nearest chair, turned to face the wall. Mike pulled his chair violently, spinning it round so he now faced him.

"Who was he talking about?"

The gunman muttered in French.

"In English."

The gunman glanced quickly at the screen, clearly encouraged by the sight of his approaching comrades. Mike estimated that less than forty-five seconds remained until they reached the control room.

Mike punched the gunman in the face.

"Call that same number. I need to speak to Maria."

Emily picked up the phone, pressing redial. Mike took the phone as it connected.

"Maria, you copy?"

"Still here."

"I just spoke to Blanco; he knows we're here."

"You made contact?"

"Never mind that right now. He said there'd been an explosion on a yacht. Someone was aboard."

Maria bowed her head, the image of the flaming wreckage once again flooding her thoughts. Looking at the screen in front of her, she saw the deck was still burning.

She'd seen no sign of life since the explosion.

"After capturing footage of Blanco fleeing the scene of the Monument, we managed to trace him to a yacht at St Katharine Docks. From there it sailed to Old Billingsgate; we think that's where the gunmen came from."

"What happened?"

"We're not sure exactly. All we know is a large group of men in arms were seen leaving it just before 22:00 hours. Grailly and Warwick were sent to check it out."

Mike sank deep into the vacant chair, his head spinning. It was as if all the air had been sucked from his lungs.

"Oh my God!"

"The Director's ordered a SWAT team to check out the wreckage." Again her gaze focused on the remains of the yacht. "Honestly, I don't care for their chances."

Mike took a deep breath, trying to make sense of what he'd just heard. He remembered his initiation; Iqbal and Sanders had been the two he'd most looked up to. Jay had been his first friend; together they'd brought him through the toughest times.

"Keep your chin up. We all know what we signed up for."

"Yeah." Mike tried hard to control his emotions. Right of his present line of vision, figures were moving across the screens. To his left, Emily was frozen with fear and uncertainty.

Another voice spoke in his ear. "Grosmont, this is the King."

"Sire."

"This is no time for self-pity. There will be a time for grieving when we're finished. We all know the way of life. If it wasn't for Fenway, you wouldn't be here." The Director sensed he was talking to radio silence. "Grosmont?"

"I hear you, sir."

"Now pull yourself together, man." His eyes monitored the semi-translucent screen. Thanks to Phil's decoder, he had a perfect view through the Tower's security cameras. "All that matters now is our capital city. Not to mention those poor hostages."

Mike took a breath, remembering. Champion was still in captivity. He prayed alive.

He looked again at the screens, noticing the gunmen had made it to the first floor. "I'm surrounded at the moment; going outside could be suicide."

"Staying where you are won't be any better."

Standing alongside him, Emily nodded, trying to calm him down. "Whoever he is, he's right. We need to get away."

Mike bit his lip, the anger inside him building. "They're not gonna get in here without the code. Even if they find it, there's nowhere for them to hide. I can take them out."

"And what if they come with explosives? Come on, Grosmont, you're better than this!"

Mike nodded, realisation setting in. The first priority was the mission. Everything else would follow.

"What are our chances?" Mike asked.

"Far better if you move out. As soon as you make it outside the barracks, resume contact."

"I will. And let me know if there's any news."

"Even if there isn't, you know your role. The City of London is dependent on our success."

"Yes, sir." Mike rose to his feet, his attention on Emily. A soft smile lined her lips. It was obvious there were things she wanted to say but that she had neither the heart nor the courage to say them.

"All right, we're moving out. Maria, what do you see?"

Maria returned to the main terminal and typed quickly at her keyboard. Within seconds, the 3D map returned. "Enemies are coming up the stairs. More are coming across Tower Green." She sighed, counting the numbers. "You're not looking at less than twelve."

"Great – I always love a challenge." He reloaded his gun. "What's my best bet?"

Maria clicked her mouse rapidly. "If you can get to the kitchen, there's another tunnel in the south wall of the cellar. Comes out in the Byward Tower."

"How do I get there?"

"Take the same stairs you came up earlier. Once you're there, you should find a door to the cellar. Look for a fireplace."

"Got it. How's the decoder working out?"

Phil beat Maria to a response. "Just like looking over your shoulder."

"Good. I'll make contact when I can. In the meantime, keep an eye on Blanco."

"Right now they're still on the roof."

"I see them. By the way, the conversation did reveal one thing. Emily was right. The hostages are below the Queen's House. Getting there won't be easy."

Maria responded, "First I suggest you worry about getting out of there. Then we can worry about the Queen's House."

Mike moved away from the screens, carrying the gunman's HT. "Take this." He asked Emily to hold it. "You never know, if we make it out of here, it might be useful."

Emily saw Mike heading for the main door, his eyes still on the screens. "You're not seriously thinking of leaving?"

"Right now, that's all I'm thinking of." He picked up the machine guns Emily had earlier collected from the dead gunmen. "You ever fired one of these before?"

"No."

"It's real easy." He gave her one. "Just aim and shoot."

He moved over to the door, removing a grenade from his belt. "You ready?"

"No!"

"Good. You're gonna need that adrenaline."

He opened the door and ran rapidly along the corridor, instructing Emily to follow. He released two grenades as he passed the top of the stairs. Gunfire erupted before they exploded.

The impact was loud, causing the floor to shake; debris ripped from the walls below. There were figures moving about midway down, clearly startled.

The explosion had bought them some time.

"Come on!"

He found the door they had used before, next came the stairs. On reaching the bottom, he came to a halt.

Beyond the kitchen, there were voices from the first-floor corridor.

"Stay here," Mike said, pushing open the kitchen door. "If you see anything above, open fire."

"What about you?"

"I'll be right back."

The kitchen was located off the main corridor, a busy area of surprisingly modern appearance. Keeping close to the central island, he crept towards the far door, expecting company.

He got it.

Gunfire.

He fired twice, both deadly; along the corridor two bodies fell to the floor. Immediately the gunfire resumed. He sensed footsteps approaching the door.

Checking his gun, he realised the magazine was empty and he had no time to reload.

In the split second that followed, his mind wandered back to the second phase of his training.

There was movement near the entry to the camp. Two flagpoles stood like twin towers either side of the exit; a Union Jack flew from the higher of the two masts. The second, until moments earlier, had displayed a different set of colours; the Star-Spangled Banner, in honour of the rulers of hell. He watched with fascination as two of the knights performed a flag ceremony of lowering the Stars and Stripes, replacing it with another. Equally recognisable.

The blue and white of Israel.

The flag went up, and silence fell. Mike sensed the calm before a storm. In the distance he heard sounds of movement: tyres, an engine; finally there were signs of life along the approach road. A solitary vehicle was approaching, six wheels, three either side; like most he had seen in recent days, its bodywork was camouflaged. He recognised it as a Nimda Shoet.

An armoured people carrier.

The strange vehicle came to a sliding halt near the head of the parade, and a man of military bearing emerged. Unlike the double act of the American naval officers, this man was alone. Like Mr Larry, his hairline was largely receding, the colour of his eyes disguised by mirrored sunglasses that did nothing to diminish the force of his penetrating gaze.

He marched briskly, taking up a position in front of the knights.

The second legionnaire from hell.

"My name is Amir Zahavi. I am from Israel. I will be training you for the next forty-eight hours," the newcomer began. "For thirty years I have learned, perfected and passed on every skill that needs to be mastered by new recruits of the YAMAM. What I will put you through will be real tough, I promise you, so be ready for action."

Standing in his position of isolation, Mike weighed up the man in front of him. The slight hint of distinguished grey invading an otherwise black hairline he associated specifically with that corner of the Middle East, whereas the olive-coloured skin and a forehead lined with deep wrinkles offered clear evidence he was looking at a man whose past fitted the profile of a career in the secret police. While his knowledge of the YAMAM was limited, he knew their fame was anti-terror, hostage negotiations, a SWAT team; they differed from the SEALs. In Israel they existed to guard the borders, weed out the spies.

The next march lasted five miles; he did it with his rifle above his head. Sanders rewarded him with extra water and a protein bar.

It was obvious from the set-up the next phase would involve unarmed combat.

"What we're gonna do here is called Krav Maga – some call it Israeli self-defence. Every YAMAM recruit is taught this; it's real hard-core, trust me, even MOSSAD train for this," the Israeli began. "Always remember, the purpose of self-defence is primarily to defend. I want to see controlled aggression."

Mike lined up opposite Sanders, for now not knowing what to expect. This was the first time he'd faced any of the Harts in combat.

He guessed Sanders was an expert.

He lost the first bout, but kept his calm. As the afternoon wore on, ten new opponents presented themselves.

It ended with a bout against Masterson.

Zahavi watched closely, the other Harts doing likewise. Kit was on the warpath. He pinned Mike to the ground. Rolling, Mike countered.

The bout threatened to get out of hand.

"Remember, controlled aggression at all times. Do not lose your cool."

Mike waited calmly behind the door, knowing contact was inevitable. He grabbed the first man as soon as he saw the door move, pinning him hard to the ground. Within seconds, another had also been dealt with.

"How the hell did you do that?"

Mike saw Emily standing on the far side of the kitchen. "I thought I told you to stay where you were."

"There were footsteps on the stairs."

Mike looked around, remembering Maria's advice about the cellar while at the same time inwardly praying that the news about Jay and Sanders wasn't true. The world was moving so fast, so erratically, his brain no longer found it easy to process what was flooding into it. He glanced at Emily, her face, her eyes; the girl was tired, her clothes still wet. Hyperthermia remained a risk.

They had to get out.

"Maria said there's a cellar here somewhere?"

"There's an old wine cellar in here!" Emily sprinted to the far wall where what seemed to be an original door concealed an entry to a pantry. Among the shelving and storage areas, a second door led down below.

Mike led the way, reloading his gun as he crossed the kitchen before doing his best to navigate in darkness. Realising visibility was gone, he pulled down his night-vision goggles, the new surroundings showing up clearly against the artificial green backdrop.

"Come on!"

At the bottom of the stairs they came to level ground, at which point the layout began to make sense. They had entered an area crammed with clutter and furniture, the majority antique and military. He turned to see Emily pressing a light switch.

"Are you crazy?"

"Relax! There aren't any cameras down here." She passed him as he removed his night visions, moving between the furniture. She continued to the far wall where an area rich in antiques partially concealed an original fireplace. "Maria said the entrance was south. It must be around here."

Mike joined her, searching impatiently for anything out of place. The fireplace clearly hadn't been used in recent years; he couldn't recall from the outside if there was a chimney.

Perhaps that was the clue.

The mantelpiece was white, decorated with emblems relating to the building's founder; everything about it reminded him of Waterloo. On the right side, a circular emblem jutted out. He turned it, holding his breath.

The rear panel of the fireplace opened.

Emily looked at him. "I can't believe you just did that."

On this occasion, his response was one of urgency. "Come on!"

In the heart of the Rook, Phil kept an eye on the screens. For the third time in recent minutes, the Director re-entered after a brief trip to his office.

"What's happening with Hansen?"

Phil offered a faint smile. "I gotta hand it to him. He sure mastered Krav Maga."

The Director watched the screens as Phil rewound the footage from the Waterloo Barracks, stopping at the point where Mike and the mysterious woman alongside him left the CCTV room. They saw Mike lead the way, passing the main stairway at pace as the onslaught began. It wasn't obvious without a slow replay that Mike had released two grenades.

Both did significant damage on the stairs.

"Who is she?" Mr White asked, concentrating on the woman alongside Mike as they made it into the kitchen and then the cellar. It was obvious from their actions she knew the way.

"Emily Fletcher, PhD, assistant curator of the Tower," Maria replied, bringing up her profile on the semi-translucent screen. "Former student of Mike's uncle. Pretty in her own way."

Phil smiled. "Apparently the lecture was her idea; ironically she's the reason Mike was there in the first place."

"Where are they heading?"

"The Byward Tower. According to this, the tunnel ends in the apartment of the Chief Yeoman Warder."

"Is he still alive?"

"Negative. He was one of the victims of the Ceremony of the Keys."

Mr White nodded, focusing on the footage. Mike and Emily had disappeared, leaving the gunmen mystified.

"Find a number for the apartment. As soon as they enter, I want Hansen back on the line."

***

The Director crossed to the far side of the room, finding Atkins seated alone at the only other terminal that was in use. "Any news on Scotland?"

"Fires are still spreading. However, I've just spoken to the First Minister. Unfortunately, there's been a disturbance at the castle."

The Director lowered his head, any feelings of surprise instantly passing. "The jewels?"

"Exact details are sketchy at this stage. Have you spoken to the PM?"

"Not since the last time, but believe me I intend to." He returned his attention to Maria. "Any news on the yacht?"

"Masterson is arriving now. You want him to enter?"

The Director saw Kit, Ward and Wilcox approaching the car park. "Tell them to start evacuating Cannon Street. Leave the investigations to the SWAT team."

47

The White Tower,
23:27

Blanco, Randek and François left the roof of the White Tower as soon as the conversation with the stranger ended. Though Randek was still unsure of the man's name, he knew he'd seen him before. He was like the one on the boat, only more junior, his face bearing the handsomeness of youth mixed with some scars of experience in combat. He remembered Everard had spoken of a man in the church, how he had been spotted and pursued before making his escape on the Underground. He smiled inwardly as he recalled his late brother-in-law's anecdote regarding his pursuer colliding with the doors to the Tube.

Maybe the lad was as foolish now as he had been then.

They made it to the heart of the arsenal, where the original six hostages were held at gunpoint.

Joining them was the governor.

"Return this gentleman to the saint's room," Blanco said to Randek, gesturing to the most senior hostage. "The rest will stay. May it act as a warning to those who seek to interfere with our plans."

"Yes, Uncle."

Blanco watched as his nephew barked orders at the governor. He grabbed the governor's arm as he passed.

"I suggest you consider my request carefully, General. Six hours is a long time. And I am a very patient man."

Blanco waited until Randek had disappeared before making his own exit. Joined by François, they took the main stairway down into the gift shop and departed the White Tower on the north side, returning to the Jewel House.

They took the main stairway through the heart of the barracks, their destination the security room. Evidence of a recent gunfight remained; even without the visual damage, he could smell it in the air. Inside the security room, five gunmen had regained control.

Besides those who had been shot, two had been killed in the grenade blast.

He found the sole survivor watching the screens. "What happened?"

The man he had earlier referred to as Christophe told him of the mysterious stranger, accompanied by the dark-haired woman. When the conversation ended, Blanco watched the entire episode as it had played out on the surveillance monitors. The man wasn't recognisable in any way except for the firearm. He looked like a soldier, probably a commando.

According to Randek, his actual employers were more elusive.

Leaning towards the screen, he watched how the man had experimented with the control centre before having a conversation on the landline.

He picked up the phone and pressed redial.

Phil watched on in disbelief as he saw Blanco pick up the phone and make a call. Within seconds the phone rang.

Maria remained alongside him.

"Don't answer." He gestured to the screen.

Maria, meanwhile, called for the Director. "Sir, you might want to see this!"

The Director returned from across the room, stopping behind Maria. The caller ID confirmed the call was coming from the same phone as before.

Watching the big screen, it all made sense.

"He couldn't possibly have got our number."

"When Emily Fletcher made the second call, it's possible she pressed a redial button. Blanco's clearly watching the same footage as us."

Without further pause the Director answered, "Monsieur Blanco, to what do I owe this pleasure?"

At the other end, Blanco's initial reaction was that of surprise. "Well, I suppose that would depend. To whom do I currently speak?"

The Director folded his arms as he watched Blanco on the semi-translucent screen; unlike the terrorist, he had a perfect view of the person he was speaking to. "Enough games. We're both far too old for such nonsense. I know what it is you want, and believe me I've already seen your nice little video. I'm sure you'll appreciate, the prime minister is very selective with whom she shares her video footage."

"Ah, then may I assume from your claims you are a member of the JIC?" the Anjouvin fished. "Or perhaps something strictly off the record."

"Who is it you're working for? You know I'll find out one way or another. I already know who's standing alongside you."

"The chip your man entered into the main console works well," Blanco conceded, quietly admiring what he was hearing. On one of the screens, he saw repeat footage of Mike leaving the room, releasing at least two grenades down the stairs and eventually disappearing through a door in the kitchen. "However, sadly for your man, he chose poorly. The passage, I fear, leads to a dead end."

"Well, I guess that's his own problem." The Director leaned over the terminal, his hands gripping the work desk, his eyes still fixed on the live footage that clearly showed Blanco seated in the security room. "Enough games, let's deal. What exactly is it you want?"

"If you truly have the ear of the prime minister, you already know the answer to this. The jewels on display are nice, perhaps even valuable. However, they are not the same as those created long ago. The choice for your prime minister is simple: relinquish the true jewels or London will burn."

Blanco hung up the phone and returned his gaze to the screens, somewhat surprised the strangers hadn't returned. At least three of his men had followed them into the cellar.

All had come back, apparently mystified.

"Make sure every inch of this building is searched. You never know, perhaps there is an entrance to a tunnel somewhere within the walls. We all know this place has many."

He left the room and marched swiftly into the office of the Chief Yeoman Warder, making himself at home. He picked up the same phone Mike had used not fifteen minutes earlier but decided against using it.

Instead he used his satellite phone.

Fieschi was seated in the same place, alongside Jérôme, alternating his attention between the French doors and the television. The experience was strange. Watching the fires as they appeared on the news while simultaneously enjoying a clear first-hand view of the actual events was uniquely captivating.

Jérôme had picked the perfect place to watch the fireworks.

Fieschi answered as soon as he heard his ringtone. "They're saying on the news that the fires have spread to the north. I must say, from here it looks like they're still to beat the wind. Nevertheless, congratulations are in order."

At the other end, Blanco showed little emotion. "What news from France?"

"As a matter of fact, I received a call from my father about ten minutes ago. All are safe and upstream. The jewels will be left in a secure place."

"They are original?"

"Unlike our British cousins, the museum doesn't seem to believe in cheating their countrymen."

Blanco could barely contain his joy. While two of the night's missions had encountered problems, another had come up trumps.

"I hope the same won't be true once this makes the news."

"Back home things like this never make the news; you know this. Even in the art world, people know how to hold their tongue. However, I'm sure it won't take long before the gendarmes are alerted."

"All of which has been planned for." Blanco rose to his feet and headed for the window. From there, the views of the city were obscured, his attention instead taken almost solely by the White Tower. "I trust the yacht will escape a similar fate."

"I've told you before, your love of architecture betrays you. However, I should warn you even if it were to lose half its stern, I doubt Robert would be willing to sell."

A wry smile. "A man who is hard to please, I think we can both agree. The duke is with you?"

"*Oui.*"

"Tell him his nephew would rather like a word."

François was waiting by the door, his usually calm face turned up in a scowl. "Uncle?"

Fieschi handed over the phone to Jérôme. "You are safe?"

"We are in the office of the chief, along with the fraudulent jewels. So far neither the governor nor the prime minister have been willing to assist our cause."

"You know as well as I, our quests for the keepsakes of our ancestors have rarely been achieved overnight. If the night allows, perhaps another perusal of Sir Walter's manuscript might serve you well."

"I have been through it many times. The picture, though elegant, is useless."

"It is at times like this I remember the words of the scientist who once lived in a building close to where you are now. Only by keeping the object of enquiry before your eyes will the cold light of day reveal her secrets."

"I admire the sentiment; that and the man who said it." The young art director remembered learning on his previous visit that Sir Isaac Newton had once lived within the Tower walls on Mint Street. "In six hours these buildings will no longer exist. It is hard to find something in such time when it has remained hidden for six months."

"Patience, François," the duke repeated. "Remember, even if the location of the jewels remains hidden from our eyes, the greatest cards remain in our hands. The threat of death is a powerful bargaining tool."

Randek led the governor as far as the final door before grabbing him by the collar. The man's earlier smart appearance, his crisply pressed white shirt a perfect complement to his recently ironed trousers, had since become somewhat dishevelled.

"Think hard, General. The fate of many great things may tonight rest on your mistakes."

Breaking eye contact, the governor kept his head bowed as he proceeded to Randek's instructions and re-entered More's room. He remembered hearing a rumour in his early days in the role that what people believed to be the real jewels were actually impressive substitutes. As the second most senior man in service, he was aware that only three people knew the true location.

Under the circumstances, he was glad he wasn't one of them.

In the lounge of the luxury apartment, Fieschi stood before a modern fax machine, holding a solitary sheet of paper in his hand. After dialling the number Jérôme had given him, he inserted it and collected it again from the other side. The display confirmed it had been sent.

Now all he could do was wait.

On the north bank of the Thames, the SWAT team prepared to explore the flaming wreckage. The fires had largely died down, leaving only a few below deck that continued to burn.

From the bank, the leader assumed recovery was doubtful.

***

Kit heard Maria's voice in his ear. "Maria, what news?"

"The SWAT team have started their search."

"Anything?"

"Nothing yet. Not even a finger. Anything that comes my way, I assure you, you'll be the first to hear of it." She delayed briefly, her eyes on her iMac. "I've got a new lead for you. Does the name Gillian McKevitt mean anything to you?"

"Should it?"

"Not necessarily, though I understand you visited her gallery today. She's Director of the National Portrait Gallery."

Kit recalled his previous visit to the gallery, a quick stop on the top floor to appease Sharon's desire to see the Tudor monarchs. It already seemed like a long time ago.

"You're very perceptive. Why's this important?"

"Grosmont managed to insert one of Phil's decoders into the main security system in the Waterloo Barracks. As well as being able to confirm Blanco and Randek, we also managed to get facial recognition on a François de Haulle. I'm guessing the name means nothing."

"No more than Gillian."

"A couple of years back, the gallery had a break-in. Two portraits were stolen: one a valuable van Dyck, the other a civil war soldier. Word has it, de Haulle was involved."

"So he's an art thief?"

"Actually, a director; not to mention one of the most renowned experts in Europe. Through his great-grandparents, he's related to Blanco. According to their ancestry, had the Revolution not taken place, they would even lay claim to Normandy and Anjou."

"Shame good old Louis lost his head, then, isn't it?"

"Right now, de Haulle is the only character we have with a clear pedigree external to Bordeaux and the only one with an otherwise flawless reputation. I have an address for McKevitt; it's in Kensington. I suggest you check it out."

Kit was livid. "Much as I appreciate the thought, Maria, might I remind you every street in front of me is currently on fire?"

"Might I also remind you what you said to me earlier about not being a fireman?" She placed her hand through her hair, tightening her ponytail. "The choppers are due in imminently; better yet, traffic on King William has cleared. You can either stay there marshalling traffic or you can find out what the hell this art director has to do with what could well be the original motive behind this attack!"

While the SWAT team continued to comb the flaming wreckage, on the south side of the river two figures made their way breathlessly to shore. Though both had suffered multiple burns, they still had use of their limbs.

Sanders was first to leave the water, inhaling desperately for air. His lungs no longer gasping, he returned to the water as the second man struggled behind him.

Together they collapsed on the bank.

In an office at Buckingham Palace, the chief of staff saw a flickering light from across the room, followed by the sound of an incoming fax. Though getting correspondence in the evening wasn't at all unusual, it was the first he'd seen in over seven hours.

Leaving his desk, he retrieved the freshly printed sheet of paper and scanned the content quickly.

Moments later he left the office and headed into the royal apartments.

48

The Byward Tower,
23:41

The passage led to a stairway. The way was dark and narrow, ending at a retractable wooden wall. Mike emerged slowly, carrying Emily, who was shaking badly from exposure to the cold passageway while still wearing the same clothes as before. Trudging through the darkness had been like a brief return to hell; at no point was the end in sight.

Mike thanked God Emily was lighter than Rawlins.

"As I told you yesterday, Special Forces is about brotherhood," the Israeli continued as he strutted the parade ground. "If someone is injured in battle, they are not left behind. No one suffers alone, dies alone. If one of your brothers is bleeding, your attitude is I'll carry him even if I have to die. Am I clear?"

"Yes, sir!" The reply shot out of every mouth.

"Captain Rawlins, I understand you were injured training with the Navy SEALs. How is your ankle?"

"Fine, sir!"

"You are not fine, you are injured." The Israeli's words delivered all eleven of the Harts into hysterics. "Lieutenant Hansen."

"Yes, sir."

"You understand what I'm saying? In battle, no man is left behind."

"I understand, sir."

"Good. Captain Rawlins, he is injured. He cannot run up that hill. Will you carry him, or are you gonna quit on me?"

Another test, again psychological. Rawlins was an ox; Mike guessed sixteen stone, perhaps three stone heavier than himself.

"No, sir. I'll carry him even if I have to die."

"Good. Put Captain Rawlins on your shoulder."

Mike picked up Rawlins and carried him up the hill. Zahavi shadowed him at every moment. As the climb continued, Rawlins' weight began to affect him.

"On your shoulder, Hansen. Keep him on your shoulder," the Israeli barked. "Are you quitting on me? Are you quitting on me?" Mike felt fists on his right arm. "Do not let him touch the ground."

He made it to the top without touching the ground. Ten minutes attempting to balance Rawlins' weight had left his shoulder and neck sore. Zahavi noticed him massage it the moment he put Rawlins down.

"What's the matter? Are you quitting on me?"

"No, sir."

"Are you sure? Are you made out of steel, or are you a pussy?"

"Steel, sir."

"Good. Stop kissing yourself better and carry him back down. On your shoulder. Come on. Move."

Standing alone on the parade ground, Mike faced Zahavi for the final time. *"I pushed you very hard; you didn't give in. You controlled your aggression. Hansen, I like your style. You've got some good qualities. Good luck."*

He found himself not in a medieval dungeon with walls showing the signs of age and decay, but a modern living room, rich in technology. Exploring the nearby bedroom, Mike saw photographs on the wall, men in uniform.

They had entered the lodgings of a Yeoman Warder.

Emily struggled at first on regaining her feet before closing off the stairway behind her to combat the wind and dampness. With the door closed, Mike found himself looking at wooden panelling, apparently part of the original décor.

"You knew about this?"

"Actually, no!" Emily replied, exploring her surroundings for the first time. "Your friend enjoy her job?"

Not for the first time, Mike sensed some hostility towards Maria. "Far as I know."

"Pity." Emily raised her eyebrow, the lines on her forehead creasing. "We could really do with someone of her knowledge. She knows more about this place than me!"

Mike smiled, half in humour, half in resignation. Though the threat of capture had for now been quelled, he found himself thinking about Sanders and Jay.

Emily picked up on his despondency. "You okay?"

Mike took a seat on the three-piece suite, knowing in all honesty it was a question he couldn't answer. Picking up the remote, he pointed it at the screen. Sky News was confirming the fires had spread to the north, the most recent starting at St Clement's Church. The breaking news at the bottom of the screen also referred to reports of bridges collapsing at the Tower of London.

"Slightly more than reports," he said dryly.

Emily was furious. "You seriously have nothing better to do than watch TV?"

"Right now, I'd say it's helpful to know what we're dealing with." He accessed his satphone, curious to see whether recent intel agreed with what was being said on the news. Sky mentioned nothing about an intrusion at the Tower, nor the hostages.

According to the presenters, the cause of the fires was terrorist related, but no one had come forward to claim responsibility.

To Emily, his response seemed inadequate. "You maybe think we can worry about ourselves first? The fires in London are beyond these walls; right now we're going nowhere. I suggest you try concentrating on getting us out alive."

Mike bit his lip, taking in her features. She was right, he knew. Even the hostages could only be helped if he had a plan. Rather than focus on the HD pictures, or worse yet his friends, the words of the Director replayed over in his mind.

The City of London depended on them.

"You're right. We need to come up with a plan. Part one of which could be to get out of these wet clothes." He left the couch, removing his black ops gear, showing no remorse for baring his muscular torso. "At least here we have a place to think. You said it yourself: there are no cameras here."

Emily agreed, doing the same, her ample breasts showing up clearly beneath her soaked blouse. Slowly, she unbuttoned it.

"You maybe not wanna stand here?" She glared at him. "Try the wardrobes."

Mike smiled, moving quickly into the bedroom, espying a double bed surrounded by the usual furnishings, the walls largely bare save a selection of replica artwork and photographs of the owner and his family. Among them, he saw an impressive framed portrait of the man he guessed was the current tenant, dressed in the famous uniform.

"This is the chief's apartment!" he said, examining the picture. Moving on, he opened the wardrobe, stunned by what he saw.

Emily entered, joining him before the open doors.

"That would look right at home on you!" She removed the famous blue undress uniform and tried it up against him. "Then again, maybe not."

"Maybe in about twenty years. And about five stone."

"You'd be lucky!" She grinned, checking the rest of the wardrobe for something more feminine. "You know the Tudor State Dress can cost over seven thousand pounds?"

Mike raised an eyebrow, surprised but not shocked. He remembered hearing once that every uniform included gilded stitching.

"He got any towels?"

Emily tossed him the first she saw. "That should do till our stuff dries."

Mike noticed a map of the Tower in a frame on the wall, every aspect perfectly outlined. He moved towards it. "Where exactly are we?"

Emily joined him, replacing her glasses and removing the frame from the wall. "We're somewhere here." She pointed at the Byward Tower. "If this is the chief's apartment, we should be right here."

Mike headed for the nearest window, hoping to obtain a view. While the flat's interior was modern, evidence of the building's dark past could be found in the metal bars crossing original windows. "Can we get to the Queen's House from here?"

"Not that I know of; then again, I've learned a lot myself tonight. Legend has it that at one time there was a connection to the Old Wardrobe, but that no longer exists."

"Where was it?"

Emily pointed to a ruined area of masonry where they'd earlier taken refuge to evade the mysterious gunmen following the abrupt ending of the Ceremony of the Keys. "There's not much left of it now."

"Is there any way out of here?"

"With the gates closed, the only way out would be through one of the windows. Even if we managed it, the bridge is destroyed."

Mike nodded, remembering. As he glanced out the nearest window, the effects became clear for the first time. Large piles of rubble could now be seen in the moat; further afield crowds continued to gather. Amongst the chaos Mike saw flashing blue lights.

The last thing he wanted was police or military action.

He left the bedroom, taking in the remainder of the apartment, finishing up in the kitchen. He flicked the switch for the kettle and went through the cupboards, suddenly aware he hadn't eaten in hours.

He tore open some biscuits, sharing them with Emily. "See what else you can find in there."

"This isn't exactly the time for a dinner party."

"We have no idea how long we're gonna be here," Mike answered as he ate. "Least this gives us something to do while we think of a plan and wait for our clothes to dry."

Emily delved deep into the cupboards while Mike continued to examine the map of the Tower. The Byward Tower formed part of the outer defences, the outermost ring of two. The Queen's House was located inside the inner ring, adjoining the Bell Tower. Getting there across open ground was impossible without attracting attention.

Their only hope was to find something below ground.

Blanco returned to the security room, finding the guards unmoved since the last time. The bodies of his men had since been removed; a trail of blood ended at a closed door.

"What's happening?" the Anjouvin asked on entering, his eyes firmly fixed on the screens. One floor below, a solitary gunman kept vigil over the kitchen; he knew several more were still searching the cellar.

"Searches of the cellar have come up empty," the bearded gunman seated before the screens confirmed, the same man who had recently had his hands bound. "There is no sign of the Englishman or his lady."

His lady, Blanco raised an eyebrow. Surely a coincidence.

Blanco re-watched the footage captured by the locked-off cameras, again seeing nothing out of the ordinary. After several seconds of silence, he raised his HT from his belt and contacted Randek.

"Fabien, do you copy?"

A response came almost immediately. "What is it?"

"Send the next six to the White Tower, along with the Ravenmaster. The hour will soon be upon us."

At the other end, Randek was confused. "Why make greater work for ourselves when six remain alive?"

"If the PM responds to our demands, it may not be necessary to kill anybody. Nevertheless, for now it will act as a reminder to the governor, no man is an island."

Randek understood. "What of the Servant?"

"No one can vanish into thin air. In time he will be found." Blanco checked his watch. "Send them quickly. I'll leave it for you to decide who shall make the walk!"

Champion saw light appear suddenly to his right. The tone was familiar, more a half-light than anything brighter; he associated what he saw with the sounds of creaking.

And also the faces of his captors.

He hadn't realised he'd been dozing. With the doors closed, the dark enclosure was barren in appearance; it was still tough to imagine anyone had once lived down here in luxury. He recalled reading once that during More's incarceration, the room had been fitted with fine carpets, the wine goblets never empty. It was a small courtesy by a giant man – one who sought to buy his allegiance.

Tonight, there had been no such offers.

Two gunmen entered, preceding the arrival of the blond man, the person he associated with a position of command. Despite his prominence, he sensed another had an altogether greater influence.

He knew he was still to meet that man.

Randek re-entered to initial quiet, the faces of those around him consumed by new terror. Champion saw him pick out figures at random, six in total; like before, he seemed content to split up families. One by one they were marched out the door, the silence broken by sounds of sobbing. Adjusting to the new darkness, realisation began to dawn. Exactly an hour had passed since the previous hostages were taken.

It was only a matter of time before his own number came up.

49

South of the River Thames, 23:45

Jay awoke suddenly, a strange tinny sound echoing in his ears. His body was sore, his head pounding, but even that wasn't the worst of it. His right arm was in agony, the skin burning as though it had recently been on fire. Rolling over and adjusting his sleeve, he saw most of his skin was absent, a red layer that had once been brown.

His right arm was heavily scorched.

He raised himself slowly, fighting the urge to pass out. There were sounds nearby: sirens, perhaps across the water; beyond the familiar whining, it was difficult to pinpoint things exactly. It was warm despite the wetness. Across the water, he could see the cause of his discomfort.

A boat was on fire, the wreckage smouldering. That was when he remembered.

He had been aboard when it exploded.

He looked around, gazing at the nearby bank, realising he'd somehow made it safely to land. Racking his memory, he had no idea how he'd got there.

He accredited it to the man alongside him.

Sanders was lying flat out with his eyes closed, his chest rising and falling slowly, confirmation he was alive. There were cuts to his face, forehead and neck; bloodstains in the strands of his beard. There were similar marks along his arms; unlike himself, his sleeves were missing.

Jay reached out to him, shaking him, calling his name. Slowly Sanders came to.

"Where are we?"

"South Bank, I think." Jay moved his head; even that was now painful. He gazed further afield, his attention north of the water. Beyond the flaming wreckage he saw the Tower, its appearance strange. Further afield, the bridge was lit up in its usual colours; to the west, far stranger and more sinister colours were visible.

Above the city's many buildings, a thick, rising smoke veiled the horizon.

Sitting up alongside him, Sanders was similarly confused. A series of strange images filled his mind; the last thing he could clearly remember had been exploring a grand stateroom like something out of Versailles.

Only the layout had been more like that of the *Royal Yacht Britannia*.

Suddenly it dawned on him. "Those bastards!" He rose to his feet, his eyes on what remained of the yacht. There were people aboard, others on nearby speedboats.

Jay noticed them.

"Hey, we're over here!"

* * *

The voice in Maria's ear caught her totally off guard.

"Hey, I hear you missed me!"

Maria felt her heart skip on hearing Jamal Iqbal's voice. "What happened?"

Jay grinned as he watched Sanders follow him off the high-powered speedboat driven by one of the members of the SWAT team. Standing on the north bank of the Thames, he surveyed with mixed emotions what remained of the yacht. What had nearly been his doom had actually been his salvation.

"Do you want the short answer or the long one?"

Maria saw the Director return from his office; he had done so regularly throughout the last hour. Rather than reply directly to Jay, she informed him, "Iqbal and Sanders are alive."

Without breaking stride, the Director tuned in to the conversation. "Grailly, this is the King."

"I honestly never thought I'd be so glad to hear that sexy voice of yours, sire."

Somehow, among the chaos, the Director managed a smile. "What happened?"

"Not sure exactly. One second we were checking out this slick dining room with gilded tableware; next I'm waking up on the South Bank, freezing my butt off but with burns all over my arms. Warwick says I owe him one."

"You can settle your debts later. Was there anyone else on board when the bomb went off?"

"Not unless we're missing something. Take one sick son of a bitch to put a stick of dynamite in his own sock. Then again, from what I'm hearing, things aren't getting much better in the city."

"You saw no sign of anyone?"

Maria had been listening in. "When Payet let off the bomb at Covent Garden, he activated it electronically. Chances are it's the same this time. Whoever set it off could have been miles away."

"If not less than a mile." The Director was now looking intently at the security scenes from inside the Tower. Blanco had left the top floor of the barracks, heading for the exit. "Where are you now?"

"Back on the north side. Close to where the gunmen were seen leaving the yacht."

"Good. In that case, report to Beauchamp and the others. The fires at Monument might be out, but the ones to the north are getting worse."

The feeling of relief was almost tangible, especially to Maria. Changing the images on the screen, she was able to see the familiar figures of Jamal Iqbal and Robert Sanders preparing to make their way north.

Burns aside, neither man appeared to have suffered any lasting injuries.

"What's the latest with Masterson?" the Director asked, standing with his hands on his hips, his eyes busily taking in images from further afield. While

Ward, Wilcox and Chambers were all accounted for, Kit wasn't.

"He's currently en route to the home address of the gallery's director."

"Get him on audible."

Maria typed rapidly at her keyboard. "Edward, do you copy? What's your position?"

Less than two miles away, the captain in the field sat in the passenger seat of a black hatchback, his tuxedo replaced by casual covert ops attire. "Just approaching South Kensington. Right now traffic is just as bad even away from the flames."

"That'll teach you to want a property near Chelsea, then, won't it? What's your ETA?"

Kit checked his watch before returning his attention to the gridlocked road. "According to the satnav, fifteen minutes. Maybe less if the traffic clears."

"Keep us posted on your arrival. Oh, and, by the way, Grailly and Warwick are alive. They just went for a little swim."

Kit had never felt so relieved. "I hope they brought their trunks. What's happening in the city?"

"The blaze at St Clement's is under control. Wish the same could be said about the buildings next to it."

"Have the choppers come in?"

"Should be any minute now."

"Let's hope they don't waste time."

The Director listened without getting involved, quietly livid that aircraft assistance had taken so long. "How long does it take to get these things?"

"They're being flown in from the West Country. Problem was none of them were nearer."

"That'll teach the Defence Secretary a lesson for being unprepared!" The Director rubbed his clean-shaven face, ruing further evidence of sod's law at work. He turned his attention back to the images of the Tower, seeing no sign of Mike. "Any update on Hansen?"

"He hasn't shown up on surveillance after he entered the cellar of the barracks," Phil confirmed; since Mike had achieved access to the screens, he'd been watching religiously. "Unfortunately there aren't cameras everywhere."

"Where exactly do you expect him to come out?"

"Byward Tower!" Maria beat Phil to an answer. "If this is correct, it should be the chief's apartment."

"Why are there no cameras?" the Director pressed.

"It's private property. Officially they're people's homes."

"What about the GPS?"

Maria checked the White Hart network, following the white dots. She saw one in the Byward Tower.

"According to this, he's made it!"

"Do we have a landline for the chief's apartment?" the Director asked.

"If there is, we should be able to find it."

"Put through a call. If we can't reach him via the satellites, maybe we can do it again the old-fashioned way."

Inside the Cabinet Office, the PM's chief of staff entered briefing room A without knocking.

"We've had further correspondence from the terrorists. This just came through to the palace."

He handed the prime minister a single sheet of paper, clearly a copy of something original. Putting on her reading glasses, she scanned the content quickly.

"What is this?"

"Received by fax at 23:31. The number has been impossible to verify."

Removing her glasses, the PM's expression was one of disbelief. Of the few lines of communication, only part was instantly recognisable.

"Get me the Prince of Wales!"

50

The Inner Ward, 23:52

Blanco approached the White Tower after leaving the barracks moments earlier. The September sky had darkened considerably in recent minutes, the peculiar cloud covering overlaid by an equally strange red tinge. There was a famous saying in England: a red sky at night was a shepherd's delight.

Tonight he knew it had other connotations.

He emerged on to the Broadwalk Steps as Randek approached from the Queen's House, his usual retinue escorting the latest batch of hostages. Joining the six was the Ravenmaster, still dressed in his famous uniform, a sad frown on his bearded face.

Blanco placed his HT to his lips as he moved.

"Where are you?"

In the heart of the City of London, away from the flames, the silhouetted figure moved rapidly through the crypt of the 17th-century church. Hearing Blanco's voice, he answered, "Everything is in place. All that remains is to ignite the fuse."

"Good. Await my signal."

Blanco slowed his pace on reaching the south lawn, pausing for the arrival of Randek. He reserved most of his attention for the Ravenmaster.

"Mr Collins!" Blanco addressed the Beefeater as he reached a point parallel to the ruins of the great hall and gestured to the ravens' cages. "If you please."

The PM paused midsentence as the flat-screen television inexplicably returned to life, providing a live transmission from the roof of the White Tower. She recognised the face of the same villain she'd seen before, alongside the Ravenmaster.

"Prime Minister, an hour ago I warned you of the penalties of not agreeing to our demands. Now you shall pay that next penalty."

The screen went blank before being replaced by a street view; it was obviously somewhere in London.

"Where is that?" the PM asked, staring intently at the screen. A tall church tower was located on a street corner, a domed apex crowning the adjoining building. Beyond it, the buildings were more modern, including a tower block.

"St Stephen Walbrook! Located on Walbrook between Cannon Street and Bank Tube stations," the bespectacled director of MI5 answered immediately.

"It looks like St Paul's," the Home Secretary added.

"Perhaps not a coincidence," the black, shaven-headed chief of police added. "Tradition has it, Wren based his design for the church on the original plan for the cathedral. One of the twenty-nine surviving Wren churches to have replaced those lost in the Great Fire."

The PM concentrated on what she saw, studying both the church and the surrounding features. The street itself could have been anywhere in London.

Indeed the baroque dome was instantly recognisable.

Off camera, Blanco placed his HT to his mouth and spoke clearly. "Richard, do you copy?"

At the other end, the silhouetted figure kept to the shadows, awaiting his instructions. He knew any passers-by were about to receive the shock of their lives.

"Ready."

"Good. The prime minister is watching."

Lingering close to the crypt, the silhouetted figure removed the small electronic device from his pocket and peered at the wall in front of him. Under the circumstances it seemed a shame such harm would come to such a fine building – it seemed like sacrilege, but not just for its religious significance.

The man who had designed it had indeed been a genius.

Ensuring he wasn't seen, he approached the walls in front of him, his thumb hovering over the strange device.

Finally he pressed it.

The prime minister was stunned. The 17th-century church, seconds earlier a sight of solitude and tranquillity, the stone of its epic façade reflecting the nearby street lighting, suddenly became consumed by a developing inner glow. Fire was taking hold within, spreading slowly but inexorably in both directions.

The picture changed, returning to Blanco. "Unless the real Crown Jewels of England and Scotland are revealed, their capital cities will burn and the Tower will be no more. Use your time wisely, Prime Minister." The Anjouvin stared deeply into the camera, the fires beyond the walls of the White Tower flickering effortlessly in the colour of his irises. "I have warned you once of the horrors that await."

The PM was livid. "Do you honestly understand what you're demanding of us? We can't just hand over the Crown Jewels of England at a moment's notice. Even if you are correct that what you've seen tonight are copies, I have no idea where they could possibly be kept."

Unlike with the governor, Blanco suspected a lie. "Fail to meet our demands and the dear old city will witness a far greater conflagration, the like of which has never before been seen." He pointed the camera over the battlements, focusing on the new fires. On the maximum zoom, the burning dome of Stephen Walbrook was clearly visible, the scenes matching those that had recently appeared on screen. "It was said on its creation that the architect simply marvelled at what he saw, for within that dome he saw an image that would one day shape his destiny."

Blanco took a step back, holding up a raven.

"I suggest you move quickly. You now have five hours!"

The raven fell dead.

The picture went blank.

A stunned silence fell over the briefing room, the faces of all present focused on the screen.

"Who exactly is this man?" The PM broke the silence.

"Bizante Blanco, born in Angers, raised in Marseille, currently believed to reside in Bordeaux," the head of MI6 began. "Uncle to well-known terrorist Fabien Randek, himself witnessed on screen tonight; also a relation through marriage of the late Everard Payet. No prior history of this sort of thing; however, he clearly shares his nephew's ambitions. Through another relative, Victor Varane, he was rumoured to have been on the fringes of the French Connection, though much of that was before his time."

The PM nodded, recalling recently covered ground with the Director of the White Hart. "Ignoring for a moment how he's achieved what he has so far, what of his demands? Is he on to something?"

"The Crown Jewels of England reside in the Tower of London and have done throughout their existence – everyone knows this," the Home Secretary said.

"Rumours of a secret chamber have long been popular among the conspiracy theorists; especially our American cousins," the Foreign Secretary agreed. "Personally, I've seen no evidence to the contrary."

"Has anyone here examined them? Possess the relevant training or expertise in fine jewellery?" The PM looked gauntly across the table. "What if he is correct?"

"Whether he is or not, he certainly believes it to be true. Furthermore, clearly at least one among his party seems to have the ability to be able to tell one from the other," the head of New Scotland Yard added. "That alone is troubling."

"Has Her Majesty been informed?" the head of MI5 asked. "Or the prince for that matter?"

"The fax we just read was sent directly to the palace," the Home Secretary reminded him. "Even if Her Majesty hasn't seen it, we must assume she isn't oblivious to her city burning."

The PM nodded, concerned there were words on the message that the terrorist was still to clarify.

"How do we know the jewels weren't replaced long ago?" the dark-haired head of MI6 added. "During the Blitz, everything was moved away; to say nothing of the turmoil of previous years. Say someone chanced upon it then."

"The Crown Jeweller is the only person permitted to assess the jewels," the Home Secretary said. "At least aside from occasions of state."

"Is he trustworthy?" the military man pressed.

"No less so than his predecessors."

"Even if the real jewels are hidden from sight, one does not simply hand over twenty billion pounds to a man starting fires and shooting ravens!" the head of police said, slightly animated. "Whatever has occurred tonight has resulted from significant funding and prior planning; hand the jewels over and we could potentially be funding an extended terror spree."

"Fail to do so, the world watches our city burn and the Tower crumble live on twenty-four-hour news!"

The PM took a deep breath, slumping back into her chair. If the jewels were fake, she knew only one other would know the truth.

That and the location of the real ones.

She looked around at all present. "First things first, let's doubly secure all roads – put the city on lockdown if necessary. No one leaves without being checked; nor under any circumstances is anyone allowed to enter it besides the emergency services. Once we've done that, get me a secure line to the palace. After that I will speak to the Mayor, the Constable of the Tower, the French premiere, the German premiere, the First Minister of Scotland; finally the Americans. When possible, get me an expert on defence and French terrorism. And will someone finally refill my coffee!"

Standing with his hands pressed firmly against the battlements, Blanco looked west as new flames crept up above the skyline. In the midst of the fires, he saw a large modern building collapse, the glass façade imploding as its structure melted.

"For more than six days and seven nights the citizens of Rome watched as their city succumbed to its apocalypse," Blanco said, sensing Randek's presence alongside him. "My father once told me it's not evil that ruins the earth, Fabien, but mediocrity. The crime was not that Nero played his violin when his city was burning. The crime was that he played it badly."

An ironic smile formed on Randek's lips. "As a master musician, I bow to your expertise. If he were here, I'm sure Everard would have seen the humour in it."

"If he were here, I'm sure so would Emperor Nero, but for completely different reasons." He moved his gaze to the frightened hostages, saving the last for the Ravenmaster. Slowly, he approached him.

"I once heard a raven happily lived here for more than forty years." He eyed the Beefeater, receiving little in the way of response. "Sadly for his cousins, I sense their time will be far more limited. The final bullet I will save for yourself. Unless you would like to take it earlier?"

The Beefeater held his tongue, hiding his aggression; inside, he felt like he wanted to explode. It seemed as though the eyes of the foreigner had been on him as long as time had existed.

Even though in reality it had been mere seconds.

Blanco turned to his gunmen. "Take them downstairs; put them with the others. Perhaps when they fail to return, it might encourage their governor to talk."

51

Central London,
00:04

The first of the six single-engined, three-bladed helicopters swooped sharply over Tower Bridge, descending close to the water. On the pilot's orders, the co-pilot activated the mechanism to drop its unique Bambi Bucket beneath the surface, hauling out over 100 gallons of river water. One by one a further five French-built helicopters followed suit before heading north over the danger area. On reaching the fire, they emptied their buckets.

Before heading in sequence back to the water.

Tommy Ward heard the steadily increasing noise of the helicopters begin to rival the sounds of the nearby inferno, prompting him to turn his attention to the sky. He remembered experiencing one of its sister crafts in his former life, tackling a forest fire out on manoeuvres in Belize.

He knew the force of the water itself was potentially deadly.

"Get down!" He grabbed Wilcox and Chambers, who were standing within metres of him on the warmer side of King William Street. As they hurried across the now deserted street, he felt the dowsing effect of over 600 gallons of water falling into the heart of the flames, successfully damping them down. Against the cloudy backdrop, a strange thick vapour enveloped the atmosphere, creating a strange rainbow across the sky. He looked at it, breathless.

Not only was he seeing the city burn but rainbows appearing in the sky at night.

He contacted the Rook via his headset. "Helicopters have arrived; they've just dropped their first buckets on St Clement's."

Watching similar footage on screen, Maria caught his every word. "How's it looking?"

Panting, Tommy Ward accepted Chambers' hand, pulling him to his feet. Though the buildings were still burning, the first pass had definitely had a positive effect.

"Seems, hopefully, to be more under control," Ward said, anticipating the choppers' return. "It's still too early to say for certain."

"Where are you now?"

"South side of King William Street. If any of that water hits us, we're gonna be swept away like the tide."

Maria concentrated on the screen in front of her, the city skyline from the Tower to St Paul's visible via distant surveillance footage. The images she'd just seen on the big screen, courtesy of Blanco's latest transmission to the Tower, made perfect sense now. "The fires are spreading to the west; the source was Stephen Walbrook. I suggest you head there now. Make sure everything beyond it is sealed off."

***

Standing in the heart of the room, the Director focused on the same images. Blanco's message had been different this time, the footage alternating between himself, the London skyline and one specific church.

"Do we have confirmation of the location?"

"St Stephen Walbrook, located close to Bank Tube Station," Phil replied. With a single click of the mouse he brought up new images.

The Director studied the pictures, seeing profile shots of the exterior in its prime alongside those of live footage of the building burning. "Where was the previous one?"

"St Clement's, Eastcheap," Maria beat Phil to a response, also bringing up fresh images alongside that of Stephen Walbrook. "Coincidentally, also a Wren church."

The Director raised an eyebrow. Both pieces of Blanco footage had been followed by a fire at a church. "Any connection?"

"Besides its creator," Maria began, "both survived damage in the Blitz and were built on old foundations."

As the Director contemplated the latest images, the face of the prime minister suddenly appeared on the flat screen.

"I assume you've seen the footage?"

The Director neglected to add he'd already seen it twice. "The helicopters have reached the danger zone; from what I'm hearing, the first buckets have already been dropped. If the fire chief is correct in his estimations, another thirty minutes should be enough to tackle the blaze."

"Assuming it doesn't get wider!" The PM's stare was cold and focused. "The church at Walbrook is within a quarter of a mile of our most vital economic asset. I can't tell you how vital it is that isn't affected."

The Director nodded, not requiring a lesson in economics to understand the pitfalls of the destruction of the UK's central bank and currency depository. "If Blanco is telling the truth and there are only five hours left, we can safely assume he'll have other targets in mind." Deep down he wondered whether the destruction of the bank would indeed be one of them. "It's time for us to show our cards, Prime Minister. Is he right?"

"I assure you I don't know what you mean."

"Villains like Blanco don't make idle threats unless they fully believe in them. Nor would they destroy priceless gems and film it if their primary purpose was to steal them in the first place. Where are the real jewels?"

The PM took a tired breath. "I've just spoken to the Prince of Wales. What I'm about to say does not leave your room."

"I understand."

"I'm warning you, Director. Perhaps it would be better if we had this conversation in private."

The Director looked at Maria and Phil, almost apologetically. "Very well." He vacated the room, climbing the stairs to his scholarly office.

The PM's face reappeared on the widescreen.

"What exactly are we dealing with?"

"It seems popular belief for once is correct, albeit not for the right reasons. Prior to the Civil War, the jewels that were kept in the Tower were the originals. However, much has changed in three centuries."

"You know of their location?"

"Not exactly, but His Highness confirmed our suspicions. Not to mention that Blanco was right."

The Director bit his lip. "A fine feat of preparation, it must be said. Clearly we're dealing with a man who leaves nothing to chance."

"Not to mention one who's willing to see an entire city burn in order to achieve a mere robbery." Her jaw tightened, the lines on her forehead deepening. "Time is of the essence, Director. I'm sure I don't need to remind you of this."

"What exactly did the prince say?"

"I'm not at liberty to disclose his exact words; however, as I'm sure you'll appreciate, Her Majesty and all the family are most concerned at this evening's proceedings."

"I take it they both realise if the fires continue, we may have no choice but to part with them."

"What are you suggesting?"

"It's a simple choice, Prime Minister. The jewels or the city."

Again the PM's expression turned hostile. "Surely after all these years you understand our policy on negotiating with terrorists."

"Surely you also appreciate the long-term ramifications of rebuilding what has already been destroyed, let alone what might be necessary." The Director felt the accumulative effect of his skin perspiring beneath his shirt, causing it to stick uncomfortably to his back. "This is far from usual procedure, Prime Minister. This is already about damage limitation."

"Even if the jewels were to be handed over, there's far more to this than just monetary value, Director. Even if we are talking well in excess of twenty billion pounds."

"A drop in the ocean compared to the cost of rebuilding our city! If we are to succeed here, I need complete transparency, as I always have. What did His Highness say?"

"If you're asking about a location for the jewels, I'm afraid we're both out of luck," the PM replied. "That's not to say I didn't ask. However, of more pressing concern, Blanco has made contact there directly."

"They've seen the footage?"

"Actually, no. A mysterious fax was sent not forty minutes ago; the number is still to be traced."

The Director guessed he knew who was responsible. "He threatened them?"

"Under the circumstances, it might be better for you to see it yourself; I'm having it sent through right now."

The Director nodded, confident in the fact the freshly printed piece would soon drop into the feeder tray in the next room. "If Blanco is intent on making threats, it might at least achieve public sympathy, especially in the UN. Then again, even his countrymen are unlikely to endorse this."

"As a matter of fact, I've already spoken to the premiere of France. He's already offered us use of his own military. Unfortunately, it seems they were also subject of a break-in tonight."

"The jewels?"

The PM nodded. "The Louvre, it seems, didn't have the same precautions in place. Unlike Edinburgh."

The Director raised his eyebrows, recalling his conversation with Atkins. "The Honours of Scotland?"

"The Provost was killed at approximately 22:00 hours, the same time as the Ceremony of the Keys was due to end here. Thirty minutes after the fires began there. I've spoken to the First Minister. All the jewels are now missing."

The Director gritted his teeth. "Were they original?"

"The prince assures me they're not."

"I assume I don't need to ask any follow-up questions."

"Not if they concern the locations. The situation in Edinburgh is building fast, but we can't fight a war on both fronts. Where are your men?"

"Somewhere on the Royal Mile. The cathedral and the parliament buildings have all been sealed off."

"Might I suggest they revert their attention to apprehending the thieves? Unlike here, there are no reports of hostages being taken."

"I assure you, Prime Minister, I'll speak to them personally."

Maria heard the fax machine in the corner of the room begin to hum, accompanied by the sight of an incoming document. She left her seat as the Director returned, and scanned it.

Immediately she was confused.

"What is this?"

"This was received by the Palace prior to the time Blanco released his latest video." The Director took possession of the single sheet of paper and looked at Phil. "See if we can get confirmation of who sent it. Check the offices for around 23:30 hours."

"Already on it!" Phil rewound the footage. There was no obvious evidence of a fax being sent from inside the Tower.

The Director, meanwhile, studied the contents for the first time. The picture, of what had originally been a large woodcarving, demonstrated five figures from astrology pouring either water or oil on to a bonfire, above which the Gemini twins were hanging upside down. Accompanying the picture were two lines of text.

Under the watchful eyes of the Gemini, the city burns to ash!
Beware the wrath of the Cardinal's Boys.

The Director viewed the strange image for what seemed an eternity, his gaze transfixed by the cryptic clues. When he'd finally taken everything in, he looked at Maria.

"Beware the wrath of the Cardinal's Boys."

Maria was confused. "What?"

"Beware the wrath of the Cardinal's Boys." He remembered Blanco had mentioned the Cardinal's Boys in his original message. Under the watchful eyes of the Gemini – he'd neglected to say that.

Ask me who we were.

Maria studied it, equally unclear what it meant. The image was clearly more historical than modern; she placed its creation in the 1600s.

"The figures are astrological," she said, slowly making sense of things. "Before the Great Fire, many soothsayers were said to have predicted the event."

"They were assumed to have been involved?"

"Not exactly." Maria shook her head. "But 666 was the number of the beast. Seems everyone associated the coming of the year with some form of great calamity. Most predictions were ambiguous – some just plain confusing."

"It seems the prince was just as confused as we are." He walked across the room, finding Atkins at an otherwise unused terminal, keeping track of activity north of the border.

"What news of Rawlins, Pentland and Pugh?"

"They've made contact with the chief of police and the fire service; unfortunately what we're looking at is a carbon copy of here. While the early fires have been extinguished, new ones are starting!"

The Director leaned over his deputy's shoulder, his focus alternating between live video coverage and a virtual map. The fires so far had all been to the east of the cathedral and were spreading in the same direction.

"Have they spoken to anyone at Holyrood or the castle?"

"As a matter of fact, both lines have been inaccessible."

The Director wasn't surprised. "Well, tell them to make their way up the rock."

"Why?"

"I just spoke to the prime minister. Turns out the Honours of Scotland have also been taken. The provost is dead."

Rawlins and the others had made it as far as Cowgate when the call came through. During the last few minutes the fires had spread, south as well as east. The A7 had been sealed off beyond South Bridge.

Above the nearby rooftops, the flames were clearly getting higher.

Rawlins heard Atkins' voice come through loudly in his ears; though the exact words were lost, he made out enough that he required an update on their whereabouts. In addition to the surrounding distractions, the Deputy Director seemed more than a little flustered.

"We're on Cowgate, just off the High Street," Rawlins replied, his voice equally loud. "The National Library is secure, but the fires are spreading. It's just taken out a nightclub on Niddry Street."

"How's the cathedral?"

"All of the important buildings are secure. I've spoken with the RAF; the choppers should be here within the hour."

"Has there been any contact with Holyrood?"

"Negative. It's like they and the castle have gone off the grid."

Atkins suspected as much. "Head to the castle. I'm afraid we've had a complication."

"What kind?"

Back in London, the Deputy Director placed his hand to his cheek, his fingers rubbing gently against the short, clean-shaven bristles. "I'm afraid the news is the same as in London."

Rawlins was momentarily speechless. "You mean?"

"Rumours right now are unconfirmed. Make your way up the rock and see what you can make out with your own eyes."

The car pulled up on an affluent street in South Kensington, away from the fires. Most of the houses consisted of three storeys, the façades clearly Victorian. The area before the entrances had a nice leafy feel, thick foliage providing a secondary layer of privacy beyond the security of the gated entrances. All of the houses had cars on the drive; more still were parked outside. Most of the light came from outside the houses, the streetlights creating a warm amber glow over the dry tarmac. It was bright in the sky, but not due to the weather.

Though the fires themselves were no longer visible, the message of hell being unleashed remained crystal clear.

Kit unbuckled his seatbelt and told the driver, "Wait here."

Gillian McKevitt hadn't been home long. The day had been hectic, as it always was on a Wednesday. The exhibition that had begun well over a year ago in acknowledgement of the purchase of a ten-million-pound self-portrait by the famous Anthony van Dyck was now only two days away from completion.

Even now, she still counted down the hours.

All in all, it had been quite a couple of years. Ever since the day of the robbery – a unique occurrence that had culminated in a bizarre series of events, initially thought to be an inside job aimed at taking an item of great value, but subsequently proved to be something of even greater significance – the exhibition had lost much of its personal appeal. Even after the portrait's return, it seemed more trouble than it was worth. In certain respects, the extra publicity had been beneficial: the number of visitors had increased to record levels, yet events had taken their toll on the staff. Even after two years, stress levels were still very high.

Gillian knew that she would never relax entirely until the exhibition was officially over and the whole episode was fully behind her.

She sat in the lounge on a three-piece suite, a recently poured rosé in a finely cut glass that had once belonged to her ex-husband. Since returning home, her concentration had been fixed on the news; it was one of those events that just didn't happen every day. A fire had broken out at the site of the famous bakery; the reports confirmed only that it was a terrorist attack. Since then the fires had spread throughout the city. Further trouble had occurred at the Tower.

There were also accounts of a yacht fire.

Seated on the couch, her weary frame sinking into the luxurious fabric, she heard her doorbell ring, twice then a third time. She wasn't used to receiving visitors so late; even when her daughter was home, it was rare. Getting up from the couch, she opened the door to be greeted by a strangely dressed man in his early thirties, his face scarred by what she guessed must have been a quite recent traumatic event.

"Ms McKevitt?"

"Yes."

Kit stood politely in the doorway, examining the woman in front of him. Her blonde hair was thick and full, the glossy conditioned effect losing some of its lustre after what he guessed might have been a hard day at the office.

Had it not been for the lines on her forehead, he could have placed her ten years younger than her true age of fifty-four.

"My name is Kit Masterson. I've been sent here from Whitehall on a matter of national importance."

Gillian was confused. She concluded that it must in some way be associated with the fires. "I'd have thought in view of what I've been seeing on television, Whitehall would have enough on its plate."

"And you would be absolutely right," Kit responded. "I appreciate you're fully aware of the current troubles in our city."

"I've been watching the news, if that's what you mean?"

"Unfortunately for dear old London, the fires are only the tip of the iceberg. There's also been activity at the Tower, and not just falling masonry." Kit removed a folded piece of paper from his inside pocket. "I need to ask you something; please think very carefully. Is this man familiar to you?"

Gillian looked at the piece of paper, attempting to focus without the aid of her reading glasses.

He was.

"The man's name is François de Haulle, an art expert from Angers in France. I understand the name is familiar to you. Along with his uncle's."

Gillian returned the paper and looked at him. "What is it you want?"

"I know it's late, but I'm afraid I'm going to have to request you open up your gallery and fill me in on a few things."

The Director of the National Portrait Gallery was stunned. "I assure you I don't possibly know what help I could be."

"Well, as a start, perhaps we can discuss the theft of the van Dyck and what happened with the de Haulles two years ago."

52

The Byward Tower,
00:11

Mike held his breath as he pushed his face deep below the surface of the water. Despite the situation, the new sensation was somehow comforting, even strangely exhilarating. After an hour in the cold, the temperature now was warm and pleasant. The first moment starved of air had again brought back memories of his training. First with Webbs.

Then Bautista.

The man in front of him was younger than his previous instructors. Unlike the others, his bronzed skin radiated the suppleness of youth with an expression that was raw with hunger and ambition. As expected from the colours of the new flag at camp, the man's features were south-east Asian, his well-honed physique like that of a highly trained and powerful Olympiad at the peak of his powers.

Mike placed him in his late twenties.

While the instructors Mike had previously met had put him through the most demanding and exhausting experiences possible, while at the same time watching over him with a degree of warmth and almost parental concern, the look in this man's eyes was noticeably different. It was somehow wilder, even primordial, like a native hunter seeking to entrap the wild animals that daily threatened his safety. His eyes and senses were constantly alert, ready to strike at any sign of danger.

Mike guessed his background before it was confirmed.

"My name is Lieutenant Bautista. I am still on active service. My unit is NAVSOG of the Philippines."

Mike nodded, satisfied his intuition was serving him well. Though he had heard of the NAVSOG – the Naval Special Operations Group – he knew nothing of their background.

Only that they'd been dubbed the Philippines Navy SEALs.

"Over the next forty-eight hours, I shall be educating you all in the arts of my unit. During this time, you may call me Sir or Tor. It is a common word where I'm from. Short for instructor – or tormentor."

Mike heard laughter among the Harts. On this occasion, he managed to keep his expression neutral.

"Lieutenant Hansen." He looked at Mike.

"Yes, sir."

"I knew it was you. Though you may all dress the same, some stick out for other reasons. Together you stand as twelve, yet there are some here who feel

you don't belong. That you should leave. Are you sure you are prepared to carry on?"

"Yes, sir."

"So be it. In NAVSOG, when instructors meet recruits like you, in order to get acquainted properly, instead of shaking hands, we do twenty push-ups. Each one must be synchronised to the same counting. All of you. Get down."

Mike dropped to the floor; bodies fell like lead around him. For several seconds, he remained poised.

"Lieutenant Hansen, please lead the count."

"Yes, sir. Everybody up. Down. Up."

"One!" the eleven replied.

"Down. Up."

"Two."

"Hold it." The tormentor wasn't satisfied. On this occasion, his complaint was with Rawlins. "What is wrong?"

"My leg is injured, sir."

He looked at Mike. "Did you know this?"

"Yes, sir."

"Then why are you going so fast that he can't keep up?"

Mike bit his lip. "I'll go slower this time, sir."

"What are you waiting for? Start again already."

"Everybody up." Mike glanced along the line at Rawlins. "Down. Up."

"One."

"Down. Up."

"Two."

"Down. Up."

"Three."

"Better," Bautista said. "What we have next is something of a NAVSOG specialty." The lieutenant led the Harts to where Atkins was standing, a quiet area close to the river. Twelve diver's masks had been placed in a large container filled with water. "For this next challenge, your team must transport a log and a casualty to the next checkpoint. Only to add excitement, you must do it wearing one of these."

Mike was speechless; so it appeared were most of the Harts. That tears it, he thought.

He was dealing with a psychopath.

"Successful completion of this task can only be achieved if you have water in your mask." He checked every man in turn. Mike pushed his away and coughed vigorously.

"Lieutenant Hansen, why is there no water in your mask?"

Mike was struggling for breath. "It felt like I was drowning."

"Look around you. See your teammates. All of them have water in their masks." He moved closer, his breath warm against Mike's face. "You do not hate water. You love water. Learn to love it."

* * *

Love the water. That was the command. There was a reason why they did all that training. *Love the water. The ocean is a bitch.*

He heard Emily enter the en suite bathroom the second he raised his head; she was dressed in a towel, recently showered.

"Shower's free if you want it," she offered, clearly feeling refreshed and warmer than before.

She looked cute in a dressing gown.

"I'll pass," Mike replied, spying on her via the mirror as she dried her hair. "Besides, I love the water."

"That because you're a honey badger?" She stared at him, hands on hips. "Why on earth do they call you that?"

"Somehow a few people got it in their heads I'm fearless!"

They returned to the living room; Emily brought out two plates from the kitchen, a small meal on both of them.

"I'm afraid all I could find were cheeseburgers." She offered him a plate with a quarter-pounder burger piping hot from the microwave. "It's the only thing they had in the fridge that was quick."

Mike smiled, imagining how different the situation might have been at another time and place. "Well, I guess it'll have to do." He took the first mouthful, relishing the revitalising properties of the fast food on his depleted energy reserves. As he washed the food down with water, his mind recollected recent events. He still felt drained, cold despite the warmth of the room, but it was another concern that preoccupied his thoughts.

Jay and Sanders were dead.

Emily noticed he was still cold. "Put this on." She brought in the Yeoman Warder's jacket, the thick material fitting snugly round his muscular physique. "If you refuse to shower, the least you can do is keep warm."

"I told you I love the water." Though inwardly he welcomed the offer. "Maybe I should take it anyway. Not often you see one of these on eBay."

"Probably because no one would ever be foolish enough to steal one."

"Either that or no one ever got the chance."

She took the first bite of her burger, her facial expression instantly revealing her dissatisfaction. Mike grinned at her.

"Find something funny?"

Mike devoured almost a quarter of his in one go, remembering as he did so a time he'd had much worse.

The march back to the camp ended at sunset; the buildings cast long shadows in the fading light. Bautista emerged from the canteen with a large metal pot.

Clearly it contained some form of liquid.

"Okay, all of you collect your metal cups. Come on. Move."

Mike lined up alongside the other Harts. One by one, they filled their cups.

Whatever the thickish liquid was, it looked revolting.

"What you see is a NAVSOG delicacy. In your language, it is fish and soy sauce. Mmmm, mmm. Tastes very nice."

The last thing Mike wanted to do was drink it. To his left, even Kit looked unimpressed.

"Once you have finished, I want everyone to put their cups on their heads. Cups on your heads. Lieutenant Hansen, you are cheating."

He was, but he knew he wasn't the only one. To both his left and right, mud-stained jerseys were now layered in fishy liquid.

"Okay, it is that time again. Drop to your chests. Lieutenant Hansen, I want them co-ordinated. First to give up and your team must pay a forfeit."

They made it to thirty before Mike was flagged up for coming out of sync.

"Lieutenant Hansen, come here. Red team, join him."

The tormentor paraded in front of them like a peacock. "I tell you already. What you do here, you do for your team. You make a mistake, your team suffers. Now everyone in red team must drink."

They returned to parade, drinking the horrible liquid on Bautista's orders. Mike finished first; again he was accused of cheating.

"Lieutenant Hansen, are you still to understand? Make mistakes, your team suffers."

Mike looked back with fire in his eyes. "Given the opportunity, sir, I would gladly drink that whole pot if it saved my team from having to do the same."

Along the line, Sanders and Iqbal stifled laughs. Even Kit raised an eyebrow.

"Day one is over. But remember, day one is only the beginning." He saluted his men.

"Gentlemen, good evening."

"All right, let's figure this out." Emily looked at Mike from across the lounge, eating her burger far more slowly. Failing to learn what had made him smile, she chose instead to concentrate on the map of the Tower. "Where do we go?"

Mike moved alongside her, again swallowing what was in his mouth. The map confirmed the Byward Tower was a safe distance from the White Tower and connected to the houses on Mint Street to the north and the outer wall to the east.

"What's in here?" he asked of Mint Street.

"Bottom floor's just a museum; there's a display there on coinage. Rooms above are just apartments."

"Any hidden passageways? Secret tunnels? Things Maria would know about but you wouldn't."

She glared at him. "Perhaps you'd like to ask her?"

He checked his phone and headset. "I would if I had any reception." He took the map, concentrating on the Outer Ward. Even without the bridge, entering the moat and escaping was possible.

But that meant leaving the hostages.

"All right, here's what we'll do. First of all, we'll head here." He pointed to the area beyond the portcullis. "Now, the bridge may be down, but if we get you to the far side of the moat, I reckon with my help we can get you up the incline."

"You want to leave?"

"This escape plan is only for one." He looked her in the eye, the clearly defined hazel irises appearing somehow lighter in the absence of her glasses. "There's no use risking both our lives. If we get you out, we can get you safe. At least you can report what you know."

"And leave you here, are you crazy?"

"You don't wanna know about my sanity." He smiled wryly – in the moment, it brought back further memories of Jay and Sanders. Somewhere on the other side, he sensed they were both looking down at him, laughing.

"There's still at least thirty armed men here. It's only a matter of time before we cross paths. It's madness you staying here."

"It's madness you staying without me."

"I'm not leaving without the hostages. Besides, if Blanco knows I'm gone, he'll probably take it out on them anyway."

"Same logic applies for me. Besides, we've already got a message out to your HQ. For all we know, they're planning something right now."

"I think right now they've got their work cut out with the fires." He looked outside, staring beyond the barred window. Though the fires weren't visible, he sensed a charge in the atmosphere. "Last thing they'd want to do is piss off Blanco further."

"So they accept it?" She folded her arms.

"Think of it more as planned negotiation. Or better yet, playing poker. They wait for him to make his move then act accordingly. Right now isn't the time to show one's cards."

He focused again on the moat, his eyes on the fallen masonry. Crowds remained gathered; a sizeable police presence joined them.

Getting there was doable.

"All right, let's do this. If you make it to the rubble, you'll become visible. The police will get you."

"I told you before, I'm not leaving you. Besides, for all we know, the terrorists have got this place covered. We could be sitting ducks the moment we enter the moat."

"I doubt it. Everyone we know is in the Inner Ward. Once I contact HQ, we could find out for sure."

"And how do you intend to do that with no signal?"

Mike took a deep breath, biting his lip. He knew he was losing the battle. "You know, for a historian, you're pretty stubborn."

She laughed for the first time in quite a while. "Well, you have to admit I do have a point. Without a visual aid, there's no way we can keep tabs on them."

A sharp crackling sound took them both by surprise. Returning to the couch, Mike reached deep into his trouser pocket, pulling out the HT he'd confiscated from the CCTV room. Suddenly he smiled.

"Maybe we do!"

* * *

Blanco watched the television on the far wall of the Chief Yeoman Warder's office as the news channel showed live pictures of the helicopters completing a further pass over the danger area. The fires had spread further since the inferno began at Stephen Walbrook, but the flames further east were lower than they had been. The dowsing effect of the Bambi Buckets had so far proven effective.

It would only be a matter of time before the fires were brought under control.

He heard the HT crackle and a voice speaking, Randek.

"Are you seeing what I am?"

Blanco answered, "If you are speaking of the helicopters on the news, yes, I am. However, you really should be more specific."

In the lounge of the Queen's House, Randek stood alone by the door, watching the news. The presenter provided a commentary as the last of the six made its way over the fires, emptying the contents of its bucket over the highest point of the flames. The overhead camera showed clear evidence that the fire was receding, the helicopter briefly hidden from view by a dense mixture of smoke and steam.

"Personally I'm surprised anyone would be foolish enough to fly so close. Then again, I suppose it is a testament to the balls of the cameraman, the lengths he will go to."

"What goes on outside these walls was never going to be within our control. Military action was always inevitable." Randek rose to his feet, his eyes on the world outside the nearest window. Though the glare of the external lights that continued to flood the courtyard, accompanying those that lit up the walls, made visibility difficult, beyond the White Tower he was able to make out small objects flying within the red cloud.

"In some cases, necessary."

Standing alone in sight of the new fires, the silhouetted figure kept to the shadows. The heat was almost unbearable, causing his skin to redden almost to the point of blistering. All around him buildings were collapsing, spewing huge amounts of debris over the roads and creating large cracks in the tarmac.

In the smoke he could also detect the fumes of melting metal.

He heard a voice come through the HT, Blanco. "*Allô?*"

"Where are you?"

"I had to move to avoid the spray of the water. The fires will not continue long if the helicopters are able to continue unimpeded."

"My thoughts exactly! Do you have your briefcase to hand?"

"You think I would be foolish enough to leave it?"

Blanco smiled. "In that case, I suggest you open it."

53

The Byward Tower,
00:17

Mike recognised Randek's voice the second it came through on the airwaves. The terrorist spoke in French; a language in which, thankfully, Mike was fluent.

The second voice was clearly Blanco's.

Discussions seemed to be centred on what Randek was seeing on the news.

Things were changing in London; it was still not easy to tell whether for better or worse. Six helicopters equipped with Bambi Buckets had arrived recently, apparently from outside London; Mike sensed he had seen them, or similar models, before.

The recent aerial strategy was proving effective in dowsing the flames.

"What are they?" Emily asked, her gaze on the screen.

"The exact model is a Eurocopter AS350; it's a French copter used to combat fires from the air," he explained, noticing that the usual grey exterior had been painted over with standard camouflage colours. "That thing it's carrying can hold up to one hundred gallons of water."

As both of them watched the pictures, Mike continued to eavesdrop, realising Blanco and Randek were discussing the helicopters. After ten seconds of heated dialogue, Blanco began a conversation with someone else.

Emily was also listening. "Sounds like they're discussing tactics."

"Also sounds like the guy he's speaking to is outside the walls."

"He's near Stephen Walbrook. He's talking about the debris."

"You speak French?"

"You're only just figuring that out?"

"In that case, there's no need for me to translate, is there?"

"Keep going. It gives me something to laugh at."

Mike smiled, noticing a soft smirk on her lips. Any other time and place, he knew things might have been very different.

The second conversation over the HT ceased, at which point Blanco resumed the first with Randek. When the sound of voices returned to radio silence, Mike and Emily gazed at one another, stunned by what they'd heard.

"Tell me I didn't hear that correctly!"

Emily bit her lip, speechless. "Actually, I think you probably did."

Below the Old Admiralty Building, Maria saw Mike's GPS was still showing up clearly in the Byward Tower.

"I've got a number for the chief's apartment," she said to Phil. "I'm trying it now."

THE CROWN JEWELS CONSPIRACY

* * *

A second noise sounded in the room, this time more melodious. The telephone was ringing on the nearby coffee table, its red light blinking intermittently.

Mike and Emily looked at one another.

"You gonna get that?"

Mike rubbed his face, the short stubble feeling strangely sharper after recent events. There was no caller ID, which made answering a risk. "If this is Blanco, we're in trouble."

"If it's your HQ, you really need to take it."

Taking a chance, Mike picked up. "Hello?"

Maria smiled on hearing Mike's voice. "Glad you decided to pick up."

He exhaled in relief. "Well, you can never be too careful. For all I knew, the chief was interested in timeshares."

"Matter of fact, he had a nice little place on the coast; used to share it with his kids." She lowered her head, the reality dawning that he'd never get to use it again. "I have some good news and some bad."

"Always start with the bad. What is it?"

"Blanco's made another video; for Downing Street's eyes only. He's also sent a communication to the palace."

"What happened?"

"The video was different. He included footage of St Stephen Walbrook south of Bank. Right on cue, it caught fire."

Mike raised an eyebrow, intrigued. "That's the second time a fire's started in a church."

"Certainly appears that way. Needless to say, the PM was not amused."

"I'd be pretty concerned if she was." Mike kept half an eye on the HT, wondering when it would once again crackle into life. "What happened with the palace?"

"A fax came through around the same time as Blanco's communication with the PM. A simple threat." Maria relayed it word for word.

Under the watchful eyes of the Gemini, the city burns to ash.

Beware the wrath of the Cardinal's Boys.

Mike frowned. "Cardinal's Boys?"

"Mean anything to you?"

"Should it?"

"Not necessarily; right now, your guess is probably as good as any."

"I'll take that as a compliment."

"The picture matches one by the astrologer William Lilly. Apparently he predicted the fire."

"William who?"

"William Lilly!" Emily was listening. "Apparently predicted the fire in 1651. Gemini is the astrological sign for London." She eyed him sternly. "Your uncle mentioned it this evening."

Maria also overheard. "At least one of you knows your stuff."

Mike cursed himself, realising how little he'd taken in of the lecture. "Well, it's a pity he isn't here right now. What's the good news?"

At the other end, Maria's face broke into a smile. "Jay and Rob are alive!"

Mike took a sharp intake of breath as a wave of relief and emotion flowed through him. "What happened?"

"Fortunately for them, they were in the best possible place. Ended up just going for a nice swim instead."

"Probably just what they needed; I hear it's warm out this evening."

"Better than a sauna. Just fortunate for them they were out of the river by the time the Bambis got thirsty!"

"Speaking of which, before we got away from the control room, we managed to get hold of one of the gunmen's communications devices. I can't be sure, as they spoke in French, but it sounded like they were planning something."

"Planning what?"

"I'm not sure exactly, but from what I've seen so far, I wouldn't put any limit on the kind of arsenal these guys might be packing."

"You think they've got heavy artillery?"

"I'm not sure. But whoever Blanco was speaking to, he was clearly under precise orders that he seemed capable of carrying out."

South of Cannon Street Tube station, just off the Hanseatic Walk located close to the Southwark and London bridges, the silhouetted figure made his way through the underpass, coming close to the Thames. Despite the recent chaos, some of the establishments were still open, a steady, high-pitched sound of hurried and anxious conversation, mainly from staff, audible from behind the main doors. Even from a cursory look, it was obvious the number of visitors was limited. It was a part of the city where visitors didn't necessarily have to rely on motor transport to enjoy a nice meal out by the river.

Being after midnight, most of the restaurants had closed.

On taking Walbrook across Cannon Street, the figure continued south, joining the walkway at the end of Cousin Lane. The views of the water were unrestricted here, the nearby streetlights coupled with those of the nearby bridges providing sufficient illumination to take in every feature. Across the water, South Bank looked as it normally did; unlike the area behind him, there were no signs of smoke rising into the heavens. Nor were there sounds of panic. He recalled reading once that during the summer of 1666, many who had evacuated the city took refuge on nearby hillsides, camping out and watching as events unfolded.

As he observed the lights of the famous towers on the skyline, he paused for a moment to wonder what was going through the minds of the residents.

The helicopters were coming in for a further pass, emptying their buckets over the latest fires. As they flew in close to the ground, he could hear without seeing the moment of release, his view of the fires now obscured by nearby walls. Returning his gaze to the water, he saw the first of the six was already losing height, lowering its bucket to be refilled.

Followed by the other five.

Waiting until the five had disappeared, he ensured he was alone before opening his leather briefcase, assembling the item within. Loading the chamber with six circular objects from the upper lining of the briefcase, he set it down on the nearest wall, composing himself.

In a matter of seconds, he knew that its capability would be visible for the world to see.

Emily left the lounge and returned to the kitchen, taking the opportunity to refill her glass with water. She gulped it down and searched the fridge. Finding two bottles of mineral water, she shoved one into her pocket.

"Take this." She offered one to Mike on returning to the lounge. "For all we know, this might be our last chance to stock up."

Mike nodded, still on the phone; Maria was talking about the fires. Most of what he was hearing corresponded with what he saw on the news.

"We can't stay here indefinitely. We really need to think of a plan." He examined the map while still holding the receiver. "Is Phil there?"

"Either that, or someone's done some great plastic surgery."

Mike laughed. "Put him on speakerphone."

Maria pressed the speaker button on her headset, allowing Mike's voice to come through.

"How are the burgers going down, Honey Badger?" Phil asked.

"Zero to tasty in ninety seconds, Phil; you know, I always wondered why people called them Beefeaters."

"Rumour has it even they don't know the answer to that. What else can you see?"

"Was about to ask you the same question. All I've got is one TV."

Phil turned his attention to the screens, clicking his mouse to alternate between cameras. "Blanco's still in the chief's office; seven more are camped out watching CCTV. Far as I can tell, they're not on to us."

"Not that it matters either way," Mike said. "You're still a long way from Kansas."

"Very true. Three more are joining Randek in the Queen's House; right now he's watching the same channel you are. Four more are roaming the Inner Ward."

"What about the hostages?"

"Can't tell, I'm afraid. Twelve are still in the White Tower, watched over by the same jerks as before. Whatever state of luxury Thomas More experienced, they never got round to fitting it with surveillance equipment."

A wry smile. "Tell me more about those roaming the grounds."

"All four are walking in two-by-two formation; they're spending most of their time around Tower Green. Still to see them leave the Inner Ward."

"Any movement on the outer ring?"

"If there is, they're wearing invisibility jackets."

"What are our options?"

The answer came from Maria. "Nearest threat is likely to come from the Inner Ward; as far as we can tell, there's no one presently in the outer. If you could somehow get the main gates open, you should be able to make your way out."

"You know I'm not gonna leave those hostages!"

"I thought you might say that. At least that could get the acting curator to safety."

"I've already made that suggestion; she didn't seem too happy about it."

"Happy about what?" Emily overheard.

"About being forced to spend the night here." He grinned.

She stared at him. "Ask if there are any further passages."

"Aside from the one you took to get there, there's nothing else on Mint Street." Maria had heard her. "Right now, your options are to stay where you are or head north to the old palace. At least then, you can make your way back to the Inner Ward."

"Staying where we are isn't an option; I can't sit by while some lunatic is starting fires and threatening hostages. Frankly, I don't feel much better about the second option either."

"I thought after all the fun you had in training, you'd love water by now."

"Water's fine, even when it is a bit sickly. I was thinking more about the fact there are seven assholes in the CCTV room, all of whom by now will have been alerted to our presence."

"Good point." Maria tapped away at her keyboard, bringing up a new area of the map. "According to this, a passage runs from the Bloody Tower underground; I'm not exactly sure where."

"What direction is it heading?"

"East. Comes up beneath the old Wardrobe Tower."

"That's where the Tower archives are kept." Emily was listening. "The original entrance was put in centuries ago."

"You have an archives beneath the ground?"

"It isn't the official archives," she replied. "Well, technically it is. As far as most people know, it doesn't exist."

Mike was confused. "You care to explain?"

"In the original castle, the Wardrobe Tower was located north of the south lawn. It's where that ruined wall was where we took shelter earlier. Once that fell, the contents were moved underground in case of invasion. Lots of stuff was lost in the Civil War."

"What's there?"

She looked at him, her expression uneasy. "Basically every royal document ever collected."

A series of thoughts went through Mike's mind: the night, the fire, 1666, the message, the Cardinal's Boys. Gemini!

Ask me who we were.

For Mike that was enough. "How do we get to the passage?"

"For starters, you'll need to find your way into the Bloody Tower," Maria said. "That means heading back into the open."

Mike studied the map, concentrating on the Bloody Tower. "Where's the entrance?"

"Here or here." Emily pointed, emphasising the door close to the Wakefield Tower. "Usually visitors enter from here."

Mike was alarmed to see it was the same area from where he'd earlier been shot at. "Phil, can I get an update on the bastards on Tower Green?"

"Matter of fact, you might just be in luck. They're all on the other side. Heading into the Martin Tower."

Keeping the phone to his ear, Mike began to change back into his black ops suit, now dry from its time on the radiator. As he was about to speak, he saw a bright explosion on the TV.

One of the helicopters had exploded.

54

Central London, 00:28

Jay and Sanders made the journey north swiftly, following the orders given by Maria. The scene at Monument had changed dramatically; the fire trucks that had previously been blocking the entrances north and south of Monument Street and Pudding Lane had vanished. Further north, the traffic remained a problem, especially on Gracechurch Street; the emergency services had reappeared there and more than thirty fire engines were combating the fires. Everything south of Eastcheap had been extinguished.

Thanks to the choppers, things were improving to the north.

They met up with Ward, Chambers and Wilcox on Cannon Street east of Walbrook. It was warm out, even without the fires; the tarmac below them felt like cooling coals.

Ward was first to greet them. "I thought you guys were dead!"

Sanders smiled. "Being honest, I just fancied getting out of the heat!" He hugged each man in turn; like himself, their faces bore the scars of recent ordeals. "What the hell happened to Kit?"

"The Director's ordered him to Trafalgar Square; apparently one of the suspects has a history with the Portrait Gallery."

"Who are these guys?" Sanders needed to shout in order for his voice to carry above the noise of the choppers.

"Aside from Blanco and Randek, we're not sure. Apparently all are French and have some kind of family tie. Whoever they are, they sure don't like us."

"And here was me thinking it was just me. What the hell's happened to Mike?"

"Haven't heard from him," Ward replied. "According to Maria, he's still on the loose inside the Tower."

"What's the deal there? When we got to the south bank, it looked like the entrance had been smashed."

"Apparently Blanco has destroyed all the bridges; even threatened the PM that if they attempt military action, they're gonna blow the place."

"The whole Tower?"

"That's what Blanco's threatened. Over a hundred hostages are currently being held somewhere inside the Queen's House."

"I don't understand," Jay said. "If all Blanco wants are the jewels, why didn't they just head in and out?"

"Apparently that was the plan. Only one thing no one counted on – the jewels are fake!"

Jay and Sanders were stunned. "Where's Blanco now?"

"Still inside; apparently twice in the last ninety minutes they've made threats direct to COBRA. If the jewels aren't brought to them by 05:00 hours, they will raze the place to the ground. Not to mention the rest of the city."

Jay was gobsmacked. "We've gotta be talking one of the biggest castles in Europe. No one has those kind of explosives!"

A deafening crash thundered through the air, followed by a blinding light. High above Walbrook, one of the helicopters had burst into flames.

It fell into a tailspin and into the fires below.

Mike was speechless. Though seeing was believing, it took him a moment for everything to register.

It seemed to be happening in slow motion. The helicopter's blades were turning, its erratic trajectory now dictated by the deterioration of its bodywork. As it fell into the flames, a further explosion went up as it hit the ground.

Even on the news the sound had been almost deafening.

Mike's eyes were fixed on the screen. Within seconds of the first explosion, another chopper hit the ground.

Maria's focus had already turned to Ward. "Beauchamp, this is the Rook! Do you copy?"

Never in any of their lives had they experienced anything like it. Within seconds of the second helicopter diving into the flames, a third followed, the sounds equally loud. It was as if the ground and the air were shaking all at once, trapping them in an invisible force field. A thin trail of light like that of a flare or a firework had been visible the moment before the third burst into flames.

It didn't require further examination to understand that the choppers had been brought down by a missile attack.

They dived to the ground close to the kerb. If anyone had heard Sanders' desperate cry to take cover, it had been superfluous.

Each man had moved instinctively.

Ward was first to crawl on to the nearby pavement, rolling on to his side. A fourth explosion had occurred somewhere over the river, followed by a mighty splash, possibly further explosions. In the ensuing confusion, he saw the final two helicopters take evasive action, turning their course immediately south. A second ray of light filtered through the smoke.

This time, it narrowly missed making contact.

Ward heard Maria's voice speaking frantically in his right ear; it was difficult to hear her exact words due to the confusion and panic on the street nearby. The firemen were still at work, combating the nearby flames from the ground. A new sounding of sirens filled the air; ambulances appeared from nowhere.

Ward feared they were already too late.

Maria continued, "Anybody, can you hear me?"

Ward answered, "Four of the helicopters have just been taken down; looks like a missile attack."

Maria was stunned. "What?"

Ward ducked as a further explosion went up from the nearby fires. "The third came down like crazy, like it was one gigantic fireball. I just saw another missile go for the fifth. I think it came down near the bridge."

On the map in front of her, Maria noted the outbreak of five new fires. The fourth helicopter was also on fire, its flaming wreckage floating on the Thames.

Sure enough, a further light became visible from near the bank.

She zoomed in. "I think I've got something, possibly a sniper!"

"No sniper could do that much damage!"

"Maybe not with a rifle." She saw movement on the screen. "Where are the others?"

Close to the pavement, the other four had risen to their feet. "We're here!" Chambers was first to answer.

"Block off all access either side of the Hanseatic Walk – head directly to the river. Chances are he's heading towards one of the bridges!"

Mike was still listening in, the phone pressed hard against his ear. Though he could clearly hear Maria talking, it was obvious the conversation wasn't meant for him.

The silence was infuriating.

"What exactly do you keep in the archives?"

Emily pondered the question. "Legal documents, anything to do with Tower history. Letters, chronicles, historical documents." She looked back blankly. "Why?"

"You said yourself there's a second way in; if we can reach it, at least it gives us access to the north side of the Tower." He contemplated what he'd just heard, Maria's words, Blanco's words. "Beware the wrath of the Cardinal's Boys."

Emily was confused. "What?"

Mike looked at her, remembering what he'd heard was officially classified; at the same time, the situation he faced was far from normal.

"Apparently whoever's behind this has made a threat to the Palace. There was a message there. Beware the wrath of the Cardinal's Boys. That mean anything to you?"

"Should it?"

"It's a phrase. Probably cryptic. You're a historian; have you heard it before?"

"Not that I can recall."

"Any thoughts on what it could mean?"

"Not exactly. Cardinals were prohibited from having kids, as it contradicted their vows of celibacy. However, that's not to say some didn't."

"You know any personally?"

"You want a list?" She raised her eyebrows, unimpressed. "We could be talking thousands. The Borgias weren't exactly advocates of the rules!"

Mike nodded, remembering seeing as much from the TV series. "What about Calais?"

"What about it?"

"You said earlier, 1347. Maybe there's a connection."

"If there is, it isn't obvious."

"How much is in the archives? Presumably it's computer indexed."

"As I said, practically every royal document is kept there. And yes, they're indexed."

"Well, maybe we can find something." Mike heard action on the phone. "Maria, are you seeing this?"

"You think I'd be watching something else?"

He let the comment pass. "What's happening?"

"Warwick and Grailly have joined Beauchamp and the others; we think there's a lone wolf acting down by the river with a rocket launcher. If he's there, they'll find him."

Mike raised an eyebrow on hearing mention of that weapon. "If the bastard's got a rocket launcher, God knows what other artillery these people are packing. For all we know, each one of these fires have been started by the same man."

"I don't think so. The footage transmitted to COBRA was strange. The last one started gradually. It was as though it began underground."

Mike remembered Kit had said the same about Faryners. "Have any of these churches got crypts?"

"Presumably."

"Maybe that's the connection. The bombs are in the crypts?"

"If this was all the work of bombs, it should have shattered the foundations. All the fires have seemed natural."

Mike bit his lip. "You got any better suggestions?"

"No, but it's not like we can investigate them now anyway."

"Maybe not. But maybe we can prepare for the next ones. Every single one of these has one thing in common."

"What's that?"

"They all involve something built by Christopher Wren."

Maria shook her head. "Apart from the first one. That was just a building."

"Maybe you're forgetting what was right next door."

Maria disconnected the call with Mike, a series of thoughts suddenly running through her mind. How the hell had she been so stupid?

The first fire had started at Faryners House; both since had been in churches. The original building had famously once been a bakery.

"Do we have a ground plan for the building at Faryners?" Maria asked Phil as she typed rapidly at her keyboard. In a matter of seconds, a 3D map confirmed the outline.

There seemed to be little below the ground.

Phil left his seat, curious. "Only what we have here."

"The original bakery probably had a cellar. Most buildings of the type did."

"The building's been rebuilt a billion times since then. After the Great Fire, the entire ground plan changed." He looked at the screen over her shoulder. "I remember reading once that construction on the new St Paul's wasn't started for nine years, partly as it took that long to level out the foundations."

Maria nodded, a light bulb flashing in her mind. "Is it possible anything still exists?"

"Does it show up on the map?"

"Not exactly," she replied.

Phil shrugged. "Then no."

As the technician left, returning to his recently vacated seat, Maria concentrated on the ground plans. Everything along Pudding Lane and Monument Street had been constructed to a consistent size, the foundations fairly level. Only one was lower.

Ironically it had also once been a church.

Mike hung up the phone on ending his conversation with Maria and took a deep breath. After two hours in the pits of hell, he craved rejuvenation. Jay and Sanders were alive.

And that was a start.

He led the way out through the front door and down the stairway to the Warders' Hall. Following Emily's directions and waiting for her to unlock doors, he immediately recognised the familiar sights of Water Lane.

It was colder than it had been, the sky darker, though strange compared to usual. He'd noticed it first on looking out of the window in the chief's office, the brightness of the raging inferno painting the clouds in a malevolent bloodlike tinge. The exterior floodlights shone brightly as before, illuminating the way and creating shadows of the imposing stonework.

To the north-east, the familiar rounded walls of the Wakefield Tower joined the archway of the Bloody Tower, the place he knew they needed to reach. Opposite it, the area around Traitors' Gate was silent, the waters below still from the lack of wind. Either side of Water Lane, the walls and towers seemed equally quiet, their imperious façades cloaked in shadow. Though more than two hours had passed since Mike had attended Champion's tour, it already felt like a lot longer, as though it had happened in a different lifetime. Whether or not he was being watched, it was no longer possible to tell.

At least not without assistance.

He removed his satphone from his pocket, checking for a signal. Finding evidence the server had updated, he retuned the radio setting on his headset.

"Looks like we're back in business, Phil."

"And not before time," Phil replied, his eyes still monitoring the screens. "The bastards on the north side have moved on to the outer reaches. Now's your chance."

"I'm on it!"

They made their way quickly to the archway of the Bloody Tower, stopping briefly in the shadows. Mike paid extra attention to the windows of St Thomas's

Tower and where it joined the Wakefield Tower, remembering a time earlier that evening when he'd been looking down from the other side.

Again the area appeared deserted.

He went under the archway and stopped on reaching the stairway to the left. Close to the White Tower, the bodies of the murdered soldiers and tourists still littered the Broadwalk Steps like the aftermath of a battle. A pungent odour filled the air; he equated it with the onset of bodily decay.

"Which way?" he asked Emily, keeping a constant eye out for the return of the gunmen.

"Up the stairs and straight ahead," she replied, keeping low. "If there are watchers in the Queen's House, we'll need to move quickly."

Touching his earpiece close to his ear, Mike contacted Phil. "Any sign of these bastards?"

"Negative, Honey Badger. Move swiftly, you're good to go. Assuming you've got a key, you shouldn't encounter delays."

"Roger that."

Stopping at the top of the steps, he looked both ways before hurrying to the nearest door. His back to the stonework, he glanced out across Tower Green. From there he saw no sign of movement.

Emily unlocked the door and hurried inside. Once Mike had followed, she locked it.

In the main security room on the top floor of the Waterloo Barracks, the leader of the gunmen noticed movement close to Tower Green. As the seconds passed, their features became clear: two figures, a man and a woman.

"It's them," the man who had earlier been tied up said, a hard, aggressive expression on his face.

Alongside him, the second gunman spoke immediately into his HT. "It's Vidal. We just got a visual.

"They're outside the Queen's House."

55

The Waterloo Barracks,
00:29

Blanco saw the light emerge from two sources, both inside the office and outside. The news cameras had captured the explosion live at the same moment it had been visible outside the nearest window. Keeping one eye on the television, he headed for the window, gazing at the skyline beyond the White Tower. A second burst of light followed; he also caught that on the big screen. A second helicopter had been hit, then a third.

The fourth explosion had been the most visible, coming down in clear view over the Thames.

The final choppers were making a hasty retreat, heading south, passing the Tower. In the moment he almost wished he'd been blessed with a second rocket launcher.

He picked up his HT, speaking quickly. "Gerard, do you copy?"

At the other end, the gunman with the rocket launcher lowered his weapon and looked to the south. His latest shot had been wild by comparison with the previous ones; he watched the rocket while it remained airborne before it came down close to the bridge, creating the first fires of the evening south of the Thames. Ignoring the crisp onset of static, a voice contacting him over the airwaves, he raised his weapon again, realising even the nearest of the helicopters had already passed out of range.

He doubted they'd be back in a hurry.

He heard Blanco call his name twice in quick succession.

"The helicopters are retreating; the remaining two have just passed beyond the bridge. I'm guessing you are already watching this."

"Even in the English castles, we are not deprived of the latest electronic technology." Blanco smirked as he watched the flat-screen television propped up against the far wall. "It seems the news reporters are in awe of your exploits. Either a testament to you or a damming assessment of them!" He paused briefly to listen in. The presenters were deeply shocked, almost speechless. All that was clear was that four of the helicopters had exploded, each incident preceded by a mysterious ray of light.

"Where are you now?"

"North of the water, close to the banks." He continued to watch the retreating helicopters. "The range is too short to reach the others."

Blanco had noticed the fifth, wilder shot on the news. "It will not take long before London's finest are out combing the streets; with the fires cooling, they will probably bring out the dogs. I suggest you do not linger. We only have thirty minutes before the next phase is due to commence."

The gunman checked his watch, glad his next involvement wasn't due for almost ninety minutes. "The walkway is limited on both sides; the exits are as we discussed. Realistically that leaves only one option."

Blanco smiled. "Then I suggest you take it. Under the circumstances, the waters will make a refreshing change from the fires."

Blanco ended the conversation and checked his watch, reminding himself of the schedule. It was exactly 00:30, the furthest time between the previous video and the next. Returning to the desk, he opened up his laptop and double tapped on the mouse pad to bring up a videoconference.

Two familiar faces appeared before him: one younger, the other noticeably older.

"The aerial attack has been successfully repelled." Blanco still had one eye on the TV footage and assumed from Jérôme's gaze the two men on screen were doing the same. "I assume you were already aware of this?"

At the opposite end, Fieschi concentrated on the view through the French doors. "As a matter of fact, I was just about to call and congratulate you. From here it's really rather beautiful."

"A similar thing was said three centuries ago; however, due to the unfortunate timing, the paper was never released – nor for that matter was the author." Blanco's expression hardened. "I assume you have received no response from the Palace."

"You honestly expected one?" Fieschi was sceptical.

"The prime minister was aware of the message; though she never acknowledged it, the clues in her sentences were easy to find. The Palace accepts there is a genuine threat. I can only speculate whether it will be enough to encourage them to accelerate their parting with the jewels. In the meantime, I suggest we widen our search."

"As I've told you before, Bizu, the map, though elegant, is deficient in the finer details. Whatever secrets it failed to disclose in six months, I find it unlikely you'll uncover them in five hours."

"Do you have any better suggestions?" Blanco asked, his expression becoming hostile. "If the Royal Family refuse to cooperate – worse still, if their ancestors took their own secrets to the grave – the journey back might be long. I did not come this far to fail."

"Admirable sentiments," Fieschi replied, showing not the least concern. "I assume the JIC were loath to see their city being destroyed before their eyes."

"No more than I if I were they; however, under the circumstances, I appreciate their tact. It's never good to show weakness!"

"Weakness, when it exists, is like a disease." Jérôme spoke for the first time, his bearded chin moving slowly in time with his lips. "Like the plague, it spreads worse than fire and seeps deep into the heart of humanity. When the original fire began, our own ancestors wrote of the selfishness and greed of the citizens.

While the houses burned, many bankrupted the unfortunate in exchange for use of a cart. I can only imagine how the taxi companies are enjoying their evening."

"If the news I'm hearing is correct, the opposite might be true. Had the traffic been moving, I might even have disagreed with you completely." He looked briefly at the TV. "What news of Paris?"

"Better news than here," Fieschi confirmed. "The yacht has left the city."

Blanco allowed himself a smile, a reminder the evening so far had been at least a partial success.

"It's still early; in the old city, the fire burned for four days. I would happily see it continue for a week if necessary."

"It will not be necessary," Fieschi maintained. "We have over five hours. By the time the fire reaches the Palace, they will have no choice but to beg their way out."

Seated at his personal terminal, Phil noticed a change come over Blanco. After restlessly pacing the office of the Chief Yeoman Warder, his concentration alternating between a large wall-mounted, flat-screen television and the action in the skies outside his window, the Anjouvin was now hunched over the desk, staring at a laptop screen.

Phil was curious and Maria had noticed. "What is it?"

"When a system's been decoded, it's usually possible to adjust the setting on the cameras." The senior technician clicked a couple of times at his mouse while tapping quickly at his keyboard. The images changed slightly.

"Eureka!"

Maria left her seat and headed towards Phil to see the new images. "Looks like he's video calling someone." She peered in closer, attempting to make out something more specific. "Any chance you can zoom in further?"

Phil tapped again at his keyboard, this time slower than before. Indeed, two faces looked back from within the 2D fifteen-inch laptop screen.

"You think we can get a match through this?"

Phil rubbed his beard, studying the screen in deep contemplation. "I don't know."

Blanco ended the videoconference and departed from the office, heading back along the corridor. He found François studying an architectural document in a second office on the opposite side of the corridor.

"What news of the Palace?"

"It is futile putting our faith in others, especially those presently outside these walls." Blanco removed a rolled-up document from his inside pocket and placed it down over the one François was reading. "In the meantime, I suggest we put our time to good use."

Recognising the photocopied document, François immediately became dispirited. "What do you think I have been concentrating my attention on for the past six months? While you and Fabien have been invading art galleries and surveying underground cities, every spare hour I have been looking!" He stared deeply into Blanco's eyes. "The plans are old; the buildings have changed. Back then these barracks didn't even exist."

Blanco's face confirmed his impatience. "Maybe. However, tonight we have something you never did."

He picked up his HT. "Fabien?"

Seated in the lounge of the Queen's House, Randek answered, "What is it?"

"I want you to check on the hostages. Tell the governor he's wanted again."

Less than two minutes later, Randek re-entered the revered chamber, pleased to discover the developing melancholy had intensified further since his last visit. Again the silence was uncomfortable, as if the hostages were afraid to speak or openly consider what fate might await them.

He found the governor seated in between a well-dressed, middle-aged man with a full head of silver hair and a Yeoman Warder.

"General, my uncle requires another word."

As the governor followed the gesturing of Randek's gun, heading towards the exit, Champion sank back against the cold stone walls, finding momentary solace in the extra legroom to his left. It was becoming a habit, he realised: victimising the governor purely because of his status. A tactic that seemed deliberately provocative.

As he readjusted to the silence, a series of unfamiliar sounds became audible from somewhere close by. Startled, he realised it was coming from his own garments.

Exploring the right pocket of his suit jacket, he felt something deep below the flaps; it was small, ear-shaped, and definitely electronic. Memories of the earlier evening returned as he realised what it was.

Emily Fletcher had given it to him on entering the lecture theatre.

56

The Bloody Tower, 00:44

Mike closed the door within seconds of entering and stepped aside for Emily to lock it. He exhaled gratefully as he heard the sound of the heavy key being withdrawn from the lock.

As far as he could tell, they had not been seen.

Once more they operated in darkness; he'd warned Emily not to turn on any lights. It was at times like this when he was particularly glad that his night-vision goggles had been in his rucksack.

With them on, he could see a small chamber with original white stone walls and an open doorway to their left. To the right was something less distinguishable.

"Don't touch that!" a voice ordered through the darkness; Mike was surprised Emily had been able to see him so quickly. The blackness seemed dense, almost tangible; there was something about the location that was particularly atmospheric. Lowering his gaze, he saw what had first caught his attention.

He was looking at a portcullis.

"Is that real?"

"Absolutely; not that it's used much anymore." Emily was moving to his left, nearly bumping into him. "We need some light."

"Trust me, I've got everything I need."

Mike grabbed her hand, monitoring her as she peered vacantly into his eyes. He touched her face, feeling the skin around her cheeks.

Even in night vision, she looked cute.

Taking her hand, he guided them through the doorway on the left, speaking as he did so into the microphone in his headset. "Maria, you copy?"

Over a mile away, Jamal Iqbal and Robert Sanders heard the transmission come through as they viewed the walkway below from Southwark Bridge.

"Hey, Grosmont, rumour has it you had to haul your ass in freezing water through a tunnel," Jay said.

In the Bloody Tower, Mike smiled wryly on hearing Jay's voice. "Yeah, well, rumour has it you two got your beards wet. Let me guess? Sitting at the Round Table got boring, so you thought you'd try the billionaire's lifestyle?"

Jay laughed; Sanders shook his head. "That the best you can do?"

Mike grinned. "Hey, Warwick, what has two legs and sawdust for brains?"

"You missed out a devilishly handsome face beneath that beard!" Sanders replied. "Where the hell are you?"

"Right now, couldn't even tell you." Mike entered the next room, surveying the surroundings. "Somewhere in the Bloody Tower. Looks like a study."

"I'll wager that would be the study of Sir Walter Raleigh."

Alongside him, Emily overheard. "At least one of your friends has a brain."

Both Jay and Sanders picked up on a female voice. "Oi, oi, does Maria know?"

Emily stared at him; somehow Mike could sense it through the darkness. "Matter of fact, the two of them have developed something of a professional rapport. If she ever leaves us, her career prospects are still looking rather tidy."

"Assuming the Tower's still there when she does," Sanders said, immediately feeling discomfort. "Where's Blanco?"

"Last I heard, still trying to get the seat adjusted in the chief's office. Where are you?"

"Southwark Bridge; looking for the bastard who brought down the helitankers." Sanders turned his gaze south, using his Phil-designed night-vision binoculars in an attempt to find signs of life. Seeing nothing, he activated the X-ray setting. "Even with the X-rays, we're coming up with nothing."

"As long as there are no fizzy Coke bottles beneath chairs!" Mike said, thinking back to his experience in the Royal Opera House six months earlier. At the same time he also recalled the manuscript the deputy PM's wife had stolen for Randek had concerned Raleigh.

"Right now, not seeing much at all. Even the bars have emptied."

"City that never sleeps, huh?"

"That's New York, but your sentiment isn't far wrong. What are you doing in the Bloody Tower?"

"Trying to avoid the bad guys." Mike stumbled against something.

"Watch it!" Emily said.

"Not to mention each other."

Again, Sanders grinned. "Well, if you get bored checking out Raleigh's study, I seem to recall there's an excellent exhibition on the princes on the top floor."

"Not to mention a rack in the Wakefield," Jay added.

"Thanks, but I think I've had my share of torture for now." He heard Maria's voice in the background. "Maria, you there?"

Seated in the same place, Maria's attention had been exclusively on Blanco. "Sorry, something just came up."

"Hope it wasn't Edward."

"Actually we don't know who they are. Cameras in the barracks just showed Blanco having an audio-visual with two others. We're trying to get facial recognition."

"You think you can get that just from the screen?"

"It's certainly worth a try; even if we can't, it's something to work with."

"Sounds like a plan; speaking of which, what's ours?"

"You looking for inspiration? I thought your acting curator wanted to check out the books."

Emily was standing alongside Mike, hands on hips. "If we can get inside, at least it should get us to the north side."

"You copy that, Maria?" Mike asked.

"Crystal clear. Where are you now?"

"Raleigh's study," he said, viewing it as best he could through his night visions. An original book in a glass display case had been placed on a wooden table, alongside items of pottery. Beyond the zoned-off area there was a 16th-century desk close to a fireplace, its inclined top covered with writing utensils, including a quill, a book and various documents. Left of the desk, some contemporary wooden furnishings were located in a niche close to the main window.

Mike ventured first into the off-limits area, examining things as he passed. "There's a desk and some other stuff, possibly a chest." He looked around. "Floor is mostly tiled. What direction is the passage?"

Maria examined the map. "East-north-east seems to head directly into the old Wardrobe. Looks like it begins in the wall itself."

Mike looked around, attempting to get his bearings. "I'm gonna check out the fireplace."

The three gunmen kept their eyes glued to the screens as the two figures quickly entered one of the buildings off Tower Green. Within seconds of reaching the door, the woman inserted a key and opened it.

Once inside, they disappeared.

"Where is that?" Christophe asked, his eyes fixed on one particular screen.

"The Bloody Tower," the man alongside him answered, also monitoring the screens. "There!"

Each screen was titled at the bottom, the room names coming up in block capitals. There were three cameras inside the Bloody Tower; what they captured was taking place almost completely in darkness. Without an IR setting, what they could see was limited.

The man who had previously been tied up raised his HT to his lips. "It's Christophe. Targets have entered the Bloody Tower."

At the other end, Randek listened in. "You're certain?"

"Who else is here?"

Randek let the comment go. "Keep watching."

He put through a call to Blanco. "The Servant and his lady have reappeared on screen; they're now in the Bloody Tower."

Seated at the desk alongside François, Blanco awaited the arrival of his nephew and the governor.

"Where are you now?"

"Just passing Tower Green. We will be with you in two minutes."

"When you reach the entrance, there will be someone there to collect the general. Then you can deal with the prince and the princess."

"Understood."

"Take this." Mike removed an item from his pocket and placed it over Emily's eyes. She kept still, breathing quickly as she felt a strange material come into contact with her face.

"What is it?"

Mike activated them; a subtle purple screen appeared almost immediately. "You should be able to see now."

She realised he'd fitted her with night-vision goggles. "You had a second pair all along?"

Mike watched her, noticing she'd become disoriented. Unlike his green-filtered lenses, the violet-coloured goggles were of a secondary quality.

"Trust me, it's not something I'm encouraged to do. Help me find the passageway."

Emily saw rapid movement to her left. The figure was of human form, clearly masculine. Though she was sure it was Mike, the room looked strange through the purple lenses.

She saw him crouch down near the fireplace, searching every corner. So far he'd found nothing.

"What exactly is it we're looking for?"

"Could be anything." Mike rose to his feet, studying the upper sections. The fireplace, though possibly modified since the tower's heyday, seemed fixed and set solidly into the wall.

Nothing appeared to move.

"There's gotta be something that triggers a release!" He spoke first to Emily, then, "Maria, where exactly does the passage begin?"

Looking at the screen, Maria answered, "The passage continues either behind or below the wall in front of you." She moved her mouse, rotating the map's axis. As the seconds passed, she realised the starting point might be where the white dot was flashing. "Check the floor directly beneath your feet. There's a cavity below you. Could be they're connected."

Mike knelt down, feeling the floor with his bare hands. Again the surface seemed to be a combination of tiling and solid brick construction; nothing appeared to move.

"Tell me more about this cavity. Where does it begin?"

Continuing to rotate the axis, Maria zoomed in, exploring the area from the opposite side. She compared what she saw to the location of the white dot.

"There's a second cavity near the window; check the floor there. The two seem to be connected."

Mike moved towards it, noticing on his night visions that light was entering through the nearby window. Below it was a large wooden chest.

Randek didn't stop till they reached the main entrance to the Jewel House.

Two gunmen were waiting by the open door; there was no sign of Blanco or François.

He spoke into his HT. "We're at the entrance."

Blanco answered immediately. "You may leave the general in the capable hands of his new escort. In the meantime, I want the Englishman found."

Randek turned away, taking his three-man escort. "Come on."

57

The National Portrait Gallery, 00:46

The car pulled up on Charing Cross Road, close to Trafalgar Square. Taking advantage of a lull in the traffic, Kit and Gillian alighted quickly, crossing the road towards the gallery. The flow of cars was limited in both directions; the same was true in terms of people. The roads had been closed east of Fleet Street, by order of the prime minister. Kit had needed special clearance to pass.

Rarely had he seen it so sparse.

It was warm out, especially for that time of night. There was a charge in the atmosphere, the usual background noise pierced by a regular clamour of sirens that echoed through the streets from the east. It was cloudy but unlike anything that either of them were used to; the usual soft cumulus cloud masked by something dense and pungent. There were other sounds in addition to the sirens, burning, possibly shouting.

Collectively it all pointed to a situation of growing chaos.

Gillian led Kit to the main entrance and unlocked the door. Doing so made her uncomfortable; even two years after the robbery, her recollection of entering work that Saturday was still crystal clear in her mind.

They took the main stairs to Room 6, Kit observing the familiar setting with imposing cyan-coloured walls on which were mounted the portraits of many of history's elite as Gillian switched on the lights.

"This was from where the paintings were taken," Gillian explained as they entered Room 5, where pictures of the nation's celebrities from the Civil War era hung proudly on the walls. The walk ended in Room 4. "This is the van Dyck."

Among the many, Kit cast his gaze over one instantly recognisable portrait located within an oval-shaped frame reminiscent of a mirror owned by French royalty. Looking back at him, the charismatic features of the famous painter Sir Anthony van Dyck appeared serene and thoughtful.

"What happened exactly?" Kit asked, his eyes on the van Dyck.

"The robbery occurred two days before the exhibition opened," Gillian replied, standing alongside him. "It was a miracle we were able to open on time. The exhibition finally closes Friday."

Kit looked at her, picking up from the heavy shadows around her eyes and the slight tremor in her voice that the weekend couldn't come soon enough.

"What else was taken?"

"A portrait of the roundhead soldier Sir Arthur Hesilrige. A rather modest piece we believe to have been the work of the artist Robert Walker." She escorted Kit back through the nearby archway into Room 5. "That was taken from here."

Kit stopped alongside her, his eyes on the wall. Next to a famous portrait of Oliver Cromwell, he saw a second, less dazzling piece titled *Unknown Man and Woman*.

"What happened to it?"

"The Hesilrige was taken at the same time; it wasn't till much later it was finally returned."

"But it was returned?"

"Eventually, yes."

Kit detected something of a backstory. "Was anything else taken?"

"As a matter of fact, this piece had been elsewhere at the time. However, we believe from footage of an attack on our storeroom, this was the final piece targeted."

Kit moved in for a closer look. At first sight the painting looked nothing out of the ordinary, but suddenly the penny dropped.

"Hesilrige?"

"Close. It was originally titled *Oliver Cromwell and his Daughter*."

Kit compared it to the painting on the left. Except for a possible facial resemblance, the famous portrait by Walker that he'd seen numerous times on television showed the former Lord Protector in a far more captivating light.

"What was the reason for their being taken? I'm guessing there was a motive."

She took Kit to the third floor, first a vaulted room deep inside the storeroom and then her office. Entering the office, Kit immediately noticed a rectangular portrait propped up against the main desk, facially similar to that of Cromwell.

"Is this it?"

"Sir Arthur in all his glory." Gillian laid out several items she'd just removed from the vaults and set them down on the desk. "These might answer your questions."

Kit joined her around the other side, studying the items laid out before him. Each was a computer printout, different versions of what appeared to be the same portrait. One was identical to what he'd seen leaning against the desk; on the final two the lighting was strange.

"What is this? Ultraviolet?"

"That and X-rays," Gillian replied. "Notice the bottom left corner."

Kit followed Gillian's directions, seeing a strange feature. "Looks like handwriting."

Gillian removed a small torch from her desk drawer and moved across the room, shining it on the Hesilrige painting.

"Perhaps you might like to see it up close."

Kit took the torch while Gillian switched off the lights, the calligraphy of three centuries earlier now showing up clearly in the darkness. Kit read it as best he could, failing to make perfect sense of everything.

Nevertheless, he'd made sense of enough to get the gist.

"I don't believe it. The Crown Jewels!"

"The original Crown Jewels of England were lost by the cavaliers in the Civil War and brought to London, where they were smelted down on Cromwell's orders – or so history tends to imply." Gillian's tone suggested some doubt and, perhaps, knowledge to the contrary. "Once Charles II took the throne, new jewels were created. What became of the originals has been lost to history."

Kit glanced at her, sceptical. "I assume from this the jewels were found?"

"Matter of fact, it's something of a long story." Gillian took a seat behind her desk, quickly looking through a plethora of documents. "Jérôme de Haulle wrote to me back in August that year, requesting the temporary loan of the Hesilrige, Cromwell and the *Unknown Man and Woman* to form part of a temporary exhibition on European history in the seventeenth century. In addition to these, he also requested three others."

"You didn't comply?"

Gillian looked back coldly. "Unfortunately over the years, my predecessor encountered first-hand the problems that can arise when paintings go out on loan to areas where their security measures fail to match our own – that's not to say, of course, our own are perfect." She raised her eyebrows. "After careful deliberation, it was decided the appropriate safeguards had not been put in place."

"I assume Monsieur de Haulle was thrilled on hearing the news."

"Let's just say he never replied to my nicely worded email."

A wry smile. "Why the van Dyck?"

"Who knows? Perhaps to ensure he got my full attention."

"I'm guessing he got it."

"Not to mention that of everyone else employed here."

"What were the other three?"

"Two were famous statesmen from the same era; however neither at the time were on display here. The third wasn't a portrait at all. In fact, all he requested was my assistance in tracking them down."

"He was more successful?"

"As a matter of fact, all three are currently on display in another exhibition in this city. Ironically, all concern the Great Fire."

Kit raised his eyebrows. "Where are they?"

Seated alone in his living room, the Curator of the Museum of London was startled by the sound of his telephone ringing. Glancing to his left, he picked up the receiver.

"Tony Green?"

"Tony, it's Gillian McKevitt here."

He recognised the voice of the Director of the National Portrait Gallery.

"Tony, I'm ever so sorry to trouble you so late. I'm afraid I need to ask rather a big favour."

58

The Bloody Tower, 00:47

"Help me move this." Mike gestured to the chest, convinced there was something to Maria's suggestion. Even in the short space of time he'd spent at the Tower, he'd already seen enough to learn never to take things at face value.

As in Edward I's bedroom, if there was an entrance, it was probably very well concealed.

Emily had also seen enough that evening not to question the possibility. Lining up opposite Mike, she placed her hands on the chest. It moved, albeit with difficulty.

Mike looked closely over the area the chest had covered but could see nothing other than plain brickwork.

"Where are we looking, Maria?"

Studying the 3D outline, Maria zoomed in further. "Seems to be a rectangular void directly to your left – could be an entrance. Try moving the chest a bit further."

Mike wasted no time, confident Emily had heard the same instructions. As the seconds passed, Mike noticed subtle differences in the patterns below; frantically, he felt them.

"Everything seems solid."

"Keep going a little further. Another eighteen inches and you should be directly over it."

Mike pushed hard, sensing Emily was tiring. With his free hand he continued to examine the area in almost microscopic detail, noticing a subtle change. He gripped it, moved it.

"I think I've found something."

Randek led the way south, passing the execution site. The entrance to the Bloody Tower involved taking the walkway between Tower Green and the wall that lined the Broadwalk Steps, ending with a wooden doorway through the inner wall.

One of the gunmen raised his machine gun.

"Wait!" Randek gripped his wrist, holding it so hard the gunman began to squirm. Slowly, he removed the gaoler's keys from his pocket, wondering which the correct one was. "Quietly!"

* * *

There was one brick that was looser than all the others. It was free on all four sides; it wasn't clear whether it was deliberate or whether it had become detached over time.

The ease with which he'd been able to remove it made Mike suspicious, as there was no sign of obvious breakage.

More suspicious still was what it covered.

He removed the brick and placed his fingers deep into the gap beneath it. There was something there, jutting out, cold, mechanical. Gripping it, he realised there was traction; he sensed it was some form of lever. He pulled it hard, at first finding no way of moving it.

Finally it came free.

A sharp noise echoed through the room, sounding as though the walls were caving in, if not the entire building. Looking in every direction, Mike could see that the walls remained as they were, the ceiling no higher or lower. To the left of the recently moved chest, a gap had appeared, revealing a clear cavity.

Inside it was a winding stone stairway.

Randek inserted the latest key, his frustration increasing rapidly as he realised he'd again chosen incorrectly. He'd already tried ten keys out of the many available.

He knew it was possible none would fit.

Mike went first, lowering himself carefully into the space. The gap was approximately a metre in length, less still in width. Adjusting the setting on his goggles, he counted that the stairwell had eight visible steps.

He looked at Emily; even in the green light, confusion was written across her face.

"Come on!"

It wasn't until the twenty-fifth attempt Randek finally found the right key. Unlike the others, it turned slowly.

He unlocked the door.

Mike grabbed Emily's hand as she edged tentatively on to the top step. He knew from recent experience that she wasn't the only person able to hear him.

Sure enough, Maria spoke again. "What's it look like down there?"

"Whatever it is looks narrow." Mike had taken five steps; he grimaced on realising there was insufficient room to stand. "Good thing neither of us is claustrophobic."

"Speak for yourself," Emily replied.

Mike focused his thoughts on the journey ahead, speaking into his headset microphone. "Where exactly does it take us?"

Maria heard the question clearly and studied the map. "Follow it to the end. It should last no longer than sixty metres."

A few steps for Usain Bolt, as Kit would say. "Any nasty surprises?"

"I guess if there are, you'll be the first to know."

Mike terminated the conversation, crouching as he concentrated on the way down. From his current vantage point, the gradient of the steps seemed to be consistent and each upcoming turn gentle.

Turning, he saw Emily had made it as far as the third step; something was clearly bothering her.

"What was that?"

Mike also heard something; it seemed to have come from the next room. A door had opened. Footsteps. Voices. Talking in French.

Emily was frozen with fear.

Mike grabbed her hand, guiding her down the previously concealed stairway. Once she'd ducked her head low enough, he reached for the recently moved flooring.

With great effort he pulled the lever quickly towards him.

Randek pushed against the door, doing his best not to attract attention. On the other side, he found his movement immediately limited by stone walls; unlike the White Hart, he wore no sophisticated night-vision equipment.

There were sounds nearby, heavy creaking, possibly another door. Finding an open doorway leading into the adjacent chamber, he saw a shimmering of light that vanished as quickly as it had appeared.

"There is no use hiding," he bellowed into the darkness before raising his HT. "Where are they?"

In the security room, the three gunmen continued to monitor the screens. In recent minutes movement in the darkness had become far more difficult to trace. "Check by the walls. There was movement there earlier."

Randek heard further movement behind him. "Turn on the lights."

Mike sensed illumination above him, the brightness creeping in through cracks in the flooring. He heard footsteps, further talking; one of the voices was clearly Randek's.

Emily was close behind him, the fear in her eyes hidden by her night visions. Mike placed his finger to his lips.

Heart in mouth, they paused.

The lights revealed an airy chamber with historical artefacts that appeared to be authentic. Beyond the long table with a pristine glass display case occupied by a well-preserved original manuscript, the furniture was in keeping with 16th-century opulence and laid out in a manner of scholarly thoughtfulness. While an antique wooden desk had been carefully positioned before a fireplace, adjacent to a wooden cabinet in a broad niche close to one of the windows, a heavy wooden chest appeared to have been randomly discarded.

Randek approached it, gun at the ready. Seeing no obvious sign of life, he addressed his retinue.

"Search every inch. Make sure he doesn't double back."

Mike heard footsteps directly above him, stopping, then resuming. Randek was speaking, ordering others to move out.

He overheard something about the floor above.

As the sounds faded, Mike inched his way forward, again sensing Emily was reluctant to move. "I think they're moving out; is there a second floor to this?"

"There's a stairway on the other side of the portcullis; leads to the second floor."

Mike sensed they had moved on.

"Come on, before they come back."

59

The Inner Ward, 00:56

Blanco looked down from the roof of the White Tower as the latest set of hostages were escorted at gunpoint from the main door of the Queen's House, heading across ground usually paraded by the silent guard. At the same time, he saw Randek reappear out of the higher of the two exits of the Bloody Tower, more than a little annoyed.

He contacted him over the airwaves. "What happened?"

Descending the stone steps that led down from the adjoining wall, Randek placed his own device to his lips. "The Englishman has a talent for vanishing into thin air."

Blanco's expression soured. "Keep looking; rip out the walls if you have to."

Randek met up with the gunmen as they approached the south lawn. Just as with the previous six, the new hostages had been picked without discrimination; there were as many women as men and all of varying creeds and age.

None were older than fifty.

He saw the Ravenmaster at the front of the seven, his uniform dusty and frayed from his time in captivity.

"Sergeant!" Randek approached him. "Let's not forget why you're here."

The prime minister watched from the same seat as before as the latest video was transmitted directly to COBRA. Just as on both previous occasions, Blanco had been specific in his demands, but less so on any other matters. For the second time that evening, he made reference to Calais and the Cardinal's Boys.

Now they had only four hours.

Less than half a mile from 70 Whitehall, the Director of the White Hart had viewed the same footage. As the sixty-second transmission came to an end with a third raven hitting the ground, the setting changed to something far darker: old stonework, clearly underground.

Within seconds flames became visible, illuminating thick walls inset with Saxon arches. As the fire began to develop, the POV changed.

To the exterior of a church.

The Director watched with folded arms as the flames he had originally seen underground began to penetrate the heart of the building above. The façade was familiar: a large tower bordering a long nave, the spire rising inwardly in equal sections.

The design was reminiscent of a wedding cake.

"Where is that?" the Director asked, knowing if anyone knew, it would be Maria.

"St Bride's, Fleet Street." She gazed in horror at the screen as the rapidly spreading inferno obliterated the upper windows. "Another Wren."

The Director digested the revelation seriously, at the same time showing little emotion. Geographically the latest fire was quite a long distance from the others.

Nevertheless, the common connection remained.

"Bring up that map."

Maria clicked rapidly at her mouse and keyboard, bringing up a 2D bird's-eye view of the danger area. The present state of the fires confirmed a clear separation between them.

Phil was next to speak. "The fires are different from the historical pattern; even if there was any truth in the firebombs legend, the original one spread north and west from the source. This is separate."

Mr White raised an eyebrow. "Firebombs?"

"Back in October 1666, Parliament set up an inquiry into what caused the Great Fire," Maria began. "Among the reports, a series of eyewitnesses referred to fires beginning of their own accord, as though they'd been started deliberately."

Mr White raised an eyebrow. Though he wasn't familiar with the account, he could see from the map the pattern was strange. "What's the latest with the other two?"

Maria made the pictures change again. "St Clement's is out, but the building is gone; Stephen Walbrook is still in the balance." She held her gaze on St Bride's, watching with sorry eyes as the wedding cake-shaped spire began to lean in on itself as though an actual wedding cake were being decimated. "I'd always dreamed of getting married there!"

The pictures changed again, the scenes of fire replaced by the face of the prime minister looking deep into the camera with a frustrated glare, the skin around her eyes darkening from increasing exhaustion.

"I assume you saw all that?"

Mr White took a deep breath, a rare delaying tactic as he attempted to allow his mind a moment for recent events to sink in. The original pattern had since been interrupted. Only one common denominator remained.

Wren.

"The church on Fleet Street is over half a mile from the previous fires." Watching the screen, the Director saw further evidence of chaos on the roads and wondered whether Blanco had planned it specifically for that reason. "All of the fires so far have occurred within the boundaries of the original event; the same is true of Edinburgh. The one thing not consistent is their progression. Whereas the fires of the past spread naturally due to the closeness of the buildings, the development here is significant. If the enemy is consistent, no fires are likely beyond the Inns of Court; nor for that matter is anything likely to occur close to the Tower itself." Inwardly he had doubts about the last point. "Assuming nobody has any tricks up their sleeves, the boundaries, it would appear, are set."

"Assuming being the correct word." The PM's mood was sombre. "What in God's name happened with the helicopters?"

What did happen? Still the culprit was yet to show himself. "The suspect was last spotted close to the Thames on the north bank, armed with weaponry that no army in Europe dishes out legally. Realistically, he only had one option. We have a SWAT team searching the river as we speak."

"You honestly believe that was his escape route?"

"It's either that or he vanished into thin air."

"It's hot enough outside as it is without your assistance, Director. You mentioned earlier you have a man at the Tower. What's his status?"

"He's alive and, so far, still at liberty; thanks to him, the number of terrorists we're facing has decreased quite considerably in the last hour. That's not to say he doesn't still face countless obstacles."

"If the helicopters can't return, there's no way the emergency services can keep pace with the development of the fires, especially with the streets still gridlocked. Time is of the essence, Director."

"I assure you, Prime Minister, I'm well aware of our situation. Our men are working round the city and the clock; it's clear from the pattern so far that the targets have all started with Wren monuments. I suggest a lockdown on all the remaining Wren churches in London."

"How many are we talking?"

"Twenty-nine," Maria answered without being prompted. "Less when taking into account those already targeted."

"Less still bearing in mind others have also sustained damage from being located in the fire's path," the Director resumed. "At this hour, all should be locked and closed to visitors; for all we know the culprits are already inside and have been for hours."

"I'll mention the matter immediately to the chief of police; the next COBRA meeting is scheduled to convene in forty-five minutes. Under the circumstances, I might have to bring it forward." The prime minister clasped her hands together tightly. "In the meantime, I suggest you brief your man at the Tower. If things don't improve during the next thirty minutes, it might be necessary to force our hand."

The screen went blank.

Maria stared inquisitively at the Director. "What did she mean, force our hand? Surely she's not talking about military action on the Tower?"

"I hate to imagine. Right now she's under extreme pressure." The Director gazed back. "Where's Masterson?"

"Just left the Portrait Gallery; now en route to the Museum of London. Said there were works of art there de Haulle had tried to obtain on loan."

"For what purpose?"

"According to Kit, they approached the Director of the Portrait Gallery a couple of years back regarding a temporary loan. At least one of those requested they later stole."

"What about Sanders?"

Maria spoke through her headset. "Warwick, this is the Rook, do you copy?"

Standing on the north bank of the Thames, Sanders heard Maria's voice come through clearly as he looked breathlessly across the water. "What's going on?"

"Too much. Any sign of the suspect?"

"Negative," Sanders replied, his attention alternating between north and south. While Ward, Chambers and Wilcox were observing London Bridge, Jay was still on Southwark. "We've combed the pond and the trenches; even with the X-ray specs, it's like the bastard has disappeared into thin air."

"I had a feeling you might say that. Where are the others?"

"Grailly's here with me; the others are combing the north bank from London Bridge back to us. If the gunner is still here, we'll ferret him out."

Maria didn't care for their chances. "Blanco has appeared again on the big screen; fires have started on Fleet Street. Looks like Blanco's not prepared to let even an inch of this city go to waste. Your orders are to head there now."

"You want us to call off the search?"

"Not call off; just reassign. We've got a detachment of river police coming in from Vauxhall. They should be with you in moments."

"By which time the target might have slipped the net!"

"Well, even if he does, maybe he'll show up on the screens. Believe me, I've no plans to stop looking." She monitored the satellite footage as she spoke. "The only connection we have is the monuments are all Wren. If Blanco keeps true to form, we've got another four hours of this."

"Any reason to doubt him?"

"I only wish I did."

"I was afraid you might say that."

Sanders ended the conversation and immediately contacted the others. "Guys, I'm guessing you got all that. Reconvene on Southwark Bridge. Keep an eye out for the bastard with the launcher."

He found Jay waiting on the north side of the bridge. "What the hell's happened?"

To the north, the nearest flames remained visible as they crept up above buildings on College Street, confirmation Cannon Street was burning.

"Not sure exactly." Sanders shook his head. "Only it clearly isn't good."

At the Rook, all eyes remained focused on the screens. In Phil's case, the images from the Tower.

"What's the latest on Hansen?" the Director asked, watching live footage from Fleet Street. Less than two minutes after the first flames had been seen at

St Bride's, the inferno had spread both east and west.

"Just lost sight of him in the Bloody Tower." Phil's response was cool. "There's still gunmen there, but fortunately he wasn't spotted. If all goes to plan, he's already on his way to the new Wardrobe Tower."

The Director hadn't heard of it. "Where on earth's that?"

"It's located underground, directly beneath the ruins of the old one."

"Any visuals?"

"Negative; if it's not open to the public, it's unlikely to be on camera."

The Director accepted the response. "In that case, keep an eye on the GPS. Let me know the moment you re-establish contact with him. If he does make it to the archives, maybe there are other ways in which he can assist."

Seated alone in his scholarly office, Ian Atkins had been watching the footage on his own screen while simultaneously keeping on top of developments in Edinburgh. During the last half hour, things had quietened.

All of the early fires had been brought under control.

While the situation in Edinburgh had improved, in the English capital the pictures portrayed a sorry sight. St Bride's was widely acclaimed as one of Wren's crowning glories, the highest of his fifty-one churches. Had the situation been different, he might have been moved to tears at the sight of its five bays with double Tuscan columns melting into the flames and for the destruction of the steeple of five diminishing octagons. In its own way, the church had been the most iconic Wren masterpiece.

One whose name and design had influenced practically every wedding ever since.

Yet as the great spire continued to crumble away, his attention switched to the right of the screen, where he could see the famous painting of the fire from the river in 1666, accompanied by the iconic photograph of St Paul's during the Blitz. If St Bride's failed to take the crown as Wren's finest construction, there was only one that could possibly surpass it.

Sadly, he feared it was only a matter of time before that too would be back in the firing line.

60

The New Wardrobe Tower, 01:04

The passage ended at what appeared to be a blocked-off wall, the exact layout difficult to determine even with the aid of his night visions. After failing to contact Maria, Mike focused solely on the obstacle.

With the arsenal he had at his disposal, he knew he could blast his way out if necessary.

Removing his night-vision goggles, he switched on his torch, pointing it straight ahead. The obstacle was of stone construction: similar, but of less density than the walls to his left and right. As he focused on it, he noticed a small shaft of light coming from the right corner; confirmation the wall didn't completely join with the adjacent stonework. Edging closer, he noticed a gap that he estimated to be about an inch in width, revealing a dimly lit enclosure illuminated predominantly by desk lamps.

He pushed hard against the wall, at first making little progress. As the seconds passed, he noticed the gap begin to increase slightly, evidence at least that he was making progress. Gritting his teeth, he persevered, his shoulder pressing with all his force against the stonework. After almost two minutes, the gap was large enough to squeeze through.

Exhausted, he collapsed on to a carpeted floor.

Almost immediately the room was engulfed in light, the cosy study-like ambience magnified more than ten times over. On the ceiling, he saw a series of lights come on in sequence, their soft glow bouncing off freshly decorated walls that seemed a world apart from the tunnel he'd just passed through.

Standing over him was Emily.

"I have to admit, I'm actually kinda impressed."

He raised an eyebrow. "Just kinda?"

She rolled her eyes. "Don't get cocky, mister. Just because you can open a door doesn't mean we're out of the woods yet." She offered her hand. "Who knows, maybe if we do get out of here, you'll win Ironman."

She noticed Mike was smiling at her.

"What?"

Mike found the Harts assembled on a lonely loch-side shoreline. It was early morning; a wintry mist veiled the chilly waters. Beyond the loch, the ice-capped peaks of nearby mountains overlooked the area like gods on thrones, the reflection of their crevices and cracks magnified in the ripples of the surface. In every direction he saw more of the same, rocky outcrops stretching out into the distance. The darkening clouds threatened rain later.

All of the Harts were wearing wetsuits, their torsos hidden by heavy life jackets. Atkins and Phil stood alongside Bautista.

The man from the Far East checked his watch.

"Lieutenant Hansen, I was beginning to think you weren't coming." He placed his hands at the at ease position. "I'm most sorry, good morning."

A wry smile. "Good morning, sir."

"Congratulations on making it this far, and to Scotland. I'm sure you're wondering why we're here already. Today we have a very special treat for you. In NAVSOG this phase is designed to test all-round strength. In English, it would be called Ironman."

Iqbal had brought Mike his own wetsuit and life jacket; the tormentor gestured for him to change.

"The waters in front of you, so your colleagues tell me, can get very cold this time of year. Right now, you're looking at about ten degrees. But consider yourself lucky – in NAVSOG, when we do this, we swim without the luxury of a float aid."

Mike listened as he undressed, getting ready in as little time as possible; even fully clothed, the westerly wind was bracing. He quietly wondered how the Filipino would fare. Even if the NAVSOG didn't use float aids, he doubted they used freezing Scottish lochs either.

"Your first task today is to swim from the first checkpoint to the next – about four hundred metres. To complete the phase, you must do it in less than twenty-two minutes – using only breaststroke. If you use any other stroke, even if only for a moment, you will be disqualified. Are we clear?"

"Yes, sir!"

On completion of the challenge Mike again ended the parade alone. At Bautista's command, the other Harts reappeared.

"We are finally at the end of our time together. May I say how much I enjoyed it."

He looked at Mike and smiled. "Lieutenant Hansen, while yesterday you were a poor team leader, today you win the Ironman. Along with your teammates here, you really worked hard. You were tough, very tough – you beat the machines, just as I asked. Throughout the day you got better. I'm impressed."

"Doesn't matter." Mike shook his head and accepted her hand, his thoughts returning to the present. "And judging from the smell, I'd say there's actually plenty of wood in here."

"Probably because we're in the archives."

He got to his feet and looked around. On every side, he could see numerous rows of bookcases and a sophisticated racking system that seemed to continue indefinitely, its contents laid out in a specific order that he guessed would make sense only to Emily Fletcher and whoever else worked there. What struck him most was the smell: heavy mahogany dowsed with a mild air freshener that, despite a slightly sweet and fragrant feminine hint, was predominantly scholarly and masculine. What also struck him about the room was its size.

He guessed he was looking at something that would rival the best libraries worldwide.

Emily led him quickly along the central aisle into the heart of the archives, heading for a brown door that clearly led to an office.

"We can get out here into my office; from there it's an easy sprint to the north side," she said, hurrying. "You'll be pleased to know there are no cameras down here."

She'd made her way to the far end where a large photocopier presently hummed on standby close to a small kitchenette that she'd last used two days earlier. Reaching the door, she turned to speak.

Only to realise her companion had disappeared.

She found him standing in one of the many long, narrow aisles with shelves filled with what seemed to be thousands of manuscripts written on anything from vellum to paper and in several different languages. Each row was titled according to subject matter; each subject was also segmented by time period.

Among the signs, a series of large labels read 1666.

Randek returned to the Bloody Tower and climbed the stairway to the floor above, his muscles aching from the effort exerted in negotiating the narrow medieval steps. Reaching the second floor, he found himself in a far emptier room containing a pantomime-style display concerning the Princes in the Tower.

On the far side was another door.

He contacted the security room via his HT. "Any sign of life outside?"

"Negative," Christophe answered. "If they'd left by either door, we'd have seen them."

Randek avoided the temptation to question the claim. Reattaching his communications device to his belt, he returned downstairs, finding the remaining gunmen exploring the study.

"Search every inch. I don't want either of them escaping."

For the last ten minutes, Phil's attention had been firmly on the offices in the Waterloo Block. While Blanco was still on the roof of the White Tower, in one of the offices, François and the governor were seated at a desk.

"What's happening there?" the Director asked Phil, now standing behind him. Though the governor was still to be tied up, the pictures confirmed he wasn't present of his own will.

"The governor's been coming and going from various places all night." Phil brushed his beard with his thumb and index finger as he assessed the incoming images from the security cameras. "Right now, I'm sure General Yates is just as confused as we are."

"Intimidation tactics," Maria said, now viewing the same footage from her terminal. "Payet tried the same thing with Mike earlier this year. By separating him from the others, he intends to try to generate an environment of fear and uncertainty."

"Sure wouldn't like to be in his shoes right now," Phil agreed.

"Something tells me the governor isn't aware the hostages taken to the White Tower are still alive."

"Nor those still in the Queen's House," the Director agreed. Within seconds he moved on, finding Atkins alone on the far side of the room.

"What's the latest in Scotland?"

Atkins spoke via his hands-free. "Fitz-Simon, this is the Rook. What's the latest?"

Standing within the outer walls of the castle, Rawlins, Pentland and Pugh all watched on, awestruck as new flames appeared suddenly at the far end of the Royal Mile, way apart from the earlier fires.

Rawlins heard the Deputy Director's voice coming clearly through his headset. His eyes on the flames, he steadied himself against the medieval wall.

"Fresh fires are starting east of the others." Rawlins stared unblinkingly into the distance, intrigued how bright they looked against the dark backdrop. "Whatever's happening, it's independent of the others."

Atkins cursed under his breath. Alongside him, the Director looked once more at the semi-translucent screen; Maria had wasted no time bringing up the latest pictures. Sure enough, whereas the previous fires had yet to pass New Street to the north, the most recent had begun south of Canongate Kirk on the Royal Mile.

"Looks like they're targeting the palace and the parliament building!" Maria suggested glumly.

"Tune me into the Edinburgh frequency." The Director's request was met instantly. "Fitz-Simon, this is the King. How far are the fires from the palace?"

Gazing east from the castle rock across the city, Rawlins attempted to make a calculation in his mind. "If it keeps spreading the same way, we could be talking less than thirty minutes."

Though able to retain an exterior of calm and composure, the Director felt his heart rate accelerate appreciably. "What's the latest on the roads?"

"Emergency services aside, roads are closed to traffic all around the city; there's flashing lights moving up the Mile as we speak." Rawlins saw no less than twelve fire engines rushing in single file, some leaving the previous danger area to combat the latest, their sirens echoing forlornly in the distance. "Unlike in London, when the helicopters do move in, there's no sign of enemy action from below as of yet."

The helicopters, he remembered. Four had been brought down, two evacuated. It would make the news channels' year if the accidents in London repeated themselves north of the border.

"Where are you now?"

"Outside the castle, awaiting entry."

"Good. Make contact as soon as you can; when you do, I suggest you concentrate every effort on ensuring the security of the palace."

Blanco left the roof of the White Tower at precisely eight minutes past one. The fires on Fleet Street had been the most distant yet; even from one of the highest buildings in the vicinity it had been difficult to see everything clearly. Nevertheless, in the last five minutes he'd seen the latest flames more than triple in height and width.

He contacted Randek on reaching the stairs, the sound of static creating an amplified, harsh vibrating echo off the medieval stonework. "Fabien, where are you?"

"First floor of the Bloody Tower." Randek had returned to Raleigh's study, eyeing the scholarly setting with an increasing feeling of scepticism. "Personally, I see little to validate the name."

"I remember hearing similar things about Sleeping Beauty's castle. Where is the Englishman?"

Randek had no answers. "We know first-hand the man has a talent for evading the net. Perhaps there are clues in the sailor's own writings."

Blanco re-entered the barracks, finding François seated alongside the governor. While his relative examined the photocopy before him with scholarly contempt, the general's mood was sombre.

"I'm most sorry to have kept you waiting, General." Blanco spun the photocopy around, allowing Yates a clearer view. "There are several matters to which, during our time together, I would much appreciate your knowledge, but perhaps we can start with the most pressing." He tapped hard against the map, his outstretched finger pointing out an area close to where they currently stood. "When the great Sir Walter Raleigh was here, he made, either with the aid of others or from the efforts of his own studies, a detailed map of the Tower. Among his observations was a tunnel connecting to the north-west from where we currently reside." Blanco's eyes were locked firmly on the former military man. "I wish to know where it starts."

Though the governor had never seen the map before, nor witnessed the tunnel, immediately his blood ran cold. If the rumours were true, the key to finding the real jewels was already within the terrorist's reach.

"I'm sorry, you must be mistaken. I've never seen this before."

Unlike François, whose pent-up emotions and heightened tension threatened to boil over at this point, Blanco remained icily calm. "Maybe it was foolish of me to expect that you would be able to provide that information without some further thought. Perhaps we might start with an easier task and instead you could identify for me how the sailor successfully travelled to and from his quarters in the Bloody Tower."

61

The Museum of London, 01:18

The car was waiting outside the gallery when Kit and Gillian departed. After locking the main doors and Gillian was satisfied that she had completed all of the necessary security measures to ensure no repeat of the break-in would be possible, they made their way east through the deserted streets, heading back into the danger area.

On taking the A40 as far as the Stock Exchange, the driver turned north towards the Barbican Centre, one of the few areas of London close to the old Roman wall. Alighting at the Rotunda, they took the pedestrian stairs to one of two footbridges and ended the walk at a glass façade.

Designated, Museum of London.

The Museum of London was one of the less famous tourist attractions in the city. Located north of St Paul's Cathedral close to the financial centre, it had been established in the 1970s to bring regeneration to an area razed to the ground during the Blitz. Though the dated building, housing over six million objects of connection to the city's social and urban past and still welcoming over a million visitors a year, had prompted plans to relocate the exhibits to nearby Smithfield, the museum was the largest of its type in the world and still famed as one of the most enjoyed attractions in the city.

Kit and Gillian hurried across the footbridge, making their way through the electronic doors. The museum was officially closed and had been for several hours, but on reaching the atrium, they were greeted by a well-dressed man in his mid-to-late fifties with balding red hair that matched the colour of his tweed blazer.

"Tony, I really can't thank you enough." Gillian hugged the curator, Kit sensed more out of professional courtesy than friendship. Judging from the man's general bearing, he guessed the thought would never cross his mind of how she could thank him enough.

"I apologise if we woke you." Kit joined the conversation. "However, unfortunately time is of the essence." He flashed an ID card.

Edward Lewis. 3/11/81.

"Under the circumstances, sleep this evening has been most uneasy to come by." The man paid the briefest attention to Kit's card before shaking hands. "Even living on the north-west side, it's not often one turns on the news to find one's city is on the brink of inferno."

"Well, quite," Kit replied, neglecting to add it was now well beyond the brink. "I'll spare you the finer details for our request tonight; last thing I'd want is to bore you. I understand from Ms McKevitt that you're currently running an exhibition on the Great Fire?"

"Yes, that's right." Green adjusted his glasses as he led them past the main reception area, his voice resonating loudly in the silence. Though there were lights on at various points, the atrium itself was largely unlit and unlikely to arouse the attention of outsiders. "As a matter of fact, we're due to close in just under two weeks."

"Well, if it's all the same to you, I'd very much like to see it."

Green led them across the main reception area and past the entrances to the gift shop and the main galleries. Kit followed quietly as the curator took them down two flights of stairs, giving them the option of heading left along a small corridor that included signs for the toilets or straight ahead where another reception desk offered access to the Fire exhibition.

"The main exhibition closes at six o'clock every day." The curator led them to the front desk. There were lights on along the corridor to their left, less so past the desk. Kit sensed the darkness was in character with the exhibition. "I wasn't sure whether you wanted to see everything, so I've taken the liberty of turning everything on."

"You're most thoughtful, Tony." Gillian smiled.

The curator led them into the exhibition, passing the front desk to where a narrow corridor had been decorated to replicate the compact streets of 17th-century London. The smouldering glow of a small oven fire offered subdued illumination, appearing convincingly atmospheric against the backdrop of several display areas and accompanied by the pre-recorded sounds of a bakery closing and the meowing of a cat. At the far end of the corridor, Kit saw a computerised map illustrating the spread of the fire, flanked by a timeline written in yellow and red against a dark background.

At the far end they made a U-turn, taking them into the next section. The exhibition was far brighter here, the text displays replaced by various items that had survived the fire and by a number of paintings, some of which were portraits of figures Kit recognised. He stopped briefly in front of the charred remains of an effigy that had once been located in old St Paul's, quietly wondering how it had survived. While Gillian chatted with her acquaintance, he continued into the final section. One article immediately caught his eye.

A stone plaque, split in two.

Here by ye Permission of Heaven, Hell Broke Loose
Upon This Protestant City From The Malicious
Hearts of Barbarous Papists, By Ye Hand Of Their
Agent Hubert, Who Confessed And On Ye Ruines
Of This Place Declared The Fact, For Which He
Was Hanged (Vizt) That Here Began That Dred
Full Fire, Which Is Described And Perpetuated
On And By The Neighbouring Pillar
Erected Anno 1681 In The Majoraltie Of
Sr. Patience Ward K$_T$

The curator appeared alongside him, noticing Kit's fascination with the plaque. "What you're seeing here was once set into the wall of the building constructed on the site of Thomas Farriner's bakery." Green stood aside to allow Gillian a view. "Back then, of course, the word among the common folk was the fire had been orchestrated deliberately by barbarous papists."

Barbarous papists. The curator quoted directly from the plaque. There were other words Kit recognised too. Blanco's first speech had been almost identical, certain words substituted.

Most obviously Everard for Hubert.

For several seconds Kit was lost for words. "What happened to it?"

"Following its removal, after the passing of the Emancipation Act, it turned up several years later in a cellar. Unfortunately by that time the damage was done." He spoke of the crack.

The split aside, Kit was impressed by its condition. "I don't understand. If the words here are anything to go by, the fire was believed to have been deliberate."

"Well, that was precisely what many writers would have you believe; not to mention what was already widely assumed by the citizens at the time. When the fire began, it was rumoured a Dutch invasion would soon follow. When a plausible suspect was found, it was only fitting, in the eyes of the authorities, that they took appropriate action. Especially as the man himself made a full confession."

Kit was surprised. He had always been taught that the fire had been an accident.

He focused on the name of the culprit.

"Who was Hubert?"

"Robert Hubert himself was a humble watchmaker's son from Normandy; contemporary accounts suggest he was something of a drifter. Following his arrest in Essex after being caught up in the general mass evacuation from the capital, Hubert recounted a story that he had been recruited in Paris the previous year as one of a gang of twenty-four who had been responsible for starting the fire."

"So the fire was deliberate?"

"Following the parliamentary inquiry that took place, Hubert was tried and hanged; however, few now take the tale seriously. Hubert's story was full of contradictions – in fact, according to the captain of the ship he travelled on, Hubert wasn't even in London that night. Nevertheless, in the eyes of the authorities, a general acceptance that the fire had been by permission of humans rather than heaven was a small comfort."

Kit listened carefully. "So you're saying he was a scapegoat?"

"He seems to have been one of many. One of the most alarming aspects of the fire is just how quick the citizens were to unleash their wrath and attribute blame on seemingly anyone with a foreign accent. There was talk of arsonists all over the city. We hear, for instance, the tale recounted by a fourteen-year-old in Moorfields of a Frenchman carrying incendiaries, which were actually tennis balls. The same boy also recounted witnessing a blacksmith walk up to a

Frenchman in the street and striking him with an iron bar. One poor woman even suffered the indignity of having her breasts removed after being the subject of mistaken identity."

Kit scowled, simultaneously concentrating on the words on the tablet for a second time. The split was clean, precise.

It seemed almost too precise.

"Who wrote this?"

"The plaque was commissioned on the orders of the man mentioned." He spoke of Sir Patience Ward. "Successor to the previous mayor, who was famously quoted on seeing the fire at Farriner's that a woman could piss it out."

"Seems the mayors had a habit of making mistakes." Kit turned his attention to Gillian, lowering his voice as the curator moved on to the nearby exhibits. "Do you still have that torch you showed me?"

Baffled, she removed it from her handbag. "Why?"

Kit switched it on and pointed it at the plaque. Immediately they both raised their eyebrows.

"Is that writing?"

Kit leaned in to obtain the best possible view. Though the room was poorly lit, it was still too bright to take in everything.

"Ask the curator to turn off the lights!"

Gillian disappeared briefly to ensure the request was met, at which point the room went dark. Leaning over the supporting table, the light of the torch focused on the heart of the text. Several previously unseen words appeared in purple.

"What's it say?" She returned, attempting to read it as best she could.

"Under the watchful eyes of the Gemini, the city burns to ash. Beware the wrath of the Cardinal's Twins."

Kit was stunned. What he read almost exactly matched the document sent to the Palace.

"There's more!" Gillian pointed, her finger floating over the third line of text. Above it was a strange symbol. "That's the symbol of Gemini."

Kit nodded, noticing the same Gemini symbol Maria had earlier sent to his satphone had been replaced by the same characters now standing upright, each holding a baby. "Should Castor and Pollux in the month of June die and their earthly offspring fall and crash, in the long-lost pages of the diarist's prose can hell's seven doors be entered in."

Kit turned to face Gillian, her tired face looking slightly gaunt against the purple backdrop. "Diarist's prose?"

"Only one diarist wrote of the fire."

"Pepys."

They returned to the previous room, finding it in darkness. Guided by the purple light, Kit noticed the familiar features of Samuel Pepys hanging from the wall on the left side.

"Was this one of the portraits de Haulle wanted?"

Gillian stood beside him, amazed. "Yes."

"I think I'm beginning to see why."

Gillian eyed him with a strange expression. After failing to get a response, she turned her attention to the portrait, noticing the UV light was revealing something.

She placed her hand to her mouth. "Oh my God!"

62

The New Wardrobe Tower,
01:22

The first thing Mike noticed among the plethora of manuscripts was a name that until an hour earlier had been completely unknown to him, despite Emily's assertion that his uncle had mentioned it earlier that evening.

"William Lilly!" Mike removed the manuscript with Lilly's name on it, inspecting the cover closely. Thanks to Emily, he was now aware that Lilly had been an eminent writer at the time of the Great Fire, later famed as one of the most revered astrologers of that century.

Only what Mike saw wasn't one of his works.

"He faced trial?"

"Not a trial exactly, just questioning." Emily took possession of the manuscript; the full title confirmed the interrogation had taken place on 25 October 1666. "According to his work *Monarchy or No Monarchy in England*, written in 1651, Lilly successfully predicted the Great Fire of London. When the fire was out, a committee was established to investigate the cause. Inevitably, Lilly was among those questioned."

"Was he involved?"

"As a matter of fact, he was found not guilty. When brought before the Commons, Lilly persuaded them his horoscope had not been specific, and even if it was, he hadn't been involved in the fire." Emily replaced her glasses and flicked through the pages, finding the diagram of the Gemini. "This was almost certainly what Maria mentioned."

Mike looked at the picture, noticing the five figures of the zodiac surrounding a bonfire. Sure enough, the Gemini hung upside down above it.

"What's the connection with London?"

"As Lilly pointed out, the exact prediction was vague. However, Gemini was regarded as the symbol of the city."

"Why was he questioned?"

"At the time, suspicion was rife that the fire had been started deliberately." Emily closed the manuscript and replaced it on the shelf before inspecting the others on that row. "Three weeks after the fire, a parliamentary commission was set up to determine the cause." She identified one book in particular, a small library-bound hardback. "This is the report of the commission's findings."

Mike was amazed. "You mean they seriously suspected it wasn't an accident?"

"From the very beginning many Londoners were convinced it was a deliberate attack." She handed the book to Mike, looking at him. "Think about it. A fire destroys eighty per cent of the city. What's the more logical explanation? That it was an accident or an act of war?"

Mike accepted the book, recognising that he had in his hand something that was hundreds of years old and probably rarely seen outside the present room. The title was self-explanatory.

A true and faithful account of the several informations exhibited to the honourable committee appointed by the Parliament to inquire into the late dreadful burning of the city of London together with other informations touching the insolency of the popish priests and the Jesuites.

He opened it to a random page. "A constable took a Frenchman for firing a house . . . There were three hundred Frenchmen that were in a plot or conspiracy to fire the city . . . We searched the fellow and found a horn of powder about him. He also had a book entitled *The Jewish Government*." Mike recited certain passages as he read them, turning pages quickly. "The people cried out, he's a Frenchman, kill him." He looked at Emily. "It's like people were looking for a scapegoat."

"Prejudice is like a virus. It can lie dormant for years, then suddenly, whoosh!" She gestured with her hands. "All hell breaks loose!"

"Kinda like the fire."

"Matter of fact, some of the accounts here really are startling; just goes to show how humans react in panic. The more the fire spread, the more mob rule prevailed." She looked philosophically at the book. "Ironically, even when the fire was burning, the greatest danger faced by foreigners in London was the English themselves."

Mike nodded, finding further examples as he read. "I apprehended a Walloon with an instrument filled with gunpowder. There were two more of the same nation in his company." He closed the book and returned it to her. "Sounds as if the blame wasn't centred on one nation more than another."

"As far as the Londoners were concerned, all foreigners were bad. The city was being razed to the ground and they were out for vengeance. Within government circles, there were only two groups believed to be guilty."

"Who?"

"The Dutch and the French."

Mike raised an eyebrow; a torrent of thoughts flooded into his mind. The reference by Blanco, the drawing by Lilly.

Ask me who we were.

Was it really possible the same people had been responsible twice?

"What evidence is there?" Mike asked, his curiosity intensifying with each new disclosure. "The uniformed ranting of the locals aside, what proof is there the fire was deliberate?"

"Accidents happen all the time, but everything about this was wrong."

"How do you mean?"

"First, it happened at the end of summer, after a long drought. The City of London was a tinderbox. In its narrow streets, it would take only a minor incident for a fire to begin."

"Surely that's an argument it was an accident. Such things happened all the time."

"Indeed they did. However, bakery fires at night were unusual. They were far more common in the morning or early evening whilst the ovens were in use. Thomas Farriner confirmed in his report the fires had been put out four hours earlier. This would have been standard practice."

"Everyone makes mistakes." Mike raised an eyebrow. "How do we know he wasn't lying to cover his back?"

"I'm sure a lot of people felt that way, and if it was an accident, it stands to reason he did that. However, it took a whole hour for the flames to spread, which allowed plenty of time to put them out.

"The location, though, couldn't have been worse. In addition to it being beside flammable materials, it also took out the great waterwheel from the Thames, which was needed to pump water."

"Meaning?"

"Meaning that the fire broke out at the worst time of day in the worst time of year, in a highly combustible area with a waterwheel that was inoperable. Added together it all looked suspiciously premeditated."

"You honestly think it was deliberate?"

"I don't think anything. However, coupled with the fact it was up a hill that had a natural draught to fan the flames, once the fire took hold, it was only a matter of time before it spread. And from an arsonist's perspective, there was one even better reason to start a fire there."

"What's that?"

"The thing that almost everyone took for granted: bakeries had a habit of catching fire."

Mike placed his hand to his mouth, stunned. "If the descendants of the group of people responsible then are responsible now, it could be they're following the same patterns." He moved from manuscript to manuscript, not knowing what to look for. "You mentioned the waterwheel was inactive, what's significant about that?"

"You mean apart from the fact that it was the only way people could get water?"

Mike realised the stupidity of the question. "How about the streets themselves, you said they were narrow?"

"You did say you did a history master's?" She stared at him sceptically through her glasses. "Matter of fact, things like that were reported to have happened a lot. Frequently as the fires were spreading, many of those fighting them or trying to rescue people caught up in the flames complained about the difficulties of gaining access to the narrow passages."

Mike frowned, realisation slowly dawning.

It was as if the culprits of 1666 had organised history's first cyber-attack.

Less than two miles from where the flames were highest, a small convoy of cabin cruisers sailed slowly towards the danger area. Unlike the yacht that had exploded earlier that evening or the similar one that had recently been present on the waters of the Seine, their dark exteriors were specifically designed for the carrying of troops and to blend in with the night.

* * *

At the same time, the man who had been last to leave Fieschi's yacht before it exploded typed quickly on the keyboard of his laptop. Hacking into the Tower of London's security system had been far from simple, but the latest task had, surprisingly, been altogether more straightforward.

He smiled with satisfaction as he watched the latest footage through one of the city's many CCTV cameras.

Just one click of the button and things would get a whole lot worse.

Seated in the same position, Maria studied the same pictures, a stunned expression on her face. The CCTV cameras showing the closed roads around the city confirmed every traffic light had changed from red to green.

63

The New Wardrobe Tower, 01:28

Mike closed the book containing the parliamentary inquiry reports and placed it down on the nearby table, glancing, as he did so, at the cover. In the last few minutes he'd scanned every page; time enough for his understanding and perception of the fire to be completely changed. For a moment, he thought back to the beginning of Champion's lecture, how his uncle had spoken in depth about the lapse in security.

It now seemed incredible that people had ever believed it to have been an accident.

He reverted his attention to the nearest bookcase, the dust-covered exteriors of over a thousand books and manuscripts lined up in front of him. Alongside him, Emily had already been through several; he'd never seen anyone read so fast. His instinctive feeling was something of importance was contained within them.

That somewhere within this extensive collection of important historical documents a vital clue waited to be uncovered.

He listened to the voices coming through his headset. Since leaving the Byward Tower, reception had been intermittent; Maria was speaking again, apparently to Sanders. All of the Harts had been given new orders to split up and cover all of the Wren churches. He'd noticed the connection himself earlier.

The questions remained: what and why?

The news from above had been predictable. Though Randek, Blanco and de Haulle were still roaming the Tower, what had become of the hostages remained unclear. The eighteen currently held in the White Tower were unharmed, despite being tied up against one of the walls and watched over by four masked gunmen. The news from the Thomas More room was no different; assuming there were no alternative exits, all remained in the same place. Any form of backup was unlikely; at least for now, Mike knew he was on his own. At least thirty gunmen controlled the areas up above, still to find any trace of him. Nevertheless, after almost twenty minutes in the strange underground archives, he was beginning to feel a little demoralised.

While he sensed the archives held something important, he knew reading manuscripts wasn't going to help save any of the hostages.

He opened the small parliamentary book a second time, concentrating on some of the claims. Besides the unsubstantiated accusations made against the unnamed French, other claims seemed to be more tangible. A Lady Hobart of Chancery Lane had written to her cousin that the fire had started in Pudding Lane where a Dutch rogue lay. Close to Westminster, another Dutchman had aroused suspicion after flames were seen coming from his own bakery. On Lime Street, a wealthy area home to several successful immigrants, a prominent Dutch family had been accused of having prior knowledge, as they had acquired several carts soon after the fire began.

Yet of all the records, one in particular caught Mike's attention. Following the fire, a Wiltshire farmer had testified against a Dutchman, saying that in the days before the fire the foreigner had threatened: *If you should live a week longer, you shall see London as sad a London as ever it was since the world began.*

"What happened to these guys?" Mike asked, showing the relevant page to Emily. "I'm guessing at least some of them faced trial?"

"With the exception of the baker and the family on Lime Street, none of the claims could be substantiated. Even in those cases, none were actually guilty of doing anything wrong."

Mike reread what he'd just been through, realising as he did so that Emily was right. "You mean it could have been made up?"

"Either that or a strange coincidence."

Mike nodded, noticing another coincidence. Whereas before the accusations had been mostly against the French, in the later pages they were predominantly anti-Dutch.

"What does this mean?" he asked about the farmer in Wiltshire. "It also suggests here the Dutchman was unhappy Londoners had been making bonfires in celebration."

"Back then it was a custom," Emily confirmed, adjusting her glasses. "When Elizabeth I died, Londoners were encouraged to light bonfires in her honour. They did the same when the Gunpowder Plot was uncovered, the first official bonfire night."

To Mike that made sense. "What exactly were they celebrating?"

"At the time, England was at war with the Dutch because of the close trade routes. The month before the fire, an English force raided a town on the Dutch coast, setting fire to ships and houses. Back in London, people celebrated with bonfires."

Mike raised an eyebrow, noticing the coincidence. Suddenly the Dutch seemed far more likely than the French.

"Was anyone tried?"

"Just one. A few days after the fire, a man named Robert Hubert was apprehended trying to flee the country at Essex. On being questioned, he admitted to starting the fire, along with twenty-three others."

"He was charged?"

"Charged and hanged."

Mike gasped in surprise. "Why have I never heard of any of this?"

"Though Hubert was tried and executed, most of those who questioned him were unsure of his credibility. Even before Hubert was hanged, the captain of the ship he'd been on even went as far as to state that he'd not been in London that night. When the Monument was created, a plaque was put nearby placing the blame on French Catholics. After the Emancipation Act, the plaque was removed. Everything that was once believed became forgotten."

Mike rubbed his fingers against his face, finding it difficult to know what to believe. Every time he sensed a new lead, he realised it was probably just another blind alley.

Moving away, he spoke into his headset. "What's the latest, Maria?"

The reply came from Phil. "Maria's tied up right now. Edward's made it to the museum. The others are taking control of the churches."

Progress, Mike sensed. "Where's Randek?"

"Currently running round the Bloody Tower like a headless chicken; Blanco and de Haulle are in the barracks with the governor." Phil leaned in close to the screen. "Blanco seems to be questioning him on some document."

"Probably about the jewels," Mike mused. "What's our best way out of here? Interesting as this place is, we can't be finding hostages cooped up here."

"It looks as though you've got two options," Phil replied as he examined the screens. "Take the usual route to the offices and come out on the north side. The other option is to go back the way you came."

"Is there a third choice?"

Phil zoomed in on the south wall. "Afraid not, Honey Badger. After that, you're on your own."

"So what else is new? What's the latest with the fires?"

"Spreading but far slower. The PM's ordered further reinforcements from the Home Counties to help police the streets. As soon as they arrive, I'll be sure to let you know."

Blanco exited the office, buoyed by the latest revelations. Though at least one of his questions remained unanswered, progress had been made on another.

He contacted Randek, using his HT. "Fabien, do you copy?"

Still in Raleigh's study, Randek replied, "I hear you."

"I have news that might help you. It seems the English sailor was most obliging in including his personal favourite routes in his map."

Randek raised an eyebrow. "He revealed the way to the jewels?"

"That route will reveal itself at the correct time." Blanco's tone was far calmer. "In the meantime, perhaps you will oblige my curiosity and pay greater attention to the floor of the sailor's study. A passage exists beneath the tiles."

To Randek the words meant nothing. "That is your advice? By the time the entrance is discovered, the Englishman could be gone."

"Sir Walter himself was kind enough to mention how to access the mechanism. The lever is located somewhere in the brick floor, close to the window. Look carefully inside the gaps."

Randek ended the transmission and turned his attention to his surroundings. There was a desk to his left, an antique cabinet against the north wall. Of all the furnishings in the room, one stood out for its awkward placing.

64

The Museum of London, 01:32

15 October 1666

Among the many who did willingly come forward to assist the parliamentary inquiry into the causes of that dreadful fire, I by chance renewed my acquaintance with Thomas Middleton, in the time of the fire, near St Bride's, who revealed in his own words information of great value that on 2 September, he did repair to the top of a church steeple near the Three Cranes in the Vintrey, where his self and several others observed the motion of the fire for two or three hours together, and all took notice that the fire did break forth out of several houses, when the houses which were then burning were at a good distance from them in every way, and more particularly, saw the fire break out from the inside of Lawrence-Pountney steeple, when there was no fire near it. These and such like Observations begat in him a Perswasion that the fire was maintained by design.

Upon Munday Middleton repaired again into the City, and found as the day before, that the fire did break forth in fresh houses at a great distance from one another. And as he was returning home, passing through Watling-Street by a Tobacco Merchants house, he saw the Master of the house come down stairs, driving a young fellow before him, saying to him, You Rogue, do you come to Rob me? What did you do in my Garret? Or words to that purpose, and pushed him out of doors. He seemed to be a Frenchman: a short fellow of about twenty-two years of Age: and as soon as he was out of the house, he having on a loose coat, in a way of Privacy, Shuffled something under his Coat, whereupon Middleton laid hold of him and said, Sirrah, what have you there? The fellow replyed, What is that to you? The Master of the House knows me: Upon that Middleton asked the Master of the House whether he knew the fellow, the master answered, he knew him not. Whereupon Middleton searched the fellow and found a horn of powder about him, and as soon as the powder was discovered, he fell a rubbing his hands, they being all black with powder: He had also about him a Book intituled The Sons of Gemini.

Kit studied the strange writing as it appeared in the purple light to the left of Samuel Pepys's face, trying hard to understand what he was seeing. The narrative was detailed and informative, reminding him of a diary entry. The previously invisible handwriting confirmed Pepys had been present at the parliamentary inquiry and spoken first-hand with an old acquaintance who had personally witnessed acts of arson separate from the natural spread of the blaze. The only suspect had been a young man, apparently a Frenchman. In the following lines Pepys recounted that the young man disappeared from gaol when it burned, presumably let free. What struck Kit most was the item that had apparently been in the young man's possession.

A book entitled *The Sons of Gemini*.

Kit lowered the torch and took a step back to appreciate the features of the portrait. In the darkness, the shape of Pepys's body, hair and face created a plain, blank silhouette; in the purple torchlight, the colours were inverted but revealed more detail. As the seconds passed, he noticed something show up on the right side.

Gillian noticed it too. "There's more."

Shining the torch to the right of Pepys's body, Kit made out additional text.

Having had the opportunity to talk over the matter with the said Middleton, some members of the inquiry wishing to speak to him privately regarding matters other than that in his statement, I made my leave and presently walked to Whitehall, and there went up into the main chamber, where His Majesty and the Duke resided. Having stayed an hour in their company, during which time I relayed the words of Middleton to them both, on hearing this, they seemed little troubled as the Duke confided in me to my surprise the fate of the young man was neither a mystery to himself nor His Majesty. Having endeavoured in ways in which he has since been notably praised in rounding up many foreigners, sparing them the wrath of London's citizens, the Duke did tell me that the young Frenchman, himself one servant of the enigmatic firework maker Belland, was in considerable want among the authorities, notably for his endeavour to acquire much pasteboard in preparation for a great display that his master had previously boasted would create a pure body of flame higher than St Paul's.

Of the exact fate of the young man and his master, I have received no further word, the Duke instead assuring me such secrecy was at the heart of dispelling the common outcry that remained rife in the city and the matter would be taken care of privately. Of the reasons behind that dreadful fire, I have been advised to keep my own counsel, the secrets being known equally by the great Architect, who has since endeavoured the great rebuilding, and in the pictures of the unknown artist.

Kit switched off the torch and took an astonished breath. The content of the second section was of particular significance: a clear reference to the foreigner who many believed was responsible for starting the fire, that the king and the Duke of York had been the first to round him up, but never allowed it to become known for fear of public outcry. Pepys suggested the royals knew the true cause of the fire.

He suggested a conspiracy.

Kit turned to Gillian. "This is incredible. It's like the portrait you showed me earlier."

Gillian was momentarily speechless. For several seconds her eyes alternated between Kit and the portrait, her pale face looking almost ghostly in the poor light. "How could he possibly have known?"

Kit had been wondering the same thing. Hesilrige, Cromwell, Pepys, the others. The Sons of Gemini. Hell's seven doors.

Ask me who we were.

"Pepys spoke of two others. The unknown artist and the architect." He remembered what Maria had said about the churches. "Wren?"

"Wren was charged with the task of designing practically the entire new city. All of the churches were in some way his doing."

Her words confirmed what Kit already knew. Reactivating the light, he focused on the final lines: *the secrets being known equally by the great Architect, who has since endeavoured the great rebuilding, and in the pictures of the unknown artist.*

"What were the other pieces de Haulle asked for?"

"There were two. One of them is over here." She led Kit to the other side of the room, where a large painting of the Great Fire hung from the opposite wall. Though Kit was unaware of the artist and title, he'd seen the picture before. It depicted the Tower of London on the right side away from the blaze, and the path of the flames that had devoured almost everything to the west.

St Paul's was both consumed and illuminated.

Kit switched on the torch, examining the picture carefully from side to side. At first sight he saw nothing.

"Do that again," Gillian requested.

Kit immediately obliged, concentrating on the central area. On closer inspection, markings could be detected under the paint.

Not text but numbers.

"What is that?" Gillian peered in for a closer look.

Shaking his head, Kit moved alongside her to concentrate on picking out the numbers. There were seven in total, developing in sequence from east to west. Number 6 was inside St Paul's itself; most of the numbers were inside churches. For the first time he noticed other markings alongside the numbers.

"They look like firebombs!" Gillian said.

"I was just thinking the same thing." Kit glanced again over his shoulder, remembering what Pepys had written.

The pictures of the unknown artist.

"What was the final painting?"

"It was a portrait of Wren."

Kit hurried off immediately, briefly looking at exhibits as he passed. Portraits of Charles II and James II while still Duke of York were hung on the wall on the left side; beyond it were kids' costumes. In the next room, he passed the plaque again, finding several documents mounted on the walls, mostly relating to the later designs for the city. As he reached the end, he saw a final portrait.

In which Christopher Wren was standing prominently against the backdrop of his famous cathedral.

Kit stopped directly in front of it and reactivated the UV torch, watching with increasing surprise as the purple light revealed the portrait's secrets.

Maria heard Kit's voice in her ear the moment she finished speaking with Jay.

"Grosmont was right." Kit's voice suggested both excitement and disbelief. "The secrets are in the churches."

Maria needed a moment for that to register. "Excuse me?"

"The works of art Jérôme de Haulle requested are all here at the Fire exhibition. Each one contains writing beneath the surface."

Maria was almost speechless. "What are you talking about?"

"The first was a portrait of Pepys. The layer beneath contains lost pages of his diary."

"Lost pages?"

"Apparently after the fire, there was an inquiry into the possible cause. Among the suspects was a young Frenchman. He was found with a book called *The Sons of Gemini*."

"He what?"

"Wait, it gets better. A near identical message to the one Blanco sent to Downing Street was written on a plaque that was once located at Farriner's. Only there's more." He recited the previously hidden message about the Cardinal's Twins in full.

Maria was lost for words. "Where are you now?"

"Just leaving the exhibition. The bigger clues were in the other paintings. The next was a painting of the Great Fire. The artist wrote seven numbers in invisible ink alongside symbols of firebombs. In the Pepys portrait, he confirms the fire was deliberate."

"Where exactly were the numbers?"

"That's the bit I'm unsure of." Still in the museum, he continued to study the elegant face of Sir Christopher Wren, concentrating on its recently revealed secrets. "The portrait of Wren contains a city layout. Like the fire painting, there are seven areas identified by numbers. It also contains a set of keys."

"Keys?"

"Doors of hell – I think it ties in with the plaque," Kit guessed. "The numbers seem to coincide with the markings beneath the fire painting."

"But the fire painting has to refer to the old city. Everything was destroyed."

"Exactly. That's what's so special about the Wren one."

Maria felt a chill go up her spine. "You mean . . ."

"Exactly. Wren planned the new city to hide the secrets the old one left behind."

65

The New Wardrobe Tower, 01:39

Mike heard Maria's voice in his ear, followed immediately by Kit's. For a moment, he didn't know who to respond to first.

"Maria?"

"The connection is Wren," Maria began. "The fires are being started in the churches."

Mike listened without offering a reply. Sure enough, every report he'd heard so far had involved a church catching fire.

Yet there'd been no explosions or signs of a culprit.

"If the fires were inside the churches, then they'd have to have been started remotely," Mike began, still curious as to the exact method. "Either that or Blanco knows a lot of people with suicide wishes."

"Actually, it's possible we were all wrong." Kit spoke up, his voice accompanied by the sound of footsteps in the background. "The words the PM heard when the building next to the Monument went up were almost identical to those written on a plaque that had once been placed on the site of Farriner's bakery. Under UV light it was also found to include other words."

"What were they?"

Kit recited the first two lines about the Gemini and the Cardinal's Twins. "Furthermore, it also said 'Should Castor and Pollux in the month of June die and their earthly offspring fall and crash, in the long-lost pages of the diarist's prose can hell's seven doors be entered in'."

Mike was confused. "Who are Castor and Pollux?"

"Castor and Pollux were the names given to the Gemini," Emily answered, eavesdropping. She showed him the picture in the Lilly manuscript again. "Here."

Kit agreed.

Mike accepted the answer. "Diarist's prose?" Again he recalled Champion's lecture. "Pepys?"

"When the de Haulles robbed the National Portrait Gallery, he specifically targeted one portrait that had writing beneath the paint layer." There was energy in Kit's voice. "Tonight I saw the three he missed out on. The designs by Wren confirm the locations of the doors of hell."

While Mike and Kit continued their conversation, Maria studied the photographs Kit had sent of the paintings. The writing on the plaque and the Pepys portrait was difficult to make out in the light; ideally it needed to be photographed flat.

Worse still was the Great Fire painting; even if the photo had been perfect, she doubted it would have shown much of relevance to the modern-day city.

Far clearer was the fourth.

Viewing the screen before her, Maria was almost overcome with surprise. The scenes she saw were instantly recognisable.

Yet never had she seen them in such a way.

"You haven't disappointed, Edward; I'll give you that much."

Kit halted his conversation with Mike. "Well, I suppose it's about time you came around."

"The diagram is Wren's original plan for London; however, it was never put in place. On the orders of the king, Wren later modified it."

"Why was that?" Mike was curious.

"Cost perhaps. Efficiency. In truth, you'd have to take it up with Charles II. Only one thing's for sure, it was never built."

Kit cursed under his breath. "So it's meaningless?"

"Not necessarily." Maria typed frantically on her keyboard, clicking her mouse. As the seconds passed, the outline of Wren's city merged with a second design.

Maria brought her hands to her mouth in disbelief. "Like I say, you don't disappoint."

"What is it?"

"The seven key symbols coincide with modern-day buildings." Maria double-checked what she saw. "Nearly all of them are churches."

"What can you see?"

She checked them off, one by one. "Stephen Walbrook, St Clement's and St Bride's are all at the exact same points. There also seems to be one under Monument."

At the other end, Mike and Kit were on tenterhooks. "What about the others?"

"St Mary-le-Bow and St Dunstan-in-the-East," Maria began. "Last is St Paul's."

A sudden realisation came to Kit. "A pure body of flame higher than St Paul's."

Again, Mike was confused. "Blanco?"

Alongside him Emily shook her head. "That was Belland."

Kit overheard. "What?"

Emily's eyes were on Mike. "Those exact words were said by the king's fireworks maker the week before the fire."

Kit recalled the second part of the text hidden in Pepys's portrait. "Grosmont, where are you?"

"Tower archives. There's a section here on 1666." Mike gazed again at the various spines as they appeared on the relevant shelves. "You oughta see this place. There's stuff here from the original inquiry."

Making his way out of the museum, Kit kept his calm. "Listen to me. There was more to the Pepys portrait than the lead about the churches. Apparently he had proof the fire was deliberate. It was seen by one of his associates. The same man even briefly caught the culprit."

"Based on what I'm reading here, there were many suspects," Mike replied. "Most of them Dutch."

"The Dutch were just scapegoats. The main culprits were the French."

"Hubert?"

"Hubert may have been responsible for starting the fire, but he wasn't the ringleader. That was a fireworks maker called Belland."

"How do you know this?"

"Pepys recorded in the lost diary pages that Belland's servant had been apprehended by the king and the Duke of York to avoid a public outcry. Appears they were tried."

As Emily began scouring the shelves, Mike replied, "You mean the king knew they were guilty?"

"Worse. The servant was found with a book entitled *The Sons of Gemini*."

Mike was incredulous. "Who were they? Who were the Cardinal's Boys?"

At the other end, Kit shook his head. "I don't know. But whoever they were, they weren't just responsible for one fire. On the plaque the word used was *twins*."

"Why's there a difference?"

"I don't know. But something tells me finding out might be important."

"Where are you now?"

"Leaving the exhibition."

Maria rejoined the conversation. "The Director's currently back in videoconference with the PM; rest assured he'll hear all about this the moment he returns. In the meantime, I'm gonna go out on a limb. I want every knight to head to St Paul's, St Mary-le-Bow and St Dunstan-in-the-East."

"What about Monument?" Kit posed. "That's still standing."

Maria nodded. "You're right. Maybe it will offer some clue as to how it all started."

"I'm on it," Kit replied. "Grosmont, you still at the archives?"

"Pretty much."

"See if you can find anything there on Belland. If we can find out who was responsible for the original, it might shed some light on who did it this time."

Kit ended the conversation as he left the exhibition. Gillian and the curator had already started to make their way up the stairs, the curator shutting up shop.

Of the three, he was clearly the most baffled.

"Who was responsible for setting up the exhibition?" Kit asked as he crossed the atrium, heading for the main doors. Seeing the three paintings Jérôme had coveted all in the same place seemed too much of a coincidence.

"The exhibition was put in place to mark the anniversary of the Great Fire." The curator struggled to keep up. "As a matter of fact, we'd been planning it for quite some time."

"How about the artwork?" Kit pressed. "Presumably they're on loan?"

"Of course. And not an easy task to get them either. We really are most grateful for the generosity of others."

"You mean you were funded?"

"The exhibition itself has been one for profit. However, that's not to say we haven't been helped."

"Anyone specific?" Kit felt his teeth were in danger of puncturing his lower lip.

"Now that you mention it, most of the funding came from the same person."

"A Frenchman?"

The curator's expression was blank. "As a matter of fact, I know little about him. Though the donation was extremely large, he wished to remain anonymous."

"You haven't met him?"

"Well, no."

Kit decided no further questions would be necessary. "Thank you for your time, Mr Green."

Kit crossed the footbridge, heading back to the road where the car was waiting. He took a seat behind the driver; Gillian got in beside him.

"If Jérôme de Haulle was responsible for setting up the exhibition, chances are he did it for one reason," Kit said. "Question is, how did he know?"

Gillian had no answers. "His knowledge of the Hesilrige was equally baffling. Claimed the secret was written in a book by Cromwell's family."

Kit watched the driver make a turn off the Rotunda. On being asked where to go, he replied, "Mary-le-Bow. Quickly as possible."

"Before you do so, might I suggest we make a quick stop at Holborn."

Kit thought he was hearing things. "What for?"

"Because if the connection is Wren, I know one person whose expertise on the subject may be of great help."

Mike searched the shelves frantically, looking for anything that might be relevant. Scanning the covers and spines, he realised, was useless.

"Just calm down." Emily replaced a manuscript he'd knocked off the shelf. "These things are priceless."

"Well, in about four hours this whole room will no longer exist." He left the aisle, looking left and right as he did so. "You said everything is indexed."

"Of course."

"You have access to it?"

She led him along the main aisle, following the lush carpet to a smart office, which she found unlocked. Entering, Emily inserted a password into the nearest desktop and brought up a secure database.

"What exactly are we looking for?"

"Belland," Mike said off the cuff, impressed with himself for pronouncing it correctly. "See if it says anything about the Gemini or the Cardinal's Boys."

She tried Belland first, finding a handful of references, most of which she recognised. Cardinal's Boys and Twins came up but with nothing of obvious significance. The same was true of Gemini.

Except one.

"There's one here that overlaps." Emily continued to type, studying the results through her glasses. "According to this, he faced trial."

"Who?"

"Belland."

Mike studied the results alongside her, noticing a similarly long-winded title reminiscent of the parliamentary inquiry.

"What does it say about Gemini?"

"The database contains scans of everything; according to this, it comes up once as a keyword." She brought up the entry. "The reference seems to mention the book your friend talked about. The one Belland's associate was found with."

Mike looked at it, noticing *The Sons of Gemini* reference. "Where is it?"

"Back where we were."

They returned to the section labelled 1666 and searched the shelves. Almost immediately Emily found it: a small manuscript with a slightly worn library-bound cover that looked as though it hadn't been picked up since the day it was published.

Mike stood alongside her as she opened it, the printed text easy on the eye. They scanned through the early pages, finding a clear reference to Belland's incarceration and confession. Within the content was a reference to *The Sons of Gemini* book and what appeared to be a facsimile of a letter to Charles II.

Emily was stunned.

"I don't believe it. According to this, Belland made a full confession." She pointed to the report of the trial and the existence of the book.

Focusing on the letter, Mike was equally surprised. In addition to the Frenchman's alleged confession, he'd threatened the fire in a letter to Charles II a week earlier unless the king agreed to abdicate. "This is incredible. How on earth was it hushed up?"

"Probably the same reason it came to be located here in the first place. It's not exactly open to the public."

"Surely some people get to see it; I mean it's not like these things are never studied."

"Matter of fact, I know a few people who would love nothing more than to be granted permission. Your uncle for a start."

"Shame he isn't here right now."

Emily placed her hand to her mouth. "Oh my, I totally forgot."

Forgetting about the book for a moment, Mike stared at her. "You feeling okay?"

Slowly, she removed an earpiece from her pocket. "I've got an idea."

Seated in an uncomfortable position against the medieval walls, David Champion again heard noise coming from his right pocket. As the volume became louder, he heard his name being called.

The voice was clearly a woman's.

Checking to ensure the gunmen were out of the room, he reached deeply into his jacket pocket and retrieved the small device Emily Fletcher had given him at the beginning of the lecture.

Discreetly, he placed it to his lips.

Almost immediately, a second voice came through. "If you're unable to speak, merely cough. Do so twice for yes, once for no."

Cautiously, he coughed twice.

At the other end, Mike heard the coughs clearly. "All right, for now just listen. I'll tell you everything that's happened. When you can, I will need a reply. Your expertise could make all the difference."

Leaning over the antique wooden chest, Fabien Randek noticed a brick slightly out of alignment with the others. The difference was subtle, miniscule; had he not been looking for it, he could have easily missed it.

He reached his hand in slowly, moving it away. Within the gap below it, he saw a small lever little bigger than a light switch. Immediately he began pulling it, bracing himself for a sudden recoil. After hauling the lever as far as it would go, he heard the sound of movement.

Within feet of him, the floor opened like a door.

66

The Bell Tower, 01:44

Champion waited until he was sure no gunmen were present before he risked making a reply. During the last few minutes, two had come and gone, each entering and then lingering briefly outside the heavy wooden door that creaked on its hinges every time it was caught by a draught. Champion could hear talking outside, clearly in French.

As long as the chamber remained silent, replying loudly would be a risk.

"Okay, they've gone."

At the other end, Mike was relieved to hear his uncle's voice. During the previous few minutes, he'd provided a full update on the fires and the situation at the Tower; he'd learned nothing new himself.

All that mattered was that no one inside the Queen's House had died.

"You okay there, Uncle Dave?"

Champion's back was sore from being pressed up against the cold stone. "Just a bit of rheumatism. Could be much worse."

"I bet even Thomas More didn't have it so bad." Emily joined the conversation. "Then again, I did hear medieval luxury wasn't all it was cracked up to be."

"You should've been with me in Scotland," Mike quipped, not elaborating. "Listen, we don't have much time. If Blanco stays to form, another transmission is due in less than fifteen minutes and, assuming the scene in the paintings is correct, the next target will be one of Wren's churches."

"If the churches were built to conceal a secret, that is certainly news to me," Champion replied, astonished at the suggestion. As an expert on the subject with over thirty years' experience, he'd never heard such a tale. "That said, not all of the churches were completely rebuilt. St Dunstan-in-the-East was merely remodelled. Mary-le-Bow still has its Norman crypt."

Mike made a mental note of the fact. "Tell me about Belland."

Champion cleared his throat.

"Everything okay?"

"Yes. Awfully dusty in here."

"All right, if any of those bastards come back, just clear your throat again and I'll know to be quiet." He took the trial manuscript from Emily. "According to this document, Belland wasn't just a suspect, he was tried and found guilty. What do you know of this?"

"As far as historical evidence is concerned, there was little. A week before the fire, he attempted to acquire some pasteboard, claiming it was for a fireworks display. When asked when it was needed, he replied that if it couldn't be delivered before the week was out, he'd have no need of it. He also claimed among his fireworks would be rockets that would fly up in a pure body of flame higher than the top of St Paul's."

Echoes of what Blanco and Kit had said. "What happened after the fire?"

"The Duke of York in particular had been riding the streets regularly throughout the fire, in part to organise action for combating the flames, but also to try to keep morale high among the citizens. When the duke witnessed the levels of distrust among the Londoners, he and his brother made it their mission to round up foreigners."

"He blamed them?"

"Officially the reason was to keep them from harm."

Mike remembered Emily had told him as much. "What happened to Belland?"

"When one of his servants tried to reach him at his residence, the gentleman learned his master had already been taken to the palace at Whitehall. When the servant arrived, he pleaded his master's case but, on speaking to Belland personally, he was assured that Belland was not a suspect."

Mike quickly read further through the manuscript, finding a date for Belland's trial, 25 September. "Three weeks later, things had sure changed a bit. This predates the parliamentary inquiry."

"A fact I'm sure Parliament were themselves unaware of; either that or something the king had planned. As I'm sure by now you're already aware, most of the conspiracies involved not the French but the Dutch. By 1681 when the plaque at Farriner's was created, the situation had changed somewhat."

"You mean it was a political move to stir up hatred against the relevant factions?"

Emily put her hands to her face. "Of course, by 1681 the Anglo-Dutch wars were over. Why risk resuming hostilities with the French in 1666 when relations between the two nations had improved?"

"What you must understand is that as soon as the flames were seen, the people of London were already intent on finding out who was responsible. Even when the site of Farriner's bakery was confirmed to be the starting place, few blamed the baker himself. When Hubert confessed, it mattered not whether he was guilty. In the eyes of the Londoners, their suspicions had been confirmed."

Mike nodded. "Were they correct?"

"For over three centuries, suspicion has refused to go away. When Thomas Middleton appeared before the inquiry, it seemed only a matter of time before the true culprits were found. Furthermore, there were other eyewitnesses. In a sense, this gave further weight to Hubert's confession. He himself mentioned he was one of twenty-four."

"Who are the Sons of Gemini?"

"I assure you, the name means nothing."

"How about the Cardinal's Boys? Or Twins, for that matter?"

The professor took a breath. "Of either, I remember hearing only a vague mention; however, I'm quite sure the time period was different."

"You mean earlier?"

"Much earlier. Back when the building in which you stand was still a palace. Think the Hundred Years' War."

"How about Calais?" Emily asked. "You mentioned the hangings in one of your lectures."

"Ah, a most ingenious point. And, indeed, whatever the exact reference to the Cardinal's Boys, I'm quite sure any answers you find will be of connection."

"Care to elaborate?"

Champion placed his hand to his mouth as one of the gunmen entered, carrying a mobile phone. He noticed the villain held it up as though taking a video.

The newcomer made a point of taking several close-ups.

At the other end, Mike picked up on the lull in the conversation, assuming a guard had returned. "If the Cardinal's Boys were at war with England in 1666, it stands to reason their formation was far earlier," he whispered to Emily. Noticing she was confused, he reopened the conversation with Kit.

"Hey, Edward, I was thinking, maybe we've been looking at this all wrong."

Seated on the back seat of the moving car, Kit's reaction was non-committal. "In what way did you have in mind?"

"Think about it. The plaque says the Great Fire was the work of papists: the culprit a Frenchman. This document confirms Belland had a trial and was found guilty. What happened to him? Who knows?" Mike shrugged. "Who was this Belland? Why is Blanco quoting him? There's stuff in that museum and in here that has probably never seen the sunlight. Yet we've found it. How did they?"

The same thought had occurred to Kit. "Even if they are one and the same, our attention must remain with the here and now. The London of 1666 burned for four days. A repeat of that and even the Home Counties will be in trouble."

"Whatever the reason, chances are there's more to it than money. The original fire was an act of war; tonight Blanco wants the Crown Jewels. Maybe there's more to it than petty theft."

"Meaning what?"

"Meaning maybe once upon a time these guys were in line to be king."

Seated in the back seat of the car, Kit turned his attention to Gillian.

"You mentioned when we left the gallery, Jérôme de Haulle valued the original jewels as though they were family heirlooms. Do you have any idea how?"

The intensity of the question unsettled her. "He mentioned something, yes. His family go back a long way."

"How far?"

"Very early."

"Normans? Plantagenets?"

"All of the above." Gillian glanced through the window; even with it wound up, the stench of smoke was becoming stronger. "Let's not forget his lineage doesn't only concern England."

A strange thought entered Kit's mind. If the story he was hearing from Maria was true, three sets of crowns had been targeted.

"I can't believe I've been so stupid."

Mike smiled wryly as he overheard Kit's voice. "That *is* unlike you."

"The thefts have been on three fronts; the Crown Jewels of Scotland haven't been used since the coronation of Charles II. If de Haulle viewed the originals as heirlooms, maybe you're right. Question is who's the link and how?"

"Been a lot of bastards in history, Edward. A lot of them were kinda messed up. Worst-case scenario, we could be dealing with something worse."

"If not someone with a better claim?"

"Like who?"

"Remember the Wars of the Roses: it was basically cousins at war. Even in this day and age their descendants may still wander the earth. For all we know, we could still be talking of a relation of the royals."

"You think the present royals are related to cardinals?"

"If we're looking back pre-reformation, the Church's position was far more prominent then. Maybe it was a guardian or something similar."

Mike looked at Emily. "That mean anything to you?"

"Does the term *needle in a haystack* mean anything to you?"

Mike bit his lip, tiredness growing. "Where are you now?"

The car made a sudden turn north. "Heading into Holborn; apparently this trip is unmissable. I guess pretty soon we'll have our answer."

Mike waited till Kit had stopped speaking before trying Champion again. "Hey, Uncle Dave, you okay?"

The professor replied in a soft tone. "The guards are extra vigilant. I fear for the consequences should I be spotted."

That was the last thing Mike wanted to hear. "Who were the Cardinal's Boys? You were saying about the Hundred Years' War."

"To receive a full answer, I fear you'll need a historian whose expertise on the matter far exceeds my own. If you can access the outside world, I suggest you attempt to make contact with Professor Richard Tinniswood. He was once a royal historian. A man of great acclaim."

"I'll be right on it. In the meantime, you just sit tight."

"Mike, whatever happens tonight, I urge you to exercise caution. If Wren was aware of subterranean passages and doors into the ground, he covered them for a reason."

Mike imagined a scenario where the famous scientist and architect had uncovered hell itself. "Don't worry. If Wren's perfect city was never built, I'm sure there was a very good reason for it."

Emily had already disappeared by the time Mike ended the conversation. He found her in the same office as before, leaning over the computer.
And typing quickly.
"What is it?"
"Your uncle said whoever the Cardinal's Boys were, he knew only the rough time period." She concentrated her search on the reign of Edward III. After finding several references to the hangings at Calais, one name caught her eye.

Randek waited until the latest gunmen had entered the Bloody Tower before ordering them into the area beneath the floor. The stairway was clearly visible with the lights on, but it was obvious the route would be confined.

Phil noticed activity on the main screens and immediately contacted Mike.
"Honey Badger, don't wish to worry you, but Randek's found your hiding place. You're about to have company."
Still in the office, Mike cursed under his breath. "How many are we talking?"
Phil counted them. "Ten – all armed. Plus Randek. Coming from the same direction you entered from."

Mike left the office, noticing Emily was on the move again. He caught up with her as she headed off the main aisle to investigate a different collection of manuscripts.
Dated 1330s.
"Listen, we have to move out; we're about to have company."
Emily scoured quickly through the middle shelf, a busy area where the documents were far older than those concerning the Great Fire. She identified one rolled-up document; Mike deduced it was vellum.
"Come on, we have to go."
"Just a second. I want to check something." She covered her hands with plastic gloves she'd picked up from the desk and unrolled it just enough to make out the title. The Latin calligraphy confirmed it was the one she wanted.
"What is that?"
"Of all the references, this was the only one that referred to the Cardinal's Twins." She looked at him. "If your uncle is right, this could be the break we need."
Mike heard Phil's voice in his ear. "Honey Badger, the enemy is closing in fast. I reckon you've got less than a minute."
He guided Emily back to the main aisle. "Which way?"
Emily answered, "Here!"

***

The Director returned to the room after yet another conversation with the prime minister had ended abruptly. Not for the first time in his career, he wished for the dissolution of the JIC.

"What's the latest?" he asked on reaching the bottom of the stairs. He found Phil shouting instructions at Mike while watching the screens; Maria was studying two sets of architect's plans.

"Kit's visit to the museum was well worthwhile," Maria began. "We've got a lead on where the fires are starting. Apparently precisely the same thing happened in 1666."

"The city that never was." The Director looked closely at the designs on the screen, immediately recognising Wren's plan for the city. "The plan never got the go-ahead."

"No, it didn't. But judging from this, he used some of it. I've ordered the knights to cover every church. Masterson is currently on his way to St Mary-le-Bow."

The Director nodded. "What's the latest with Hansen?"

"About to have a reunion with Randek if he isn't careful."

The Director reattached his headset and spoke to Mike. "Grosmont, this is the King."

Mike had made it halfway along the main aisle, worried gunfire was imminent. He heard the Director's voice intermittently and answered as he moved.

"I've managed to make contact with my uncle. All the hostages inside the Queen's House are okay. He was relieved the others weren't dead."

His words weren't news to the Director. "What about Blanco?"

"Haven't seen him recently; though Phil assures me his nephew is hot on my tail. If my uncle's correct, Edward's latest lead on the Sons of Gemini could be crucial."

"Never you mind about that. All that concerns me is the here and now."

"Right now, I'd be worried about both. What Edward discovered from the pictures could run pretty deep. Whoever Blanco is, or whoever he's working for, seems to go back a long way. The archives have proved that much."

The Director was intrigued. "You've discovered a reference?"

"Right now it hasn't been possible to read everything." Again he checked over his shoulder, doing his best to hurry Emily along. "All we know is that once upon a time the Sons of Gemini apparently did exist. My uncle confirmed that much."

"He's an authority on the matter?"

"Right now, the best he could do is recommend one of his friends. Some royal historian. Name of Tinniswood."

The Director's response was interrupted as a volley of gunfire echoed throughout the room; Mike instinctively dived out of the way. Directly behind them, shelving and manuscripts were being decimated.

He knew they'd waited too long.

* * *

Standing alongside Maria, the Director was relieved to hear Mike was still alive. As the seconds passed, Phil took over as the main contact.

Mike had counted eleven, including Randek.

"All of the knights are covering a different church, awaiting instruction," Maria addressed the Director.

The Director nodded. "I want every gate and doorway monitored. Any sign of anything suspicious, I want them to close in. In the meantime, I want a helicopter outside as soon as possible."

Maria was confused. "You've been summoned to COBRA?"

"No." The Director's face was stern. "I merely need to pay a visit to an old friend."

67

The New Wardrobe Tower, 01:49

Momentum took them along the main aisle before diving into the nearest row to the left. Mike felt Emily's hand come loose as they hit the ground, rolling into the surrounding furnishings. There were voices shouting in French somewhere behind them; thanks to the layout of the archives, whoever was responsible was no longer visible.

Which meant for now, at least, they were hidden.

Mike hurried quickly to his feet, finding Emily a few metres away, terrified. He whispered her name as he pulled her to her feet, ushering her further out of the path of the latest spray of bullets. Beyond the nearby wooden racking, a series of minor explosions drowned out the sound of shouting.

Looking across the main aisle, Mike realised several racks had collapsed due to the gunfire.

Mike removed his USP45 from his belt, replacing the magazine, arms out ready to fire.

He spoke into his headset. "What am I looking at, Phil?"

Eyes on the screens, Phil had no definitive answers. "CCTV doesn't spread this far south, Honey Badger. Last I saw of Randek, he was leaving the Bloody Tower the same way you came."

Mike cursed under his breath, realising Phil was right. "How about a satellite link-up?"

"All I can tell you right now is there's gunmen on Tower Green, but no one's on the roof."

"How about infrared?"

Phil tapped quickly at his keyboard, causing the pictures on the big screen to change from ordinary satellite footage to a red and black background. Over twenty metres below the ruins of the old Wardrobe Tower, he saw figures moving in what appeared from the new view to be a 2D maze.

"Think I've got you. You've got ten enemies to the west." Averting his attention to Tower Green, he saw others approaching the Bloody Tower. "Can't promise there won't be more to come."

"Just my luck." Mike fired in the direction of the noise, unclear for now whether or not he had hit any of his targets. "What are my options?"

"Right now, you're still looking at the main offices. If you're smart, you'll use the racking for shelter."

The noise of bullet impacts peppered the rack in front of him. "Thanks!"

Edging closer to the main aisle, Mike exhausted the rest of his magazine, aiming again at where the gunfire was coming from. Out of the corner of his eye, he saw two gunmen hit the ground, wounded, possibly worse. Reaching deep into his belt, he reloaded.

"What's the quickest way out of here?" The question was for Emily.

"The main exit is next door to the office we just entered." Emily's face was pale with concern. "The way there is largely uncovered."

"Let me deal with that."

Mike grabbed her hand and led her through the maze of nearby racks and bookcases, doing his best to avoid using the main aisle. The sound of gunfire had faded now; in its stead the staccato pitch of panicked voices was accompanied by a lingering smell of smoke.

He glanced back at the first opportunity, using a bookcase for cover. No less than three rows of them had been decimated; again the gunfire had been muffled. They'd reached the far end of the archives, separated from the main offices by less than twenty metres. Their only chance was to sprint for it.

Emily grabbed his hand tightly. "You're not seriously thinking of doing this!"

Mike removed a small canister from his belt; unbeknown to Emily, it was a smokescreen. "You just worry about directing us out of here. Let me worry about keeping us alive!"

He looked her in the eye for what seemed like an eternity. The pretty make-up she'd worn at the start of the night had smudged from water and tears; at no point had she attempted to rectify it. She had pretty eyes, with or without her glasses, the warmth of her hazel irises a brief comfort even at the brink of death. As he tightened his grip, he saw her smile.

"You ready?"

She wasn't, but she nodded anyway.

"Don't stop running till we get there."

A deafening explosion knocked them both to the floor; Mike felt his knees buckle before stumbling to his right. A blinding flash had preceded the sound; within seconds, the light became lost in a dense cloud of smoke. It wasn't until it cleared that Mike was able to ascertain the cause – not that he'd been in any doubt. A series of grenades had obliterated everything in their path.

Behind them, the gunfire had resumed.

Mike rolled to his left and got to his feet, reaching out for Emily's hand, guiding her out of sight. Across the archives he could see that at least four bookcases had been destroyed, their contents floating lightly through the cloudy air.

Emily was horrified. "If we survive this, I'm so getting fired."

Somehow Mike found the energy to smile. "Hey, Phil. You copy?"

An answer came immediately. "What the hell is going on down there? I'm seeing fires."

"You're not the only one. Traditional way out is kinda blocked. Worse still, I've got bogies on my tail." Mike waited for an instant response that never came. "You got any ideas?"

Phil scanned the map rapidly, seeing no obvious solution. Leaving his seat, he moved over to Maria's terminal; in the Director's absence, she was organising a guard on every Wren church highlighted in the Wren portrait from her new position close to the Round Table.

He brought up the same 3D map as before, rotating it with the cursor. Aside from the stairway into the offices above, he saw only one option.

"Think I've got something. An old passage – looks like it comes up in the Fusiliers' Museum."

"Where am I looking?"

Phil alternated his glance between the terminal and the screen. "Five rows back, it should be somewhere inside the wall. I can't tell the exact entrance from here."

"I'm on it!"

Mike ducked as a second explosion rocked the nearby racking, again overwhelming other sounds. As the noise died down, he heard voices shouting, a clear instruction from Randek to surrender.

Ignoring the demands, they returned the way they'd come, ending in the row designated 1460s.

"Are we there yet?"

"You're very close. Look for something in the wall," Phil responded.

Mike hurried to the far end, standing in between two sets of racking filled with manuscripts from the 1460s and 1470s. The wall was painted white, with a rectangular fresco of a Yeoman Warder from the 1400s at the centre; feeling it, he sensed it was older than the paintwork suggested.

Emily was standing behind him, leaning over a nearby table. He noticed she'd retrieved the two manuscripts they'd previously been reading.

"What, are you crazy?"

"If the Gemini and the Cardinal's Boys are behind this, these could be the clues we need."

"You wanna maybe concentrate on getting us out of here first?" His attention returned to Phil. "I'm not seeing anything here, Phil."

Gripping the desk in front of him, Phil searched frantically for answers. The 3D outline confirmed a tunnel beyond the wall; it was less clear how to enter.

"Phil?" Keeping low, Mike gestured Emily to join him, deciding against restarting the gunfight. Randek's voice sounded above all others as he continued his attempts to convince Mike to surrender.

"Apparently there's a doorway here."

Emily joined him, feeling the wall with her free hand. Immediately her face became despondent. "I don't see anything."

"Keep trying," he yelled into his headset. "Phil?"

Rotating the cursor sideways, Phil noticed something. "You notice an area where the wall overlaps?"

Confused, Mike continued his search. On closer inspection, he saw the area where the painted Beefeater was angled inwards slightly.

"I see it."

"Pull on the corner."

Mike pulled hard at the left corner, attempting to get a firm grip. Failing, he tried again. "It's not working."

"Try the other side."

He did, no better. "I'm fast running out of time here, Phil."

Phil was also running low on ideas.

As Mike returned to the left side, he gripped hard, pulling harder still. He felt a slight gap, possibly a thin wooden frame between the painting and the surrounding wall. Whatever he was pulling wasn't moving.

Searching it up and down, panic led to prayer; all the while he realised the noise behind him was getting louder. There was nowhere to run, nowhere to hide.

When Randek appeared, the game would be over.

He saw Emily pushing the painted area alongside him, desperation etched across her face. He'd failed her, failed Champion. Perhaps he hadn't been worthy of sitting at the Round Table.

Randek's voice spoke clearly again. Turning his attention to the end of the rack, Mike held out his firearm, back to the wall. As he sought to fire, he felt himself falling.

Instead of standing facing the main aisle, he was now lying on his back in darkness.

68

The New Wardrobe Tower, 01:53

The last thing Randek had been expecting to see was a deserted row. There were manuscripts untidily scattered on the left-hand side; the right was far neater.

It was clear from their condition they had not been damaged.

Recent sounds had emanated from there, he was sure of it; he'd heard them not ten seconds earlier. Already once that night, the Servant had slipped the net.

He was damned if he'd allow the same thing to happen again.

"There is no use trying to escape. We have you completely surrounded. Come out now; no harm will come to you." Randek checked the magazine of his Heckler & Koch. "If you refuse to comply, I'm afraid the penalties will be most severe."

Lying on his back, Mike noticed a presence nearby, a familiar perfume in the air. "Emily?"

"Shhhh." She placed her index finger to her lips. "He'll hear us."

Randek marched up and down the aisle designated 1460–70s, finding nothing amiss. He searched everywhere from the racks to the wall for signs of hiding places before moving on to the surrounding rows. He radioed in to the CCTV room, ruing the response that the area had no cameras.

Without surveillance, there was no way of pinpointing their exact location.

"Keep searching. I want no stone left unturned."

Blanco was in the security room when Randek made contact. The cameras in the Bloody Tower confirmed the entrance had been found; at least eleven gunmen had since disappeared beneath the floor.

Including his nephew.

"Fabien, where are you? What has happened?"

Hearing his uncle continue the conversation, Randek replied, his words corrupted by interference. "The passage came out in an archives. The Englishman was here."

Blanco centred in on the final word. "What do you mean, was?"

A brief pause preceded the reply. "Don't worry, he will be found."

Ignoring his uncle's venomous reply, Randek marched quickly along the central aisle, concentrating now on the offices. The grenade damage had been substantial; even five minutes later the stench of smoke still lingered.

He knew his targets would have had no chance of reaching the offices unseen.

"We know first-hand these walls conceal secrets. He cannot hide forever."

Blanco spoke to the gunman nearest him. "Watch these screens like a hawk. Contact me immediately when he reappears."

"Yes, sir."

Blanco left the CCTV room, resuming his conversation with Randek as he headed for the main stairway. "How many are with you?"

"Eight. Two are down."

Blanco avoided the urge to curse. "Station three men at both exits. When you've done that, return to the Queen's House. The prime minister will be expecting another video."

Mike sensed the voices on the other side were fading, as were other sounds. For now at least they had not been seen.

He felt a slender hand guide him to his feet. Rising, he saw the familiar outline of Emily's slim frame alongside him; in the current passageway, it was difficult to avoid coming into contact.

Her face appeared in the torchlight. "I guess your friend was right after all."

Mike grinned, at the same time hearing a second voice in his ear calling his name. "You sure as hell don't disappoint, Phil. I guess I owe you one."

At the other end, Phil exhaled in relief. "Under the circumstances, I'm prepared to put it on the tab. What do you see?"

He avoided the temptation to say Emily's face. "Right now, we're pretty enclosed. Which way are we heading?"

"Follow the passage the same way, it comes out in the Fusiliers' Museum."

"Anything I should be worried about?"

"You mean besides a bill from the archivist?" Phil smiled as he shook his head. "Enemies are currently congregating around the barracks and the Queen's House. The museum is unguarded, albeit mostly on camera."

Mike guessed as much. "Any movement from the hostages?"

"Negative. Furthermore, all in the White Tower are still to move."

"How about outside the walls?"

"All the knights have been ordered to home in on the churches." He checked his watch. "Right now I guess it's only a matter of time."

The car pulled up outside a period apartment block in the heart of Holborn. Exiting via the rear doors, Kit followed Gillian to a black front door framed by a classical white archway.

Despite being close to the main roads, it was a street of quiet and grandeur.

"Someone here's not short of a bob or two."

Glaring back at him, Gillian pressed the doorbell for flat 3. "I suggest you let me do the talking. It's not often he's visited by men from the military."

Nathaniel Johnstone had been up since 7 a.m. Despite being retired and with an early appointment tomorrow, bed was now the last thing on his mind. With fires raging in the city, some now visible in the distance from the lounge window of his three-bed flat, sleep was no longer possible.

Like most of the city's citizens, he had remained glued to the television since 9 p.m.

He heard a buzz at the intercom, late by all standards. Waiting till a second sounded, he rose from his sofa and answered.

"Yes?"

"Nat, it's Gillian."

The voice confirmed the identity of his former colleague. "Gill, what is it – it's almost two in the morning."

"I'm well aware of the time, Nat. I'm afraid I have another great favour to ask. And it involves François de Haulle."

Johnstone appeared at the front door within two minutes, smartly attired as though ready for an appointment with an old acquaintance or former client. He recognised the familiar face of his successor as Director of the National Portrait Gallery.

Less so the man in dark clothing alongside her.

"Nat, this is Captain Kit Masterson. He works for British Intelligence."

Johnstone didn't bat an eyelid. "How do you do?"

Kit accepted his hand. "Mr Johnstone, I have it on good authority the name de Haulle is not unknown to you; nor do I doubt you're unaware of the problems currently facing our city. Our intel advises us that the threats seem to be connected to the buildings designed by Sir Christopher Wren. Gillian tells me you're something of an expert on the subject."

The comment caught Nat off guard. "I give tours occasionally. My book came out last year."

"Perfect. We believe the latest to be targeted is St Mary-le-Bow. You know it?"

"I could walk it blindfolded."

"Perfect," Kit repeated. "Let's get in the car. As Gillian says, time is of the essence."

Less than two miles from the flat in Holborn, a silhouetted figure ghosted his way through the heart of the Norman crypt, knowing both internal and external surveillance was unlikely. Glancing at his watch, he saw that time was still on his side.

In less than seven minutes, for the fifth time that night, history would repeat itself.

69

The White Tower, 01:56

Blanco watched again from the roof of the White Tower as Randek began the familiar walk from the Queen's House, joined by seven others, including the Ravenmaster. At the same time, he concentrated on the laptop in front of him as it played recent footage taken by one of the gunmen of the remaining hostages crowded together and practically unmoving in the chamber once inhabited by the former Chancellor of England.

In his mind he pictured the PM's response on viewing the footage.

He saw Randek lead the way to the ravens' cages, opening one of them. "Which one did he choose?" Blanco asked over the airwaves.

Twenty-seven metres below, Randek answered, "Ivanhoe. The gentleman seems determined to sacrifice the older birds first."

"A man of great integrity perhaps." Blanco changed frequency and called Alain.

Approximately ten metres below the famous streets in the heart of the Scottish capital, the younger brother of François de Haulle took the call.

"*Allô?*"

"What news from the north?"

"The fires have spread to within one hundred metres of the palace." Alain paused as he heard further sounds of sirens from somewhere above, the road noise clearly audible despite the heavy stone surrounds. "Soon it will be fifty."

"Any word from the castle?"

"Not besides calling 999."

The Anjouvin smiled before making a similar call to Paris. "Sébastien?"

In the galley of the luxury yacht, the famed Parisian antiquarian heard Blanco's voice come through clearly. "I'm here, Bizu."

Blanco felt a twinge of relief on hearing the antiquarian respond. "And where exactly is here?"

Peeking out through a gap in the curtains, the old man concentrated on his surroundings, the banks of the river floating by like soft clouds on a summer's day. With the lights of the city now far behind, the countryside was shrouded in almost total darkness.

"We are out of Paris. The journey should be over by dawn."

Blanco changed the frequency a third time. "Patrice?"

Seated at the helm of one of ten cabin cruisers moving east along the Thames towards the heart of the city, the younger brother of Fabien Randek took the call.

"Yes, Uncle."

"What is your position?"

"The convoy is currently west of the capital," the shaven-headed man replied, the lights of Craven Cottage reflecting softly on the waters in front of him, the nearby buzz of the city overwhelmed by that of three large helicopters approaching from directly behind them. "The choppers will be with you in moments."

Maria saw unidentified objects show up on radar, flying in a V-formation towards the city.

"We've got three helicopters coming in over Hammersmith." She brought up live footage via a series of locked-off street cameras. "Whoever sent these forgot to ask for ones with buckets."

Standing alongside her, the Director viewed the same footage, concerned that the next stage of the enemy's attack was about to be put into operation.

"Inform the Cabinet Office things are building." He looked at Phil. "How are we looking with the latest road closures?"

"Traffic system is wreaking havoc throughout the city." He clicked through a range of CCTV cameras, all of which showed green lights. "Luckily for us, the city centre is already closed off – except, that is, for the cars already stuck there. The news is advising drivers to stay away from the centre."

The Director avoided the urge to respond. "What news on the knights?"

Maria spoke through her headset. "Warwick, this is the Rook. What's your position?"

Standing in the shadow of the Monument, Sanders and Jay approached the main entrance. It was strange under the circumstances, forlorn, almost ghostly. The temperature was warm for the time of night, the charred remains of the nearby buildings giving off a strong heat that showed no signs of cooling anytime soon. The nearby fires had all been extinguished, the surrounding buildings razed to the ground. The only sign of life came from the main entrance, the person's features obscured by the thick shadow of the 202-foot-high Doric column.

"We're just approaching the Monument." Sanders made eye contact with the man by the door. "Looks like our escort has already arrived."

"Roger that. Keep us posted on your findings."

Within seconds of ending the conversation, Maria put through a call to Wilcox.

"Stafford, this is the Rook."

*　*　*

In the public garden of St Dunstan-in-the-East, Wilcox heard the familiar voice of Lieutenant Maria Lyons buzz lightly in his ear. "I hear you, Maria."

"What's the latest?" she asked.

"Beauchamp and I have set up guard in the gardens," he said, his eyes fixed on the illuminated façade of the ruined church, the tall, typically Wren tower rising well above the nearby greenery. "No sign of anything."

"Keep us posted if anything changes." She put through the final call to Chambers. "Stapleton, this is the Rook. How's things at Mary-le-Bow?"

Seated close to an airy forecourt outside a closed Costa Coffee, Chambers and Dawson blended in well with the crowds. It was busy out despite the roads being closed; traffic was non-existent bar the comings and goings of the emergency services. Ten fire engines had taken up position on the double yellow lines; others waited a short distance along the street.

He estimated there were no less than thirty policemen in the immediate area.

"Entrance to the church is covered; March is on the crypt." Chambers spoke of Dawson. "No sign of anything suspicious. Nor the Black Prince for that matter."

"Trust me, he's wishing he was there. How are the walkways?"

"Police are currently patrolling both ends. Even an insect would struggle to get through undetected."

"Let's keep it that way."

Maria disconnected the call and turned to the Director. "All of the churches in the portrait are covered, plus all the others, at least by civvies. If Blanco starts anything from there, we'll know soon enough."

The Director took a deep breath as he gripped the desk in front of him. Under the circumstances he decided no response was necessary.

If Blanco was on schedule, he'd be making himself heard in less than thirty seconds.

Blanco waited until the last of the hostages had made it to the roof before preparing the latest transmission. He watched as the Ravenmaster took his usual position alongside him, his terrier-like scowl now seemingly a permanent feature.

The PM was alone in COBRA when the pictures on the screen changed. Unlike the previous two occasions, the first thing she saw was a dank prison packed with worn-out hostages.

Blanco's voice spoke over the footage. "It was once said that in opposition to the fat king's split from Rome, the Chancellor of England did willingly suffer at

his tormentor's hands, viewing it as a small price to pay for eternal salvation."
The cameras zoomed in randomly on certain faces, the majority of whom were women. "Watch how they cry."

The PM watched uncomfortably as the footage ended, replaced with a close-up of Blanco's face. In his hand, he carried another raven.

"I understand from the Ravenmaster that the bird's name is Ivanhoe. As a child, I remember reading a novel of the same name, thinking what genius the author must have been for creating a story, though historically incorrect, capable of captivating my young mind, forever inflaming my passion for history." He held the bird up to the camera. "Who knows? Perhaps in my own way, I achieve the same."

A humoured smirk was gone in an instant.

"Since we last spoke, Prime Minister, the rules have not changed. Five hours have now passed. Only three remain. Use them wisely."

The video ended with a gunshot.

The footage came through on the wall-mounted monitor at the very moment Blanco signed off. No sooner had that finished did the PM appear.

"The condition of the hostages makes for especially unpleasant viewing." She eyed the Director via the technology, inwardly furious that Blanco had made such a bold gesture. "A quick headcount tells me the number of hostages is now down to the fifties. If the trend continues, we could be looking at a fifty per cent casualty rate."

The Director was far cooler in his response. "Intercepted security footage from the Tower confirms that, up to this point, no hostages have been killed. Right now, the original eighteen are still being held safely in the White Tower." Mr White broke eye contact to watch the latest six being led down from the roof. "In a few moments, that number will be twenty-four."

"How are they looking?"

"Like their counterparts in the Queen's House, most are experiencing the early stages of mental and emotional exhaustion. None appear to have been physically hurt. Right now, Blanco seems content to play with the power of suggestion."

The PM neglected to add it was a powerful play. "We can't delay any longer, Director. Every hour that passes is another closer to the end. For over a thousand years, leaders of this country have overseen the safety of its shores. I will not be the one who oversees its destruction."

"The options right now are clear to us, Prime Minister. The Tower is surrounded on all sides. Escape for Blanco is almost impossible. That said, I fail to see him negotiating on his demands." He looked firmly at the PM. "He will not cease the fires until he has what he requires."

"I have told you already, I have no idea where the jewels are located; nor am I willing to initiate a search for them."

"May I assume Her Majesty has been informed?"

"Once again, Director, I must request you respect your station. Just because

I place in your hands the power to protect this country does not mean you have permission to rule it."

"The fate of the jewels, Prime Minister, is inconsequential. Even if Blanco obtains them, he has no chance of escaping. Right now, over one hundred lives are under extreme threat. Not to mention those at risk outside the Tower walls. In order to bargain, we first need a chip."

"You're actually suggesting we hand them over?"

Glancing quickly at the surrounding screens, the Director observed footage of the fires. So far nothing new had materialised except for the natural spread of those already burning.

"Right now, I'd be prepared to consider any option to halt the destruction of our capital city."

"A role in which I already employ you." The PM's stare was cold, stern. "What developments on the fires?"

"Thanks in part to the Director of the Portrait Gallery and the Curator of the Museum of London, we now have possible intel on the key locations. The terrorists, as we've long suspected, have been following a historical pattern, concentrating their attacks on churches. I currently have men assembled at each location."

"Might I remind you, Director, that we're currently undergoing the greatest crisis in living memory. I'd trust the leader of our most elite line of defence would have more sense than to put his faith in history books."

"On the contrary, Prime Minister. In my experience the past often fuels future developments and events." Quietly the Director prayed Kit was right. "As a precaution, we have a barricade set up outside each of the remaining churches, not to mention several other locations throughout the city. When Blanco strikes, we shall find him. By cutting off the root, the plant will fall."

"And what if you're wrong?" The PM's stare was piercing. "Half our city has already been destroyed."

"You know Blanco's terms, Prime Minister. If the Jewels of England are to remain in our hands, we have to wait for this to play out. The connection is there, I'm sure of it."

"I hope to God you're correct, Director."

Maria spoke as soon as the screen went blank. "Your helicopter is waiting on Horse Guards. The pilot has been briefed."

The Director put on his jacket as he prepared to leave. "Keep in contact with the others. Let me know if the fires spread further."

"Yes, sir."

Mr White found Atkins on the opposite side of the room. "You're fully up to speed with developments. In my absence, you have full authority to act on my behalf."

"Just like the old days." Atkins showed no obvious sign of concern. "Give the old boy my regards."

"That will depend on whether he gives us any answers."

THE CROWN JEWELS CONSPIRACY

* * *

Within seconds of touching down, an identical helicopter to that which had earlier transported ten of the Harts from Charlestown to Whitehall set off again, heading east.

Seated behind the pilot, the Director of the White Hart stared forlornly across the skyline. From the air, the prominence of the fires hit home; even at a height of over 10,000 feet, the tail of the flames seemed peculiarly close, some reaching the height of the dome of St Paul's. It was surreal, strangely peaceful. With the heat no longer noticeable, the flame-coloured cloud had a more artistic aura about it, as though the evening was indeed a shepherd's delight.

Yet within the image, he saw extreme danger: a picture from history, captured by both photographers and artists. The PM had been wrong on at least one point. No matter where he looked, the facts were clear.

Past patterns were repeating themselves.

Turning his head in the opposite direction, the west side of London revelling in its usual illuminated aura, a series of thoughts filled his mind. Whatever the truth behind the origins of the Gemini and the Cardinal's Boys, their lineage had been ongoing throughout the centuries, lying dormant like a volcano ready to spew lava. If the answers to stop them were to be found, it wasn't just going to come in the form of heavy artillery.

It would be done so in history books.

Standing behind his desk, Ian Atkins again found himself looking at the two works of art displayed on his otherwise bare walls. For over fifty years, he had been captivated by the brushstrokes of the unnamed artist who had captured an image in time that had the power to send shivers down the spine of an onlooker centuries later.

Never during that time had he imagined it would also be the secret to it.

Moving his attention from the artwork to the photograph, he remembered what other secrets had been found beneath the painting. Of the seven doors to hell, one was right in front of him.

If the chain remained unbroken, it would only be a matter of time before it would be opened once again.

70

Whitehall, 02:03

Maria saw the clock on the dashboard tick a further minute past the hour and braced herself as 02:03 moved another minute into the past. The pattern for the last three hours had been clear: the fires at St Clement's, Stephen Walbrook and St Bride's had all occurred at three minutes past the hour. Only Monument had been the exception.

Every raven so far had been shot at one minute past the hour. Almost exactly one minute after Blanco's transmission had begun.

On this occasion, Blanco seemed to be running late.

Her eyes on the screens, she concentrated on the view closer to home. The Director's helicopter had taken off from Horse Guards Parade; she watched it rise slowly into the night air, quietly ruing the fact the forecast for the next few days was to be dry.

For once the English weather was letting the city down for the wrong reason.

In the corner of the room, Atkins was on the phone to Edinburgh. With the Director gone and the Deputy concentrating on events north of the border, Maria knew the task of operations management again rested predominantly on her shoulders.

She spoke clearly into her headset. "All Harts report in. Warwick, what's the latest?"

Sanders followed Jay up the stairway of the Monument, hearing the noise in his ear at the same moment a brown-haired man explained the layout.

"Chap is just showing us up the Monument." He smiled at the employee.

"Were you the same guy on duty here earlier?" Jay asked.

"Yes," the man answered, slightly nervously.

"What happened?"

"The Monument is open daily, nine thirty till six. Anyone can climb it. Today, my supervisor told me he had an important visitor coming over. Wanted to climb it."

"At night?"

"Not exactly normal practice. Supervisor said I'd be paid double time."

Sanders smiled philosophically, realising that the employee had just been doing his job. "Was this the man you saw?" He flashed him a printout of Blanco.

"That's the guy. Must be someone of importance. I've worked here eight years, never once been asked to reopen except for group tours."

"Where did you take him?"

"Follow me. I'll show you."

*　*　*

Wilcox and Ward were still in the garden of St Dunstan-in-the-East, their eyes closely monitoring the odd mix of greenery and ruined walls. Both heard Maria's voice come through at the same time.

"What's the latest?"

Ward beat Wilcox to a response. "Garden is absolutely scenic. Tower isn't bad either." He kept his eyes on the ruined arches, anticipating a moment something could appear from within. "Streets are quiet."

"Let's hope it stays that way."

Ending the conversation, Maria put through a call to Chambers and Dawson. "What's the latest at Mary-le-Bow?"

Seated at a metallic table in a relatively quiet area between the coffee house and the west side of the church, Chambers took the call while the lightly bearded Jack Dawson sampled his black coffee.

"Emergency services are all set on the front. Bobbies are still parading everywhere from Bow Churchyard to Crown Court."

"Any sign of anything inside the church?"

"Negative." Chambers glanced across the paved and tarmac surfaces, taking in everything from the brick façade to the imposing Portland stone tower that adjoined it on Cheapside. Due to the surrounding darkness, he could see through the windows that there was no sign of any obvious light. "If the bastard starts lighting fires, we'll see them."

Below the crypt of the church, the silhouetted figure watched the scene in front of him as the recently lighted embers began to take on a life of their own. As the seconds passed, the flames reached heights of over ten feet, coming close to touching the stone ceiling.

Not for the first time that night, he rued the necessity to vandalise such fine architecture.

As the flames began to spread in both directions, he left through the fifth door of hell, returning to the Norman crypt.

If he timed it well, he knew he wouldn't be seen.

The car had reached Gresham Street, passing the London Wall. The traffic near Mary-le-Bow was far heavier than on the previous roads; though the traffic lights were still green, almost every entrance had been barricaded.

Kit heard Maria's voice addressing him. "What's the latest?"

"We're approaching the church now; traffic permitting, we should be there in less than three minutes." He wiped his eyebrow clean of sweat. Despite no obvious signs Mary-le-Bow was in any imminent danger, he was concerned that picking up Johnstone had left them very tight for time. "What's the latest on Grosmont?"

"Right now, he's still to resurface." She glanced at the map on the screen, noticing that his GPS position indicated he was somewhere below ground. "At least his dot's still moving."

"What about the other bastards at the Tower?"

She glanced first at the security images Mike had earlier tapped before doing the same for those transmitted back from the main satellite. "Blanco and Randek are still on the roof of the White Tower; the hostages are presently being taken down below." She focused on the pictures caught on the Tower's CCTV, noticing Blanco and Randek were once again staring deep into the fires. She'd seen them do the same thing already that night.

Their presence was usually a precursor to new outbreaks.

"Right now, we're still to see anything."

Sanders was first to emerge at the top of the Monument, barely fatigued from the 311-step climb. On passing through the door on to the observation deck, he looked east across the city before doing a 360-degree walk around the central column.

Never had London looked like this. Countless buildings to the north were largely in ruins – only now was the impact becoming clear. To the north-west, beyond Monument Station, a crane stood at an odd angle above the charred remains of a scaffold where building work had been carried out. A similar situation applied in the west even though the flames had generally been less intense in that area. The fires were still burning to the north, where the nearby buildings were engulfed in thick clouds of smoke that also seemed to be appearing from cracks in the road. There was a heavy smell in the air, burning but not just that. The destruction had been indiscriminate: houses, shops, every industry and sector devastated. It was as though the charred remains of every possible produce and substance was being cooked in one almighty barbecue.

Never had any human witnessed such smells.

Sanders moved to the east side, taking a moment to look at Tower Bridge. Just to the left, the Tower gave off its familiar aura, its famous walls presenting their usual image of strength and impenetrability. Behind the walls he knew much was unfolding: no less than eighty people were imprisoned like the traitors of old, while others were working hard to save them. He thought of his friend, then the villain responsible. Singling in on the White Tower, he removed his field glasses and gazed in that direction. There were figures on the roof, looking in his direction. Ironic thoughts occurred to him as he imagined staring them out across the city. Gritting his teeth, he reflected ruefully on the reality of the situation.

If only his firearm were capable of making the shot.

While Sanders stood on the east side, Jay did the same for the west. Through a narrow gap in the smoke, the familiar façade of St Paul's could be seen rising impressively above the surrounding debris, its epic dome illuminated by the strange combination of floodlights and flames. When viewed from so high up, the fires appeared both closer and further away, a strange sensation that Jay attributed to a combination of tiredness and the distorted effect their present height and heat had on his distance perception.

Sanders joined him, noticing the employee standing by the door. "This the only place you showed him?"

The employee shook his head. "On the way down, he asked to enter the cellar. Had written permission from the managers."

Sanders raised an eyebrow. "That usual?"

"Only area open to the public is the observation deck."

"What's in the cellar?"

"Nothing much. Apparently Christopher Wren once used it to conduct experiments."

"Show us."

Just as Sanders prepared to move away from the west side, there was a flash of light midway between the Monument and the cathedral. Across the city, the view of the dome of St Paul's had become obscured by more flames, creating the impression that the cathedral itself was on fire.

Maria saw the flames on the screen and, at the same time, noticed Kit's GPS dot move into the area.

She recognised the latest fire was at St Mary-le-Bow.

"Stapleton, what's happening?"

Through the nearest window of the church, a light orange glow had preceded the appearance of something far greater. Wasting no time, Dawson had risen to his feet, setting off at pace towards the fire engines.

"There are flames inside the church," Chambers replied. "I didn't hear a thing."

"There was no explosion?"

"If there was, the sound was muffled by something."

Maria caught the sarcasm; the lack of sound was consistent with the other fires. "What's happening?"

"Marchie's calling the shots out front; the fire trucks are about to get the hoses out."

Watching the fire on the screens, Maria noticed the highest flames were already threatening the buildings either side. "Get it under control quickly, it may be possible to save the church. Any sign of activity?"

"Negative. Emergency services aside, it's like a bleeding ghost town."

As the fires encroached into the Norman crypt of St Mary-le-Bow, the silhouetted figure took the steps back to street level, re-emerging into the open air of Bow Churchyard.

The crowds had diminished since his arrival, but activity was at fever pitch. Even without paying close attention, he was aware that there was fresh smoke in the air and the exterior surfaces of the nearby buildings were developing dark scorch marks in the intense heat.

Once again he felt a sense of satisfaction as he quietly slipped away.

Chambers listened inattentively as Maria began a conversation with Dawson. Out of the corner of his eye, he saw movement close to the outer stairway to the crypt. A figure was leaving, heading south, apparently oblivious to the surrounding flames.

Ignoring Maria as she asked another question, he set off in the same direction.

71

The Fusiliers' Museum, 02:06

The passage came to a dead end, just as Mike had feared. With the night-vision setting on his eyewear activated, he'd been able to follow the consistent pattern of the brickwork that had lined the way.

There was light penetrating from above, far from bright but clearly noticeable. Concentrating on where it appeared brightest, he could see a strange, grid-like pattern, clearly some form of grate. Stretching, he felt for it, sensing it was loose but possibly covered over.

He was slightly too short to get a proper grip.

"See if you can reach this." Mike made a cup with his hands. Guided by her own eyewear, the purple shades showing up very differently to Mike's, Emily placed her left foot on to his hands, bracing herself for the moment of contact. Mike felt her legs brush up against his chest, her perfume again a soft intrusion on the otherwise dense air. Looking up, he saw her place her hands cautiously on the bars, discovering they were of iron construction.

Slowly she pushed upwards.

She emerged through the opening quickly, into an area shrouded in darkness. Exploring the vicinity through her night visions, she could see what appeared to be a museum-like arrangement with exhibits in glass display cases surrounded by cream-coloured walls and ceilings that seemed to reflect the darkness. Either side of her, red carpet had a slightly abrasive feel against her soft skin.

Mike followed her up, accepting her hand while also pulling against the bars of the grate to aid his climb. Rolling to one side, he realised they had indeed come up in the Fusiliers' Museum, the visual history of the regiment's last 150 years surrounding him like a moving picture screen. Out of the corner of his eye, he saw the famous features of George V looking down his nose at him, his face caught in a permanent sneer. Nearby was a portrait of a lance corporal from 1914–19, alongside other memorabilia from the Great War.

"Wow, Kit would love this," Mike muttered as he rose to his feet and began exploring the hallways, discovering they had come up in the heart of the exhibition. A large square-shaped tear could be seen where the lifting of the grate had damaged the red carpet.

Emily was horrified by its appearance. "I'm seriously getting fired for this."

Mike smiled, checking his gun for ammo. Including what remained in the bullet chamber, he estimated he had less than forty bullets.

"We might be in trouble unless we get some more ammo." He turned his attention to his headset. "Rook, this is Grosmont. Have just come up in the Fusiliers' Museum."

Maria had noticed movement on the screen shortly before hearing Mike's voice. Her conversation with Chambers had ended abruptly; the satellite link confirmed he was running south at pace, apparently in hot pursuit of a second figure.

Alongside her, Phil had also picked up on Mike's emergence. "Was beginning to think you were gonna see out the close of play in the tunnel, Honey Badger." He glanced from screen to screen. "So far there's been no change in the activities of either the gunmen in the security room or those patrolling the Inner Ward."

"You know me, Phil. I'm always one to do things the hard way. How are our chances?"

"Right now, I'd say flip a coin. Not that I'm expecting that to remain the case."

"They have cameras in here?"

"If you look up to your right, you can wave to me."

Mike glanced up at the corner of the room, noticing the electronic eye pointing down at him. "If you can see us here, they can see us in the CCTV room." He led Emily from room to room, quickly taking in everything he saw. Almost directly opposite the main entrance, a glass door was code-operated, clearly not part of the tour.

Emily punched in the code, pushing the door open. "Most of this and upstairs are offices. They don't have cameras in the staff areas."

"Good enough for now. What are my chances of getting some ammo?"

"Maybe upstairs."

On the second floor of the Waterloo Barracks, the leader of the three watchers saw two figures moving quickly through the heart of the Fusiliers' Museum, stopping outside a door that required coded access. He saw the woman enter the code before proceeding to move out of sight.

Blanco heard Christophe's voice come through as he watched the new fires. Within seconds of the flames appearing, they became significantly brighter, extending to the buildings either side of the church. The new light had a strange distorting effect, especially on the dome of St Paul's. It reminded him of the famous painting, how the old cathedral had been swept away in the merciless inferno, the molten lead flowing down the streets like lava.

He removed his HT from his belt and answered, "What is it?"

"The Englishman and the woman have reappeared. They're currently inside the Fusiliers' Museum."

Blanco raised an eyebrow, shocked they'd managed to travel so far. "You see them?"

"They've entered the offices upstairs. There are no cameras there."

Blanco walked quickly to his right, not stopping till he reached the east wall. Directly below him, the imposing neo-gothic façade of the museum caught the surrounding lights, its appearance reminiscent of a smaller version of the barracks. From there, it was unclear whether there was anyone in the museum.

"You want us to check it out?" Christophe pressed.

Overhearing, Randek beat his uncle to a response. "Stay where you are. I shall deal with this one myself."

Emily led the way to the first floor, stopping at one of several offices whose workspace appeared primarily intended for civilian use but surrounded by decorations that were largely imperial.

Mike rummaged through the desk, looking for anything that might prove interesting.

"Yo, Edward, you copy?"

Approaching St Mary-le-Bow where Gresham Street met Wood Street, Kit's primary concern was the surrounding blaze.

"This had better be important."

"Matter of fact, I'd consider less than forty bullets to last me the night particularly important. Especially with at least half that many enemies still unaccounted for."

"Where are you?"

"The Fusiliers' Museum. I must say, even in the dark it really is most compelling. Guessing you've been here a few times?"

"Far more than once, I assure you. Tell you the truth, I lost count after twenty."

"Maybe you could give me the complete tour one day. Preferably in daylight. Don't suppose any of your visits included the back areas?"

"I suppose it helps having an all-access pass. However, being a Fusilier did have its advantages."

Mike saw Emily look at him, clearly overhearing. "In that case what are my odds of increasing my stash?"

"I'd personally say very good. Though I suppose it would largely depend on your preference."

"What did you have in mind?"

"Whatever you prefer? A Lee-Enfield or a Martini?"

A wry smile. "I kinda feared you might say that." Mike turned his attention to the windows, seeing no sign of life on the east side. "Hey, Phil. How we looking?"

Monitoring the screens in the Rook, Phil's enthusiasm had wavered at the sight of Fabien Randek leading a group of ten gunmen down the stairs of the White Tower.

"Hate to break it to you, Honey Badger, but I think you might be about to have company."

"Anyone I recognise?"

"Everything except for his hair colour." Phil remembered footage of Randek six months earlier with a completely shaven head. "Randek's currently leading a posse down the main stairs of the White Tower."

"How long have I got?"

"I'd say forty-five seconds before you hear a knock on the door. After that, it depends how good you are at hide-and-seek."

"We still on camera?"

"Haven't been able to see you since your curator tapped in the code."

"In that case, maybe we can lie low for a bit. What are our options?"

"Again, you know I hate to be the bearer of bad news."

"Break it to me gently, Phil."

"Right now, if you're not into hide-and-seek, your best bet is to learn to fly."

Mike smiled. "No secret passages. No escape doors. Nothing Maria would recognise in a heartbeat but you're just not bright enough to see."

The bearded IT analyst laughed. "Sorry, Honey Badger. Randek's just made it to the bottom of the White Tower. You should be hearing that knock any second now."

The stairway beneath the Monument ended after precisely 155 and a half steps, exactly half the number that led to the area above. The stairway wound in the same direction; lower down, the stonework appeared more primitive, like that of a church crypt. There was a foul stench in the air, smoky and damp. Whatever was down there, Sanders sensed it hadn't been disturbed for centuries.

Until, perhaps, earlier that evening.

Alongside him, Jay followed the employee to the very end, where he could see an impressive opening beyond a narrow archway. A variety of icons decorated the area on the way down, ending with a series of carvings that were clearly medieval Christian. Beyond the archway, the walls were further apart, the stonework blackened, charred.

Side by side, Jay and Sanders stared in disbelief.

Emily decided to take Phil's advice, even if Mike wasn't convinced. She led them to the furthest of the offices, locking the door from the inside. There were no cameras; she was sure of that. Phil had confirmed the same.

Nevertheless, the last thing Mike wanted was to attract attention.

"What, are you crazy?" He immediately switched off the desk lamp, the low light of the forty-watt bulb enough, he feared, to be visible beyond the door.

"We don't know when will be the last time we get to see this." She unrolled the parchment she had taken from the archives, ignoring the feeling of guilt she felt handling something of historic value without the appropriate gloves. Spreading it out across the desk, Emily waited until she had enough space before again switching on the light.

Mike watched over her shoulder. "What are we looking at here?"

"Shhh!" She replaced her glasses, doing her best to concentrate on the Latin calligraphy. "I really wish we had more time to study this."

Moving alongside her, Mike removed his phone and took a snapshot, ensuring the whole thing was captured. "Phil, I've got something coming your way."

Within seconds, Phil noticed a message come through. "Parchment?"

"We found it in the archives; it was the only thing that contained reference to the Cardinal's Twins. I'm gonna do the same for the second one."

Page by page, Mike photographed the book concerning Belland's trial, his tired mind still trying to understand the connection. The king and the duke had been rounding up foreigners, one of whom was tried. The book implied the culprit had been found guilty, later executed. The plaque fifteen years later had placed the blame firmly on another man.

The son of a watchmaker.

"You got everything?"

"Unless there's something you're not telling me," Phil quipped.

"Trust me, there's plenty I'm not telling you." Mike returned his gaze to Emily, his concern growing. "What are we dealing with?"

"This is so strange. It's a letter from Edward II to his son, the future Edward III, apparently written in Italy." Emily read it as best she could. "I honestly don't understand; it seems to be cataloguing a trip he made. It refers to the prince's brothers, which doesn't make sense."

"He had no brothers?"

"Edward II had five children. The eldest, Prince Edward, went on to become Edward III; he was one of the most famous kings of England."

Mike nodded, neglecting to inform her the man had also founded the White Hart.

"John of Eltham died in 1336, almost forty years before his brother. The other two were sisters."

"Any illegitimate offspring?"

"Yes, Adam Fitzroy also died young. The identity of his mother was never known."

"You sure he had one?"

Emily frowned. "This is very odd: it refers to a trip to the north of Italy, to the Abbey of Sant'Alberto di Butrio in Ponte Nizza."

Mike's attention sharpened at the reference to the abbey. "Where is this abbey?"

"North Italy. It's in the diocese of Pavia."

"Does it mention a cardinal?"

"Matter of fact, it mentions several of the religious life from monks to papal notaries. Even confirms the letter was sent courtesy of one Manuel Fieschi."

"Who was he?"

"The Fieschi family were prominent in Italy. According to this, Fieschi was a papal notary."

"Why's any of this important?"

"I honestly have no idea; clearly whatever had transpired beforehand was well known to both of them."

"Meaning there were other letters before this one?"

"Presumably. I guess it depends on what the date was."

"Does it say?"

Emily scanned the content, looking for a date. Finding one, her expression became even more confused.

Randek was first to depart from the White Tower, heading swiftly towards the entrance to the museum. Finding it locked, he shouted instructions to the nearest gunman.

"Blow the door."

Mike heard, more than felt, the explosion. The tremors in the floor, though noticeable, had been reassuringly weak; Mike attributed it to the strength of the foundations.

The noise, on the other hand, had been almost deafening.

Recovering his bearings, he spoke via his headset. "Phil, what's the latest?"

"Didn't I tell you to expect a knock on the door?"

"Maybe next time they could ring the bell."

He edged towards the door, pushing it open a few inches, just enough to make out sounds. There were voices coming from below, footsteps sounding on the stairs.

Both almost drowned out by the noise of gunfire.

Mike shut the door behind him, locking it again from the inside. The sounds had reawakened the warrior in him, filling him with the inward desire for combat he secretly lived for.

He looked at Emily.

"Gonna need some proper advice here, Phil."

Watching the screens, Phil's attention alternated between the security images and the satellite link-up. "You remember your experience up in Scotland with Colonel Radchenko?"

"How the hell could I forget?"

"Take a look at the left pocket of your belt. You see a coil with a hook on it?"

Mike reached deep into the pocket, finding it. "Yep."

"You're clear on the north side. Head down, you should be free all the way to the Hospital Block."

Mike hurried to the window behind the desk, raising the blinds and forcing it open.

"Come on, let's move."

Emily was terrified. "You're not being serious?"

"Trust me, it'll be just like taking an abseil."

Mike attached the small grappling hook to a secure part of the wall, remembering Phil's instructions from training. He fixed the other end securely to a belt placed around Emily's waist, guiding her to the open window.

He looked down, searching in both directions. "We still clear, Phil?"

"Go for it. Just be quick."

Mike guided Emily to the ledge, talking her through the following steps. "Okay. Take it slow. I'll guide you down."

Completely unwilling, Emily took a seat on the ledge, placing her legs over the side. Almost immediately she felt her balance go.

"It's okay, I got ya." Mike gripped hard against the coil, the line burning against his hands. Almost five metres below him, he saw Emily had found her bearings. "One step at a time, just imagine you're walking – only vertically."

Dangling to a standstill, Emily breathed in deeply, placing the soles of her feet against the walls. Slowly she made her way down.

Within seconds she reached the bottom.

She detached herself and ran quickly to the rear of the Hospital Block. Pulling it back up, Mike attached the line to his belt, preparing to begin his descent.

Outside the room, the sound of voices was getting louder, threats aimed at him. Taking a deep breath, he recalled the advice of the Ukrainian.

Suddenly he wished he were wearing a helmet.

72

St Mary-le-Bow,
02:07

Chambers left his seat the moment he saw the figure pass beyond the stairs. He called out within seconds of seeing him before doing so again as he turned left, heading from Bow Churchyard into Bow Lane. As the stranger disappeared, his dark frame shielded by the position of nearby buildings, the White Hart's first black agent accelerated into a sprint, following the curvature of the pathway. In Bow Lane he re-established visual contact.

Less than fifty metres in front of him, the man was also sprinting.

The cabin cruisers had docked close to Blackfriars, approximately midway between the two nearby bridges. The vans were waiting on White Lion Hill; within seconds they sped off, heading north-east along Queen Victoria Street.

The journey ended on Watling Street, close to St Mary Aldermary.

All of the roads had been closed for over two hours, the lanes heading into the city presently clear of traffic; in some cases the tarmac was melted and cracked from a combination of earlier flames and fallen debris. A police checkpoint had been set up where Queen Victoria Street crossed Cannon Street; all the traffic lights were on green.

Like every element of the project, the plan had so far been implemented perfectly.

As the first duty police officer walked towards the vehicle on its approach to the recently erected barricade, informing him the road was closed, the driver showed a recently forged identity badge indicating his profession was counterterrorism. When the policeman refused to grant immediate access, they proceeded with plan B.

Like the ceremonial guard who had recently paraded on the Broadwalk Steps, within seconds the policeman's body had been shredded to pieces by muffled gunfire.

The car in which Kit was travelling turned left on reaching the end of Wood Street, heading east along Cheapside before stopping in a loading bay directly opposite the church.

Even from inside the vehicle, Kit could see the flames. He got out through the rear offside door, crossing the road just as the latest fire truck passed. The noise levels were high, sirens sounding from all directions; either side of the church, the latest fire engine was already dealing with the blaze in the neighbouring buildings.

"Maria, it's Edward. I'm outside the church."

***

Maria saw Kit appear via the satellite link-up. Since the last time she'd seen him, he'd finally replaced his smart tuxedo with something more suited to the task in hand.

"What's it look like down there?" she asked.

"Well, compared to other things we've seen tonight, I'd have to say we're looking at a marked improvement."

He began in Bow Churchyard, investigating the west side of the church, his attention turning next to the tower. While it was obvious from the steady orange glow that shone through the stained-glass windows the interior was alight, the exterior was, as yet, undamaged.

"Where are Stapleton and March?"

A response came from Dawson. "Top of Bow Lane, by the fire truck."

Kit saw him before needing to respond. Like himself, Dawson was dressed in full field gear, the predominantly black attire not dissimilar to those used for black ops missions, but casual enough to avoid suspicion.

"What the hell's been happening?"

"Fires either side are already largely out of control. The chief's tackling the church from both the front and the churchyard, but they can't get anything in this side." He pointed to the narrow area along Bow Lane. "With fires on both sides, right now the smoke's too thick to see exactly where it's coming from."

Kit had been thinking the same thing. Standing close to the doors, he noticed the inverse L-shaped area of Bow Churchyard was crammed with three fire engines. "Have you been inside?"

"Negative. Even outside the doors, it's so hot in there you could boil lobsters."

Kit moved quickly towards the main entrance, doing his best to catch a glimpse inside. Though the main door was open, no less than three fire hoses disappearing within, a sudden cloud of dense smoke made it impossible to assess just how bad the blaze actually was.

He heard Maria ask for an update.

"The yellow helmets are heading inside; looks from here like they might soon have it under control." Kit moved past Bow Churchyard, noticing another fire engine had recently arrived. From the west side, the fires appeared smaller.

As did those of the neighbouring building.

"How did it happen?" The question was for Dawson.

"Haven't the foggiest. One second AC and me were sitting here pretending to enjoy a coffee. Next, the building next door spontaneously combusted."

Kit looked around, suddenly confused.

"Where is AC?"

Chambers followed the passageway round to the right, heading along Bow Lane. Like many of London's quaint side streets, a plethora of designer shops boasting famous labels lined the way that was far too narrow for vehicle access. There were lights on inside some of the establishments despite the lack of customers.

Even in the absence of nearby lampposts, it was strangely bright out in the city.

He sprinted south in the direction of Watling Street, sighting an inn in the distance on the corner. The street curved from right to left, the angle of greater benefit to the pursued than the pursuer. On reaching the crossroads, he came to a halt, seeing no sign of life in any of three directions. As instinct guided him left, he saw five white vans parked outside the church of St Mary Aldermary.

Within seconds, he realised he was heading into an ambush.

Kit heard the gunfire the moment it began. A pulsating echo resonated from somewhere south of St Mary-le-Bow; even with the sirens roaring, he heard it clearly.

He heard Chambers swear in his ear.

Forgetting about the fire, Kit sped off along Bow Lane, following it to the end. After a couple of hundred metres, he saw a figure crouched down low on the corner, dressed almost identically to himself.

The gunfire was coming from the left side of the crossroads.

Kit joined him, followed by Dawson. "What the hell's happening?"

Since dashing for cover, Chambers had taken refuge behind the nearest wall as glass fell like rain from the windows of the building in front of them. "God knows, bro. I just saw some turd weasel out of the crypt. Drew me straight into an ambush."

Keeping low, Kit spoke into his headset. "Maria, we're in trouble. What can you see?"

Maria watched the screens in astonishment. The doors of the vans had opened, no less than thirty men spilling out. Each carried automatic weapons, their faces covered by ski masks.

"You might have picked the wrong place to get lost, guys. There are five white vans blocking the road by the church; at least thirty are packing something heavy. The leaders are coming towards you."

Kit grabbed two grenades from his belt, removing the pins and tossing them behind him. "Any sign of the suspect?"

Maria rewound the footage, finding a solitary runner baiting the unsuspecting Chambers. "Matter of fact, he's just entered the van at the end. Get the feeling a few of these guys aren't planning on sticking around too long."

Kit braced himself as the gunfire resumed, ending with the dual explosion of grenades. In the distance he could see evidence of destruction beyond the smoke, the façades of nearby shops becoming partially obliterated.

Fortunately they'd managed to avoid damaging the church.

"We're gonna need guidance here, Maria. If these bastards encroach on us, without shelter we're sitting ducks. To say nothing of these fires."

Maria frantically studied the map as the three knights tossed further grenades in the direction of the vans, the sounds of explosions for a short time drowning out the gunfire. Beyond the smoke, the noises of commotion were becoming louder, panicked instructions, clearly not in English.

Two of the vans reversed out on to Queen Victoria Street and drove away at high speed.

Kit waited until the smoke began to clear before reloading, edging towards the corner. The pub on the opposite side was covered with bullet holes; at least two of the windows were smashed. Further along the street the same was also true; the church was no longer visible, so thick was the smoke.

Moving forward slowly, keeping close to the entrances of the shops on the left, Kit pulled his gas mask from his belt and placed it over his face as he approached the smoke.

At the heart of it, two vans were on fire.

He opened fire again; Chambers and Dawson did the same. A further brace of grenades left their hands, both exploding on impact. Themselves aside, the guns had been quiet for several seconds now.

Slowly they advanced, Kit taking the lead, finding shelter where possible. With the cessation of the enemy's gunfire, the noise of developing fires was now audible both in front and behind them, accompanied by the constant drum of pressure hoses from the vicinity of Mary-le-Bow. The heat was becoming unbearable, his skin breaking out in blisters.

Spreading out, they passed the first van, finding it deserted and engulfed by flame. Beyond it, the same was true of the second.

Five metres on, the third was still unaffected, the doors open, the cockpit empty. Nearby lay a number of dead bodies, some clearly missing limbs. Among them Kit saw movement.

Gunfire.

Maria heard the gunfire resume and immediately feared the worst.

"Edward?" She heard no response, nor from any of the others. Trying again, the result was the same.

Finally Kit responded.

"Vans are empty. All around them are dead. Two we saw speed off."

Maria had seen everything on the screens. "I see them. They're heading north. With the streets closed, we won't struggle to find them." She saw on the satellite footage that the three Harts had made it back to Mary-le-Bow. "How's it looking there?"

"Better," Kit replied, now reaching the top of Bow Lane. "Something tells me Blanco won't be quite as happy as before."

"Let's hope it stays that way." She contacted the Director. "Eagle one, this is the Rook. We ran into a spot of bother, but things are under control."

Seated behind the pilot in the single-engined helicopter, Mr White looked out across the city. The fires had spread in recent minutes, yet they were still to reach new heights of scale or intensity.

Viewing a combination of intel and news footage on his tablet, he was prepared for the worst. "You know, Mary-le-Bow has always been one of my favourite churches. I hope to God it fares better than it did at the hands of the Luftwaffe."

"Right now, I can only speculate on that. I'm sure the Black Prince will provide a more informed report." She tracked the movement of the white vans on the screens. One had stopped briefly close to the city walls. Since then, all had moved on. "Enemies are heading north after attempting an ambush and picking up the arsonist. We believe the troops originally arrived by river."

"How in God's name did they pass the roadblocks?"

"Sadly thirty armed men against one copper wasn't much of a challenge." Maria looked at recent footage of the policeman's murder. "The fires at Mary-le-Bow are nearly out. A full search should be possible soon. In the meantime, what are your instructions?"

The Director took a deep breath, finally diverting his attention from the fires to concentrate instead on an open patch of greenery ahead of him that belonged to a small village on the outskirts of the city.

"Five places on the map have been targeted. That leaves only two. Ensure the knights have every angle covered. If even an ant gets into the crypts, I want to know about it. And keep an eye on those helicopters."

"Yes, sir."

Sanders was almost completely speechless. Even after five minutes in the strange undercroft beneath the Monument, he struggled to digest what he was seeing. Nothing of the sort was known to exist in the modern day.

Least of all in London.

He heard Maria speak to him once again, asking, "What's your position?"

"It's really difficult to put into words right now." Again he stared at his surroundings. In every direction he'd looked since passing the strange archway, the expected sight of drainage or depleted walls, perhaps illustrating the effects of past bomb damage, had actually been something far more intriguing.

"What do you mean?"

Sanders struggled to put it into words. "It's like I'm looking at an underground catacombs."

That was the last thing Maria had expected. "Any sign of damage?"

"Could say that."

"What happened?"

Sanders laughed. "Even you would struggle to make sense of this one."

"How do you mean?"

Sanders knelt down, re-examining the area where the foul stench appeared to be strongest. "We got this all wrong. They're not using modern explosives, it's gunpowder."

Maria was speechless. "Gunpowder? But . . ."

"And unless I'm very much mistaken, I also sense the presence of tar, timber and some form of petrol." At the other end, Sanders noticed the silence.

"Explains everything. Why they weren't seen. Why the explosions weren't heard above ground. Perhaps even how they managed to create so much damage six months ago." He smiled to himself. "They've been building bonfires beneath the city."

Maria shook her head, amazed. "You might have to talk me through this."

"Look forward to it. How are things above ground?"

"The latest fire was at St Mary-le-Bow. Also had a little company, but both are under control. Targets now are St Paul's and St Dunstan-in-the-East."

"The cathedral?"

"If the terrorists are following the pattern of history, St Paul's might be next. I suggest you head there now."

"We're on it!"

Maria returned her attention to Kit. "How's it looking down there?"

Kit replied immediately, "Would you like the short answer or the long?"

"Maybe another time. The vans are heading north. Police have the area under control. I suggest you divert your attention to St Paul's."

"Maybe later. Right now, I want to check the area below ground."

"You want to enter the crypt?"

Kit crossed the road, returning to the car. Gillian and Nat remained in the back seat. "I currently have with me, on the recommendation of the Director of the National Portrait Gallery, one of the foremost experts on Wren architecture. Let's find out what he has to say."

73

Highlands of Scotland, Twenty-One Months Earlier

The journey ended after twenty minutes; again the destination was in the mountains. Mike disembarked from the mini bus on Masterson's orders; as usual when an instructor left, the uniforms worn by the Harts changed. For now, Mike couldn't quite place what he saw. It was whiter than usual, the colours blending well with the surrounding frost. It seemed all-purpose.

Mike assumed it meant further cold.

They lined up in three ranks of four and marched in formation to Masterson's commands along a bumpy country road. Some 800 metres from the minibus, he noticed signs of life, a solitary figure standing on a small mount.

What Mike saw left him speechless. Even from a distance it was clear the man was staring in his direction. A cold, hardened glare originated from what appeared to be dark, colourless eyes whose ferocious appearance seemed to be greatly intensified in their sunken position deep within a bald, partly shaven head, that had almost the appearance of a lifeless skull. Though Mike guessed the man was in his early fifties, a more informed assessment from his gaunt features alone was difficult, especially when considering the physical stresses to which the man had clearly been subjected during his years of service. It was a face that appeared haunted by the demons of the past, a past devoted to war, a face itself capable of telling a story of conflict, yet unhindered by the curse of self-conflict; instead, that of a man who had seen everything there was to see and wasn't afraid to revisit it.

As Mike drew nearer, he was able to detect colour in the eyes, a subtle shade of blue, engaging, with a clear, questioning quality about them that he found strangely disturbing. In his mind, the words of his previous tormentors replayed: he'd been sent to hell and kept there. Yet while the others had only reached the gates, there was something about this one that tugged deeper at his anxiety levels, as though looking into those eyes would provide a glimpse of what existed beyond the gates. If he had indeed been taken to hell, the being that he looked at now came directly from there. Specifically for the purpose of completing his training.

Or finishing him off completely.

As the nervous lieutenant finally managed to break free of his new tormentor's penetrating gaze, other clues to his identity became apparent. Replacing the desert-storm, camouflage-style combats favoured by his previous tormentor, the attire of this man was of a more plain and basic fabric, in a lighter shade of green of the kind associated with the Great War of a century earlier.

From battledress to outer garments, his appearance was every bit military, but unlike the previous instructors, indicative of a man who had risen high in the service ranks. Now more so than ever, the look in the man's eyes was clear. He had led not only men, but leaders of men. He was in the presence once more of someone from the east, yet not so far east as Bautista. This man was a veteran of SPETSNAZ. A former soviet.

If he'd lived thirty years earlier, Mike knew he'd be looking at a member of the KGB.

The Harts came to a halt at the bottom of the mount; on Kit's command, they stood to attention. For the first time Mike noticed a flag flying from a low pole directly alongside the new tormentor; he'd been so engrossed with the man's appearance, the colours had failed to register till now. Though Mike was certain they had never met, it was clear to him the man was targeting him specifically, as though he had studied profile photos of him beforehand and committed his appearance to memory.

"For the next two days, every step you take, every breath, will be evaluated," the tormentor began, his eyes firmly on Mike, his accented English providing further evidence of his nationality. The blue and yellow patterns on the flag confirmed his initial suspicion. He was looking not at a Russian.

But a Ukrainian.

"Whatever fears you have previously been hiding, I promise you now, I will dig them out. It is never wise to hide from fear. Accept it. Embrace it. Feel it. Face it. Overcome it. Once our time together is over, one of two things shall be clear. You will have passed or you will have failed. If you pass, you will continue on to the next phase of your selection. If you fail, you will go home."

The tormentor descended the mount. "Lieutenant Hansen, come with me, please."

The man's name was Colonel Igal Radchenko; as Mike had anticipated, he'd worked in Ukraine's SPETSNAZ. Like all of the tormentors bar Bautista, the man had retired from active service.

Mike guessed that at one time, the former Soviet would have been fighting on the opposite side from his forebears.

Radchenko led Mike on a slow march several hundred metres up the nearest mountain. On reaching a cliff top, he saw two specialists preparing equipment for an abseil.

The eleven Harts had assembled below.

The Ukrainian sat down on a jagged piece of rock and picked up a clipboard.

"Lieutenant Hansen." His gaze alternated between Mike and the text. "You are currently with the Parachute Regiment, is that correct?"

"Yes, sir. Five and a half years, first battalion."

"Good. Then you are no stranger to heights."

"No, sir, my personal record currently stands at two hundred seventy-one successful jumps. Including two in Afghanistan."

"Two-seven-one." The Ukrainian raised an eyebrow, be it doubtful or impressed, Mike couldn't tell. "What we have here is a simple task. It's about facing fear and overcoming it." He looked at Mike sternly with those same penetrating eyes. "Tell me now. Are you afraid?"

"No, sir."

"You do not fear death?"

"I acknowledge death is a possibility. After over five years in the Parachute Regiment, I've learned not to be overawed by heights."

"You've abseiled before?"

"Yes, sir."

"It's different from a parachute, no?"

"Yes, sir, but my feeling towards heights remains the same."

"As a red beret, you have the luxury of a second string. Here you only have one."

A wry smile. "I put my trust in the man who prepared my rope. In the regiment the same is true of whoever packs my chute."

The tormentor smiled. "Okay, very well. Get ready."

Mike allowed the specialists to prepare the line. Once they'd finished, he moved to the edge on Radchenko's instructions.

Radchenko watched on with folded arms. "When you're ready, I want you to walk slowly backwards and descend the mountain. At halfway down, you will be required to make a thirty-foot leap. You will see when you reach it how the cliff separates."

"Yes, sir."

"At every point, I want you to keep hold of your helmet. Keep your hands on your helmet at all times and you will pass this task. You understand?"

"Yes, sir."

Mike moved slowly to the edge of the cliff and slowly began his descent. He moved his feet one at a time, a slow vertical walk. As his legs became completely horizontal, he pushed off, using the rocky exterior for leverage.

It was cold out on the cliff front, the wind bracing; even dressed in heavy layers, he could feel it penetrating his hands and chest. The air seemed thinner, his breathing tighter, sounds seemed excessively close as the wind distorted his hearing.

At forty feet down he saw the cliff had separated, the area Radchenko had warned him of. From somewhere up above, he heard a call, confirming he'd reached the point he needed to reach. In his mind, he counted down to impact. One, two, three. Bounce.

One, two, three. Bounce.

One, two, three. Bounce.

The next would be the hardest.

One, two, three. Bounce.

He felt himself falling, the bare crags moving quickly across his eye line. His legs gave way to jelly; his body lurched forward, expelling every last morsel of air from his lungs.

His training had prepared him for this. Everything: the fall, the impact, the last resort if he hit the ground.

He wouldn't fall – he reassured himself. He wasn't being murdered. The man's purpose was clear.

To instil the fear of God deep into his heart.

He straightened his legs and closed his eyes, both hands pressed tightly to his helmet. He felt contact with the cliff face against the soles of his feet. Then again. Then a third time. The air seemed to be passing slowly against his face, his movements more precise. Velocity had returned to normal.

He'd passed the point where Radchenko instructed him to jump.

The Fusiliers' Museum,
02:11

Mike waited till Emily was out of sight before returning his attention to the office. Beyond the door, the sounds of shouting had become louder, confirming the enemy was fast approaching. With his gun at hand, Mike frantically attached the coil to his belt, satisfied it would hold. With the ties secure, he placed one leg outside the window, his attention briefly turning to the ground. The area at the foot of the museum was presently uninhabited, the walkway deserted from the Constable Tower to the Broad Arrow Tower, from the museum to the New Armouries Restaurant. There was a chill in the air, but nothing out of the ordinary; he heard no sounds to combat the silence. Emily had made it to the rear of the Hospital Block, accessing the nearest door.

All that remained was to follow her.

The sounds outside the office were getting louder, a clear contrast to those outside the window. He saw the door rise suddenly off its hinges, a figure in black appearing, evidently armed. Letting off lead, Mike watched the figure fall to the floor, the shouts and gunfire clearly a cause of alarm to the others nearby. As the sound of running along the corridor increased, he removed a grenade from his belt and tossed it through the doorway.

Pushing off, he fired wildly at the door.

"Tell me now. Are you afraid?"

"No, sir."

"You do not fear death?"

"I acknowledge death is a possibility . . ."

"You've abseiled before?"

"Yes, sir."

"It's different from a parachute, no?"

"Yes, sir, but my feeling towards heights remains the same."

Mike held his breath as he quickly found his rhythm, the soles of his feet bouncing against the museum's exterior. In his mind he recalled his conversation with Radchenko; not for the first time that night he wondered whether providence had trained him especially for this one night. Directly above him, the sounds of consternation were continuing to brew, becoming ever louder as the gunmen approached the window. From the room he had just left, he heard sounds, urgent voices, instructions given in French.

Without warning the window lit up with a fiery light.

The explosion was visible even on the way down, the impact testing his balance. He felt the line pull suddenly to his right, causing him to fall faster.

"*At every point, I want you to keep hold of your helmet. Keep your hands on your helmet at all times and you will pass this task. You understand?*"

"Yes, sir."

Again, Radchenko's words replayed in his mind. Holding his breath as he bounced against the wall, he felt his momentum begin to slow, as though he were moving underwater. His fingers on his head, he concentrated on his surroundings.

Without warning, he hit the ground.

He tied off quickly, realising retrieving the hook would no longer be possible. His bearings recovered, he darted south. The rear door to the Hospital Block was open; Emily's face peered out from inside. Like the museum, the Hospital Block consisted of three storeys, its construction far more recent than the medieval towers.

"Come on!"

He heard Emily's call, followed by other noises. Sparks appeared nearby, eerily silent.

Gunfire.

He changed direction instinctively and headed east, finding himself entering a wide archway, the illuminated stonework much older than that he'd recently seen. Guided by instinct, he'd entered the lower section of the Constable Tower, a sturdy refuge if not a dead end.

He realised his only option was to stand and fight.

Edging back towards the archway, he looked out across the concrete. The Fusiliers' Museum was directly in front of him now, the Hospital Block alongside it to its left. Emily's face was still visible, an expression of concern etched across her features. He gestured for her to get inside.

Getting there was now a problem.

A second set of sparks appeared against the nearby walls, the closest they'd come so far. He estimated from their trajectory that they'd come from both above and directly in front of him; sure enough, he could see movement through one of the windows in the room he'd recently vacated. Two gunmen were firing at him, missing only by inches.

He dived deep into cover.

Replacing the depleted magazine on his USP45, he moved with his back to the stonework, awaiting the moment the sparks would stop. No sooner had they than he took aim and fired, dispatching one of the gunmen. Over the coming seconds, the pattern replayed itself.

He calculated he now had thirty-three bullets.

Taking a deep breath, he saw new sparks; they disappeared after five seconds of ferocious onslaught. Chancing the merest inch of exposure, he saw a second figure in the window; again the sparks resumed. Biting his lip, he calculated his next move. The longer he stayed there, the worse his chances.

At least for now, Emily was safe.

His arms extended, he fired quickly at the window from which he'd jumped, watching one of the gunmen fall to the ground, his body smashing down on a wooden bench close to the museum's rear wall. Depleting his magazine, Mike saw a third man had also appeared; he was down to his last two magazines. Reloading, he waited for the sparks to return; when they did, they ended suddenly. Without taking breath, he made his decision. Removing a smoke canister, he threw it across the concrete, sprinting and taking aim.

Without being able to see whether his latest bullets had hit their mark, he ran at full speed up a set of steps and across the concrete before bursting through the open door into the Hospital Block.

74

Whitehall,
02:16

Phil breathed a sigh of relief as he saw Mike disappear through the rear door of the Old Hospital Block, leaving a cloud of smoke in his wake. From a combination of satellite imagery and the nearby CCTV footage, he was already aware that no less than two gunmen had been taken out, their bodies lying crumpled in a heap outside the Fusiliers' Museum.

"Hansen's made it safely inside the Hospital Block," Phil confirmed, quietly ruing the fact there were no cameras inside there.

"Was the curator with him?" Maria asked, her own focus now on Edinburgh.

"How else do you think he opened the door?" He smiled.

From across the room, Atkins returned, his footfalls echoing off the hard flooring.

"What's the latest in Edinburgh?"

Maria replied, "The fires on the Royal Mile are subsiding. There's been nothing new for over an hour."

Atkins replaced his headset. "Put me through to Rawlins."

Rawlins heard the Deputy Director's voice come through clearly, asking the same question recently asked by Maria. "Fires near Holyrood are all but out. So are the ones down the road."

"Anything new?"

"Negative. Every road in the city is now closed; you couldn't get a gerbil through without being seen."

"What about the castle?"

"Salisbury's still there; de Courtenay's with me." He spoke of Pentland and Pugh. "Salisbury's already spoken with the curator."

"To what effect?"

"We have confirmation. The jewels were fake."

Atkins was relieved but unsurprised. "Any news on the culprits?"

"Negative. CCTV had been sabotaged. Whoever did this clearly had insider access. The head of the guards confirmed the jerks responsible weren't official military. Apparently they entered and escaped through a subterranean tunnel somewhere inside the old palace. Clearly this was better planned than we thought."

Atkins was concerned. "Where was the last explosion?"

Rawlins looked across the city, the lights of the palace commanding his attention as its illuminated exterior glowed among the fading fires. "Pretty much directly in front of me. We're over one hundred yards from the palace."

"Any leads on what caused them?"

"It's like London all over again. It's as if they came up from a hole in the ground."

In an ancient tunnel beneath the city, Alain eyed the strange cave-like enclosure around him, awaiting the moment the next phase would begin.

He put through a call, Blanco answered. "*Allô?*"

"Preparations in Edinburgh are ready."

A delay preceded the reply. "Let them have it."

Rawlins saw new fires ignite suddenly to his right, approximately midway between where he was standing and the palace. The flames were visible on the north side of the Royal Mile, taking out a pub and a tearoom.

On the opposite side, the walls of the Scottish parliament building reflected their yellow tint.

The shaven-headed White Hart looked on in disbelief. "You seeing this?"

At the other end, Atkins saw everything on the screens. A sweeping inferno had engulfed the north side, the worst attack yet. He estimated less than 120 metres separated it from the palace.

Less still, the parliament building.

"Get every fire engine in the city to the top of the Mile now. You hear me? Everything else pales into insignificance."

"The engines are already on the Mile; the choppers are still on their way." Rawlins looked north, noticing the emergency services had wasted no time. "We can't use resources we don't have."

"It's at times like this that we learn to improvise!" The Deputy Director's gaze was stern, his mind picturing images from the Blitz. "I don't care how you do it. Be it helicopters, hoses, even kids' sandcastle buckets, I don't want a single flame touching the key buildings. You hear me?"

Equally stern-faced, Rawlins nodded. "I hear you, sir."

Maria watched the screens as the images changed abruptly, footage of the fires replaced by that of the prime minister. "Sir, the PM is on the videoconference."

Atkins had already noticed. "Prime Minister?"

"Where is the Director?"

"The Director is currently en route to Surrey, personally following up a new lead. I understand the instruction was left with your secretary. In his absence all communication goes through me." Atkins' response was calm and confident. Though he'd only met the prime minister a handful of times, he knew his identity would be well known to her.

"The situation in our capital is escalating. Though the fires are slowly being extinguished, I'm hearing new reports of gunfights on the streets and rioting in the outer perimeters." The PM's face was deadly serious. "Furthermore, in the last few moments I'm also hearing reports of new fires in Edinburgh."

Atkins waited till he was sure the PM had finished. "I've just got off the phone to Edinburgh. The emergency services were already on the scene; fortunately, on this occasion we were prepared. The fires won't reach the key buildings."

The PM didn't buy it. "I'd hate for your confidence to be misplaced, Deputy Director. That the latest fires have begun in an area already recently affected can be considered either good luck or bad, but on no occasion have any of the fires been predicted. Time is running out – we cannot continue to rely on chance alone."

"Our latest intelligence confirms the terrorists are following an historical pattern; the blaze at Mary-le-Bow has already been put out, along with those of the neighbouring buildings. The gunmen on Watling Street have been partially neutralised; the vans are being trailed as we speak. Believe me, Prime Minister. If the vans do open their doors again, we'll be ready."

"I hope for all our sakes, your judgement is correct." The PM leaned forward, elbows on the table. "If word of the riots spreads, we know from recent history it takes only one moment of madness to escalate a major crisis. Our resources are already stretched near to the limit."

"In cases of national emergency, Prime Minister, might I suggest a curfew? The streets of the city are already largely empty; the traffic problems have been resolved. It's in the people's own safety that they remain indoors."

"Martial law, you mean?" She contemplated the possibility. "And what do you suggest we do if citizens refuse?"

"You're the leader of the nation, Prime Minister. And in times of crisis, the call is for desperate measures."

"What are you saying?"

"Perhaps under the circumstances, it's time to take a leaf out of Blanco's own book."

Kit completed two circuits of the church, delaying his entry. According to tradition, the church was an important feature of local folklore, as only a true cockney could be born within the sound of its bells. According also to tradition, the same bells had persuaded the then unknown Richard Whittington to turn back to the capital.

Kit hoped they would have the same effect on Blanco.

He entered through the main entrance off Bow Churchyard alongside Gillian and Nat, the noise of the recent gunfight still echoing in his ears. Though a crime scene had already been set up around three of the vans, the blazes extinguished, the fact that two had been able to drive off still irritated him.

He knew from Maria they were being watched.

Inside, the main aisle was busy with people, the majority heavily suited with protective firemen's overalls and strong yellow helmets. It was wet underfoot, the chessboard-style flooring darkened and cracked by the recent flames. The interior was different to what Kit had expected. While the 224-foot-high steeple, crowning a tower of Portland stone below a slender obelisk atop two balustrades surrounding thin columns and two rotundas, gave off an appearance that many considered to be typical of Wren, the brick-built main structure demonstrated a notable change in appearance.

The floor aside, the interior had survived relatively well. The glass of the three round-headed windows that formed part of the central bay and the blue and white of the barrel-vaulted ceiling had become blackened with smoke, but all were structurally intact. Of the three, Nat had been paying most attention.

"Bet it looked far worse after the Blitz."

Kit remained tight-lipped as he turned to view the back of the church, noticing the imposing organ case over the arched entrance. Though he'd never been inside the church before, the baroque interior reminded him of St Paul's.

He heard Maria ask, "How's it looking in there?"

"You want the short answer or the long?"

"Let's just focus on the damage."

"There are cracks in the floor, but it's tough to tell the full extent with the water level so high. It seems to be seeping somewhere below."

"There's a crypt directly below it," she replied, remembering what Chambers had told her before the gunfight. "According to Stapleton, it was from there he saw a figure climbing the stairs."

"Where's the entrance?"

"Outside. West side. Another exists inside the church."

Kit ended the conversation and found Chambers close to the organ. "Whereabouts did you see the guy?"

Chambers pointed through the wall. "Bastard was showing up just as the fires started."

Kit nodded and headed towards the altar, where Nat was standing below an ornate crucifix that had somehow survived unscathed.

"I understand there's a crypt below here; my colleague saw a figure leaving the external stairway just as the fire started. Can you show us the way?"

"Of course."

"Good." He spoke again through his headset. "I'm about to take Mr Johnstone and Ms McKevitt downstairs."

Back at the Rook, Atkins was first to respond. "How's it looking in there?"

"I've seen worse," Kit replied. "A quick lick of paint and a few mops and buckets, we could even be in shape for Sunday's service."

"Good. If the situation here is anything like that at Monument, there's some form of subterranean passageway directly below you. If Stapleton is correct in what he saw, the crypt would make perfect sense."

"My thoughts exactly."

Atkins immediately proceeded to contact Wilcox and Ward. "What's the latest at St Dunstan's?"

***

Crouched down in relative obscurity within the church gardens, Ward responded, "All quiet. No one has entered the churchyard."

Satisfied by the response, he enquired of further west.

"What's the latest on Fleet Street?" Atkins eyed the semi-translucent screen that once again was streaming new pictures.

"Fires have reached Ludgate Hill; they've spread past City Thameslink." Maria also watched the footage as it came through live. Like the earlier fires on Eastcheap and Cannon Street, what had originally been a minor blaze had developed into a raging inferno.

"Show me on the map."

Maria typed quickly at her keyboard. Within seconds, a 2D map came up, confirming the pattern of the fire.

"How's it compare to the historical fire?"

Maria brought up a second map alongside it. "In 1666, the fires spread gradually from east to west. This is different."

Atkins watched quietly as the two patterns appeared one on top of the other. While the fire in 1666 had developed gradually, destroying everything in its wake, what he currently saw was clearly by design.

"How long until the fires reach the cathedral?"

"Based on the current spread, even if St Paul's isn't the next target, it could be knocking on the door come 03:00 hours."

The Deputy Director paced the floor, his focus intense as he considered the options. "If the fires near Mary-le-Bow aren't checked, we could already be fighting its spread on three fronts." He turned his attention to those on Cannon Street. If the pattern continued, the cathedral would be surrounded on all four sides around the same time. He thought back to the words recited by Blanco.

A pure body of flame higher than St Paul's.

"This has to have been their plan all along."

Leaning over her terminal, Maria watched the same pictures, her attention on the pattern of the 1666 fires. "They haven't touched anything north of Lombard Street. Since the fire reached St Mary Woolnoth, no fire has encroached on to Cornhill. In 1666 that was one of the first places affected."

Adjusting his glasses, Atkins considered what he'd just heard. He realised from the map one area was indeed being left untouched.

Away from the fires in London, the single-engined helicopter came down in the grounds of a luxury estate. Leaving his seat, the Director of the White Hart made his way rapidly across the perfectly manicured lawns, heading in the direction of a period mansion whose interior appeared shrouded in gloom.

On reaching the rear of the property, he found a butler awaiting his arrival.

"I'm here to meet Sir Richard."

The butler's demeanour was cold. "At this late hour?"

Mr White decided not to elaborate on the nature of his visit. "I'm afraid under the circumstances, I had to leave London immediately."

A change in the butler's facial expression suggested his words struck an immediate chord. "Your visit is expected. If you'd like to follow me, the master is currently at work in the study."

75

The Old Hospital Block,
02:17

Mike kept running until he was through the door, oblivious to everything beyond it. He saw Emily blocking the way as he approached; at first she'd shown no signs of moving. As he got within ten metres, he saw a look of panic in her eyes, the promise of a collision finally registering.

Move!

He hit the ground with a thump, his instincts returning him to the moment. The floor was soft, carpeted; he'd narrowly avoided colliding with a wall. Emily was standing inside the door, fumbling with the keys. Even with the door now closed, the stench of recent gunfire poisoned the air; the noise of impact off the concrete and stonework still rang loudly in his ears. From somewhere outside he thought he heard the sound of shouting, orders being barked.

As the seconds passed, other sounds faded.

Mike got quickly to his feet, gun at the ready. Taking in his surroundings, he could see a pleasantly furnished setting with white walls and doorways to a kitchen, lounge and bathroom.

"What is this place?"

"The Old Hospital Block."

Mike was confused. "Looks more like flats."

"That's because they are." She focused on Mike's face and arms; both were bleeding from recent falls. "That said, let's hope there's something here to deal with these."

The Old Hospital Block was one of the more modern areas of the Tower. Originally constructed as two houses in 1718 to provide accommodation for ordnance clerks, the three-storey buildings of Flemish bond brickwork were later merged into one and converted into the garrison hospital. While the north part of the building had since been dismantled following damage from the Luftwaffe, what remained had since been converted into homes for Tower officials.

Emily found a first aid kit in a cabinet in the bathroom and immediately set to work on cleaning Mike's wounds. "Hold still!" She dabbed him lightly with a wet wipe, persevering till the blood was removed. She did the same for his face and arms. He smiled.

"What?"

"You get much practice doing this?"

She ignored his glance. "Only when it involves my nephew. Why? You get much practice getting cut up?"

A wry smile. "You say this used to be a hospital?"

"Once upon a time. Not exactly one of the places on the average tour."

"I'll say. Who lives here?"

"Probably one of the Beefeaters." She finished the job, putting two plasters over the biggest cuts on his arms. "There. I'd say all of them working together couldn't have done a better job."

"Yeah, well, I guess Humpty Dumpty has one over on me."

"That and all the horses." She laughed as they looked one another in the eye. A peaceful silence passed between them, ending as the static of the HT they stole from the barracks crackled through the air.

Mike spoke first. "We got cameras on us?"

"Don't you get any ideas, mister!" She raised her eyebrows and smiled. "But since you ask, we're currently in the clear. It's just like the Byward Tower."

Mike assumed that meant the Rook were no longer watching him. "Hey, Phil. You copy?"

"That was some mighty fine smoke work, Honey Badger." The IT technician's response was instant. Seated alongside Maria, his eyes remained on the surveillance footage. "For a second, you almost had me worried."

"Well, you know me. I love to put on a show."

"I did say almost."

Mike laughed. "What's been happening out there?"

"Randek and the others are just leaving the Fusiliers' Museum. I have no idea what exactly you did up there, but at least one of the windows is gonna need a paint job."

"Well, let's just hope they have insurance. You're not gonna tell Edward, are you?"

"You know he can probably hear this, right?"

Another smile. "Well, right now I'd settle for a quiet night. Any advice?"

"Maybe *The Book Thief*."

"Thanks, I was really thinking something more historical. Better yet, anything where the bad guys get killed."

"Something educational, then." Phil's eyes remained on the screen. "Right now, I'm afraid I can't help you. Unfortunately we don't have footage where you are."

"Just imagine a nice cosy apartment, only the lights are out."

"Sounds very cosy."

"Last thing I'd want is a bastard like Randek joining us. At least one of them saw me entering. We can't stay here indefinitely."

"Right now, I suggest you bide your time. Maria's working on your escape route."

"In that case, tell her I'm already working on her thank you card."

He found Emily seated in the lounge, the dim glow of a forty-watt table lamp the only light. While he was satisfied the location wasn't under electronic surveillance, he guessed from the curtains that light could attract attention from the outside.

He found her leaning across a nearby coffee table on which the manuscript she'd been reading in the Fusiliers' Museum had been laid out in full. With her glasses on she was studying the content carefully, her expression incredulous.

He still had no idea why.

"What exactly is that?" He took a seat alongside her, his gaze on the quill-written Latin. "You were saying about Edward II having kids."

Emily shook her head. "History recalls Edward II had five kids, four of which were legitimate and two of which were sons. One of whom later succeeded him as king; the other died shortly after he did."

To Mike the connection meant nothing. "And?"

"Edward II was dethroned in 1327 after a coup by his queen, Isabella of France, and her lover, Roger Mortimer, Earl of March. After that, it's widely recorded that Edward died during his imprisonment in Berkeley Castle, some say after having a hot poker pushed up his bum."

"Guess it beats being shot in the dark." Mike grimaced. "What's so important?"

Emily pulled the document nearer. "The commonly accepted date of death for Edward II is around 21 September 1327; at the time the government was at Lincoln. Have a look at this."

Mike leaned forward, attempting to make out the Latin text. "1336?"

"Exactly. If this is true, Edward II was still alive nine years after he was dethroned."

Mike looked at her, their gazes locked. "Meaning?"

"Meaning that in the eyes of the people, England may possibly have had two kings during that period."

Mike allowed a moment to pass, attempting to make sense of everything. As a history lover, he was aware Edward II had been regarded as one of England's weaker kings, unlike his father and son.

"You said he was dethroned. What happened?"

"You did say you had a master's in history?" Emily's expression was no longer playful. "By 1326, Isabella finally lost patience with her husband. Whereas Edward I had consolidated much of England and Scotland, Edward II had undone it by losing at Bannockburn. Unbeknown to her husband, Isabella entered into an alliance with Roger Mortimer and had Edward imprisoned and dethroned, with Edward III replacing him under Isabella and Mortimer's supervision."

"So Edward II was alive but no longer king."

"In the eyes of the government, no, but there was still the problem of Avignon. Edward was highly thought of by the papacy."

Mike raised an eyebrow. "So according to this he survived?"

"According to this, not only did he survive, but he also had kids."

Mike bit his lip, the penny slowly beginning to drop. "So in the eyes of Edward III . . ."

"Exactly! He now potentially had pretenders to his own throne."

* * *

Champion waited until the two gunmen left the chamber before clearing his throat in accordance with the instruction he'd just received in his ear. To his left, the governor had once again been marched in at gunpoint, his weary frame clearly suffering from recent ordeals.

Champion sensed his suffering was more emotional than physical.

He heard his nephew speak a second time, enquiring of his health. "Well as can be expected. Which is more than I can say for some of the others."

At the other end, Mike remained calm. "You just sit tight; help is on its way." He slowly removed the headpiece. "Listen, Uncle Dave, I don't really know how to explain this. We found something down in the archives that we think is important."

He passed it over to Emily.

"Professor, I appreciate you might not be able to respond, so I'll talk briefly. The archives database gave us one lead for the Cardinal's Twins. It was a letter from 1336 concerning Edward II. It was sent by a papal nuncio named Fieschi."

Seated against the cold wall, Champion felt a sudden burst of exhilaration. "The Fieschi letters, of course. Later Bishop of Vercelli. My dear, you really have excelled yourself."

Emily refused to let the compliment go to her head. "You've heard of this?"

"Back in 1878, a bizarre discovery in Montpellier became a source of intense controversy as what appeared to be a letter written by a Genoese priest at Avignon to Edward III made the startling claim that not only had Edward II cheated death at Berkeley Castle, but he'd since made it across France and into Italy, where he'd been living as a hermit."

Emily had never heard of it. "Was it genuine?"

"That was indeed the point of contention. Though the letter itself was clearly a copy, the content, we have reason to believe, was potentially original save, of course, the common assumption, including that written in the Patent Rolls, that Edward had died around 21 September 1327 and been buried at Gloucester Cathedral. Unfortunately at the time, confirmation of the king's death cannot be proven conclusively. Nor, however, can this claim."

Quietly Emily felt her heart palpitating wildly as she considered the potential ramifications. "Let's say it was genuine. What could it mean exactly?"

"It means precisely what it says. Edward III, king for almost nine years, was very much alive, as was the father he had seen buried. Whereas the act of entitlement had been placed on him thanks to Edward II's dethronement, in the eyes of the papacy, Edward II remained an anointed king."

Emily nodded, making sense. "So Fieschi told Edward III his father was alive?"

"Assuming the letter was indeed delivered, Edward, it appears, was told. There is also a later story that the pair met, Edward II disguised as a hermit. By then over ten years had passed since they'd last seen one another."

Emily returned her attention to the Latin manuscript, her eyes panning over the detail. "The letter I have here was written later in 1336. According to the content, Edward II wrote it himself, addressed to the king. He talks about his stay in Cecima and also about his boys being looked after by the cardinal." Emily hesitated. "It speaks as though the king had brothers. Not necessarily by the same mother."

"It gives them names?"

"Unfortunately not. Only that Fieschi was their godfather."

Champion placed his hand to his mouth in disbelief. "My dear, this is incredible. This could be firm proof the king survived."

"But the Fieschi letter already does that."

"If it's genuine, yes; however, what makes this unique is this is the first definitive piece of evidence we have written by Edward II himself. Meaning, if the old boy was alive and indeed a father, Edward III potentially faced the possibility that in the eyes of Avignon, his father was still king."

In the main security room in the Waterloo Barracks, Christophe re-watched the footage caught on the CCTV cameras of Mike leaving the Fusiliers' Museum through an office window, taking refuge briefly on the ground floor of the Constable Tower.

Before disappearing in a cloud of smoke into the Old Hospital Block.

He put through a call to Randek. "The Englishman has entered the Hospital Block."

Leaving the Fusiliers' Museum, Randek answered, "You see him?"

"No. There are no cameras inside."

Randek stopped east of the White Tower, his eyes on the entrance. "Leave it with me."

76

Somewhere in Surrey,
02:20

The walk took place in silence, during which time the Director was granted a full tour of the downstairs. Though he had seen the building many times before, the setting seemed different at night. A melancholic mood pervaded the air, suiting the lack of light that he sensed went deeper than the lateness of the hour. It was quiet, strangely antagonizing, as though one step on a creaky floorboard would bring about frowns of discontent. Besides the gentle chimes of a distant grandfather clock, he sensed little beyond the footsteps, such was the butler's mood. On heading up a banistered staircase to the second of the period mansion's three storeys, a short walk along the carpeted hallway ended with a wooden doorway sited close to a suit of chain mail armour and a painting from the Jacobean era.

The Director knew from past experience, it would mark the end of the journey.

Without awaiting a response after knocking on the door, the butler opened it, admitting the Director into a room that was familiar to him. At this hour it was illuminated only by the dim light of a single desk lamp, the glow of which barely extended beyond the mahogany table on which it rested. Elsewhere in the room, oak and mahogany were recurring features, with several recently varnished wooden bookcases blending comfortably with the oak floor. Like the corridors he'd just seen, works of art hung from the oak-panelled walls, the subjects predominantly military.

And historical.

While the room itself, despite the varied assortment of family keepsakes, could be defined by a sad feeling of emptiness, within that loneliness he sensed the heart of the melancholy. Seated at the desk, a figure of possible aristocratic leanings glanced up from his reading, paying the Director attention for the first time.

Reminiscent of their last meeting, a once handsome face now ravaged by time peered sternly at him through dark-rimmed lenses resting on the bridge of a nose that had become increasingly crooked. Behind the thin layers of glass, the deep blue eyes, once so full and engaging, had something of a lost look, the melancholic impression intensified by the rather haggard appearance of the man's facial skin. Despite the hour, his dress was impeccable, his trademark blazer a non-spoken message the meeting was indeed to be taken seriously.

The Director addressed him, "Richard, it's been a long time."

The historian studied him at length before finally responding. "Time. It can mean many things to many people. We all have our own ways of handling it.

How else could one arrange a reunion at such an ungodly hour?" He dismissed the butler and watched him leave. "Tea, I'm afraid, will have to wait. The liquids don't sit well with me this late these days."

The Director smiled. "Another thing we all have our own ways of handling."

The butler closed the door as he departed. In silence, the old acquaintances watched one another.

"I must say, the timing of your coming is strange to say the least." The historian moved away from his book, his weary frame becoming fully visible for the first time. "I'd have thought you'd currently have bigger things on your mind. Unless, of course, you've retired and not told me about it."

"One does not simply retire from the pinnacle of government service. I'd have thought of all people you'd understand."

"I understand a lot of things, or at least I did. Once upon a time, people came from all around, sometimes at these same ungodly hours, asking questions that only made sense to those doing the asking. These days, the telephone rings far less."

The Director sensed the melancholy had deepened. "I really am most sorry about Julia."

The historian's tone became increasingly sombre. "So what brings you here? As I say, I'd have thought under the circumstances, your need might be better served elsewhere."

"Unfortunately, these things are rarely straightforward." Mr White removed a copy of the fax received by the Palace from his inner pocket and showed it to the historian; he could tell from Tinniswood's expression that he understood. "For one night, perhaps you could humour another old man and come out of retirement."

The historian gazed at the fax, his curiosity clearly piqued. "Of course, the anniversary. You know they've been talking on the news for hours about the latest threats. Seldom have I heard any mention of the date. It was an act of terror, they say. Back then it was a far more complicated affair. The houses of the old city were an accident waiting to happen; even a badly discarded match could have brought the old city to its knees. Only it never did. No matter how dry the summers."

The historian adjusted his spectacles, concentrating on the image of the Gemini. He noticed the words alongside it.

"The image is different from the one in most history books." He eyed the Director. "It's no coincidence, of course."

"Well, that's perhaps something you'd understand better than I." The Director considered his words, remembering the historian had no military clearance despite a long history of being trusted by the royals. "The paper you see was faxed to the main office at Buckingham Palace earlier this evening. I shan't bore you with the details. There are some, it seems, who believe there to be a connection between the catastrophe unleashed upon our city tonight and that over three hundred years ago. The question is, are they right?"

The historian placed the fax down on the desk and walked towards the nearest window. Beyond the mullioned design, a full moon shone down brightly across the countryside; they were now a long way from the fires.

"When the bright summer moon of 1 September glowed powerfully over the chilly waters of the North Sea, it was said the night watchman on the *Royal James* was taken by a sudden flash of light in the distance. As the seconds ticked by, sound rumbled like thunder. Then a further flash of light. For the captain of the *James*, one of over a hundred British warships patrolling that five-mile stretch of water at the time, he judged them to be the first sign that a Dutch fleet was fast approaching. However, little did they know, whatever caused the bizarre flashes had occurred neither at sea nor by the Dutch."

He returned from the window, drawing the curtain. "Even before the time of the Great Fire, few believed 1666 would be destined to pass without a significant happening of some type. London's role in the fall of Charles I had already been the subject of many a doleful ballad even before the mathematician George Wharton had written his own prediction: 'now sixtene hundred sixtie six is come, when as some say shall be the day of doome'. In post-Restoration England, people had a tendency to take the portents seriously. Wharton was far from alone in his doom mongering. When in 1658 the royalist mystic Walter Gostelo wrote of lights illuminating the ruinous condition of the cathedral, it seemed only a matter of time till judgement was upon us. Lilly, of course, had already beaten him to it."

He returned to the fax. "In addition to the watchful eyes of the Gemini, a second illustration had shown a far more foreboding image of a city burning beside a river. Perhaps most telling were the visions seen through the eyes of baker-turned-astrologer Richard Saunders after perhaps as many as three comets were seen falling through the heavens from 1664 to April the next year. Like those seen through the eyes of Harold Godwinson, such sights were rarely viewed with great optimism."

The Director folded his arms, listening with mild fascination as the former royal historian set the scene. "Be they portents of doom or not, tonight we have reason to believe the gentlemen responsible for our current problems are following a similar pattern." He removed a further two sheets of paper, one containing Kit's photograph of the plaque, the second of Pepys's portrait. "Perhaps this might mean more to you than it does to me. I must remind you, discretion is of course expected."

"You think I'd consider betraying you?" The historian seemed almost offended before examining the content through his glasses. His expression fast became one of disbelief. "Where did you get this?"

"The pieces are currently on display at the Museum of London. It seems the perpetrators of all this knew something we didn't. Before tonight, I had no reason to suspect the Great Fire of London had been anything more than an accident in a bakery. Tonight, I'm told it's not simply a case of is there a connection, but what." He allowed the historian a moment to finish reading. "I'm prepared to leave no stone unturned, Richard. Tell me, what in God's name happened in 1666?"

The old man removed his glasses and shook his head. "Even without the concerned antics of the soothsayers, prediction of the fire was by no means uncommon. Nor was the parliamentary inquiry set up after the fire slow to point the finger at England's innate areas of prejudice. A woman questioned informed Parliament that in April earlier that year in response to a quarrel with a French servant, he did reply, English maids will like the Frenchmen better when there's not a house remaining between Temple Bar and London Bridge – an event that would come to pass between June and October. To say nothing of the actions of Monsieur Belland."

White was now familiar with the story of the French fireworks maker. "The man responsible?"

"Without question, the man Parliament later found guilty of being responsible, even though details never emerged in the public domain. Should news have got out, successful identification of the true culprit was never likely to do the royals any favours, especially as Belland was himself employed by the king."

"So it wasn't the Dutch?"

"It would have made sense, wouldn't it? Especially after the bonfire fiasco following the invasion of Terschelling. Economically, Holland was thriving; worse, as the commercial trade routes overlapped, war became inevitable. However, in the eyes of the people really responsible, the Dutch were the perfect people to frame. At least until poor Hubert came along."

The Director sensed the end was in sight. "Who were the Cardinal's Boys?"

"Essentially, they were merely godsons. Something their real father undoubtedly chose very carefully."

"Who are the Gemini?"

"Ask me who they *were*."

Echoes of what Blanco had asked. White's expression hardened. "Very well. Who were they?"

The historian gazed upon his old acquaintance with a smile of soft pomp. "Some things are better seen than heard."

77

The Waterloo Barracks,
02:20

Blanco returned to the barracks on leaving the White Tower. He found François in the same room as before, the governor now absent.

"What's the latest from Edinburgh?"

"Fires have spread along the Royal Mile." François had been watching the news on the wall-mounted flat-screen TV, his expression one of mild amusement. "You might say, all going according to plan."

Blanco contacted Alain on his HT. "Alain, do you copy?"

Making his way calmly past the cathedral, one of many who had congregated close to the churchyard, Alain heard him. "*Oui.*"

"Where are you?"

"En route to the latest checkpoint. There are helicopters approaching in the distance. Unfortunately, the emergency services are getting better at dealing with the blazes."

To Blanco, this was no surprise. "The first phase was only intended as an hors d'oeuvre. Perhaps things will be different when we serve them the main course."

Blanco re-entered the chief's office and activated another video call. Within seconds, he saw Fieschi and Jérôme appear at the other end.

Fieschi responded first. "I was beginning to think you had forgotten about us."

Blanco smiled, the lines on his face thinning and lengthening as he gestured. "The fires at Mary-le-Bow have already been quelled; it seems London's finest are improving with practice." His words echoed those he'd just heard from Alain.

"Nevertheless, they continue to burn." Fieschi watched the fires both on the screen and as they appeared in the distance. "I must say St Paul's really does look beautiful all lit up."

"The prime minister is due to receive her final warning." Blanco's expression hardened. "If the answer is not as we require, soon the modern-day Christopher Wren will have his chance to excel."

"I know many even in our own country who would love the opportunity to achieve such fame." Jérôme spoke for the first time, the taut skin around his chin making his face look bizarrely distorted on screen. "Have you spoken to the prime minister?"

"No. Not that I gave her much chance. But rest assured, I am preparing my speech."

"Spoken like a true orator." Fieschi remained composed. "Nevertheless, the British are not the fools we sometimes paint them to be. They can see the conundrum they face. Yet who knows? Perhaps very soon, fortune will shine on us."

Jérôme was far more sceptical. "They are talking now about clashes on the streets. Several gunmen killed."

Blanco's expression hardened. "The action at Mary-le-Bow certainly did not go according to plan. Our losses were great."

"How great?"

"Fifty per cent."

Jérôme remained unmoved. "Where are they now?"

Blanco checked his watch. "If they have progressed as scheduled, they will reach the cathedral on time. Perhaps on this occasion, they will have greater success. Who knows, if the mob's thirst for blood isn't quenched, we may soon have reinforcements on our hands."

Less than four miles away, in the heart of the Rook, Phil and Maria once again focused their attention on the aquiline features of Bizante Blanco as he commenced a videoconference call with the two unknown recipients.

On this occasion, the camera view was better.

"Pause that," Maria requested; Phil obeyed without hesitation. The audio continued as normal, but the pictures now showed a frozen view of the two unknown faces.

"Did we get a match?" Phil asked, watching Maria attempt to get facial recognition.

Within seconds they did.

His conversation with Fieschi and de Haulle at an end, Blanco clicked rapidly on the mouse of his laptop. Over the coming seconds, he re-watched the footage filmed in Thomas More's room, his attention fixed firmly on the expressions of fear in the faces of those held captive.

As the footage played out, something caught his attention. Amongst the motley assortment of foreign tourists, military or ex-service attendees, one of the few of civilian status whose appearance suggested English nationality could be seen moving his lips slowly, his face partially hidden behind his hand. Though it was largely concealed, Blanco could see that the man was holding an object of some kind.

Placing his hand to his chin, Blanco looked a second time as the camera panned past the man.

Unmistakeably, he was communicating.

78

The Old Hospital Block, 02:23

"There will always be unpleasant things you must deal with. In times of war, it is always your duty to remain strong, remain stable and able to function. No matter what you face, your job is to complete your mission."

The words of his Ukrainian tormentor echoed in Mike's mind; they had done so consistently in recent minutes. Abseiling from the Fusiliers' Museum had been easy in terms of the height of the drop but far less so in the circumstances in which it had to be done. Making a forty-foot jump in Scotland had been terrifying in the moment, especially when the man who had set up the harness was a stranger.

Tonight it had paled into insignificance compared to doing twenty feet while being shot at by terrorists.

Emily had ended her conversation with Champion. The look on her face was a mixture of shock and enlightenment.

Behind it, Mike still sensed fear.

He returned to the lounge from the kitchen, taking the opportunity to raid the fridge. In the time Champion had been talking, he'd devoured a bottle of mineral water and almost everything in the fruit bowl.

He feared he still had a long night ahead of him.

"I still don't get it," Mike said on returning to the lounge, investigating every table drawer and cabinet for signs of a firearm or weapon of any description. The best he found was a steak knife. "Even if Edward II did survive, he'd already been dethroned. What's so important?"

Emily had also grabbed some of the fruit, taking small mouthfuls in between sips of water. "Edward III became king by conquest. Though the invasion was largely under the command of Mortimer and Isabella, Edward II's forces had deserted him, leaving him no choice but to abdicate. When news came of Edward II's death, there was no longer a problem concerning Edward III's legitimisation. As eldest son and already crowned monarch, he was free to rule unopposed.

"Should Edward II have lived, the potential for a coup would always have been there, not that Edward II necessarily had that ambition or support among the barons. Nevertheless, there have been plenty of examples throughout the Middle Ages of similar things. Richard II was dethroned and killed; Henry VI was dethroned and later restored. The same would potentially have been true of the Princes in the Tower."

"All of which came after Edward II."

"True, but just because it hadn't happened in England didn't mean it wasn't possible."

Mike could see that she had a point. "So let's say Edward II lived. The letter makes no reference to any intention to reclaim the throne. For all you know, Edward III was happy his father was alive."

"In some ways, he probably was. By 1336, Edward II would have been over fifty. It does seem unlikely he'd have been in any way excited about a lengthy military conflict, especially against his beloved son. However, what Edward III might not have considered was the possibility of his father going on to produce further offspring. With a different mother, the boys were potentially claimants in their own right after Edward."

"But not before him?"

"No, but put together a heavy invasion force, who can say the same thing that happened to his father wouldn't have happened to Edward III? Especially if Edward II's younger children had the papacy's support."

Mike took a seat alongside Emily as she unpeeled an orange and hungrily devoured the first segment. "So let's say you're right. Would they have been legitimate?"

"I guess that depends on who was the mother. Interestingly, after Mortimer was executed as a traitor at Tyburn, Isabella never remarried despite her husband's alleged death. Instead, she went into quiet retirement. Normally, it would have made sense for her to be bonded in marriage to a powerful lord."

Mike immediately understood her point. "So how could Edward II have remarried if he and Isabella were still married?"

"The question really comes back to what Edward II was doing in Avignon and Italy. As England was under the guardianship of the papacy, any support Edward II had would have been crucial."

"I thought you said he was unlikely to want to launch a campaign."

"No, but if his marriage with Isabella was dissolved and Edward remarried, any children he then had, particularly if they were boys, would have been heirs to the throne."

A curious smile lined Mike's face. "I think I'm starting to see why you quit sports science."

Emily lowered her head, smiling before resuming eye contact. In the silence, the pause was strangely tantalising.

A loud voice in Mike's ear interrupted the silence. "Honey Badger, I hate to break it to you, but I think you're about to have company again."

Mike jumped to his feet, his eyes on the hallway. As far as he could tell, the front door led to a communal atrium, off which were several neighbouring apartments. Without the worry of nearby security cameras, he knew Randek would have no chance of finding them immediately.

"What am I dealing with, Phil?" Mike edged closer to the front door of the apartment. Unable to see outside, he had no idea of the layout beyond.

Phil watched Randek and the others as they appeared on screen. "Ten of the bastards are just passing the railings outside the blue door. Prepare for a knock."

"Let me know when they enter."

"Trust me, you'll know."

* * *

Kit left the church with Nat and Gillian and made his way along the west wall to where metal railings protected a stairway that headed below ground. He took them at a steady pace, stopping at the main door.

Unsurprisingly he found it unlocked.

He entered quickly, finding himself staring into a dark enclosure smelling of fire and damp. Within seconds, the area was illuminated from above; already Nat had proved his worth. In the light, he found a small chapel with several wooden chairs circling a small altar situated beneath a stone archway and before a brick wall with a round-headed window in which there was an ornate crucifix. Beneath the glorious white vaulted ceiling, the chapel was surprisingly bright.

Moving on, he could see that part of the crypt was used as a café.

"What is this place?"

"The crypt of the original eleventh-century church. It was actually the first arched crypt found in London." Nat gestured to the nearby surroundings, doing his best to avoid either soaking his feet on the drenched stone slabs beneath him or inhaling the smoky air. "As a matter of fact, the name le-bow derives from these arches."

Kit avoided any temptation to ask him to elaborate. "So you're saying this was all here before the fire?"

"Absolutely."

"Was there anything Wren changed?"

Johnstone considered the question, walking slowly through the chapel, into the café. There were slabs on the floor with writing on them. For the first time, Kit noticed the presence of graves.

"Both the north aisle and the eastern section has Norman masonry interspersed with brickwork once used by the Romans." He led Kit to a rectangular doorway cut into the stonework. "This was where Wren blocked off a Norman stairway."

Kit was immediately interested. Entering the empty space, he pushed hard against the wall.

Inexplicably it moved.

"That usual?"

Nat was stunned. As Kit ventured beyond the doorway, he noticed a stairway heading down.

The smell of smoke was simply horrendous.

"Get the fire chief. It's possible we still have areas on fire."

Maria heard Kit's voice speaking frantically in her ear. "We've found the passage below the crypt."

"Already?"

"Turns out Gillian McKevitt isn't just a pretty face after all. Nathaniel Johnstone has been worth his weight in gold."

Maria was shocked. "Where are you?"

"The crypt at Mary-le-Bow actually survived the Great Fire. Wren later used it as part of the new church. There's a Norman stairway that the great man blocked off. Only today it's accessible."

To Maria that made sense. "What's it look like down there?"

Kit proceeded cautiously. "The crypt itself is largely okay, aside from the water damage. The fires themselves don't seem to have touched it, which suggests what lies beneath isn't directly so. The fire chief is leading the way; judging from the smell, I'd say fires are still burning."

"If these fires are where you think they are, that confirms beyond all doubt the painting was correct."

"I think we're already past that stage. Only question is, where are the ones at St Dunstan's and St Paul's?"

Maria had been thinking the same thing. "Talk us through what you see when you get there. Maybe if we can make it before 03:00 hours, we can stop this thing once and for all."

"My thoughts exactly."

Kit waited until the chief emerged from the previously blocked stairway, giving him the all clear. Wasting no time, he activated his breathing apparatus and began descending the winding stairway. He followed it for over ninety steps down to a floor leading to a wide archway.

On the archway, he saw a series of symbols.

Sanders and Jay had reached the cathedral by the time they heard Kit speaking in their headsets. The car had stopped on the south side, the great dome looming above them like a gigantic harvest moon against the black backdrop.

"This what you saw beneath the Monument?"

Both of them checked the recently sent image on their satphones. "Mate, it could be a carbon copy," Sanders replied. "Where are you?"

"Mary-le-Bow, just under the crypt." Kit's voice echoed against the strong air pressure of his breathing apparatus. Beyond the archway, the scene was like that of a subterranean city. "I bet even Churchill didn't witness the likes of this."

"Just be careful, mate. Even when we went down, the ground was still smouldering. If you're not lucky, you might run into another bonfire."

"I won't be that stupid! If the pattern continues, chances are St Paul's will be next. Judging from the designs in the portrait, the keys were on the south-east side. That's also where the crypt is."

"You just leave it to us, mate. We're on it."

Over 330 miles north, Rawlins waited until the recently arrived helicopters passed overhead, bringing the latest fires under control, before heading for the parliament building. He found Pugh by some fire trucks that had been parked close to the entrance.

Learning quickly from past lessons, neither were taking any chances.

Rawlins gestured him over to the nearest police car and opened a map of the city on the bonnet. "Copper just gave me this." Outlines of the old vaults could be seen in all areas of the city. "If the fires in London are being started underground, they might be using any one of these up here."

Pugh studied the layout for several seconds, quickly seeing the pattern. "Where's the nearest entrance?"

"Only known ones are here." Rawlins pointed to the entrances to the Edinburgh Vaults.

Pugh nodded. "What say we split up and try them both?"

Less than half a mile away, Anthony Pentland circled the now empty display case that had once contained the Honours of Scotland. Everything except the Stone of Destiny had been taken.

Even the jewels on the side were missing.

As he studied the walls around him, he remembered overhearing the conversation between Kit and Maria about the terrorist in London and the portrait gallery. A sudden thought came to mind.

Maybe Jérôme de Haulle's list was not confined solely to works of art in England.

79

Surrey,
02:28

Tinniswood led them to the upper storey and along a further corridor to the far side of the house. Like the downstairs, the upper levels were themselves depositories of valuable artwork of various genres and eras. As the walk continued, the Director sensed a gradual evolution, as though the majority were sorted chronologically rather than by subject. Ignoring his surroundings, he focused instead on the reasons for his visit. The direct answers he needed.

Who were the Cardinal's Boys?

Who were the Gemini?

"If there is one point on which most historians agree, it is that Edward II was one of England's least effective rulers," Tinniswood resumed on approaching the end of the corridor, at which point the white, painted walls, complemented by a rough blue-coloured floor covering, ended at a heavy set of double doors. "While his father will always be remembered as the Hammer of the Scots, it would perhaps not have been unjust had his son been dubbed with the epithet hammered *by* the Scots. It was his own reckless planning and military ineptitude that resulted in defeat at Bannockburn and saw the rise of personal favourites, thus alienating his wife and the barons."

The historian stopped outside the doors. "But exactly how Edward died will always be a point of contention. The chroniclers at the time were largely consistent in claiming the former king had died, but descriptions of how varied. According to most, he succumbed to illness, helped in no small part by usurpation at the hands of his estranged queen and her lover." The old man looked at the Director, stern faced. "Because of this, such errors of fact have been misleading both scholar and layman ever since."

The Director watched as the historian opened the doors, revealing a surprisingly grandiose chamber, equally rich in artwork and memorabilia. The lustre of the walls he'd just passed had been dimmed with age and wear and adorned with a miscellany of paintings that were instantly forgettable. In this room the bright purple shade that reflected the overhead chandeliers was ornately regal and the artwork far more recognisable.

In keeping with Tinniswood's former profession as a royal historian, portraits of every monarch from William the Conqueror to the present monarch completed a visual timeline rather like the walls of St Paul's Basilica in Rome.

The Director was speechless.

"In medieval times, descriptions of Edward II's demise were clouded in confusion. By the mid-1330s, reports of a grief-stricken end had been replaced with claims that he had been tortured and killed by the insertion of a metal rod into his hindquarters. A decade later the reference to the metal rod had changed to one of a red-hot poker." The historian adjusted his glasses. "No matter what the story, or the teller, the only real outcome of that was to prolong the inaccuracy. Perhaps that was the intention."

Tinniswood led him to one portrait among the many. Like a good number of those on that area of wall, the subject was bearded. He had a light shade of brown curly hair and was wearing a small gold ringlet that included four fleurs-de-lis. His face suggested a clear family link with the subjects of the portraits on either side with possible evidence of a slight droop on one eyelid.

His robes of state, orb and sceptre confirmed his royal lineage.

"Incredible, isn't it? Each person here in their own way played their part in shaping the future of this green and pleasant land for better or worse. Irrespective of their faults and failings, I for one have always been grateful. It never serves well to look negatively on the past. If that had been different, who knows how it would have affected our lives today."

"Said like a true historian." The Director focused on the pictures, with an uneasy feeling that it might be the darker secrets of the past that were affecting London's future tonight. Elsewhere in the room, a number of wooden cabinets and display cases, the majority holding manuscripts and historical memorabilia, covered a large portion of the purple-carpeted floor.

The Director faced the historian. "What was so important about Edward II?"

"Living in the present day, one often forgets the things that have gone before it. History itself is nothing but a recording of the present long gone. It is like a chain, a story. Every life lived, whether in fame and public scrutiny or anonymity. A wise man once said one can ignore history: But one can never ignore the consequences of ignoring history."

The historian returned his gaze to the portrait of Edward II. "Be it by fate or design, Edward II's legacy was never destined to be distinguished. By 1326, he had alienated almost all his barons and was loathed by his queen. In January 1327, he became the target of a coup, which saw his reign cut short, despite the fact he lived on beyond that time. By September that year, news of his death began to circulate; indeed, a funeral later took place at Gloucester Cathedral. On receiving the news of his father's death from Lord Berkeley, the new king understandably accepted that it had been presented in good faith.

"Yet good faith and fact aren't always the same thing. When Berkeley was questioned about the king's death three years later, he testified he had only learned of it at the subsequent Parliament – a strange contradiction. That same year, the then Archbishop of York wrote of how he had received certain news that the king was still alive and that he had attempted to rescue him. Similar bids are also recorded of one Lord Pecche, previously constable of Corfe Castle in Dorset, the very same castle in which Edward was said to have been staying. Such news on reaching the ears of Edward II's respected half-brother, the Earl of Kent, led to the Earl's own imprisonment after he initiated a number of failed attempts to rescue Edward. Eventually Kent was executed on charges of treason against the new king."

The Director listened with folded arms. "Who's to say the information was correct? For all we know, they were just the victims of Chinese whispers."

"Perhaps a valid observation, had it not been for the supporting evidence. Since that time, only three documents have surfaced that shed light on the true circumstances. The most famous was the Fieschi Letter, named in honour of its mailer, one Manuel Fieschi, relative of a former cardinal in Genoa. Unlike the other two documents, Fieschi traced a full account of Edward's life from his imprisonment: how he escaped from Berkeley to Corfe Castle; how he was aided by a gaoler who dressed him up as a pilgrim; then, on reaching Avignon, he travelled to Brabant after spending two weeks with the pope; and from Brabant on to the shrine of the Magi at Cologne before heading to Milan and eventually an abbey further south, at which point Fieschi wrote the letter." The historian paused.

"A second document appears in the form of an account from the royal wardrobe that confirms a meeting took place at Koblenz between Edward III and a certain William le Galeys. Of le Galeys we know nothing, nor do we possess any portraits of him. All that is known is that he claimed to be the king's father."

"Surely even after so many years, the king would have recognised him?"

"Evidence of which can perhaps be found in the knowledge le Galeys was entertained at royal expense and a sizeable advance made to his keeper." The historian moved towards the far more magnificent portrait of Edward III immediately to the right of Edward II, his white-haired, bearded and purple-robed appearance reminiscent of King Arthur or Charlemagne. "The third document is far more obscure. I myself was most fortunate even to gain a glimpse of it. Its location isn't easy to find, even for one of my former profession."

"The Tower holds many secrets." The Director's look was stern. "Who were the Cardinal's Boys?"

"The third document expands only on the plausibility that the meeting in the second document had indeed occurred. Here, we find the only written evidence Edward II wrote to his son personally; we cannot account, of course, for any oral communication or indirect communication that occurred before or after that time. By 1338, Edward II had become accustomed to life in Genoa, so much so there is evidence he'd taken a new wife. There is also mention of two sons, perhaps twins. After 1341, we have no evidence that Edward was still alive, or what became of the boys. Only according to Manuel Fieschi, the man later to become Bishop of Vercelli, he had replaced the late cardinal as their godfather."

A sudden thought struck the Director. "Twins? Gemini?"

The historian nodded sagely.

"There is no further mention of them?"

"The answers cannot be found in any document I know of. Whether Edward III ever regarded them as part of his family is a matter of speculation. What would have been on his mind, I'm sure, was that due to his father finding favour in Avignon, the threat of invasion would have been increasingly likely. With French support and a French pope on their side, any excommunication of the king's mother for the part she and Mortimer played in Edward II's dethronement would have been almost inevitable."

The historian led him to another part of the room, stopping in front of a large painting in between Edward III and Richard II. "It's possible the twins fought at Crécy. One thing we know is that when Calais was taken in 1347, Edward demanded hostages to come forward and offer their lives for the safety of the city. When six men came forward, Edward ordered their execution, only to be dissuaded by his queen at the eleventh hour. What Edward may or may not have known is what was later recorded, but omitted, by the work of Froissart. Among the six was one of the godchildren of the late Luca Fieschi."

The Director bit down on his lower lip. "Go on."

"I assure you, I would love nothing more. If only I knew the facts."

The Director was disappointed. "You must know something."

He led the Director past the portraits of the Tudor monarchs, stopping in between Charles II and James II. Amongst the paintings was one on the Great Fire.

"Exactly what became of the boys is a matter of conjecture. Legend has it one was named Richard, the other John – both after Plantagenet ancestors. In time, the boys married and produced offspring of their own. The family names are not specifically recorded; perhaps they became Fieschis themselves. In Genoa the family thrived beyond the Reformation, at all times remaining close to the papacy. When the Hundred Years' War ended, little more was heard until late in the reign of Elizabeth I. The English papists tried everything to avoid the coronation of the petty little man from Scotland. When that failed, they looked to a new saviour, one who would rewrite the history books." He gestured to a portrait of Cromwell. "Whether the Protector really knew the truth behind the people fate had put him on side with, again one can only speculate, but when Charles I was beheaded, it potentially opened the line of succession for the return of the Cardinal's Boys."

The historian turned to face him. "Until they were themselves deceived."

They left the large study and entered a small side room. Inside, Mr White observed a drab and poorly maintained setting that absorbed much of the light from the solitary light bulb.

"Understanding allegory in art is not usually the province of the traditional historian; however, through association with the subject over many years, I have inevitably acquired a certain level of knowledge."

He led the Director through a part of the room that was cluttered with various, apparently discarded, antique artefacts towards a bare part of a wall on which was hung a single painting.

The Director studied it. "What is this?"

"This image depicts the unfortunate pattern of events that followed the execution of Charles I. If you look carefully, you can see that within the painting there is a second work of art – inception at its very best."

The Director turned his attention to the right side of the painting where a strange group of animals surrounded a second picture: this one of an execution scaffold.

"I don't understand," the Director said.

"The painting itself was a work by the Flemish artist Jan Brueghel the younger of Antwerp, who died in 1678. You will, I'm sure, notice the inaccuracies in the way in which the artist has represented the grisly execution of Charles I and the view of the Banqueting House in the background. In the main picture we find a masked fox with an axe and cooking pot, almost certainly a reference to Cromwell's Ironsides. Alongside the horrid creature is a hound, perhaps Fairfax. On the floor around them are the works of Luther, Calvin and Machiavelli, not to mention the laws of England, all of which lie discarded. Further afield, we see reference to the horrors of war. Notice also how London burns in the background."

The Director stared at the familiar scene of the old city burning. "Why are you showing me this?"

"The image itself was sent to Charles II less than two weeks prior to the fire, along with a stark warning. This is a copy, but on the original there was said to have been written, in invisible ink, a sinister warning: beware the Sons of Gemini."

Echoes of what Mike had found in the Tower archives. "Who were the Sons of Gemini?"

"Tradition has it, Edward II was buried in Cecima around 1341 and later exhumed at the King's request – at which point his body was returned to England. As for his twin sons – if indeed they were twins – they remained in France with their wives, almost certainly taking more interest than most in England's progress in the Hundred Years' War. Of the activities of their descendants prior to the rise of the virgin queen, one can only speculate. When the English Civil War was over and the Protectorate established, it was the view of the majority in England that the time of the monarchy was over. When Cromwell donned the purple robes of state himself in 1653, it was apparently the view of those both at home and who had assisted him from overseas that he had overstepped the mark. On hearing of plans for a foreign invasion and an alliance with foreign lords, the Protector acted. Doing what he did best, before the seeds of rebellion could be sown, the enemy was crushed. So too were the Gemini."

The historian again looked closely at the strange painting. "When the Protector again put on the purple robes for his second inauguration in 1657, he did so secure in the knowledge the final obstacle had been removed. Yet as Charles II would subsequently learn, whispers from the underworld spoke of an altogether more real threat. The original Gemini may have gone, but their offspring remained far and wide."

"Who are they now?"

"I'm afraid there your guess is as good as mine." The historian walked him out of the room, closing the door behind him.

The Director's frustration was building. "The City of London is burning. The threats of the past, it seems, have resurfaced. Whoever the Sons of Gemini were, others have since replaced them or attempted to copy them."

"As I've told you already, history is nothing more than a chain of events from the past to the present. None of us can escape it. Every family has a past."

In the Director's mind, the significance of the jewels now took on extra meaning. "Even for kingdoms long lost?"

"Ah, so it is the same old threat. I had assumed from the action at the Tower their intention was merely the theft of the jewels." The historian looked questioningly. "Or perhaps they found more than they were bargaining for?"

"There are certain things that cannot be said."

The historian sighed. "You came here seeking my help. If you're a sensible man, you might get it. In many ways our jobs weren't so dissimilar as we might care to pretend. The true answers to one's questions often rely solely on asking the right ones to begin with."

The Director relented. "Where are the real jewels?"

"Ah, so it is as we feared."

"Time is of the essence, Richard. Their threats are clear. Unless the Crown Jewels are handed over, the Tower of London will fall, the pièce de résistance at the end of the show." There was urgency in his eyes. "For almost forty years you served the royal family. If anyone knows the location, it's you."

"You honestly believe it's that easy? That I would readily turn my back on those who trusted me?"

"It's on such judgements that kingdoms are won and lost. When the original fire burned, the people of London celebrated the bravery of the king and the duke as they rode forth into the city. Tonight, the Palace has remained quiet. If an answer fails to come soon, the time for drastic measures will be upon us." The Director's gaze was stern. "I came here for your help. Do not disappoint me."

The historian's expression relaxed slightly. "The location of the vault was mentioned only once; never even with my supposedly unrestricted access was I invited to see it with my own eyes. It was created in 1681, around the same time as the Monument. Incidentally, by the same creator."

"Wren?"

"One of his less acclaimed works, but in its own way magnificent. If it still exists, it can only be found from one entrance. The very same one from which the duplicates are found."

"The Jewel House?"

The historian nodded.

"You've seen the document?"

"So have you. Only perhaps back then you didn't have the eyes to see."

The Director was unclear of his meaning. "What about Scotland?"

The historian sighed. "My oh my, you really do need my help, don't you?"

"What of the jewels in Scotland?"

"If my understanding is correct, you will find everything in the same place."

"One document? Take me to it!"

"You won't find it here, yet that's not to say I haven't seen it myself. Fortunately, though, a timely word in the right ear may provide the answer."

* * *

On the second floor of the large estate in the heart of Somerset, the owner of the property took the late-night phone call and made the short journey from his grand bedroom into the library. Making his way along one particular row of bookshelves, he removed the article that had been requested, noting the title, *The Ocean to Cynthia*, by Sir Walter Raleigh.

Strangely, it was the same manuscript that had been stolen from the property six months earlier.

Opening it to the final page, he glanced with disinterest at the blank setting. Unlike the earlier pages, the copied prose had come to an end; a series of smudges marked the page at irregular intervals, suggesting something included in the past had been later erased.

If the historian from London was right, it was a secret only heat could expose.

80

The Old Hospital Block, 02:29

Randek was first to reach the front door. After brief thought he decided not to waste time trying to find the right key amongst the large number on the gaoler's keyring. Even if one of them worked, he doubted he would find it quickly.

He waited till the nearest gunmen caught him up. Unlike himself, all were armed with explosives.

"Break it down!"

The door to the third apartment came down with the sound of a loud crash, just as the others had. Randek's view was poor; it took several seconds for the smoke to clear.

The interior was almost identical to the others he'd seen, the modern furnishings completely at odds with the historic nature of the Flemish brickwork. Like the apartments in the Byward Tower, they had been refurbished for comfort.

Finding no obvious signs of life, he ordered four of the gunmen to continue their search of the ground floor while he led six others to the floor above.

As Randek trod heavily on the carpeted stairway, one of the four ordered to remain on the ground floor took a more thorough look inside the third apartment. Finding nothing in the lounge or the bedrooms, he went into the bathroom.

The bathroom was in darkness, just as the others had been. Pulling the cord, the overhead lights revealed a similarly modern interior with a bathtub and white wall tiling.

Immediately he became drawn to the bath; unlike the others, this one was filled with towels.

Approaching, he peered inside.

Mike saw movement above the makeshift blanket of towels and sprang forward from his hiding place beneath them, gun at the ready. Deciding against wasting precious bullets, he disarmed the unsuspecting gunman and slammed him hard to the floor, knocking him unconscious.

At the same instant, he heard movement outside the apartment.

Collecting the gunman's firearm, he left the bathroom and opened fire, aiming through the open doorway into the communal atrium that was now occupied by several gunmen. Two hit the floor immediately, a third followed; within seconds the previously pristine white walls were splattered in blood.

He darted towards the door of the apartment; voices spoke quickly outside. Taking shelter behind the adjacent wall, he opened fire again, watching two more hit the deck, blood pouring over the carpet. The next voices came from the stairs; he tossed a grenade and dived into the living room.

The explosion was deafening.

He waited till the sound of ringing in his ears subsided before speaking quietly into his headset. "How am I doing, Phil?"

"Beautiful, Honey Badger. Not that I can see your face. Judging from the infrared, six out of ten are down." Phil grimaced, his attention on the main hallway. "One of the bastards on the stairs is still moving."

"Maybe I should put him out of his misery." Mike moved cautiously back towards the door, seeing that the hall was now thick with dust and smoke. He saw movement at the bottom of the stairs, a figure in black, clearly armed.

Mike raised his weapon and fired.

"What's the latest?"

Phil monitored the screens. "Three more on the stairs. They're coming right at you."

Mike waited, hearing footsteps and voices before seeing figures. With the stairs partially destroyed, he sensed accessibility would now be far more difficult.

A canister landed in the middle of the floor.

He dived.

The scene Randek saw was one of chaos. The stairway, perfectly preserved not a minute earlier, was now all but demolished. As the smoke cleared, he realised the wooden banisters had been completely destroyed from the bottom half up, the carpet smouldering, setting off the alarms. As he reached the midway point, he stopped, gesturing those behind him to do the same.

The final six steps had disappeared.

Mike collected a second gun from the nearest of the dead gunmen, finding the magazine filled close to capacity. He recognised the weapon as a Heckler & Koch G3; like the AK-47s he'd seen earlier that evening, it was another gun he didn't associate with the French military.

He kept close to the apartment's main doorway, finding the area beyond the nearest bodies hidden behind a cloud of smoke. There had been no recent explosions as far as he could tell, informing him he was looking at a smokescreen. Experience taught him it usually meant only one thing.

Gunfire.

He dived to his right, finding himself back in the lounge. Rolling on impact, he took shelter behind the couch, his aim on the door.

A figure appeared through the smoke, he fired, connected. He heard further voices close by and lobbed a second grenade in the direction of the sound; it exploded on impact.

"Nice job, Honey Badger." Phil saw the explosion on the IR. "Seven more are coming from the White Tower. Look lively."

"Copy that," Mike replied.

Leaving the couch, he tiptoed through the hallway, creeping again towards the front door and the smouldering atrium. Outside the apartment, several doors were open, providing the briefest glimpse into the neighbouring apartments; as far as he could tell, all were empty.

Considering his options, he retreated along the main corridor of the current apartment, opening the door to the airing cupboard.

Emily was crouched down with her hands over her head. "Is it over?"

"Not exactly. Stay here. I'll be right back."

He closed the door and sprinted through the hallway, stopping briefly for shelter in the lounge. Edging towards the apartment's front door, he saw another doorway partially hidden by the smoke.

Unlike the others, it led outside.

He sensed movement behind him. "I told you to stay put."

"I can't just stay there."

Mike noticed she was holding a firearm. "You know how to handle it?"

"You already showed me."

He recalled the Waterloo Barracks; much had happened since. He took the gun off her. "Safety toggle, single fire, automatic fire." He checked it for bullets. "Brace yourself. It might have a kick to it."

She kicked him in the shin. "Kinda like that?"

He smiled. "Come on!"

They left the apartment quickly, heading immediately for the next one on their right. Finding it deserted, Mike ushered Emily into the lounge; again he took cover close to the door.

"What's the latest, Phil?"

"One more on the stairs. The others are just approaching."

Outside the main door of the Hospital Block, Mike heard further movement. "I hear them."

He edged closer to the door and stared across the atrium. The sight in front of him was a sorry one. At least eight men in black were sprawled out on the carpet, blood pooling; in certain cases they were missing limbs. Beyond the stench of smoke, another poisoned the air, instantly recognisable.

Once again that night, his mind wandered back to his training.

81

Highlands of Scotland, Twenty-One Months Earlier

Mike unzipped his sleeping bag and quickly left the tent. The parade ground was illuminated again, the high-powered beams of the overhead lights appearing heavily distorted as they glimmered through large droplets of rain. In the last few hours the rain had fallen heavily, the grassy surface covered with large puddles. Two large objects had been placed there, their interiors a mystery below waterlogged tarpaulin. All of his teammates from the previous challenge were lined up facing the two objects, their combats absorbing the rain.

"You may think you know what hell looks like. Believe me. You have absolutely no idea." Radchenko marched slowly before his men. "I didn't come here to offer praise and blow sunshine up your ass. In Ukraine, we are used to the wet, the cold; these conditions are like heaven to us. In SPETSNAZ, you learn to make your home amongst the worst – living with the worst when necessary. We are here to pull you out of your comfort zone."

He stopped in front of Mike, his deep-set eyes penetrating his inner being like a spectre intent on capturing his soul. "If you are going to proceed, there are certain questions I need answers to. Are you prepared to accept what needs to be done – do it without overthinking it? What I'm looking for is attitude, a steely determination even in the most grave of circumstances. I need a will to survive."

Mike wasn't sure whether the question was real or rhetorical. Before he had a chance to answer, the tormentor ordered them into push-up positions. Unlike the NAVSOG tormentor, the only instruction was to hold the position. As the minutes passed, the rain became heavier, the faintest rumble of thunder evident from the north.

"You're fortunate you're on a soft surface," Radchenko said after several minutes of silence. "This exercise is not intended for a soft surface. Keep your spines straight, your hands flat, your arms still like statues. Lieutenant –" he knelt down, his mouth close to Mike's ear "– I need you to listen carefully. What happens tonight is going to make you or break you."

Mike took a breath, an alternative to answering. His body was tired; the accumulated fatigue now seemed like a never-ending torture. Even after two minutes, his arms were still shaking.

The Ukrainian resumed his speech. "In life, many people you meet will consider themselves fearless. Laugh in the face of danger. Talk of shit. When their bodies are put to the limit, these same people will give up mentally long before their bodies reach their limit. That is comfort. In war, comfort kills – it sacrifices friends and family. In life, most heads are weak. It is always your heads that give up before your bodies do."

For fifteen minutes no one fell, each man winning the psychological battle and keeping their arms straight. The first to go was Cummins, then Rawlins. Mike focused solely on each subsequent sixty seconds, counting each second down; with his eyes closed, he blocked out both Radchenko and the rain. The thunder had come close before receding.

"Okay, everyone on your feet," the Ukrainian commanded. "I want you all to take three steps forward. Move!"

Mike jumped to his feet and moved forward, trying in vain not to shiver. Either side of him, Rawlins and Masterson stood with determined expressions.

Everyone was suffering from the cold.

Radchenko walked breezily before the parade, concentrating on the large objects in front of him. "Captain Cummins, in making amends for giving way first, please reveal to us what's beneath the covering."

Mike watched uncomfortably as Cummins removed the puddle-ridden tarpaulin. A sharp clap of thunder was the fitting prelude to what lay beneath.

He was looking at a bath filled with blood and animal entrails.

Even Masterson looked ready to vomit.

"Inside this bath, we have many unpleasant substances," Radchenko began, his morbid expression disguising any secret pleasure. "In war, it is essential you learn to accept your reality. There will always be unpleasant things you must deal with. In times of war, it is always your duty to remain strong, stable and able to function. No matter what you face, your job is to complete your mission."

The former SPETSNAZ operative moved across the line, stopping in front of Kit. "Captain Masterson, take a bath."

Kit took a breath and entered immediately, placing everything but his head beneath the surface. After a minute of exposure to the air, the stench had already begun to travel.

At least Masterson was suffering.

After five minutes he was called out. "Get out of the filth. Go take a shower and change your clothes. After that, you may return to your bed." The tormentor looked at Chambers. "Captain Chambers, take a bath."

Mike watched on as the five Harts all completed their turns. Finally it was left to him.

"Lieutenant Hansen, are you scared?"

A loaded question. "I was with the lightning. Electricity and liquid aren't supposed to be mixed."

The Ukrainian laughed. "You think I would risk anyone's life?" He shook his head. "Come on. Take a bath."

Mike held his breath and took the plunge, doing his best to ignore his mounting problems. The chill factor was nearly unbearable, like entering an ice bath unprepared. The stench was overwhelming; it was like something from a peat bog.

He immediately fought the urge to regurgitate.

"Put your hands inside," Radchenko instructed, monitoring Mike like a prison warden. After ten minutes, Mike was still there; he'd already done double that of the others. He sensed the blood was beginning to solidify around his body, creeping into every orifice.

The Ukrainian smiled, lowering himself close to the edge of the bath. In the poor light, the veteran's masculine musk failed to register.

"Are you afraid, Lieutenant?" he asked, his eyes their familiar unrelenting stare. "Would you sleep in something like this for an hour?"

Of all the things Mike had faced so far, the promise of that was by far the worst. *Show no fear. Soon it'll all be over.*

"Would you?"

"Are you asking me to, sir?"

Radchenko watched him closely, his gaze penetrating the cold. Suddenly he relaxed and smiled. "Good answer."

82

The Old Hospital Block, 02:34

Randek heard the sound of the new arrivals outside the revamped apartment block before seeing his reinforcements appear. They paused outside the main doorway, entering on Randek's command. By the time they'd arrived, the smoke had cleared.

Gunfire greeted them from one of the apartments.

Mike opened fire the moment he saw movement, keeping his finger on the trigger till his magazine was spent. Tossing the empty gun to one side, he exhausted the supply on the next before unleashing a further grenade.

As it left his hand, he hit the floor, diving for cover.

Outside the apartment, all had gone quiet.

Randek waited till the sounds faded before making his way to the bottom of the stairway, using the recent smoke as cover. The floor was crowded with the bodies of his men; finding a safe footing was difficult. He'd seen no sign of movement since the gunfire ceased. Of the latest arrivals, only two were still alive, both on the floor. He saw them rise gingerly to their haunches, their gunfire met with counter fire coming from one of the doorways.

Immediately he opened fire.

Mike felt a sudden pain in his left thigh. The impact caused his momentum to shift, first backward then forward; somehow he managed to remain on his feet. The pain was dull, numbing; he saw blood oozing from a hole in his black ops uniform.

Till now, he'd never experienced a bullet wound.

A sudden yellow flash appeared immediately to his right; ducking into cover, he waited till the sounds of bullets tearing strips from the wall stopped before returning fire. He knew instinctively he'd hit one; a second followed almost instantly. A third flash was visible by the stairs; he aimed and fired, each time narrowly missing the targets. Doing his best to ignore the increasing pain in his thigh, he kept his finger on the trigger till he was out of bullets.

A second round of shots originated from close by.

Randek felt a sharp impact close to his shoulder, a second narrowly missing. With the smoke beginning to clear, he realised he was a sitting duck.

Swiftly, he made it through the front door.

Watching from the CCTV room, Blanco was furious. He'd already seen no less than sixteen of his men disappear without a trace, depleting his remaining resources by almost half.

On camera, Randek was clearly wounded.

"What the hell's happening?"

Struggling with his shoulder, Randek answered his HT with his weaker hand. "The Englishman is inside one of the apartments; he's stronger than we thought!"

Blanco swore violently. As he did, he saw another explosion close to the main door, knocking Randek off balance.

Dropping his HT, Randek scrambled away, clearly injured.

His gaze on the screen, a sudden onset of frustration overcame Blanco. For over two years he had been planning this mission.

Only one eventuality had he failed to allow for.

In the grounds of the historian's estate in Surrey, the Director of the White Hart re-embarked on the helicopter and secured his seatbelt while the pilot went through the usual preflight checks. As the craft lifted off and gained height, he glanced down at the period mansion, the windows of which were now cloaked in darkness.

After the night he'd had, he knew Sir Richard Tinniswood had earned his rest.

Once the view of the estate disappeared into the distance, he spoke into his headset. "Maria, what's the latest?"

Seated at her terminal, Maria replied, "The fires at Mary-le-Bow are out; just as we thought, they were started under the crypt. According to Edward, the layout is just like the one at Monument."

After speaking with Tinniswood, that was no longer a surprise. "What's the situation with the other fires?"

"Everything is out east of St Clement's; although Mary-le-Bow has survived, those near it are still spreading. Fleet Street is all but gone."

The Director bit his lip, fighting the urge to swear in frustration. "How about at the Tower?"

"Better. Blanco made another video call to the same men as earlier; on this occasion, we saw far more."

"Their faces were on file?"

"Oh yes."

"Who were they?"

"The first man was Jérôme de Haulle, uncle of François. The same man the Director of the National Portrait Gallery claimed to have been behind the van Dyck theft."

"And the other?"

"Gabriel de Fieschi. A powerful wine magnate and billionaire from Bordeaux. Blanco's first cousin. Also a distant cousin of de Haulle."

The Director gritted his teeth on hearing the name Fieschi.

Beware the Cardinal's Boys.

"Any trace of their location?"

"Negative, but rest assured, searches are under way."

The Director shook his head, quietly appalled. Mention of the name had made his blood run cold. "Where are the others?"

"The Deputy Director has departed for St Paul's; Warwick, Grailly, Stapleton and March are with him. Edward is clearing up the mess at Mary-le-Bow. Eam has joined Stafford and Beauchamp at St Dunstan's."

The Director nodded, *leaving just one.* "How about Grosmont?"

Emily saw Mike stumble and reached out her arm. She caught him on her strongest shoulder, both pleased and surprised that she'd managed to take his weight.

"How bad is it?"

"It's okay," Mike replied, straining. "I just need something to strap it."

He rummaged deep into the left side of his belt, sifting through the contents. Eventually he extracted a small plastic bag and tore it open as he struggled to lower himself down on to the couch.

"You need any help with that?"

Removing the bandage, he smiled. "Relax."

The last thing she felt like doing was relaxing. "If that isn't dealt with properly, it could go septic. Last thing we need is you getting infected."

Mike smiled wryly. "Trust me, I've done this before."

"In war, it is not only about dealing with casualties when you're with your comrades. Sometimes, you find yourselves in the most isolated situations possible. There, you have to fend for yourself." Radchenko looked at Mike and his five teammates from the bloodbath.

"You thought last night was hell. Believe me, we're just getting started."

They took a hike up the nearest mountain, five hours with little food. On reaching flat ground, they came to a large area of shelter, its stone exterior resembling a small cottage.

Mike instantly twigged it was a bothy.

Though the walls were intact, inside it was dilapidated. The windows were broken, the chimney demolished by the gales; if anything, it was colder inside than out. There was something about the house that suited the Ukrainian. It was like a hunter's cottage in Siberia; a man would have to be stronger than the wild animals to survive the prolonged tortuous effects of cold and hunger. To Mike, the only reason for the building's existence was pain. If it hadn't been for the remote location and exposure to the extreme elements, the damaged condition of the interior could have been attributed to bomb damage.

Radchenko led him as far as the doorway. "Stop here, please." The tormentor turned to Masterson and once again Mike found himself reacquainted with the soft, dark-coloured fabric of a sack as it was placed over his head.

He was taken to what he guessed was a low area of wall, probably close to the fireplace. The ruined stonework felt harsh to the touch, and after so many days in the wintry conditions, his hands were numb with cold. With his vision restricted, other sounds began to register with him: the howling of the wind, creaks in the floorboards, dogs barking in the distance. As the seconds passed, he sensed they were getting nearer.

Then inside the bothy.

The former SPETSNAZ operative had returned.

"Your next task is this." Radchenko spoke from the point where Mike had judged that he would be. "You are currently being held prisoner in the middle of nowhere. You have two men watching you that you know of; whatever the location is, guard dogs protect it. You are the only member of your team to have been taken that you know of; they have no idea where you are. You have a serious gunshot wound to your upper left thigh – 762 by 39 calibre. You are suffering severe arterial bleeding; in moments you will enter the early stages of irreversible paralytic shock."

The Ukrainian placed something in Mike's right hand.

"In this small pouch, you have everything that is required for you to survive. But time is ticking. You have three minutes. The exercise will begin at the first blast of my whistle."

The pouch was slippery, almost impossible to get open. The strange wet coating also had a tacky feeling about it; it reminded him of the texture of drying blood. The dogs were barking wildly; he estimated there were at least three inside the bothy. Radchenko was also barking.

For all Mike knew, there could have been three of him as well.

There were other noises in the background: precise, controlled; dialogue, clearly military. It reminded him of something from a mission briefing; he realised he was being played intel. The task clearly had a secondary purpose; under the circumstances, listening to intel seemed far less of a priority. Nevertheless, he realised that it was vital.

Wars had been won and lost on a person's ability to remember.

"You are bleeding! You are dying!" Radchenko's voice carried above the barking of the dogs. "Your body is going into irreversible shock!"

Opening the pouch was a slow process; finally he resorted to biting down hard on it with his teeth. Inside was a large roll of bandage; just as the tormentor had promised, it included everything he needed to stem the bleeding.

Mike tore at the bandage rapidly and tied it tightly round his upper thigh. Drowning out the sound of the Ukrainian and his horrible dogs, he concentrated on the recording. The enemy had a convoy of twelve, the majority armoured cars. Over fifty armed men were already on hand; a potential 150 would later join them. The orders were to hold a bridge and, if possible, take down a Food Aid truck.

Further supplies would come at sundown.

Radchenko monitored the time down to the last second. When three minutes had elapsed, he ended the exercise.

"Okay, I want you to stop and raise your hands."

83

The Old Hospital Block, 02:37

Mike adjusted his position on the couch to make himself as comfortable as possible, again declining Emily's offer of help. The painful throbbing sensation he'd experienced in his left thigh moments earlier had reduced slightly, the sensations like those of a dead leg. The blood flow was alarming, but he sensed reversible, at least if he acted quickly. He remembered Radchenko telling him irreversible paralytic shock would be unavoidable if left untreated.

At least it had only been a flesh wound.

He rifled through the contents of his belt, his attention also partly on the door to the lounge behind him, which Emily had since closed. She approached him cautiously, wanting to help but unwilling to intrude.

She watched him rip open the pouch.

"You sure you don't need my help?"

Mike grinned at her as he unfolded the bandage, wrapping it tightly around his ripped trouser leg. He saw Emily sit down alongside him, mopping away the excess blood, her hand brushing delicately over his leg.

In another time and place, he knew his reaction might have been far different.

He wrapped the bandage tightly, ensuring he'd got the pressure and the positioning correct. He could see that the bleeding had reduced.

Removal of the bullet would have to come later.

He smiled, doing his best to relax. "This a typical night after work for you?"

She eyed him inquisitively. "Even in the tourist season, things aren't usually this hectic." She continued to clean the area around the bandaging. "You take a master's in first aid too?"

"Not exactly. Just practice."

"You make a habit of this?"

"On the bright side, at least I don't have to listen to soviet intel this time."

Emily was confused. "What?"

"Nothing."

He struggled to his feet, accepting Emily's hand. Walking was difficult, but he forced himself to move. Opening the door slightly, he looked across the grenade-damaged hallway, finding it deserted; the smoke had largely cleared. Opening the door fully, he made his way as best he could to the building's main door, investigating each apartment as he passed. The stairway was also deserted, the lower part destroyed.

Climbing it was now impossible.

He stopped on reaching the outer doorway, his attention on the area directly beyond the door. As usual, the White Tower dominated the view; the area surrounding it appeared to be deserted.

He spoke into his headset. "Phil, what are you seeing?"

Phil heard Mike's voice come through clearly. "Matter of fact, it's all gone rather quiet. Blanco is still in the barracks along with most of the other bastards. Rest are in the same place."

"How about Randek?"

"Returned to the Queen's House. I don't know what you did to him, but he sure didn't like it."

"Nothing to do with me. You can thank the acting curator."

Emily tugged at him and whispered in his ear, "Are you out of your mind? I can't admit to using a gun."

"I take it back, it was all me." He smiled wryly as Emily rolled her eyes. "Where am I heading from here?"

"Right now, I'd say you've got two choices. Not convinced you're gonna like either."

Crouching down on one knee, the pain in his thigh throbbing wildly, Mike concentrated on the area outside the door. "Doors to the White Tower appear to be closed; getting there unseen could be doable on the south side, but the north would be a problem." He considered the location of the barracks. "If the majority of the hostages are in the Queen's House, I've got to reach them at some point. Any ideas?"

Just as Phil sought to respond, the Director's voice cut him off. "Grosmont, this is the King."

"I hear you, sire."

Seated behind the pilot of the helicopter, the Director spoke into his mouthpiece while viewing the sights of the city in the distance. Just as before, gigantic flames pierced the skyline, creating thick smoke across the cosmos. In one of the rare gaps, the moon appeared red like blood.

"What's the latest?"

Mike filled him in on recent events, ending with his belief Randek had taken one in the shoulder. How he had taken one in the thigh.

"How bad is it?"

Mike decided to be liberal with the truth. "Thanks to the teachings of Colonel Radchenko, I'm unlikely to enter paralytic shock."

"Is the curator with you?"

He retreated to the nearest apartment, taking a seat at a dining table. "Yes, sir. She can hear your every word."

"Good, as this probably concerns both of you. The documents you discovered in the archives were more important than you could possibly know. Along with the paintings Edward found, they've blown this thing wide open." The Director paused, uncharacteristically cautious. "Until now, I'd never believed what we now know to be possible."

Mike felt his heart rate begin to increase, whether a response to the wound or the news he was unsure. "Who are these people?"

"According to the royal historian your uncle mentioned, they ceased to exist around the time of the English Civil War, thanks in no small part to Cromwell. However, clearly the iron man didn't wipe them out completely."

"So they're descendants of royalty?"

"Exactly who they are and where they've been hiding for the past few centuries is unclear, even to Professor Tinniswood. That the fake death of Edward II has conned historians for centuries it now appears was indeed part of a deliberate master plan that has succeeded in confusing historians and every monarch since. That the king survived and his descendants are behind this now seems highly probable. Irrespective of their godfather's plans."

Mike realised he was talking about the Italian cardinal. "So we're dealing with former royalty?"

"From what I've learned during my absence, the Fieschi name is still prominent in the south of France. During his time in the Tower, Blanco has been recorded having no less than two conversations with gentlemen up to now unrecognisable. However, facial recognition technology has enabled us to identify them."

"Who are they?"

"Gabriel de Fieschi and Jérôme de Haulle. Both, so Maria tells me, distant cousins and of revered ancestry, especially in the Anjou and Aquitaine areas of France. De Haulle is a prominent art collector and director; Fieschi an influential business magnate, particularly in the wine industry." The Director paused for thought. "Had the French Revolution never taken place, both would have had strong claims to the French throne."

Mike raised an eyebrow, Emily more so still. "They're both on record?"

"On record, but neither have any criminal activities noted against them. Further checks have revealed blood links with Blanco and Randek."

"Sounds like one big happy family." Mike bit his lip. "What are my orders? Last thing I wanna do is complain, but standing still isn't gonna help my wound."

Maria beat the Director to a response. "Right now there are twenty-four hostages in the White Tower and only four gunmen. Getting there on the south side might be possible, but only with a key."

Emily shook her head. "It probably wouldn't make a difference. The doors can be bolted from the inside."

Mike figured as much. "On the other side, the gift shop is too close to the barracks. One alert gunman and we'll be sitting ducks."

"Ten gunmen are still in the barracks; the rest are split between the Queen's House and the Martin Tower." On the screen, Maria hadn't seen any sign of guards patrolling the grounds since Randek was shot. "Your best bet is probably the south side."

"Even if it's not bolted, chances are that those in the Queen's House have the entrance covered. That still leaves the same problem." Mike's frustrations were increasing. "There must be another way into the Queen's House."

Maria studied the 3D map on her iMac. "There's a passage from the Salt Tower into the crypt of St Peter ad Vincula." She rotated it on its axis. "If you can get to the Beauchamp Tower, there's another passage to the Bell Tower.

That connects directly to the Queen's House."

"That sounds more like it." He asked Emily for the map they'd taken from the Byward Tower and began studying it. The Salt Tower was accessible, but there would be a problem on the other side. "Getting from the chapel to the Beauchamp Tower won't be easy."

At the other end, Maria gritted her teeth philosophically. "Right now, I don't think you have much choice. It's sure gonna be better than passing the White Tower."

Mike agreed. "All right. Where are we heading?"

Emily realised they had a straight choice. "It's either the wall walk or we make a run for it across open ground. With your injury the way it is, both options have their problems."

"What's our best choice?" Mike asked Emily, having terminated the conversation with Maria. Once again that evening, he was unclear about the layout.

"Our destination is here." Emily pointed to the Salt Tower located in the south-east corner of the inner wall and forming part of the famous wall walk. She rued the fact that the New Armouries Restaurant blocked the path. "We need to enter it here."

Mike realised she was gesturing to the lower floor. "Can we get in from the upper storey?"

"Unfortunately not." She recalled the upper section, famous for its wall markings made by Catholic martyrs. "If we took the wall walk, we'd have to start again here at the Martin Tower and follow it round. Our first chance to return to ground level would be the stairs here." She pointed to the stairway outside the Lanthorn Tower.

Mike realised that would take them well out of the way. "What's the short way?"

"Here!" She mapped out the route from the Old Hospital Block to the lower entrance to the Salt Tower. "Distance is less than a couple of hundred metres. Problem is, it could leave us exposed."

Moving his leg, Mike grimaced in pain. "Is there no way around?"

"No. Unfortunately the restaurant backs on to the inner wall."

Scanning the map, Mike realised she was right. The choice was simple, stairs and a slow walk or a mad dash across open ground.

He left his seat and moved towards the outer door, his eyes on the outside world. Apart from a replica of a heavy gun, a bench and some trees, there was little in the way of shelter.

"What are my chances, Maria?"

Watching the satellite footage, Maria responded, "The grounds are clear; the gunmen remain in the same place. If you're gonna do it, do it now."

That was all the advice Mike needed. He grabbed Emily's hand. "You ready?"

Emily nodded.

"Let's do this!"

Christophe noticed movement near the Martin Tower, first inside and then on the steps. The quartet of gunmen who had earlier assisted Randek in emptying the display cases of the once-jewel-encrusted crowns were now making their way back to the barracks via the Flint Tower, marching in two-by-two formation.

Inside the White Tower, the twenty-four hostages remained packed tightly together, the faces of those who had been there longest appearing increasingly haggard. The four gunmen maintained their silent vigil, their eyes never leaving the captives. The same was true in the Queen's House, where the remainder of the party kept guard by the doors, some watching the news in the lounge.

The rest he knew were in the barracks.

As he concentrated on the whereabouts of his comrades, he failed to notice the two figures leaving through the front door of the Old Hospital Block.

84

The Bell Tower,
02:38

Champion glanced to his right on hearing the door open. Light flooded into the dark interior; against the bright backdrop, he saw the bulky frame of the man he now identified as the most senior in the building – the second in overall command. As before, the angle of the light caused heavy shadows across the man's stubbled face and blond hair, creating an imposing silhouette against the nearby stonework.

Unlike before, however, the man was now heavily bandaged around his shoulder.

And holding a camera.

Randek entered the Thomas More chamber slowly, his eyes on the nearest hostages. After over four hours in captivity, he sensed things were beginning to take its toll on some of the older people, especially the women. He'd learned on arrival that one of the women was pregnant; on Blanco's orders, she'd since been moved into the lounge. The latest order was to allow toilet breaks every thirty minutes, but under no circumstances would the doors be permitted to close.

Handbags and mobile phones had all been confiscated.

He held the camera in his weaker hand, relaxing the shoulder that was heavily bandaged beneath his dark jacket. He concentrated on each face in turn, ensuring he obtained at least a second of clear footage, long enough for his uncle to judge each person's general state of mind while also striking fear into the heart of his potential victims. Though it was not yet time to pick a further six, he knew the hostages would be wondering who would be next.

He completed a pass of the room and departed through the same door. Once outside, he spoke to Blanco over the airwaves.

"You see him?"

Watching the live footage as Randek streamed it through to his laptop, Blanco concentrated on the face of the man he had earlier seen whispering into his hand. Whereas the tired-looking Beefeater alongside him was struggling to stay awake, the silver-haired man's physical condition seemed stronger than those around him, including the governor's, who coincidentally was seated to the left of him, seemingly seething with rage.

Focusing on the silver-haired man, Blanco paused the footage and zoomed in for a close-up of the man's face and head. On this occasion, his eyes were closed, his head bowed as though in prayer. Whereas earlier his hands had been joined together, now they were visible and clearly hiding nothing.

Blanco heard Randek's voice. "You want me to bring him up?"

"Not yet. The time is not right." The Anjouvin left the office and entered the CCTV room. "Any sign of the Englishman?"

Christophe shook his head. "The Hospital Block has been quiet since the last explosion." The gunman shrugged. "Who knows? Perhaps the blast killed them."

Blanco was sceptical. "Keep searching. I refuse to allow the fate of our mission to be compromised by one tourist."

Mike took a deep breath and uttered the words, "Let's go," as they took the first step out into the open. He led the way, darting quickly to his left, down a short flight of stone steps to the lower ground, before making his way in front of the New Armouries Restaurant towards the Salt Tower.

The Salt Tower was located beyond the restaurant in the south-east corner of the Inner Ward, a tall circular structure with a combination of ecclesiastical-style and narrow arrow slit windows set deeply into the medieval stonework. Mike saw the entrance at the bottom of a small set of stairs, located left of a large archway that formed part of the wall walk from there to the Lanthorn Tower.

Emily reached the door and unlocked it, maintaining a firm grasp of Mike's hand until they were both inside the tower and the door secured once again. The interior was dark, the rectangular lantern-style light overhead turned off; the last thing Mike wanted was to switch it on.

With his night-vision goggles reactivated, he explored the chamber carefully, identifying a small enclosure with pointed archways and a few small windows. The floor below had been constructed using stone slabs; if Maria was correct, their escape route was somewhere beneath them.

He limped to one of the archways, taking a seat on a stone slab. Satisfied the bandage continued to hold, he spoke into his headset.

"We've reached the Salt Tower."

Phil had been watching everything. "Gunmen haven't moved since before; if the cretins in the CCTV room have seen you, they haven't acted on it yet."

"Let's hope it stays that way." Mike took a deep breath. "Where exactly is the passageway?"

Maria had been studying the map. "Seems to go directly below where you're seated. Judging from this, it was once part of the drainage."

Emily grimaced on overhearing Maria's response, though partially reassured by the knowledge the moat had been drained well over a century ago and the royal privies were no longer in use.

"The area was possibly once a garderobe." Emily pointed to another of the archways, examining the stone seat with her hands. Mike did likewise, similarly finding it sealed tight. "Just think, back in the Middle Ages, this would probably have been used every day."

Mike shrugged. "Where exactly does this lead?"

"Directly below where you're standing." Maria continued to study the 3D architectural outline. "If a garderobe once existed there, it's almost certainly some way down."

"I was kinda afraid you might say that." Mike studied the area below him carefully, finding the stonework sealed on every side. Rummaging through his belt, he explored his kit and found a small jemmy. He lined it up with the far wall and snapped back sharply.

Almost instantly the slab broke in two.

He did the same thing a second time, removing the broken masonry. As the slab came free, he heard sounds of rubble falling below him, a prolonged echo followed by a deep splash. With the slab now absent, he had an unrestricted view down to the bottom.

Emily moved in alongside him, almost lost for words. "This won't be easy on your leg."

Mike smiled wryly. "Trust me, I've done far worse."

The blond-haired Sean Cummins completed his sprint from Cannon Street to the gardens of St Dunstan-in-the-East. Panting from fatigue and the heat, he negotiated his way through the greenery, finding two men of similarly dark attire exactly where he'd expected.

Ward was the first to notice him. "Here was me thinking you'd got lost."

Cummins grinned. "What's been happening?"

"Couple of bird calls, bit of movement among the trees. But enough about us." Ward smiled. "What's it look like over there?"

"Word on the street says Mary-le-Bow has been salvaged. Wish the same could be said for Cannon Street."

Wilcox lowered his head. "How about St Bride's?"

"You ever seen a burnt wedding cake?"

"Once. It didn't end well."

"Wish I could say the same about Fleet Street." The newest arrival checked his watch and contacted Maria. "This is Eam. Am in position."

"Any sign of life?"

"Negative," Ward beat him to a response. "It's like a ghost town."

"Good. Let's hope it stays that way."

Outside the great hall of Edinburgh Castle, Pentland put out a call using his satphone. Within seconds he received a response.

Masterson.

"I hear you've done some sterling work this evening. Never realised you were such a man of the world."

Back in the crypt of Mary-le-Bow, Kit sensed the question had little basis in military protocol. "May I assume, as it's you, you're talking about paintings?"

Pentland grinned. "The fires in Edinburgh are getting worse. There's a pattern, just like in London." His expression hardened as he saw the city from the castle. Along the Mile, the fires were getting brighter. "The jerk behind this clearly had an interest in art with good reason. Is the Director of the Portrait Gallery with you?"

"Absolutely."

"May I speak with her?"

Standing by the café in the crypt, Kit passed his phone to Gillian. "One of my associates would appreciate your input on an art problem."

Gillian accepted the phone, equally confused by both its appearance and the request. "Hello, Gillian McKevitt."

"Ms McKevitt, I understand from my colleague that you've been very helpful in disclosing the secrets behind the artwork at the exhibition."

"Well, I wouldn't really go that far . . ."

"Your assistance has been most helpful, thank you. Right now, we're faced with a similar situation in Edinburgh."

Mention of that concerned her. "Look, whoever you are, I assure you I know little about the city."

"And I know little about art, which makes you the perfect person to ask. Tell me, Ms McKevitt. The pieces you saw in the museum tonight were requested by Jérôme de Haulle; that is correct?"

"It is."

"In addition to the works in London, can you recall whether the curator from Angers requested anything from Edinburgh?"

Gillian considered the question. "As a matter of fact, I remember one."

At the other end, Pentland exhaled gratefully.

That was exactly the answer he'd been hoping for.

In Tudor Street, on the roof of a building that had once been the headquarters of the *Daily Mail*, the Deputy Director of the White Hart stared across the flaming skyline. The fires were getting brighter, the menacing light having a strange effect on the cloud that, had it not been for the imminent danger, might have appeared strangely transfixing.

The view itself was familiar, even though he'd never stood on that roof before. He remembered the story of a man who had done so over seven decades earlier, a man who had taken a photograph that would later become famous worldwide. Surrounded by the fiery light, the dome of St Paul's seemed to take on new heights, as though he was watching the clouds of heaven breaking through hell. He had thought similar things many times seated at his desk and often considered how the course of history had been plotted by those brave enough to take decisive action when it was really needed. History was strange; rarely could anyone imagine that actions they were about to take would impact dramatically on future generations.

Staring intently across the skyline beyond the dome, he made a decision.

Like the brave men who had lived through the Blitz, his duty was now. One day, perhaps the mighty cathedral before him would fall, be it in a cloud of smoke or brick by brick. Only one thing he was now sure of.

It would not fall on his watch.

85

Chapel of St Peter ad Vincula, 02:41

The passageway led to a crossroads, just as Maria had predicted. The water level was low; unlike their trip from St Thomas's Tower to the Constable Tower, negotiating it hadn't involved swimming.

The area directly above them matched the condition of the walls. The tunnel had clearly been dug out of the earth, almost certainly for purposes of drainage. The water was cold, non-salty; Mike reasoned they were probably dealing with overflow from the Thames.

At some point, he guessed it would merge with the tunnel they'd taken from the king's bedroom in St Thomas's Tower.

Proceeding on foot, he switched off his night visions and examined the area around him in the torchlight, watching Emily as she did the same. The cold was having its familiar numbing effect, particularly noticeable around his wound; he knew the longer they remained in the water, the greater the risk of hyperthermia. With every second that passed, he felt his body become more and more drained, as though an invisible weight was pulling at him.

In his mind, he recalled the advice of the Aussie.

Mike awoke to a familiar sound, a coarse voice barking out instructions against the background of a metallic drumbeat. Outside the tent, the Harts had already assembled; today it had been Chambers' turn to bang the drum.

Another individual was also present, the light-green colour of his combat uniform distinguishing him from the Harts. The man carried himself with an air of authority similar to that of the previous tormentors but equating more, in Mike's view, with the former SEALs than Zahavi or Bautista. Two well-defined biceps showed clearly through the folds of his sleeves that Mike guessed were capable of benching at least 120kg at max output, an extension of at least 30kg on his bodyweight. Like Webbs, the man seemed particularly pumped, with a demeanour that was pure no-nonsense. If the situation was required, Mike didn't doubt he'd quite happily wrestle a cougar with his bare hands and back himself to come out on top. Dark haired, with still youthful features and penetrating eyes, his face radiated a powerful message of experience; that of eyes that had seen death and been responsible for it. Yet when it had happened, there had been no joy or remorse. What had been done had been solely in the line of duty.

"I don't care what you've already been through or what you will encounter later. I'm in charge now, and for the next forty-eight hours that will be your only concern." The man stood rigidly on the spot, his arms by his sides.

"During this time, you will be constantly monitored and assessed – and on that you can trust me completely. I don't care what previous instructors have told you, good or bad. Over the next forty-eight hours, what I see is all that counts. If I feel you're failing any task, you're mentally not up to it, or worst of all not giving one hundred per cent at all times, I'll cut you right there and send you home. Is that clear, Lieutenant?"

"Yes, sir!" Mike nodded, his eyes looking deeply into those of his new leader like a small child caught in a spell. The first thing he'd noticed apart from the man's expression and uniform was the sound of his voice; clearly not from the UK but of a Caucasian origin. As he watched the returning Chambers, his first sight of the new flag above the training camp confirmed his suspicions. Though he saw a Union Jack, it appeared only in one corner. The rest was made up of stars on a blue background.

The new leader relaxed his posture to the at ease position and began to strut slowly in front of the Harts. "As you've no doubt deduced from your quick glance at my national flag, I'm from Australia – Adelaide to be precise. Until six years ago, I served for over fifteen years in the Australian SAS. My name is Major Malcolm Waugh. Spelt just like the cricketers. You like cricket, Lieutenant?"

"Yes, sir. I like most sports."

"Well, you've certainly got the physique for it. Just remember, the lifestyle of some sportsmen has no place here. At best it can retard, at worst destroy. Do you understand me?"

Again Mike nodded and replied, "Yes, sir!"

Waugh walked a few paces to a large kit bag, opened it and showed Mike the contents.

"I'm sure you'll be pleased to hear that I've got some brand new clobber in here just for you. Your current stuff is beginning to get a bit smelly, mate. So strip yourself bare and get yourself clean."

Mike stripped to his underwear and began pulling on his new uniform. After a week of training and a lack of nutrition, his body was clearly showing signs of wear.

"You've got a few marks coming out there, Lieutenant. Gotta warn you now, next few days, it's unlikely to get any better."

"I understand, sir." Mike attempted to avoid giving an answer with chattering teeth.

"I should hope so, too. Now hurry up and get that on. The longer it takes you to get dressed, the longer you're exposed to the cold. And that ain't gonna help the healing process."

Waugh returned to the head of the parade. Mike stood in his new uniform; dressed in the fine material, he felt even less equipped for Scotland than the NAVSOG gear.

The officer from Adelaide removed a folded piece of paper from his pocket and opened it up.

"Unlike your previous encounters, today we have one major difference. Look inside your right pocket, Lieutenant."

Mike zipped up his new combat jacket and felt deeply into the right pocket, finding that it contained a similar piece of paper.

"Care to read that out for us, mate?"

Mike speed-read the content before doing so. The pause infuriated Waugh.

"Afraid that's an order, Hansen."

"This is to confirm that after pitting my wits against the best and failing, I hereby withdraw from the process and therefore desert my colleagues despite being sound in the knowledge that my doing so may result in any one of them suffering serious injury as a direct response of my act of cowardice."

The reactions of the Harts varied from shock to stunned laugher. Waugh's expression remained unflinching. "You gonna sign that today, mate?"

"No, sir."

"You sure?"

Rather than reply, Mike ripped the declaration into quarters and threw it away. Of all the Harts, it was difficult to tell whose jaw had dropped lowest. Masterson appeared strangely satisfied.

The day had been the toughest yet. Humping over 400kg of weaponry even just short distances had been a strain unlike any other. Even for the likes of Rawlins, walking had become tough.

They'd had no meal for almost fourteen hours.

They found Waugh waiting in a deserted field, warming his hands by a campfire. On delivering the weapons, Mike ordered the men to fall out. For the first time since the process had begun, he felt burnt out.

Waugh sat down alongside him. "I know you're feeling pretty tired and maybe even a little sorry for yourself right now," *he said, speaking quietly and close to Mike's ear.* "Getting into the Australian SAS is a tough process – even the most hard-core recruits struggle at some point. The selection course is one of the hardest of all the Special Forces. Carrying a lot of weight over pretty amazing distances. At times it can really suck."

He got comfortable alongside Mike, a thoughtful smile on his face, almost parental in nature. "Selection for the SASR usually lasts about twenty-one days. Now, just for a second, I want you to imagine that. Really imagine that. Three weeks of nothing but this. Of course, the reason for it, you already know. In times of war, there is no respite. To ensure the right people are selected, you need to replicate those same conditions, take away the light. No matter how strong you are, stuff like that's gonna mess with your mindset. In times of war, when those kind of things happen, you're gonna get broken down. Life's gonna get tough. If you're a commanding officer and part of the selection process, you're gonna need to know the people you're selecting are still gonna be able to perform." *He allowed a moment for everything to sink in.* "At the end of the day, it's that perseverance, that will, and that forged toughness through this extraordinarily hard training that's gonna pull you through. So that when war does come, you're gonna be ready."

Mike nodded, listening to every word. Looking around the makeshift campsite, it was obvious everyone there had gone through the same process. He had been to war, passed P Company, been dropped out of a plane ready to carry out missions that would strike a firm blow for his country's cause. Under the circumstances, life suddenly seemed simpler.

"Thank you, sir."

Together they pushed on, Mike doing his best to ignore the pain. However long remained between now and the end, it was unlikely to last twenty-one days.

"The signal is gone." Mike tried speaking through his headset, concerned they might be trapped. Of equal concern was the lack of visual clues. If Maria's information was correct, the entrance to the chapel would be from below ground level.

Meaning the likeliest escape route would be directly above them.

After almost four minutes of wading through knee-deep water, Mike noticed a small gap in the stonework above them, seemingly manmade. "Hey, check this out."

Emily added her torchlight to his. She made out the area to be rectangular, perhaps large enough for her to fit through. At the very top was what appeared to be a stone slab.

Removing the slab was difficult, especially trying to balance on Emily's shoulders. Using the same jemmy as in the Salt Tower, he was able to loosen the stone above him and move it, revealing their exit.

Climbing out, he leaned into the space beneath him and pulled Emily up. In the torchlight, he could see a cavernous area with a white ceiling and surrounding walls on which numerous plaques had been fixed.

The layout reminded him of a crypt or subterranean bunker.

"Where are we?"

"It's the crypt of St Peter ad Vincula," Emily replied, both relieved and impressed that they'd managed to locate it. "You know, some of the most important people who ever lived are buried down here."

"Maybe some other time," Mike responded; even out of the water, the cold and bullet wound were a lethal combination. "How do we get out of here?"

Emily led them out of the crypt and through an arched doorway into the chapel above. In the darkness, Mike made out the familiar outline of the 16th-century church as external light shone through the stained-glass windows, illuminating several rows of wooden seats either side of the stone pillars that had something of a haunting effect on the paved flooring.

They continued all the way to the main door. Emily quickly opened it and edged her way up the steps to look out across what had once been the scaffold site.

As far as they could tell, the area was deserted.

"They have cameras in here?"

"No cameras are allowed inside the church." She returned to the chapel and pulled the door to. "That said, the possibility that they're watching from the outside can't be ruled out."

Mike tried his headset again. "Maria, you with me?"

This time a reply came immediately. "Just as I was starting to fear you weren't coming." She saw from the GPS they had made it inside the church. "How was it down there?"

"Now that you mention it, it was kinda cosy. Albeit more than a little wet." He glanced at Emily, biting his lip as a response to the chill.

She looked cute when she was cold.

"How we looking?"

"The tunnel from the Beauchamp Tower to the Bell Tower is accessible via the top floor," Maria replied. "Your only chance is to cross open ground."

"You heard of this one?" he asked Emily.

The acting curator nodded. "The passage is famous. Assuming we can reach it, getting in shouldn't be a problem."

Mike spoke again into the headset. "Where are the others?"

"Gunmen are in the same places as before, except for those that were outside the Flint Tower."

"Where are they now?"

Alongside her, Phil monitored the same footage. "Outside the Martin. Right now they seem undecided whether they wanna take a leak."

Mike glanced at Emily. "Whereabouts is the Martin Tower from here?"

"Other side of the Jewel House." She got out the map they'd taken from the Byward Tower. "If they're here, we should be free."

Mike agreed with her logic. "What do you reckon, Phil?"

"I'd say now's as good a time as any."

Blanco watched the original footage for the sixth time in as many minutes, pausing it in the same place. The silver-haired man had definitely concealed something in his left hand, possibly electronic. The movement of the camera seemed to have caught him unaware, perhaps even interrupting a conversation.

Either that or he was talking to himself.

In the CCTV room, Christophe saw a strange mist emerge around the scaffold site, slightly unnerving him. He remembered learning during their reconnaissance missions that the area was infamous as a site where many important executions had taken place; over the centuries it had become widely regarded as being haunted.

Within the mist, figures were moving towards the stairway that led down to the Beauchamp Tower. One was clearly a woman.

Unlike the spirits of the past, the man alongside her was clearly armed.

Standing outside the Martin Tower, the leader of the four heard Christophe's voice come through clearly over the airwaves. Within seconds, they began making their way between the Jewel House and the White Tower, heading for the scaffold site.

THE CROWN JEWELS CONSPIRACY

* * *

Mike heard a sudden crackling sound coming from the HT he'd earlier taken from the gunman inside the CCTV room. He saw Emily startled by the sound.

"You get the feeling that might be for us?"

"Uh-huh."

Mike heard voices close to the Jewel House, prompting him to increase his pace. "In that case, I really hope you have the correct key."

The pathway led from north to south, following a metal railing that separated the cobbled surface from the grass. To his left, Mike noticed a square that was inset into the greenery on which a display had been erected in honour of past executions; to their right another building, a private residence with a blue door, was in darkness alongside the Beauchamp Tower.

Entering the Beauchamp Tower required descending a stone stairway. Mike made it to the highest step and ducked instinctively, taking the stairs as fast as his wounded leg would allow. On reaching the fifth step, a series of sparks came up off the concrete behind him, more still off the tower wall.

The near miss preceded shouts in French.

They hurried to the bottom, at which point the entrance became clear: a strong wooden door in the stonework. Directly adjacent, a modern toilet had been put in at the foot of the steps.

Emily fumbled with the keys, doing her best to insert one into the lock. To her horror, she realised she'd picked the wrong one. Attempting to remain calm, she tried again. Mike's attention turned to the top of the steps. In the silence, the sparks resumed.

"Come on, they're getting closer."

"Don't rush me."

Biting his lip, Mike made his way tentatively back up the steps, realising an attack was imminent. Reaching into his belt, he grasped his penultimate grenade and threw it beyond the stairway. As the door opened, he ran and dived for cover inside.

No sooner had he made it, an explosion went up from close to the scaffold site.

Blanco banged his fist against the nearby surface, furious. The images on the screens confirmed the Englishman and the woman had reappeared suddenly on the opposite side of the Tower, on the grassy area around the former execution site. In the following seconds, he'd seen them make their way down the adjacent stairway, struggling with the door to the Beauchamp Tower before finding a way inside.

Within seconds of their disappearance, he saw two more of his gunmen taken out in a cloud of smoke. As it dispersed, he could see that the monument to the executions had been all but destroyed.

Randek's voice on the airwaves ended the silence. "What has happened?"

Immediately Blanco responded, "I think it's time I have a conversation with the man seated next to the governor. On this occasion, only one hostage will be necessary."

Champion saw the door open for a second time in quick succession, the blond-haired villain returning. Just as on most previous occasions, the newcomer's focus centred on his side of the room, the side where the governor sat.

Unlike last time, he paid the governor little attention.

Watching the footage as it played out on the semi-translucent screen, Phil groaned as the silver-haired Professor Champion was escorted from the dingy chamber up into the heart of the Queen's House.

Alongside him, Maria placed her hand to her mouth. "Oh my God!" She looked at Phil, suddenly worried. "You think we should tell Mike?"

Phil knew it was an awful question to answer. "Right now, there's no way he could get there."

Nodding, both watched on as the figures headed out the main door, crossing Tower Green towards the Jewel House. So far that night none of the hostages had been executed.

Quietly, they both feared that was about to change.

86

St Mary-le-Bow,
02:47

Kit left the crypt, astounded at what he'd seen and furious that so much damage had been caused on his watch. The discovery of the secrets within the paintings that offered a detailed insight into future events, he had witnessed with his own eyes.

Once more that evening, his frustrations were mostly with himself.

He put through a call to the Rook. "What's the latest?"

Maria responded just at the moment Randek and Professor Champion disappeared inside the Jewel House.

"The Director is on his way back from Surrey. The Deputy is already at St Paul's with the others. Your orders are to join him."

"I'm on my way," he replied as he got into the car through the rear right door, Nat and Gillian doing the same from the left. He knew the journey would only take a couple of minutes along Cheapside.

The car set off, heading west. On the north side of the road, the buildings were mostly undamaged, a stark contrast to what he saw to his left. Every spare inch of road was filled with fire engines, each one attempting to tackle the escalating furnace. Even with the car windows closed, escaping the heat was impossible.

While St Mary-le-Bow had been lucky, other buildings had not.

The threat from Blanco had been that a display would occur that would illuminate St Paul's; Belland had used the very same words in 1666. As they reached the end of Cheapside, the car turning left on to New Change, the famous dome of the cathedral towered over the churchyard like the rising of the Third Temple in Revelation.

Kit feared even if the surrounding fires didn't reach this far, it wouldn't be long before new ones began.

It was busy around the churchyard. Crowds swelled from Paternoster Row to the gardens on the south side, occupying seemingly every inch of available ground. There was an air of pandemonium, fear in the expressions of the onlookers. It was as if the whole city had come out to watch, everyone afraid they would become engulfed in the flames if they looked away.

In the crowds, he could see people praying.

His attention returned to Johnstone. "You've been right so far about the crypts. If there is something here, we can be sure the enemy are going to use it." He grabbed Nat's hand and looked earnestly into the man's eyes. "Think hard, Mr Johnstone. What, if anything, still exists of the original foundations?"

Peering back with a stern expression, his experienced face now partially covered by windswept hair, Johnstone answered, "If you're talking about the previous cathedral, practically nothing. A small manhole exists on the south-east side."

That sounded exactly what they needed. "Where is it?"

"I shouldn't get too excited. It's only about a human's width on either side. Not exactly easy to get into." Nat was already aware that what Kit sought would be very similar to that beneath Mary-le-Bow. "Wren's new building, magnificent though it is, was built to different specifications. If anything, the work here is almost all his own."

That was the last thing Kit wanted to hear. "Its inclusion in the two paintings shows a clear match; there must be something if only small." Beneath his covert ops gear, Kit felt his pulse quicken. "A place like this must hold many secrets."

"Secrets and age don't always go hand in hand. When old St Paul's burned to the ground, much of the damage occurred when the lead roof melted. When work began to level out the foundations, the builders were faced with significant difficulties. When Wren himself attempted to oversee the construction, it was discovered that the ground beneath was rich in clay. If work had continued, the new build would inevitably have collapsed in a very short space of time."

"How about the crypt? The churchyard? Even the main body?" Kit looked him deep in the eye. "Think about Mary-le-Bow. What possible things could they have in common?"

On this occasion, Nat was stumped. "The markings on the Wren portrait suggest the door is somewhere in the south-east side, which clearly points to the crypt. If there is anything similar to Mary-le-Bow, it could be lower still."

Kit checked his watch, frowning. "Well, let's just hope what's been hidden for over three hundred years has actually been hidden in plain sight."

Outside the cathedral, fear and anticipation were reaching fever pitch. Though Atkins was sure awareness of the next intended target couldn't possibly have reached the public domain, it was obvious from the approaching flames that the cathedral was in imminent danger. He remembered reading how in the early days of the Great Fire, many had brought their prized possessions to the cathedral, placing them away securely in the old vaults. It had been confirmed time and again in numerous historical accounts.

In times of crisis, the sheep flocked back to the pen.

He stood on the steps outside the great west front, watching Sanders and Iqbal approach.

"What's the latest?" Sanders got there first.

Arms folded and jacket now discarded, the Deputy Director replied, "Fire engines are on standby on all sides; all that can be spared are heading here now. The fires east of Mary-le-Bow fortunately are nearly out."

"How about Fleet Street?" Jay asked.

"The only good thing is that it doesn't seem to be spreading further west."

Sanders couldn't believe his ears; further proof the terrorists were following the paths of history. "Where are the others?"

"Dawson and Chambers are positioned on the north side, keeping an eye on the Old Bill. With that in mind, I suggest you both concentrate on the south. Masterson, when he arrives, can take the east."

"How about the interior?"

"The second these doors open, there'll be a stampede. If hell is on the other side, opening it could kill us all, including whoever is stupid enough to do the opening."

Jay scowled, his eyes on the nearby crowds; never had he known such widespread panic. Further afield, the sirens were sounding once again; in the last hour, he'd seen no vehicles other than those with flashing red and blue lights. "What do we do if the fire does begin?"

Atkins took a deep breath, contemplating the events of the Blitz. "I guess we'll just have to pray it doesn't."

Close to the original London wall, three dark vans were heading south on St Martin's-le-Grand in the direction of the cathedral. Unlike the five white vans, three of which had been abandoned or reduced to burnt-out shells blocking the entrance to Watling Street, none of these were associated with criminal activity, nor was the identity of their drivers known.

On passing another roadblock unchallenged, the driver of the first put his foot down as he approached the churchyard.

In a closed section of the National Gallery of Scotland, Anthony Pentland shone a UV torch at the masterpiece in front of him and was amazed by what he saw. The picture, entitled *Edinburgh from Calton Hill*, by Alexander Nasmyth, was one of the gallery's treasures; one of the few that portrayed both a realistic and romanticised view of the city.

And also the only one that had been coveted by Jérôme de Haulle.

Close to the entrance to the Edinburgh Vaults, Pugh and Rawlins heard a voice in their earpieces. "Turns out we might actually owe the Black Prince a beer. The portrait gallery director came up trumps."

Rawlins was confused. "What are you talking about?"

"The key was in the painting de Haulle missed. It's given the location of everything. The only two areas not used so far are Market Street and Holyrood Road."

"Where are you?"

"Just leaving the National. The next entrance is via Mary King's Close."

Rawlins checked his watch and exchanged glances with Pugh. "We'll be with you in five minutes."

87

The Beauchamp Tower, 02:48

Mike felt his left leg buckle as he desperately tried to duck below the latest stream of bullets. Passing through the open doorway, he felt it go completely on impact with a new timber surface, causing him to lose his footing and crash down heavily.

Under the circumstances, he was grateful it wasn't stone.

He rolled on to his back, crying out in agony; in the dim light of the otherwise deserted chamber, he'd seen enough to know the bandaging was still secure, despite the increased throbbing. Behind him, Emily was standing close to the door. With shaking fingers, she reinserted the key into the lock, turning it.

Within seconds, a further volley of bullets peppered it from outside.

Mike heard the sound of keys hitting the floor; against the green backdrop of his night visions, he saw Emily searching for them, finding them and putting them back in her pocket. As the gunfire stopped, they looked at one another, their features appearing strange in the artificial lighting. While Emily had returned to her feet, Mike remained on the floor.

Standing was suddenly difficult for him.

"How's your leg?"

Sitting up, Mike inspected the wound; seepage appeared minimal. "I think I'll live." He held out his hand; with Emily's help, he was able to get back to his feet.

He took a couple of paces to his right, into the main chamber. Like the lower part of the Salt Tower, the room was arranged in a rough circle, the exterior a combination of white plastered brickwork intercepted by archways at regular intervals, some of which contained narrow windows. At the centre of the room, an exhibition on past prisoners had been attached to an iron cage arranged in the form of a prison cell.

Mike recalled the Beauchamp Tower had once been the state prison.

Using the bars for support, he spoke into his headset. "We're inside."

Maria exhaled in relief. "You both okay?"

"Just about," Mike replied. "I take it from the welcome we were seen."

"Your grenade took out two of them – not to mention the display on the executions." She monitored the surveillance footage, observing that the surviving gunmen were laying charges outside the Beauchamp Tower's door. "The others are still outside. You'll need to get your skates on."

"We're on it." He turned to Emily. "Where are we heading?"

"Upstairs. The passage is behind one of the walls."

***

Blanco monitored the screens as the more senior of the two gunmen set the charge outside the door. Though the Beauchamp Tower housed at least two locked-off cameras, viewing motion was difficult in the dark.

Nevertheless, he was able to detect some movement on the stairs.

"The English are heading to the upper floor," he said into his HT. "Whatever you do, do not lose them."

Outside the main door of the Beauchamp Tower, the second gunman lit the charge and followed his accomplice up the steps, waiting until they were at a safe distance before stopping. Seconds later, they heard an explosion from the bottom, wood clearly splintering. As the smoke cleared, both investigated the damage in frustration.

The door remained intact.

Mike felt his leg give way once more as the explosive impact hit the outer door. Finding his footing, he held his breath, grateful that the charge appeared to have been badly laid and had not achieved its purpose.

Luck for now seemed to be back on their side.

They followed the winding stairway to the very top, finding themselves in a chamber of similar appearance to the one downstairs, the rugged exterior of the archways replaced by one with white paintwork partially covered by graffiti left behind by prisoners from the Tudor era. Four benches had been placed in the centre of the room, arranged in the shape of a cross. Despite the lack of artificial light, the room was partially illuminated by a ghostly pale light filtering through the narrow windows.

Mike took a seat in the centre of the room, carefully examining the walls without his visual aid. The graffiti was eye-catching, due more to the designs than the surrounding names. As in the Salt Tower, the carvings were protected by transparent pieces of plastic.

He recalled that Sir Robert Dudley had been one of the tower's famous occupants.

"Where exactly are we heading?" Mike noticed a small doorway in the far corner, close to the nearest window. Set into one of the walls was a fireplace.

Immediately he was suspicious.

"Not this time, buster." Emily had turned her search to the graffiti left of the fireplace. She concentrated on what appeared to be a cross of St John protected by a plastic covering. With considerable effort she removed the plastic protection and tossed it across the floor.

Mike rose to his feet. As Emily pressed against the stonework with her hands, a small cavity appeared in the wall inside the nearest archway.

Through which she could see the top of a narrow stairway.

***

Champion complied with the blond man's orders and continued up the stairs to the top floor. Though the distinguished academic had never visited the military section of the Waterloo Block before, he was certain the layout wasn't set up to appear bomb damaged.

He turned left as Randek instructed, heading along the main corridor, passing several open doors. On reaching a smart office, he entered to find a dark-haired man hunched over a laptop.

The figure immediately ceased what he was doing. "You are Professor David Champion of the University of Nottingham." He held the man's confiscated wallet aloft. "There is no point attempting to deny it, we know exactly who you are."

On seeing the well-spoken villain for the first time, Champion realised he was looking at the same man whose face had earlier been obscured by a ski mask; the man he sensed was the blond man's only superior.

"What do you want with me?"

Blanco rotated the laptop, allowing Champion a perfect view. The footage captured over an hour earlier inside the Queen's House was still playing, the camera coming close to Champion's face.

Blanco hit the pause button.

"Whereas your fellow visitors seem quite content in passing the time in quiet reflection, you seem much more engaged." He walked towards Champion, stopping a short distance in front of him. "What was that device in your hand? Who were you talking to?"

Champion remained silent.

"Search him."

Randek frisked him violently, checking every pocket. Aside from a packet of tissues, he carried nothing.

"I will advise you not to make things difficult for yourself. We are all civilised men. With your compliance, resort to force will not be necessary." Blanco stared menacingly at the professor again, his face so close Champion could feel the heat of his breath. "Unless, of course, you have a wish to join the others at the top of the White Tower?"

Champion's expression hardened. "Whatever you do to me, it pales into insignificance compared to what will later be done to you."

Blanco laughed sarcastically; at the same moment, Randek pistol-whipped Champion on the back of the head, drawing blood. "Search him again. We might have missed something." Randek frogmarched the helpless captive through the door. "While you consider your situation, perhaps you would like some refreshment. It must be thirsty down there in the dust!"

88

The Beauchamp Tower,
02:50

The passage behind the wall was smaller than Mike had anticipated, a narrow arch-shaped space that barely reached head height. The width was equally restricted; it made sense to proceed sideways.

After ten metres of winding stairway, the floor levelled out, at which point the gap became narrower still, the surface of the stonework on either side painfully abrasive. He felt it tear at his combats, cutting uncomfortably into his skin. Being so cramped, the air was heavy and filled with choking dust.

Even his joke about people in the Middle Ages being smaller than those in the modern day failed to lighten the mood.

The light was fading, especially after closing the entrance behind them. They decided to make use of their night visions, finding them a better option than the torches. Emily had gone first, but even her slight, five-foot-six frame was confined for space. As the passageway progressively reduced in size, their fear increased that it would eventually become impassable or end entirely.

And they'd both be trapped inside.

As the ceiling closed in further, Mike lowered himself to a squat position, placing his arms out to both sides for support. The cramped conditions would have been difficult even without the wound; even Emily had to resort to a kind of waddling motion to make progress. The pain in Mike's quads and calves was excruciating now; every fibre of his being was calling on him to give up. In his mind, he thought back to the sixth section of Hell: his school days in Charlestown.

Mr Masterson as headmaster.

"Who gave you permission to sit?" Kit asked, unimpressed. "Get up and into a waddling position. Now move."

Mike obeyed, struggling to catch his breath. After ninety minutes cross-country, squatting felt like agony.

"Come on, Hansen, you've had your reward. Ten days you showed your mettle, now you can't even move after an hour and a half." Kit was on his toes. "Stay down. Keep moving."

Mike lost his balance and fell over. Pain shot through his quads.

"Please do not give birth on my parade square – this is a school, after all!" Kit's voice boomed with venom. "Are you sure you still want to be here?"

Right now, he just wanted a bath. "Yes, sir."

"Then get back on your feet and waddle like a proper duck. Quack. Quack!"

The pressure then had been relentless: psychologically and physically. He remembered Kit had made him waddle for almost an hour, the constant pain compounded by continuous abuse. Of all the days, that one had felt the longest, the one time he had considered lashing out. Mental strength was the key – that was the true essence of the thinking man's soldier. There was a reason only 2,000 Navy SEALs existed at any one time.

A similar one that only twelve sat at the Round Table.

Mike felt the air become dustier, making breathing ever more difficult. In front of him Emily was coughing; in the green light he could clearly see the debris that was poisoning the air.

"Come on, it's just a little further." The words were just as much for his benefit as hers. He attempted to contact the Rook through his headset, receiving only static.

Once again, they were on their own.

They continued onward, each step torturous. After what he guessed was ten metres of constant crouching, the walls narrowed further, the ceiling now less than four feet in height. There was a restriction ahead of them, the exact opposite of light at the end of the tunnel. Under the circumstances, Mike found it almost a blessing.

Only by reaching a wall would the end be in sight.

They came to it suddenly, the way apparently shut off on every side. Mike eyed everything before removing his night visions, activating the torch. Just like at the beginning, the wall ahead appeared white in the torchlight; its surface was smooth, brick as opposed to stone. Those on either side had also become smoother; the change had come suddenly.

He sensed there was a reason.

Emily removed her night visions and began feeling frantically for clues on all sides.

"What are we looking for?" Mike asked, realising changing positions would be impossible.

"I'm not sure." Emily turned her attention to the ceiling, shining the light into every nook and cranny. She coughed as dust filled her mouth and nostrils; the air had become far worse as the passageway became smaller.

"You've never seen it before?"

"Not like this."

"But you knew it existed?"

"The passage itself is legendary." Emily looked at him, her eyes appearing ghostly white in the torchlight. "After the White Tower, the Bell Tower is the oldest we have. Like the Beauchamp, its prime purpose was incarceration."

"Then why the passage?"

"Originally it was to facilitate quick distribution of food; most likely carried in by a child," she answered sharply, her frustrations primarily with herself. "Of course, it can't be ruled out that the former governors used them to spy on their prisoners."

To Mike that made far more sense.

"So what exactly are we looking for?"

Emily was becoming increasingly desperate. "Anything that might trigger a release."

Outside the main door of the Beauchamp Tower, the two surviving gunmen laid the charge a second time before hurrying away up the stone steps back towards Tower Green. The quantity they'd used was greater this time; on the previous attempt the door hadn't shifted.

On this occasion, it had the opposite effect.

Mike and Emily both heard a distant crash. Even inside the concealed passageway, neither of them needed visual confirmation that the door of the Beauchamp Tower had been breached.

The sound spurred Emily into overdrive. "Come on, they could be right on us."

"You honestly think they could find us?"

"The Beauchamp Tower has cameras everywhere. Even if they didn't see where we went, it's a risk I'd rather not take."

Mike prayed his decision not to use the lights when searching for the tunnel would now pay off.

He moved as best he could alongside Emily, for now alternating between his night visions and the naked eye. The wall in front of him was indeed smoother than the early sections, reminding him of what he'd seen in the upper chamber of the Beauchamp Tower.

The clue outside had been the graffiti; he saw markings on the left wall. Close to the wall was a small cross.

He pulled it.

The door had disappeared by the time the smoke cleared. Where exactly was anyone's guess.

Not wasting time, the two gunmen made their way inside, contacting Blanco. "We're in."

Back in the Waterloo Barracks, Blanco had returned to the CCTV room, for now leaving his latest hostage in the company of his nephew. The surveillance footage from outside the Beauchamp Tower confirmed the door had been demolished.

What was happening inside was less clear.

He heard the gunman's voice come through clearly.

"Make sure you cover every area. Who knows what other secrets can be found within the walls."

* * *

It opened slowly, like a portcullis that hadn't been used in centuries. The smallest crack of light began to materialise, becoming ever brighter as the seconds passed. Mike felt that they were returning to civilisation; that there were people beyond the wall.

He quickly realised it had been an illusion.

Emily was first to emerge from the passageway, holding her hand out for Mike. Once again darkness surrounded them, any slight improvement simply confirmation that it had earlier been pitch black. The walls around them were also stone, the setting reminiscent of the Beauchamp Tower. Light was entering through a narrow window. Against the far wall he saw a four-poster bed.

For a moment it reminded him of St Thomas's Tower.

"Where exactly are we?"

"Beneath the Bell Tower and the Queen's House," Emily answered, clearly familiar with the layout. "Legend has it this room was once used to imprison Bishop Fisher. Another victim of Henry VIII."

Mike nodded. "What's in this place?"

"This room was apparently put in for the king in case of siege; it's also possible the governor used it during the air raids in the war. The tower itself was used as part of the outer defences." She gestured towards the ceiling. "There's a small bellcote on the roof. They still use it at closing time."

As far as Mike could tell, he'd never heard it before. "Where's More's chamber?"

"The Queen's House is directly adjacent; we have to enter from the floor above." She looked at Mike, her breathing slowly returning to normal. "If your uncle's where I think he is, he should be almost directly above us."

Mike accepted her explanation without further inquisition. He sensed from the noise in his ears that reception had also improved.

"Maria, do you copy?"

Back in the Rook, Maria heard his voice clearly. "Where are you?"

"Inside the Bell Tower. Somewhere below ground. How's everything looking?"

Maria turned to the CCTV footage. "Hostages are still in the same place – all we can see is the entrance."

"How many gunmen?"

"At least ten."

"Seems par for the course tonight," Mike replied. "How about Blanco and Randek?" He checked his watch. "I'm guessing it's about time for another hostage taking."

"Both in the barracks." Maria bit her lip, her heart sinking as she considered telling him about Champion. "I guess we're gonna just have to wait and find out."

Mike ended the conversation, his attention returning to Emily. "Where are we heading?"

"This way." Emily closed the secret door and headed in the opposite direction. "We can enter the Queen's House directly from here."

Mike checked his ammo, finding far more in the Heckler & Koch than his pistol. "Great. Last thing my leg needs is another hike."

***

The lower chamber was deserted, as were the stairs. On examining the upper chamber, the gunmen found no sign of intrusion.

Blanco's voice came through over the airwaves. "What's happening?"

The leader of the two was afraid of answering. "Both chambers are clear. He must have found a way out."

At the other end, Blanco exhaled furiously, fighting the urge to take out his aggression elsewhere. After the night he'd had, he knew it would only be a matter of time. Patience would win the race.

Eventually.

As he concentrated on the screens, he saw Christophe pointing. "Look!"

Following his direction, he looked at the screens, astonished. The Englishman and the woman had appeared on one of them, about to open a door. Only they were no longer in the Beauchamp Tower.

But below the Queen's House.

89

St Paul's Cathedral, 02:52

The car stopped at a red light at the south end of New Change. Though the road was officially closed and the traffic lights no longer in use, it was clear from the volume of people present that Cannon Street was presently inaccessible. The crowds were at their largest on the south side, the numbers spilling back into Distaff Lane, which was itself densely covered in scaffolding.

Kit knew the car was no longer of any help.

He got out from the right side, holding the door open for Gillian and Nat. The pathways were jammed all the way to the south entrance; further crowds covered both the concreted area and the greenery of the festival gardens.

Despite the late hour, he'd never seen the area so busy.

Kit led the way west through the festival gardens and past the south door, following the natural curvature of the road until he could see the statue of Queen Anne outside the great west front. The cathedral's famous twin-towered façade glowed angelically in the floodlights, the epic pillars creating strong shadows across the stepped entrance and paved approach. For the briefest of moments, he found himself concentrating on the stone faces of the saints looking down as they had for three centuries. Like the building itself, they had become symbols of permanence and of London.

Yet according to the famous clock on the south-west tower, time was something they were running out of.

The entrances had been cordoned off on every side, the 'do not cross' tape completing a full perimeter of the building and extending all the way to the pavement. He found Atkins at the top of the steps, the way to him blocked off. As Kit ducked underneath the tape, he caught the attention of two duty policemen.

Atkins saw him from the steps. "Let him pass!" he instructed, at the very same moment as Kit flashed his identity card; it was obvious that the policeman, under strict instructions to exercise extreme vigilance, hadn't been in a hurry to accept it. On receiving permission, Kit passed, Gillian and Nat following close behind.

They met Atkins on the steps.

"What's the latest?" Kit caught his breath, his attention turning to the main doors. From the outside it wasn't clear whether the cathedral was open or not.

"The gunmen you ran into in Watling Street are rumoured to have abandoned their vans for something that will blend better with their surroundings." He kept his voice low, ensuring only Kit heard the words. "Maria and Phil are trailing them."

Kit sensed the gunmen's reappearance would be inevitable. "Where are the others?"

"Sanders and Iqbal are taking the north side; Chambers and Dawson the east and south. Right now, there's nothing they can do except assist the Old Bill if the crowds get out of hand."

Beyond the Queen Anne statue, Kit noticed the general atmosphere was more one of shock and concern than possible violence.

"Let's hope this evening our citizens continue to behave themselves." He turned his attention beyond the statue, focusing on Ludgate Hill. Behind the guild church, the fire continued to roar vigorously, its voracious onslaught devouring everything in its course. It was now starting to spew out on to the roads; like the others he'd seen recently, the lack of traffic seemed strange. He judged from the visual evidence that over a hundred buildings might have been destroyed since the fire at St Bride's; even with the benefit of height at the top of the stairs, it was unclear how far it had spread in the other direction.

Directly above, dark smoke covered the night sky; though starlight was always a rare sight in the city, tonight electric light pollution was not the primary cause. Even with the aid of the floodlights, a unique gloominess hung over the city, matching the sombre mood that prevailed. In his mind, Kit recalled a story Atkins had once told him, a photograph the man had once shown him. Once more this evening he had the feeling that history was repeating itself.

As in the Blitz, Londoners had come out in great numbers in a bid to save St Paul's.

The vans pulled up at the traffic lights where Cheapside met New Change to the north-east of St Paul's Churchyard. Though the crowds were dense and the cathedral clearly in view, it was the one place where the grounds were richly covered in trees.

Alighting in an area otherwise devoid of cars, the twenty-plus survivors of the gun battle at Watling Street spread out as they headed towards the greenery, machine guns at the ready.

On reaching Paternoster Row, they began firing wildly into the air.

Sanders had been standing on a pathway close to the gates; like most parts of the north-east corner, it was currently cordoned off and empty of people.

Of all the Harts currently present, he had been stationed closest to Paternoster Row.

He heard the screams come up from the road in the split second that followed a sudden burst of gunfire. As the seconds passed, the firing became louder, multiple bursts; as it did, the screams became more panicked.

Passing the restricted area inside the churchyard, he ran along the pathway, approaching the gates. Less than forty metres away, he saw no less than twenty figures in black stationed in the middle of the road, firing wildly into the sky.

So far there had been no victims.

***

Kit heard Sanders' voice come through at the same moment it was heard by the others. Standing alongside him, Atkins paused mid-sentence, his thoughts chaotically disrupted.

It was obvious to Kit that what Sanders described was the same as Kit had seen earlier with Dawson and Chambers.

"All men report to the north-east corner. The same applies for all armed police." Atkins gestured to the nearest police, all of whom were marshalling the crowds.

Kit joined him as he sprinted north. "Pound to a penny they're the same bastards we saw near Mary-le-Bow."

"Pound to a penny they don't have blanks in their gun chambers either. Let's just pray they don't open fire on the crowds."

"They won't." Kit was confident, remembering his experience with Everard. "Even at Covent Garden, Everard had been unwilling to deliberately target civilians. Apparently it's one of the conundrums of the moral criminals."

"In that case, let's hope none of them get caught in a crossfire."

They headed east on passing the north wall, negotiating their way through the heart of the churchyard. The gunfire was audible here; whatever Sanders had said next had been drowned out. The crowds were scattering towards the nearby establishments, mostly heading north into Paternoster Square; so far the fires hadn't reached there.

Atkins was relieved the crowds were dispersing.

Further screams came from the east side; when Sanders spoke again, he confirmed there had been casualties. Reloading his gun, Kit prepared to move on.

Atkins grabbed his shoulder. Checked the time.

Only six minutes remained until the hour passed.

"You mentioned the man with you was an expert on Wren."

"Well, he was right about Mary-le-Bow."

Atkins looked at his watch again, satisfied at the sight of several armed police descending on the north side.

"We have less than nine minutes before the next fires are due. If this is the next target, we haven't a moment to waste."

"Even if it is, we have no idea where we're looking." Kit considered Johnstone's response about the crypt. As the seconds passed, it dawned on him. "You think this is a diversion?"

"In its own way, perhaps even a timely one." Atkins' gaze was stern. "There's more at stake here even than lives. If the cathedral falls, the terrorists have won."

"The fate of one building can never define victory or defeat. Even if it is St Paul's."

Atkins glanced up at the dome, recalling a memory from the past. A footnote from the Blitz. As the tired inhabitants of London re-emerged from their underground shelters, among the dust the great dome remained intact before them.

And the city was still standing.

"Maybe. But not today." He looked Kit in the eye, his expression like that of a proud father imparting knowledge to his son. "If the former director was right about one, he might be correct again."

Atkins continued along Paternoster Row, heading east through the churchyard. Sanders, Chambers, Iqbal and Dawson had already assembled close to the exit, the way currently blocked by a combination of trees and over twenty armed police.

Beyond the greenery, a gunfight had spilled out on to the road.

"What's happened?"

"Five of the villains are already down, as are a couple of coppers," Sanders replied.

"How about civilians?"

"Unfortunately there are a couple who might have wished they'd stayed home."

Atkins cursed under his breath and spoke into his headset. "Maria, this is Atkins. Get me the chief of police."

"Right now he's locked in a COBRA meeting," Maria responded immediately. "The Director's on the line with the PM as we speak."

"Well, I'm afraid you might need to break in. We've a gunfight in progress outside St Paul's."

He ended the conversation, his focus returning to the road beyond. Behind the policemen, the gunmen were spreading out, some taking shelter behind their vans.

One exploded before their eyes, the sounds deafening.

All five ducked for cover. "If we're not careful, this whole thing could escalate out of all proportion," Atkins said as the sounds died down. "The people are spooked enough as it is. The last thing we need is a bloody riot."

Keeping low, Chambers agreed. "Worse still, this could be like Mary-le-Bow. Maybe it's just a ruse to distract attention while someone else sets fire to the crypt."

Atkins had been thinking the same thing.

Iqbal noticed one man was absent. "Where's Kit?"

Kit returned to the great west front, taking the steps to the main doors. He found Nat and Gillian in the same place as before.

"How far's the crypt from here?"

"South-east of the altar through the main church." Johnstone checked his watch. "Unfortunately it won't be open at this time."

"That's what they said about Mary-le-Bow." Kit pushed the main doors, relieved to find them open. "Come on. If we're not quick, this whole thing could be on its last legs."

In a dark enclosure beneath St Paul's, the silhouetted figure waited until Blanco's voice fell silent before offering a reply, keeping his responses calm but clear.

Of all the orders he'd received that evening, he was facing the one he'd least wanted to carry out. He remembered hearing a story from the end of the war, that when the Nazis abandoned Paris, undetonated explosives were discovered at Notre Dame.

When it came to the crunch, the soldier assigned the task of setting off the bombs couldn't bring himself to destroy such works of history.

Taking a deep breath, he composed himself, preparing for the moment that would follow.

Unlike those during the war, he knew he wouldn't fail.

Rawlins and Pugh had reached the main entrance to St Giles; on Pentland's instructions they'd proceeded back down the Mile.

They found him on the west side, his phone in hand. "The painting was in the gallery, exactly as the director in England suggested." He showed them a photo taken on his satphone, the UV outlines showing up beneath the artwork.

Rawlins addressed him first. "Looks like the Mile."

Pentland nodded. "You were right about the Vaults. Only thing you missed was the final location." He pointed to the various entrances concealed within the painting. "All five fires have started at the same places. That only leaves two."

Pugh nodded as Pentland pointed to the remaining two; the reality wasn't lost on learning what would follow. "Just like in London."

"Come on." Pentland led the way towards Mary King's Close. "If we're not quick, this place could be gone within minutes!"

90

The Inner Ward, 02:53

Blanco watched proceedings intently as the two silhouetted figures came quickly into focus on the screens. Like most older parts of the Tower at night, light was almost non-existent, the ghostly outlines of the duo's presence given off by a combination of natural light filtering in through the medieval windows and anything artificial carried, or worn, about their person. Once more he was able to detect soft green and purple hues glowing from around their eyes, confirming his earlier suspicion that they were in possession of specialist equipment to aid their night vision.

They had entered the foundations of the Bell Tower, which was bad news for many reasons. Although that tower was technically separate from the old lieutenant's lodgings that had once existed on the site of the Queen's House, in actuality the two were adjoined. Worse still, the entrance to More's chamber was also in the Bell Tower.

Blanco placed his HT to his lips, his eyes never leaving the screens. "Come in, Queen's House."

He got a response immediately; the CCTV footage confirmed the recipient was standing close to the main entrance.

"Get everyone to the Bell Tower. The Englishman has been spotted."

Mike followed Emily through the subterranean passages below the Bell Tower, doing his best to keep to the shadows. As the light went, his night visions once again becoming an essential tool, he focused on the surrounding walls, looking for any clues as to their destination. Judging from the Norman foundations, it was clear he was dealing with one of the oldest areas of the Tower.

Emily had already told him the Bell Tower had been the first part of the Tower to be built following the White Tower.

"Where are we heading?" he asked, inspecting the gaps between each archway as he passed. It was unclear from the outlines whether he was looking at foundation stones, an area that could once have been a prison or, perhaps, both.

"The Queen's House was built on the medieval foundations of the old lieutenant's lodgings," Emily said, not willing to waste time. "How's your leg?"

Mike had been trying not to think about it. "Peachy. Just so I'm prepared, what are we going to come to?"

"You honestly asking me that?" She looked at him through her purple lenses, doing her best to dismiss any nerves from her mind. "More's prison should be directly above us. We won't have to enter the main part of the Queen's House yet."

Mike bit down on his lower lip. "Let's hope they don't either."

Blanco continued to monitor the screens as the shaven-headed gunman left his position by the main doors, heading firstly into the lounge and, secondly, the dining room. Over the coming seconds, Blanco saw no less than eight gunmen leaving the Queen's House, taking the underground passage below the Bell Tower.

Despite being rarely open to the public, he was pleased to see the area wasn't totally devoid of cameras.

The intruders were making their way along the main passageway; he could tell from the layout that they were fast approaching More's prison. As the seconds passed, he saw movement on the nearby screens was getting faster, a conflict imminent.

Without warning a sudden blaze of yellow flooded across three of the screens.

"Get down!"

Mike grabbed Emily's midriff and fell sharply to his left, crashing hard on to the floor. He felt a sudden twinge go up from his left thigh; the pain had escalated from a dull throb to the intense, stabbing sensation of a sharp needle. He felt Emily come down on top of him, partially breaking her fall. He heard her mutter, "Thanks for that."

The yellow flash came almost immediately; he hadn't seen it until after he'd made the dive. The decision had been instantaneous, based solely on sound rather than sight.

Rising slowly against the nearest stone pillar, he muttered, "Thanks, Phil."

"Don't mention it." Phil's attention had moved from St Paul's to the Bell Tower; Maria's remained on the former. "Looks like you've got eight of the bastards blocking your way."

"Story of my life." Mike saw further yellow flashes appear from the far end, followed by several more. Amidst the constant eruptions, he sensed panic in the air, nervous shouting, as though whatever happened next would define their futures.

He guessed Blanco was watching.

"Stay back!" He gestured to his left, shielded by the pillar, Emily now directly behind him. He brought the Heckler level with his eye line and held the trigger till the magazine was empty.

He rued not having any more bullets.

"Give me your gun." He traded weapons with Emily, concerned shortage of ammunition was becoming a problem. He guessed from recent sounds he'd possibly dispatched two with his latest volley.

The last thing he wanted was to rely on his pistol.

He fired between the archways, aiming wherever he saw movement. In the brief, random illumination of yellow light, he saw a further two figures hit the floor. Whoever remained had retreated slightly.

Nevertheless, the gunfire continued.

He removed another grenade from his belt; immediately he felt a hand on his wrist.

"Are you crazy? You could bring this whole thing crashing down."

Immediately he realised she was right. "You got any better ideas?"

"Just one."

He followed her around the other side of the pillar, moving on quickly to the next. The layout, he realised, was strangely ecclesiastical, the pillars forming Romanesque arches where they joined. Removing a smokescreen from his belt, he tossed it into the main aisle; gunfire followed immediately.

Sticking to the walls, he fired where he saw the latest light from the gunmen's shots, dispatching two for sure. As the gunfire continued, he moved rapidly from pillar to pillar, taking shelter behind each one.

He stopped, holding his breath.

"How are we doing, Phil?" The words were forced out of his mouth, the air almost trapped in his windpipe. "What can you see up there?"

Phil had been able to see everything clearly. "Looks like one more bastard on the far side, currently hiding in the shadows. The rest are toast."

Mike exhaled, partially relieved. "One's sure better than two."

He crept round to his right, then left, his eyes staring into the darkness.

A sudden burst of yellow caught him unawares.

He dived to his right, again hitting the floor. His skin felt warm on his right side; thankfully it was just a graze. As the seconds passed, the gunfire resumed; he felt it pass just over his head. Guided by his instincts, he moved till he collided with the nearest pillar; sparks burned his skin.

Stopping suddenly.

Emily appeared through the empty darkness. "Come on!" She offered her hand; Mike was confused.

"Stay down!"

He heard laughter in his right ear. "That curator of yours is more than just a pretty face, Honey Badger."

Mike raised an eyebrow, noticing the gunfire seemed to have permanently ceased. "You're telling me this now?"

Phil's laughter carried clearly. "Hey, if she does get fired, we might even have a job for her."

He looked up at Emily, her night visions now absent; in the grisly conditions her hair had become flat, the earlier glossy sheen dulled by dust. She looked tired and emotionally drained.

But still cute.

"I'll be sure to pass on the message."

He ended the conversation; Emily stared at him. "What did he say about me getting fired?"

Mike laughed, his first for a while. The sudden flood of emotions joined with the dusty conditions forced him into a coughing fit; the pain in his thigh was simply horrendous.

He removed the water bottle he'd taken from the Hospital Block and poured it over his face, sharing some with Emily.

"You okay?"

He looked at her. "Trust me, we're both gonna be fine!" He accepted her hand and got back to his feet, moving as quickly as possible to where the gunfire had come from; it seemed every pillar hid something new.

"They dead?" she asked.

Mike shone his torch at each one, double-checking with the naked eye. "Sure as hell not alive." He looked at her. "Where are we heading?"

"Follow me."

Blanco had never felt so angry. It was as though the veins in his neck were in danger of popping, every last ounce of patience well and truly exhausted.

Randek had appeared alongside him, a venomous look on his face. "I will take care of him myself."

As he sought to leave, Blanco grabbed his arm. "Wait!" He looked his nephew in the eye, the hatchings of a plan continuing to form. "Bring me the historian."

They stopped on approaching the door to More's chamber, finding it slightly ajar. Two gunmen were keeping watch from the outside; Mike opened fire instantly.

Both fell to the floor.

The sound of gunfire had caused consternation behind the door, confirmation the hostages were definitely within. Stopping outside the door, Mike's eyes focused on the adjoining passageway. He realised he had finished off the last of the gunmen.

He nudged the door open, gun at the ready.

The shouts of consternation had become louder; he knew from his appearance that it wouldn't be obvious what side he was on. Entering, two gunmen had control over the room; gun raised, Mike ordered them to surrender, the clarity of his words echoing.

"Drop your weapons! Do it!"

Both obliged, raising their hands. Neither had been able to aim their guns in time.

Emily entered behind him, heading straight for the governor's wife. She hugged her tightly, allowing the woman to break down in tears against her chest. Within seconds, Emily had moved on to her daughter.

Mike continued to focus on the now unarmed gunmen, his eyes piercing with aggression as he watched them walk slowly towards the nearest wall. "Keep going. Hands on the wall. Backs to me. Move!"

Both obliged, taking up a position that had earlier been reserved solely for the hostages. As both men surrendered, Mike stepped forward, his eyes turning to Emily.

"Keep them covered."

He frisked them one at a time, removing a handheld transmitter; neither carried further weapons. Retreating, he eyed Emily, finding her gun raised; he could tell from the look in her eye she would no longer hesitate should the decision be required.

His eyes turned to the rest of the room. "Where's Professor Champion?" He realised to his horror his uncle was missing. "Has anyone seen Professor Champion?"

A voice echoed within the static interference, a quick command over the airwaves.

He realised instantly it was Blanco.

Blanco spoke into his HT a second time, the same words as before. If all was as it should be, there were still two gunmen in More's chamber; without CCTV footage, he couldn't see exactly what was happening.

He repeated the same words a third time, an instruction for the gunmen to reply. On the fourth occasion he named them.

"Wrong again, jackass!"

Blanco lowered his head, recognising the Englishman's voice from earlier. "Who is this?"

At the other end, Mike held the HT close to his lips. "I'll leave the introductions till later. Right now, all you need to know is that the Queen's House is once again under Her Majesty's command."

"I'm sure Her Majesty will be only too pleased to hear that. Who knows, if you make it out alive, you might even have the honour of receiving a personal thank you." Blanco allowed himself a smile. "Then again, it wouldn't be customary, would it, a servant being invited into the house of royalty?"

Mike raised his eyebrows, recalling his strange conversation with Blanco earlier that evening and the even stranger one with Everard six months earlier. "Rather than spoil the surprise, perhaps it would be more fun to leave this one to your imagination. In the meantime, let's talk about more practical matters. All of your men I've encountered so far are either dead or captured; thanks to their failings, I have over forty Yeoman Warders and Queen's Guards back in a job. Between you and me, I don't particularly rate your chances."

"Games of chance are really more of an English custom. In France, we tend to deal more with facts. Better yet, a true Frenchman will neglect to trouble himself with things that may or may not come to pass. There is a saying in my country: *c'est la vie*."

"Yes, there are a few in my country as well. Perhaps you'd like to hear one of my favourites. Where are the rest of the hostages?"

"As a man blessed by wealth and technology, I will spare you the insult of pretending I know nothing of what you speak. Think carefully, however. So far, the spilling of innocent blood has proven unnecessary. It would be a shame for such goodwill to be shattered so late on."

"Spoken by a man apparently oblivious to what's happening outside his very window!" Mike left More's chamber, entering the adjoining Queen's House. He found himself walking on Tudor-style floor boarding leading to a quaint living area that juxtaposed both original furnishings and modern technology. As Phil had already indicated, those who had been stationed there had been watching the news all night. The presenters were reporting gunfire in the streets. Civilian casualties. Further afield the armed police had been put out to combat potential riots.

"You've had your fun, Blanco; better yet, you might have even made your point. Finish this madness before the irreparable happens." Mike's eyes focused on live footage of St Paul's. The pictures confirmed that flames were approaching it from two sides.

He feared from what he'd learned earlier from Kit that the cathedral itself would soon be the subject of a direct attack.

"There are over three thousand people in the streets; your gunmen are losing the battle. Pretty soon you'll lose the war. It's time to bargain."

At the other end, Blanco let out a deliberate sigh. "What did you have in mind? A state pension? A desk job in the service? Or merely my choice of lead in the prison musical?"

"If it were up to me, any of the above. I do, however, have the authority to bring you in on my terms. Play straight with me now, perhaps we can talk face to face."

"What did you have in mind we talk about?"

"How about the release of the twenty-five hostages currently unaccounted for."

"What makes you so certain there are so many?"

"You're forgetting, I was on this tour myself. I count twenty-five missing. Including the lecturer."

"Ah, of course. The rogue schoolchild. How I admire him; perhaps in a way, you and I are not so unalike. You know, even back then I was more interested in what was happening in my uncle's wine cellar than I was learning about adverbs."

"A common predicament, I'm sure we can both agree." Mike saw the seconds tick closer to 03:00. "What say you, then?"

"Tempted as I am, I think I must pass. However, I'm sure before the evening ends our paths will cross."

"Even if you burn the rest of London to the ground, you can't leave here, with or without the jewels. Release the hostages."

"Perhaps you might humour me by choosing the first? Better yet, the last to die."

"What are you talking about?"

Alongside Blanco, Randek had returned. Along with one other.

Blanco eyeballed Champion. "I have with me a man I think you might recognise. He would rather like a word."

Mike held his breath as his heart pounded violently in his chest, taking his mind off the pain in his thigh. As the seconds passed, he felt an increasing tightness. Through the static he heard a voice speak, tired, frail.

Champion had avoided the temptation to name Mike directly.

Mike did the same. "Professor, are you okay?"

Blanco's face exploded with venom. "Perhaps it was foolish of me to believe a man such as yourself would be capable of anything beyond professional decorum. However, unfortunately that time has now passed. So far, loss of life has fortunately been unnecessary, but under the circumstances, things have changed. You said it yourself – time is ticking."

"Dammit, Blanco, you're surrounded on all sides. The location of the jewels is too well guarded; believe me, I'd give them to you myself if I could. End this now, this is madness."

"Madness it was that made this necessary in the first place. Madness was the actions of those who came before us who were too weak or perhaps just too naïve to understand. Madness built this country, this continent. Educated us in the ways that will guarantee our children's doom. This is not an end but the beginning."

"Continue with this and you won't leave this building alive."

"Perhaps so, perhaps not. No cause is without loss. Nor sacrifice. Thanks to you, the fate of the latest hostage is now decided."

The line went dead.

91

St Paul's Cathedral, 02:57

A great fireworks display would take place, and that it would culminate with a pure body of flame higher than St Paul's.

Blanco's words echoed in Kit's mind as he entered through the main doors and sprinted past the reception desk. The lights were on, something that he knew had occurred very recently; even when he'd arrived, the interior had been in darkness.

Though Atkins was no longer present, Kit knew the Deputy Director was still directing operations.

He led the way through the heart of the nave, grateful that the cathedral Wren built was far shorter than its predecessor. Though the 574-foot-long body from the portico of the great west door to the east end was far from small, the cathedral that had burned had been the third longest in Europe.

In the circumstances, Kit almost considered it a blessing.

A pure body of flame higher than St Paul's – similar words he now knew had been said before. The man responsible for the original statement had indeed been a fireworks maker; behind the closed doors of Whitehall he had been tried, convicted and executed. In hindsight, the actions of the king had been prudent; had the truth been made known, war with France might have been unavoidable. The fireworks maker had been sacrificed for the greater good.

So, ultimately, had the cathedral.

The cathedral at St Paul's was the fifth incarnation to have stood on Ludgate Hill. After both successors to the original had burned down in 962 and 1087, it had been the fourth one that the young Christopher Wren had been introduced to; indeed, the building had later inspired his crowning glory. Even prior to 1666 plans had been put forward for a dome to replace the spire that had been struck by lightning a century earlier. In its 1,400-year history it was a building plagued by fire.

A perfect place to hide a door to hell.

Kit raced through the heart of the nave, his footsteps echoing on the hard floor. Reaching the area directly beneath the dome, he gazed in awe at the incredible baroque architecture that surrounded him, intent on ascertaining the layout. The design had been produced in five stages; it was not till 1710 that the final stone was laid. What had once been intended as a rebuild for a depleted shell later gave way to something totally new. Whatever was left of the old cathedral had been recycled indiscriminately.

Kit knew little, if anything, survived of the charred remains.

Nat was first to join him under the dome, his eyes looking upwards to the heavens. As a regular tour guide, he knew as well as anyone that the dome had been an ingenious piece of architectural design where triple domes fitted inside each other like boxes within boxes. The steep core of brickwork was hidden on both sides by an outer shell, supported on a timber frame, and an inner dome that was decorated by eight monochrome paintings depicting the life of the famous disciple. Within the rotunda, he made out the first of its three famous galleries, surprised to find it busy with people.

He contacted Atkins via his headset. "This is Edward. I thought the cathedral had been evacuated."

Standing among the gardens, the Deputy Director responded immediately. "Evacuated of all except those who can't be spared."

"I don't follow."

"The dome of St Paul's is a complex structure; if the timber supports catch fire, we could have a firebomb on our hands capable of taking out half the city this side of the water," Atkins replied, satisfied to see the last remaining gunman had been taken down, the second van exploding amidst the onslaught of gunfire. "The job of fighting the fires is best left for those who know it best."

Kit recalled the story Atkins had taught him on joining the Harts: how the task of protecting the dome had been left to a loyal band of volunteer architects, affectionately known as the St Paul's Watch.

"Let's hope their expertise won't be necessary."

He waited for Gillian to catch them up before returning his thoughts to the present. Through the windows behind the altar, an ominous glow was becoming brighter.

He prayed the famously thick walls would hold.

"Which way to the crypt?"

Nat led them to a quiet area in the south-east corner, accessible through an open doorway flanked by several statues. A stairway ended at a narrow passageway below the cathedral. As the floor evened out, he saw a well-lit repository of plaques, keepsakes and other memorials, all presented in a catacombs-style layout located between a small side chapel and an area that was now a restaurant and gift shop.

Kit navigated the vaulted chamber, investigating the chapel through the gated entrance and immediately becoming sidetracked. Between the chapel and the gift shop, the imposing monuments of Wellington and Nelson rose above the patterned floor like ancient sarcophagi, the names standing out in eternal glory.

He saw no sign of the creator.

"Where's Wren's tomb?"

"East end, south aisle," Nat answered instinctively, taking him to a simple stone slab close to where they'd entered, surrounded by white walls and several plaques.

Kit looked down, discovering it to be surprisingly basic, raised slightly above those near it. He read the epitaph quickly, finding proof that it belonged to the architect.

"Funny, I always imagined his monument would be more spectacular."

Nat pointed to a plaque on the wall. "A point well made. In Latin it translates, *Reader, if you seek his monument – look around you.*"

Kit gazed at the writing, finding himself able to translate it. Looking around, he sensed a subtle rise in temperature; he put it down to his own stress levels more than anything more threatening.

"Keep your eyes peeled. The entrance could be anywhere."

He set off immediately, passing Nelson and Wellington, finding himself in the gift shop, the lights to which had now been extinguished. It was lonelier than he remembered it, haunting almost; the sound of their footfalls carried, as did voices.

He spoke into his headset, relieved he still had reception. "We've made it to the crypt. What were the layouts on the portrait?"

Maria examined the photos of the paintings Kit had earlier sent her. "The markings are definitely south-east of the nave. Judging from this, it could be near Wren's grave itself."

Kit returned to Wren's tomb, feeling its chilly exterior, taking in the words. Unlike the previous churches, the layout of the crypt was potentially ambiguous; he knew any leads might be false ones. As his watch bleeped the coming of the hour, he felt his heart miss a beat.

Be it externally or internally, he knew the fires were closing in all around him.

Atkins ended the conversation with Kit as the final van exploded. He exhaled with relief as he saw the flames go up, the sights and sounds inevitably causing further concern among the nearby crowds and convincing some of them to finally leave the area.

He found Sanders and Iqbal along New Change; Chambers and Dawson joined them from the south. Of the four, only Sanders had fresh injuries.

"What happened?"

"Relax. It's just a flesh wound." A bandage had already been strapped round his shoulder. "According to Maria, the vans were swapped over a few miles away; the first ones have been left abandoned near an area of rioting to the north. Apparently the helicopters and cabin cruisers might have brought some reinforcements. For now at least, I think that's all of them."

Atkins nodded, his attention taken by what he could see along New Change. A fire engine was travelling at high speed along Cannon Street, the latest of a number that had put out the fires around Monument and St Clement's.

At the top of the street, the police had retaken control.

"How many casualties?"

"Four, all of them coppers." Jay's words were filled with sympathy. "Unfortunately there were some civilians in there too."

"How many?"

"Possibly six."

Atkins grimaced. "Masterson has made it to the crypt; we've got volunteers patrolling the galleries." He looked up at the dome. Though the fires along Cheapside had spread, only a heavy wind could possibly endanger the roof.

"Let's just pray the wind remains in our favour."

Chambers was more concerned with the other side. "Even if that holds up, we've still got Ludgate to contend with."

Hurrying to the bottom of New Change, the four Harts joined the Deputy Director in a steady jog as he reached Cannon Street, hoping for a clear view into the distance. In both directions the fire continued to move closer, the smoke swirling ominously around the cathedral.

Even where they were standing, they could feel the heat on their bodies and the smoke in their lungs.

"The fires on King William are all out; the trucks will be with us in moments," Jay said. "Maybe it's time to bring the helicopters back."

Atkins agreed. "If they're able to get back in time. But maybe it's also time we took a leaf out of our predecessors' book."

Sanders was confused. "What's that?"

"Tear some of these obstacles down."

High above the city, the Director of the White Hart looked down at the developing inferno either side of the famous dome. There was something about the view that just didn't seem real, as though he were reliving a moment from the past or perhaps obtaining a glimpse of one from the distant future. Both east and west, the fires were growing in strength; the smoke and colour gave the cathedral a strange aura, as though it were itself rising out of the pits of hell.

If the pattern remained unchecked, he knew it would soon be incinerated.

He heard Atkins' voice come through urgently, the request equally clear. Like most of the man's requests, the words were sensible.

"Put her down where you can." The Director avoided the temptation to request a return to Whitehall. Ending his short conversation with the pilot, he accepted the Deputy Director's suggestion, quietly confident it would achieve the desired result.

Not for the first time in his tenure, he was confident he'd made the correct appointment.

In the voids beneath the cathedral, the silhouetted figure heard a melodious bleep from his wristwatch, confirming the hour had come. The green light of the LED symbols aside, visibility was limited; of all the locations he had visited that night, this was the darkest.

The previous onset of fires had come later than usual on the last occasion; the one time tonight Blanco had been off schedule. He knew that in their world snap decisions were sometimes needed, compromises had to be made; every eventuality had been discussed and considered in depth during the preceding months.

HT reception at the other locations had been clear enough to allow operational communication, but here it was unreliable. He knew from his research the fact could be blamed on the geography, indirectly the fault of the previous fire. Due to the condition of the foundations after the lead from the original roof had melted, it had been impossible to build again without a thorough excavation. He had to hand it to the architect.

He really had thought of everything.

Standing in the heart of the old ruins, he again checked his watch, wondering what Blanco was thinking.

With no way to seek instructions, he had to make the decision himself.

While the black vans burned to shells on Cheapside, the final survivor of the original attack made his way east on foot, passing Bank Tube station.

Unlike the places he'd been through recently, this one had so far evaded destruction.

Avoiding the glances of those piloting passing fire trucks, he continued south, heading to his final destination.

92

The Queen's House,
02:57

Mike left the lounge the moment Blanco's voice went dead, and dashed along the hallway, heading for the front door. He opened it without hesitation and took the first step across the concreted area outside, heading slightly right of Tower Green towards the White Tower.

Within seconds, sparks of muffled gunfire illuminated the area, the impact knocking him off balance, causing his knee to buckle and the pressure on his wound to extend deeper into his leg. Stumbling, he somehow managed to keep his feet, making a turn, lunging for the door. He heard voices nearby: Emily; others further away, speaking in French.

Clearly Blanco had left the Waterloo Barracks.

Emily had followed him all the way to the door, leaving seconds later. She saw a posse of armed gunmen approaching from the north, halfway between the barracks and the White Tower. The barrels of their weapons became lit up in a collective yellow blaze; the only sounds came from their mouths.

On seeing the sparks and Mike falling in front of her, she reached out for his hand, grabbing it, pulling hard.

On returning inside, the door closed behind them.

Emily came down hard on top of him and rolled on to the hard oak flooring, remembering for the first time in recent minutes that she'd acquired her own share of injuries that night. As she caught her breath, she realised Mike was struggling, yet somehow managed to return to his feet.

Outside, gunshots continued to be targeted on the cottage-style façade.

"Just calm down!" She dragged him back to the ground, coming down on top of him.

Mike's face was red with anger, his eyes oozing venom that she had not previously seen that evening.

"You getting killed isn't going to help anyone. If Champion has any chance, he's going to need you fully functioning." She pushed him down, placing her hands to his face. "Will you listen to me?"

He heard the words clearly, more so than before. His heart was racing, fresh air flowing; the pain in his thigh had become increasingly unbearable. It was like being back at training, yet somehow the intense fatigue seemed insignificant by comparison.

He felt as though his entire leg was seizing up.

"Mike?"

He looked at her: her eyes, her face, the dishevelled hair that had been perfect not five hours earlier. It was the same face he'd once known, spoken to, secretly fancied.

Now he heard the voice of common sense.

"I can't just leave him."

"No one's asking you to." She turned her stern gaze to the area outside the window. She saw movement on the south lawn, approaching the main steps to the White Tower.

Without warning, further sparks appeared close to the glass.

Instinctively she hit the floor.

Mike scrambled to the nearby stairway, climbing it one step at a time. He spoke into his headset as he regained his footing, stopping by a small original window on the landing.

"Phil, we're in the Queen's House. They've got Champion."

Seated side by side, Maria and Phil took a collective breath. "I see him, Honey Badger. They're currently entering the White Tower. Same way as before."

Tentatively, Mike rose to eye level with the window and stared out across the lawn. There was movement on the White Tower stairway, others on the lawn. Randek had reached the ravens' cages; four of the gunmen patrolled the green area.

"How's he looking?"

Phil concentrated on the satellite footage. "Looks okay from here; the other twenty-four are still in the same place. So far Blanco has yet to kill anybody."

"Let's hope it stays that way." Mike saw Emily appear beside him, peering out through the next window. "What are my chances of getting up there with him?"

"You want the honest answer?"

"Actually I was kinda hoping you were gonna tell me what I wanted to hear."

Blanco watched from the relative security of the entrance to the White Tower as Randek crossed the south lawn, carrying one of the three surviving ravens. He had been hoping to allow the Ravenmaster the honour of once again participating in the event that would follow, but under the circumstances that wasn't presently possible.

He waited till Randek joined him before entering the White Tower. Champion followed, escorted by four gunmen. A further four remaining on the green, along with those already in the White Tower and the four occupying the barracks, now made up his entire force.

He contacted the White Tower via his HT. "Robert, do you copy?"

On the second floor of the White Tower, the leader of the four gunmen answered, "*Oui.*"

"Pick five hostages and join me on the roof. We will be with you in under one minute."

Alone in the office off the second-floor corridor of the barracks, François finally saw the light. The images he had been studying almost constantly for the last six months, currently laid before him in photocopy form, now made perfect sense. Sir Walter Raleigh had been a genius in many ways, not to mention a generous one.

Even in death he continued to impart his wisdom to the believers.

Grabbing his HT, he contacted Blanco. "We've had a development."

Blanco responded quickly. "Later. It's time for the transmission."

On this occasion François refused to let the rebuke bother him. "Perhaps you might pass on a message and tell the PM I have discovered the location of the jewels and plan to enter the vault with or without her cooperation."

Blanco's face broke into a smile. "I will be glad to tell her personally."

"Randek and Blanco have just disappeared inside." Phil watched the pictures as they appeared live, relaying what he saw to Mike. "Something tells me they didn't exactly leave it unlocked."

Mike stared again through the window, finding the wooden stairs deserted. Four gunmen still guarded the lawn, their Heckler & Kochs aimed at the windows and doors.

Without warning, one of the nearby panes of glass shattered.

Mike removed the grenade he'd saved in the Bell Tower and tossed it through the window, no longer concerned about what damage it might cause. As the pear-shaped explosive did its job, he expelled what remained of the shattered glass from the broken pane and fired rapidly across Tower Green. Two further bodies hit the ground; the others started to scatter.

"I'm really gonna need a plan here, Phil; Maria, you listening?"

"What else would I be doing?"

He avoided the temptation to say 'not listening'. "Two gunmen are down; if I leave now, I think I can make it. Only problem is running across the uneven ground and stairs."

"How's the injury holding up?"

"Bandage is fine; leakage is minor." He groaned, quietly praying the time would come when he would be lying in a hospital bed. "I don't think I can take the stairs. Least not in time."

"How you fancy a different tactic?" Phil posed. "One from your training?"

Mike instantly twigged what he had in mind. "Let's do it!"

93

Charlestown,
Twenty-One Months Earlier

School reconvened at 08:30, first thing after breakfast. Kit again led the parade; the remaining Harts watched on through light rain.

Kit walked the parade ground confidently before coming to a standstill. "How have you enjoyed your first week at school?"

Mike hid a smile by biting his lip. After two weeks in Masterson's company, the loaded questions were no longer a surprise.

"It's been educational, sir."

Some of the Harts did smile.

"Take a look around you. Soak it in for a moment. These walls are old. They have seen much, educated the best. These walls will be here far longer than us." He marched smartly, his eyes switching between Mike and the wet ground. "Here, school is just like any other. We begin Monday and end Friday. Sometimes we go in Saturday; however, there can often be time off for good behaviour."

This was it, Mike thought. At last, the killer requirement was inevitable.

"Yesterday we set you a task. Today, you will repeat it. School is all about repetition. It is the mother of all skill. The woods you ran yesterday were dry. Today they are slippery. Even a slight drizzle can add an extra two kilograms to your kit. Do not underestimate the power of the water." Kit looked at him, a steely expression in his eyes. "Any further questions?"

"No, sir."

"In that case, you may begin."

The journey to the final checkpoint took almost exactly twenty minutes, a decent showing, he considered. The final surprise now awaited him.

He looked at it, shell-shocked.

Beyond the last perimeter of the area of greenery, strong outer curtain walls rose out of the ground like a medieval citadel. Behind them, a tall, imposing keep could be seen above thick battlements, its glass windows looking out like gigantic eyes maintaining perpetual surveillance of the surrounding countryside. A solitary flag flew high above the roof, its fabric folding and unfolding erratically as it caught the rain-soaked breeze. Mike focused on the patterns; its designs were similar to those he'd seen at the camp at the beginning of the week.

On closer examination, he also recognised the walls.

The outer curtain walls were surrounded by a moat; it was semi dry, clearly drained but susceptible to collecting rainwater. What remained in it at present had become stagnant, giving out an unappealing stench. There was evidence of dead insects floating on the top; more inevitably lay beneath the surface. There was no lowered drawbridge from the barbican; it was unclear from the outside whether it was ever opened, even if it was genuine.

Mike sensed he was looking at a trap.

He circled the castle once, keeping to the shrubbery where possible. As often before in his training, he felt exposed, that the eyes of his enemies were on him. The only way inside was an arched wooden door on the west side, rugged, dilapidated, clearly the postern. A sign had been placed over the heart of the wooden exterior, seven simple words.

ABANDON ALL HOPE YOU WHO ENTER HERE

Mike approached it cautiously, taking care not to lose his footing as he negotiated a dry path through the moat. The door moved with difficulty. As the last opportunity to turn back passed, he ignored the warning and entered.

Once inside he stopped.

Looked around.

Wondered.

There was something about what happened next that simply refused to compute. After the episode at Windsor, he was aware that appearances weren't always what they seemed; after a fortnight in the company of the White Hart, he expected the unexpected.

Nevertheless, the actuality of his new situation, even after everything he'd been through, he never believed could be possible. Sure enough, behind the strange door was a great many other equally strange things, all accessible across what appeared to be a medieval courtyard.

Unlike the parts of the castle he'd already seen, this area appeared more authentic; surely too old to be a folly. The inner walls displayed evidence of disrepair; there were huge cracks in the stonework, indicating they'd either been adversely affected by neglect and long-term exposure to the elements or damaged by military action at some time in its history. There were no information points or eye-catching billboards like those typically seen at tourist sites; in fact the only modern additions seemed to be those currently about his person. The layout was symmetrical. That was when he noticed the keep's true area of significance.

Like the lost tower at Windsor, its design was round.

And it was presently under armed guard.

Kit was waiting alongside Sanders, his arms folded, his gaze firm. Their modern appearance was out of keeping with the medieval surroundings.

"You might remember I warned you earlier today about taking things at face value. Clearly you didn't take my advice."

Mike approached cautiously, still sensing he was walking into a trap.

"Captain Chambers gave me the checkpoint, sir; said it would be my final challenge." He thought back to the warning sign outside. "Besides, I figured the sign was only advisory."

He looked up at the surrounding walls, reminding himself of what he knew of England's history and what he had seen at Windsor. Three days earlier, he'd taken a history class.

The signs pointed to Arthurian legend.

"I don't believe it. Camelot?"

Sanders smiled. "Be careful what you choose to believe, Lieutenant. There's still much you don't yet know about our world."

Mike nodded; clear in his mind the castle was too modern for any connection with an historical King Arthur.

"The Round Tower. It's just like at Windsor. Only above ground."

"You seem insistent on reciting useless facts. Perhaps if things fail to work out, you could retrain as a tour guide. What we have here is called the Accumulator." Kit spoke of the strange building behind him. "Legend has it that when the original knights of Camelot were brought together for the first time, the king and his wizard designed a challenge that only the wisest and strongest could ever hope to conquer. Only twelve ever passed."

Mike raised an eyebrow. "So you're telling me Camelot was real now?"

Kit's gaze was stern. "Whether it was or was not, what you see before you was created post-Restoration. Tradition has it it's based on old designs. But I digress. The reason you're here is for the ultimate challenge. In here, your strength will be tested to the utmost. Next, it's about skill and intelligence. Finally, the true test will be one of will. I will give you one piece of advice only. When you're going through hell, you must keep going."

Mike stared hard at Kit for a long time before turning his gaze to Sanders. Behind his beard, the Hampshire-born former SBS sniper gave nothing away.

"There is no time limit. Nor will you receive any assistance. This is your final chance to turn back. If you do enter, just remember one thing. There is more than one layer to hell. Good luck."

Kit blew his whistle.

And disappeared with Sanders across the courtyard.

There was a moment when Mike was genuinely unsure what to do next. Ever since his arrival in this strange part of England, if indeed it was still England, there was only one thing he'd been sure of – eventually it would end and he would emerge victorious. Even in the cold waters, the chilly caves, the endless runs that seemed designed only to torment, he knew the light at the end of the tunnel would eventually illuminate the way. Even if things reached a serious point, he was never in physical danger.

Suddenly he felt danger. Even if it was an illusion, it seemed totally real. Masterson had succeeded.

He was closing in on the breaking point.

He took a deep breath and looked around. It was quiet everywhere, disturbingly so. Moments earlier, the sound of the woodland had been loud, comforting, like taking a run through merriest England. The rummaging among the foliage seemed distant now, the birds no longer singing. Even the skies above seemed bizarrely ominous; whatever flew above him seemed to circle the haze in a menacing fashion. He recognised shapes: ravens, perhaps crows.

Everything about them signalled his doom.

He had one decision to make, continue or turn back. To turn back meant defeat; the only logical reason was fear. Fear was the key – the SEALs had lectured him on it for what seemed like hours. Radchenko had taught him he had no idea what hell even looked like. The only way to overcome fear was to embrace it. The quote he associated with Churchill. It had helped win a war. Perhaps many. That was it, he'd decided.

He'd enter.

94

The Queen's House, 02:58

The captain of the Queen's Guard looked both ways before leaving the Queen's House, sprinting in the direction of the White Tower. He darted to his right on reaching the lawn, taking the wooden steps to the main entrance.

Pushing and pulling against the door, he found it locked.

He turned to face the Queen's House, shaking his head.

Mike didn't need a transmitter to be able to understand the message. Though the two remaining gunmen had disappeared, almost certainly regrouping inside the barracks, Blanco had left nothing to chance.

Even blowing the door wouldn't help.

In his mind Mike recalled another memory from his training, one Kit called the Accumulator. The situation had been similar, the tower round instead of square. The objective was exactly the same.

Entry.

Emily checked her watch, becoming ever more frantic. "We've only got two minutes before the video will be sent; even fully fit, you'd be pushing it."

Mike nodded, aware of the time. He had only one shot.

It had to be perfect.

"What's the quickest way on to the roof?"

"What?"

"Don't question it, just answer."

"The loft is on the top floor. You can get out through the windows."

"Show me."

She led Mike up two further flights of narrow stairs, culminating in a loft area with cramped rooms and low ceilings. She led him across the uneven flooring, the floorboards creaking and moving as they took their weight. She stopped on reaching a window and opened it.

Slowly she climbed out.

Mike took her hand, glad of her help. Once outside, he found himself standing on a tiled roof, the slope forty-five degrees in two directions.

Almost immediately he lost his footing.

"Careful." Emily reached out for him, clearly the more balanced of the two. The temperature was still warm, but the wind had picked up; even the slightest breeze could now potentially upset their balance.

Mike looked north-east to the famous Norman citadel that had survived unscathed for almost 1,000 years. He estimated the gap to be at least 100 metres in length, more still in height. He knew his capabilities would be pushed to the utmost.

Emily gazed at him, suddenly confused. "What exactly are you intending to do?"

The keep contained two doors on the ground floor, both of which were locked. After circling it once, his newfound loneliness was unexpectedly broken. A figure was standing before him, his hands placed deep in a thick leather jacket.

Unlike Masterson and Sanders, this man was not of military experience.

"If you're to successfully scale the tower, you'll be needing this." Phil removed something from his right pocket, handing it to Mike. On inspecting it for the first time, Mike saw it was a small pocket gun.

Opening the gun chamber, he discovered its true purpose.

He looked quizzically at Phil. "You're being serious?"

"What we're talking here is approximately twenty-seven metres elevation, perhaps thirty trajectory to get you a good angle." He gestured to the medieval walls with his free hand. "Now pay attention, as this is the one thing you need to do flawlessly."

"Only one, huh?"

"Failure to hit your target and this will recoil automatically; however, make a mistake, you'll need an instant detachment. You do this by firing again." He gestured to the trigger. "Once a successful attachment is made, you'll learn its best feature." He pointed out the side clips. "Now, unlike your experience with Colonel Radchenko, there's no safety net here. However, use this properly, you'll never need one. Just fire the gun and let it do the work."

"Let it do the work." Mike turned his attention to the roof of the keep. It suddenly felt a long way up. "You're serious?"

"Aim just beyond the nearest turret. You can set the sights with this." He clicked a small button on the side, activating a scope from within the body. He looked through it, seeing the walls become magnified, the centre designated by a large X.

It reminded him of a sniper rifle.

"Hold it like this." Phil gestured for both hands to be placed together, gripping the gun on either side. "Push down slowly. Just like squeezing a lemon."

Push down slowly, Mike thought, just like squeezing a lemon. *Aiming through the scope, he directed the X to where Phil had recommended, extending his arms. Breathing in slowly, he exhaled deeply.*

He pressed the trigger, sensing the chamber had become lighter. A large coil ejaculated, the end disappearing over the battlements. As it became attached to something immoveable, he felt heavy ties encircle his wrists like handcuffs.

Next thing he knew he was airborne.

Mike reached deep into the right pocket of his belt, finding what he was looking for. The gun was smaller than he remembered, at least compared to the Heckler & Koch. The surface was smooth on both sides, the scope intact. He raised it level with his eye line; focusing on the White Tower was difficult, so great was the surrounding light. Adjusting the sights, he concentrated on the four turrets. The nearest was located at the south-west corner, one of the three that were square rather than round.

He estimated the distance to be approximately 100 metres. Perhaps another ten in height.

He knew further pain was unavoidable.

Emily realised what he was holding. "You're not seriously thinking of doing what I think you're doing, are you?"

"It's a little late for turning back now."

Emily's jaw dropped as she realised why he had gone up to the roof. "Are you crazy? Making it even with careful planning would be hit-and-miss. You're acting on impulse with a bullet in your leg."

Mike smiled, anything to psych himself up. He knew he had only seconds to make the call. With the X aimed beyond the nearest turret, he considered squeezing the trigger.

Pausing, he looked away.

"The Queen's Guard are now back in control. So are the Yeoman Warders. Stick with them. If you can, contact my HQ – it's the same number I showed you. Whatever you do, don't tell anyone else. Promise me."

Emily looked at him, now with deep concern. "But?"

"Promise me, Emily. Even if I had time, I couldn't go into detail." He looked her up and down, focusing on her face. Beyond the fear, he saw strength.

Perhaps love.

"For the first time tonight, we have the upper hand, but this can only end with Blanco and Randek gone. If I get this right, they could be eliminated in seconds."

"Get it wrong, you're gonna need wings."

He laughed, knowing the moment of their parting was at hand. Looking again through the scope, he prepared to fire, confident the line would carry him to his target, provided that the hook attached properly.

"As soon as you can, I want you to get out of here. I'll take care of the hostages; if I fail, you'll have support very soon."

Attempting to reply, Emily felt the words choke in her throat. As Mike sought to fire, she grabbed him.

"Wait!"

He felt her warm lips move bashfully against his, her hands gripping the back of his head, her tense body rising and falling against his. Briefly he forgot about his physical pain, losing himself in the moment. It was different to the others he'd kissed, the others he'd been with.

Only now wasn't the time to enjoy it.

As their lips parted, he saw the fear in her eyes had returned, the love somehow stronger. In less than six hours, he knew the complexion of her life had changed; never could it be the same again. Pressing the trigger, he saw her face before him, then vanish in a blaze of light. Over the coming seconds, he saw the light change several times, his view becoming obscured by the speed of his movement through the air. The White Tower was getting nearer, the Queen's House now a vortex of fast-moving light. Whatever was on the roof behind him was out of focus, but instinctively he knew she was still there.

And that somehow he would find his way back to her.

95

Central London, 02:59

The Director watched from the skies as the pilot of the helicopter plotted their landing. With the fires on both sides moving ever nearer, an attempt to land close by would be a risk not worth taking. With the churchyard off-limits and everything west of Ludgate in flames, the only realistic place to put down was closer to the river.

After the incident with the rocket launcher, it potentially opened up the greatest likelihood of exposure.

He heard a recurring bleeping sound on his portable tablet, an incoming message: Maria.

He answered.

"Sir, the PM is on the line. Wants to speak with you now."

"Put her through."

The Director watched as the image changed from Maria's face against the backdrop of the Rook to that of the PM still seated inside COBRA.

If Blanco continued on schedule, less than a minute remained before he was due to transmit.

"You're aware of the time no doubt, Director, so for now let's make this brief. I shall not witness one of England's finest landmarks fall this hour."

Fully aware of the scenes beneath him, the Director kept his eyes on the screen. "The identity of the terrorists is now known to us. Though their organisation has evolved in the modern day, as previously believed, its existence goes back much further. All the key players believe themselves to be of royal lineage, and not just in France. The event in 1666 can no longer be considered an accident. It seems that tonight the past is catching up with us."

"I've told you once before, Director, tonight my only concern is with the present. If Monsieur Blanco were the son of the president, it would make no difference." She stared at him with a cold, penetrating look. "What's happening at St Paul's?"

"All of the gunmen have been neutralised; sadly there were also unavoidable civilian casualties. The fires on Cheapside and Fleet Street are currently being combated; if necessary, preparation is in place to take down buildings. I've also spoken to my colleagues in the RAF. The Bambis are on their way back; they'll be here in under five minutes."

"What of the cathedral itself?"

"The building is currently under lockdown, inside and out. I've got men in the crypt; others are patrolling the outer galleries. If any fires are started from within, they won't last long."

"I wish I shared your optimism, Director; unfortunately tonight, fortune has not been kind to us."

"The alternative has been in plain sight all evening, Prime Minister. Unless the Tower is retaken, I fear Blanco will not hesitate to carry out his threats."

"You know my views on negotiating with terrorists, Director."

The Director frowned, the memory of his recent conversation with Tinniswood still fresh in his mind. "The location of the jewels has recently become known to me." The coldness of his own gaze now matched that of the PM's. "Time is very much against us. Neither of us want to wake up tomorrow to find that what is left of our city has been reduced to ashes. It's time to make the call."

The PM's response was calm, calculated. "You're not the only person capable of making phone calls, Director. Having spoken with Her Majesty, she acknowledges if the terrorists aren't apprehended within the next hour, there may be no choice but to surrender the jewels. The fires will eventually burn out; what's been lost will be rebuilt." She took a deep breath, exhaling with a sigh. "Whatever happens, the Tower and the cathedral must not fall."

The Director nodded, his face for once failing to hide his personal torment. The fate of the city was worth far more than mere jewellery, even that which represented the most famous institution in the world. Yet despite his agreement, his anger was rising. He was paid to lead the best; tonight they had already excelled. The youngest was in an excellent position to strike the enemy.

He just wished they had more time.

Blanco emerged first through the door that led out on to the roof of the White Tower, and headed along the walkway to the west wall. The fires had spread since he'd last looked; a wall of flames now closed the route between all of the areas level with London Bridge and Blackfriars. Beyond Mary-le-Bow, the dome of the cathedral was draped in an ominous shadow, its façade obscured by flame. The image was strange, unique but not entirely unfamiliar. Looking through the nearby flames, against the lighted, yet smoky backdrop, it was as though two of history's famous pictures had become merged. Both had captured iconic moments in history.

Now he sensed he was about to witness a third.

Randek joined him, peering out over the parapets; behind them, several more people were present. Looking to his right, he saw the tired frame of the man he now knew as Professor Champion, one of six hostages who feared their time was almost up. Of the six, he noticed Champion carried himself best; his eyes were dry, his natural demeanour, he sensed, loath to succumb to melancholy or self-pity.

In different circumstances he might have respected him.

"When the great city was destroyed at the end of that hot seventeenth-century summer, it took a man of special genius to rebuild what had been lost. The architect, in many ways, was himself a phoenix – a man who had known many beginnings and ends." Blanco turned to face the hostages, his focus particularly on Champion. "Who, I wonder, will take on the task of rebuilding what has tonight been lost?"

Choking back his urge to reply, Champion remained quiet. From his recent conversation with his nephew, he knew no hostages had yet been harmed.

He prayed that wasn't about to change.

"In a few minutes, we will see the grand finale; at least, the last you will see." He moved ever closer. "Who, I wonder, will be the first to volunteer?"

Champion recognised the Calais reference.

Blanco smiled. "As you wish. We will leave that decision to another."

Leaving the office in the Waterloo Block, François hurried down the stairs, heading into the heart of the Jewel House. Ignoring the display cases that still contained their exhibits, he hurried through the crown room, taking the stairway below ground level.

Once more that evening, he found himself in the jeweller's workshop.

The photocopied diagram confirmed the passage existed on the north side, beginning in the heart of what had once been storehouses. By 1688 the buildings had been destroyed and construction of the new storehouse begun.

In time that too had been replaced by the barracks.

Exploring the room, he continued to the east side, using the GPS on his phone for bearings. He remembered seeing something earlier that night, located beyond the workstation. It was dark with the lights off; not knowing the location of the switch, he activated the flashlight feature on his phone.

Continuing, he headed for the wall, attempting to find anything that revealed the location of the tunnel entrance. Quickly he discovered that the original walled surroundings led to a doorway; unsurprisingly he found it to be locked. Retrieving the keys that had been taken from the Jeweller, he tried them in the lock, eventually finding the correct one. Opening the door, discovering another black void thickly filled with cobwebs, he ventured forward, shining his light in every direction. He had entered some kind of vault, possibly the start of a tunnel.

Judging by its condition, it hadn't been used in recent years.

Holding his breath to block out the musty smell, he edged his way in the direction of a small circular shaft of light that he could see in the distance, a light that would reveal the Tower's greatest secret yet.

Possibly the greatest secret he had ever uncovered.

The PM waited until the hour was on them before abruptly ending the conversation with the Director. They'd both agreed they would reconvene shortly; as before, she knew Mr White would be watching.

The PM saw the pictures change the moment the clock struck 03:00. From the familiar position on the roof of the White Tower, she saw the instantly recognisable skyline to the west becoming rapidly enveloped in the constant pall of smoke now blocking out the usual glow of artificial street and building lights.

The view centred on what remained of Cannon Street where, whether by luck or design, the fires had seemingly split in two. Beyond that street, the familiar dome of St Paul's rose magnificently above the burning rubble, its famous features partially obscured by the distorting heat waves of the distant fires.

Concentrating, she realised to her relief the appearance of the burning cathedral was just an illusion.

The focus changed, the view returning east where Blanco himself was standing. For the fifth time that evening she found herself looking deep into his dark-brown eyes, eyes that seemed to have an almost hypnotic effect as they looked back into hers.

"At the end of that hot summer of 1666, it was reported in the parliamentary inquiry that the fireworks maker to the king had been frustrated in his attempts to bring in new supplies of pasteboard, materials that he needed within the week if they were to be of any use to him. When asked of the need, he replied that he planned a great display that would illuminate St Paul's. Little did those he spoke to at the time understand the full extent of his intentions."

Watching from different places, both the PM and the Director of the White Hart felt a sudden twinge of anticipation on hearing Blanco repeat words he'd said four hours earlier; words that were historically attributed to Monsieur Belland.

Having spoken to Mike and Tinniswood, the Director no longer doubted he was listening to the disciple of the man responsible for the Great Fire.

A true Son of Gemini.

Blanco stared closely into the lens, so much so that features that had not been clearly visible before were now for the first time. The man's nose was slightly crooked, indication perhaps of a past break. There were scars on both cheeks, more so the right, further evidence of an eventful past. Yet behind both they saw certainty, the firm beliefs of a man intent on carrying out his purpose.

"Prime Minister, time is passing. In only a few moments, a fireworks display like no other will commence; so great will it be that St Paul's will inevitably be consumed in flames for the second time. The hour is upon us. After which only two ravens shall remain."

"You honestly believe killing a few birds will make the slightest difference?" Concentrating hard on the screen, the PM feared herself beginning to show weakness. She realised the answer to the problem had already been given to her by the Director of the White Hart. "The city itself will be rebuilt; whenever crisis hits, opportunity beckons. Sadly for you, I fear your own end will be much more gruesome."

Blanco laughed wryly. "My dear, it appears I overestimated you. I warned you earlier this evening that it is unwise to try my patience. When the night began, I told you of my willingness to show clemency. Now, alas, the time for that has passed."

The PM leaned forward as she saw Blanco gesture to one side, bringing forward a hostage, a man in his fifties or sixties. "When the King of England was asked to offer clemency for those who readily offered their lives for the greater good, he agreed only when his queen begged on their behalf." Blanco stared hard into the lens. "Will you not beg for them now?"

"The fate of this city and its citizens cannot be forged by violence alone. End this madness; perhaps I will let you leave with your life. Should any harm come to any of these hostages, your negotiating position will be lost."

Watching on his tablet, the Director spoke frantically to Maria.

"Maria, this is a last resort. Put me through to the PM."

Seated in the same position as she had for most of the evening, Maria shook her head. "Sir, I'm trying, but I'm getting no response."

The Director felt his desperation was starting to get the better of him. He knew if news of even one murdered hostage got out, it could initiate the start of a battle they couldn't win.

Blanco smiled into the camera as he placed a welcoming arm over Champion, guiding him into view. He felt his resolve strengthen as he saw the PM's face looking into the lens as though it were the barrel of a gun.

"The days of the Hundred Years' War are over. In the spirit of our present age, and perhaps in honour of the last man to be executed here, I will offer a more civilised method." He waved his gun in the hostage's face.

The PM's expression hardened further. "I warn you now, lay one finger on this man, there will be no negotiation."

"The time for negotiating is over; it ended long ago. Perhaps if you had been willing to talk earlier, you would have found me in a more forgiving mood. Now, the price is firm. Now I will make you listen."

The PM gripped hard against the table as she saw Blanco raise his gun, aiming it at the man's temple, his finger closing on the trigger. As the Anjouvin briefly looked away from his intended victim, the sound of a bullet pierced the air.

Fired from somewhere behind him.

96

St Paul's Cathedral, 03:00

For what seemed like an eternity Kit felt his body go limp, as though time had stopped, his life and soul caught in suspended animation. From up above the toll of the bells confirmed what he already knew; the hour was upon them, the next phase nigh. For over five hours Blanco had kept the world waiting.

Despite having found the correct place, Kit knew he currently had no way of preventing the next fire.

He moved quickly around the tomb, examining the slab in almost microscopic detail. Although noise continued outside, a strange quietness came over the crypt, somehow more depressing and melancholic than before, almost as though the building itself were weeping for a tragedy that could no longer be avoided. He imagined the spirits of the famous figures buried down there wandering the narrow passages with him, attempting to impart words of wisdom, encouragement, direction – anything that could delay the inevitable. The key was in the crypt; the story had been the same in every building so far, including the Monument. Whoever was starting the fires had been using ancient intelligence.

All the signs pointed to the one great architect.

He returned his attention to the south aisle, circling the tomb frantically, knowing there must somehow be a connection. After rereading the wording on the slab, his attention returned to the Latin epitaph on the wall.

Reader, if you seek his monument, look around you.

He looked again at the slab. "He has no monument."

Johnstone was now less than five metres away, his attention on the grave of Sir Joshua Reynolds. "That's the ambiguity. His monuments are all around us. You're currently standing inside the most famous."

Kit shook his head, his thoughts racing. If you seek his monument, look around you – he cursed himself for not seeing it before. Maria herself had confirmed the location was there.

Looking around in every direction, he saw the Wren slab was one of the most basic.

Nat walked over to him, the same air of desperation gnawing away at him. "I couldn't tell you the number of times I've been down here. There is no such stairwell."

"At least not in clear sight." Kit eyed the epitaph again, then another on the wall close by.

Remember the men who made shapely the stones of Saint Paul's Cathedral.

He knelt down beside the slab, feeling it all the way round. While the head and foot were attached to the floor below, on exploring the left side he noticed a gap; he placed his hand beneath it. As the seconds passed, he observed a slight change in the depth of the ground below. Getting down on his chest, he realised to his surprise that there was an empty space beneath the slab.

"That supposed to be this way?"

"What?"

Pulling hard at the left side, Kit felt movement, enough to convince him that the slab was not fixed securely. Gripping harder, he pulled again with all his might, willing it to come free. As the seconds passed, he felt it loosen further.

Before opening like a door, revealing a dark void in the floor.

Atkins heard Kit's voice come through clearly, a calming breeze in the gathering storm. The words confirmed he'd achieved the impossible.

He'd found the entrance before the cathedral caught fire.

"Where are you?" Atkins asked, his pulse rate increasing in anticipation that at last some significant progress was about to be achieved.

"Still in the crypt. The entrance is beneath the tomb."

In the north-east section of the churchyard, Atkins came to a sudden halt, his tired mind attempting to digest what he had just heard. Dumbstruck, he found himself almost subconsciously reciting the words he knew appeared on Wren's epitaph.

"You see the monument?"

"I guess I'll have to let you know." Kit looked into the space under where the slab had been. Within it, stone steps descended into darkness. "I have no idea what I'm gonna find down here. Request assistance; whoever can be spared."

"Very well." Atkins gestured Sanders and Chambers to come over, the nearest of the four Harts. "Warwick and Stapleton will be with you shortly. You have my permission to proceed by any means necessary."

Within seconds of hearing the Deputy Director's command, Sanders and Chambers sprinted across the deserted Paternoster Row, changing direction on reaching the great West Front. Entering through the right of the epic doors, they ran along the nave, through the archway in the south-east corner, and down to the crypt.

They found the recently disturbed grave with the slab removed and the steps leading down into darkness.

Sanders removed his torch. "Come on!"

Less than twenty metres below the tomb, Gillian and Nat stood in shocked silence as their eyes accommodated to the new surroundings. In the half-light of their respective torches, what they saw was difficult to comprehend.

But to Nat everything told a story. "This is incredible!"

Kit walked slowly around what appeared to be an irregularly shaped, underground chamber, its purpose difficult to determine. The surrounding walls were richly hung with paintings and at the centre of the main space a large sepulchre-style tomb rose above the otherwise flat ground like a medieval altar.

On closer inspection, Kit realised the layout was like that of a church.

"The great Greek cross!" Gillian exclaimed with a look of stunned surprise.

"The great what?" Kit was confused.

Within seconds of hearing the words, Nat realised she was right. "Good heavens! The original design."

Kit stared at Nat from across the chamber. "What are you talking about?"

"Wren's original design for the cathedral was based on a Greek cross," Gillian replied, realising as she looked around more closely that the surrounding artwork had almost certainly been influenced by the architect's travels. "That was turned down in favour of a traditional cross."

Studying the flooring, Kit could appreciate that the floor plan was indeed cross-shaped, though clearly far smaller than the cathedral above. Beyond the tomb, a doorway led further afield.

He spoke into his headset. "I understand now, Maria. Everything Wren had designed was used. Only beneath the surface."

Studying the UV designs Kit had captured in Wren's portrait, Maria was struggling to get the latest developments clear in her mind. The great original design had indeed been created.

Beneath the surface.

"This is incredible!"

"Not nearly as incredible as what might be about to happen." Footsteps on the stairs caught Kit's attention. Out of the darkness, the familiar faces of Sanders and Chambers came quickly into view. "You see us on the GPS?"

Maria saw three white dots close together, clearly below the crypt. "Yep!"

"Good. If we're not quick, we might need guiding out of here pretty sharpish."

In a similar area in a previously unknown part of the city, the silhouetted figure saw the time on his watch move ever closer to 03:03. Failing again with his HT, the transmission dead, he put his faith in Blanco. The plan had been discussed in detail; only something catastrophic would cause a change.

As the seconds ticked closer to the next minute, he prepared to light the fuse.

Almost a hundred feet above the strange chamber, Atkins watched from the great front steps as the iconic stone building north-west of the cathedral fell violently to the ground, its foundations ripped apart by the planned explosion. On the opposite side of Ave Maria Lane, the rapidly moving flames had already consumed every building east of the guild church. Destruction of the latest building with its renowned arcades had been necessary to create a firebreak. With the surrounding fires dying, he prayed it would be the last one that would be needed.

Switching his attention to the other side of the road where St Paul's Churchyard met Ludgate Hill, he saw that the inferno that had lately taken out the Tokyo Stock Exchange and everything else on the building west of Dean's Court had now spread to the adjacent building, consuming it rapidly.

Unlike on the north side, the fires on the south side showed no signs of abating.

Around the Queen Anne statue, where crowds had been impossible to shift, a sudden gasp went up, the already widespread panic escalating further. Leaving the steps, Atkins headed beyond the taped-off section, his eyes turning to the roof of the cathedral. A strong wind continued to blow to the north, fanning the flames on the south side, extending their reach ever further.

At precisely 03:02, fire was seen coming from the dome of the cathedral.

97

The White Tower,
03:00

The rush of air was familiar, but at the same time different to anything Mike had experienced before. It was like being thrown out of a plane, the moment before pulling the ripcord, only never had he done so with the lights moving so blindingly around him. He had used the device Phil had dubbed the Rocket Climber only once; even now, the experience differed from that day at Charlestown. Though the objective was the same, he'd never done it injured.

Or at night.

As the force of the coil pulled him forward, another blinding flash of light distorted his vision. He could make out the White Tower yet less clearly than usual, like looking through the lens of a camera obscura. Over the coming seconds the famous walls came quickly into focus, the south-west turret now the sole area of his attention. It was obvious from the trajectory of the wire that he was heading right for it.

Worse still, heading into it.

He grimaced as he anticipated contact; sure enough it came. Hitting the wall with bent knees, he braced himself as pain shot through both legs, the impact worst around his wounded thigh. Flying rapidly through the air at intense speed merely seconds earlier, he saw the world around him was now moving in progressively slowing circles as he lost momentum. On gaining his bearings, he realised he was still moving upwards, coming closer to the crown of the nearby turret. Reaching out, he touched it, finding the hook lodged securely against the stonework on the far side. Exhaling in relief, he knew he couldn't have aimed any better.

By hook or by crook, he had made it to the roof of the White Tower.

Securing himself against the battlements on the south side, he looked back in the direction he had come from, his attention on the roof of the Queen's House. Emily was still there, clearly recognisable. He sensed from her movement that she was close to tears, possibly out of concern, possibly joy. Raising his thumb, he grinned at her.

In the dim light, he saw her wave.

Turning around, he climbed over the nearest battlements, stepping carefully on to the lead panels. He moved extra slowly, knowing that any sound he made might be overheard. Near the west wall to his left, he saw several figures standing overlooking the city; one voice in particular carried on the wind. His tone was antagonising.

Mike knew he'd arrived in the nick of time.

***

Blanco ducked instinctively. The second gunshot had come from somewhere other than the first; both had been from behind him. A third came from his left; a voice was crying on the wind.

The words for the attention of the hostages.

Blanco saw shapes moving across his eye line, sparks flying at his feet. The gunman alongside him had hit the floor, his Heckler & Koch setting off on impact, the bullets narrowly missing him. Within seconds, a second gunman had fallen; the two around him were firing back, their bullets causing sparks off the opposite wall. From where he stood, he couldn't see who was responsible.

Only that they were clearly on the roof.

Seated in their respective positions in the COBRA and in the passenger's seat of the helicopter, the PM and the Director of the White Hart observed, with varying levels of disbelief, the frenzied events on the roof of the White Tower. Mixed in with the sounds of gunfire, screams were clearly audible, the latest drowned out by other surrounding noises. While Blanco had initially remained in shot, the camera had since been knocked off balance. Below the lead panels, the hostages had thrown themselves to the ground, lying with their heads covered; everyone in view clearly feared for their lives. Further back, a gunman dropped to the floor, wounded, almost certainly dead.

Closer to the camera, the raven had flown free.

Alone in the cabinet office briefing room, the PM moved closer to the wall-mounted flat screen for a better view of what was presently unfolding. Balanced on the edge of her seat, she could feel her heart racing as the man she knew as Bizante Blanco revealed clear signs of losing control, his position sorely compromised.

The question was how.

At the same time, the Director of the White Hart looked on with equally intense scrutiny. At least one gunman had been taken down; he guessed from the panic in the words he was hearing that a second might have joined him.

In total, he had only seen four on camera.

None of the hostages appeared to have been harmed.

Focusing on the screen of his portable tablet, he contacted Maria over the airwaves. The satellite footage confirmed everything he had expected.

Mike had made it to the White Tower roof.

And was now on the warpath.

***

Mike continued to fire until he'd exhausted the penultimate magazine of his semi-automatic pistol, simultaneously rolling to his right. On the far side of the tower, he saw a third gunman fall lifelessly to the floor; it was the last thing he picked up on before he rolled below the lead panels on to the surrounding walkway.

He had made it to the north-east wall, one of only three areas that were easily accessible, one of only three that didn't involve walking on the raised areas of lead. Reloading his pistol, he peered towards the battlements on the west side, in front of which the last remaining gunman was firing wildly in his direction. Blanco was crouched down low alongside him; the hostages were no longer visible. He sensed from the sounds they were still alive.

"Maria, you copy?"

Back at the Rook, Maria was watching everything. "You're certainly not dull, I'll give you that."

Taking cover, Mike smiled wryly. "If we get out of this, I'll let you congratulate me in person. What's left?"

"You're down to the last gunman apart from Blanco."

"How are the hostages?"

"All seem to be alive; they're currently crouched down by the west wall."

Mike listened extra carefully, pleased to hear everyone was still alive. "I'm running real low on ammo here, Maria."

"Good thing for you, you're an awesome shot, then."

He ended the conversation and headed north, his path covered only by a circular turret; he realised its door would probably later be his escape route. Chancing a better view, he saw the one remaining gunman had once again opened fire, his bullets causing sparks to fly up off the lead panels. Keeping low, he reached deeply into the pockets of his belt, assessing the contents.

Removing the one remaining smoke canister, he tossed it across the lead surface.

And ran hard in the opposite direction.

Emily heard a voice coming from the nearest window the moment she saw smoke appear above the White Tower. For the briefest of moments she felt herself unable to respond, unable to look away; it seemed inevitable from the smoke that the building would soon be enveloped in fire.

"Miss Fletcher?"

On hearing the voice again, she moved quickly to the same window she'd previously used to get out on to the roof, recognising the face of one of the Queen's Guards. She accepted his hand as he helped her back inside.

"There's a telephone call from Whitehall. Asking to speak directly to you."

Gazing once more at the roof of the White Tower, she saw the smoke had faded to a light, ghostly mist.

Suddenly, she no longer cared if she was fired.

They took the narrow stairways to the ground floor, at which point she entered the lounge. She found that order had been largely restored; the Yeoman Warders and the Queen's Guard were seeing to the hostages, bringing in drinks from the kitchen.

She found the captain of the Queen's Guard on the phone when she entered; she recognised his blond, balding appearance from their previous meetings. Like most of the soldiers, he was dressed in full uniform.

"She's here now," the captain said to the unknown caller before handing over the receiver. "It's from Whitehall; asked specifically for you."

"Thank you." She brushed her hair to one side, answering, "Hello? Emily Fletcher."

Maria replied via Bluetooth. "Thank goodness you're okay. The captain's filled me in on everything. You've really been amazing tonight."

Emily recognised the voice she'd overheard several times through Mike's headset. "You know I was actually about to say the same thing about you. At some point, I'd really like to meet up and trade stories."

Maria smiled. "Sounds like a date. How's your bodyguard?"

"Well, five minutes ago he was flying through the air on some form of glorified zipline. Last I saw, he'd made it up okay and the roof was smoking."

"Sounds like our boy." Maria continued to watch Mike's progress via the satellite footage. "Don't worry, by the way; if you do get fired, there's a job here waiting for you."

"I guess we'll have to see if the White Tower is still here tomorrow." She looked around, pleased to see life inside the Tudor cottage was showing some signs of returning to normal. "What do we do now?"

"Captain Hansen is on the roof of the White Tower, as is the man responsible for all this. The other hostages are alive, although those on the second floor of the White Tower are still under close guard. The only other gunmen are in the Waterloo Barracks."

"You suggest we start a gunfight?"

"Any form of counter-attack, you can leave to the regular forces; from what the captain tells me, most of their weapons are back in the barracks."

"The Queen's Guard have already collected everything left behind by the terrorists here and in the Bell Tower, but I doubt it'll get them far. What do you suggest we do?"

"Right now I suggest you barricade yourselves in and make sure any bullets you do have are put to good use. If things don't get worse, there'll be an opportunity to bring in troops from outside."

"And what if they do get worse?"

Maria gritted her teeth. "Then I guess our prayers will be with Captain Hansen."

* * *

Mike jumped back on to the lead roof panels the moment the smoke began, keeping low as he sprinted to the north side. He caught a glimpse of the final gunman firing through the smoke at the position he'd previously vacated and immediately pulled the trigger, catching the man squarely in the chest. He watched him hit the ground, his firearm becoming detached.

Blanco aside, the last obstacle had now been removed.

Staying low, he changed course, diving across the lead panels and sliding on to the walkway on the west side. Cries of panic went up from those on the ground; he counted six hostages, recognised one of them.

"Uncle Dave." He hurried to Champion, looking deep into his eyes. Exhaling deeply, the professor embraced his nephew tightly.

"Michael Hansen, I've never been so glad to see anyone before in my life."

Holding him equally tightly, Mike felt a sudden onrush of relief throughout his body that evaporated as quickly as it had come. Despite recent successes, there was much still to be done.

He looked around, his eyes on the nearby stonework. Suddenly he was concerned.

"Where's Blanco?"

Turning in every direction, there was no sign of the terrorist. Close to the wall, he saw the camera was gone. Observing nothing to the south, he reverted his attention to the north, then the north-east.

The door to the rounded turret was swinging on its hinges.

Randek watched the events taking place on the roof of the White Tower through the screens in the CCTV room. Since the moment he first saw the gunfire, his concern had been steadily mounting.

He placed his HT to his lips, putting out a call to Blanco. Though he received no response, he could see from the cameras that his uncle was rushing down the main stairs, clearly with other things on his mind.

Failing to get Blanco's attention, he attempted to reach François.

"This is Randek. Do you copy?"

Three storeys below, François tried the latest key in the older of the two doors, amazed to discover another perfect fit. His heart racing, he turned it slowly, finding the heavy iron begin to move, albeit with difficulty.

Pushing hard, he felt the door creeping forward inch by inch. He sensed from the resistance it was catching on something; it seemed too slow to be restricted by weight alone. When the gap was wide enough, he passed through the doorway, his torchlight focusing on what lay beyond.

Standing in the darkness, he smiled.

"François? This is Randek. Do you copy?"

He heard Randek's voice come through twice in quick succession. "Fabien?"

"Where are you?"

François re-emerged into the light of the jeweller's workshop. "Come downstairs. I have a surprise for you."

* * *

On the rooftop helipad above the tower block south of the Thames, the single-engined helicopter came in to land. Behind the seclusion of the French doors, Gabriel de Fieschi and Jérôme de Haulle both watched expectantly as the motors stuttered to a standstill, preceding movement from inside the cockpit.

Fieschi was first to leave the apartment. He opened the door behind the pilot, finding his father unbuckling his straps.

"Gabriel?" The pair embraced. "You are well?"

"Quite so." Fieschi gestured to the nearby walls, his attention on the city below, the dome of St Paul's occupying centre stage between two gathering clouds of dense smoke. "Come. You are just in time. Very soon the illumination will begin."

98

The White Tower,
03:02

Mike passed the north-west turret and turned east along the north wall, heading for the door. He entered to find a stairwell in darkness; pulling down his night visions, he was quickly able to take stock of his surroundings and determine his way forward. He followed the stairs to an open doorway, at which point artificial illumination returned.

He found himself in the heart of the Tower's arsenal.

"Maria, where am I heading?"

Maria watched his progress on the CCTV screen. "Blanco has made it to the bottom; if you stay on this floor, you should find the hostages."

"Where are they?"

"Looks like the Chapel of St John."

"I'm on it."

He left the great stairway and entered a grand chamber where wooden pillars supported the boarded ceiling. The room was lit by a combination of internal lighting that shone down from where the stone walls met the ceiling, and external from a series of rounded windows. Passing several wooden benches and wall displays, he found himself nearing the chapel.

As he approached the entrance, he saw sparks fly up off the nearest wall.

Blanco waited until he'd made it to the basement before finally replying to Randek's radio message.

"Where are you now?"

Heading quickly across the ground floor of the barracks, Randek replied, "Heading for the jeweller's workshop. Are you safe?"

"For now!" Gazing around the medieval armoury, Blanco realised he had a decision to make: leave via the gift shop or re-enter the tunnels below. "I heard the Englishman on the stairs. Soon, he will be with me."

Entering the Jewel House, a plan began to hatch in Randek's mind. "The passage to the jewels is here, inside the tower. It looks like it comes out in the same passage we walked earlier."

Listening, the same thought had already entered Blanco's mind. "Be ready when I come out."

Mike saw the sparks before hearing any sound; not for the first time, he realised he was dealing with weapons that were fitted with silencers. Instinct had taken him deep into the nearest archway, his body shielded behind the stonework.

He spoke into his headset. "Maria, I'm gonna need you to be my eyes and ears. Where am I heading?"

Maria felt her heart skip as she saw Mike disappear inside the nearest archway, a single flare of yellow aimed clearly in his direction.

Within seconds, further gunfire followed.

"There are three gunmen aiming at you; ten o'clock from where you're currently looking." She checked the chapel screen. "Final one is still in the chapel."

"Roger that."

The sparks were still flying, causing debris to fall from the surrounding stonework. Gripping the Heckler, he waited till the sparks had stopped before firing rapidly across the chamber, bringing glass down from the nearest display cases.

As he ceased firing, he realised two gunmen were down.

Taking refuge again within the archway, he examined the gun chamber: only seven bullets remained. Inhaling deeply, he waited till the next round of shots died down before glancing over his shoulder. He found the next gunman partially shielded by a wooden pillar and caught him as he reloaded.

Keeping low, he dropped the Heckler as he passed the first dead gunman and picked up an identical weapon. Finding it recently reloaded, he pressed on towards the chapel, moving slowly as he drew close to the doorway. Glancing inside, he raised his weapon, firing once, hitting the final gunman in the centre of his chest.

As he did so, the room was once again filled with sounds of panic.

"Keep calm," Mike instructed, lowering his gun and doing his best to communicate with the hostages. He counted nineteen; the correct number, he mused. Twenty-four had earlier been there, his uncle becoming the twenty-fifth.

Five had been escorted to the roof within the last ten minutes.

Along with his uncle.

"Relax." Mike did his best to reassure them, struggling to make himself heard. All nineteen were seated facing the altar, their features illuminated by a mixture of natural light from the clear, round-headed windows and artificial from the surrounding wall lights. Even at night, the stonework of the Romanesque chapel reflected the light well, making it appear spectacularly bright.

"All right, just stay calm. The Tower is back under official control. Nothing will happen to you. Just stay here until I say otherwise."

He pushed on, passing several suits of armour and weapons in glass display cases.

"Gunmen are down; hostages are freed." He spoke to Maria via his headset.

As usual, Maria had seen everything as it had appeared on the screens. "How is it in there?"

"You know what they say, a picture paints a thousand words." He grimaced as the effects of his injuries again caught up with him, the short lift of adrenaline subsiding. "I can't watch them and chase Blanco. What are my orders?"

Maria frowned, a quick smile fading. "Blanco's made it to the basement. If you hurry, you might find him among the souvenirs."

"I'm on it."

On the roof of the White Tower, David Champion gazed across at the five hostages, recognising all of them from his lecture earlier that evening.

It was difficult to tell from their appearances how fluently they spoke English.

Urging them to their feet, he led the way down the main stairway, moving slowly in the darkness. On finding the interior brightly illuminated, he took the risk of crossing the chamber and found the hostages in the chapel and the dead bodies of the gunmen nearby.

Again he recognised faces.

"Where's Mike Hansen?" He addressed two hostages as he entered the chapel. Among those present, he recognised a couple he'd spoken to earlier. "What's happened?"

Over the coming seconds, four of the hostages filled him in on recent events.

"Where is Mike Hansen?"

One of the four answered and pointed, "He went through there."

Champion followed their directions, soon finding himself in the heart of the arsenal. Ignoring the items in glass display cases, he walked on the wooden flooring to another stairway and through the heart of the exhibition, passing displays on the Tower Records Office and the Royal Mint. At the far side, he found another stairway that memory told him would take him to the basement.

Tentatively, he started down.

99

St Paul's Cathedral, 03:02

The door beyond the tomb led to a lightless passageway similar to the one Kit had already seen beneath Mary-le-Bow. Entering alongside him, Sanders looked around in the light of his torch.

"This is just like what we saw beneath Monument."

"Was just thinking the same thing about Mary-le-Bow," Kit replied before attempting to contact Maria through his headset. Though he was certain Maria had heard him, the reply was instantly cut off.

He returned his gaze to Sanders. "Looks as though we're on our own."

The options were left and right; in both cases the passage continued in a straight line with several offshoots heading in various directions. Kit noticed the layout was identical on both sides; it was strange, almost like a network of streets.

It seemed incredible he was looking at something so real beneath the surface.

"If we're gonna stand any chance, we'd best split up." Kit pulled on his night visions, seeing his two associates as they showed up against the green backdrop. "Rob, you and AC take the right." He turned to Nat and Gillian. "You two come with me. If I tell you to get out, you do so. That clear?"

The two civilians nodded.

"Good." His gaze returned to Sanders and Chambers. "Eyes peeled, boys. Any sign, shout!"

The silhouetted figure counted down the seconds, knowing the moment was at hand. Blanco's timing was like clockwork. The raven would have been killed a minute after the transmission began. The fire would start within two minutes. A minute later it would be visible inside the cathedral.

Leaving him less than two minutes to make his escape.

Atkins held his breath as he negotiated the last of the stairway's 257 steps, exhaling on reaching flat ground. The short, wide stairs that revolved anticlockwise from the south aisle to the base of the dome were notoriously difficult to climb even at a steady pace, but sprinting up them was exhausting. The harder he climbed, the more focused his thoughts became, the more he realised only one option remained.

In a matter of minutes, time would be up.

He entered the Whispering Gallery and started to make his way round to the other side. As he scoured the left side of the inner dome, he became aware of the view below, the majesty of the great interior set out before him. At 111.3m in height, the dome of St Paul's was famous for being the second highest in the world, eclipsed only by the Vatican. At 257 steps, he'd made it up only thirty metres.

After completing the journey to the first level of the triple dome layout, he prayed that ascending all three would not be necessary.

Beneath the streets of Edinburgh, Alain checked his watch as he prepared to ignite the fire. All five so far had gone off like clockwork; if all went to plan, only two remained.

Counting down the seconds, he felt deep into his pocket as he got ready to light the fuse. Even compared to what had already occurred that night, he knew what he was about to do would leave a deep mark on the city forever.

Just north of the cathedral on the opposite side of the High Street, Pugh, Pentland and Rawlins stopped as they reached the entrance to the Real Mary King's Close.

Strangely, it was unlocked.

"All right. Tony and me are gonna take this way; Danny, you head back up the Mile," Rawlins said. "Try to establish contact with the Palace."

Receiving no objection, Pugh raced across the tarmac towards the Royal Mile while Rawlins and Pentland started down the stone steps, entering the subterranean passages. If the information in the famous painting was correct, somewhere beneath their feet lay the final clue to all of their outstanding problems.

Three hundred and seventy-six steps up, Atkins attempted to catch his breath again as he headed out on to the outer dome. Inhaling fresh air, he paused briefly against the nearby parapets and looked upwards.

The flames he'd seen before entering the cathedral had escalated in the last two minutes, spreading ever closer to the Golden Gallery. From the view he had, he could see two people already up there, dowsing the flames with fire hoses; at least ten others were doing the same from the present level.

He knew that the fire had not yet reached the interior.

Taking a deep breath, he walked over to the foot of the nearby stairway and began the climb up the final stage of the cathedral's 528 steps.

After splitting up, they moved off quickly: Kit taking the left passage, Sanders and Chambers the right. From the left side a harsh cacophony of sounds could be heard; Kit put it down to a combination of the unusual acoustics and the abnormal events taking place above ground. As he continued along the passage, it occurred to him that they might have been designed deliberately to allow sounds to travel in the manner of some of the great churches.

Everything he saw was baffling.

"Why the hell create something like this below the surface?" He eyed Nat as he ran. He could tell from Gillian's expression that she was equally confused.

"If something like this existed before the fire, Lord knows what it was used for." Johnstone's breathing felt restricted in the claustrophobic environment. "For all we know, people may have lived down here."

Kit remembered something similar existed in Edinburgh.

He increased his pace, investigating every passage as he passed. From one of the openings on the left side, he noticed a peculiar smell that didn't seem entirely natural. It reminded him of something he'd experienced recently.

Beneath the crypt of St Mary-le-Bow.

In the green light of his night visions, features showed up clearly. The designs on the wall were elaborate in comparison with those he'd previously seen. The ceiling was ribbed and vaulted. A series of tombs lined thick stone walls on both sides, some more elaborate than others, the exteriors charred and burned. Heading to his right, he noticed one name stand out above the others.

John of Gaunt, 1st Duke of Lancaster.

Nat read the name. "Impossible!"

Kit was intrigued. "Why?"

"John of Gaunt was buried in old St Paul's. His tomb was destroyed during the original fire."

Kit raised an eyebrow, rather less surprised. He tried Sanders and Chambers, getting nothing but a dead line.

"I'm going to need you to locate my two colleagues – tell them to come here now." The message was for both Gillian and Nat. "Go!"

Both hurried off, leaving Kit alone. As he continued to walk, his gun raised, more tombs came into view along with several wall decorations. At the far end, he observed another tomb of particular importance, the effigy raised several feet above the ground. Before it he saw movement, a figure praying.

He aimed his weapon at him. "Don't move a muscle!"

The figure turned slowly, clearly caught off guard. In the green light, making out features was difficult beyond the fact he was human. As the figure moved his right hand, Kit saw a series of lights around him.

The area by his feet became engulfed in flame.

100

The White Tower,
03:04

The stairway ended in what had once been the storage basement, another area that now housed exhibits of the Tower's arsenal. There was a sign in bright white letters on an aqueous background, confirming its purpose – the storehouse. Whereas the stairway leading down had been shrouded in darkness, the efficiently arranged displays of historical cannons, body armour and rifles were brightly illuminated by a unique selection of LED lights shining down from replica candle holders that hung from the ceiling on metal chains.

As Mike passed the gift shop, he saw a wooden stairway heading upwards. There had been no sign of Blanco since leaving the roof. Phil was calling frantically in his ear.

"I'm in the gift shop, Phil. Where is he?"

Phil had been watching closely while Maria focused solely on St Paul's. "He disappeared just back where you came from, somewhere among the cannons."

Mike stopped as he approached the stairway, secretly pleased that he might not need to take the steps. Looking down, he saw the flooring was mostly paved, the light colouring reflecting the overhead lights. In an area between a display of rifles and bayonets, close to the cannons, he could see that the floor had been disturbed.

"This what you had in mind?"

Watching on the screen, Phil nodded. "Have your wits about you. We don't have cameras below the floor."

Dropping down into the dark void, Mike reattached his night visions.

"I'm on it."

The gap was small, just wide enough to get through; Mike had calculated the drop from the storehouse was less than three metres. The floor beneath was flat, possibly stone; for once he wouldn't be descending into water. The lack of light in both directions confirmed the absence of torchlight; as far as he could tell, Blanco had worn no night visions. Had he done so, the subtle signs were likely to present themselves.

For now, he saw nothing.

He landed as lightly as he could, ready for action if the need arose. With his USP45 almost empty, he continued to rely on the Heckler; the final magazine was likely to last him ten rounds. Turning in both directions, he saw no sign of life.

Instinct guided him to his right.

The passage was wide and curved slightly right to left. There were pictures on the wall, faded but still visible. To Mike, the feeling was one of déjà vu. Like the strange, cave-like system he had discovered beneath the castle in Charlestown during the trials, he realised he was witnessing something original, something lost to history. Only by following the subtle signs could he make his way through. Kit's words replayed over in his mind.

When going through hell, just keep going.

He found a doorway in the walls. Entering, he found himself in a similar passageway, the layout uncannily identical to another he'd seen once before. In his mind Maria's voice replayed her message from the trials: *The first circle. It is here the punishments of hell begin.* After the night he'd experienced, he feared the punishments would never end.

The throbbing in his thigh continued, the pain now almost unbearable. It felt as though a knife were being twisted, only one that had itself been forged in hell. His hand on his thigh, he breathed deeply as he realised the seepage was still minimal. If the bandage had been applied correctly, he knew he still had a few hours of reasonable strength. Radchenko's words now began to haunt him.

You are now half dead.

Standing in the fifth passage, Blanco came to a sudden standstill, his eyes on the surrounding artwork. Never in his wildest dreams had he imagined something so depressing could exist in the modern day: a real circle of hell beneath the place famed by many to be hell on earth. The story of their creation was equally legendary. If it were true, the present passages were reserved solely for the most sinful of prisoners, the ultimate form of solitary confinement. He recalled learning as a child how his ancestor had once begged for execution, the wish finally granted, not on Tower Green or Tower Hill but within the tunnels he currently walked.

Revenge was long overdue.

Waiting in the shadows, he listened as nearby footsteps became louder: running, panting, the sounds of a man clearly lost. Gripping his firearm, he moved slowly into the next section.

One closer to the centre.

Champion left the chapel and hurried through the remainder of the exhibition, taking the main stairs to the ground floor. On reaching the area now designated the storehouse, he hurried through the large collection of heavy artillery, remembering the area ended with a gift shop.

He passed through the gift shop and took the stairs, finding the door locked. Beyond it, the famous neo-gothic walls of the Waterloo Barracks were cloaked in obscurity, the yellow stones absorbing more light than they reflected. By the main entrance, he saw no sign of movement; the Queen's Guard adorning the famous uniform of a redcoat was still lying in a heap, his dead body yet to be removed.

He felt his heart sink on seeing the poor victim lying lifelessly before the black sentry box.

Finding no way of getting out, he headed back the same way, taking the stairs down into the storehouse. On reaching the cannons, he stopped, his attention on the floor.

Part of the flooring had been removed.

101

Below St Paul's Cathedral, 03:04

The scene Kit saw was simply impossible to comprehend. It was like being in the middle of a vast crypt, but unlike any he had seen in his lifetime. In his mind, he found himself revisiting sights from his past: Windsor, Charlestown, scenes from his own training. He recalled his own experience in the Accumulator, taking immense satisfaction in watching Mike Hansen nearly lose his mind on coming face to face with images that had almost scared him to death five years earlier. The village of Charlestown held many secrets, the castle, the inn, the church; even now he knew there was far more to discover.

Yet seeing what he saw now was stranger still, as though every single one of those had been rolled into one, all for one extreme purpose. The effigies, be they of real men, their remains long since decayed in their tombs, or just for show, he was now unsure. Only one thing he was sure of. He had found a door to hell, whatever indeed hell was.

And one among the dead was clearly living.

Kit deactivated his night visions, pushing them up on to his forehead. With the lighting of recent fires, coupled with the additional illumination of several fiery torches, they were currently unnecessary. Even from a distance, he realised what he saw was self-explanatory. The man was of indeterminate age, perhaps closer to thirty than forty, his expression resentful, as expected of a man who hadn't anticipated getting caught. Though the lines on his face were distorted by shock and surprise, the rest of his features were easier to define. It was like looking at a man he knew well, or at least knew of. Without question he was looking at a man he had seen before.

Had been partly responsible for his death.

"You?"

The man who knelt alongside the grandest of the tombs lowered his hand, the lighted torch creating ethereal shadows across the surrounding stonework. Inexplicably, his expression softened.

"I knew you'd come. Had you done so a few moments later, you might have been too late." He rose to his feet and walked forward, his face becoming clearer still. "It would have been a shame, I must say. After all, it's not often one gets the chance to gaze upon such majesty."

Kit gritted his teeth, his gun still raised. Unlike his last meeting with the arsonist, he needed no excuse. "An even greater shame to decimate such priceless antiquities."

The arsonist lowered his head. "Ironically, it was much to the endeavours of my forebears they survived at all. As far as history is concerned, the effigies of

Gaunt, Ethelred the Unready and every one of the others buried here were destroyed along with the old cathedral. Truth be told, I'm not entirely sure what inspired them to be saved at all."

"A misplaced sense of conscience perhaps."

The stranger shrugged. "Regardless of the motivation, few over the centuries since are likely to have benefited from their generosity and viewed them with their own eyes. Even those who knew, I sense had better things to do. Sadly, there is always a price for life's most demanding endeavours. There is an old saying in my country. A desperate disease requires a similar remedy."

Kit felt his blood run cold. "I seem to recall hearing you say something similar once before."

"Me?" The Frenchman shook his head sombrely. "I think you mistake me for someone else. A brother of mine perhaps. It's often been said we share the facial resemblance of our forebears."

Stepping forward, Kit focused on the man's face, concentrating on things besides the man's beard. He looked like Everard, yet on closer inspection, he sensed this man was slightly taller, a subtle difference, obvious only now he looked closely. Different too was the weight, although much could change in a year. Other features were very similar, particularly the voice.

And the cruel way in which he spoke.

"I must apologise for mistaking you for something so foul and degrading." Kit bit his lip, his grip on the gun tightening. "Then again, there is something to be said for judging a man on the conditions in which one finds him, not to mention the company he keeps. I hear Everard passed away."

The Frenchman bowed his head solemnly. "You knew him well?"

"Well enough to know the bullets I fired weren't as accurate as usual; then again, under the circumstances he proved most useful – dare I say, most willingly cooperative."

The Frenchman frowned, his grave expression replaced by one of anger. "I suggest you choose your words a little more wisely. Even the bravest usually know when not to tempt fate. There is another famous saying in my country. It is better to prevent than to heal."

"Yes, I know a few sayings in my own country too; I must say, under the circumstances Everard might have wished he'd taken his own advice. For what it's worth, I didn't know he was dead till quite recently."

"A most terrible day for all in my family, but far less terrible, I should imagine, than today will be for those who brought it about. Had the actions of your countrymen been more understanding, perhaps the events of tonight might not have been necessary."

"Don't give me that twaddle. Operations like this are never about petty revenge." Kit walked on slowly, keeping his distance from the Frenchman before stopping by the same effigy at which Everard's brother had previously knelt. "Edward II." He looked at the inscription. "A blessed king indeed to have two tombs."

The Frenchman smiled. "The grave at Gloucester, though elegant, was not only superfluous, but many years too early."

"Unnecessarily elaborate too, I should have thought, for a servant." Kit stared at the effigy, focusing on the head, where long locks were partially covered by a crown. In the inscription he saw he'd died 17 July 1341. "I take it back, perhaps it does make sense you being here after all. Had it not been for him, your organisation would never have existed. I suppose it's quite a conundrum for you. Only by destroying the bones of your forefather can you truly replace him."

"Everything in life is dust and eventually to dust it shall return. It is perhaps for that reason I have always been fascinated with fire." He moved his hand quickly, bringing the torch down, the flames creating shafts of light in the darkness. "It is impossible for one to illuminate without also burning. So too, it is better to burn out than to rot, no?"

"Perhaps that might also explain why your brother didn't wish to be buried. I'm most sorry I couldn't attend the service myself; I understand there was one."

The Frenchman bowed his head again. "We are digressing. And the hour is getting late. Soon the cathedral above us will be consumed in flame, and both us and all within this room along with it. There is no avoiding the consequences of history. Only the lessons it serves to teach us."

"Spoken like a true revolutionary. I've always wondered how one lives with oneself after bringing death and hardship to so many."

"A strange question coming from a man aiming a gun at an unarmed man."

Kit lowered his weapon. "That make you feel better? Make you more interested in answering the question? My dear sir, you disappoint me. For a man whose sole motivation is the destruction of a great cathedral, I thought at least you might stand by your convictions."

"I take no pleasure," he said, his gaze now firm, his jaw tight. "Nor does it please me that such things are necessary. Had the circumstances been different, perhaps the building above us might never have existed; instead we might have been looking at something far longer, the steeple even higher; the tombs you see surrounding us still interred in the same positions as before."

"You think this is solely about architecture?" Kit walked away from the tomb, forcing the arsonist to back into a corner. "You said it yourself, what is lost is always replaced. It might interest you to know, Wren spoke of a dome even before the fire. I'll wager in a few centuries, very little of what exists now will do so then."

The Frenchman smiled. "As an Englishman educated in your modern ways, I'm sure you're unfamiliar with the name Yves de Bonaire..."

"You can spare me this one. My colleague once heard the whole thing from your brother."

"Ah, so it was not you he enjoyed his chat with in the church of St Mary's?"

"No. I seem to recall we had a far less enjoyable one at the Opera House. Ironically I was there earlier this evening." Strangely, it already seemed like a long time ago. "You know, being there now, you'd never know there was any damage. Except, of course, for the plaque of remembrance."

"Another of humanity's great gifts, especially for the English: to sweep the past under the carpet."

"Enough of this garbage, not to mention all the other stuff." Kit tightened his grip on the gun, his expression hardening. He continued forward, not stopping until the arsonist's back was pressed against the wall. "The location of the seven doors of hell are now known to us; the only point of confusion is why their discovery took so long. The fires above will soon be out; the cathedral itself is safe. The other passages are known. Your friends at the Tower are on borrowed time."

"All of us, monsieur, are on borrowed time. In the past, people were more accepting of their mortality. I have often thought it a sad feature of the modern day, how death has become something to be feared. That life has become something no longer lived."

"Said like a true poet." Kit's face broke into a smile. "You really are a man of many faces; I bet even the Scarlet Pimpernel didn't possess such talent. Perhaps under the circumstances, not fearing death might be in your best interests. It's a long walk back to the surface. Drop the torch. It's time to end this."

The Frenchman continued to edge his way along the wall, not stopping till he reached the far corner.

Then to Kit's horror, he realised he'd just made an unforgivable mistake.

The reflection of the fire in the Frenchman's eyes seemed brighter somehow, as though it were illuminating a part of his soul. "When the original architects of the Great Fire came to London in 1666, they had access to neither mortar bombs nor Molotovs. Rather, they had to rely on techniques that had been trusted for years. He bent down, his light revealing no less than thirty wooden barrels. "The train, when lit, runs quickly. Only a man with a death wish or a good escape plan would dare take the chance."

"So which category are we in?"

"Perhaps you'll do me the privilege of putting away your gun and together we shall learn our fate."

A series of echoes from the nearby passage confirmed running in their direction. Two figures emerged; in the fiery light Kit recognised Sanders and Chambers.

"Don't you move a muscle!" Sanders spoke first, edging closer to Kit and whispering in his ear. "Reports are the dome may have caught fire. They're attempting to put it out as we speak."

"You've managed to make contact?"

"Negative. But I've sent the gallery director and her friend back upstairs."

Though the Frenchman was out of earshot, he sensed from Sanders' face the news wasn't ideal.

"My friends, the hour is late. It is time to decide."

"Enough idle threats, jackass. Just remember what's currently being pointed at you!" Sanders' gaze was stern.

"My friend, you disappoint me. Like many of your countrymen, your concern is never beyond your own doorstep. But just remember, it is in the nature of every man to see first what is on his own doorstep. And for every man, noon soon comes upon them, even the dead."

"Drop that and noon will be upon you even sooner!" Since learning of fire reaching the dome, Kit's irritation had increased rapidly. "Your order has been practically wiped out. Surrender now; at least you'll leave here with the dignity of being the one sensible enough to turn away."

"A most sobering proposition, but the Sons of Gemini was never about survival alone. It was instead a sign. One of togetherness and continuous rebirth." The Frenchman smiled sombrely, shaking his head. "No matter how great the disease, the cure can always be found."

Kit aimed squarely at the man's chest. Looking deep into his eyes, memories of Everard continued to haunt his thoughts: the risk of shooting a man currently holding a detonator.

Again history repeated itself.

"Enough games!" Kit resumed, inching ever closer. "One way or another, we're leaving this place. I'm prepared to give you to the count of five." He began the countdown, each word clear. "Three. Two."

Gripping his weapon, he saw no sign of surrender.

"One!"

As the count ended, the Frenchman dropped the torch; the silence was broken by gunfire. As the burning wood hit the floor, it bounced once, coming to a standstill.

Beyond it a second set of flames flared into the darkness.

102

St Paul's Cathedral, 03:08

The recurring sound of an incoming helicopter could be heard over the wind as it came in from the east. Atkins heard it before he saw it. Despite having the current benefit of being the person in the highest point in the cathedral, right now possibly the highest in London, with the fires on the outer dome still raging, a thick blanket of cloud had temporarily obscured his view. At eighty-five metres up, standing in the heart of the Golden Gallery, the highest of the dome's three galleries, the views on a clear day were famously stunning; it was a rare place in the city an onlooker could be treated to a complete panoramic view of the surrounding area. Making it to the top, the 528-step climb causing havoc with his quads, had been exhausting in itself; even on a calm day, it was never a climb to be taken lightly.

Today, it had been necessary.

He stood with his body pressed against the stone supports, continuing to point the pressure hose against the outer dome below. The flames were particularly dense when the wind picked up; the north-easterly breeze laden with smoke now badly affected his breathing.

Of the three men with him, he was the only one not wearing the proper safety equipment; there hadn't been time for such preparation. On both sides, two men of lean build directed their hoses at the nearest flames. In addition to the smell of the smoke, another strange odour now pervaded the air; clearly caused by the fire but out of the ordinary, like something melting. Covering his mouth with his weaker hand, he did his best to concentrate.

Secretly, he feared the blaze would soon be out of control.

A voice called him from the nearby stairs. "Sir, the flames are seeping through into the inner dome. Any second the timber supports could catch fire."

The timber supports. Located at the heart of the inner dome – the place that could cause the most damage. The area that had been marshalled so well during the Blitz.

The Deputy Director's response was immediate. "Get your men to it as soon as possible. Any damage to the main beams, we'll all be cut off."

Down below, the masked man shook his head. "The smoke is rising; go in there, you'll be asphyxiated."

Keeping one eye on the blaze, Atkins forced himself to think. The helicopter he had heard less than sixty seconds earlier had taken a course close to the river, descending in height briefly before re-emerging, its Bambi Bucket filled to the rim, dripping slowly over the nearby buildings.

He braced himself as the chopper came overhead, releasing its contents at the vital moment. He held his breath as the recently collected water spilled like a tidal wave down on to where he was standing. As he opened his eyes, he saw the fire had receded significantly. While the chopper made a full circle of the dome, making its way back to the river for a refill, he heard the noise of a second engine approaching from the same direction.

He guessed that less than four buckets might be enough.

He retreated from the Golden Gallery and started down the stairway, recalling anecdotes he'd heard from veterans of the St Paul's Watch. They had survived the Blitz despite the same problems.

If it was possible then, it was possible now.

"Show me."

The masked man led him down the tight metallic stairway, heading back into the inner dome. The smell of smoke was indescribably strong, although somewhat less than he'd experienced at the top.

Stopping close to the wooden supports, he saw the way blocked by two masked firefighters, both of whom were attempting to direct their fire hoses at the timber supports beyond metal fencing. Although the infrastructure was still intact, flaming embers that had floated down from above were smouldering in the centre of one of the beams. As the seconds passed, he became aware of falling water and further debris.

He concluded from the noises above that the contents of a second Bambi Bucket had been discharged over the dome.

Standing in silence, he studied the smoking wreckage, attempting to make sense of the chaos. Accurate targeting of the hoses and the Bambi Buckets to where they could be most effective was achievable more by luck than judgement. If fortune didn't favour them, the pressure of the water from the Bambi Buckets could actually endanger the timber supports.

Causing the dome to collapse.

A voice called out from the top of the stairs. "The fire on the dome is almost out, sir."

Atkins heard the words clearly. "Get on the radio to the pilots. Tell them to divert to the nearby buildings. We'll finish the job here."

"Sir, the fire is nearly out; one more bucket could finish it."

"No!" Atkins' face was stern. "Any further drop from above could take out the entire infrastructure. The dome will be lost."

"Sir?"

"Get on the radio now." Atkins rolled up his sleeves and headed rapidly for the nearest beam. Taking a deep breath, he climbed the fencing and scrambled on to the beam, holding them both tightly for support. "Give me your jacket."

The man alongside him was hesitant. "Sir, it's too risky!"

"Not doing anything is too risky. This dome represents the heart of this city. Its survival won us the war!" His expression was clear, his resolution absolute. Despite the mental exhaustion from an already tiring day, the late hour, the thickening catarrh on his lungs, his heart still beating uncontrollably from the

528-step climb, adrenaline had reinvigorated him, giving him fresh hope and optimism. He felt that the heroic spirit of those who had fought the flames during the Blitz was with him, guiding him to stand up and be counted in the country's hour of need.

The patterns repeat themselves.

Over 100 feet above the dome, the two helicopters changed course as directed. The fire on the dome was far less of a threat now, the smoke almost non-existent. Where the blaze had been strongest, a thick black mark now scarred the outer shell. Within it, the pilot saw several small gaps had appeared in the structure.

Whoever gave the instruction to redirect had been dead on, he mused.

Completing his circle of the dome, the pilot of the first helicopter flew away over the Thames, coming in for a further refill. The fires on the north side had been practically extinguished.

All that remained was the south side.

As the second helicopter completed its pass, heading towards the Thames, Phil and Maria watched in silence, concentrating their attention on the multitude of images that filled the semi-translucent screen. The flames on the dome had receded significantly and were now confined to an area of less than ten metres just above the Stone Gallery, which was presently being tackled by firefighters.

Two others were doing the same from the Golden Gallery.

"Sir, this is the Rook. Do you copy?" Maria's question was intended for Atkins. Beyond the sound of shallow breathing she received no response.

"Edward, this is the Rook. Do you copy?" Phil addressed Kit. On this occasion the line was dead.

"Grosmont, this is the Rook. Do you copy?"

The next five passageways passed by quickly, the duration becoming shorter each time. Visually the surroundings were strangely familiar to him, but even after less than five minutes navigating them in the darkness, Mike was finding it difficult to trust his own judgement.

The illuminated dials on his watch confirmed over five hours had passed since the terrorists' arrival, over two hours since his meal with Emily in the Byward Tower. Though functioning efficiently with injuries had become a regular occurrence in recent times, doing so under extreme pressure with a gunshot wound was a completely new experience. Fatigue was coming on quickly, worse still coupled with the pungent air. In the darkness, he feared exhaustion could overcome him rapidly.

When going through hell, just keep going.

The persistent stench of damp and water that he had become accustomed to in recent hours returned in the fifth passage, although on this occasion the water level failed to rise above ankle depth. The artwork continued, yet whatever the pictures were portraying was now impossible to comprehend. The sixth passage was little better, the bitter air poisoned by a strange incense that seemed to complement the illusion of hell. He cursed Blanco. Cursed Masterson.

Just like his experience beneath Charlestown, he was undergoing the ultimate test.

He made it into the seventh passage, eyes peeled, gun at the ready. The height of the floor changed slightly; he picked up the pace as the air became fouler still. His mind continued to replay the events of two years earlier; he heard another voice in his head, Kit's.

Last chance to quit!

When going through hell, keep going.

The final passage was located on the far side of the eighth, accessible through an iron door. Approaching, he pushed it, finding it swinging on its rusty hinges. On the surrounding wall, the scene differed from any he had seen before. In addition to the faded artwork, heavy chains and manacles had been hammered into the stonework.

Unlike in the tunnels beneath Charlestown, he realised that at some time this area really had been used to administer harsh and cruel punishment.

He moved slowly across the scene of torture, concerned Blanco would be waiting somewhere in the shadows. He took a deep breath, doing his best to concentrate on his surroundings – anything to take his mind off his memories. Being here was strange, different yet similar to his experience in the trials. He had finally reached his lowest ebb, the moment he'd strived to avoid. During the trials, Masterson had repeatedly said breaking a man was not only useful but necessary; only by finding the limits did one really know the measure of the man.

For the second time in his life, he had found it.

He picked up his pace, moving as fast as his injury would allow. The end was visible now, the way clear. Whereas in Charlestown the trial had ended in a thick area of woodland, today he found himself at another crossroads, sounds coming from either direction. Taking a deep breath, he focused on the sounds.

One wrong turn and he knew there was a danger he'd be stuck down there forever.

Maria shook her head as she looked at Phil. "Still no news of Mike."

Phil checked the GPS. "Least he's still moving. I guess there's no reception underground either."

Maria clicked her mouse, bringing up pictures of Edinburgh. "De Courtenay, do you copy?"

Standing outside Holyrood Palace, Pugh shook hands with the chief fireman as the final flames were doused.

"Fires on the Royal Mile are completely out." He paused for breath, his eyes still focused on the iconic 16th-century palace. Unlike St Paul's, so far it was still unmarked.

"Where are Fitz-Simon and Salisbury?"

"Just entered Mary King's Close. If the painting is correct, they should be nailing the bastard any second."

In another part of the city, Pentland and Rawlins ran flat out through the subterranean passages. The first thing that struck them was how gimmicky the place was, how every nook and cranny was filled with costumed props, all aimed at heightening the atmosphere.

Taking the narrow passageways deeper beneath the city, they kept their eyes on the adjoining doorways, searching every room.

"Any sign?" Pentland asked.

"Negative." Rawlins exited the latest room. "Let's keep going. He must be here somewhere."

Less than two hundred metres away, Alain sensed what he was sure was the sound of muffled voices, the noises echoing from the nearby stonework. Last time he'd checked, both his accomplices had been in a different part of the city.

Above ground.

He put his HT to his mouth. "David, do you copy?" he asked, receiving no reply. Experience told him that meant one of two things.

Neither of which was necessarily good.

Standing as quietly as possible in the small room directly under the cathedral, he checked his watch, knowing the time was at hand. Placing his hand into his pocket, he removed his firearm.

Before moving deeper into the darkness.

103

Beneath St Paul's Cathedral, 03:11

Kit saw a series of sparks go up from the ground, accompanied by a strange hissing sound. As the noise of the gunfire died down, the surrounding flames became brighter, illuminating the far wall behind the tomb of Edward II.

Only then, to his horror, did he see the full extent of what it hid.

Chambers was the first to break the silence. "Yo, please tell me that isn't what I think it is."

Kit noticed over a hundred previously unseen wooden barrels stacked up in rows, accompanied by a harsh smell of what seemed to be petrol. "Whatever it is, it probably isn't apples."

Sanders dropped his firearm and sprinted for the barrels, his torch aimed at the ground below. The brother of Everard Payet had alluded to a train, almost certainly a reference to gunpowder.

Sure enough, a steady path of illumination burned across the stony ground.

Kit felt himself momentarily frozen to the spot. Being underground, the nearby gunfire had echoed excessively loudly, the force causing tremors beneath his feet. Seconds later, he could still hear the ringing in his ears. With his dying breath, the brother of Everard had dropped the lit torch in his left hand, his aim both deliberate and accurate.

As his bullet-ridden body hit the floor, he collapsed, spread out in a heap.

Chambers' reactions had been quickest, following the shaft of light as it sped towards the wooden barrels. Diving at full stretch, he came down hard on the stone surface, smothering the gunpowder.

As it hit his midriff, the light became brighter.

And exploded against his chest.

Atkins held his breath as he made his way on to the beam, crawling ever closer to the source of the flames. Rising to his haunches, he placed both arms out wide for support, doing his best to concentrate on his feet while avoiding the temptation to look down. Exactly how far the fall was, he no longer knew. From his position well above the Stone Gallery, he knew it would be in excess of fifteen metres and any mistake would surely prove fatal.

Gaining his balance, he made his way along the lengthy beam as quickly as he could, his concentration now solely on the developing flames. In recent seconds, the pall of smoke had become greater still, the poisonous air and enclosed space now a lethal combination. The one positive was that the light had improved.

With the flames becoming brighter, it was possible to see without a torch.

Holding his breath, Atkins approached the end of the beam. He crouched low as he sensed further water and debris coming down from above; being close to the centre of the infrastructure, at least he had something to hold on to. As the shower of debris ended, he continued to the far end and reached the fire, starving it of oxygen by stamping on the flames. Wiping the soles of his shoes across the beam, he exhaled shallowly as the dying embers floated down into the void below.

Composing himself, he focused again on the beams, doing his best to maintain his balance. With the fires out, the light had gone; he called out, hearing a reply from the far side.

As he turned back, he came to a sudden stop; a second flicker of light had caught his attention.

Another ember had burst into flame on the next beam.

Rawlins paused on approaching yet another doorway, taking refuge behind the supporting wall. Directly above him, costumed props had been placed on a washing line, furthering the illusion of 18th-century squalor. Despite the dry conditions, the smells were strange. A strong musk came up from the stonework; the stench was old, clearly authentic. There were other odours too, even less appealing, but more modern: a perfume of some kind, possibly masculine.

Moving alongside Pentland, he placed his finger to his lips.

Crouched down against the far corner, Alain gazed across the otherwise empty chamber. Through the red-coated lenses of his night visions, he sensed movement outside the doorway, possibly just a shadow.

Gripping his firearm with his outstretched hand, he squeezed the trigger, the silenced shot creating a spark off the far wall.

All around him, the corridor had become silent.

Kit saw the sparks rise clearly, making contact with Chambers' chest and burning brightly into his black ops kit. Where the powder train disappeared, he saw his colleague roll on to his stomach, crying out in pain as he sought to smother the flames. Despite the interruption of its progress, the train was now continuing on the other side, less than ten metres from the barrels. Wasting no time, he dived to the ground, reaching out towards the powder and creating a clear gap between it and the barrels.

He exhaled in relief as the flames died.

The only way Atkins could get to the adjacent beam was by using the sloping wall for assistance. Making it back to the start of the first beam, he gripped the supporting wall with both hands, regaining his composure. With the light almost gone, maintaining balance was difficult. In the darkness to his left, he heard voices, saw lights.

Torchlight was being pointed at the walls.

"Mr Atkins?"

The Deputy Director recognised the voice of one of his colleagues. "I'm here."

"Sir, fire's out on the roof; they're already reporting it on the news."

Atkins held his breath, inching slowly forward. He prayed it wasn't a false dawn.

"Sir?" the voice repeated.

"I'm going to need your light." He glanced over his shoulder to the point from where the lights were shining. Shielding his view, he realised the wall sloped to an angle of approximately twenty-five degrees. Attached to the wall were a number of metal pipes. The burning embers were about ten metres away, directly in front of him; they had fallen further than any of the previous ones.

The area was also far darker.

Gripping the surface to his left, he moved slowly along the supporting wall, using the pipes for a foothold. Taking a deep breath, he completed the manoeuvre in one swift movement, coming down on the second beam.

He estimated eight metres now separated him from the flames.

Movement was becoming difficult despite the light of the torches. The smoke was rising in front of him, partially hiding the exact location of the fire. Closing his mouth, he held his breath to avoid inhaling the toxic air, doing his best to shuffle across to the source of the burning, anything to reach it in time.

Little by little he was getting there, inch by inch, millimetre by millimetre, but with each movement the blaze was becoming stronger. As he concentrated on the beam, he realised it was in severe danger of becoming unstable.

He feared only seconds remained.

Increasing his speed, he reached out, his bare hand gripping the wood. The closer he got, the warmer it became; sweat poured down his forehead, the skin on his arms tingled. Moving forward again, he touched the flame, recoiling. Despite the pain, he willed himself on, knowing only seconds now remained before the strength of the supports gave way. Biting down hard, he kicked firmly against the burning embers.

And watched them float away into the void below.

Lying on his back, Kit peered up at the nearby barrels, finding them all intact. As the seconds passed, the situation remained unchanged; even in the total darkness, there was only one logical conclusion.

The fires were out.

Rolling to his left, he could see Sanders patting frantically at Chambers' chest. Though alive, it was clear from Chambers' face that he was in great pain.

Kit rushed to his feet, investigating the damage. There were raw scars on Chambers' chest where the powder had burned through his clothing. In one particular area of about three inches in the centre of his rib cage, the black skin was deeply cut and had become purple.

"Life in the old dog yet!" Kit smiled.

Chambers smiled back. "Bro, that's exactly what she said."

Shaking his head, Sanders burst out laughing. In the setting that had earlier been filled with panic and destruction, there was now an air of relief and optimism.

Finding no source for the recent disturbance, Alain rose to his feet, moving carefully towards the doorway. He looked down at his feet as he moved, knowing one wrong step could give away the game completely.

Reaching the doorway, he looked out in both directions through his red lenses. The passage sloped downwards to his right, upwards to his left; metal railings provided support on both sides. The clothes line above was empty, the costumes piled up to one side. *Strange*, he thought.

He didn't recall it had been that way on entering.

Holding out his firearm, he heard a clicking noise close to his head.

"Don't even think about it."

Atkins accepted the hand of the nearest firefighter and immediately took the stairs down to the Stone Gallery. Though the air was pungent, he inhaled it gratefully, knowing a few more seconds on the smoking beam might have been enough for a lack of oxygen to cause permanent damage.

Looking up to the dome, he focused on the area that had previously been on fire, noting the white steam rising from the curved exterior. Close to the dome, the air was particularly bad, contaminated by smoke and something else that Atkins put down to melted metal. He recalled the famous story from 1666 that when the lead melted, it poured away down the streets, creating rivers in the flames.

He exhaled in relief, knowing a similar outcome had just been avoided.

For several seconds, he stared at the damage. What had been traditionally white was now scarred by blackness. As he reflected on the scene before him, he recalled the words of its creator.

The secret of architectural excellence is to translate the proportions of a dachshund into bricks, mortar and marble.

What was presently scarred would one day be repaired.

Moving away from the dome, he turned to view the broader skyline. The fires were now out on the north side; further west, those on Fleet Street had been dowsed by the efforts of the returning helicopters. Moving on to the south side, the fires that had spread to the dome were also out; the same was true to the east. Watching on in silence, a strange feeling of pride came over him as though whatever had recently transpired, it wouldn't be forgotten anytime soon.

Like the heroes of the Blitz, the heart of the great city was still beating proudly.

104

Beneath the Jewel House, 03:12

Randek and François returned to the jeweller's workshop, passing through both of the previously locked iron doors. What they had seen of the passageway so far had gone on for around a hundred metres; if the plans photocopied from the Raleigh manuscript were right, the route would end after almost a mile.

On reaching the jeweller's work desk, they re-evaluated the photocopy. Whatever the exact location of the Tudor storehouse, Raleigh's map confirmed the tunnel had been dug directly beneath it.

Unquestionably they had found it.

A sudden blast of static erupted from Randek's HT; answering, he realised it was Christophe.

"What's the latest?"

In the CCTV room, the leader of the three gunmen answered while monitoring the screens, just as he had been doing throughout the evening.

"The hostages in the White Tower have all been liberated; as have those in the Queen's House." He watched with mild irritation as four members of the Queen's Guard entered the White Tower through the south door; at least one of the hostages had been smart enough to open it from the inside.

One by one, they were discovering the charges.

"Ten minutes' time, you might not get another chance at this."

Randek listened carefully. "Relax. Our intention was never to destroy the building unless it was completely necessary." He glanced again at the first of the previously secret doors. "Besides, all plans are subject to change."

Ending the conversation, he looked again at the photocopied plans, trying to establish exactly where their route would end. In addition to what appeared to be a rounded chamber at the end of the passageway was a second tunnel, its appearance almost a mirror image of the first.

"What direction is that?"

"South-west," François responded. "If everything is to scale, the end will be somewhere close to Blackfriars."

"Assuming it hasn't been blocked." Randek placed the HT again to his lips. "Where is my uncle?"

"I haven't seen him since he returned to the tunnels," Christophe replied. "Nor the man who followed him."

Randek bit his lip, his anxiety increasing. Twice in recent minutes he had failed to receive a response from his uncle. "Let me know as soon as he returns."

"I will. Oh, and the news outside isn't good. The fires are fading. The cathedral is saved."

"As I've told you already, plans are subject to change."

Randek changed the frequency and tried again to contact Blanco. "Bizu, this is Fabien. Are you receiving me?"

Blanco heard his nephew's voice come through clearly on his frequency. He slowed his pace on leaving the ninth passage, at which point his eyes were once again dazzled by the bizarre layout.

A prisoner could easily have lost their mind down here, he mused.

"What is it?" he answered, at the same time discovering the next option was left or right; from earlier enquiries, he knew the correct direction was right.

Randek exhaled with relief. "We have found the passage. Just as we suspected, it begins in the jeweller's workshop."

Alone in the darkness a broad smile appeared on Blanco's face. Keeping his eyes on the area where he had just walked, he anticipated the moment he would no longer be alone. "You have seen it?"

"The original doors still exist. The passage continues beyond. Continue your current course, eventually you will join it."

Blanco's smile widened further. While his left hand gripped his communications device tightly, with the right he did the same with his firearm.

"Where are you now?"

"The workshop. The first door was hidden behind the old man's tools."

Blanco laughed wryly; just like the antiquarian in Paris, the sly old fox's intelligence was practically unrivalled. "Are you alone?"

"François is with me. Aside from the barracks, the Tower is lost."

"How many remain?"

"Eleven, including us."

Blanco bowed his head; fifty-four had entered, less than a quarter now remained. "How about outside?"

Randek paused. "I understand from the news, the cathedral has been saved."

"Have you contacted Pierre?"

"*Oui*." He spoke of Everard's brother.

"And?"

Again Randek delayed. "There was no response."

Blanco nodded, realisation dawning. "Let us concentrate on what remains in our control. Our only concern now is the jewels."

Maria breathed a sigh of relief as she finished her conversation with Atkins. The Deputy Director was still alive, the fires inside the cathedral successfully quelled. Like the exterior of the dome, the damage was repairable.

Within seconds of finishing the conversation, another voice came through, Kit's.

"Rook, this is Edward."

"Receiving you, Edward; and right on cue."

"Just what on earth is that supposed to mean?"

"I guess I'll have to tell you sometime." Maria smiled; following her recent conversation with Atkins, she felt suddenly exhilarated. "What's been happening?"

"Would you like the short version or the full?"

"Short – orders of the Deputy Director. The long might have to wait until the victory party."

"So there will be one?"

"I guess that depends. Where are you guys?"

At the other end, Kit was first to re-emerge through the false façade of Wren's tomb. He found Nat and Gillian close by; Gillian hugged him warmly on his return. "We're back in the crypt."

"Any scars?"

"I thought you were only interested in the short version?"

Another smile. "In that case, I'll definitely look forward to hearing about it."

Blanco waited until he was sure the passageway behind him was empty before placing the HT to his lips. Though he was waiting alertly for the moment his pursuer would emerge from the centre of hell, the last thing he wanted was to be caught off guard.

He adjusted the frequency for Edinburgh.

"Alain, do you copy?"

Phil recognised Rawlins' voice come through just as Maria took the call from Kit.

"How are you guys?"

Speaking from an otherwise deserted chamber off the Real Mary King's Close, Rawlins answered via his headset while both himself and Pentland kept their guns trained on the recently apprehended Alain de Haulle.

"Mary King's Close. Directly north of the cathedral."

Phil raised an eyebrow. "I never had you down as one for the tourist sites."

"What can I say? I'm always discovering new things about myself." Rawlins looked hard into the eyes of the recently apprehended arsonist, sneering as he smiled. "Tell the Director we have some good news. The cathedral will be open as normal tomorrow."

Failing to get a response from Alain, Blanco turned his attention to another part of the city.

"David, do you copy?"

Situated high on a grassy area on Arthur's Seat, the cousin of Fabien Randek took the call.

"I'm here."

On this occasion, the feeling of relief was particularly strong. "And where exactly is here?"

"Outside the city." He checked his watch, realising he still had over forty minutes to reach his next destination. "The hour is early."

"Where is Alain?"

"I've received no contact." He gazed out across the city, concentrating on the cathedral. "The fires are all out."

Blanco ended the call, again checking he was alone.

"Sébastien, do you copy?"

In the centre of Paris, the noise of sirens blared as seemingly every police car and boat covered every inch of the city, searching for any sign of the jewel thieves. Despite the late hour, there were lights on in many of the establishments.

Almost thirty miles south of the French capital, the antiquarian was roused from his slumber by the harsh tone of his employer's voice as it crackled through the handheld transmitter. Switching on the nearest light, he looked across the living quarters of the small yacht, relieved to find the nearby contents unmoved.

"Sébastien, do you copy?" the voice repeated.

He answered, "Don't you ever sleep?"

Blanco smiled. "Where are you?"

"Where should I be?"

"There are reports reaching the English news of a disturbance in the museum. The police are out searching the capital in force."

"But we are not in the capital, Bizu; you have known this for some time."

Beyond the slight antagonism, he detected confidence in the old man's voice. "You are safe?"

"Safety, as Einstein would once have said, is relative. Compared to an innocent man, perhaps not. Compared to those poor souls in the city, I'd say so." The old man switched on the news; even in France, the reports were almost exclusively focused on London. "And are you?"

Blanco neglected to answer. "Stay where you are. The helicopter will be with you soon. We will discuss things properly in Bordeaux."

Emily was still waiting by the phone when it rang a second time. She picked up the receiver, anticipating the caller.

"Hello?"

"We really need to get you a headset."

Emily smiled on hearing Maria's voice. "For what it's worth, I understand using a landline to the Tower is fairly inexpensive at this hour. And if it makes you feel any better, I promise to call home before I leave. That way, they'll never be able to trace you."

"You honestly think we're stupid enough to leave a trace?" Maria smiled as she glanced at her surroundings, knowing that even if the woman's charm and beauty had led Mike to reveal any of the organisation's secrets, she would never believe a word he said. "How are the hostages?"

"Well – all things considered." She looked around the lounge; every hostage from the White Tower had returned.

Bar one.

"One's still missing. Professor Champion. Mike's uncle."

Maria glanced at the security pictures on the semi-translucent screen, but found no obvious sign of movement in the White Tower. She didn't remember seeing him since he'd left the roof.

"He can't have gone far." She continued to explore the live footage. Strangely, Mike was still to resurface. "What's going on out there?"

"The Queen's Guard and the Yeoman Warders are in conference with the governor in the Council Chamber." She spoke of the room where famous prisoners had once been interrogated. "Besides the weapons recovered from downstairs and in the White Tower, we're not exactly well equipped."

"Well, just sit tight for now; last I counted, there's only eleven of them, so you're probably punching above their weight."

"Any further advice?" she asked, traces of anxiety now detectable in her voice.

"Right now, all you can do is sit tight. And pray the Queen's Guard manage to locate all the explosives."

Blanco held his breath as he anticipated movement from the passage behind him. Though visibility was poor, the acoustic effects of the vast, enclosed surroundings were misleading, almost like the noise equivalent of a mirage in the desert. The sounds Blanco was able to hear gave no clue as to their location but confirmed one thing.

Somewhere, someone was moving.

Inching ever further along the wall behind him, he kept his eyes on the entrance to the passageway, gun at the ready.

Even if the Englishman had visited the area before, he knew he would have no chance of catching him off guard.

In the fourth passage, Professor Champion gazed in shock as he realised he'd entered yet another area once used as part of a subterranean prison.

Using a small light attached to his keyring to guide him, he headed into the next passageway, wondering how many more separated him from the end.

"Mike's uncle is missing and hasn't been seen for over ten minutes." Maria left her seat and moved behind Phil, watching the footage on his screen from over his shoulder. "What is that?"

Allowing the footage to run, the IT specialist concentrated on the locked-off camera in the cellar. Blanco had been the first to leave the White Tower from there, lowering himself into a void within a display of historic cannons. Mike had followed him three minutes later; Phil remembered guiding him down there himself.

Then, something unexpected happened.

After less than two minutes, the void was entered a third time.

The exit from the ninth passage was different to what Mike had expected. He was presented with a straight choice: left or right; up ahead was a dead end. After trying the right, he discovered a similar decision would be necessary.

Without further guidance, he realised he was lost.

Instinct guided him right, then left. A second time, the pattern repeated. On reaching a crossroads, he stopped. Listened. Getting through to Maria or the others was still impossible.

He realised he was on his own.

Heading right, he heard sounds in the distance, a cough, footsteps, clearly running. He hurried off in the direction of the noises, on guard in case of a sudden attack. As he reached the far end of the tunnel, a figure became visible against the green backdrop of his night visions, staring back from what appeared to be a doorway into somewhere far brighter.

Removing his night visions, he concentrated on the source of the movement.

Blanco was standing before him.

Unarmed.

The first thing Mike saw was a shadow to his right, moving swiftly across the treeline. Within a second, the same thing happened to his left; his senses told him only that the figures were male. Listening carefully, he detected sounds: heavy boots, voices, whispered commands. One voice he recognised.

Masterson.

He hit the ground violently, momentum forcing him into a forward roll. His initial reaction was to fight, but he forced himself to hold back, knowing resistance against such numbers would be useless. A barrage of insults flew like bullets around his ears; after over twelve hours underground, his senses tingled. The shouting seemed all the louder, the force of the heavy impact punishing.

As they pulled him to his feet, he felt his energy sap.

"Welcome to the foot of Mount Purgatorium. For over two thousand years, pilgrims have been coming from all over the world to discover this holy place." Blanco's voice echoed off the surrounding stonework, his smile widening as Mike approached. "I really must congratulate you. Few are both brave and smart enough to find their way out first time."

"Nor stupid enough to venture down here alone in the first place." Mike crept forward, gun at the ready; his eyes darted side to side, anticipating a possible ambush. After his rude awakening at Charlestown, he was unwilling to make the same mistake again. "Truth be told, I'd actually been thinking the same about you. Throughout history, would-be thieves have been thwarted in their attempts to infiltrate the Tower, not to mention burn the city to the ground. Somehow you've managed to achieve both in the same night."

"You are most generous in your praise, albeit perhaps not entirely sincere."

"On the contrary. Should he have been alive today, even the genius of Waterloo would surely have paid tribute to your ingenuity. The wisest commanders rarely make predictions; those that do successfully often wish they were wrong. Then again, what is life but a test of one's limits? Personally I'd rather be Phaethon than Plato."

"A man of great intellect, I see; my nephew was quite correct about you."

"I'd rather been hoping to catch him myself. Where is he?"

"He will be here soon enough; perhaps in time, he too will learn a similar appreciation, but I digress. As you rightly say, in life we all have our strengths and purposes. We cannot all be philosophers."

"Nor poets for that matter. I must say you had us slightly stumped earlier, at least for a while. Right now, I'm sorry to say your luck's out."

Blanco appeared confused. "I'm sorry, I do not follow."

"The Sons of Gemini. It's brilliant, really. Unknown sons of Edward II. A rogue Italian cardinal. Up until now, no one picked up on the connection; not even with the modern-day descendants. You only made one mistake, Blanco." Mike stepped forward, gun still at the ready. "Only an arrogant man celebrates victory before he's actually won."

The sound of fast-moving footsteps in the passage behind him caught Mike unaware. As the figure emerged into the light, he recognised Randek.

"Wise words indeed. One day I really hope to make use of them." Blanco walked forward, not stopping till he was only inches away. "Tie him up!"

105

St Paul's Cathedral, 03:14

The helicopter came down at the point where Paternoster Row met Ludgate Hill. During the day, landing there would have been practically impossible; the location – famous for being the main area of traffic south of the cathedral, heading either east into the city or west out of it across the box junction and along Fleet Street – had been officially closed to pedestrians since the gunfight began and to cars for much longer. In the absence of crowds and vehicles, the pilot knew he had only one major obstacle to overcome.

Thanks to the recent destruction of buildings north-west of Paternoster Row and the fires to the south, the challenge was to find an area free of debris.

He came down approximately midway between the zebra crossing and the statue of Queen Anne, judging everything to near perfection. On touching down, the Director wasted no time before alighting, ducking his head on making his way quickly under the force of the slowing rotor blades before reaching the off-limits area around the great steps.

A quick showing of his ID card was enough to convince the duty police, each man clearly exhausted from recent challenges, that his clearance was legitimate. One had been looking out for him.

"Mr Atkins is expecting you, sir."

Stooping low under the cordon tape, the Director hurried inside, saving but a passing glance for the great west front that loomed over him. Whereas the sights around the cathedral were largely of mass destruction, the scenes somewhat reminiscent of archive footage taken at the height of the Blitz, the building he entered was largely unblemished. Apart from the thick soot-like stains on the dome on the far side, the structure remained intact.

Despite the best attempts of both the Luftwaffe and the Sons of Gemini, the building was still standing.

He entered the cathedral and proceeded quickly through the nave towards the altar, his eyes distracted by the surprisingly spotless interior. On approaching the altar, reaching a point almost directly under the dome, he slowed, his attention on the pictures of the cathedral's saint of dedication that decorated the inner dome, the famous monochrome paintings and gilded niches remarkably untainted. A few feet away, a man with his back to the nave carried out a solitary vigil, his appearance far different to that he had presented earlier. The trademark white shirt, rimless glasses and well-polished shoes were still present but each heavily stained by smoke and dirty water.

Evidence of a man who had fought fire with fire.

Exhausted, the Deputy Director turned from the dome to face the Director.

"Two hundred men." The words barely escaped Atkins' mouth; the Director sensed he was talking about the war. "Tonight we had seventeen."

The Director looked around him, observing that the floor was also unmarked. He recalled another story from the Blitz: how an incendiary fallen from the roof had damaged much of the floor. Only decades later was the story finally released.

"Even the cleaner couldn't have kept the floor so spotless." Mr White stood alongside him, gazing again up at the images of the saint. "Throughout everything, you're both still standing. A lesser man wouldn't have ventured close to the beam."

The Deputy Director looked Mr White in the eye: tired, uniquely forlorn. Though the dome was still standing, the external scars were clear.

In his mind, he had failed.

Footsteps sounded loudly from the south-east corner as several figures appeared. At the head of the group of five was Masterson.

"Fires below ground have been extinguished." Kit addressed both men; like Atkins, his face was blackened by dirt and smoke, his usually smart hair dishevelled.

"The entrance was here?" the Director asked.

"Access below ground was directly through the crypt; more precisely through what the architect designed to be viewed as his grave. There's a great many more things below the surface; another day, I'd almost recommend a visit."

"What of the culprit?"

"Dead. His identity might surprise you." Kit filled him in.

On hearing the news, both were surprised but not shocked. "Presumably that just leaves one?" the Director asked.

"Ward, Wilcox and Cummins already have St Dunstan's covered. If he enters externally, they'll find him. Same if he tries to escape."

"In that case, let's hope he doesn't use any other way." The Director's mind was racing.

"Surely all the more reason to get there early," Sanders observed, his appearance equally scruffy, the scars from the explosion on the yacht and during the shoot-out clearly visible. Just behind him, Nat and Gillian remained quiet.

"Sir, this is Gillian McKevitt, the Director of the National Portrait Gallery and her predecessor, Mr Johnstone. Their input this evening has been most valuable."

The Director offered his hand to both. "You know the church at St Dunstan's?"

"These days it's just a ruin. The area was reopened as a public garden," Nat responded. "Unlike here, the area never had a crypt."

"Good. In that case, I think your work here is done." He turned his gaze to Chambers. "What on earth happened to you?"

Chambers' bare chest was still partially visible from where the gunpowder had burned his top. "Well, you know what they say about playing with fire."

"Get yourself properly attended to by the medical people. On your way, please escort Mr Johnstone and Ms McKevitt to the car." He waited till the civilians departed before addressing the others. "What's the latest elsewhere?"

"I think you may be more up to date than us," Kit responded. "Reception down there was almost non-existent."

"Fires are almost out; only a few on Cannon Street and Fleet Street remain," Atkins answered. "We know of the next two targets."

"What of the Tower?"

"Maria's confirmed the hostages in the White Tower have been returned to the Queen's House; with the exception of the Waterloo Barracks, the Queen's Guard and the Yeoman Warders have resumed control."

"You've spoken to Mike?" Kit asked.

"Unfortunately no. Intelligence says he followed Blanco underground. Hasn't come up since."

"What of Edinburgh?" Mr White resumed.

"One down, one to go. Rawlins and Pentland apprehended de Haulle's brother in one of the vaults beneath the city. Fires on the Mile are out."

Kit adjusted the frequency on his headset, trying to get through to Mike. Getting no reply, he contacted Maria.

"What's the latest on Grosmont?"

Listening in, Maria shook her head. "I honestly don't know what to tell you. GPS confirms movement; although others are alongside him." She turned to the satellite footage. "Judging from the infrared, signs are he might have been apprehended."

Kit cursed beneath his breath. "Where is he?"

"He entered the area beneath the basement of the White Tower. The GPS is strange. He could be somewhere beneath the Jewel House."

"You've had contact with the Tower?"

"Affirmative. The governor is briefing the captain of the Queen's Guard and the Yeoman Sarjeants as we speak. All but one of the hostages are accounted for."

"Who's the exception?"

"CCTV footage showed the lecturer followed Grosmont down. So far, he hasn't reappeared."

"What about the girl Grosmont was with? The curator."

"You mean acting curator?" She smiled wryly. "She's fine. Just worried."

"Keep in contact. You never know, she might still come in handy."

Kit ended the conversation as they moved towards the main exit, his attention again on the Director. "Sir, request permission to relocate to the Tower. Captain Hansen has disappeared from all platforms."

"There's been no contact?"

"Not from his end. IR coverage indicates he may have been compromised. Request permission to go after him."

"Negative, Captain." The Director shook his head. "You know the rules of our organisation. The mission comes first."

"Sir, with respect, this could affect the very outcome of the mission. The fires are dying. Blanco is underground; indications are Randek and de Haulle are two of only eleven that remain. If Blanco is down there, capturing him could see the end of all this."

The Director eyed him sternly; the fatherly bearing that Kit had seen so many times before returned. "The terms Blanco set out earlier were straightforward. Any attempt to infiltrate the Tower could send him into overdrive. We can't risk the lives of Hansen or the others by one drastic movement."

"Sir –"

"The artwork in the museum confirms there is one site remaining on the list; that same one, if what I understand is correct, could be the key to unlocking any further doors."

Sanders was stunned. "Surely you're not suggesting what I think you are?"

The Director nodded. "Randek's interest in the Raleigh manuscript six months ago, it seems, had a firm purpose after all. Enter the final crypt, we might just make our way into the Tower anyway."

Keeping to the shadows of the church of St Magnus the Martyr, the mysterious figure listened again to his HT, confused by the recent quiet. Though periods of radio silence had been consistent all night, it was rare for his employer to remain out of contact completely.

Passing the site where the famous monument was surrounded by white-hot debris, he continued past the church, making his way east towards the Tower. Even if he received no updates, he knew the plan was unlikely to change.

Standing in the shadows, Professor David Champion felt his heart beat ever faster as he heard a conversation involving several voices from within the ancient passages. Against the strange backdrop of the grim, soulless walls, the sound seemed deeply threatening, like a demonic presence intent on sapping his soul. Though speaking in English, he could make out the familiar tones of a European accent.

After his experience earlier that night, he was in no doubt of their identity.

Remaining silent, he waited until the noise died down, doing his best to hear every word. There was one voice among them that didn't belong: a calmer voice, an English voice.

Heart-wrenchingly familiar.

He waited till the conversation ended before continuing along the passageway, finding it more brightly illuminated further on. Though he couldn't see clearly into the area beyond, he determined from what he knew of the building above that it could only be one place.

Noiselessly, he turned away from the light and proceeded back the way he had previously come.

106

Charlestown,
Twenty-One Months Earlier

Mike felt the heavy presence of no less than six hands shepherding him through the woodland. With his eyes covered, his hearing became more acute; at least eight of the Harts were present, whispering, their heavy feet treading a combination of muddy path and dry twigs.

After a while the talking stopped, the walk continuing in silence. His senses tingled to the feeling of hot and cold, any warm stimulation from close contact offset by the brisk chill of the winter's evening. There was rain in the air, a light drizzle interrupting the near freezing stillness; he could hear it falling into nearby puddles. The waters of a river or stream were creating a cascading effect as they fell energetically from a higher level.

The group stopped without prior warning, clearly close to the water. A brisk shove in his back preceded the order, "On your knees."

Following the command, he heard the sound of shovelling from directly in front of him, large pieces of earth being removed from the ground. He felt some of it lightly brush against his hands, like sand caught in a breeze.

The sounds stopped, the busy hands again pressing down hard on his back. For a fraction of a second, the sack was lifted before being immediately replaced.

It was time enough to see he was looking at a shallow grave.

Beneath the Tower,
03:16

Mike felt several pairs of hands grab him heavily from behind, pushing him fiercely in the back.

On stumbling to the floor, he was immediately pulled back up.

The light had improved significantly – strong, warming. He'd come up in a room that had the appearance of a tradesman's workshop. There was a plain, unremarkable door at the end, clearly closed. Directly in front of it was a large workbench on the top of which were several crowns.

Instantly he realised that he was in the jeweller's workshop below the Jewel House.

Figures moved around him, six Heckler & Kochs aimed squarely at his face or torso. Among his captors, he recognised two faces.

One in particular.

Randek stepped forward and punched him hard in the nose. "You made a big mistake coming here tonight. Any more will be your last."

Mike felt blood flow from his nostrils and down into his mouth. Coughing vigorously to avoid choking, he endeavoured to control his breathing, knowing it was even more important with two injuries than one. Like the tightening of his thigh, his nose instantly felt smaller, the pain numbing.

Randek stood with folded arms, examining Mike's face. "You were there on the docks in Scotland that night." He leaned in closer, touching Mike's hair, pulling it extra hard. "And in Paris, by the river outside the museum." He tried to recognise him. "You are different to the man on the boat."

Spitting bloody saliva on the floor, Mike neglected to add he'd been responsible for the capture of his brother-in-law. Immediately Randek went for his injured thigh.

Grabbing it.

"I'm sure by now you know the truth of what happened to your comrade, how he begged for death when he was captured in the south of France." Randek's grip tightened further still, increasing the pressure like a knife digging in ever deeper.

"Fabien!" Blanco ordered him to stop.

Relaxing his grip, Randek spat in Mike's face and moved to the other side of the room, joining Blanco in examining the photocopied map.

"The longer the Englishman remains alive, the longer our mission is jeopardised." Randek addressed his uncle with fire in his eyes. "We must kill him now."

"Always so rash. Always so unprepared." Blanco looked back with a hard expression, his eyes confirming the message: *Do not question me.* "If the vault is as well protected as we expect, he may be the bargaining chip we need."

Breaking eye contact, Blanco returned his attention to the map, concentrating on where the passageway ended. From a bird's-eye view, the outline of the final chamber appeared to be circular; a second tunnel existed on the far side.

He removed his HT to contact Fieschi.

Seated alongside his father and relative, Gabriel de Fieschi heard a sharp sound from the handheld communications device.

"Receiving loud and clear."

Blanco recognised Fieschi's voice. "The vault has been discovered. We are moving in now."

Fieschi felt his heart miss a beat. "You've seen it?"

"There are many doors and many keys." Blanco jangled the iron keys in his hand. "Soon we will know which work and which do not."

Fieschi's instincts guided him to his feet, his movements light as though wind lifting a feather. Heading for the French doors, his gaze fell upon the city. Under the circumstances, the sight of the dying fires no longer appeared so disheartening.

"If the passage exists, the end is in sight." He concentrated on the dome of the cathedral, the only illumination coming courtesy of the floodlights. "Pray this is good news."

"It is only good if the vault can be accessed. Until it is, we must assume there will be obstacles along the way." Blanco's gaze turned to Mike. "Negotiation at this point might still be necessary."

The Plantagenet heir nodded, his gaze now on the Tower that had once been the residence of his ancestors. "The fires are dying. It will not be long till the prime minister moves her focus off the streets. You must hurry."

Blanco ended the conversation. "I'm entering the passage as we speak."

Trapped in the room's far corner, Mike concentrated on his breathing as the recently tied rope cut uncomfortably at his arms and torso.

Blanco and Randek had disappeared, heading through the far door; surprisingly it was already unlocked. As the posse of gunmen departed, Mike found himself alone with one other, the gunman's firearm still trained firmly on his torso.

He guessed from Blanco's commands, he wouldn't be leaving anytime soon.

In the silence, he heard a voice in his ear: Maria; as the seconds passed, he also heard Phil's, then Kit's. Taking a deep breath, he cleared his throat, making a habit of doing so at regular intervals. As he asked for water, the gunman pistol-whipped him hard over his head.

Maria had all the information she needed. From the cough alone, the message had been obvious. The gesture was itself a secret form of communication: something that could mean different things to different people.

In the line of duty, the challenge was making do with what was at your disposal.

Her eyes on the semi-translucent screen, she saw from the GPS position that Mike was back on the grid, located in a lower level of the Waterloo Block. The blueprints confirmed only two underground sections existed for either the barracks or the Jewel House: the cellar Mike had earlier escaped from and the Crown Jeweller's workshop.

Neither contained CCTV, as neither was open to the public.

Concentrating instead on the IR footage as it appeared from the satellite link, she saw two figures in the same room, both largely stationary. One appeared to be seated by a wall, the other watching over him, apparently armed. The message from the cough was clear: three dots, three dashes, three dots.

SOS.

107

The White Tower,
03:21

Champion headed back the same way he'd originally come, negotiating the strange passageways in the opposite direction.

In less than five minutes, he'd found himself back at the start.

The gap in the floor of the storehouse he'd used to enter reappeared as expected, the lights from above guiding his way. Whoever had cut the original hole had clearly done so with access in mind. The gap in the ceiling was inclined, allowing a person to climb it easily. Jumping to the lowest section, he rested against the flat stonework, wriggling his way up back into the White Tower.

Phil thought he was seeing things. "Champion has reappeared on camera. Exact same place." His words roused the attention of Maria, who had been concentrating solely on Mike.

"How the hell did he manage to get out of there by himself?"

"Goodness knows." Phil had been wondering the same thing. "Take a pretty big fool to underestimate him though."

Maria tapped quickly at her iMac, putting through a phone call. Again the person who answered was Emily.

"David Champion is alive; he just showed up on camera."

Standing by the couch in the living room of the Queen's House, Emily breathed out, relieved. "Where is he?"

"White Tower basement. Exactly where he disappeared." She watched his progress on the screens. On making it into the gift shop, he took the stairs to the exit. Again, he stopped short of trying the door.

"You have any Queen's Guards still out there?"

Emily walked over to the window, glad the phone was cordless. "Two are guarding the White Tower. I can't see inside."

Maria noticed them on screen; sure enough, the only guards still in the White Tower were examining the explosives Blanco's men had laid on the top floor.

"Tell them to pick him up. For all we know, he might have information that could be valuable to us."

* * *

Emily relayed the message to the first Queen's Guard she came across, a young man whose best friend had earlier been killed in the Ceremony of the Keys.

Within seconds of hearing the news, he left through the front door, continuing up the south stairs to the White Tower.

Champion heard the sound of movement somewhere among the cannons. From a distance, it wasn't obvious whether they were English or French.

Taking shelter close to the till in the gift shop, he heard his name being called, clearly in English. As the seconds passed, he recognised three members of the Queen's Guard who had recently joined him in More's chamber.

He emerged, hands up.

The nearest guard approached. "Professor, are you all right?"

"I'll live, at least a few more minutes." He walked to the other side of the gift shop. "There's a secret passage beneath the floor. The man making the threats used it to make his escape."

The Queen's Guard immediately put through a message using his handheld transmitter. "Captain, contact has been made with the missing hostage. He is safe. Possible location on Blanco. Over."

A response came immediately. "Bring him back to the Queen's House; I'd rather like a word myself."

Champion followed the recently rescued guards through the cellar area, passing the site of his recent escape. On taking the main stairs, he soon found himself at the far door.

Fresh air had never felt so good.

Emily was waiting by the front door of the Queen's House when Champion emerged. Unlike the last time she'd seen him, his smart silver suit had become noticeably unkempt, his trousers and jacket covered in stains, some of which she feared was blood. While the dishevelled condition of his hair was nothing out of the ordinary, she saw heavy bruises and cuts around his eyes and cheeks.

She hugged him immediately. "I'm so glad you're okay."

The force of her embrace caught him briefly off balance. "I'm quite all right, my dear. There are far worse things to deal with in life than the need of a new suit."

He looked at her as they separated, taking particular notice of the look in her eyes. Much had changed in recent hours.

Emily found the energy to smile. "What happened up there?"

Maria heard Emily's voice for the first time in over five minutes. Rather than disconnect the call, they had kept the line open.

"How is he?" Maria asked of Champion after hearing her confirm news of his return.

"Under the circumstances, he's done remarkably. I've just fetched him some

OJ and biscuits. Poor thing hasn't had a drop in over six hours."

"Give us another two, he'll be able to have all the steak dinners he wants. May I speak with him?"

"I'll call him in when he's back; right now, the governor and the captain of the Queen's Guard are questioning him."

"When he gets a moment, I'd rather like to do the same thing."

"On the way in, he told me the passages ended with a bright chamber."

"He couldn't place it?"

"No, but I think I can. It sounds like the jeweller's workshop."

Maria took a moment to allow the information to sink in. Potential confirmation of what she was seeing of Mike via the satellite footage. "Did he see anyone?"

"Yes." Emily swallowed hard, choking back her emotions. "They have Mike."

Actual confirmation of what she was seeing. "Just stay calm. I've got visual and audio footage. He's still alive."

"You see him?"

Maria noticed the relief in Emily's voice. "Our intel confirms there's at least one other keeping guard, not to mention two others in the CCTV room. Right now, they're watching your every move, so any attacks won't exactly be a surprise. That said, it's not as though they have the manpower to launch any counters."

"How about Blanco and the others?"

"Right now, I'd say there's only one likely place they're at."

Emily listened carefully, remembering what Champion had told her moments earlier. "You think the tunnel exists?"

"I'd have thought that you of all people would know the answer to that."

"I honestly didn't know about the other secret passages."

A sudden thought entered Maria's mind. "Well, good thing you do now. I'm going to need you to show the Queen's Guard how to use them."

Alone in the CCTV room, the two remaining gunmen saw further activity outside the Queen's House. Leaving through the main doors, the woman who had successfully evaded capture all night led the way as three fully armed and uniformed Queen's Guards and a further eight Yeoman Warders followed the steps down from Tower Green and along the passage that connected the Broadwalk Steps to the Bloody Tower. On reaching the end of Water Lane, they entered the Byward Tower.

Communicating among themselves, both men watched with concern as the figures disappeared off camera. The last time the woman had been seen inside the Byward Tower was after her disappearance from the barracks.

They feared the tide was about to turn.

Maria heard confirmation that the group had made it into the Byward Tower. If everything ran to plan, they would re-enter the Waterloo Barracks in four minutes.

Ending her latest conversation with Emily, she put through a call to Kit.

***

Kit watched from the window as the helicopter made its ascent before heading east over the cathedral. A strange feeling of melancholy overcame him as he saw for the first time the true extent of the battering the city had already taken that night. While the fires were slowly dying, the scenes of destruction were almost indescribable.

He heard Maria's voice in his ear, realising from the frequency that it wasn't intended for him alone.

"David Champion is alive and well; furthermore, he had some interesting news. The tunnels beneath the surface lead straight to the jeweller's workshop. It's the same location where Grosmont appeared on camera."

"How is he?"

"Still moving." Maria watched the footage. "In the last ten minutes little has changed. If he's still there in four minutes, he might have company."

"Where is Blanco?"

"Right now, I couldn't tell you. From what I understand, there may be a tunnel that leads beneath the Tower. Based on what Emily has told me, I think I know where its entrance is."

Alongside Kit, the Director listened attentively. "How many gunmen are still in the barracks?"

"Two on the top floor; one with Mike. Unless Blanco and the others return, the Queen's Guard should get a fairly quiet welcome when they reach the end of the passage."

The Director nodded, remembering the words the historian had left him with.

The right answer is invariably the most sensible.

"Has there been any contact?" Kit asked, quietly worried.

"Besides his ability to cough in sequence, no. When he asked for water, he got a smack over the head." She continued to watch the IR images. "I'm guessing he'll have a mighty headache right now."

"Keep watching," the Director said. "Our ETA at St Dunstan's is under three minutes."

"Yes, sir."

Kit waited until Maria's voice fell silent before speaking to the Director. "If Blanco's off the radar, this is the perfect time for us to enter."

"As I told you before, our plan is to enter. But first, we need to secure the church."

"Finding the area beneath the crypt could be a matter of chance. If we're not lucky, it might take well over an hour."

"It won't."

"You can't be sure of that!"

The Director peered through the window, concentrating on the damage below. Despite the widespread impact, one area was surprisingly intact. "As I've

told you many times before, the best secrets are often those left in plain sight."
He spoke again to Maria. "Maria, do you copy?"

"Yes, sir."

"Get me a line to the chief of police. I want every available squaddie to converge on the following point."

Maria heard the reference clearly. Checking the map, she realised it was the one location reached by the historical fire but not touched on this occasion.

108

Charlestown,
Twenty-One Months Earlier

Mike felt something soft touch his left cheek. A light wind was blowing, accompanied by small spots of drizzle. He had a piercing pain in both of his legs; he was becoming used to getting pins and needles from time to time, but what he felt now was more intense.

He kicked out, trying to force the issue, but to no avail. Opening his eyes fully, the darkness of the head sack further frustrated him, reminding him he'd recently been captured. Where was he? Why was he there? He'd dreamt he'd been running through the centre of hell, his weary body chased through the underworld by a horde of demons led by knights in black. Masterson's voice was barking at him, his expression snarling; joining him were the Ukrainian, the Israeli, the Americans, the Filipino, the Aussie. No matter how close he got to the gates, there was simply no way out. The dream ended with a fall close to the void.

And darkness.

Again he kicked out, his inability to move now troubling. Something was weighing him down, trapping him like cement. His attempted movements caused new sensations against his skin, a soft tickling feeling; again he felt water. The head sack felt damper than usual. Close to his ear he felt a light pattering sensation, like a drumbeat caused by the treading of insects. He felt cold, especially on his neck; what felt like water seeping down. That was when he realised. When it all made sense.

The last thing he remembered was being ordered into a shallow grave.

By Masterson.

He shuffled for comfort, doing his best to remain quiet. He assumed someone was still close at hand; indeed, he heard voices from somewhere behind him. Two males were engaged in conversation; though he couldn't pick up on their exact words, he recognised the voices of Dawson and Pugh. One of them was leaving, one relieving the other.

As he slowly moved his head, he saw daylight outside the head sack.

He listened as attentively as possible, able to pick out isolated words. Most of the conversation seemed trivial, non-military, as if the two friends were enjoying a chinwag. He smiled to himself beneath the bag, quietly excited.

Suddenly, he had an idea.

Dawson had been alone for almost ten minutes – ten minutes too long. The rain had worsened the moment Pugh left; he knew him well enough to know an escape from the cold was as good a reason as any to return to base. Secretly, he'd have done the same thing.

The only thing worse than boredom was boredom in the wet.

He'd taken up a position ten metres from the shallow grave, under partial cover of the trees. The coverings were sparse, typical winter; at least it offered something without losing the benefit of being able to observe the surrounding area.

The man dubbed the Poet had excelled in recent days; the time in hell bettered his own by almost an hour. Only the best were awarded the honour of sitting at that table.

Secretly, he had already accepted Hansen as a knight.

He watched the pit, doing his best to concentrate. The lad had made subtle movements since Pugh had left; he remembered from his own experience, keeping still wasn't easy. The rainfall had increased, creating small puddles around his head, the droplets pooling on his clothes.

If the lieutenant was asleep, he knew he'd wake soon.

Twenty minutes in, he saw movement. Hansen was shaking, possibly convulsing. Masterson had warned him to be on the lookout for anything suspicious.

The red beret was struggling.

He ran forward, machine gun at the ready, keeping an eye out for sudden movements. Hansen was shaking uncontrollably, his body fighting the weight of his incarceration.

"Hansen?" Hearing no response, he leapt down into the pit. He leaned in close, taking care not to leave himself exposed. The convulsions looked disturbingly genuine, as though the boy were choking or suffering some form of epileptic fit. With one swift movement he yanked away the head sack.

Hansen's eyes were closed, his mouth salivating.

Dawson's reactions were immediate. "Hansen! Hansen!" He threw his weapon to one side and unzipped his combat jacket. Among the various devices and ammunitions Phil had installed on the belt, each man was equipped with both a battery-operated defibrillator and five millilitres of adrenalin.

"Mike, Mike!" He tapped the red beret's face, his movements achieving little more than spilling saliva. "Hold on, buddy. I've got this."

The instructions he'd received in training were clear – crystal clear. Any sign of a convulsion, roll the patient on to his side and, if there's no sign of a pulse, strike the device directly into his chest.

And to repeat if necessary.

Dawson tore rapidly at Mike's torso, clearing a path to his chest and inadvertently freeing topsoil from his legs. As the lieutenant's body came free, he spread his arms out wide, double-checking for a pulse.

Mike waited till the last moment before springing from the trap. He could sense from Dawson's movements that he was preparing something; Phil had told him during the first phase that protocol was standard in the event of medical emergencies.

He rolled the unsuspecting Hart to one side and pinned him hard to the ground. He smiled wryly on spitting the built-up saliva from his mouth.

"No funny games, Jack. This is nothing personal. I'm afraid I've just had quite enough of water."

Dawson was furious, clearly angrier with himself than with Mike. He attempted to fight back, but Hansen had the advantage.

"Easy, Jack. It's not gonna be easy without this." He glanced at the machine gun. With both their eyes on the firearm, Mike's upper body came down hard on Dawson's. He rolled away. Collected the gun.

And aimed it.

"No funny business. Last thing I want to do is actually use this. On your feet."

Dawson rose slowly, threatening to toss the defibrillator away. Exhaling, he regained his patience, his eyes on Mike.

"Very clever, Hansen. Dare I say, ingenious." He spat on the floor, his expression sour. "But it's one thing beating one of us. The other ten are another matter."

Mike smiled, his first genuine one for as long as he could remember. The onset of emotions was so great he felt the need to both laugh and cry. He composed himself and did neither.

"You've got me all wrong, Jack. I don't intend to beat anyone. How about we march back to the canteen and we can all have some lunch together?"

"You think it's that easy?" Dawson's resolve had steeled. He laughed; the increasing downpour was now starting to flatten his smartly combed dark hair. "What makes you think I'll come? You honestly think we'd be reckless enough to load that thing?"

Mike looked at the weapon, deciding against inspecting the drum. Any sudden movements, he knew Dawson could regain the upper hand.

He placed it on its automatic setting and aimed it at the man's heart. "Then I guess you won't mind if we walk like this, then."

The remaining ten were seated at the Round Table, chatting over lunch. Most of them were eating soup, mopping up their bowls with bread rolls. The main course was cooking nearby; it smelled like chicken.

On seeing Mike enter, the room fell silent.

He had come in behind Dawson. After deciding on making a joke about being a late guest, his mind suddenly went blank. Seeing Masterson and the other Harts guppy mouthed was just too much for his tortured soul to take in.

"Mmmm." He inhaled the various aromas. "I must say, that chicken really does smell delightful."

Seated at the round table, the stunned expressions lightened into something better humoured. Jay and Chambers laughed loudly, the others not sure what to do. Shaking heads were replaced with smiles.

Finally, everyone except Masterson burst into applause.

109

The Jewel House,
03:29

Mike awoke suddenly, aware of a series of sensations close to his face. The room was spinning, his head pounding; just moving it created an overwhelming desire to vomit. As his vision began to focus, he saw he was in an underground room; he recalled seeing it earlier that day. Then he recalled other things.

The nightmare in his mind was real.

There were noises occurring somewhere around him, most of them directly in his ears. Someone was speaking, a soft voice, clearly female.

Maria was calling his name.

His only response was to clear his throat.

Maria turned to Phil. "Mike's awake."

"You spoke to him?"

"Not exactly." She glanced again at the IR footage. As before, two figures were still positioned in the same room.

The second no longer paying him attention.

Mike's sight was clearing now. His position was unchanged, though his guard was taking the time to enjoy a cigarette close to where the fake crowns were now on display. The downside was that being awake again brought with it consciousness of his pains, all of which seemed to have escalated. The throbbing in his thigh had worsened considerably; proof, he prayed, that it was starting to heal. The impact of Randek's punch had caused numbness and swelling so that he was unable to feel his nose. Trying to swallow, he could feel a build-up of saliva and hardened blood in his mouth, restricting his ability to breathe.

His eyes on his onlooker, his mind began to recall past memories, one from his training coming instantly to mind. What worked once could always work again.

Cautiously, he closed his eyes and allowed his mouth to fill up.

A sudden, urgent sound of coughing caught the final gunman off guard, so lost had he been in his thoughts. It was coming from the Englishman; he'd pistol-whipped him so hard, the last thing he expected was for him to awaken before dawn.

He found him still strapped tightly to the chair, his back arched, his eyes closed. There was foam seeping from his mouth, possibly mixed with blood.

He immediately picked up his HT, but received no response.

Placing it back down, he raised his gun, his mood anxious. The Englishman's movements were becoming ever more erratic, like someone undergoing shock treatment. The spillage from his mouth was worsening, his face locked in a tight grimace.

Whatever had brought on the convulsions, he feared the man was ready to choke.

Unsure how to proceed, he moved nearer, his gun still trained on Mike. He grabbed his shoulders, pressing down hard; in desperation, he attempted to pat his back. He considered shooting him, but remembered Blanco's orders: *make sure he stays alive*. Banging his back ever harder, he opened the prisoner's mouth, considering artificial respiration.

With that the figure burst from the chair.

Maria watched developments closely over the infrared communications link. The two figures, previously well over five metres apart, were now within touching distance. Listening in on Mike's frequency, she heard what sounded like desperation and straining.

The volume was loud enough to unnerve Phil.

"What is it?"

"I don't know; sounds like he's having a convulsion." She spoke quietly into Mike's earpiece, fearing being overheard. Her eyes on the screen, her concern increased.

Mike waited until the last second before lunging at the gunman. While he'd been unable to free himself from his bonds completely, the sharp movements had loosened them sufficiently for him to lift the chair off the floor. Spitting out the sickly liquid that had threatened to choke him, he turned sharply left and then right. As the binding loosened from around his arms, he heard a sound of wood crashing, then a second time, after which he was able to move freely.

Expelling the remainder of the liquid from his mouth, he looked down to see his captor unconscious within a pile of wood.

Maria heard Mike's voice within seconds of seeing the previously still figure moving. "What's the latest?"

She exhaled in relief. "For a minute, I thought you were having a serious episode."

"So did Jack Dawson." He grinned to himself, rearming himself with his captor's Heckler & Koch, which he saw was fully loaded. "Blanco and the others disappeared behind a door." He headed towards it, opened it. "Looks like another passageway."

"Not just any passageway. If this goes where I think it does, it could be the most important yet."

Immediately the penny dropped. "Where's the Director?"

"In the helicopter. He's currently in videoconference with the PM."

"What about the Deputy?"

"Currently being checked out by the medics, along with Chambers."

"They okay?"

"Let's just say it got pretty hot at the cathedral for a while."

"In that case, who is in charge?"

Kit heard Mike's voice coming through clearly in his ear. "I hear you've just got a promotion."

"The captain in the field must always be flexible when it comes to making decisions," Kit replied, secretly relieved. "What's happening? I heard you were taking a nap."

Mike smiled wryly, completing a double take of the workshop. The stairway came up in the jewel room. At the far end, the door was unlocked and heralded the beginning of a passageway.

"Matter of fact, I dreamt I was back in Charlestown, seeing the look on your face when I escorted Dawson in from the shallow grave." He moved slowly along the passage, reattaching his night visions. "I think it must have been a premonition."

"Well, you'd know all about that kind of stuff, wouldn't you? Where are you now?"

"Somewhere beneath the Jewel House – looks like a workshop." He moved on, opening the second door, the hard iron shell turning slowly against its supports.

As he did, he sensed the reception go.

"Grosmont?"

Mike returned to the workshop, at which point Kit's voice came through clearly again. "Blanco, Randek and the others have all disappeared; there are two unlocked doors – appear to be part of a longer passageway. It's possible it might lead to the real Crown Jewels."

"What do you mean, might?"

"I don't have all the answers right now; I just know that wherever it leads, I intend to follow it." He strapped on his gloves again, checking himself over. Under the circumstances, he'd felt worse. "Unless I have orders to the contrary."

"Negative. You follow it and you find those SOBs. Rest assured, we'll be right there behind you."

"Understood."

Over half a mile from the beginning of the passageway, in the strange gothic streets beneath the City of London, the walk continued in silence.

From out of nowhere, a loud crackle of static came up from Blanco's HT.

"What is it?"

In the CCTV room, the two gunmen saw activity on the ground floor. "The

Queen's Guards have entered the barracks. We can't hold it, just the two of us."

Blanco scowled, frustrated but far from surprised. "Very well. Reassemble in the workshop. When the reinforcements come, make your way down the passage."

While the two gunmen made their way down the main stairs, changing direction on entering the Jewel House, the arsonist heard a similar sound come through on his own device.

"*Allô?*"

"Where are you?"

He recognised Blanco's voice. "I have just arrived at the ruins."

"Good. As soon as the hour is upon us, you may activate."

In the vaults beneath Edinburgh close to Holyrood Palace, the cousin of Fabien Randek received a similar order. It would no longer be practical to rely on further conversation.

Instead, the final stage would be initiated the moment the hour chimed.

Just north of the Royal Mile, Pugh waited for Pentland's instruction before entering the underground vault. The secrets in the artwork had already served them well once that evening.

He no longer doubted the same would be true again.

110

Central London, 03:32

The helicopter landed in the middle of Lower Thames Street, directly adjacent to St Dunstan's Hill. Like all roads in the city, it was closed in both directions, its carriageways devoid of traffic.

On touching down, the doors opened immediately. Kit and Sanders wasted no time in getting out and heading north up the hill. The spire had been the only part visible from the road, peeking up discreetly above the surrounding trees.

Reaching the road, they split up, Sanders taking the left, heading for the tower. Kit went right, following the road as it curved around, connecting with Cross Lane to the east.

As well as the main entrances to the church.

St Dunstan-in-the-East was the most easterly of Wren's churches. Built around 1100, it was one of the few credited to Wren that had escaped complete destruction in 1666 and hadn't needed to be entirely rebuilt. Re-opened in 1671, the iconic steeple was added to the unique design of four smaller spires surrounding the central spire in 1698 and somehow survived a bombing raid by the Luftwaffe that gutted the main body of the church. Despite never being rebuilt, the surrounding area instead reopened as a garden.

Kit entered the garden through the main gates at the same moment that he received confirmation Sanders had done the same at the other side. The south walls loomed large above him, the iconic archways creating dark shadows from the nearby street lighting. He took a further flight of steps through the first archway of the south wall immediately to his right.

And found the bearded figure of Tommy Ward in the garden area close to a number of benches.

"What's the latest?"

"All quiet. So far no sign."

"Where are the others?"

"Cummins is covering the porch on the north-east; Wilcox, the tower."

Kit moved off, crossing the burnt-out nave that was now overgrown with green plants and creepers. Passing the north wall, he turned east and saw Cummins among the trees.

"Any sign?"

"Negative," the blond-haired Cummins replied, his eyes peeled on the nearby doorway. "Haven't seen a single soul."

"Let's hope it stays that way." Kit headed west, following the north wall towards the tower. Sanders was already speaking with Wilcox.

"Any sign?"

Wilcox shook his head. "The gates close at nightfall. The tower is headquarters to some charity."

What Kit heard confirmed the intel. "Keep where you are. Rob, take the road outside."

"What are you gonna do?"

"Same as what I always do. Take a walk in the park."

The helicopter was airborne again by the time Kit returned to the road. He heard it without currently being able to see it; even with the fires out, the skyline remained obscured by smoke.

"Church garden is covered," he said over the airwaves. "Any sign and we'll find him. Even if he enters the tower."

Watching the city from the window of the helicopter as it headed back towards Whitehall, the Director heard every word through his headset. "Good. Whatever you do, make sure you keep him alive until you learn the precise location of the crypt."

"Yes, sir."

Kit headed back north, circling the churchyard once before re-entering, passing his comrades a second time. Seeing no sign of anyone else, he took up a position among the trees on the site of what had once been the nave.

And contacted the Rook.

"Rook, this is Edward. Churchyard is currently clear; all angles are currently covered."

An answer came from Phil. "Roger, Edward. May I say you're all showing up beautifully in IR."

"I'll be sure to pass that one on. What's happening at the Tower?"

The next response came from Maria. "I've just spoken to the professor. Thanks to his earlier look around, he's volunteered to act as a guide for the Queen's Guard."

Kit couldn't decide if that was good news or bad. "Where are the villains?"

"Two are still in the barracks; though presently making their way downstairs. The curator and the Queen's Guards should be entering the cellar any second now."

"Well, tell them to stay safe. If the White Tower is still rigged, one wrong move could see the whole thing crashing down."

"You don't have to remind me."

"How about Grosmont?"

"No signal." Maria's eyes turned to the GPS. "According to this, he's still moving."

Mike gritted his teeth in concentration as he continued along the passageway, fighting the increasing pain in his face and leg. Behind the second door, what had started as a straight tunnel was now curving and sloping slightly; he sensed that he was gradually descending.

Listening through his headset, he realised that the progressively weakening signal had now gone completely, leaving him without any line of communication. Once more that evening the reality dawned on him that everything that followed would be entirely in his hands.

Emily saw the cellar wall in front of her, just as she had done several hours earlier. After everything that had happened since, it seemed like a long time ago; it was strange approaching it from the other side.

The escape lever was obvious on her side; it had been far less so earlier when examining the fireplace. Grabbing the head of the metal mechanism, located on the bottom right corner of what was clearly the rear outline of the fireplace, she pulled down hard, holding her breath as a sharp sound followed.

The wall spun ninety degrees on its axis, opening up in front of her. Crouching down, she entered first, finding herself in familiar darkness. Reactivating the night visions Mike had given her, she led the way through the cellar, the torches of the Queen's Guards and the Beefeaters clearly visible behind her.

Tentatively, she entered the kitchen.

The captain of the Queen's Guard heard the update clearly through his HT.

"Waterloo Block is clear. Come on!"

Within seconds of giving the command, he and the five remaining Queen's Guards departed from the Queen's House, heading for the Jewel House. Entering, they swiftly spread out in both directions, finding the lower floor completely deserted.

While the six Queen's Guards headed for the main entrance, a second company of ten made up of David Champion and nine Yeoman Warders made their way up the external steps, back into the White Tower. On reaching the basement, they entered the underground passages.

The group left the cellar through the kitchen, at which point Emily hung back slightly. On receipt of confirmation the lower floor was clear, she joined her unit in taking the concealed stairway to the top floor.

Reaching the CCTV room, they found it empty.

Emily picked up the phone, pressing redial. Sure enough, the person answering was Maria.

"They're not in the CCTV room, or anywhere else on the ground or top floor. The guards are currently checking the first."

"They won't find them there either." Maria watched the barracks via the IR footage. "Both are currently in the jeweller's workshop. Must've seen you coming."

"Quite possibly. Where are the others?"

"They'll be joining you any second. If you can reach them, tell them to head to the workshop."

Mike came to a standstill as the pressure on his thigh continued to escalate. Running on the uneven ground was difficult enough in the dark without an injury; even the slightest uneven step made it difficult to maintain his balance. The pain in his head had cleared slightly, but the swelling on his face was becoming worse. Every drop of saliva continued to mix with blood.

Every impulse in his body told him to lie down.

Pushing on once more, he continued along the passageway, using the wall on his right for support. Their appearance so far had been flat on both sides; there were no nooks or niches, nowhere obvious to hide. Blanco was accompanied by at least eight men; if he encountered them, Mike knew there would be nowhere to run.

Coming again to a standstill, he felt deep into his belt to assess its remaining contents. As he did so, an idea struck him.

Even if he did reach a dead end, he still had one remaining trick up his sleeve.

As the Queen's Guards completed their repossession of the barracks, the two surviving gunmen descended the stairs into the jeweller's workshop, finding it deserted. Following Blanco's directions, they passed the jeweller's worktable, discovering a door in the far corner of the room.

Tentatively, they entered.

Maria heard Kit's voice again through her earpiece. "What's the latest?"

"Governor is currently on the phone to the PM. I've already told him help's on the way."

Crouched down low in the heart of the church garden, Kit listened to the surrounding sounds. It felt strange being among so much greenery in the city centre, yet also so quiet.

"Wish I could say the same for us."

"Just hang in there, he's not due till 04:00 hours."

Looking at his watch, Kit realised they still had over twenty-four minutes to wait.

"That's what worries me. What's the latest with Grosmont?"

"You know, I'm sure he'd be touched just how concerned you are." A soft smile lined Maria's lips. "GPS confirms he's still moving. With any luck, he should be closing in on them."

Kit took a deep breath and looked around. As he did so, his mind wandered back to his time as Mike's tormentor.

111

Charlestown, Twenty-One Months Earlier

Mike walked in silence, in the company of his two-man escort, down to the main hall. Like most parts of the school he had seen so far, it was dark by comparison to most modern buildings, the dim shade of mahogany adding to the gloom. All of the lights were on when he entered, the thick velvet curtains that lined the east side giving off a peculiar smell in addition to keeping in the light. Mixed with the dense aroma of the wooden surroundings and chalk from an unused blackboard, it really felt like a school.

The sound of hard shoes on the wooden flooring drew his attention. Masterson entered from the far doorway, dressed in combat bottoms and a white T-shirt.

His attire was as informal as Mike had seen from him.

"You can dispense with the hand waving, Lieutenant." Kit dismissed Mike's salute. "As I've told you many times, we don't go in for formalities here. It's initiative we like to reward. And heaven knows, we've seen enough of that from you recently."

"I aim to please." Mike lowered his salute. "I trust Captain Dawson is recovering okay. I didn't mean to throw him to the ground so hard."

"He suffered no permanent physical injury, if that's what you mean? You needn't worry about any threat of court-martials either. That's one of the benefits of being in the White Hart. Personal pride is a different matter. I daresay we won't allow him to forget it in a hurry."

Mike grinned, detecting a lighter atmosphere than usual. For the first time since his arrival, an audience with Masterson felt distinctly non-military.

"Guess I could get used to that. What are the negatives?"

"You'll receive no rewards either; not that a true knight would covet them. All in all, I'd say personal glory is a subjective thing."

Echoes of what Atkins had already told him. "According to my granddad, being mentioned in despatches isn't worth the paper it's written on."

Kit laughed, clearly genuine. "Well, he would certainly know. He's really rather well thought of around here."

"As he is at home. Not that any of them know of this. I thought he spent most of the war in North Africa."

"Who's to say he didn't? Receiving conflicting reports doesn't necessarily mean that neither of them are true."

Mike raised an eyebrow; he assumed it was code for a cover story. "Either way, it's been something of a surprise. Especially as at least one other member of my family also served."

"As I understand it, you're in line to be the fourth, though I'll leave it to Bennett to fill you in on the details. Personally, I've never been much of a biographer."

"In line to be the fourth?" Mike detected a slight question mark over the phrase. "Does that mean I've passed?"

"Unfortunately the process isn't quite over yet, nor is the decision up to me." Kit placed his hands briefly on his hips before returning them to the at ease position. "The final decision must come from the top. All we can do is advise."

Mike frowned, not shocked, but still unclear. "For a minute you had me worried. I was actually starting to think I wouldn't get the chance to continue all this fun I've been having."

"Well, you certainly haven't been shy dishing it out, least of all this week. For the first ten days, I was worried. I actually thought we might have recruited a proper soldier."

A wry smile. "Don't let the uniform fool you. Saluting and dressing up like chocolate is a small price to pay for the buzz of being alive."

Kit's lips again curled into a smile, the pause strangely tantalising. "I dare say, there's probably a part of you that still doesn't know exactly what to think of all this. I'm damn sure after I'd escaped the Gates of Hell, I didn't know what to think. Of course, at the same time, I was still in the grave."

"Can I take that as a compliment?"

"If it gives you motivation. We're all human here. Doing drills till the soul loses all feeling may work for the chaps on parade, but the White Hart were never formed for conventional warfare. As I told you before, among our ranks you'll find some from the Oxbridge select, but just as many from elsewhere. Not that you're likely to see many from broken families. We're not the SAS."

"Tell you the truth, I was starting to wonder. All these Special Forces instructors coming in. Must be a reason for it."

"We face the same obstacles. When the knights of old were founded, only the cream of the crop were selected. Only the dates have changed."

"But they were knights. Something must have changed?"

"All your questions and more will, I'm sure, be answered. But first, let's not forget where we are. We still have a process to complete."

Mike nodded and looked down at the floor. As he reconnected with the former Royal Fusilier, he sensed a strange wave of sympathy. "So what happens now?"

"You've just completed phase six. The sixth circle, if you like. By now I'm sure you'll appreciate what that means."

Mike smiled ruefully. The Accumulator had clearly spoken of nine circles of hell.

"So same time tomorrow, then?"

"Not exactly. Phase seven is usually when the fun begins. You've passed initiation, winning the approval of outsiders. Today, with the exception of one small dent to Dawson's pride, you've done the same of the knights." He shuffled from foot to foot. "Each circle you pass brings you one closer to the beast. It's those at the top you have to win over before victory is complete."

Mike nodded, his mind ticking over. Maybe it was the adrenaline or the lack of sleep affecting his thinking, but he suddenly had a renewed willingness to keep going.

"So when do we reconvene? Don't tell me, you're sending me to purgatory?"

"Like every good school, we give weekends off – today is Saturday, in case you've forgotten. Phase seven will commence early Monday morning." This time Masterson held a straight face. "I should warn you, the day off can either help or hinder. It's incredible how easily the mind can switch off."

"Not to mention how the absence of adrenaline can make old wounds feel creaky again."

"Well, I'm afraid there I can't help you. Just remember, with every circle completed, the next gets smaller. I think it's fair to say, the worst is possibly already gone."

"Then why the great delay? Surely if it's easier, the point of testing is over."

"I said the worst is gone, not the most important. Ultimately, a candidate can achieve everything he needs to. It all comes down to one important question."

"What's that?"

Kit's expression was stern. "Would I die for this man and would he die for me?"

The pair's eyes became locked as if carrying on a conversation without spoken words. Somehow, in the moment, Mike sensed a connection he'd missed till now.

The realities of the White Hart suddenly stood out clearly before him.

"If that's what my country asks of me. You can rely on nothing but."

Kit's expression turned non-committal. "You'll be pleased to hear you'll be returning tonight to your room in the inn. Your stuff hasn't been moved since Christmas. Get a good rest; eat as much as you can without getting stomach cramps. The challenge that awaits, you'll need to prepare for."

Mike nodded. "Yes, sir."

For several seconds they stood in silence, the strange awkwardness remaining. Lost for options, Mike saluted, the gesture on this occasion returned. As the two-man parade ended, they parted with a handshake.

Then, like brothers, they embraced.

112

Somewhere North-West of the Jewel House, 03:36

Blanco brought proceedings to a halt as they headed deeper into the underground vault. He replaced his HT on his belt after taking the call from Christophe; the last stronghold above ground had officially been lost.

Authority had been restored at the Tower.

Holding his flashlight, he returned his attention to the photocopy of Raleigh's map, comparing it to what he'd already seen. So far, it had been entirely accurate – even to the slightest curve, the famous sailor had pinpointed everything. Assuming his bearings were correct, they were within a quarter of a mile of the end.

Blanco resumed the walk. "Come on!"

Emily paid extra attention to the screens as the second detachment of Queen's Guards closed in on the barracks, spreading out across the bottom floor. As far as she could tell from the images, it was likely they would find the area deserted.

A voice crackled from the HT of the guard alongside her.

"Jewel House is clear."

She picked up the phone, speaking to Maria. "Second detachment has cleared the Jewel House. There's no one there."

The figures Maria had recently seen had already disappeared from view. "They must have taken the passage. Tell the guards to descend to the jeweller's workshop. If Blanco tries a U-turn, at least we'll have him covered."

In the tunnels below the White Tower, David Champion continued to lead the way. In the light of ten torches, the way ahead was far more visible this time.

Entering the next passageway, he recognised features from before.

If all went to plan, they would reach the end in less than two minutes.

In the shadows of two large buildings on St Dunstan's Lane, the arsonist took a left turn towards the gateway into the garden of the ruined church. Ensuring he was alone, he moved quickly past the tower and into the north section of the ruins.

* * *

Maintaining his position behind the shelter of the nearby trees, Kit noticed movement close to the tower. Keeping his voice at whisper level, he spoke through his headset.

"I see movement."

Phil looked closely at the satellite footage. In addition to the five Harts, he saw a sixth figure.

"Target is moving close to the north wall."

Moving cautiously, Kit ran to the nearest tree, ensuring he remained out of sight. As the seconds passed, he saw the figure head up on to raised ground.

Inexplicably, he saw him remove a block of masonry.

And disappear down below.

Kit wasted no time. Confident the person wasn't about to double back, he approached the raised platform. His gun at the ready, he approached the ruined window.

Even in the dull light of the moon, he could see a dark, empty space.

He sensed movement around him: Ward.

"Go and get the others. This time, I'm not leaving anything to chance."

Mike battled on, doing his best to ignore the pain. Feeling in his left leg was almost non-existent now; he feared the wound might no longer be operable. In his tired and dazed state, he focused on the way ahead, praying for the moment darkness would give way to light.

Without a map, he had no idea how far the passage would continue.

Intuitively he felt he was close, every step a new victory. It reminded him of the trials, how every breath brought new agony, how even what had earlier been the smallest task became a huge obstruction. In the darkness, old memories swirled around in his battered head, conversations that might or might not have taken place. He saw the Ukrainian, the man from the Far East, the man from Israel, the SEALs, the other Harts. Of all he'd come across, the tormentor he remembered best was the Aussie, particularly the conversation in the field. Twenty-one days was a long time. The light at the end of the tunnel might never be visible. That was how they were trained.

There is no respite in war.

The decline started to steepen slightly, taking him ever lower into the earth. Directly above him, the height of the ceiling also seemed lower. As the seconds passed, movement became easier, gravity now helping him. He felt his momentum building, his pace increasing, filling him with renewed hope that as long as the slope remained consistent, he would soon be guided to the end.

It curved again to his right, more acutely, a clear change in the direction of the pathway. He sensed new odours around him; what had earlier been typical stonework was now mixed with something more iron based. He became aware of different sounds directly above him, possibly traffic; surely it was too early for the roads to have reopened? Concentrating, he also made out other sounds, possibly talking. Holding his breath, he slowed his pace as he followed the wall and the slope, down and right.

Suddenly he came to a stop.
Up ahead, there was light at the end of the tunnel.

Champion led the Beefeaters right on leaving the ninth passage, remembering the route from earlier. There was light beyond the area where he had last seen his nephew; he walked into it, finding it deserted. It was less bright than it had been, indicating a light had been turned off. Venturing onwards, he found an iron door blocking the way.

Exchanging glances with the leader of the Beefeaters, he pushed hard and forced it open.

Another door appeared at the end of a long passage to the right.

The workshop was deserted as Emily had expected. The images on the security screens had confirmed as much.

With the exception of the early sections, the jewel room had been emptied. All of the crowns had been removed from the long display case at the room's centre, leaving only the altar plate and wedding banquet undisturbed. Entering the workshop, Emily found everything apart from the Imperial State Crown intact; she had heard from Maria that Blanco had dropped it off the roof of the White Tower. She investigated the crown of St Edward first, gradually moving along the line.

To her they looked genuine.

The doorway was located on the far side of the room; although it wasn't her first visit to the workshop, she had never ventured beyond the iron door. As she sought to enter, she sensed movement on the other side; inexplicably the door opened. Her Heckler & Koch at the ready, those of the Queen's Guards alongside her also aimed at the door, she saw the man facing them was not a terrorist.

But a historian.

Emily exhaled in relief. "I thought you were him."

Champion's confusion ended immediately. "The passage also headed in another direction. Quickly, they may yet not be far ahead."

Kit was first to enter the opening. Guided by the light of his torch, he saw a series of stone steps, rather like those he'd seen beneath Wren's fake tomb. Waiting until he'd safely placed his foot on the fifth, he switched off his torch and reactivated his night visions, the stone surrounds showing up clearly against the green backdrop.

The stairway ended after thirty steps. He had entered a crypt more reminiscent of what he'd seen at St Mary-le-Bow than St Paul's. The area to his left was a dead end, but it was more open in the opposite direction. Tombs that had been damaged by past weathering had been left unattended and were no longer arranged in any clear order. The walls were of stone construction, any markings or artwork on them faded long ago.

Sanders entered alongside him. "Not quite what I had in mind."

Kit nodded. "Come on. Let's see where this leads."

The route ahead was blocked; Blanco was the first to notice. Ordering his men to a halt, he approached cautiously, unclear for now what was causing the obstruction. The walls on both sides had been identical throughout, their condition largely like that of the Tower's outer ring. The construction of the ceiling similarly was consistent with the age of the walls; the paved layout of the floor he guessed also dated from the same era.

What he saw in front of him was different.

"Get out the lamps."

Randek joined him, as did François, the combined light of their torches added to that of several portable halogen lamps removed from the rucksacks of the gunmen. The light confirmed their suspicions. The article in front of them was not stone, but steel, designed to prevent entry to anyone without appropriate authority.

Judging from its appearance, it was impossible to breach by use of force.

Mike could hear voices ahead of him, transmitted by the acoustic properties of the confined space. Coupled with the lack of light, the effect was very powerful, strangely disorientating. He recognised voices rather than words; understanding what was being said was impossible being so far away.

The passage continued downwards, curving right to left, the opposite of the previous section. Against the green backdrop he could see at least eight figures, none of which seemed to have noticed him.

Instead, their attention was fixed on what appeared to be the entrance of a bank vault.

The door was moulded of special concrete and clad in stainless steel. The round shape was familiarly iconic, reminding him of a bank vault from the early 20th century.

Blanco guessed it probably dated from that period.

Examining it in the torchlight, the Anjouvin observed several massive metal bolts extending into the frame that was set into a surrounding concrete wall. The door was secured by a substantial and clearly very sophisticated combination lock.

After several seconds of close study, Blanco concluded that it was dual control.

Meaning they needed not one combination but two.

He took a step back, surveying the exterior in the lamplight. The reinforced door was clearly impenetrable. He reasoned it would take the explosive force of a large bomb to dislodge the door; there was more chance of taking out the walls. Digging was also out of the question.

He placed his HT to his lips. "We've found the chamber."

The sound of Blanco's voice cut the air like a clap of thunder in the dead of night. Though the television was on, the atmosphere in the room was quiet, subdued. Earlier successes had been reversed. The news presenters and reporters confirmed the situation was coming ever more under control.

The mission now rested on a knife-edge.

Fieschi was first to respond. "You've seen it?"

"*Oui.*" Blanco paced the tunnel, wall to wall. If his judgement was correct and the interior was constructed of reinforced steel, realistically they only had one option. "The final door of hell will shortly be opened; though the church no longer exists, that doesn't mean its crypt doesn't still harbour secrets. The prime minister will return once more to the negotiating table. Failure to hand over the combination and the Tower will fall."

Fieschi heard every word carefully. "It isn't breakable?"

Blanco inspected the dials once again, realising the chances of breaking two combinations were almost impossible.

"Time is no longer with us. At the appropriate moment, we will take our intentions before the royals themselves. That, I will leave to you."

In that very moment, Fieschi felt as though his dreams were coming true. "In that case, I'd better prepare a speech."

Kit came to a sudden stop, raising his gun instinctively. There was sound nearby; the others heard it too.

Sanders was first to step forward. "Come on."

Blanco heard the arsonist's voice come through clearly, confirming his location.

"The time is upon us. Light the fuse now and make your escape. I will deal with the Tower myself."

"Not if I have anything to do with it."

The sound of an unknown voice threw the gunmen into chaos; a rogue gunshot went off, then several more, all from close by.

Blanco raised his hand, calling halt; immediately the gunfire ceased. His attention on the passageway, he saw shadows moving against the walls, a human figure emerging.

Both hands raised in surrender.

Blanco lowered his HT. "Only a foolish man would enter a dark passageway just to surrender. An inch lower, you could have been shot."

Limping, Mike emerged into the lamplight. "Now wouldn't that have been unfortunate."

Gazing upon the newcomer, Blanco's face was frozen in shock. What he had assumed to be a gesture of surrender was anything but.

Concealed in both hands, the Englishman carried two grenades.

113

Charlestown, Twenty-One Months Earlier

Mike stood with his eyes on the Harts, intrigued by the impeccable stillness that defined their postures. On Masterson's command, Chambers and Dawson left the line and marched swiftly to the approach road, stopping at the base of the flagpole. From somewhere nearby the haunting sound of a bugle resonated across the otherwise quiet parade ground, heralding the arrival of the next distinguished guest. With military precision, the two Harts lowered the flag of the White Hart before raising a new one, the new material swaying gently in the morning breeze. Everyone watched and listened as a camouflaged RV motored along the approach road before circling the parade ground. With seemingly pinpoint timing, the new flag rose up the pole, flying at full mast. A tinge of electricity pulsated through Mike's veins as he saw its colours. Red, white and blue.

The Union Jack.

The vehicle came to a stop close to the Harts just as Chambers and Dawson returned. The bugler ended his tune to take his place quickly as the fourth member of a guard of honour. Another of the four opened the rear door as Kit ordered the Harts to attention, the movement of their feet sounding in unison. He paused midway through the next command as the passengers prepared to alight.

Whoever they were, Mike could tell from the ceremony they were among the most important of the important.

Three men got out from the rear left door of the vehicle. The first he recognised instantly. Atkins was dressed in his usual style, an impeccable dark suit partially hidden beneath a long overcoat.

The second man was of similar standing, yet different attire: like the bodywork of the car, his uniform indicative of a military background. Similar to the Ukrainian tormentor, his face and head bore the proud bearing of a bald eagle, the creases on his forehead providing unspoken confirmation he had lived through the worst and become stronger because of it. Also, like Radchenko, Mike noticed his gaze was reserved solely for him, as though he had decided on his prey in advance and would not let up till the time of reckoning was over.

The crown and three pips on his shoulder confirmed the rank of brigadier.

The final man was dressed in black, following Atkins and the brigadier in a solemn walk towards the Harts. Unlike the brigadier, Mike had seen him once before.

In the churchyard for Fenway's burial.

As the three-man party passed the escort, the bugler resumed his rendition of the "Last Post", its melancholic notes sounding hauntingly in the drizzly conditions. On approaching the Harts, Masterson's voice echoed like mortar fire; on his command each man offered their firearms at the present.

The brigadier spoke first.

"Right, a very good morning. My name is Brigadier Sir Anthony Stokes. Prior to my retirement, I spent over thirty-two years in the British Army, over fifteen of which were in the White Hart. I was one of the youngest members to join at the age of twenty-nine. Quite simply, we are the best in the world."

The brigadier took a few paces forward, now standing with his hands down by his sides. "I understand from my recent briefing that you have now participated actively in sixteen days of training, including ten delivered by other Special Forces' experts. While admirable it may be that you've passed them all, I don't care about that training. I'll be watching you from now on. As far as anyone here is concerned, your training process starts now."

Mike nodded, taking every word seriously. As much as he respected the tormentors of previous weeks, there was something about this one that just commanded complete respect.

"Now, to be a member of the Special Forces requires a keen sense of observation, not only when on duty but at all times. The most effective tool in the enemy's box is to catch you off guard. Nobody ever intends to be kidnapped.

"The purpose of this exercise is to see how you fare when facing a formidable foe. You've been dropped off behind enemy lines; the object of which has already been realised. Unfortunately, however, the enemy have got wind of your presence, and you are now being held at gunpoint.

"I understand in recent days you've been successful in giving your enemies the slip once already. However, being in your chosen career sometimes means being faced with challenges you'd rather avoid. The purpose here is to measure how you fare under interrogation.

"Every successful Special Forces recruit must have the following attributes," the brigadier continued. "An unyielding will to live, to achieve, to win, to help his fellow comrades even in the event of certain death, and, perhaps most important of all, the will to get to somewhere no matter what the difficulties are. Mental endurance is absolutely pivotal, no matter what the mission."

Somewhere beneath the Tower, 03:43

The memory of Stokes's words echoed in Mike's ears. Of all the tormentors he had suffered in training, now it was the voice of the White Hart legend that came through most clearly. Whatever had taken place during those three weeks in Charlestown and the Highlands of Scotland, he knew had been just practice for the real thing. The scars of the trials had faded, along with the memories; when he thought of them now, he did so with pride, even humour. He had kept his word to the Israeli, to the others, to Kit. With adversity came great triumph and desire.

Even now in the depths of hell.

He stopped within ten metres of his recent captors, close enough to make out their features. Something about their faces seemed different in the new light, as if the orange shades of the halogen lamps cast them in a fiery glow, ironic on both accounts. At the centre of the eight, Blanco's expression was scornful, yet less so compared to Randek's. In the light, his short blond hair seemed to have acquired a bizarre red tinge.

A fire that reflected in his eyes.

Blanco stepped forward, his features becoming more visible. In the better light, his face seemed uncharacteristically gaunt, yet still possessing an indefinable noble quality that had also been visible in the CCTV footage. The eyes were deep and possessed of great concentration, like a great artist preparing to add the final brushstrokes to a nearly completed masterpiece. He no longer doubted he was looking at a Cardinal's Boy.

A disciple of Luca Fieschi.

"It must be very difficult standing with such a terrible wound, especially with your hands aloft." Blanco's attention centred on the items in Mike's hands. "Come, sit a while. Maybe in time you will begin to understand."

"Matter of fact, I've heard it's better for the healing process to keep the blood moving; probably the reason I never cared for commercial jets." Mike noticed movement from Randek, as though he were preparing to remove his firearm. "I wouldn't recommend that. We're on a slope. Shoot me; I'll fall forward. Along with the potato mashers."

Blanco raised his hand, a gesture intended for Randek. "A man who has thought through every move, I see; also one not frightened by the spectre of death." The Anjouvin smiled. "I'd always thought the reputation of the Servants was one that belonged only in folklore. I see now that I was wrong. The stories of my niece's husband were perhaps worthy of respect I never before offered. It's funny, no, how only when it's too late are the real lessons learned?"

Mike remained unflinching. "Fortunately, I've always been a fast learner."

"Perhaps in some ways we are not so different after all. But fast learner or not, it takes a special kind of man to carry out such things and also hold his hands so high for such time. I am a patient man; we are all patient men. Perhaps you would care to reconsider."

"Matter of fact, I was about to make you the same offer. Seventeen minutes is a long time to wait for further fires. An hour and seventeen longer still to wait for death. Fortunately, I have nowhere else I need to be. And don't worry about my arms." Mike thought back to his time with the Israeli. "I'm a quick learner in other ways too."

* * *

"Everywhere these days there are spies; sometimes it is difficult to know where to look," Zahavi began. "As a master, you learn to see things that might otherwise look normal. If you want to work in anti-terrorism, you work when they work. And if you want to work, first of all you're gonna need a weapon. You're gonna have to carry it at all times."

He presented Mike with a M4A1 carbine; it reminded him of the M16A2 assault rifle he'd carried during training in the 1st Battalion.

Strangely, it had no strap.

"Now listen to me very carefully." The Israeli returned to the head of the parade. "I want you to take your rifle in your hands and hold it up." He gestured above his head. "I want you to keep it there."

Mike obliged, stretching out his arms, the firm exterior of the foreign weapon bracing against his raw fingertips.

"Feeling comfortable?" Zahavi watched with folded arms as Mike fought hard to maintain his position. "Now, I want you to bring your arms forward ninety degrees. Straighten them up. Don't move!"

Again Mike followed the YAMAM veteran's orders. Maintaining the new position was difficult, the pressure particularly hard against his triceps and below his shoulders. Almost immediately he began to struggle, his body straining. It was obvious Zahavi was satisfied.

"My training is real hard core. No pink flowers, no Brylcreem. There'll be no bitching and whining, no shoe shopping, no crying to your mother." He pushed his sunglasses back up his nose. "Straighten your hands, I said!"

"If there's a hidden meaning, I'm afraid I must have missed it." Blanco's stare was inquisitive, his voice low, each word precise. "Seventeen minutes is really very little time. In another time, I'm sure we'd have so much to talk about."

"You mean about how you razed half of this city to the ground just to become the world's greatest jewel thief?"

"You believe that is why we're here?"

"Your words, not mine. Your demands of the PM seemed quite clear."

The Anjouvin smiled. "You know it was Edward II's secret ambition to do away with the Crown – at least the institution of it. He realised, as many do today, that the plight of the nobility and the common man are not so inseparable. Instead, our lives are very much intertwined; success for one often means the same for the other. It was perhaps Roger Mortimer's greatest shortcoming he failed to see this. But to his credit, he did at least see reason in keeping the king alive."

Mike took interest in what he heard, recalling the documents in the archives. The letter to Charles II. The confession of Belland. Fieschi. Le Galeys. The Sons of Gemini.

Ask me who we were.

"I guess under the circumstances, the wish came true. I seem to recall it was during his reign that Parliament created separation between the king and Crown. Then again, I never did pay much attention in class."

Blanco's smile widened. "You are far more intelligent than you care to let on; Everard himself spoke of such things. I'm guessing it was you he spoke to inside the church six months ago."

"You seem to base a lot on guesswork."

"You think we're guilty of despicable crimes, don't you?"

"I'd hardly describe the murder of innocent people and the destruction of historical property in peacetime as justified."

"So the rules are different in wartime?" The Anjouvin shook his head. "You think this makes us murderers? Architects of genocide? Earlier tonight, you uncovered the secrets of history for yourself. The truth that your government and even schoolteachers are too corrupt, afraid or simply too stupid to understand. You saw the documents that reveal the true cause of the fire. You said it yourself; it was not permission of heaven but others. For the false rulers who sat on the throne without claim, the story of an accident in a bakery was plausible but also convenient. Without revealing the identity of the real enemy, there was no need for war, nor fear of uprising. In his wisdom, the Protector realised this many years before and used it to his advantage till it no longer suited him. Then, like the slaughter of the sheep, he did away with us."

"But some of you survived?"

"By the beginning of the English Civil War, the network of the Sons of Gemini set up by the godsons of Cardinal Fieschi had extended, not only back into France, but far across the Papal States. There was hardly a village or monastery in Anjou or Gascony that failed to benefit from their wisdom. In their own wisdom, the kings of France and the papacy saw the benefits of mutual cooperation; it is perhaps thanks to them more than any that the Protectorate failed. Had the circumstances been different, perhaps there would have been less need for civil war. Any advantages the Protector gained would have become unavailable the moment he rose above his station."

Mike was speechless. "You spread this chaos? Why?"

"Perhaps you've already answered your own question. The government of England, previously a product of Plantagenet efficiency, had become contaminated; bastardised not by the rightful heirs but those who desired illegal self-promotion, actions seen by many as dangerous even in their own time. When Edward III's son died early, the case of rightful succession was at last brought into question. When his grandson was dethroned, whatever right of succession once existed had itself been thrown into chaos. Over time, the impotency of the chosen few saw succession fall not only out of France but also out of England. Into Wales."

"You're talking about the Tudors?" Mike picked up on the reference to Henry VII. "This was centuries ago."

"The information is at your fingertips, yet you fail to grasp it. The word you used was *chaos*: throughout history, it has been a valuable tool of kings and governments, but also instrumental in their fall. The monarchy of England is obsolete; like those of France, it should have ended long ago. Still the actions of Parliament remain. The only remedy to chaotic government is neutralisation. Sadly, the only way for this to be achieved is equal chaos."

Mike couldn't believe what he was hearing. "You mean terrorism?"

"In the hot summer of 1666, if a man was asked about terrorism, he would have failed to recognise the term. Educate him about the concept, perhaps he might have listened. If he were a man of reason, he would surely have agreed. The primary role of government has evolved only to protect the rights of the minority. Consider the city you once saw. The eighty-seven churches have become twenty-nine. The workplaces of the humble have been replaced by monuments to decadence. The streets you walk serve only for the ultimate benefit of the wealthy. The only failing of the Sons of Gemini was that they failed to rebuild what was there to rebuild."

"So your solution once again is to burn everything to rubble."

"Our answer is to revisit what once worked and do away with what has since failed. Take a look around you. Perhaps in your great haste, you never truly saw what existed in the city you mourn for. If the City of London had one weakness, it was its willingness to prey on the weak. The corrupt abbot and tavern keepers may have long since gone, but look what took their place: the banks and the financial institutions that brought ruin to themselves and many; the halls of the liars and the judges whose own freedoms could be bought and sold like the stocks. The steeples exist still, not that you would recognise them. Some say the gift of London is its willingness to accept outsiders; yet when the fires burned, those who took to the streets did so not to help save the city from inferno, but to find foreigners to blame."

Mike realised the words contained more than a kernel of truth. "Even if you're right, what separates it from any other city in the world?" He shuffled his feet, keeping his arms still. "What takes its place? What replaces the shops? The government? Feudalism?"

"If by feudalism you mean a new wave of men of reason, then yes. Men who understand the true world we live in, while understanding the same of those who came before us. The Plantagenet age was the most prosperous in English history. It was the age of the gothic cathedral, the mighty castles, the origins of democracy. Imagine if we could start again, one blank canvas. Imagine had the sons of Edward gone on to rule when the fat king and the virgin queen failed. England itself could have been the home of the Renaissance. The original sons of the sea. The nation always offers so much but fails to deliver."

"If we're talking about football, I'd probably agree with you."

The Anjouvin broke into a harsh laugh, shaking his head. "You waste your time with scepticism and sarcasm, yet you yourself are a victim of what since has been lost. When the order of the servants was first established, the twelve sat in equality. All were knights. Each had land. Each was honoured with the freedoms of the kingdom bestowed upon them. Take a look at yourselves now. Your missions are run by corrupt government officials who have themselves never visited a war zone. Your salaries fail to match incompetent bureaucrats whose only path to office was sycophancy. Your land and titles have been lost to celebrities who spend their ill-earned status snorting cocaine. Think hard, Son of the Servants. The government of England has failed you."

Mike arched his back, both shocked and startled. How on earth did he know of the White Hart?

"Personally, I never went in for all that king rubbish. My only ambition was to enter the military."

"And why? So others could shoot at you while you faced a court martial should you dare to shoot back without command?"

"You mean like if I should drop these?" Mike gestured to the items in his hands. "Sorry to disappoint you. I never did show much regard for the rules."

"A blessing on two accounts. Even if the slope took the grenades to the door, by the time they exploded, I doubt the ceiling would survive. Drop them and kill us you may; however, rest assured, whatever dies here tonight, it will not be our principles or beliefs. As you are clearly aware by now, the Sons of Gemini has survived all this time." He checked his watch. "Another twelve minutes. You're quite sure I can't tempt you to sit down?"

"I've got a far better idea. Contact your men. Tell them to call off the fire at St Dunstan's. We already know the location. End it now, I might even get you diplomatic immunity. But end this madness."

"Do not test my patience. Whether you drop the grenades or not, the new society is already with us. It will function competitively and fairly without the need for future violence. The attacks tonight have laid bare for all to see the impotence of the British government; had it not been for you, they would have fallen far more quickly. I really am most sorry your name will never be known; in your own way, you really have been most heroic."

Blanco pulled his HT from his belt, calling Fieschi. "The link-up will be made shortly. I hope your speech is ready."

An answer came immediately. "It was ready the day I was born."

Blanco laughed beneath his breath and replaced his HT on his belt. As he did so, he noticed Mike was struggling.

"I told you before, seventeen minutes is a long time."

"And an hour longer still." Mike smiled wryly. "You honestly thought I entered with an escape plan?"

"Perhaps the credit I gave you was undeserved. Perhaps you yourself are just a servant."

"Your word. Not mine."

"Once upon a time, a man of your order would have been worthy – a man who sensed his own value. One unlikely to give his life so needlessly."

"You think stopping you isn't needless?"

Behind him, Mike heard a shuffling of feet. "Do not move!"

Grimacing, he saw Blanco's smile widen. "Remove those things from his hands!"

114

Beneath the City of London, 03:51

Mike anticipated the punch before it came; the malice in Randek's expression suggested he had been saving it for some time. The terrorist had waited till the grenades were taken, placed carefully in the hands of those who surrounded him.

After almost ten minutes standing completely still, Mike no longer felt in control of his legs.

"Get up!" Randek spat. On turning over, Mike saw the wound was bleeding again; further blood trickled down his face.

His nose was now so numb the recent impact had been almost unnoticeable.

"Get up!" Randek repeated.

Attempting to raise himself, Mike realised getting up was currently not an option. The longer he struggled, the more Randek's anger escalated.

"Leave him." Blanco opened his laptop, typing quickly; it seemed incredible to Mike that he had a signal so far below ground.

"I guess that's one thing they didn't have in the 1600s. Imagine what else could have faltered under the Norman Yoke."

Blanco seemed interested in the comment. "Do my views offend you?"

"Only because I'm on the opposite side."

The Anjouvin laughed. "And suppose you were to change sides. Your opinion would also change?"

"You offering me a bribe? A piece of what's in there?" Mike gestured to the vault. "Sorry, but even if I were so inclined, I don't particularly care for your chances of getting in."

His eyes locked with those of the Anjouvin. "I wouldn't be so sure if I were you."

The PM saw Blanco's face appear suddenly on the same screen as before. For the first few seconds she was unsure what she was looking at; like most of the videos that had come through that evening, the footage had not begun with the sender. The light was the poorest yet; she detected the area was underground, the ceiling vaulted. A strong, round door indicated he was inside a bank.

She didn't recognise the specific location.

Within seconds, the angle changed, the terrorist's face again taking centre stage. His features looked different than before: paler, tired. His hair had become dishevelled, his forehead covered with sweat.

Despite the tiredness, he smiled.

"I have kept my end of the bargain. Your hostages are unharmed; soon they will be free, as I said they would. The fires that have devastated your city need not continue. Time is precious to me, madame." He checked his watch. "I ask for the final time. Tell me the location of the jewels."

The PM lowered her head, taking a moment to compose herself. Though she didn't recognise anything of what she saw, she didn't require verbal confirmation the terrorist had discovered where they were housed.

"As I've told you before, the location is unknown to me."

Blanco's laugh returned, echoing, almost hyena-like. "Perhaps under the circumstances I have been unkind to you, madame. Throughout history, the pattern has been the same; never should a commoner be entrusted to do a king's job. I apologise for burdening you with tasks above your level."

Beneath her calm demeanour, the PM felt her blood boiling. "The fires in our city are almost fully extinguished. Command of the Tower has been restored. Whatever elements of waste still wander the sewers are unlikely to last longer than the tide." Her expression hardened, her eye contact fierce. "I warned you at the start, Monsieur Blanco, our government has never negotiated with terrorists."

"Your government, as you call it, is obsolete. Tonight we put you to the test and you failed. The City of London burns to ash around you. Throughout the night all you did was fiddle."

"The horror that has befallen our city is the work of evil and evil alone. Had it not been for the bravery of our emergency services, we would also be adding genocide to your list of atrocities. The time for playing games is over, Monsieur. Rest assured, I will find you."

"My own fate is no longer of consequence. The truth of history lives, just as it has all these years. The inability of your government to function has been exposed; it can no longer remain. If it does, your nation will not see through the next century. Nor your city through the night."

Holding his electronic tablet, the Director of the White Hart watched with deepening concern as Blanco turned the camera to the object at his feet.

Under the lamplight, he saw a device that had no place in Blanco's arsenal.

The PM's expression turned to that of horror at the sight of the same item.

"Take a look around you, Prime Minister. Just for a second, look out beyond your window." Blanco's tone had become intensely antagonistic. "The fires that have consumed your city may have destroyed the surface, but it is not always the surface that matters. As is often the case of history, the deepest truth lies far beneath the surface. It is there where the source of the disease lingers."

The PM was lost for words. "You wouldn't dare. Detonation of such a device will cause the destruction of everything in the capital. Not to mention the deaths of millions of innocent citizens!" She gazed at the screen, wondering how something so sophisticated had been brought into the city unnoticed. "Even Hitler wasn't so barbaric."

"Maybe he just wasn't finished."

The words appalled her. "I completely misjudged you, Blanco. Earlier tonight, I assumed you were to be taken seriously. A genuine pioneer. Now I realise you're just evil."

"You may dispense with the insults; they are unnecessary. My position has always been clear. Tell me now, the location of the jewels."

"You bring death to millions, including yourselves, for a few pieces of jewellery!" The PM shook her head, unsure what to do next. "I've told you several times, I do not know!"

The Anjouvin's expression lightened. "Then perhaps it is time I spoke to someone who does."

The Director saw the images change, the layout becoming split screen. Two further rooms appeared, Blanco disappearing. Alongside what appeared to be a modern apartment whose decorations were notably affluent, he saw a second room, almost immediately recognisable. Surrounded by cyan-coloured walls, hung with famous paintings from Turner to Gainsborough, was a luxurious three-piece suite on which a man of instant recognisability was seated.

The footage was coming from inside the Queen's private chambers at Buckingham Palace.

The Prince of Wales rose hesitantly to his feet, his attention on the flat-screen television that had recently been placed on the famous desk. He walked towards it slowly, studying the features of the man who had appeared on screen, contemplating what he would say. The situation was strange: both surreal and complex. The face was familiar, like looking at a long-lost relative, though not necessarily one he regarded with any favour.

"Gabriel?"

Fieschi answered immediately. "My dear cousin."

The prince approached the desk; due to its height, he found himself looking down, a position he'd decided to adopt in advance.

"My chief of staff told me of a document received earlier this evening. At first, I didn't believe it. I thought they must have been mistaken, perhaps victim of a bizarre joke. I know few with such a sense of humour. Strangely you were the first to come into my mind."

"Your thoughts serve you well." Fieschi stared deep into the screen of his laptop; unlike the prince, he remained seated. "It really has been too long."

"Perhaps in a world of opposites." The prince shook his head, quietly coming to terms with the situation that had befallen him. "You know, ever since receiving the fax, I had a feeling this conversation would come. The only thing I failed to anticipate was the consequences."

"Inspiration for our writers to make our communications clearer perhaps. Though after all this time, I must confess I might have thought you'd no longer be in doubt of our intentions."

"Razing a city to the ground? Murdering the Queen's Guard and our Yeomanry. Causing chaos among our citizens. You know, I always suspected you'd cheat your own museums; even turn a blind eye if an electronic payment ended up in the wrong hands. But mass destruction?" The prince shook his head. "Why now?"

"I suppose an equally reasonable question would be, why did we wait?"

"You honestly expect me to believe this has been in the offing for some time?"

"You can believe what you want!"

"Enough of this rubbish." The prince's face reddened with anger. "I've seen the pamphlet, not to mention the other documents held in our archives. You know, at one time, it didn't even occur to me to take them seriously. The whole thing reeked of propaganda; in truth, I'd seen more realistic threats in the caricatures. The stories from 1666, foreign firework makers attempting to obtain new quantities of powder, it all has a certain Guy Fawkes ring to it."

"Perhaps next time you'll take them seriously rather than dismiss them with an ostentatious wave of your royal hand."

"I'll ask you politely not to sneer." His eyes locked with Fieschi's via the screen. "You never did answer my question. To what purpose?"

"You mean besides those that have already been made clear to you?"

"No!" The prince waved his finger. "The period of justified violence for lasting peace; the calm before the storm. You can't lure me in with this virtuous rubbish. Even if you were so inclined, you're likely to find no government of honour shirk their responsibilities in times of crisis."

"Nor those who lack honour." Fieschi lit a cigarette, inhaling slowly. "Should you do so, that would make our job far easier. Perhaps even unnecessary."

"You mean tonight isn't just a glorified excuse at trying your hand at robbery? Not exactly what Cardinal Luca had in mind."

"You might be more right than you know. Had Edward II been a stronger man, Mortimer's overthrow could not have been achieved. Yet I've often thought in certain ways, history tends to have a sense of humour. Only by overthrowing the man who made you can you really replace him."

"My God, you make it sound like a Greek tragedy."

"Under the circumstances, credit really must be given where it's due; your initial guess was much closer than you think. The intention of Edward II was to bring commoner and noble together, replace the old with a far more even playing field. In time, one might even argue it occurred, albeit far from the way he intended. His dream was to destroy the corrupters in government, rid the feudal system of avaricious profiteers. The critics mocked and abused him, accused him of weakness and nepotism. Yet was it really a mistake to promote the few he trusted? He gave us a dream; it was for that reason the papacy loved him. All that was needed was a platform to put it into practice."

The heir to the Duchy of Aquitaine paused to flick ash into his ashtray. "I must admit that in the eyes of his onlookers, such views would have seemed strange rather than enlightened. However, I'll leave it to the historians to scoff. The dream still lives inside each and every one of us. After seven hundred years we have found it. A chance to save England from itself."

Watching on his tablet, the Director was speechless. He put through a communication to the Rook.

"Maria, are you watching this?"

At the other end, Maria and Phil eyed the screen, equally dumbfounded. "Every word."

"Get a message through to Masterson and the others. Whatever they do, they must locate the vault."

Making their way along the tunnel beneath St Dunstan's, the five Harts heard Maria's voice come through clearly.

Kit sensed the end was in sight. "Come on. Quietly."

The prince gazed silently at the screen, his eyes suddenly struggling to focus. He was tired, but not solely because of the hour, the effects of which no longer felt physical. The words Fieschi spoke, though said convincingly, were those of a maniac, perhaps the leader of an entire group of madmen, capable of cold, calculated dialogue but ultimately ruled by something far more maverick. Like the fires that had affected the city, he was an inferno ready to be unleashed.

And one that only effective planning could counteract.

"What do you want?"

"My demands are clear and have been for some time," Fieschi said as he lit a fresh cigarette from the dying embers of his last one. "Had you only been willing to listen, you could have been part of this. Dare I say, a useful consultant, if not a full partner. Instead, you proved to be just like the others. An obstacle. A man never to be trusted."

"Strange words for the associate of convicted criminals," the prince replied.

"Trial by association; I should have expected so much. Are you not guilty of the same? Perhaps involving those closer to home? In truth, you are only partially to blame. The true disease lies in the past, to my shame even with my own ancestors."

"Your what?"

"Do not look so surprised. The human capability for failure affects us all. Imagine what could have been achieved in 1666 had the true vision been implemented. Wren's original designs could have given birth to paradise; even Paris would have trembled in her wake. It was a city of grandeur in the making; the new dawn set out before us. What has really been lost tonight? Monuments of corporate debauchery? Retailers whose own desire for greed would leave its citizens penniless? The opportunity is here for new beginnings. This is the opportunity to build the city Wren was never trusted with."

"If that's your agenda, surely it's a case of job done. What else separates you?"

Fieschi's smile widened. "The obstacles made of stone may have fallen, but others remain. For almost a thousand years, the Crown Jewels of England have represented more than just material wealth. They are the symbol of the monarchy. Just like the Tower, whoever holds them holds the kingdom. It is time for you, respectfully, to stand down."

"My God, you really are mad!"

"I'd urge you not to try my patience any longer, Cousin!" Fieschi's expression hardened. "Already once tonight, you've been offered a glimpse of what we're truly capable of."

The prince's gaze remained unwavering. "And if we refuse?"

The images on the screen changed; Fieschi disappeared, replaced by Blanco. Clearly in shot was the bomb.

"Do not forget what has already occurred here this evening. Nor attempt to sweep it away like the tide on a beach." The camera moved suddenly, focusing on Mike. His face was bloody, his nose swollen.

Blanco asked, "Do you have a message for your future king?"

Mike stared hard into the camera. "I do not fear death."

The footage ended with him being punched in the face.

Maria flinched, her hand coming level with her mouth. For the first time in over twelve hours she saw Mike's appearance, his usually handsome face disfigured with recent cuts and bruises.

"Oh my God!"

The Director shook his head, completely lost for words. Every thought that had previously entered his mind had been replaced by one almighty fear. It wasn't just about the life of one of his men.

One wrong word and it could be the end of London forever.

Fieschi reappeared on screen. "The terms are clear. Abdicate, or we all die."

The prince took a seat, his face level with the screen. Up close, he saw Fieschi was doing the same.

"All right, Gabriel. Let's dance. You yourself are heir to one of the wealthiest estates in all of France. Even if you get your wish, it's only a matter of time before evidence links you inextricably with the monstrous deeds that have been perpetrated tonight. Think of your son. Think of your family. See reason now and their futures at least can be assured."

"I'm afraid already that time has passed. The network of Cardinal Luca and the Avignon popes was never intended to belong to one alone. My father is an old man – and a dying one. With his dying wish, I too yearn for him to see his dream of the better world that I also wish for my own children. The last act of violence will be done away with, paving the way for rebuilding like the phoenix atop the mighty cathedral." The Frenchman shook his head. "Many times, I attempted to barter. Now there will be no deal."

"Mighty cathedral," the prince muttered under his breath, boiling with indignation. "A building you yourselves sought to destroy."

"Even the greatest eventually turns to ash. Every day we are dying a long, slow death. Act now and you can prolong the lives of others. Right what for so long has been wrong. Take heed, son of Henry." The Cardinal's Boy's voice was firm, cruel. "The hour is close at hand. Destiny is almost upon us. The Tower created by both our ancestors will be no more. It will act as a sign. The coming of the end of the kingdom. In time, the rubble will be replaced, but the stories will last far longer. It's decision time, Highness. Do not make the mistakes your forefathers made."

Staring hard into Fieschi's eyes, the prince saw a bold resoluteness that passed beyond the earlier ravings of possible insanity. Whoever the true leader, whatever the true purpose, the reality was upon them.

The Tower would be the last stand before the city.

"What is it you want?"

Fieschi's face relaxed slightly. "The vault beneath the Bank of England is known only to a few; the combination to fewer still." The Frenchman edged closer to the screen. "Entrust to me the way in. Then, and only then, will the destruction of the Tower be averted."

The prince took a tired breath, his heart pounding relentlessly beneath his regimental uniform. "And the second bomb?"

"With confirmation of your family's abdication made known to the world."

Biting his lip, the prince nodded. "So be it."

The PM and the Director watched with shocked expressions as the prince rose to his feet and walked behind his desk, the sounds indicating he was searching through drawers. Almost immediately he returned.

"The code is two-part; it must be entered simultaneously."

Outside the round door, François and Randek took up positions either side, awaiting the numbers.

"The first is the date of birth of the designer," the prince resumed. "The second is the date the vault was originally created."

Fieschi nodded. "Who was the designer?"

"The same man who designed the city."

Fieschi nodded, Wren. "And the date of its creation?"

The prince lowered his head. "The day of the coronation of Edward II's successor."

The Cardinal's Boy's face broke into a wide grin.

* * *

Somewhere below the crypt of St Dunstan-in-the-East, Kit stopped suddenly, gesturing Sanders to join him. For the first time since his arrival, he sensed movement up ahead.

A figure was moving in the darkness.

The layout was different to what he'd seen below the cathedral and the church. Though it contained a street system, the options had been one of two.

Thanks to Ward, Cummins and Wilcox, the other way had been fully searched.

He spoke clearly, quietly. "This is Edward. State your location."

The response came from Ward. "The tunnel forks into two. GPS states we're below St Margaret Pattens."

Kit checked it against his own position. The figure ahead was below an inn close to the Tower. "Roger that. Retrace your steps. The bastard's right where he should be."

***

The arsonist checked his watch for the umpteenth time, waiting for the seconds to tick down. He'd felt the anticipation build ever since Blanco's last message; within seconds, his final task would be complete. The news above ground had been more positive for the city; the fires were almost out, order restored.

Glancing at the barrels of tar and gunpowder along the wall, he imagined the reaction when it went off, a second stab of fear entering right into the hearts of the citizens as a further wave of destruction was about to be unleashed.

Standing by the far wall, he again checked the coloured LEDs. One minute closer.

In less than two minutes, he would ignite it.

***

Kit sensed the presence of the other three returning alongside him.

"Target's in sight," he said into his headset. "Moving in!"

He waited for Maria's response before turning his attention to his colleagues. "On the count of one. Ready?"

"Ready!"

"Good. One!"

115

Below the Bank of England, 03:58

François and Randek entered the combinations carefully: day, month, year. As they simultaneously completed the task, they stood back as the cogs turned, the locks separating.

The door opened slowly as if the flow of time was stalling. The harder they pulled, the more swiftly it came, the momentum turning the weight into an asset. Its movement was fast now, swinging backwards on secure hinges. When it passed halfway, they retreated quickly, avoiding contact.

As it crashed against the surrounding wall, it became clear that the weight was capable of crushing any human in its path.

Blanco waited until the door was fully open before daring to approach the vault. Alongside him, François was more cautious, as though afraid the door might swing back. On Blanco's orders, the gunmen remained where they were.

Randek's attention had returned to Mike.

It was dark behind the door, so much so that even the torchlight failed to provide assistance. Carrying the nearest lamp, Blanco passed beyond the seal, holding it aloft. The new light confirmed his next fear.

A secondary door, iron bars crisscrossing in a recurring pattern, cell-like in appearance, provided the final obstacle.

François was furious. "He lied to us."

"Try the keys!" Blanco studied the keyring in François's hand. "If it doesn't work, we can always resort to more experimental measures."

Kit saw light ahead of him, shining down from above. Removing his night visions, the effect was less clear with the naked eye – whatever caused it was bright enough to make out details on the walls.

Like the passageway he had entered, its construction appeared medieval.

He stopped where the light was brightest, his attention on the area directly above. The ceiling was more open than before, a clear gap interrupting the otherwise recurring stonework.

Using the natural incline, he climbed it, pulling himself up.

He found himself in a room with paved flooring, illuminated by artificial light. The bulbs, though bright, were strange in way of arrangement, the holders like candelabra from a great hall. Surrounding him was a display of cannons.

"We've just entered the Tower," Kit said into his headset, pulling Sanders up as he spoke. Within five seconds, Wilcox and Ward followed, both taking stock of the surroundings.

"We see you," Maria advised them before she returned her attention to the Queen's House and the barracks. "Head to the Jewel House. Quickest way is through the gift shop."

"Roger that."

Kit led the way through the gift shop and up the nearby stairs. On reaching the far side, he saw a door, beyond it a large neo-gothic building with twin towers.

Immediately he recognised it.

"We're at the door. Any enemies?"

"Negative. You're the only ones left."

"Roger that."

Kit pushed against the outer door of the White Tower and sprinted towards the main entrance of the Jewel House.

While Maria passed directions to Kit, less than five feet away Phil's attention had turned to Edinburgh.

"Fitz-Simon, this is the Rook, what's your status?"

In the vaults beneath the Scottish capital, Rawlins, Pentland and Pugh hurried through the narrow tunnels, paying close attention to their surroundings. Unlike the costumed props and tourist set-up at Mary King's Close, what they saw now appeared to have been undisturbed for centuries.

"GPS confirms we're almost directly under the palace," Rawlins replied as he ran. "If he tries to double back, he'll only have one option."

Directly beneath the cellar of the old palace, the cousin of Fabien Randek heard Blanco's voice come through clearly. Alain had been detained; the attack compromised.

Thanks to the concession of the prince, the final detonation would not be necessary.

The key turned swiftly as if it had been made recently, the slow creaking of the opening door preceding the movement of feet.

Blanco was first to enter, followed by François. One by one, the gunmen followed, the accumulative light of half a dozen lanterns creating an atmospheric glow across the 17th-century walls.

The ceiling was vaulted, the designs reminiscent of both a church crypt and a bank's strong room. Any decorations on the walls were hidden by a series of wooden ornaments; Blanco guessed they might be some form of safe deposit boxes. Moving to the centre of the room, he saw more of the same; it reminded him of the long display case he'd seen in the Jewel House. Cautiously, he attempted to open it, again finding it locked. Searching the keyring, he looked out the smallest key, discovering it to be the right one.

His heart was palpitating wildly now, anticipating that the next moment would define the rest of his life, every life. Slowly the case opened, the weight again restrictive. He peered inside, his eyes alight at the sight of the object before him. His smile widening, he reached inside, removing it carefully.

He held the Imperial State Crown of the United Kingdom.

Outside the vault, Mike fell to his left as a second blow struck him hard across his right cheek, courtesy again of Fabien Randek. Through numbing pain, he heard him ask the same question as after the first punch.

"Where are the rest of you?"

Spread out on the floor, Mike ignored the question, concentrating instead on his latest wounds. Behind him, he sensed Randek drawing closer before repeating the same question.

Again that night, his mind returned to his training.

When the head sack was removed, Mike found himself standing in a rectangular room; other than its shape, its only characteristic was whiteness.

A four-legged table of the same colour was surrounded by three chairs, one of which was vacant. The occupants of the other two were clear. The man, heavyset, bearded and bespectacled, stared icily into a slimline computer, while the woman, older, motherly, was far more interested in Mike.

"Take a seat," the woman offered.

He did so, finding it initially difficult to adjust to the sudden onset of light. The man at the computer typed quickly at his keyboard, the regular adjustment of his spectacles the nearest he came to communicating. The woman rose to her feet and circled Mike slowly, her attention alternating between him and the floor. The sound of her footsteps and the way she walked was almost hypnotic.

Mike sensed she did it to create a pulsating echo with her heels.

As his eyes continued to adjust to the brightness, Mike noticed other features, subtle, more innocuous. A large mirror covered the far wall, the corners of which were layered in plaster. A long electrical cord ran along the tiled floor; the electrical sockets were located in the same wall. Staring beyond the two strangers, he hid a smile; there was nothing here he hadn't seen before.

Behind the glass and the plastered corners, he knew both people and cameras were watching him.

The woman completed a third circle of Mike before finally stopping in front of him. Like the man at the desk, the colour of her clothing matched that of the walls, a pristine lab coat that for some reason Mike thought was more in keeping with a surgeon than a scientist. The woman smiled coyly at him, provoking a strange sexual feeling that rather disturbed him. Her brown, shoulder-length hair, presently tied in a bun, fitted the mould of an RAF intelligence girl from the Second World War, while her strong, no-nonsense demeanour indicated experience of exercising authority, perhaps as a headmistress or a mother of teenage children.

The woman's smile came and went, always carrying a strange sense of warmth.

"How are we, dear? You feeling okay?"

Mike kept quiet, monitoring the woman closely. Experience taught him the worst thing he could do was antagonise his captors.

"I can't answer that question, ma'am," he eventually replied.

"Of course you can't. I know how well you boys are trained." She walked towards him, circling him again, only now anticlockwise.

"What did you say your name was?"

"Michael Hansen, ma'am."

"That your full name?"

A slight pause. "Michael Ashley Hansen."

"Very good. How are you, dear?" she asked again.

"I can't answer that question, ma'am."

The woman moved closer, touching his cheeks and face. Even after several minutes in the room, the light still felt painful on his eyes.

"It's okay. Allow yourself time to get used to the light. Can you see okay now?"

"I can't answer that question, ma'am."

"I see. Remind me again. Your full name."

"Michael Ashley Hansen."

"And what's your occupation, Michael Ashley?"

"I can't answer that question, ma'am."

"You're freezing, aren't you?" She saw him shiver slightly. She rubbed his shoulders gently. "Would you like a blanket?"

"I can't answer that question, ma'am."

"Well, I'm afraid I might have to make things even colder for you. When were you born, Michael Ashley?"

"Seventh of June, nineteen-eighty-seven."

"And how old are you?"

"I can't answer that question, ma'am."

"You just told me your date of birth." The woman's patience was thinning. "What religion are you?"

"Catholic, ma'am."

"And your blood group?"

"O, ma'am."

"And where did you go to school?"

"I can't answer that question, ma'am."

Mike coughed as he slowly rose again to his haunches, touching his face with his left hand. Though all feeling had seemingly left that part of his body, it was obvious from inspecting the palm of his hand the recent assault had drawn fresh blood.

"Where are the rest of you?" Randek looked down with malice. "Speak!"

Mike looked up at him, spitting on the floor. "I can't answer that question."

116

Beneath the Bank of England, 04:02

Kit turned left on passing the main door of the Jewel House, relieved to find those beyond it open. The way ahead was well lit, the replica lanterns illuminating a passageway lined with medieval ornaments of obvious connection with a coronation. Following the passageway, he found himself in the main room, where the fake crowns were usually located in a long display case in between two travellators.

The first thing that struck him was that they were empty.

A Yeoman Warder was standing at the far end, clearly awaiting their arrival.

"Where's the workshop?" Kit's words spat out like bullets.

The Yeoman led them down the stairs, entering the workshop. Twelve crowns were located on a long workstation covered with tools and fluids; among the crowd of people he noticed a brown-haired woman in her late twenties, her face and hair clearly suffering the effects of a recent ordeal.

He didn't need a nametag to know he was looking at Emily Fletcher.

"Where's the tunnel?"

Emily saw the quartet emerge, taking the stairs two by two. The first thing she observed was how they dressed; she had seen an almost identical uniform once already that evening.

"The vault is located somewhere beyond this door. I don't know exactly where."

Kit followed the instruction and spoke quickly into his headset. "Grosmont, this is Edward. Do you copy?" he asked to no response. "Rook, this is Edward. We're outside the tunnel."

"Copy that, Edward," Maria replied. "You are to proceed by any means necessary."

"Roger that!" He turned to Emily. "When was the last time you saw him?"

Emily struggled to gather her thoughts. A series of images passed through her mind: a rooftop, the White Tower, a zipline – it seemed like something out of a dream. "Around 3 a.m. Just before he made it up to the roof of the White Tower."

"Have you heard any word since?"

"Only from your headquarters."

"Stay here; we may need to contact you."

Emily watched the men in black disappear through the doorway. "Is he okay?"

"He was never okay." Ward eyed her as he entered last. "But at least he's alive."

***

Mike held his head as the blond-haired villain's fist made further contact with the side of his face, sending him crashing down hard on the slabs below. He felt his eyes close instinctively as he caught his temple on a jagged edge; even before he reopened them, he was aware of blood pouring from the latest wound.

Less than three metres away, he saw Fabien Randek looking down at him with an expression of pure malice that threatened to escalate further as Mike attempted to regain his feet. Of all the hits he'd taken, the latest had been by far the most damaging. Objects seemed blurred; rings of light distorted his vision. A sudden wave of nausea came and went instantly; the pain in his head felt worse than being pistol-whipped.

Concentrating on his breathing, he spat at the floor, his blood-tainted saliva now alarmingly solid. Without water, his throat felt that it was in danger of closing, his breathing about to cease. *Mental endurance is absolutely pivotal, no matter what the mission.*

Again Stokes's words continued to run through his mind.

Randek stood with his feet comfortably apart, his arms down by his sides. In the dim light, his eyes had a strange, venomous quality that reminded Mike of a serpent.

"Where are the others? They have deserted you, no?" He looked deep into Mike's eyes. "What is your name?"

Mike spat at the floor. "Dennis the Menace."

"You think it's wise to antagonise your captor?"

"Doesn't matter, shithead, I'm already dead."

Randek stepped forward, his latest blow taking Mike to his knees. With one swift movement he removed his gun, pointing it at Mike's head.

"Soon, you will be."

Each cabinet was filled, as were individual shelves. What they contained was of profound importance both to a coronation ceremony and the mission. One by one, Blanco and François gazed at them, awestruck, before passing them on to the nearest gunmen.

After less than a minute the holdalls were full.

Leaving the large cabinet in the centre of the vault, he looked around to satisfy himself that they had found all that they had come for. Everything in the original collection had been there from altar plate to the Honours of Scotland, their appearances dazzling even in the half-light. Once he was sure every item had been accounted for, he returned his attention to the two main items of importance: the Imperial State Crown and that of St Edward. He focused first on the Imperial Crown, carefully examining the important stones. Even without the extra inspection, he could tell that the glow was brighter than the crown he had damaged, the stones clearly of rare magnificence.

Alongside him, François studied the jewels with his jeweller's glasses.

"Well?"

The expert nodded. "They are good."

Blanco exhaled with relief. In the same breath, he picked up his HT, contacting Fieschi.

"They are good."

At the other end, Gabriel de Fieschi and the two men alongside him heard the words clearly.

"You have seen them?" Fieschi answered.

"Seen them and packed them safely away."

Fieschi allowed himself a moment for the reality to dawn. The words of the Prince of Wales had proven true.

The Crown Jewels of England had been returned to their rightful owner.

"The last men on the streets are presently returning to the river. The cruisers are presently departing from Blackfriars. After that, I will send the helicopters."

Blanco replaced the HT on his belt, his attention returning to François. "Show me the map."

François removed the A3-sized photocopy from his pocket and spread it out across the now empty wooden cabinets. The tunnel in had proven clear, as had the design of the chamber. The entrance had been from the south-east.

The exit was south-west.

Blanco examined the nearby wall with the aid of both torch and lamplight. Among the heavy wooden furniture there was a metal door.

Again, it required opening with a key.

Less than a quarter of a mile from the strange vault, the four Harts led by Kit Masterson made their way speedily along the deserted subterranean passageway. Against the green backdrop, he made out figures in front of him, army uniforms, other regalia more unique.

He addressed the captain of the Queen's Guard. "Captain Roberts?"

"You must be the men the woman from Whitehall told us of."

"Let's leave the introductions till later, shall we? The terrorists have ascertained the combination for the vault. Unless we're quick, your employer might soon be out of a job!"

Blanco picked up his HT and tried calling his men at St Dunstan's and Edinburgh in turn. Failing first time with both, he tried St Dunstan's again.

"Lillian, this is Blanco. I repeat, you may proceed immediately."

In the now closed public gardens of St Dunstan-in-the-East, Sean Cummins escorted the arsonist out at gunpoint, directing him beyond the south wall. On reaching the gate, he found an unmarked police car parked next to the kerb.

Within seconds it drove away.

In Edinburgh, the cousin of Fabien Randek heard Blanco's voice come through clearly. Deciding against replying, he switched off the device. The noises he'd heard merely moments earlier had clearly come from outside the room; what he'd initially taken to be footsteps was accompanied by something else.

Whispering.

Removing his firearm from his belt, he focused on the nearby doorway, extending his arms.

Randek reloaded his pistol, watching the empty magazine bounce up off the floor. Down on his knees, Mike did the same, quietly ruing the fact his own weapon was presently lodged in the same man's belt.

Gathering each last ounce of his remaining strength, he raised his head, his eyes meeting with Randek's. Though the light faded when the halogen lamps were moved, the distant glow from their new position inside the vault had no impact on the serpent-like look he presented.

If anything, the darkness intensified it.

Mike heard Blanco call Randek's name, telling him to make haste. The second door had now been found and opened; only one tunnel separated the terrorists from their escape. Hearing his uncle's command, Randek extended his hands, the end of the gun coming hard into contact with the centre of Mike's forehead. Instinctively he blinked, now staring down the barrel, his eyes locked with those of the serpent.

Blanco called out again. "Enough. You can see him in hell."

At that moment, Randek's face formed a manic smile; somehow Mike felt the energy to replicate it. He remembered what Kit had told him on joining the White Hart.

On entering the centre of hell, you will remain there for the remainder of your life.

He held his breath, awaiting the inevitable, feeling rather than seeing Randek's finger close in around the trigger. He saw the villain bite down on his lower lip; even the way he did so appeared strangely reptilian. Blinking again, he exhaled as he saw movement from the man's index finger, followed by sound: an echo of further gunfire. A sharp yellow flash appeared quickly from his right, taking him off balance. Falling to the floor, a blaze of shots came from Randek's gun.

Only none of them were aimed at him.

117

Beneath the Bank of England, 04:05

The entrance to the vault showed up clearly against the green backdrop of Kit Masterson's night-vision goggles. Other sights did too; an initial glance hadn't been enough to take them all in.

The open door was circular, perhaps spherical; the depth of the opening, although clearly in proportion to the door, created an optical illusion that made it appear peculiarly deep. Inside the vault, he heard voices, saw movement: shadows, human shapes, things which had no right being there. There were similar movements in front of the door; two silhouettes cut very contrasting figures. One was kneeling, his head raised; opposite, the second figure had a gun pointing downwards, execution style. Among the outlines he saw other features: certain things a man could instinctively recognise in the dark. The body language of the pair confirmed their identities in subtle ways. The way the attacker stood was antagonistic; even his hairline was unmistakeable. The same was true of the man on the ground. He had seen him before, lived with him, watched him go through hell and back.

Mike Hansen was seconds away from being shot.

Kit's actions were instinctive, clinical. Raising his weapon, he fired twice; backup gunfire came from behind him. The first bullet had been successful, albeit not deadly.

Even with the night visions it was too dark to see exactly where Randek had been hit.

Mike rolled to his right, his hands coming instinctively over his head. Rummaging through his combats, he realised he had no weapons but his hands, and only a fool would turn up bare fisted to a gunfight. The recent onslaught had monopolised Randek's attention, but Mike knew he wasn't out of the woods.

He scrambled his way along the wall to his right, focusing on where the gunfire was coming from. Pulling his night visions back down over his eyes, he realised it had come from five sources: all of whom were White Harts. Kit had taken the lead; Sanders, Iqbal, Ward and Wilcox followed. Each man was lined up in cover formation; he saw Wilcox take one in the shoulder, losing his weapon.

The others, for now, were largely unhurt.

Beyond his five teammates, he saw further movement, voices speaking in English. He made out uniforms, two kinds. In addition to the Queen's Guard were Yeoman Warders.

In total he counted over ten.

Staying low, he crawled towards them, doing his best to ignore the pains that pounded through his head and thigh. Close to the door, Blanco was shouting, his words drowned out by gunfire. Beyond the door, Mike saw him disappearing through the second door; François and the others followed closely behind. When nine had passed, the firing ceased.

Randek had been left on his own, clearly bleeding.

The initial gunfire had been of no concern to Blanco; nor had it been to anyone else inside the vault. The jewels had been packed away, the escape door opened.

All that remained was to execute the hostage.

The second wave had also initially failed to rouse any deep concern; Blanco knew his nephew well enough to know the line was easily crossed. Desecrating the corpse of the man who had brought about his brother-in-law's downfall was less likely to be considered barbaric in the family circle.

The concern only came when it was clear his nephew was injured.

Heading for the main door, he ducked immediately, the sparks of countless shells reflecting back off the reinforced steel. As the seconds passed, he sensed a further onslaught coming fast above his head; the cabinets behind him splintered under the impact of machine gun fire. Edging closer to the door, he called Randek's name, repeating it twice. Amidst the chaos, he saw him fire wildly before taking one in the shoulder, then a second. In what appeared a moment of time distortion, Randek dropped his gun, losing his balance.

Blanco called out again.

And hurried to the exit door.

Mike saw the weapon drop from Randek's hand, clattering down on to the floor. In that moment, the gunfire stopped, the erratic yellow blazes disappearing along with the sounds. Within seconds, the Harts descended on him, Kit the first to arrive. Mike saw him look at Randek from a distance before coming ever closer. Even in the darkness, hatred defined the terrorist's features, coupled with a developing sense of resignation.

For several seconds Mike watched on as the two enemies remained locked in unspoken conversation. On approaching the vault, Kit removed his night visions, looking Randek coldly in the eye. Aided by the nearest halogen lamps, Mike saw he was bleeding on both sides, wounds which were unlikely to be fatal.

Scornfully, Kit turned to those behind him. "Cuff him."

Within moments of receiving the call, the Harts descended on the vault, the Queen's Guard on Randek. Jay hurried towards Mike, his familiar handsome face looking down compassionately.

"You okay?"

Mike answered through the pain. "Blanco's disappeared into the left wall. Must be a side passage."

Smiling, Jay squeezed his shoulder before joining Sanders, Wilcox and Ward in the vault, Wilcox clearly nursing a throbbing shoulder. Kit joined them after looking briefly at Mike to check on his condition; any outer concern as usual masked by the imperatives of urgency and duty.

He ordered the Queen's Guard to clean up the mess.

Down on his knees, Randek looked up to see the man he'd tussled with six months earlier on the boat in Paris begin to walk away, his attention turning to the vault. He heard the commands to cuff him coming through clearly; equally clearly, he was now outnumbered.

He could see ten armed men descending on him.

As he watched the leader of the Servants pass him by, he reached down below his right legging, removing a semi-automatic pistol.

Raising his hand, he went for the trigger.

Mike's reactions were instinctive. Unarmed, unable to move, he called out to Kit, warning him of impending danger. Turning on the spot, he saw Kit aim his weapon just as Randek attempted to make his shot. The sound of gunfire once again filled the passage, blood spilling from Randek's skull. Beyond the gathering of Queen's Guards, a man adorned in a far grander uniform looked down the barrel of his firearm.

All eyes fell on the Ravenmaster.

"That'll teach you to mess with my bloody birds!"

The second passageway was like the previous one in every way, from the patterns on the walls to the height of the ceiling. On reaching the other side, Blanco pushed the door, hoping desperately that Randek would be able to join him.

He called him via the HT. "Fabien? Fabien, come in."

Kit heard the request clearly. Picking up the HT, his eyes focused on the lifeless face of Fabien Randek, his blood-soaked carcass spread out across the floor.

"You're wasting your time with this one. Turns out the ravens aren't destined to leave just yet."

Blanco's face flushed red with fury, creating a pressure that caused the veins in his forehead to bulge. He took a deep breath, his eyes on the passageway. Less than five metres away François stared at him, his expression grave.

"Delay now and they will get us."

Blanco turned around, his focus on the door. He inserted the key, taking a further breath. Ignoring the temptation to take one last look, he locked the door as quickly as he could and sped away along the previously concealed escape route.

118

Beneath the Bank of England, 04:10

Ward was first to reach Blanco's escape door. Pushing it hard, he encountered resistance.

"Locked, dammit!"

Kit entered the vault alongside him, his attention drawn briefly to the damaged furnishings before switching his concentration to the door. Attacking it with his shoulder, he met the same resistance.

"Blow the lock!"

Beneath the Scottish capital, the sounds in the nearby passageway were getting louder. The arsonist detected three sets of footsteps, at least two voices.

His arms outstretched, his fingers itching for the kill, he saw the light change in the backdrop of his night visions and squeezed the trigger.

Rawlins fell immediately, a sudden piercing force striking his shoulder. The impact was high; another inch up and it would have missed him.

Two inches lower, the body armour would have absorbed the impact.

Pugh and Pentland reacted immediately. A yellow flash had showed up clearly in the green light, surprisingly noiseless. Taking shelter behind the walls, they waited for the firing to stop. A clear sound ensued of a gun being reloaded.

Moving as one, they rounded on the gunman.

And watched as his weapon dropped to the floor.

The direction of the second tunnel appeared to be almost a mirror image of the first. From the map, both passages formed a perfect triangle, with the apex at the vault to the north. From where the first tunnel began beneath the Jewel House, he calculated the second would end somewhere near Blackfriars, although the exact location was difficult to determine.

Blanco hurried on, ignoring the threats from his nephew's killer as they came through on Randek's frequency. He estimated the length to be no more than a mile; reachable, depending on how long it took his pursuers to break the door.

He sensed from the noise on Randek's HT that they were preparing to blow the lock.

"Turn on the lights," Blanco ordered, deciding on reflection that with the aid of the night-vision technology his pursuers possessed, it would make little difference.

If the exit came into view suddenly, the extra light could be helpful.

Kit ordered the others to take shelter as the electric current met the plastic explosive, causing a sudden flash from inside the vault. The ground shook far harder than Kit had expected; a deafening echo filled the locality.

As the smoke cleared, Kit entered first. There was debris on the floor, dust in the air; something had caused the wooden cases in the middle of the room to split.

Soon he saw what.

"Rob – you, Tommy and Jay come with me. Marcus, stay here."

"I can still run!" Wilcox protested.

"No. You take care of Hansen." Kit caught Mike's eye as he struggled towards the vault. "Keep in contact. Queen's Guards and Yeoman Warders, follow me."

As Kit departed through the second door, Mike limped into the vault, holding his gaze till he disappeared. Though nothing was said, it was an expression he'd seen many times before.

Don't you go dying on me!

Mike stepped aside as the Queen's Guards and Beefeaters followed, pursuing Blanco along the second tunnel. He found Wilcox nursing a wounded shoulder, bloodstains covering much of his left side, partially staining his blond hair and beard.

"What the hell happened to you?"

"Was about to ask you the same question." Mike's battered face broke into a grin. Within seconds of entering the vault, he saw the device Blanco had shown on camera to the PM still on the floor among the display cases.

Quickly he searched his belt for wire cutters. "Come on, before that asshole tries to detonate it!"

Blanco placed the HT to his lips, again trying St Dunstan's and Edinburgh. Just as before, he received no response.

He feared the worst.

Giving up, he put through a different call. "This is Blanco. We'll be with you in two minutes."

Close to Blackfriars Bridge, the three single-engined helicopters hovered over the north bank, their blades causing ripples in the waves below. On hearing Blanco's voice, the pilot of the first responded.

"Everything is in place. The choppers will be waiting."

***

Kit upped the pace as the passageway began to slope upwards, doing his best to fight off the ever-increasing fatigue. He'd noticed that although the previous passageway had sloped down, both curved from right to left; he put it down to the surrounding geography.

As the passage continued, so did the pattern; the GPS had placed the vault directly under the heart of the Bank of England and approximately half a mile under the ground. He remembered what Maria had said earlier about how the areas to the north, despite being taken out by the original Great Fire, had not been affected tonight.

He guessed that was no coincidence.

The GPS now placed them south of St Paul's Churchyard, close to both the Thames and the River Fleet. He could hear water nearby, possibly on both sides; that too he thought was no coincidence.

Speaking into his headset, he called the Rook. Failing the first time, he tried again.

His ears buzzed with the tone of a dead line.

The map confirmed only that the tunnel ended. Exactly where was unclear. From earlier experience of the passageways, it seemed likely that the exit would almost certainly be underground and medieval. Anything different, Blanco dreaded to contemplate.

Whatever happened now was in God's hands.

He sensed the tunnel was becoming brighter, the hypothetical light at the end drawing nearer. Extinguishing the torches, he realised there was no mistake; whatever the source of the light, it was enough to illuminate the way. The closer he got, the more he felt the light was unlikely to be natural, but probably from outside the tunnel.

Within seconds he had his answer.

Kit saw the light at the same time as the others. Guided by the brighter illumination, he saw the slope of the pathway continued to steepen, the increase in incline further testing his tired limbs. Following it further, he realised the light was artificial and from outside the passageway.

Beyond the walls there was an open doorway, a possible means of return to the outside world. Passing through it, he found himself among a strange collection of statues, possibly effigies.

Switching on his torch, he immediately recognised his location.

"Rook, this is Edward."

Maria heard him reconnect; the GPS confirmed his location. "What the hell happened?"

"You want the long story or the short?"

"Humour me."

"The passage came out in the crypt of Temple Church." A famed society of bankers and another church developed by Wren – it annoyed him he hadn't predicted it.

On entering the crypt through a gap in the walls, Kit hurried up the stairway, finding it ended just outside the main doors of the church. Once outside, he looked up at the 12th-century walls that were lit with a warm yellow glow by the surrounding floodlights. "We've lost sight of them!"

Maria's attention focused on the screens. "Targets are heading south through the inner court gardens. Looks like they're heading for the river."

Wasting no time, Kit led the group south through the Inns of Court to Middle Temple Lane. After passing the iconic archway, they stopped on reaching the gates, finding them locked and too tall to climb. Choosing to tackle the fence, Kit accepted Jay and Sanders' assistance and scrambled over, ignoring the incessant pain where the spikes stabbed his thighs. Crossing the main road, he made it to the north bank, his eyes scanning the river in both directions. Both east and west, the lights of the city were reflected in the gently bobbing waves.

Like a thief in the night, Blanco had vanished.

119

Charlestown, Twenty-One Months Earlier

The brigadier stood with his arms by his sides, his focus on Mike. Atkins was alongside him, the mysterious man in black absent.

"Good morning, Lieutenant."

"Good morning, sir!"

"I've just come in from a debrief with your interrogators. I'm pleased to inform you they were very impressed by the way you handled yourself. You managed to resist interrogation admirably – far better than most in the forces, including many past members of our organisation. Congratulations, you have passed the seventh circle."

Mike nodded. On hearing the words *seventh circle*, he suddenly felt tired. He couldn't remember the last time he'd eaten.

"You now have one final challenge remaining. For myself, you might say a personal favourite. Ever since its creation back in 1941, the spiritual home of the Special Forces has been the Brecon Beacons. Your final challenge is an endurance march across the national park. It will be done under timed conditions." He tapped his stick against a nearby blackboard, a 2D map outlining the route. "Your challenge is to get from point A to B. This must be completed in under three hours and forty-five minutes."

Mike raised an eyebrow, the lines on his forehead causing a deep crease. He'd seen the route before, recently; he'd created it himself. The final pieces of the puzzle fell into place. The people who had been watching him, the reasons for their interest.

It all came down to one almighty test.

The irony wasn't lost on Mike as he saw his starting location. The car park was deserted, the approach road closed. The official reason was potholes.

It was quiet on the hills. The helicopter completed two full circles of the route before landing; instructions from Sanders bellowing in his ear, barely audible over the sound of the motors. If there were people present, they would arrive later; it was impossible to close the entire park.

Mike guessed if there had been a way, the White Hart would have found it.

The brigadier was waiting by the car park exit, a pathway that led to both Pen y Fan and Fan y Big.

"You okay, Lieutenant?"

The question sounded genuine. "Yes, sir."

"You understand your objective?"

Though Mike understood every word, the target seemed impossible. "Yes, sir."

"Now, as I've mentioned before, the importance of these assessments cannot be overemphasised. In war, sometimes you have to cross large areas of undulating terrain and still have to face your enemy on the other side. Just like the earlier tests, it's up to me whether you pass or fail, so do your best."

Mike made a strong start, deciding to proceed at his usual pace. It felt strange operating on so little energy; his previous trips had been well planned. Until now he'd never trained more than twice a month.

At least now he'd had breakfast.

He followed the stone path to the bottom of the valley where the two Fans met. He found Chambers waiting at the bottom – the first checkpoint.

The knight smiled at him. "Everything okay, bro?"

Mike eased to a standstill. "You don't have to guide me, I already know the route."

"I'm glad to hear it. Unfortunately I do have to ask you a question."

He should have known. "Okay, fire away."

"In what year was the Battle of Crécy?"

A White Hart history question. "1346."

Chambers winked at him. "Good job, bro. Give me a wave when you reach the Big Fanny."

After two hours, he found himself on a familiar road that intersected two areas of woodland. The reservoir was to the north now; the way back to the start would involve a jog in that direction before heading east again across the next area of woodland. He entered the woodland when the road came to a crossroads, and headed east, uphill. The woods were deserted, the trees bare; even the birdlife seemed eerily silent.

There was smoke rising from somewhere; he smelled it before he saw it. Two silhouetted figures were moving beyond the flames, their muffled voices lost in the wind. They were dressed in military combats: he felt sure that he knew them. Since meeting Chambers, he'd encountered all but one of the Harts.

He sensed the next checkpoint was near.

He made it to the fire, finding it deserted. There were animal bones scattered around; their arrangement seemed deliberate.

Kneeling down, he laughed as he saw they were artificial.

"What time do you call this?"

Masterson was standing behind him, dressed in combats. Like the majority of the Harts he'd seen at the various checkpoints during the last few hours, a warm woolly hat covered his smart locks.

Mike instinctively checked his wrist before remembering his watch had been confiscated. "I understand you have a question for me."

"You understand correctly." Kit folded his arms, no sign of a clipboard. "Do you want to be a White Hart?"

"What kind of question is that?"

"One with a yes or a no answer." Kit eyeballed him, humour now absent. "Think carefully."

What kind of question was that? It wasn't as though he had a simple choice. Did he?

Over the last three weeks he'd been through the mill. Injured every part of his body. Worked through the pain. Entered the Devil's personal playpen and walked out of the gates of hell. He'd passed every segment. Proved himself to the SEALs, YAMAM, NAVSOG, SASR, SPETSNAZ, even to Masterson. All that remained were those in charge.

And the mysterious man in black.

He looked at Kit, focusing on his eyes. He saw a change in him; he'd noticed it on completing phase 6. The man was mellowing, slowly becoming convinced.

"Well, I didn't come this far to turn back now."

Kit's hard façade softened, melting into a smile.

"All right then. I suggest you prove to the brigadier that you're fast enough."

The helicopter touched down in the heart of the parade ground. Mike was unsure of the time; the only clue was, it was dark.

One by one, the eleven members of the UK's oldest and most secretive elite taskforce made their way across the grass-covered ground and into the mess. Mike followed, slightly unsure of himself. Stokes and Atkins had disappeared.

He still had no idea how he'd done.

"Now, tonight is a very important occasion." Sanders rose to his feet, clapping his hands together to get everyone's attention. Though the plates were all full, no one had started to eat. "Today, Lieutenant Hansen completed his final task as a poet. We all remember what it's like to get to the centre of hell. Lieutenant." He picked up his metal cup and saluted Mike. "I tip my hat."

"Yeah!" Everyone slapped their hands against the table, the vibrations causing the plates to move.

Ward noticed Mike was quiet. "Everything okay, bro?"

"Being honest, I'm not quite sure. I still have no idea what my time was."

"Don't worry about that, bro." Chambers started his food. "They deliberately don't tell you. Besides, it's not about time anyway. Not completely."

Mike raised an eyebrow. "But the brigadier said . . ."

"The brigadier told you only what he wanted you to know." Kit had started to eat, his eyes firmly focused on his plate. "Do you honestly think we'd waste all that time training you for the possibility of one little mistake?"

"To be honest, I hadn't thought about it," Mike replied.

"The important thing is, are you one of us?" Sanders looked at him. "I think you've proved that."

Mike stared back before facing the others in turn. All looked at him, Kit still concentrating on his food.

Strangely, he could no longer imagine life without them.

"So what happens now?"

"Same thing that always happens," Sanders said. "Your future will be discussed at board level. Then they'll make a decision."

"So in a way this was all for nothing!"

"No, not at all. It just means there are bigger questions. Fortunately for you, you've got some influential supporters."

Mike smiled, knowing the praise was genuine. "Well, whatever happens, it's been a blast. I'd love to fight with you guys."

"We'll all be interviewed," Ward added. "After that, it's out of our hands."

All of the Harts added similar words of comfort; Kit again was the one exception.

"The important thing is you can get back to normal," Sanders said. "The trials are over. Tonight you can relax. And in your honour" – he glanced at Iqbal – "we've prepared this for you."

Jay smiled and broke into song. Laughing, the rest of the Harts joined in with the chorus of Hanson's "MMMBop".

Activation of the camp floodlights coincided with the end of dinner. Mike went his separate way as they re-entered the parade ground, taking up his usual solitary position looking back to the head of the parade. The eleven stood behind Atkins and the brigadier, their elegant postures almost mirror images despite different attire. Both men had auras about them, although the military veteran was more charismatic. He returned Mike's salute before lowering his muscular arm.

Mike hoped he'd look as good in thirty years.

A pause in proceedings followed as the mysterious man in black came to a halt close to Stokes. Again what struck him most was the impeccable timing of the Harts' salutes.

It reinforced the view that the stranger was the most important of all of them.

The brigadier stood at ease and addressed Mike in a friendly tone. "Well, firstly, Lieutenant, well done. I know it's been a gruelling few weeks, and probably not something you'll be hoping to repeat in a hurry. Nevertheless, what we've seen has been very informative. In times of war, there is no escape, so it's important when we recruit that we take on only the best. I know as a member of the Parachute Regiment, you're already quite experienced in operational requirements, but take it from a veteran of nearly forty years, in the days when the light at the end of the tunnel goes out, you have to work that extra bit harder."

Mike nodded, maintaining a neutral expression. He didn't doubt it for a second.

"I have the results of your run today. Your target was three hours and forty-five. You completed it in just under five hours." The senior officer handed his clipboard to the bugler. "While you didn't complete it in the time set, in truth there was much more at stake here than the time. The time we set, so my experts tell me, was an unrealistic expectation, especially with the weight you carried and after the stresses you've put upon your body. Therefore the key things are, A – you completed it successfully. And B – despite perhaps feeling the temptation from time to time, you saw it out and never gave up. That's very important."

Mike allowed himself a smile, remembering Sanders and Kit saying as much. Both looked on with controlled expressions.

"I will now go away and have a little chat with the people who know you best, and discuss the results of the last week. Together they'll decide on the best way forward. However, I want you to rest assured you have successfully passed the eighth section of your training. You are therefore now eligible to be considered for selection for any out of the SRR, the SBS or the SAS. Congratulations."

As those on parade went their separate way, heading apparently for a remote part of the White Hart Inn, which Mike guessed was of significant importance to the organisation, Mike climbed the creaking stairs and entered room 5.

It was warm inside with a strong smell of appetising food. A large dining platter had been placed on a portable trolley, an ice bucket with bottles of beer alongside it. He lifted the lid and saw everything from chicken on skewers to sirloin steaks.

Training, it appeared, was officially over.

As the man referred to in recent days as the Poet lay down on his bed, the scars of recent exploits showing clearly as he threw off his clothes, a strange moment of reflection followed. What had been normal before was normal no longer, and all that he had just experienced, itself far from normal, felt surreal. Shattered as he was, the way of life had grown on him. It had become the norm. He doubted whether life would ever be the same again.

Part of him hoped not.

Reaching over to his food, he sampled the chicken then the beer, savouring the taste of both. After three weeks in hell, he'd finally reached the centre.

And even though the physical tests were over, he knew he wouldn't rest easy until he'd climbed out of the tunnel.

While the man referred to in White Hart lore as the Poet trudged his way wearily up the stairs to his quaint hotel room, every other person involved in the parade made a walk down a different, more rustic-looking stairway and into the cellar of the inn. Within an hour, the meeting came to an end.

The opinions of all present had been unanimous.

120

Beneath the Tower of London, 04:48

A warm wind blew softly along the passageway, making a slight whistling sound as it penetrated the gaps between the stonework. Mike hadn't noticed it the first time; he reasoned his attention had been on other things.

The vault he'd just left had been breached in two places; the doors, as far as he knew, were still to be secured. He could feel that the wind was coming from behind him, indicating the vault was probably the source; a sealed airtight area opened for the first time in a long period would inevitably create a current of air. The breeze was a welcome benefit, gently pushing him forward like unseen hands. After a night in the depths of hell, he could think of much worse things.

Remembered much worse.

The light was becoming brighter, confirming he was drawing close to the exit. He made his way slowly along the passage, gratefully accepting the support of a Queen's Guard to his left and Wilcox to his right, himself still nursing a bleeding shoulder. Re-entering the jeweller's room, with the fake crowns still lined up on the work desk, he saw an elderly man, perhaps in his seventies, hard at work, polishing the exterior with a moist cloth. Eyeing the man, he smiled wryly.

While the genuine crowns had been extracted from their secure location over a mile away, as far as the British public was concerned, business would continue as usual.

Leaving the Jewel House, his movements becoming ever slower from tackling the stairs, he came out on to Tower Green, the familiarly imposing four-turreted White Tower looming high above, as it had for so many centuries. Figures moved rapidly on the south side, the majority in the same uniform as the man to his left.

One approached, saluting his captain. "Explosives have all been neutralised, sir. The Tower is no longer in danger."

The captain of the Queen's Guard returned his salute. "Make sure every area is triple-checked. We can't afford any slip-ups."

Mike took the opportunity to free himself of his helpers, stumbling forward a few steps before taking a rest on Tower Green. He frowned as he looked to his left, seeing the bomb-damaged execution monument, reminding him he'd come to rest on a site famous for taking lives. For the briefest of moments, he felt the pain in his head return, along with the nausea. As he concentrated on his breathing, the feeling passed, the strange light-headedness replaced by a sense of peace and solitude he hadn't experienced recently. It felt different, strangely reassuring. The tower in front of him was still standing; those he'd fought for were alive.

Even though he was still to see them.

Lying on his back, the sky above still tainted by a strange redness that he realised was more due to an impending sunrise than any further fires, he noticed movement within the clouds, accompanied by a loud buzzing sound. As the seconds passed, he saw something come into focus, its features becoming instantly recognisable as it circled the White Tower.

On the south lawn, the official helicopter of the White Hart was coming in to land.

It touched down near the wall of the Inmost Ward, close to the ravens' cages. The first thing Kit noticed as he disembarked was the small number of birds present; he counted two with a third presently hopping along in the ruined masonry.

In the circumstances, the image seemed peculiarly ironic.

He headed west, passing the steps to the White Tower and then north along the Broadwalk Steps. The sights that befell him defied easy explanation. There were bloodstains on the walkway all the way to the archway of the Bloody Tower, providing clear evidence of the atrocities that had taken place within the last six hours. By the wooden steps, he observed a large collection of electronic equipment; from a distance it could have been anything from stereo speakers to heavy communications devices. It wasn't until he got up close he realised he was looking at some form of explosives.

The freshly cut wires confirmed the threats had been neutralised.

He moved quickly to Tower Green, passing the Queen's Guards who were either removing the remaining dead bodies or combing the grounds for any further evidence. One man he saw clearly not on duty was lying on his back on Tower Green.

As he approached, he saw him move upright.

"Don't strain yourself. After all, it would be a shame after everything you've gone through if you suffered a hernia trying to sit up." Kit stood with his hands on his hips, looking down at his colleague, taking in every aspect of his appearance. The strapping round his left thigh had lasted well under the circumstances; he sensed the bloodstains were probably older than newer. The same was true of his face, where two black eyes featured in mirror image, creating the illusion of an eye mask. Further down, his cheeks were covered in a dirt-infested purple crust that extended to his ears and neck. His nose was out of shape, possibly broken; the same was true of his jaw. His lower lip, chin and black ops gear were all liberally covered in dry bloodstains.

Unlike the rest of him, the remainder of his clothing had lasted well.

"How am I looking?"

Kit folded his arms. "Normally, I'd say not as handsome as I am. I won't ask if you agree."

Mike grinned, a sudden coughing fit causing extra pain in his torso. Sipping from the water bottle he'd acquired inside the Old Hospital Block, he looked back at Kit, focusing on his appearance. The black ops suit, operative gloves and combat boots matched his own appearance, although the battle scars were different. While there were no gun wounds to his legs, Mike detected evidence of burn marks, dirt and grime on his face indicative of time spent underground.

"You look like hell."

On this occasion, Kit smiled.

On the south lawn, the helicopter's remaining passengers alighted slowly before taking the same route as Kit towards the Broadwalk Steps. Following Jamal Iqbal and Robert Sanders, Andrew Chambers was also strapped up, his chest covered with three layers of bandaging. The same was true of Atkins, who was dressed far more casually than usual.

As always, the Director wore a trademark black suit.

Mr White climbed the steps that led up to Tower Green, changing direction, his eyes on Mike.

"How's the leg?"

"Moving," Mike replied, his numbed mouth struggling to swallow water.

"Consider yourself lucky. Few people who choose to play Virgil end up leaving hell."

Mike nodded; the choice of words seemed peculiarly ironic.

"What happened down there?"

On the helipad on top of the high-rise skyscraper, one of the three helicopters touched down softly on the tarmac, its doors opening immediately to allow its esteemed passengers to enter.

Fieschi was second to board, waiting for his father to take a seat. Alongside him, Jérôme de Haulle finished his cigar, stomping it out with his leather size nines.

Blanco was seated behind the pilot, opposite François. Both carried a crown on their laps.

The Anjouvin waited until all were aboard before giving the pilot the instruction to take off, the sound of the muted conversation overwhelmed by the force of the blades. As Blanco passed the Imperial State Crown to the Duke of Aquitaine, he looked out over the city below, the fires now smouldering among the ruins. In the distance he saw the Tower, the famous walls illuminated in a dreary half-light, the effects of the floodlights softened by the faint promise of dawn.

Like the buildings to the west, it had suffered little damage.

As the chopper headed west, his concentration turned to a different set of buildings, one in particular. Located at the head of the Mall, the palace had also suffered no physical damage; the area around Whitehall remained fully intact, just as it had in Pepys's day. In his mind, he imagined the conversations presently taking place within its walls and how they would differ from those alongside him. It had taken seven hundred years, but they had done it.

The Cardinal's Boys had knocked a pretender off the throne of England.

* * *

A sixth person left the helicopter, sprinting across the greenery towards the famed execution sight. Even from a distance, Mike had no problem recognising Maria Lyons, her ponytail swinging in the breeze.

"We've tracked the helicopters south of the water. One just touched down on a helipad on one of the skyscrapers."

All present listened with intense interest, the Director's expression remaining peculiarly calm. "Keep track of it. The PM has already been on the phone with the premiere of France. If it does touch down south of the channel, the gendarmes are under orders to arrest everyone on board."

"What if they head elsewhere? If I were responsible for stealing three national sets of Crown Jewels, I'm quite sure I'd be heading a long way from here."

The Director remained unmoved. "I'm sure a word in the ears of many of our friends and allies overseas would have the desired effect, don't you?" He returned his attention to Mike. "Where's the governor?"

"Probably in the Queen's House." He accepted Kit's hand, forcing himself to his feet. At that moment, he saw the door open, someone exiting.

Champion hurried towards him.

Mike approached him gingerly, embracing him in a tired hug. "Thank God. For a moment, I thought I'd lost you."

"No, just his walking stick."

Mike grinned at Kit, releasing his uncle. As he limped on, he saw a second person had left the Queen's House, her appearance by comparison far more glamorous. Much had changed since he'd last seen her. The soaked and stained designer suit had been replaced by something far more glamorous; he guessed the wardrobe of the governess prepared for every occasion.

Likewise, he'd changed too, not necessarily in a good way. As she hurried across Tower Green, he saw her place her hands to her mouth, emotion overcoming her. As she tried to speak, he saw her lose it fully, her eyes streaming. For what seemed the longest of moments, he felt unsure of the cause, whether the tears were for him or the occasion.

Maybe after all, she had been fired.

Beyond the pain, he found the energy to smile. Behind the veil of tears, he saw her laugh; after a night in hell, the sound felt like an angel calling him on the wind. As though concerned that even the slightest force would bring him to the ground, she embraced him softly, the faintest brush of her raven-coloured hair bringing a familiar tingling feeling to his face. When their eyes met, she placed her fingers to his cheeks, massaging everything that hurt. For a moment, he thought he was going to cry too; under the circumstances, he couldn't place the cause. With each moment, the pain seemed to dry up; finally the same became true of her tears.

She touched him in the one place that didn't hurt. And lost each other in their touch.

121

3 September, 08:30

A red sky rose over London that morning. The same was recorded in 1666 but for a different reason. The Great Fire that had ravaged the capital's tinderbox houses for four successive days, finally brought to an end by the demolition of buildings to create firebreaks and early autumn rains, in the modern day had ceased within seven hours, thanks in part to a similar combination. The rain, when it came, was little more than a drizzle.

It was as though the heavens themselves were weeping rather than intervening.

Throughout the nation, a period of mourning was already under way, especially among the Londoners. Those who remained in the capital were encouraged not to leave their homes; those who had already left, advised not to return for the present. For many, there was little to return to; like the inferno of 1666, the fire had been indiscriminate. It was estimated over 3,000 homes had been lost, the number of businesses far greater. Ever since the fire started, numerous estimates of the likely insurance settlement costs had been put forward. Even without the theft of the jewels, it was impossible to put a definitive figure on the true damage.

Not once so far had the projections been less than eighty billion pounds.

There was a saying in England about red skies in the morning being associated with warnings, but on this occasion it seemed unlikely that anything further could be worse than what had already taken place. In reality, the rising of the sun was only one reason for the redness. Although the inferno had been dowsed, flames remained visible, especially on Fleet Street and north of the Monument, where steady lines of smoke continued to rise above what remained of the skyline.

What remained varied according to what one looked for, or from where. A citizen or employee at work in one of the tower blocks south of the river could see much compared to one exiting a Tube station on the north side, but both in their own ways could offer uniquely different insights into the city's present condition. As always, the best views came from the television coverage, but while a bird's-eye view could tell a lot about a situation in terms of the area affected, capturing the atmosphere was never fully possible through a glass lens. One or two reporters appeared live on air, providing a dramatic insight into developments from the fiery streets, but they were in the minority. The roads nearest the damage remained off-limits; if one or two attempted to brave the cordons, they were usually met with short shrift from the police. Exactly how long the roads would remain closed was uncertain. One thing was undeniably clear.

What remained of the great city was a sorry sight, from any angle or perspective.

Most of the damage had followed the historical path. What had begun in the hot summer of 1666 in a bakery on Pudding Lane had last night begun in a bank in the same location. For the conspiracy theorists, the location was especially apt; even if those responsible had chosen it primarily for its historical connection, the choice of the bank could have had secondary purposes. On every side of the Monument, what had once existed now did so only in charred remains. In the hub of the original blaze, the famous column had become blackened by soot, the stonework slightly cracked and distorted by the heat. If any daring tourist felt motivated to climb to the top to take in the views across present day London with their own eyes, they would have found it presently off-limits. If the fires had lasted even an additional twenty minutes, the fate of the Monument could have been considerably worse.

Unlike in 1666 when a new city started to rise like the phoenix from the ashes, for now Wren's symbol of remembrance continued to stand.

North of the Monument, the sights were equally sorry. A depressing gale blew along Cannon Street and Gracechurch Street, the areas where the fire had done the most damage. A vile odour permeated the morning air, still heavily polluted by a combination of burning materials and melting metals, coupled with smoke still rising from the charred stonework in the areas where the fires had begun. Whereas the Great Plague of 1665 had been linked with rats, today the dirt in the streets was made up predominantly of the remains of broken windows; for those who walked the streets in official capacity, escaping them was impossible, just as it was for drivers.

The injury count from exploding windows alone was estimated to account for over a quarter of all those being treated for their injuries, numbers of which ran into thousands. Every hospital within a hundred-mile radius remained on red alert; every volunteer and extra staff could make a difference. Many on leave had agreed to come in, some cutting short holidays, offering their services for no pay. Those with minor injuries had generally been redirected to the chemists, others to makeshift medical centres, mostly set up in schools, halls or scout huts. Like calculating the total insurance bill, putting an estimate on the total number of injured was almost impossible.

There was, as yet, no announcement of the official death toll.

Further along Cheapside, the damage was more varied, ranging from minor cosmetic marking to complete obliteration. On the south side, the famous tower of St Mary-le-Bow was one in the fortunate former category; from the outside, few could be aware of the scars that now disfigured the interior. The same was true of the Tube stations, most of which had suffered damage only to their exteriors.

Be it by luck or design, the communications lines had remained largely intact.

In the west part of the city, the damage was more scattered. Whereas St Mary-le-Bow had escaped largely unscathed, the situation was very different in Fleet Street. Amidst the chaos, the long-revered façade of St Bride's survived only as a shell, the great steeple mutilated like a charred wedding cake. In keeping with the historical pattern, the fire had ceased around the Golden Boy of Pye Corner; just as in 1666, the famous legal buildings of the Inns of Court continued to stand tall, the great chambers already a hive of activity.

As always, the first process of rebuilding from the ashes involved contacting a lawyer.

While the scenes of loss were plentiful, others focused on what remained. North of Lombard Street, close to Bank Tube station and Cornhill, the modern headquarters of the Bank of England continued to stand, looking out over the crossroads, its elegant Palladian façade showing no signs of damage.

From its location between St Mary-le-Bow and St Bride's, Wren's magnificent cathedral continued to occupy centre stage at the heart of the city's skyline. A fine dust swirled in the local air, as it had since the early hours, if anything made worse by the rain; even the lightest touch had a tendency to disturb what was underneath. Like St Mary-le-Bow, the damage to the outer structure had been relatively minor. A series of black scars marked the dome like acne on the face of an unfortunate adolescent, but there was nothing that couldn't be replaced or repaired. Inside, the condition was better still, any evidence of debris long since cleared.

Like the second great fire of London, St Paul's had survived the third against all odds.

West of the city, life went on more or less unaffected. Around Westminster, the traffic moved slower than usual, drivers honking their horns, venting their frustrations in response to the numerous road checks. Close to the Commons, the entrance of Westminster Hall was busy with MPs arriving to discuss recent events. In the far corner of the building, Big Ben chimed the hour with its usual precision, its melodious tone sounding sombre on this occasion as it rang out across the depleted skyline. Further west still, crowds gathered outside Buckingham Palace while watching the Queen make her speech via their smartphones. Since the early hours, speculation had been rife that threats had been made against the royals. In recent hours, rumours had been spreading faster than the flames that the Queen herself would abdicate.

Exactly who was responsible was a matter of speculation. According to the news, the fires had indeed been a terrorist attack, a fact endorsed by the PM. In certain circles, ISIS were already taking responsibility, but such claims were taken with a pinch of salt among the political commentators. Opportunism was a curse that clouded the facts, especially to those who had taken the trouble to acquire a good knowledge and understanding of the events. The video footage captured at Watling Street and later off Paternoster Row confirmed the gunmen were white and had European accents.

While the palace remained undamaged, its famous walls shielding meetings of potentially utmost importance, east of the historical fires a different mystery was developing. Close to Tower Bridge, currently closed and devoid of traffic, the Tower was also alive with activity, mostly in the vicinity of the ticket offices. As in other areas in the city, the building was presently not open to the public.

Though not directly affected by the fire, the large pile of fallen masonry in between the Byward and Middle towers was worthy of investigation. Whether its destruction, along with the other approaches, was in any way connected to the attack or a second one was a matter of uncertainty. The official line was that tremors from the earlier explosions had caused the medieval bridge to collapse, but such an explanation failed to satisfy the sceptics. Since 06:00, a photo had been doing the rounds of what appeared to be the Imperial State Crown in a heap, close to the White Tower, but that had already been dismissed as a fake. A PR shot of the real crowns had recently been put out; the date authenticated. Whatever the cause of the rumours, they were merely that – rumours.

Exactly who had started the fire, for the time being, remained a mystery.

Over sixty miles from the scene of devastating destruction, beneath the quaint inn in the village of Charlestown in Suffolk, a meeting of a different kind was already under way. Behind the retractable wall, its external appearance typical of a foundation wall from the 17th century, the concealed room filled with both modern and historical features was alive with the sound of countless voices coming in over the vast collection of electronic devices, the most prevalent being the semi-translucent screen that had the appearance of floating in mid-air between the far wall and the large green and white round table, most of whose chairs were presently occupied.

As they had from the start, the occupants were looking intently at the screen where Sky showed live footage of a podium outside Downing Street, where highlights of the prime minister's earlier speech immediately began to play out. In keeping with that of the Queen before her, despite her well-presented appearance, the PM's eyes revealed the dark shadows of stress and fatigue.

"Our hearts go out to the citizens of London, especially those who suffered deep personal loss or who even now are fighting for their lives or recovering from their injuries in our many hospitals. From every corner of the world, tributes have been pouring in, in recognition of the outstanding efforts and response of our emergency services, a tribute I would like to echo as we reflect on the enormous challenge of fighting for the preservation of our city when under attack at so many levels. As a nation, we are never stronger than when we are threatened, and in times of great need and pain, we demonstrate great resilience. It is a firm testament of our ability, both as a nation that has endured past invasion and heartache, but also a leader on the world stage, that we continue to learn and open our hearts to all in times of need, despite feeling such grief ourselves. We live in a dangerous world and, as the search for those responsible for this appalling attack goes on, it remains imperative that we uphold the ideals and values that have shaped this country's past so that we can move forward with fortitude and confidence in the rebuilding of this great city."

"Speaking from outside her official home at 10 Downing Street, the prime minister refused to comment on whether or not she would resign in the wake of the most damaging terror attack ever witnessed on British soil, nor was she able to confirm the identity of those behind the attacks both here and in Edinburgh, which is now believed to have killed at least sixteen people," the Sky News presenter continued. "On her arrival at Westminster, the PM took no further questions besides confirming she expected a busy day for Parliament; items to be considered including increased security throughout the UK and the emergency clean-up operation that is due to take place in both cities. Although the rebuilding of the cities is not likely to be given high priority in the early weeks, it is expected that it will be mentioned in PM's Questions this afternoon. The leader of the opposition, meanwhile, wasted little time this morning in calling for strong leadership in trying times and commented that the disaster was an important learning curve in our handling of the war on terror and an opportunity for renewal and replanning."

The Director of the White Hart swiped his hand across his portable tablet and the images faded. As the screen vanished before them, he turned to face the round table.

"The prime minister is due at Buckingham Palace the moment Parliament is adjourned; under the circumstances, fixing an exact time is unlikely to prove possible, at least before eleven. Rumours of abdication are unlikely to remain rumours for long. Though Her Majesty avoided the topic in her morning address, clarification is expected before the end of the day."

"Do we know of her decision yet?" Sanders asked, his dark hair and beard appearing far neater than they had a few hours earlier, despite clear cuts and burns to his face and arms.

"In truth, I expect she's still to decide fully herself; whatever her exact plans prior to meeting the PM, it's fairly safe to say she'll be taking advice from her trusted confidants." The Director slumped slightly into his chair; though his appearance seemed fresh, it was clear to those nearby that he had not slept since the trouble began.

"The attack may be over, but the threat of another looms large. The prime minister has called for extra vigilance throughout the United Kingdom; had it been possible, I'm sure she would have created a new level of alert above Critical. Had Blanco been apprehended, of course, this might have been very different. If pictures of the device found in the vault below the Bank of England come to light, it won't take long before Parliament starts to demand an inquiry."

"Presumably there'll be one?" With the exception of the beard, Kit's appearance was similar to that of Sanders.

"A full investigation into the cause of the fires is to begin immediately; Scotland Yard, as usual, have first refusal on the matter. Priority is expected to be given initially to the crypts of the churches; in the interests of national security, sharing what we know isn't something I feel should be denied, especially as the artwork is already in a public place. Exactly where the PM got her intelligence from, however, will remain restricted. As far as the world knows, we were not present last night. Nor did the attack on the Tower occur."

"Surely it's only a matter of time before people start opening their mouths." Kit was sceptical. "Over eighty hostages aren't going to find it easy to keep their mouths shut – especially with rumours appearing all over social media."

"Rumours of the hostage situation is likely to be confirmed later today; as I understand it, any press conference, just like the mopping up, has been assigned directly to the constable and governor. The party line, as I understand, is an unsuccessful jewel heist; the same is to be true of Edinburgh. As luck would have it, the false honours showed up near Arthur's Seat. According to Randek's cousin, the plan had been to throw them in the Leith."

"So it was a family affair?" Wilcox posed. Like Chambers and Sanders, his right shoulder was heavily bandaged.

"I expect a full report as soon as our men return." The Director spoke of the empty seats. In addition to those belonging to Rawlins, Pentland and Pugh, the seat designated Grosmont was also vacant. "As I understand it, they're due to return very soon. Right now, all three are in conference with Scotland's First Minister. The culprits are currently safely under lock and key."

"How about those in London?" Kit asked, a venomous expression on his face.

"The body of Fabien Randek has already been removed, along with those of his comrades. The exact manner of their disposal is still up for debate; however, unlike with Payet, there's little chance they'll show up south of the channel. On the subject of Payet, a body was found below St Paul's in the location you mentioned." He gestured to Kit. "Facial recognition software confirms he was a brother of Payet. The only men to suffer arrest are the two at the Queen's House and the man brought in by Cummins at St Dunstan's. Besides being another relative, little is currently known."

"Where is he now?" Dawson asked; despite suffering clear cuts to his face, his body appeared in better condition than most.

"Right now, that isn't important. He's locked away, you can rely on that." The response came from Atkins, who had stood attentively throughout. Like most, his torso was heavily bandaged. "Due to the sensitive nature, news of his arrest is unlikely to be made public anytime soon. However, from what I'm hearing, it's one of the usual places."

For Kit that was motivation enough not to ask any further questions. "How about those who got away?"

Maria was also standing near the table. "Satellite and GPS tracking confirmed the helicopter that landed close to the Inns of Court touched down on a rooftop helipad at South Bank within two minutes of taking off from north of the water. Following its second take-off, our satellites tracked it to the Angers region of France; incidentally the castle is credited as being property of the de Haulles."

"How about the apartment?" Sanders pressed.

"No firm connection, but one worth investigating. The penthouse was owned by the former business partner of the man who had owned the yacht you visited."

"The yacht I visited." Sanders raised his eyebrows. After everything that had happened, it already seemed like a long time ago. "So there was a vast network involved. Or at least a conspiracy?"

"Our visuals confirm Fieschi was on the chopper, along with his elderly father; had history been different, the man would currently be Duke of Aquitaine. Something similar I understand is true of de Haulle. Both he and his nephew were on the chopper. As, of course, was Blanco."

"What of their whereabouts since?" Jay spoke for the first time.

"We're still tracking them. A warrant to search the penthouse at South Bank has already proven fruitless, not that any of us considered it likely that the jewels would remain in England. An exact itinerary of what existed below the Bank of England is likely to prove helpful in due course; however, whether or not the family feel it's in their best interests to share it is another matter." The Director exhaled deeply.

"So just what exactly are we dealing with here?" Masterson's expression had hardened. "Was this really some ridiculous, yet heavily funded attempt to overthrow the British government, or was this merely Thomas Crown with an arson fetish?"

"It is unlikely these questions will be answered anytime soon, even if the gentleman apprehended at St Dunstan's and those in Edinburgh feel like talking." The Director cupped his hands together, his expression haggard yet thoughtful. "We all knew Randek's feeling towards us; based on the video footage from the White Tower, it's clear where he got his hatred. Whether the attempt to rid England of its royalty was in some way opportunistic or part of a greater plot, perhaps with historical connotations, for now I'm afraid I too must plead ignorance. Though Hansen brought us back some interesting documents, I'm not the person to interpret them – not that there is any shortage of willing candidates."

"I can think of one for a start."

Kit's comment brought a smile from most.

"Whether the Sons of Gemini ever existed, or even if they still do, it doesn't change the fact that those responsible for last night's events are humans living in the here and now. If there was a conspiracy involving a one-time king, if not several, it doesn't change the facts. The culprits are known to us; even if there were others involved, it's safe to say we know who the ringleaders are."

"What of France?" Ward asked, another whose appearance was heavily bandaged.

"From what my sources are telling me, a break-in at the Louvre did occur, almost certainly involving the same people. Unlike here, the crowns were taken, but replaced; news of their success is unlikely to be made public, not that it needs to. The PM is due to speak to the French premiere at the first available opportunity; with the exception of their chat last night, it hasn't been possible for her to do so today. Assuming pressure from the opposition doesn't turn her head, news of the foiled robbery in France could encourage mutual sympathy and cooperation. Here, the real crowns will be back on display at the time of reopening; by real, of course, I mean the ones that have always been there. As far as the public are aware, not to mention many of its employees, nothing has changed. The bridges that were destroyed will be rebuilt, as will be the city."

"So who gets the blame? Assuming the real culprits aren't brought to light." Sanders crossed his arms.

"In addition to her duties in the Commons and conversations yet to take place both at the palace and with the premiere of France, a further COBRA meeting is scheduled for later this evening. ISIS have, of course, already used the opportunity to claim responsibility. As those in the know are already aware, they rarely need much excuse, yet as far as the public are concerned, any answer is better than none.

"As far as we're concerned, the duty of rebuilding the city and interrogating its many criminals is a task designated to others. Our sole concern, as it always has been, lies with ensuring the safety of our borders. This is where our priorities must lie, in addition to ensuring those absent from this table regain their rightful place as soon as possible."

122

Berkshire,
Twenty-One Months Earlier

The driver of the bulletproof hatchback checked his rear-view mirrors before making the final turn-off. The route was familiar. As the official chauffeur of the former undersecretary of state for the Ministry of Defence, the destination was one of his regular ones, often at odd hours. In recent weeks, the passenger's duties had taken him to far more obscure places.

It was part of his job not to ask questions.

Making the turn that brought him back on to the B470, familiar sights could be seen ahead. Heading west along by the Thames and north of the Home Park, the magnificent walls of Windsor Castle looked out majestically over the landscape like the opening sequence of a fairy tale. Even in the mist, the medieval fortress had a presence about it, like an omnipresent deity keeping guard over its realm. As usual, the undersecretary had chosen a time that avoided the worst of the traffic.

It was closer to dawn than dusk.

Checking his mirrors once again, he caught sight of the undersecretary seated quietly on the back seat, showing little interest in his surroundings. Though the driver knew Atkins had seen them all before, today he sensed his quietness was also out of respect for the man alongside him. The second passenger was far younger, his bearing unquestionably of military standing. He remembered driving him before; back then the young man had been blindfolded. Today there was no such restriction on his vision, yet even now the man was still unlikely to have been aware of the route.

Even the speed humps had failed to wake the drained red beret.

Mike heard the sound of two doors closing in quick succession, then another opening. The sound seemed distant, like a TV playing in the background.

The only thing not distant was the cold.

He opened his eyes as he felt a second draught pass in front of his face, the drop in temperature causing him to shudder slightly and a prickling sensation to develop on the skin of his arms. The driver of the car was enjoying a cigarette by the bonnet; the undersecretary was standing by the door.

"Look alive, Hansen!" Atkins ordered. "We're here."

Mike unbuckled his seatbelt and left the car, stifling a yawn. The instruction to get into the car had come precisely at 03:00; he'd slept through most of the journey.

Despite the tiredness, he was in no doubt of the location.

It was starting to get light outside. The nearby wall lamp cast the medieval stonework in a hazy half-light, its powers of illumination weakened by a combination of approaching daylight and mist. It was quiet out, visitors clearly absent; it would all change later, he mused.

Nothing that was about to follow would occur in the public view.

He followed the undersecretary across the Lower Ward, just as he had four weeks earlier. On the north side of the courtyard, the Chapel of St George appeared to be empty; unlike his previous visit, there was no sound of angelic singing within, no well-dressed individuals paying their respects to a loved one, no circle of eleven mourning a brother lost.

South of the courtyard, two figures were walking his way; it wasn't until they approached that he realised who they were. Ward and Dawson both smiled at Mike, saluting Atkins.

"The Director is expecting your arrival, sir," Ward confirmed.

Atkins returned their salute. "Very well." He looked at Mike, forcing an awkward, almost apologetic smile as he removed the familiar head sack from his smart jacket. "But first, Lieutenant, I'm afraid I must trouble you one last time."

When the head sack was removed, Mike saw a poorly lit chamber, the sights recognisable from before. Unlike his previous visit, there had been no great performance involving him being carried down the stairs.

Physically little had changed, but the atmosphere seemed different somehow. It was lighter, calmer; like visiting a relative's home for the first time in months. As his eyes adjusted properly to the new surroundings, he realised he was in the chamber that housed the round table, the twelve seats again unoccupied. Light reflected from the impressive, highly glossed surface like a sunrise on an ice rink. He walked towards it, touched it; a soft, sweet smell confirmed it had very recently been polished. The green and white pattern that had caught his eye weeks earlier, visually almost an exact replica of the famous table housed in the great hall at Winchester, seemed brighter than he remembered, as though the colours had been touched up by recent brushstrokes.

Moving around the room, he noticed things he hadn't before. The oak-panelled walls were more modern than he'd once assumed, although presented in the same style, possibly an upgrade on something older. The paintings that covered large sections of it seemed more relevant now; he'd heard stories of the knights of old, met some of them first-hand. There were names inscribed beneath; he recognised one in particular.

Edward, the Black Prince.

In all his glory.

Circling the table, he concentrated on the other seats, feeling the backs as he passed. Each was old, antique. The wooden structures were hard, even compared to those he'd faced during interrogation; the elegant frames clearly built more for substance than comfort. There were carvings on the back of each, all differing slightly.

For the first time he realised they carried the coats of arms of the original twelve.

He stopped behind the one once belonging to Grosmont, wondering what kind of man he'd been, what kind of men had succeeded him. Recent experiences had told him the facts, but more importantly to know life was never learned through a history book. Only one conclusion was clearly evident.

Like the men who had sat alongside them, they were the best.

"It'll be yours soon enough."

A man had entered, somewhere in his mid-to-late sixties with a full head of short-cropped, spiky hair that, although fallen grey in the autumn years of his life, had barely receded a millimetre since entering the military. As the newcomer stepped further into the light, Mike saw the hard, angular features that had first drawn his attention the day he'd first arrived in Charlestown, then again the day he'd met the brigadier, were on display once again. He knew nothing of his real name, nor his story. He recognised him only as someone he'd seen on parade.

The man whose opinion counted above those of all others.

The Director of the White Hart smiled softly as he circled the table, deliberately walking anticlockwise, which took him to the opposite side from Mike.

"There are always twelve. Never more, never less." *He stopped on reaching the throne.* "A seat here must never be left empty too long. Emptiness causes dust. Ever since our organisation's beginnings, the process has remained very much the same. When an old friend passes, be it into the world beyond or into the peacefulness of retirement, the spirit of the founder must go on. As you can see, even those lost long ago are never truly forgotten."

Mike saw him gesture to the paintings as though he were speaking of old friends. Something about the man's manner immediately captivated him.

"I'm most sorry I've been unable to meet you properly till now. The customs of our order are old and permanent. Just like this table, they were made long before me. Like you, I'm just the latest in a long line. Nothing lasts forever."

"I was beginning to think this process was about to last forever. You certainly haven't made it easy."

"Did you expect anything different? Over four hundred can be a member of the Regiment at any one time. Here we have only twelve. Being granted a seat at the king's most prestigious table was never for the faint-hearted. In these modern, uncertain times, perhaps there's even less room for leeway. After all, technology changes. Susceptibility to corruption by the promises of unworthy suitors was far less likely in a world without instant communication."

Mike raised an eyebrow, understanding the point. He chose his next words carefully. "Matter of fact, I almost feel I ought to thank you. Even three weeks ago I'd never have dreamed I could accomplish so much. The challenge was unexpected. Not unwelcome."

The Director's lips displayed a hint of a smile. "Twelve seats. One vacancy. To become a full knight, a squire must earn the loyalty of his brothers. At the time of our foundation, when a knight owed a debt of thanks to another, it was customary for that man to hand over his sword, a symbolic gesture taken to represent unequivocal loyalty. This very table, be it based on mythology or something more substantial, to this very day represents that same loyalty. Only when a squire receives the swords of a full brother can he take his place." He gestured to Grosmont's seat.

Mike watched the Director as he moved to within touching distance, stopping by the next seat. He noticed it was the seat of the Black Prince.

Currently the seat of Masterson.

"So I guess this means training isn't over?" Mike shook his head, exhaling quietly in frustration. "I'm beginning to wonder if this will go on forever. When this whole thing began, I wasn't exactly offered an instruction manual."

"As I'm sure you realise by now, any document concerning our existence is unlikely to be found by anyone outside the locations where they can be securely stored. Reference to us won't be found in any history books. According to the chroniclers, an order of the Round Table had been put forward in 1344. If the same writers are to be believed, its creation never actually occurred.

"Winchester was the first." He tapped gently against the table, a tinge of pride evident in his otherwise unflappable features. "There have been many since, usually replacements. Any that once existed survive no longer. Try as you might, you're not going to find reference to us in any filing cabinet in Whitehall either, or any other facility you can think of. The budget is strictly black ops." He caught Mike's gaze, preparing to make his final point paramount. "Even in the twenty-first century, there are some things that transcend the powers of the Freedom of Information Act."

Mr White moved quietly away from the table, stopping before one particular portrait. While the others all appeared noble, the person in this one was far less dignified, more like a theatrical villain. The malevolent smirk on the man's face seemed to have been put in for comic effect; it reminded Mike of Shakespeare's portrayal of Richard III.

"In almost seven hundred years, rarely has a candidate been identified and then walked away without taking the chance to accept their reward. Fewer still have turned their back on their reward after passing all the necessary qualification steps."

Mike looked the Director in the eye, knowing he only really had one choice to make. "I want to sit at that table, but only if the other eleven want me to."

The Director eyed him with a proud expression, as though a father casting a thoughtful look over a son. "In that case, I suggest you follow me."

The Director led him through the underground complex, keeping further talk to a minimum. As in the chamber Mike had just left, he recognised things from last time, other features he hadn't taken in properly. He sensed from the layout that the new additions had been made with full respect to the old as though it would be considered sacrilege for anything original to be altered.

They stopped outside an arched doorway with a strong wooden door. He remembered entering it before.

And falling silent as he witnessed the secrets of Richard II.

"Before initiation is considered, an oath of allegiance must be taken by every brother before the high altar. Once taken, it cannot be undone." He looked Mike directly in the eye with a serious and intense expression. "You're quite sure you wish to enter?"

Mike was sure.

"Very well then."

And within those following moments, Mike knew his life would never be the same again. On entering the chapel, the sombre silence that had filled the medieval corridors since the days of its founders was replaced by the sound of enthusiastic cheering and applause as the man dubbed in the trials as the Poet completed his final journey.

Separating him from the five rows of pews that covered the floor of the medieval chapel from west to east and separated by a long aisle that led to the altar, where the treasures of Richard II still lay, each knight of the White Hart stood together, lined up as if to provide a guard of honour. Though the faces were as he remembered, each bearing the scars of war and entrusted with the secrets of the past, glossed over by childlike humour that he'd witnessed in full flow less than a day earlier, they were now attired in a manner unlike anything he had ever seen in real life.

Replacing the usual military-style combats, dark jackets, slick military-style marching boots, belts fitted with anything from semi-automatic firearms to sophisticated tracking equipment, each man stood in the dress of centuries past, a secret uniform he knew he'd only now earned the right to see. Impeccable white mantles hung proudly around dark tunics that matched the leggings and footwear, which, he could now see, were modern replicas of medieval tights and buskins. A unique logo was emblazoned on the centre of the mantle. He'd seen it before, three times: on a sign outside the inn, at the centre of the round table, and on the suits warn by Masterson, Sanders and Iqbal the day he'd first visited the castle.

Today it needed no explanation. The final test had been passed. He was at the centre of hell, knowing he was within seconds of beginning his return to the surface.

The Director of the White Hart walked alongside him, regarding his men proudly. Each knelt as though addressing a king; in that moment it almost felt as though he were witnessing a scene from the past.

Under the circumstances, Mike found it strangely fitting.

"Once again, here we are." The Director looked at the knights as one. "For forty days there have been eleven. Never before has more time passed. As you all understand of our customs, the willing squire can only rise to the rank of knight with the brothers' agreement. Gentlemen, I must ask you now to make a decision. And if you so choose, hand over to the squire your sword."

In what seemed one swift movement, all of the knights unsheathed their swords and formed a line. Each man raised his sword at the hilt and thumped it once against his chest in a sign of allegiance.

Ward found himself at the front. He banged the sword to his chest a second time. "My sword is yours, good squire."

In a moment of disbelief, Mike accepted Tommy Ward's sword in his outstretched hands, the blade potentially capable of thousands of kills reflecting the overhead lights like a mirror. Within moments of receiving the first, Rawlins did the same, as did Cummins, Pentland, Wilcox, Dawson and Pugh.

He grinned as he saw a wry smile on Jack Dawson's lips.

Chambers followed, then Iqbal, both smiling ear to ear. Though never as a child had he envisaged the knights to have been anything other than white skinned, both men looked resplendent, as though the attire had been designed for them alone.

Sanders came one from last, his bearded face beaming with pride. Of all the eleven, he wore the uniform with the greatest dignity, as though he were revisiting a scene from a past life. He smiled warmly at Mike and jokingly threatened an execution before placing the sword down with the others, uttering the same words.

Ten swords Mike now carried, the collective weight beginning to feel uncomfortable. The Director had been clear in his instructions.

Only with all eleven could he ever dream to sit at the Round Table.

Last in line was Masterson, who carried himself in a quietly dignified way with an inner conviction that was different to the others. Whereas Sanders could easily have looked at home in a previous life, for Kit, clearly, this was his life.

Mike felt his heart rate rising rapidly, the realisation quickly dawning that despite all of the trials and tests that he had endured, the future that he now coveted more than anything in the world now rested on the actions of one man. He was looking at a man he feared, briefly hated, strangely admired, could never understand. There was something about him that marked him out from the rest, made him stand out in ways most soldiers could only dream of. There was a reason the captain in the field was appointed; to Mike, those reasons had never been a mystery. He was looking at the strongest of the eleven. The bravest. Most resilient.

Most unpredictable.

Kit stopped in the same place as the others. His pause was the longest yet, but strangely Mike felt prepared for that. He was looking at a showman, a great manipulator, but not an evil one.

Kit Masterson raised his sword, bringing the blade slicing through mid-air as he juggled it into position. Like the knights before him, he raised it slowly, refraining for now from pumping his chest. As he slowly brought the hilt in line with his heart, Mike locked gazes with him, his poker face still giving nothing away. In that second, it felt as though his whole world had ended, that the process he'd given his all to had been for nothing. His future was *disappearing, disintegrating in a cloud of smoke in the centre of hell.*

Then, as the captain of the White Hart raised his sword a second time, Kit's face broke into a satisfied smile.

"My sword is yours, good squire."

A sudden burst of adrenaline pummelled through Mike's body as the extra weight of the heaviest of the swords joined the pile, further testing the strength of his arms. At that moment, a chorus of loud cheering and applause once again broke the quietness in the chapel.

"Lieutenant Hansen."

The Director's words brought new silence. Only then did Mike notice three others present. Atkins was standing to the Director's right, wearing his usual immaculate suit and the highly polished shoes that reflected the light. On the other side, Brigadier Stokes was equally smart, his officer's uniform decorated with the medals of service, each one sparkling as they hung from just above his left breast.

The identity of the final man left him speechless. Though he had seen him before, nothing had prepared him for the moment he sensed was due to follow. Like the brigadier, he wore an officer's uniform, the area above the left breast glistening with the shine of numerous medals, only, unlike the military commander, some of which were honorary. There was the slight hint of a proud smile on his lips that like the rest of his face possessed a clear noble bearing, one Mike knew was famous worldwide.

He was looking at the Prince of Wales.

"By tradition, only a captain can be made a knight of the Order of the Round Table." The Director gestured to Stokes. "Anthony."

The brigadier walked towards Mike and revealed a small item in his hand. "By the authority placed in me by Her Majesty's government, I'm delighted to inform you that you have been promoted to the rank of captain."

Further applause followed from among the knights, enough time for Mike to investigate the item that was now in his hands.

Sure enough, he had been presented with a brace of pips.

The brigadier stood to one side as the Prince of Wales walked forward. Mike felt the air in danger of leaving his lungs as their eyes became locked for the first time.

"Captain Hansen, by jove." The heir to the throne looked him up and down. "As is customary of our traditions, laws and by-laws, any new addition to the Order of the Round Table must abide by the following oath. Are you willing to take that oath?"

Mike struggled to get the words out. "Yes, sir."

"Very well. Do you, Captain Michael Ashley Hansen, swear to be faithful and bear true allegiance to Her Majesty the Queen, her heirs and successors, according to law. So help you God?"

Though Mike heard every word, what the prince said barely registered. He simply replied, "I do."

"Take a knee."

The prince removed his own ceremonial sword, placing the tip on Mike's left shoulder.

"Arise, Michael Ashley Hansen, captain of the 1st Battalion of the Royal Parachute Regiment. In accordance with our traditions, laws and by-laws, I hereby bestow on you the honour of Officer of the Knights of the Garter and 515th Knight of the Order of the Round Table." He then placed the sword over his other shoulder. "You may stand."

A unique barrage of emotions hit Mike all at once as the small chapel erupted with the loudest cheering yet. Without having a chance to look again at the prince, he found himself being mobbed by the knights, the regal face of the heir to the throne vanishing behind a sea of far younger faces. Each man grabbed him and offered their congratulations, many hugging him, almost depriving him of air. Among the feelings of an adrenaline rush, fear, confusion, warmth, hope, expectation, excitement and pure exhaustion, he felt something deeper and greater still, something he couldn't quite put into words. As the faces of his recent tormentors looked back at him, it was different than before. He was looking at his closest friends. Lifelong friends. Family. He was looking at the faces of brothers he'd never had.

And he knew each one of them would always have his back.

123

Charlestown, Suffolk, Modern Day

The churchyard was deserted except for him. Even when it wasn't, it was the kind of place that had that feel. The acre-sized lot that surrounded the quaint, white-stoned edifice to the north-west allegedly dated back to the Norman era; most of what surrounded it hadn't changed much in the centuries since.

The town itself was located east of the river; even the tops of the tallest buildings were shielded by the surrounding hillside. The sea, too, was invisible from where he stood, despite the recurring sound of the tide lapping against the rocky shore. From the top of the tower, it was possible to see everything up to twenty miles away, but he hadn't been up there recently. Most of the land was farmland. It was a place of seclusion and solitude; right now he felt a need for both.

That and reflection.

Mike was standing in the most open part of the churchyard, about twenty yards from the south wall of the church and away from the nearest trees. The plot, used for burials since the time the church was built, was as abundant in vegetation as it was graves; according to the parish vicar, the oldest of both dated back to around the same time. A large gathering of oak trees lined the north side; it was there the oldest stones existed, the surfaces most weathered. Though the writing on most was illegible, certain features repeated themselves, especially symbols. Even from the earliest days, remains were still there, dates from the 14th and 15th centuries easily found. Most of the founders were buried elsewhere, but those who were there had pride of place. Rumour had it a fine vault existed below the crypt; even in recent days, he'd not been tempted to visit it. Areas below ground seemed strangely confined these days.

On rare sunny days, the churchyard was an oasis of calm.

He stood beside one grave in particular, his attention on the lettering. Like most he'd seen, the writing made up only part of the decorations. Above the man's name, a shield-shaped emblem was etched into the polished exterior, the triple lion design like that on the coat of arms of a prestigious medieval family but also matching one of those found at the round table. The seat belonging to Grosmont, once Earl of Lancaster.

His seat.

While many Grosmonts lay within the greenery, just as did his eleven comrades, the stone stood out for two reasons. The dates were modern compared to most, the date of death by far the most recent. It was the stone whose existence had led to his own journey to Charlestown.

The only knight he had witnessed being laid to rest.

For several minutes Mike Hansen stood in silence, leaning his bodyweight against the crutches that he gripped tightly with both hands. His hands felt stronger than they had in recent days, despite the clear scarring, the appearance of which paled almost into complete insignificance when compared to his more serious injuries.

The operation to remove the bullet had taken place the same night as the attacks. He'd been asleep when it happened; even without the general anaesthetic, he doubted he would have awakened. Movement was freer now. There was a tingling sensation in his thigh, a pleasant feeling compared to what he'd been through that night at the Tower. The stitches were concealed beneath his jeans; the scar would heal in time. Unlike those on his face, a part of him wanted them to stay. A glorious reminder of what had happened. Even if Chambers was wrong and chicks didn't dig scars, it acted as a reminder, an event that had shaped his past and would define his future.

Like the Monument to the Great Fire, he was looking at all that remained of a night he would never forget.

He heard the sound of movement from the bottom of the hill, the lychgate opening and closing. Along the pathway a figure was approaching, his movements far less restricted than his own.

Even in the bright sunlight, he could tell who it was.

"So this is where you are," Kit called out as he approached. "I'd have thought after everything, you of all people would be wanting to avoid this sort of thing."

Mike smiled wryly. "Matter of fact, I was just thinking that you of all people would want to avoid churches. Then again, as far as I'm aware, this one's never caught fire."

"No. At least not by intent." Kit stopped alongside him, looking down at the writing on Fenway's grave. "Then again, personally I seem to recall he wasn't the greatest fan even before the fires."

Mike's smile widened. "What was he like?"

Kit shrugged, his expression suggesting he was unprepared for the question. "Much like the others, really. Besides Sanders, he was the most senior; other than Wilcox, he was the oldest." Kit's expression softened, as though revisiting an old pain. "Never cared much for authority. Especially when he was threatened with court martial."

"Sounds like your kind of guy."

"Didn't always play by the rules, that was for sure. I remember one occasion out in the North Sea near Holland, the Deputy Director ordered he abort a mission aboard an oil refinery after learning it had caught fire. Needless to say, the bastard he killed probably wished he had obeyed the order."

Mike nodded, attentive. "I never asked how he died."

A lengthy pause preceded Kit's reply. "There are certain things one shouldn't ask."

"There are certain people who don't have a right to know." Mike raised his eyebrows; though the scars had faded slightly, it still caused minor discomfort.

"Since you ask, it was outside a castle in France." Kit bit his lip, his head lowered in either sadness or respect. "Even before your time, Jérôme de Haulle wasn't completely unknown to us."

Mike nodded, a moment of quiet passing. "You know, in all the time I've been in the military, I don't think more than four people I served with have been killed by enemy fire. Even in Helmand, I can only think of two unlucky enough to be taken down." He raised his head, moving it from side to side. "That night at Covent Garden aside, I can't think of a single time when I actually thought one of us was going to die."

"Oh, don't get all sentimental on me now, Mike. We're soldiers, after all. I remember when I was at Harrow, we were learning about Louis XIV. I'll never forget our teacher told us his last words. He said, 'Why do you weep? Did you think I was immortal?'"

Mike smiled.

"It's one of the strangest aspects, I think, about being a White Hart. Though the names on the seats remain the same, no less than forty different knights have sat in each one. Ask me to name them all, in truth I wouldn't have the slightest clue; but their stories do exist if I choose to search for them. It never does well to dwell too much. I think that's another requirement of a knight that isn't necessarily given scrutiny in training. After all, how does one respond if his order was to leave his best friend to die in order to complete the mission?"

Mike raised an eyebrow. "Well, you said yourself, even Captain Fenway wasn't always one to follow orders."

"Nevertheless, he knew what was right. He saw no less than three Harts die at different times, watched their bodies come back in the choppers. They're all buried here somewhere; you come here often enough, you see the families from time to time." He glanced down at the date on the slab, noting it was almost Fenway's birthday. "I'm quite sure if you're here in a few days, Tracy herself might put in an appearance."

Mike nodded, remembering seeing the man's widow himself the day he arrived. Under the circumstances it seemed sad. Almost forgotten.

"It's not a lot really, is it, when you think about it?"

"How do you mean?"

"When I was outside the vault, Blanco said that the knights of old were among the most revered of their day, the next to the king himself. Now we exist in anonymity; do so on a pittance. The knights of the past had titles, land." He looked at Kit. "Makes you think."

Kit's expression turned scornful. "I never had you down as a mercenary."

"Nor am I. Just makes you think. All this time we were out busting our asses trying to save buildings the employees would never save, protecting jewels that could take millions out of poverty. Is it worth it?"

"And what do you imagine possessed the founders to join the order in the first place? After all, what you say is correct. They had the status, they had the lands, they had the titles, they had the ladies of the court going spare over them. But despite all that, they risked everything they had to sit at that table. If you look at the Templars, each knight was required to give away his lands, estates often worth millions in today's money, for the honour of joining. Why did they do so?"

Mike's lips curled into a grin. "You know, my granddad often told me every boy is a little wild at heart."

"You should really go have a cup of tea with that man more often. At heart, a man's true purpose is to be victorious. Even if not straightaway. The end game is never about the lands, the status; if anything, that's just a way to keep score." He turned to face Mike, his eyes looking deeply into his. "Even for the founders, being at that table was never about the status. It was about honour – and in turn being honoured. The real test of a man isn't so much his insignia. It's what's in his heart."

Mike smiled. "I suppose they teach some useful things at Harrow."

Kit's expression hardened. "There and other places."

Mike's smile widened. "It makes you think though. When I was down there, Blanco attempted to justify what he was doing. Questioned what had happened since the original fire. You know, in some ways I think he was right. The opportunity to build a better world was lost." He balanced on his crutches. "Are you honestly telling me this was what Wren imagined? Tower blocks as far as the eye could see. The great spires and architecture replaced by bank buildings?"

Kit shook his head. "You really are a doughnut sometimes, you know that? Wren himself was a capitalist, just like every successful person involved in the Restoration. He not only lived through the turmoil and profited as a result of it, but continued to be revered throughout the reigns of six monarchs since. Few, if any, people in history can say the same. The London we lost then, perhaps it did look a bit prettier, its steeples more iconic, but look at what's really happened since. Had it not been for new London, England might never have ruled the waves. Had it not been for the fire at Parliament, the world would never have heard Big Ben. The actions of over three centuries' worth of operations have been conducted, during which England has conquered the world and saved it from being conquered."

"You're not gonna start singing 'Rule Britannia' on me, are you?"

Kit laughed. "It takes a certain type of people to rebuild something lost in such ways. Perhaps you're right: perhaps to some extent construction has gone overboard. It would be nice if a few more hanging gardens could spring up and a few less office blocks, but I guess that's the challenge of transition. If you look at Wren's original drawings, I think that was what he tried to achieve."

"You could achieve a lot more if the jewels were just sold in the first place."

"You honestly believe that?"

"A week ago, I'd have said no. But when you think about it, all they do is sit in a vault all day."

"And even if they do, there's a reason people go to see them. It's not just about how brightly they shine. Perhaps that is the one thing Blanco did get right. The jewels aren't just about the authority of the realm or twenty billion pounds' worth of jewellery. They encapsulate an enlightened history of the English people." Kit's expression hardened. "And that is something always worth fighting for."

Mike raised an eyebrow, smiling.

"Besides, even if you could, just think of all the money the tourists bring in."

They took the pathway back across the river and then among the hills. On reaching the circular courtyard, the twelve houses surrounding it like knights seated at the round table, Mike stopped at the top of his driveway.

"There's one other thing that gets me. Edward II."

"What about him?"

"Just something else Blanco said. People criticise him because he was unlike his father and son – a softer man, more artistic, concerned for the rights of the commoners. In his own way, maybe he was a pioneer."

"And maybe Blanco just told you what he wanted to, to get you on side. At the end of the day, it's one thing to be a philosopher, quite another to be king. As I've told you before, some men are born to be leaders, others born to be led. Besides, it's common knowledge Edward III was the greatest king in English history."

"Because he founded us?"

"I guess that does work in his favour. In your free time, I suggest you look into it yourself." He glanced up at Mike's bedroom window, noticing someone looking down, body draped in a dressing gown.

"Or better yet, just ask the historian."

Inside the house, the trimmings of history gave way to the sleek and modern. A plush, carpeted lounge ended at a luxurious kitchen with views across a garden that extended into the nearby countryside. Up the stairs, four perfectly proportioned double bedrooms offered little insight into the occupant's personality, a reminder to Mike it had been redecorated since Fenway's death. There were no longer any traces of children's toys, unique wall decorations, photos in frames; if the young widow and children he'd seen at his predecessor's funeral had once lived there, any sign had since been removed. As he left the final bedroom, the words of the Director echoed in his ear.

Nothing is left empty for long. Emptiness attracts dust.

Off the lounge, an area one could immediately assume to be for storage turned out to be something far more appealing. A snug, rectangular entertainment suite had been done out with two rows of leather, reclining chairs, a seventy-two-inch cinema system, with surround sound speakers built into the wall. Adjacent the room, a home gym set-up occupied a second room, directly below a hydro gym, together forming part of a recent extension. On the top floor, another room had been fitted with a pool table and a small bar area with a second large television, crowning the perfect bachelor pad.

Returning to the heart of the house, a large study, also on the top floor, was the one room out of keeping with the rest, the oak flooring and antique trimmings instead suiting the mood of a university professor. He remembered learning the day he moved in that the desk would be key; that it was here above all else where the heart of the order's secrets could be found.

The signs were found inside the desk.

Emily was staggered. Seated behind the desk, her eyes alighted on the surrounding decorations, where various artwork covered oak-panelled walls, reminding her of the stately homes she loved to visit on weekends. Throughout the visit, Mike had been hardly explicit when it came to answering her questions.

Each room had prompted more questions than answers.

"Told you I liked history."

She smirked. "So I suppose all this belongs to you? You didn't inherit anything from the previous owner."

"I think maybe he might have left the Jane Austens."

She rose to her feet, a wry smile on her face as they left the room to view everything else on the top floor, ending with the final room overlooking the garden. As the sun began to set, long shadows crossed the lawn as the light hit a line of ancient oak trees that shielded the garden from the surrounding fields. There was a pub in the distance, partially hidden by the trees. An artist's painting of it also hung on one of the walls, along with a variety of new age art, posters of rock groups and memorabilia ranging from music and sport to Mike's earlier days in the military.

She looked at him, sitting down at the end of the king-sized bed, the thick duvet creasing beneath her.

"I told you you'd never believe me if you saw my bedroom."

Her smile widening, she raised the duvet.

Mike had been dozing when he heard a knock at the door, loud and persistent. A voice was shouting, apparently through the letterbox.

He rolled to one side, extricating himself from the bedclothes, taking a second to look back at the bed, for once not empty.

Emily smiled at him. "Tell him to leave the champers by the door and come back in a few weeks."

Mike laughed. "I'll be right back."

Kit was standing outside, dressed in full battle ops uniform, his expression no-nonsense. "Get your arse in gear."

"What's up?"

"Fieschi and Blanco have been spotted in France. We're moving out."

Epilogue

Angers, France, 22:30

The phone had been ringing for quite some time. It was a familiar ring, tinny with a hint of an echo. It had been the same when he was young, very young even. After all these years he viewed it as iconic. Part of history.

His heritage.

Jérôme de Haulle exhaled on his cigar and reached for the phone. *"Allô?"*

"It's Gillian."

The Frenchman felt a twinge of apprehension. "Ah, Madame, is this to be my one phone call?"

"Relax. If I'd have wanted to call the police, I'd have done so by now."

He flicked ash into an ashtray, its metal frame elegantly embossed in black and gold with a lion's head to denote the Plantagenet coat of arms. "For that I am grateful. So, Madame, to what do I owe the pleasure?"

"Actually, I wanted to thank you."

"I see."

"It arrived the day of the grand opening. I'm most grateful."

Jérôme smiled. "Yes, I recall seeing an article in the newspaper."

"You get English newspapers where you are?"

A wry smile. "No. But my laptop is most useful. I love the Internet. Particularly in the mornings. It keeps me company as I take in the view."

There was silence at the other end, a welcome pause. He detected disappointment, as if she was trying to dream up a question that would leave him stumped.

"Madame, I trust the portrait will be back on the walls soon?"

"Yes. As a matter of fact, it already is."

"Ah, I did wonder..."

"About what?"

"About whether it might be kept aside. For tests possibly."

Another delay. "The portrait of Sir Arthur is one of the finest in our collection. Not only a terrific example of the talents of a remarkable man, but a captivating period in history. It deserves pride of place."

"A remarkable man. Are you talking about the artist?"

"Of course."

"Forgive me, I merely wondered..."

"Wondered?"

He laughed, this time loudly. "I appreciate your courtesy, Madame. May I wish you every success with your continued exhibition."

The line went dead, silence then a disconnection. Jérôme replaced the phone, smoked, and walked slowly into the corridor.

***

Gillian McKevitt replaced the phone carefully, her eyes focusing on the display as the base set sat on the coffee table of her lounge. Taking a deep breath, she picked it up again and put through a call to the number she'd been given.

A woman answered.

"It's done."

Beneath the White Hart Inn in the heart of Suffolk, Maria, the Director and Atkins sat quietly, watching the screens. The castle appeared quiet from the outside, any sign of movement accessible only via the IR setting.

As expected, Jérôme de Haulle was present in his study. Gabriel de Fieschi and Blanco were all in different parts.

Maria spoke into her headset. "Edward, this is the Rook."

Crouched low on a rocky outcrop in sight of the 11th-century chateau, Kit Masterson and Jamal Iqbal watched the rounded towers through their field glasses.

Kit responded immediately. "Hearing you loud and clear."

"The baby is napping. Now's your chance."

"Roger that."

Kit moved closer, targeting one area in particular. The reconnaissance mission the night before had been useful.

Entry would not be a problem.

Turning around, he eyed his nine accomplices. "Right, let's move."

The lady wasn't there today; she had spent a lot of time there in recent days. There was something about the corridor that was different to every other part of the chateau. The grand cream walls reflected the moonlight-like water from a crystal-clear lake, an ideal backdrop for the exquisite collection of artwork that would be the envy of almost any gallery in the world. Jérôme's father and grandfather had often recounted to him the stories of how the kings of old had claimed and conquered what was theirs to take, and built an empire, a dynasty, whose actions had shaped many courses of history. He stopped at the lady's favourite. The hero of Agincourt. An English hero, but an Anjouvin one too.

A famous king.

Wearing a famous crown.

Jérôme followed the corridor to the north, the oldest section of the castle. A series of archways, intercepting a vaulted ceiling like that of a mighty church or cathedral, continued to the far end, where several large chambers offered views of the hills. Large double doors were closed but not locked, their heavy frames knocking together under the strength of the breeze coming in from an open window.

He stopped and tapped lightly against the wooden frame. The lady would be present, he imagined; if she wasn't in the corridor, she was usually there. Entering, he saw her standing in the centre of the room, her feet resting on the fine woollen carpet that had been in the family as long as the artwork. Other fine portraits lined the walls, men, women and children, their character unquestionably regal. Items of regalia also hung on the walls, whereas others were on display in containers in the centre of the room. The lady was looking at one in particular, a heavy glass display case like those in the Jewel House at the Tower of London. She had been looking at almost nothing else all week.

Not that he blamed her.

He stood alongside her, studying her features. There was a distant look in her eye that he'd seen frequently of late. She was lost in a dream, a fantasy, as if her soul had returned to a bygone era. He placed his hand on her shoulder but saw no movement or acknowledgement. It was as if she were in a trance. Lost to the world.

Jérôme smiled at his mother and joined her to admire the objects in the glass. He had done so frequently in recent days, but this was his first visit for several hours. It was a sight he was still to grow bored of. Would never. It was not only how it appeared but what it represented. The history of a family and a nation. Gold and jewels.

Together for the first time in three centuries.

He took in the sight, glowing inwardly with anticipated satisfaction and the pride of possession. As the seconds passed, the smile faded, replaced by a sense of dread and panic. The view of the crowns, lined up alongside each other as in their heyday, had been replaced by a different one: velvet with four imprints.

Velvet and empty cases.

Their glass doors swinging gently back and forth in the breeze.

Sanders was waiting on the north side, the opposite from where Kit and Jay had entered. After almost an hour he saw movement in the moat, a series of ripples disturbing the water.

Within seconds, he saw two men emerge.

"Over here." He gestured them over, watching as two became ten. Other than himself, only one had not entered.

His eyes immediately focused on the holdalls they carried. "Did you get them?"

"Everything is here." Kit gestured to the bag he carried.

"Even the French jewels?"

"Even the original English ones; I'm quite sure Mr Johnstone will find some interest in them. Call it a thank you for showing me the crypts."

Sanders smiled and spoke through his headset. "Rook, this is Warwick. The doctor has left the crèche."

* * *

Maria had been watching everything on the screens. "Roger that."

She changed frequency. "Grosmont, this is the Rook. The doctor has left the crèche."

High up on the west side, Mike Hansen viewed the outer curtain walls through the magnified scope of his recently assembled weapon.

Unlike the firearms he was used to, he knew it was capable of packing a punch.

"Roger that." He adjusted the sights, focusing on the window of one tower on the north-west side. After seeing little movement through the window, he activated the X-ray setting he'd first been introduced to seven months earlier at Covent Garden.

"I've got four of them together in the north-west tower. One of them appears to be in a wheelchair."

"That would be the duke." Maria was watching similar footage courtesy of the satellite link-up. "His son is with him. Along with de Haulle and his nephew."

"Where's Blanco?"

Maria swiped her hand against her portable tablet. "Heading your way now."

Blanco moved quickly along the narrow corridor, heading for the far end. His footsteps were heavy on the wooden flooring, causing loud echoes off the original stone walls. On reaching the door, he found everyone was already present, looks of concern crossing their faces.

"What is it?"

Fieschi turned to face him. "The jewels are gone!"

Maria saw Blanco enter the room. "He's there."

Mike saw the same thing via the X-ray setting. Locking on to the centre of the room, he squeezed the trigger.

A bright yellow flash shot out from the end of his weapon, the first light of a trail that lit up the night sky. On approaching the tower, the object veered suddenly left, picking up speed.

Without further warning, the medieval tower erupted in flames.

The explosion was clearly visible via the satellite footage, the moment of combustion so bright it was almost painful on the eyes. As the seconds passed, the graphics came more clearly into view, the layout visible despite the heavy smoke. Three bodies were scattered across the floor; a fourth then appeared.

* * *

Watching from high above, Mike alternated his sights between the telescopic zoom and Phil's custom X-ray setting. In the normal light, the heavy smoke blocked out the view, giving confirmation only that the tower was burning.

Inside, the same was true.

He heard Maria's voice in his ears. "The duke is down, along with the de Haulles." She paused, contemplating what she was seeing. "At least one other is down."

Mike continued to watch, examining the chamber through the X-ray setting. As the smoke began to clear, he saw a large part of the wall had been destroyed, allowing a clear view. Returning to his telescopic sights, he moved up to higher ground, heading further south. There he viewed it again.

Five bodies were now visible across the floor.

Maria's voice spoke again in his ear. "Grosmont, this is the Rook."

"I hear you. I see five bodies. All KO'd."

His words resonated clearly to all present. "You see Blanco?"

Mike nodded, the terrorist's body clearly lying still alongside Fieschi's. "Mission accomplished.

"The king is dead!"

JOHN PAUL DAVIS

The Facts Behind My Fiction

Of all the books I've written so far, without question this one has taken me on the most varied journey. During the last fifteen months, I've visited places I never knew existed, read books I'd never heard of, and discovered tales from England's bloodiest past that I never would have believed could possibly be true.

Many of my experiences along the way turned out to be of great consequence to the story you have just read, whereas certain parts I owe more to the experiences of others. In many cases, the story was influenced by genuine historical events and set in real-life locations; at other times, it was completely made up.

Thank you for reading. For those of you who are interested, what follows is an insight into some of the research that took place and how it fitted into the story.

The Tower of London

The Tower is, of course, a real location. With an estimated 2.5 million visitors every year, it remains one of the most popular tourist attractions in the world. Since the creation of the original 'White' Tower around 1078–1100, under the guardianship of Gundulf, Bishop of Rochester, to help consolidate William the Conqueror's dominion over London, a further twenty towers (twenty-one including the now demolished Lion Tower) have been added to create two surrounding walls in addition to countless other buildings, some of which no longer exist.

With the exception of the underground New Wardrobe Tower that housed the archives, all of the buildings mentioned in this novel do exist. The subterranean foundations of the Bell Tower that Mike and Emily used to enter the Queen's House are fictitious, and the same is true of the many secret passages. While it's possible – in fact, heavily rumoured – that several tunnels were created either as escape passages or for incarcerating prisoners, hard evidence of their existence is difficult to find.

Similarly, as there are many areas of the Tower that are off-limits to the general public, it was not possible to see everything first-hand.

The Queen's House does exist: built on the orders of Henry VIII as a present for Anne Boleyn, it is currently used to house the resident governor. The chamber in the Bell Tower once used to incarcerate Sir Thomas More also exists and is now highly revered due to More's later canonisation. The Waterloo Block is used for both military and civilian purposes, but for this novel I've taken liberties with its interior. The same is true of the Old Hospital Block, the Well

Tower, the apartments in the Byward Tower, upstairs in the Fusiliers' Museum and the various other buildings used as residences/offices for Tower officials. The crypt of the chapel of St Peter ad Vincula is also at least partly made up. Descriptions of the Yeoman Warders' Club, appropriately named The Keys, I believe to be accurate, though I've personally never had a drink there!

Every character of connection to the Tower mentioned in this book has been made up, though the real-life military and officials inspired many. While most of the thirty-seven Yeoman Warders are stationed there permanently, the military personnel are rotated regularly, much like the Changing of the Guard at Buckingham Palace. The Ceremony of the Keys is a real ceremony and has taken place every night for at least five hundred years – possibly seven hundred. The Chief Yeoman Warder and the Yeoman Gaoler are regularly involved in proceedings – though not necessarily at the same time. In addition to military officials, many civilians are employed at the Tower, notably historians. Lectures are often given on site; however, the lecture theatre mentioned in the Welcome Centre I have made up.

Most areas of the Tower mentioned in this book are open to the public and are well worth a visit.

The Ravens' Legend

Mentioned prominently in the book, the legend of the ravens is a real one. The account of Charles II's astronomer is believed to have occurred – unquestionably, the observatory was moved from the White Tower to Greenwich. Though the first records of ravens kept purposely at the Tower apparently only dates from around 1880, there are earlier stories, most notably concerning the executions of Anne Boleyn and Lady Jane Grey, of ravens being among those observing the grisly events.

Unlike today, ravens were common in England in the Middle Ages and were undoubtedly attracted to the Tower due to the regular number of executions having occurred there and the castle's general condition. Interestingly, another story suggests large numbers of ravens scavenged the ruins of London following the Great Fire!

In light of the stories, today a minimum of six ravens are housed inside the Inner Ward.

The Crown Jewels of England

As discussed in some detail in my earlier thriller *The Cromwell Deception*, the history of the Crown Jewels of England is arguably every bit as colourful as the gems themselves. While the original crowns, plate and regalia are believed to have been smelted down and destroyed or sold off on the instructions of Oliver Cromwell following the execution of Charles I, a new collection was subsequently created, apparently using gold from the previous jewels, for Charles II's coronation in 1661.

The present collection, which consists of approximately 140 different pieces, including 13 crowns (sovereign and consort), 66 items of plate and various other ceremonial objects and vestments, is predominantly kept on display in a purpose-built bank vault inside the Jewel House of the Tower of London – the exception being five of the older crowns, which make up the heart of the display in the Martin Tower. Descriptions of both the key locations and the pieces mentioned in the novel are based on primary and secondary research and I believe them to be accurate. According to the staff, the current collection is worth an estimated £20 billion and is genuine!

The Crown Jeweller is the role given to the person charged with the task of maintaining the jewels. The workshop beneath the Jewel House does exist. The tunnels beyond it, almost certainly, do not. Understandably, the exact security measures and technology in place isn't widely broadcast. Though I did try asking one of the Beefeaters, all that was really achieved was a laugh at my expense!

Only once in its history has the collection been the subject of an attempted theft. While kept in a locked storeroom in the Martin Tower in 1671, the then custodian of the jewels often showed them to visitors for a small fee, only to be attacked on one fateful occasion by a hot-blooded Irish-born military officer by the name of Colonel Blood, who attempted to make off with the crown of St Edward, the orb and the sceptre. Though considerable damage was done to the crown and sceptre, fortunately everything was recovered.

In light of this narrow escape, an armed guard has looked after the jewels ever since.

The Crown Jewels of Scotland

The oldest survivors of the UK regalia, the Honours of Scotland, were shaped in Scotland and Italy during the reigns of James IV and his son James V and first used collectively at Stirling Castle for the coronation of Mary, Queen of Scots, in 1543. The crown, itself a remodelled version of the original, was first used by James V in 1540, four years after the remodelling of the sceptre that Pope Alexander VI had presented as a gift to James IV. The final item, the Sword of State, was also a gift of a pope, in this case Julius II in 1507, and the famous break is believed to have occurred when the honours were smuggled out of Dunnottar Castle in 1652.

Following the Acts of Union in 1707, the Honours were locked away inside the Crown Room in Edinburgh Castle for more than a century until it was reopened, apparently by a group that included the novelist Sir Walter Scott, with permission of the future George IV. They were used for the final time during the coronation of Charles II at Scone in 1651 and are currently on display inside the same room at Edinburgh Castle.

The Crown Jewels of France

Last used to crown a king in 1825, what was once a vast collection of items dating back to 752 is no longer used for official purposes.

Today, very little remains of the original selection. Despite the recovery of most of the jewels following their theft in 1792 when rioters looted the Royal Treasury, at least two of the famous pieces, the Sancy Diamond and the French Blue Diamond, have never been located – interestingly, the latter is alleged to have been recut and is reputedly a bad luck charm.

Of the items that were returned, the establishment of the 'Third Republic' led to the controversial decision to sell off most of the jewels, predominantly to private collectors, around 1885. Most of those that survive are housed in the Louvre's Galerie d'Apollon and are kept purely for their historical value. Like their English cousins in the Martin Tower, they no longer contain their original diamonds.

The Hundred Years' War

Generally dated 1337–1453, the Hundred Years' War was a succession of conflicts between the English House of Plantagenet and the French House of Valois over the succession to the French throne. As inheritors of the holdings originally owned by William, Duke of Normandy (later, the Conqueror), and augmented by Henry II's Angevin Empire that by 1337 consisted only of Gascony, the Plantagenet Kings of England had long ruled over large areas of France as vassals of the French King.

When Charles IV died with no male heir surviving into adulthood, and thanks also to a principle established in French law that no female could succeed to the throne, Charles's sister, Isabella, widow of Edward II of England, attempted to seize the throne for her son Edward III by right of blood succession as nephew of Charles IV and grandson of Phillip IV. Although her motion was rejected by the French, leading to count Phillip of Valois – grandson of Phillip III and nephew of Phillip IV – being accepted by the English as King of France, Phillip's meddling in Edward III's war with Scotland saw Edward reassert his claim.

Despite the great victories at Crécy, Poitiers and Agincourt that paved the way for Henry VI of England to become the disputed ruler of France 1422–53, the large number of French resources eventually led to Valois dominance and the end of the war.

JOHN PAUL DAVIS

Edward II of England

Son of Edward I, father of Edward III and ruler of England 1307–27, Edward II's claims to fame are few. Humiliated by the Scots at Bannockburn, it's perhaps not unjust to say his reign is one that is often submerged within the great sea that is England's history.

In recent times, this has changed slightly. In addition to a, largely fictitious, portrayal of him as heir to the throne in *Braveheart*, interest in this king has also increased as a result of questions that have been raised about the exact manner of his death, something which was of key importance to this story.

And something which even now remains a matter of some controversy.

Of Edward II's life, much is known. Born at Caernarfon Castle in 1284, the prince accompanied his father on many of the Scottish campaigns throughout his late teens and early twenties, leading to his being knighted in 1306 before taking the throne a year later. On marrying Isabella, daughter of Phillip IV of France, in 1308 as part of an attempt to pacify the rift between the two nations, much was expected of Longshanks's successor. Yet any chance that England might have enjoyed a continuation of his father's dominance was plagued by regular run-ins with his barons.

Of Edward's performance and personality, most notably his sexuality, debate has been ongoing since his coronation. His fathering of four children with Isabella, in addition to a lack of personal accusation by his rivals, suggests he was unlikely to have been gay, even if he was bisexual, but what cannot be disputed is that his tendency to promote personal favourites like Piers Gaveston to roles of prominence proved a cause of great political unrest, eventually resulting in a series of reforms, most notably the Ordinances of 1311, which further curbed the king's absolute authority.

Though success in achieving the new legislation and the execution of Gaveston a year later was undoubtedly viewed with much initial optimism by the barons, sadly for Edward the worst times remained ahead of him. His crippling defeat by Robert the Bruce in 1314, despite a numerically superior English force, saw a drastic shift in the war with Scotland, following which widespread famine further tested the patience of his people. Even after Gaveston's death, his willingness to empower personal favourites remained, resulting in the rise of the Despenser family, who in time would take their rightful place among history's controversial figures.

Despite initial success revoking the reforms of 1311, his uneasy truce with Scotland saw opposition to his regime intensify significantly, and when his furious queen allied herself with the exiled baron Roger Mortimer, the writing for Edward was on the wall. As his regime collapsed, he fled into Wales, where he was eventually captured and forced to abdicate in January 1327. According to most contemporary chroniclers, he died eight months later at Berkeley Castle, be it of a grief-stricken illness or a painful murder.

However, in recent times, much of this has been brought into question.

The Fieschi Letter

Discovered in the French city of Montpellier in 1878, the Fieschi Letter is one of those 'is it?/isn't it?' documents, the veracity of which could change everything we know about Edward II's final days.

As the key facts of the letter have already been discussed at length in the novel – and seeing as Emily Fletcher and David Champion are far better historians than I'll ever be! – further analysis of the content is largely unnecessary. What is perhaps worthy of discussion is what that content could mean in terms of our understanding of Edward II's life.

The letter itself is believed to be a copy of an original and was discovered by an archivist in an official register once belonging to the Bishop of Maguelonne. Despite being a copy, as the register concerned files dating before 1368, its authenticity has never been seriously doubted.

Instead, the key questions seem only to relate to its accuracy.

In his books on Edward III and Roger Mortimer, in addition to his articles in *The English Historical Review* and the *BBC History Magazine*, the historian and author Ian Mortimer put forward a convincing case in favour of the letter's reliability. Fieschi's account of Edward II's escape from Berkeley Castle can potentially be backed up by the activities of the former constable of Corfe Castle – to where Edward apparently next travelled – and would also make sense of the Earl of Kent's subsequent attempts to rescue Edward. Interestingly, critics of the letter tend to argue that Roger Mortimer fabricated news of Edward's survival in order to persuade Kent to support a plot against the new regime.

In addition to the letter, there are other interesting things to consider. In the small town of Cecima in northern Italy there is a long standing tradition that a King of England was buried in one of the abbey tombs – today, the tomb in question is open, apparently due to it being exhumed on the request of Edward III, who later had his father's body brought back to England. Even without Lord Berkeley's inconsistent claims regarding the former king's death in 1327, further questions arise over the viability of eyewitness accounts. Though many dignitaries paid their respects to the king before he was buried in Gloucester Cathedral, reports suggest the body had been embalmed by then; coupled with the fact Edward had been imprisoned since his dethronement, it's unclear how many had seen the former king recently. Similarly, this was the first occasion the body of a post-Norman king was not paraded through the streets on a bier – a wooden effigy was used instead. Incidentally, the name William le Galeys, apparently the name of the man Edward III met in Koblenz, translates as William the Welshman – a Welshman by birth, Edward II was also the first Prince of Wales since the eradication of the line of Welsh princes. Equally curious is the fact that Isabella never remarried, unlike many previous consorts.

While all of the above can be considered as possible evidence in favour of

Edward's continued existence, unfortunately there is little that can be considered definitive; above all there is a distinct lack of corroborating evidence. Was the copy transcribed correctly? Was Fieschi telling the truth? As a regular visitor to England, one could argue his supposed knowledge of Edward's survival could have been used as a source of blackmail, but there is nothing to indicate that he personally profited from it – as mentioned in the novel, le Galeys' agent appears to have been voluntarily entertained at royal expense.

A second theory is that the letter was an attempt by the Bishop of Maguelonne to undermine Edward III's position with the Holy Roman Empire. Without question that might have weakened Edward III's status in Germany, but the author's consistent tendency to name specific locations could call this into question. After all, if Fieschi were lying, a quick search of Cecima would surely prove or disprove his deception.

Or at least his accuracy.

A key matter to consider might simply be whether Edward's survival really mattered. Despite his forced abdication and imprisonment leading to various plots to rescue him during the last six months of his recorded life, come 1337 the situation in England was far calmer. After ten years away from the throne, being over fifty and long believed to be dead, there is little to suggest the previously weak king would have had any serious chance of regaining power. Whether he died or not, the Fieschi Letter perhaps instead provides an interesting insight into the minds of the powers that be. If Edward did die in 1327, its suspicious timing could indicate he was the victim of a plot. If he didn't, it might just be that by 1337 the English lords no longer saw him as being important enough to merit further investigation.

The Sons of Gemini

The villains of the piece and completely fictitious.

The case for the existence of this organisation hinges on three possibilities: firstly, that William le Galeys was indeed Edward II; secondly, that Edward II's marriage to Isabella was annulled and, thirdly, that he in turn later remarried and had children with a new bride.

This is important for many reasons. At the time of Edward II's abdication, England was still a papal fiefdom following King John's surrender to the papacy in 1213. Over the years there have been various discussions over when this arrangement formally ended. Though the final break may have occurred during the Reformation, the last official payment to the papacy was recorded as having been made by Edward III in 1333, thus confirming papal superiority over England was still in place shortly after Edward II's alleged death. Had Edward II survived, an anointed king in the eyes of the Church, pressure on Edward III could have been strong from Avignon, despite his position being secure at home. In theory, a similar argument could then be put forward regarding

Edward II's offspring, especially as an annulled marriage – in no small part due to Isabella's adultery with Mortimer – would have rendered all of Edward II's children, including the present king, illegitimate.

Should Edward II have fathered children with a new wife, it would stand to reason the Fieschis would, in turn, have become their guardians and thus watched over any descendants. By 1347, it's possible the eldest could have been present at the siege of Calais. The story of the Burghers of Calais is a real one, at least with the exception of my reference to the Cardinal's Boys. The astrologer William Lilly did make some form of prediction of the Great Fire in 1651, and drawings, which include the Gemini twins above a bonfire, were created for his publication *Monarchy or No Monarchy*.

As mentioned in the *Facts Behind My Fiction* section of *The Cromwell Deception*, there is nowhere in the world that has been responsible for more Kings of England than the County of Anjou. In 2012 a petition was put on the City of Angers' website that the city demands the crown jewels, if not a similar monetary sum, to compensate them for their lost revenue over the centuries.

Three years after that book's release, the City of Angers is still to prize the Crown Jewels away from England!

The Great Fire of London

Prior to 1666, should anyone have mentioned the Great Fire of London, one would immediately have assumed they were referring to an event that took place in 1212 south of the river, if not another fire that occurred in 1135. Bearing this in mind, it would not have been unreasonable had the Great Fire of 1666 been forever remembered as the second great fire of London – if not simply one of several.

Much of what happened during those four days in 1666 is well documented. What began in the early hours of Sunday 2 September had by Wednesday 5 destroyed approximately eighty per cent of the old city, including 13,000 houses, 87 churches and, most famously, one of the largest cathedrals in Europe. Had the fire lasted a further day, depending on the direction of the wind, it could potentially have posed a severe danger to Charles II's palace at Whitehall and the Tower of London, at the time England's principal gunpowder depository.

That the Great Fire began in an area of London known as Pudding Lane is indisputable. That the bakery owned by one Thomas Farriner was the first building to be destroyed is also well documented. Of Farriner's family, only their maid failed to make it out alive, the first of the fire's six definite victims. Records from the time confirm Pudding Lane was renowned for connecting the River Thames to the various butchers in Eastcheap – pudding was the medieval word for offal, which was well known for falling from the carts. The records also confirm Farriner had a contract with the Royal Navy to produce ship's biscuit, a long-lasting bread that was a popular choice during the Anglo-Dutch Wars.

Most references to the Great Fire in this book are based on historical accounts. That the Great Fire was an accident, began by a stray burning ember, has long been accepted as fact.

Though that wasn't always the case.

The Arson Theory

Suggestion that the Great Fire was originally by design is surprisingly easy to find. Indeed, there are so many recorded claims it wasn't necessary for me to make much up. The one exception is the lost pages from Pepys's diary, which itself relies heavily on Thomas Middleton's account before the parliamentary inquiry.

As indicated in the novel, and inspired by the real words that appear on the plaque from 1681, one Robert Hubert, a watchmaker from Rouen, did willingly admit to starting the Great Fire and was subsequently executed after a ludicrous trial brought about primarily from an indictment against him backed by seven signatories, three of which were Farriners. Intriguingly, while much of Hubert's testimony was inconsistent, on being asked to point out where he started the fire, he was successful in locating the former position of Farriner's bakery – curiously, he'd previously said the plan had been to raze Whitehall to the ground, which was one area the fire never touched despite his claim he'd thrown a fireball near the palace. Adding to the intrigue, he originally stated he was one of a group of twenty-four that included one Stephen Peidloe about whom nothing is known. Nor is anything known of his other, supposed, accomplices.

While Hubert was exonerated of blame by the captain of the ship he'd travelled on who reported that Hubert wasn't even in London at the time, the French watchmaker was by no means the only person who could, possibly, have been responsible for starting the fire. Among the most striking claims, as also mentioned in this book, is the testimony of a Wiltshire farmer regarding the English response to something later known as Holmes's Bonfire.

At the time of the fire, the second Anglo-Dutch War had been raging for about eighteen months. Two weeks earlier, Rear-Admiral Robert Holmes of the Royal Navy had inflicted a hammer blow on the Dutch by destroying a fleet of 140 of their warships, followed by the burning of the coastal town of West-Terschelling.

Whereas the Dutch inevitably reeled from the surprise attack, back in England, news of the event was received with great celebration; so much so that Charles II decreed in Holmes's honour that the traditional custom of lighting bonfires would be observed – something that was recorded in a contemporary poem:

Where are those boasting boors, what are their names?
That swore they blockt us up i'th River Thames
Brave, were it done: I must confess the Hogan
Was very willing, but wanted Mogan
Our streets were thick with bonfires large and tall
But Holmes one bonfire made, was worth 'em all
Well done, Sir Robert, bravely done I swear
Whilst we made bonfires here, you made 'em there!

If the attack itself caused outrage in the Dutch Republic, the English celebrations went down little better. In his hometown of Chippenham, the farmer told the inquiry it had been said to him by a Dutchman, 'You are brave blades at Chippenham. You made bonfires lately for beating the Dutch. But since you delight in bonfires, you shall have your bellies full of them.' Later on he was also reported to have added, 'If you should live a week longer, you shall see London as sad a London as ever it was since the world began.'

The coincidence here is seemingly astounding. The same could be said of the testimony of one Elizabeth Styles that a French servant had boasted to her back in April that English maids will like the Frenchmen better when there's not a house remaining between Temple Bar and London Bridge – an event that would come to pass between June and October. Based on such reports, it seems highly probable that the fire resulted from a French or Dutch conspiracy, if not a joint effort. Proving it, however – or even verifying the claims, or who made them – proved anything but straightforward.

Of the motley collection of candidates, only one had a tangible background and connection with the city. The fireworks maker mentioned in this book, one Monsieur Belland, was a real person – records confirm he was in the king's employ. Though Belland apparently proved his innocence, his actions in the build-up to the fire were suspicious to say the least. When some pasteboard that he ordered was delayed in its arrival, he was reputed to have retorted – sources vary whether he spoke to the stationer who provided the materials and one of the stationer's neighbours or just the neighbour – that if it didn't arrive by the following week, he'd have no need for it. During the same conversation, he was also quoted as saying the fireworks he was making included rockets which 'fly up in a pure body of flame, higher than the top of St Paul's, and waver in the air'.

What feelings must have been going through the mind of the questioner a week later on witnessing such bodies of flame from his boat on the Thames, we can only imagine. When the Frenchman's servants, followed by a duo of concerned citizens – apparently the stationer and the questioner – attempted to locate Belland, by which time the fire was threatening to destroy St Paul's, they found him and his son safely inside the Palace of Whitehall, one of a number of foreigners rounded up to escape the wrath of angry citizens. Whether the Frenchman was guilty or not, or if there was anything at all in the arson rumours, remains unclear.

Other than being able to pinpoint where it started, exactly what caused the Great Fire of London remains a mystery.

JOHN PAUL DAVIS

Christopher Wren and His Monuments

It was famously said that 'Clever men like Christopher Wren only occur just now and then'. When taking full account of Wren's achievements, it would probably not be unjust to say he was a complete one of a kind and appeared exactly when London needed him.

As conducting even a brief overview of Wren's complex life would require every bit as much research as was necessary for this entire novel, not to mention be completely superfluous considering the excellent biographies already on the market, I will forgo anything of the kind here, and instead suffice to say that of all the historical characters I've researched or drawn upon over the years, this gentleman truly takes some beating. Famed for his role as architect of the new St Paul's Cathedral, credit must also go to Wren for his contributions to much of the new City of London.

Born around October 1632 and consistently in favour throughout the reigns of six monarchs before finally passing away at the incredible age of ninety – his tomb says ninety-one – Wren, though chiefly remembered as an architect, was not only a jack-of-all-trades, but also a master of many. After achieving notable recognition early on in his career, in particular for his work on astronomy, he was later a founder member, and even president, of the Royal Society and a well-respected scientist and mathematician, his work earning praise from esteemed contemporaries such as Sir Isaac Newton.

Of his life mentioned in this novel, I've attempted to stay close to the facts. That his original designs for both the layout of the city and St Paul's really included doors to subterranean passages is highly doubtful. What cannot be doubted, however, is that when the designs were implemented – both of which were amended, almost certainly for cost purposes – the completed buildings, many of which continue to stand to this day, were widely esteemed and celebrated.

Indeed, 'never a cleverer dipped his pen'.

Of the many monuments/buildings that Wren is credited as having designed, or been involved in, during the course of his long and illustrious career, only a handful were mentioned in this book.

The most notable, of course, is St Paul's Cathedral. The edifice that currently stands on Ludgate Hill is the fifth cathedral to have been built there and is without question Wren's finest work. Every mention of the cathedral in this book I believe to be accurate, with the exception of what lies beneath Wren's own tomb. Of the fifty other London churches Wren is credited as having designed – usually with the help of others – twenty-nine still stand. All of the churches mentioned in this novel are described accurately – again, with the exception of what lies beneath. St Mary-le-Bow, for example, does have a Norman crypt, which now includes a café. One of the stairways Wren did block off, though not necessarily because it concealed a 'door to hell'.

The Monument, which stands at the site of old St Margaret's, New Fish Street, is described as it appears in real life. Though off-limits to tourists, there is a laboratory beneath it, which Wren and co-designer Robert Hooke put in to conduct experiments. Due to the increase in traffic, it's apparently no longer used.

Historical Characters

Many of the characters mentioned in this book really existed. Samuel Pepys was famously a diarist, perhaps best remembered for his writings at the time of the Great Fire. The missing diary content secretly transcribed within his portrait is fictitious but, as previously mentioned, based heavily on Middleton's recorded observations.

Sir Walter Raleigh, mentioned far more prominently in the book's prequel, *The Bordeaux Connection*, was a famous explorer and courtier, who spent many years of his life in the Tower, primarily due to his alleged treason against James I. During his incarceration in what was then the Garden Tower, Raleigh was given many freedoms and even had his lodgings upgraded to house his family. While it is known that Raleigh was a prolific writer during this time and would have been more familiar than most with the Tower's layout, there is no evidence he created a map or had any rare connection with the jewels. The poem *The Ocean to Cynthia* is believed to have been written for Elizabeth I.

Jan Brueghel the Younger was a Flemish painter and the work mentioned in this book is real. The same is true concerning Edinburgh-born Alexander Nasmyth. Every artwork mentioned in the book does exist but, as far as I'm aware, the artists included no secret writing beneath the top layer!

All the characters mentioned with connection to the fire also existed, most notably Thomas Farriner, Monsieur Belland and Robert Hubert. The same is true of the various monarchs, noblemen and mayors of London, though some of those have been used fictitiously, most notably Charles II and James II's secret knowledge of the cause of the fire and their execution of Belland. Charles and James were both praised for their efforts in combating the fire and for rounding up innocent immigrants, but there is no proof they oversaw any clandestine trials. Henry III and Edward I were primarily responsible for the development of the Tower of London.

There is no evidence they ordered the creation of the aforementioned tunnels.

JOHN PAUL DAVIS

Real-life Locations and Vaults Beneath the Surface

Many of the locations mentioned in the novel do exist. In London, general descriptions of the city are based on how it is in real life. The National Portrait Gallery and the Museum of London are described as they appeared during my visits – unfortunately the excellent Fire exhibition has since closed. Temple Church and the Bank of England are both real locations. Though it survived the fire, Christopher Wren was also involved in the refurbishing of Temple Church – as far as I'm aware, he added no tunnel. The Bank of England building post-dates the fire. It is possible vaults like the one mentioned do exist – indeed the Bank was briefly home of the Crown Jewels after the Second World War – but any connection with Wren is made up.

Descriptions concerning Edinburgh, most notably Edinburgh Castle and the other important buildings, are also based on how they truly appear. The Ceremony of the Keys as described at Edinburgh Castle is fictitious, though it is based on a similar ceremony that takes place at nearby Holyrood Palace every July. In Paris, the Louvre and the Métro are, for the most part, described accurately. The exception is the passageway into the former bedroom of the king, which is unlikely to exist.

Throughout the centuries, tourists and citizens of all three cities have been enthralled by dark, but often thrilling, tales concerning life beneath the streets. In Edinburgh, the existence of concealed passages is well known. The nineteen arches of the South Bridge famously contain underground chambers – known today as the Edinburgh Vaults – which for some thirty years in the late 1700s were the homes of several taverns and tradesmen, in addition to potentially hundreds of poorer members of society. A similar tale is true of the Real Mary King's Close located beneath the Royal Mile.

Both are now open as tourist attractions.

In London, what lies beneath the streets is perhaps less famous. Many of the churches in the city were fitted with crypts or undercrofts similar to that of St Mary-le-Bow, and can be visited today. Military citadels and subterranean bunkers also exist in large numbers, thanks in no small part to Britain's involvement in the Second World War and, subsequently, the Cold War.

The most famous of these are the Cabinet War Rooms, at least part of which are now open to the public. Whether a similar facility really exists beneath the Old Admiralty Building is anyone's guess. That a communications facility was constructed under Whitehall is fact. Whether or not the widely speculated Q-Whitehall is its official name has never been confirmed or denied. In 1980, a journalist named Duncan Campbell writing for the *New Statesman* magazine – and subsequently in his own book *War Plan UK* – claimed to have found a closed entrance to the facility beneath Trafalgar Square, having followed the tunnels used to house BT cables. While no official evidence has ever come to light concerning tunnels beneath the Tower of London, the nearby London Bridge Experience and the London Tombs are both located beneath the surface and confirm tunnels from the correct age do exist in the city.

Windsor Castle and Buckingham Palace are famously the principal residences of the Royal Family and, besides the secret chambers below Windsor, descriptions of them are accurate. Most of the places mentioned in connection with the White Hart do exist, at least in some form. My descriptions of the Brecon Beacons are based on how they really appear – the training is also based loosely on what is really encountered by recruits/potential recruits to the Special Forces. Most of the vehicles/weaponry mentioned do exist in some form. RAF Brize Norton is a real base and the HQ of the parachute training school, though my descriptions of the mess do stretch a point. The base in the Highlands of Scotland and the village of Charlestown do not appear on any maps...

The White Hart

The chief protagonists of the piece and the current incarnation of an exclusive and ancient order formed to serve the ruler of England.

Many 14th-century chroniclers record that an Order of the Round Table was proposed. Inspired by his grandfather's fascination with the Arthurian romances, it was Edward III's intention to establish an order of up to 300 knights that would meet every Whitsun at Windsor Castle for a grand tournament. Construction of a round tower at Windsor is recorded as having begun soon after, only to be abandoned and destroyed prior to its completion. It is commonly assumed Edward III's founding of the Order of the Garter in 1348 took place instead.

It is unclear whether the Order of the Round Table was ever created...

Further Reading

As this book is a work of fiction, again I have decided against including a full bibliography. For those of you who are interested in learning more, however, I would recommend the following:

Arthur, Max, *Men of the Red Beret – Airborne Forces 1940–1990*, London: Hutchinson, 1990

Ashcroft, Michael, *Special Ops Heroes – true stories of exceptional bravery behind enemy lines*, London: Headline, 2014

Barber, Richard, *Edward Prince of Wales and Aquitaine – a biography of The Black Prince*, London: Penguin, 1978

Campbell, Duncan, *War Plan UK*, London: Hutchinson, 1982

Carpenter, D.A., *The Reign of Henry III*, London: The Hambledon Press, 1996

Christopher, John, *Wren's City of London Churches*, Stroud: Amberley Publishing, 2012

Davis, John Paul, *The Gothic King – a biography of Henry III*, London: Peter Owen Publishers, 2013

Hanson, Neil, *The Dreadful Judgement – The True Story of the Great Fire of London 1666*, London: Corgi, 2002

Jones, Nigel, *Tower – An Epic History of the Tower of London*, London: Windmill Books, 2012

Leasor, James, *The Plague and the Fire*, Cornwall: House of Stratus, 2001

Lewis, Jon E., *The Mammoth Book of Special Forces Training – physical and mental secrets of elite military units*, London: Robinson, 2015

Lewis, Jon E. (editor), *SAS: The Autobiography – the bravest of the brave in their own words*, London: Constable & Robinson, 2011

Morris, Marc, *A Great and Terrible King – Edward I and the forging of Britain*, London: Windmill Books, 2009

Mortimer, Ian, *The Greatest Traitor – The Life of Sir Roger Mortimer, 1st Earl of March, Ruler of England 1327–1330*, London: Vintage, 2010

The Perfect King – The Life of Edward III, Father of the English Nation, London: Vintage, 2008

Parker, John, *Royal Marines Commandos – The Inside Story of a Force for the Future*, London: Headline, 2006

Porter, Stephen, *The Great Fire of London*, Stroud: The History Press, 2009

Prestwich, Michael, *Edward I*, London: Yale University Press, 1997

Rideal, Rebecca, *1666: Plague, War and Hellfire*, London: John Murray, 2016

Saul, Nigel, *Richard II*, London: Yale University Press, 1999

Tinniswood, Adrian, *By Permission of Heaven – the story of the Great Fire of London*, London: Pimlico, 2004

His Invention So Fertile – a life of Christopher Wren, London: Jonathan Cape, 2001

In addition to the above, key secondary sources included the souvenir guides of the Tower of London, the Crown Jewels, St Paul's Cathedral, and Edinburgh Castle, Pitkin's *Under London*, *National Geographic vol 184, no 4* and Ian Mortimer's articles on the Fieschi Letter in *The English Historical Review* and the BBC History Magazine's collector's edition: *Medieval Kings & Queens*.

Acknowledgements

Books like this can never be completed alone. For their assistance, I'm indebted to many people who have kindly offered their advice and guidance, most notably the staff, including the Yeoman Warders, at the Tower of London and the staff and guides at St Paul's and many other locations throughout London. The same is particularly true of Edinburgh, and in certain cases my gratitude also extends to historical visits.

In addition to this, as always, I'm particularly grateful to Karen Perkins and Pauline Nolet for their dedication and diligence as copy editor and proofreader respectively, and, on a personal note, for their continued enthusiasm towards my writing. A special mention must go to my incredible family and friends, whose support has always been there through the good times and the bad. The most special thank you goes to my parents, especially my father for his continued patience and selflessness in helping me pursue my dreams and for his pivotal role once again in designing the cover.

The final thank you I reserve once again for you, the reader, without whom my life would be very different. Thank you for continuing to invest your time and money in my work. I hope you enjoyed the story. If you did, please check out my other titles and stay tuned for further adventures involving the White Hart!

Fiction

The Templar Agenda, 2011
The Larmenius Inheritance, 2013
The Plantagenet Vendetta, 2014
The Cromwell Deception, 2014 (a prequel to this novel)
The Bordeaux Connection, 2015 (a White Hart prequel to this novel)
The Cortés Trilogy: Enigma, Revenge, Revelation, 2016

Non-fiction

Robin Hood: The Unknown Templar, Peter Owen 2009
Pity for the Guy – a biography of Guy Fawkes, Peter Owen 2010
The Gothic King – a biography of Henry III, Peter Owen 2013

For more on me, please check out my websites, www.johnpauldavisauthor.com and www.theunknowntemplar.com.
All my books above are available on Amazon.

If you have any questions or you would like to get in touch, please feel free to email me using the contact me sections of my websites or at jpd@theunknowntemplar.com. Constructive comments are always appreciated, as are reviews on Amazon and Goodreads. You can also follow me on Twitter @unknown_templar

Printed in Great Britain
by Amazon